The Sackett Novels
of
Louis L'Amour

THE SACKETT NOVELS
OF
LOUIS L'AMOUR

Volume III

The Sackett Brand
The Lonely Men
Treasure Mountain
Mustang Man

NELSON DOUBLEDAY, INC.
Garden City, New York

THE SACKETT NOVELS OF LOUIS L'AMOUR, VOLUME III

Originally published as four separate works
THE SACKETT BRAND
Copyright © 1965 by Bantam Books, Inc.
ISBN 0553-27685-9

THE LONELY MEN
Copyright © 1969 by Bantam Books, Inc.
ISBN 0553-27677-8

TREASURE MOUNTAIN
Copyright © 1972 by Bantam Books, Inc.
ISBN 0553-27689-1

MUSTANG MAN
Copyright © 1966 by Bantam Books, Inc.
ISBN 0553-27681-6

Published by arrangement with Bantam Books

PRINTED IN THE UNITED STATES OF AMERICA

Contents

Foreword

The pioneer period in America is without doubt the best documented period in history until, perhaps, 1900. There is little need to surmise what took place for in most cases we *know*. There is still room for learning, and there are gaps in our knowledge, but generally speaking we have first-hand glimpses of what was happening.

Aside from official records of one kind or another, it seemed that at least one person in every party coming west kept a diary. Fortunately, many of the diaries have survived, and they are invaluable to the researcher.

We not only know what was done but how, where, and when it was done. We know what the pioneers wore, what they ate, how it was prepared, how they travelled, and how they entertained themselves or were entertained. We have literally thousands of day-by-day accounts to guide us.

A friend of mine who began listing the journals of wagon-train crossings of the plains over the overland trail had, at last count, listed more than four hundred. This says nothing of the Santa Fe Trail, the Oregon Trail, or the many others. Diaries were kept by cowboys, army officers' wives, businessmen, Indian agents.

Without a doubt there are hundreds of diaries still lying in dusty attics, or tucked into the bottoms of old trunks or cartons. Often they have little or no monetary value, but historically speaking they are always important.

Many of the Army officers serving in the West were men of broad vision and understanding. Although they often had to fight Indians they respected them and some warm friendships sprang up between them. The journals they kept are informative, usually entertaining, and often touched with wry humor.

Much of the best knowledge we have of Indian life and villages comes from Army men, but even more comes from mountain men who lived with Indians, and from the Indians themselves. Generally speaking we know a great deal about the life of the Indians of various types. Contrary to what some might think there were enormous variations in the manner of living from one part of the country to another, and even from one tribe to another. Of course, as an Indian friend of mine said to me, there are some things no Indian would tell a white man.

History is a vast jig-saw to which we are forever fitting pieces. The recovery and recording of history is disturbed by the casual pot-hunter who digs into an Indian mound or grave site and in so doing destroys any chance of accurate dating.

At this point we know very little about the early history of our continent and every site is of importance. For effective research the archaeologist must find the site either undisturbed or relatively so. Scattered over every state are sites that need to be studied.

Scholars themselves have often been at fault when they attempt to fix the dates when men first arrived on this continent. With each succeeding year man's presence here is moved back further and further into the past, and we have not yet seen the end.

We who write about the frontier write for an audience that is expert in various technical aspects of our history. There are groups who shoot black powder guns, others who have re-formed old cavalry units, or who drive stage coaches, and they can judge the accuracy of what we are writing about.

Every few days a letter comes from some old-timer, man or woman, who gives me the greatest reward I can receive. They say, "Yes, that is how it was. I remember . . ."

THE SACKETT
BRAND

To Jud and Red,
at Tucumcari and Santa Rosa,
a long time ago. . . .

Chapter 1

Nobody could rightly say any of us Sacketts were what you'd call superstitious. Nonetheless, if I had tied a knot in a towel or left a shovel in the fire nothing might have happened.

The trouble was, when I walked out on that point my mind went a-rambling like wild geese down a western sky.

What I looked upon was a sight of lovely country. Right at my feet was the river, a-churning and a-thrashing at least six hundred feet below me, with here and there a deep blue pool. Across the river, and clean to the horizon to the north and east of me, was the finest stand of pine timber this side of the Smokies.

Knobs of craggy rock thrust up, with occasional ridges showing bare spines to the westward where the timber thinned out and the country finally became desert. In front of me, but miles away, a gigantic wall reared up. That wall was at least a thousand feet higher than where I now stood, though this was high ground.

Down around Globe I'd heard talk of that wall. On the maps I'd seen it was written Mogollon, but folks in the country around called it the Muggy-own.

This was the place we had been seeking, and now I was scouting a route for my wagon and stock. As I stood there on that high point I thought I saw a likely route, and I started to turn away. It was a move I never completed, for something struck me an awful wallop alongside the skull, and next thing I knew I was falling.

Falling? With a six-hundred-foot drop below me? Fear clawed at my throat, and I heard a wild, ugly cry . . . my own cry.

Then my shoulder smashed into an outcropping of crumbly rock that went to pieces under the impact, and again I was falling; I struck again, fell again, and struck again, this time feet first, facing a gravelly slope that threw me off into the air once more. This time I landed sliding on a sheer rock face that rounded inward and let me fall again, feet first.

Brush growing out from the side of the mountain caught me for just a moment, but I ripped through it, clawing for a grip; then I fell clear into a deep pool.

Down I went, and when I thought to strike out and swim, something snagged my pants leg and started me kicking wildly to shake loose. Then something gave way down there under water, and I shot to the surface right at the spillway of the pool.

My mouth gasped for air, and a wave hit me full in the mouth and almost strangled me, while the force of the water swept me between the rocks and over a six-foot fall. The current rushed me on, and I went through another spillway before I managed to get my feet under me in shallow water.

Even then, stepping on a slippery rock, I fell once more, and this time the current dropped me to a still lower pool, almost covered by arching trees. Flailing with arms and legs, I managed to lay hand to a root and tug myself out of the water. There was a dark hole under the roots of a huge old sycamore that leaned over the water, and it was instinct more than good sense that made me crawl into it before I collapsed.

And then for a long time I felt nothing, heard nothing.

It was the cold that woke me. Shivering, shaking, I struggled back to something like consciousness. At first I sensed only the cold . . . and then I realized that somebody was talking nearby.

"What's the boss so wrought up about? He was just a driftin' cowpoke."

"You ain't paid to question the boss, Dancer. He said we were to find him and kill him, and he said we were to hunt for a week if necessary, but he wants the body found and he wants it buried deep. If it ain't dead, we kill it."

"You funnin' me? Why, that poor benighted heathen fell six hundred feet! And you can just bet he was dead before he even started to fall. Macon couldn't miss a shot at that distance, with his target standing still, like that."

"That doesn't matter. We hunt until we find him."

The sound of their walking horses faded out, and I lay still on the wet ground, shaking with chill, knowing I'd got to get warm or die. When I tried to move my arm it flopped out like a dead thing, it was that numb.

My fingers laid hold of a rock that was frozen into the ground and I hauled myself deeper into the hole. The earth beneath me was frozen mud, but it was shelter of a kind, so I curled up like a new-born baby and tried to think.

Who was I? Where was I? Who wanted me dead, and why?

My thoughts were all fuzzy, and I couldn't sort out anything that made sense. My skull throbbed with a dull, heavy beat, and I squinted my eyes against the pain. One leg was so stiff it would scarcely move, and when I got a look at my hands I didn't want to look at them again. When I'd hit the face of the cliff I'd torn nearly all the skin off grabbing for a hold. One fingernail was gone.

Somebody named Macon had shot at me, but so far as I could recall I had never known anybody by that name. But that sudden blow on the head when I started to turn away from the cliff edge must have been it, and that turn had probably saved my life. I put my fingers up and drew them away quickly. There was a raw furrow in my scalp just above the ear.

The cold had awakened me; the voices had started me thinking. The two together had given me a chance to live. Yet why should I try? I had only to lie still and I would die soon enough. All the struggle, all the pain would be over.

And then it struck me.

Ange . . . Ange Kerry, the girl who had become my wife. Where was *she?*

When I thought of her I rolled over and started to get up. Ange was back up there on the mountain with the wagon and the cattle, and she was alone. She was back there waiting for me, worrying. *And she was alone.*

It was growing dark, and whatever search for me was being carried on would end with darkness, for that day, at least. If I was to make a move, I had to start now.

Using my elbow and hand, I worked my way out of the hole and pulled myself up by clinging to the sycamore. At the same time I kept my body close to it for concealment.

The forest along the stream was open, almost empty of underbrush, but the huge old sycamores made almost a solid roof overhead, so that where I stood it was already twilight.

My teeth rattled with cold, for my shirt was torn to shreds, my pants torn, my boots gone. My gun belt had been ripped loose in the fall and my gun was gone, and with it my bowie knife.

There was no snow, but the cold was icy. Pounding my arm against my body, I tried to get the blood to flowing, to get some warmth into me. One leg I simply could not use, but from the feel of it I was sure it was not broken.

Shelter . . . I must find shelter and warmth. If I could get to the wagon, I could get clothing, blankets, and a gun. Most of all, I could see Ange, could be sure she was all right.

But first I must think. Only by thought had man prevailed, or so I'd heard somewhere. Panic was the enemy now, more to be feared than the cold, or even that nameless enemy who had struck at me, and now was searching for me with many men.

Who could it be? And why?

This was wild country—actually it was Apache country, and there were few white men around, and nobody who knew me.

So far as I knew, nobody was even aware that we were in this part of the country. . . . Yes, there was somebody—the storekeeper in Globe of whom we'd made inquiries. No doubt others had seen us around Globe, but I had no enemies there, nor had I talked to anyone else, nor done anything to offend anyone.

Now, step by careful step, I eased away from the river and into the deeper forest. The sun was setting, and gave me my direction.

Movement awakened pain. A million tiny prickles came into my numbed leg, but I kept on, as careful as I could be under the conditions, wanting to leave no trail that could be followed.

As I crawled up a bank, my hand closed over a rounded rock with an edge. It was a crude, prehistoric hand-axe.

I remembered that Leo Prager, a Boston college man who had spent some time on Tyrel's ranch near Mora, had told me about such things. He had spent all his time hunting for signs of the ancient people who lived in that country before the Indians came—or at any rate, the kind of Indians we knew.

For several weeks I'd guided him around, camped with him, and helped him look, so naturally I learned a good bit about those long-ago people and their ways. When it came to chipping arrowheads, I was the one who could show him how it was done, for I'd grown up around Cherokee boys back in the Tennessee mountains.

What I had found just now was an oval stone about as big as my fist, chipped to an edge along one side, so I had me a weapon. Clinging to it, I crawled over the bank and got to my feet.

I could not be sure how far downstream the river had carried me, but it was likely no more than half a mile. And I knew that after I left Ange and my outfit I had ridden five or six miles before reaching that point where I'd been shot.

So I made a start. Under ordinary conditions I might have walked the distance in two to three hours, but the conditions were not exactly ordinary. I was in bad shape, with a game leg and more hurts than I cared to think on. And with every step I had to be wary of discovery. Moreover, it was rough country, over rocks and through trees and brush, and I'd have to climb some to make up the ground I'd lost in the fall.

How many times I fell down I'll never know, or how many times I crawled on the ground or pulled myself up by a tree or rock. Yet each time I did get up, and somehow I kept pushing along. Finally, unable to go any further, I found a shallow, wind-hollowed cave almost concealed behind a bush, a cave scarcely large enough to take my body, and I crawled in, and there I slept.

Hours later, awakened by the cold, I turned over and worked myself in a little further, and then I slept again. When at last the long, miserable night was past, I awoke in the gray-yellow dawn to face the stark realization that I was a hunted man.

My feet, which had been torn and lacerated by the fall and the night's walking over rocks and frozen ground, seemed themselves almost frozen. My socks were gone, and probably the shreds of them marked my trail.

Numb and cold as I was, I fought to corral my thoughts and point them toward a solution. I knew that what lay before me was no easy thing.

By now Ange would know that I was in serious trouble, for I'd never spent the night away from her side; and it could be that my horse had returned to the wagon. My riderless horse could only mean something awfully wrong.

From the trunk of a big old sycamore, I hacked out two rectangles of bark. Then with rawhide strips cut from my belt with my stone axe and my teeth, I tied those pieces of bark under my feet to protect the soles.

Next, I dug into the ground with the hand-axe and worked until I found a long, limber root, to make a loop large enough to go over my head. Then I broke evergreen boughs from the trees and hung them by their forks or tied them to the loop, making myself a sort of a cape of boughs. It wasn't much, but it cut the force of the wind and kept some of the warmth of my body close to me.

With more time, I could have done better, but I felt I hadn't time to spare. My right leg was badly swollen, but nothing could be done for it now. By the time I finished my crude cape my hands were bleeding. Using a dead branch for a staff, I started off, keeping under cover as best I could.

If I had covered one mile the night before, I was lucky, and there were several miles to go. But I was sure that at first they would be hunting a body along the river—until they found some sign.

By the time the sun was high I was working my way up a canyon where cypresses grew. On my right was the wall of Buckhead Mesa, and

I'd left Ange and the wagon on the north side of that mesa. I thought of the rifle and the spare pistol in that wagon . . . if I could get to it.

Then, far behind me, I heard a loud halloo. That stopped me, and I stood for a moment, catching my breath and listening. It must be that somebody had found some sign, and had called the others. At least, I had to read it that way. From now on, they would know they were hunting a living man.

If they knew of the wagon—and I had to take it they did—they had little to worry about. How many were hunting me I had no idea, but they had only to string out and make a sweep of the country, pushing in toward the wall of the mesa. Using the river as a base line, they could sweep the country, and then climb the mesa and move in on the wagon. It left me very little chance for escape.

My mind shied from thinking of my condition after that fall. I knew I was in bad shape, but I was scared to know how bad, because until I reached Ange and the wagon there was just nothing I could do about it. Right then I wanted a gun in my hand more than I wanted medicine or even a doctor. I wanted a gun and a chance at the man who had ambushed me.

Using the stick, I could sort of hitch along in spite of my bad leg. It didn't seem to be broken, but it had swollen until the pants seam was likely to bust; if it kept on swelling I'd have to split the seam somehow. My hands were in awful shape, and the cut on my skull was a nasty one. I had a stitch in my side, as if maybe I had cracked some ribs. But I wasn't complaining—by rights I should have been dead.

When I was shot I had been standing on a point on Black Mesa, which tied to Buckhead Mesa on the southeast. The canyon where the cypress grew seemed to reach back toward the west side of Buckhead, and from where I was now standing it seemed to offer a chance to follow it back up to the top of Buckhead. So I started out.

You never saw so much brush, so many trees, so many rock falls crammed into one canyon. Fire had swept along the canyon a time or two, leaving some charred logs, but the trees had had time to grow tall again, and the brush had grown thicker than ever, as it always does after a fire.

One thing I had in my favor. Nobody was likely to try taking a horse up that canyon, and if I knew cowpunchers they weren't going to get down from the saddle and scramble on foot up the canyon unless all hell was a-driving them.

A cowhand is a damned fool who will work twenty-five hours out of every day if he can do it from a saddle. But put him on his feet, and you've got yourself a man who is likely to sit down and build himself a smoke so's he can think about it. And after he thinks it over, he'll get back in the saddle and ride off.

It was still cold . . . bitter cold. I tried not to think of that, but just kept inching along. Sometimes I pulled myself along by grasping branches or clutching at cracks in the rock. Cold as it was, I started to sweat, and that scared me. If that sweat froze, the heat in my body would be used up fighting its cold and I'd die.

Once I broke a hole in the ice and drank, but most of the time I just kept moving because I'd never learned how to quit. I was just a big raw-boned cowboy with big shoulders and big hands who was never much account except for hard work and fighting. Back in the Tennessee hills they used to say my feet were too big for dancing and I hadn't any ear for music; but along about fighting time I'd be there—fist, gun, or bowie knife. All of us Sacketts were pretty much on the shoot.

By noontime I was breasting the rise at the head of the canyon. Only a few yards away the rock of the mesa broke off sharply and dipped into another canyon, while the great flat surface of Buckhead lay on my right. It was several miles in area and thickly forested.

Crawling back into the brush, I settled down to rest a bit and to try thinking things out. My head wasn't working too well and my thoughts came slow, and everything looked different somehow. I kept passing my hand over my forehead and scowling, trying to rid my eyes of the blur.

Near as I could figure, Ange and the wagon were now about three miles off, and moving as I had to, it might take me to sundown to cover that distance. Long before that, every inch of the mesa top would be scoured by riders who would seek out every clump of brush, every tree, every hole in the rocks.

Nobody ever denied that I was a tough man. I stand six feet three in my socks, when I own a pair, and I weigh a hundred and eighty, most of it in my shoulders and arms. I ain't what you'd call a pretty-built man, but when I take hold things generally move.

But now I was weak as a sick cat. I'd lost a sight of blood, and used myself almighty bad. The way things stood, I couldn't run and I couldn't fight. If they found me they had me, and no two ways about it . . . and they were hunting to kill.

There was no way across that mesa but to walk or crawl, and there was no place a rider couldn't go. It looked to me as if I needed more of a weapon than that hand-axe I had in my pocket.

Turning around, I crawled deeper into the brush and burrowed down into the pine needles. My head ached, my eyes blinked slowly. I was tired, almighty tired. I felt wore out.

Ange, Ange girl, I said, *I just ain't a-gonna make it. I ain't a-gonna make it right now.*

I was trying to burrow deeper, and then I stopped all movement when I heard a horse walking on frozen ground, but the sound faded off in the distance.

My head felt all swelled up like a balloon, and I couldn't seem to lift it off the ground.

Ange, I said, *damn it, Ange, I . . .*

Chapter 2

Leaning my shoulder against the rough bark of a tree, I stared at the empty clearing, unwilling to believe what my eyes saw.

The wagon was gone!

Under the wide white moon the clearing lay etched in stillness. The surrounding trees were a wall of blackness against which nothing moved. Within the clearing itself, scarcely two acres in extent, there was nothing.

To this place I had come after hours of unconsciousness or sleep, after hours of fitful struggle for some kind of comfort on the frozen ground, in the numbing cold.

Only when darkness had come had I dared move, for riders had been all about me, searching relentlessly. Once, off to the right I heard faint voices, glimpsed the flicker of a fire.

How many times they might have passed nearby I had no idea, for only occasionally was I even fully aware of things around me. Yet with the deepening shadows some inner alarm had shaken me awake, and after a moment of listening, I rolled from the pine needles in which I had buried myself, and taking up my stick, I pushed myself to my feet.

All through my pain-racked day I had longed for this place and dreamed of arriving here. In the wagon there would be things to help me, in the wagon there would be weapons. Above all, Ange would be there, and I could be sure she was all right.

But she was gone.

Now, more even than care for my wounds I wanted weapons. Above all, I was a fighting man . . . it was deeply grained in my being, a part of me. Hurt, I would fight; dying, I would still try to fight.

A quiet man I was, and not one to provoke a quarrel, but if set upon I would fight back. I do not say this in boasting, for it was as much a part of me as the beating of my heart. It was bred in the bloodline of those from whom I come, and I could not be other than I am.

This it was, and my love for Ange, that had carried me here. Ange, who had brought love and tenderness to the big, homely man that I am.

Ange knew me well, and she knew I was not a man to die easily. She knew the wild lands herself, and she would have believed that she had only to wait and I would return. She would not willingly have left this place without me, knowing that even if I suffered an accident I would somehow return.

And now a curious fact became evident to me. This place, to which I would be sure to come back, was not watched. None of the searching men were here in this most obvious of places. Why?

The simplest reason was that they did not know of it, though a wagon is not an easy thing to conceal, nor are the mules by which it was drawn, nor the cattle. But now they were not here.

Hesitating no longer, and using my staff, I limped into the clearing and stopped where the wagon had stood.

There were no tracks.

I looked to where the fire had been, and there were no coals, no ashes. The stump that I had dragged up for a backlog, which should have been smoldering yet, was gone.

Had I then come to the wrong place? No . . . the great, lightning-struck pine from the base of which I had gathered dead branches and bark to kindle our fire stood where it had been. The rock where I had sat while cleaning my rifle was there.

But the wagon was gone, the mules, the cattle . . . and Ange.

Ange, whom I loved. Ange, who was my life; Ange, whom I had found in the high mountains of Colorado and brought home to the ranch of my brother, in Mora.*

The numbness seemed to creep into my brain, the cold held me still. Leaning on my crude staff, hurting in every muscle and ligament, I looked all around me for a clue, and I found none.

I knew she would not have left without me, and if someone or something had forced her to leave, there should still have been tracks.

Horror crept over me. I could feel its ghostly hand crawling on my spine and neck muscles. Some awful thing had happened here, some terrible, frightful thing. The ruthless pursuit of me, the wiping out of tracks here, all of it spoke of a crime; only I refused to allow myself to think of what the crime might be.

Stiffly, I began to move. I would find the camp of those men and see if

* *Sackett*, Bantam Books. 1961.

Ange was there; in any case, I would see who my enemies were. The wagon and the stock must surely be there.

Turning, I started with a lunge, only to have the end of my staff slip on the icy ground. I fell heavily, barely stifling a scream. My hands fought for a grip on the frozen ground and I struggled to get up, and then I must somehow have slipped over on my face and lost consciousness, for when I awoke the sun was shining.

For a time I lay there, letting the sun soak away the chill in my bones, but only half aware of my surroundings. Slowly realization came to me: I was a hunted man, and here I lay almost in the open, at the foot of a pine tree.

Carefully, I started to turn my head. A wave of sickness swept over me, but I persisted.

My eyes came to a focus. There was no sound but the wind in the pines. The clearing was there before me, and it was empty.

My mind was alert now, and in the broad daylight I carefully skirted the clearing. There were no tracks anywhere, none to show our arrival, none to show how the wagon had left. It had simply vanished.

I was without weapons, without food, without clothing or shelter, but all I could think of was Ange. Somebody had been so desperate to have her disappear that every evidence of our presence there had been wiped out.

An hour later, I was at the clearing where their camp had been the night before, but now all were gone. At least a dozen men had slept there, and there were tracks in profusion. Cigarette butts were scattered about, a coffeepot had been emptied, and a crust of bread lay upon the ground.

But there were no wagon tracks, no tracks of small boots for which I searched. And knowing Ange, I knew that she would somehow have contrived to leave a track. She knew me, knew my methods, knew my thoroughness when on trail . . . and yet, there was nothing. Wherever she was, Ange had never been in this camp.

How could a wagon loaded with more than a ton of supplies, drawn by six big Missouri mules, disappear from a mesa that offered only two or three possible ways by which a wagon might leave it?

Somehow my impression was growing that these men knew nothing of Ange or the wagon. So what then? What had happened? Where was Ange? And who had shot me, and why?

And with these questions there were the others: Why were these men hunting me to kill me? Had they gone for good? Or would they be back?

My hunch was that the search had only begun. Such a desperate search would not be ended that quickly.

I moved off through the trees, hobbling painfully, crawling over fallen logs, occasionally pausing to rest.

When I had left the wagon to scout for a route off Buckhead Mesa, a route into the Tonto Basin, I had skirted the mesa itself and had seen a deep canyon leading off to the southwest. It was all of five hundred feet deep, and it appeared to be wild and impassable, but there was a creek along the bottom. There would be water there, there would be game, there would be fish.

I could no longer look to the wagon for relief. From now on I was completely on my own, alone and without any possible help. And I was surrounded by enemies unknown to me.

By nightfall of a bitterly long day I had found a cave under a natural bridge. The bridge was a tremendous arch of travertine at least a hundred and eighty feet above the waters of the creek, and the cave was a place where a man might hide and where no trouble would come to him unless from some wandering bear or mountain lion. It was a place hidden by brush and the rock slabs all about, a place littered with dead trees brought down by flash floods.

Using the bow and drill method, I started a small fire, and felt warmth working into my muscles. The warmth of the sun had brought some relief from the chill, but not very much.

Making a basin by bending together the corners of a sheet of bark, I heated some water and carefully bathed my hands, then lowered my pants and looked at my leg. It was almost black from bruising, and it was swollen to half again its natural size. For perhaps an hour I sat there, soaking my wounds with a washcloth made from the remnants of my shirt. Whether it would help I did not know, but it felt good.

Then after carefully extinguishing my tiny fire, I put together a bed of evergreen boughs and crawled onto it. I fell into a fitful, troubled sleep.

Hunger woke me from a night of tormented dreams, but first of all I heated water and bathed my leg again, and drank warm water to heat my chilled body. It began to seem as if I would never be warm again, and though I was hungry, what I longed for most was clothing—warm, soft, wonderful clothing.

Sitting there, applying hot cloths to my wounds, I got to thinking on the reason for that attack on me.

As a general run, motives weren't hard to understand there on the frontier. Things were pretty cut and dried, and a body knew where he stood with folks. He knew what his problems were, and the problems of those about him were about the same. A man was too busy trying to stay alive and make some gain, to have time to think much about himself or get his feelings hurt. It seems to me that as soon as a man gets settled down, with meat hung out to smoke and flour in the bin, he starts looking for something to fuss about.

Well, it wasn't that way on the frontier. A man could be just as mean as he was big enough to be; but if he started out to be bad he'd better be big enough, or tough enough, if he figured to last. Such folks were usually given time to reach for a gun or they were tucked into a handy noose. I've noticed that the less a man has to worry about getting a living, the more time he has to worry about himself.

Folks on the frontier hadn't any secret sins. The ones who were the kind for such things stayed close to well-populated places where they could hide what they were. On the frontier the country was too wide, there was too much open space for a body to be able to cover anything up.

But now somebody wanted me dead, and it was apparently that same somebody who had taken my wagon away, and Ange with it.

I could understand a man wanting a wagon, or a man wanting Ange, and it wasn't ungallant of me to think it was more likely to be the wagon and outfit than Ange. And there was reason for that.

One thing a man didn't do on the frontier was molest a woman, even an all-out bad woman. Women were scarce, and were valued accordingly. Even some pretty mean outlaws had been known to kill a man for jostling a woman on the street.

Pretty soon my leg was feeling better. It was easier to handle, and some of the swelling was gone.

Toward noontime I found me a rabbit. I twisted him out of a hole with a forked stick, broiled him, and ate him. But a man can't live on rabbits. He needs fat meat.

Several times I saw deer, and once a fat, healthy elk, a big one that would dress two hundred and fifty pounds at least. But what I hunted was something smaller. I couldn't use that much meat, and anyway, I had nothing with which to make a kill.

The afternoon was almost gone and weariness was coming over me when I fetched up at a rocky ledge below a point of Buckhead Mesa. Pine Creek and its wild canyon lay north and west of me, the mesa at my back.

Night was a-coming on, and I wished myself back at my cave. Just as I was fixing to turn back, I smelled smoke. Rather, it was the smell of charred timber, a smell that lingers for days, sometimes for weeks after a burning. That smell can be brought alive again by dampness or rainfall. I knew that somebody had had a fire, and close by.

The ledge was behind some trees and close against the face of the cliff. At this point the cliff was not sheer, though it was very steep, and ended in a mass of rubble, fallen trees, brush, and roots.

I started working my way through the trees. The smell of charred wood grew stronger, and with it the smell of burned flesh.

For the first time I felt real fear, fear for Ange. And with the fear, came certainty. I was sure that when I found that fire, when I found that charred wood and burned flesh, I would find my wagon, and I would find Ange.

Chapter 3

The wire-like brush was thick, and there was no getting through it in my present condition, half naked as I was, without ripping my hide to shreds. What I had to do was seek out a way around and through, and finally I made it. My heart was pounding with slow, heavy beats when at last I came in sight of the burned-out fire.

I had found my wagon, and I had found my mules. But there was no sign of Ange.

The wagon and all that was in it had been burned. The mules, I discovered, had each been shot in the head, then dumped over the cliff one by one. Afterward, somebody had come around and piled brush over the lot, then set fire to it. The killing of those fine big mules hurt me . . . there'd been no better mules west of Missouri, if anywhere.

A fine gray ash had been left by the burning of desert brush. And it was obvious that anything that scattered when the wagon struck bottom had been carefully picked up and thrown on the heap.

Whoever had done this had made a try at wiping out all sign, just as no tracks had been left on the mesa top. Suddenly it occurred to me that whoever had done this might well come back to make sure the destruction had been complete. If they returned and found me, I would be killed, for I was in no shape to defend myself, nor had I any weapon.

For several minutes I stood there, trying to think it out, and studying that heap of charred wood and burned mules, trying to figure out who could have done this, and why.

The destruction was not total, for all the work somebody put to make it so, and in thinking about it I could see why. This had been a hurried job.

Careful to disturb things as little as I might, I worked my way around the fire. A big wagon like that, made of white oak, doesn't burn so easy, in spite of the dryness of the wood. The hubs of the wheels were solid, the wagon bed was strongly made. . . . And then I thought of our secret place.

It was a box hollowed out of a block of six-by-six timber and bolted to the underside of the wagon, and in it we kept a few odds and ends of keepsakes and five gold eagles for emergency money. By lifting a wooden pin inside the wagon-box a section of the bottom lifted out. It made a lid for the box.

The canvas top of the wagon and the bows were gone, of course; the wheels were badly charred but almost intact, the body of the wagon was largely destroyed. Poking around in the mess that remained, I found the box, charred, but still whole. Breaking it open, I found the gold money, but whatever else had been inside was charred to ashes.

Poking around where the grub box had been, I found a can of beans that had tumbled from the box when it busted open, and had rolled down among the rocks. And there was also a charred and partly burned side of bacon. What I had hoped to find was some kind of a weapon—a kitchen knife or anything—but whatever there was must have been buried in the rubble.

There was no telling when the ones who had done this might come back, for they had been bound and determined to destroy all sign of me and my outfit, and I was feeling convinced they would return to make sure the job had been done. I'd been taking care all the time to leave no tracks; now I took a last look around.

There lay the ashes not only of my outfit, but of my hopes as well. Ange and me had planned to start a ranch in the Tonto Basin, and I'd spent most of what I had on that outfit and on the cattle to follow.

It was plain to see from the way things had been piled up that somebody had stood here, carefully putting into the pile everything that was scattered, and it made no sense. In this wild country, who would ever know about what had happened here? Many a man had been murdered and just left for the buzzards, and nobody was the wiser. No, whoever and whatever, they not only wanted me dead, but everything wiped out to leave no slightest trace.

So what did that spell for Ange?

Always she was there in my thoughts, but I kept shoving those thoughts of her to the back of my mind. There was nothing I could do to help her, or even to find her, until I could get a weapon and a horse. To think of her was to be frightened, to let myself waste time in worrying— time that I'd best spend doing something. One thing I'd learned over the years: never to waste time moaning about what couldn't be helped. If a body can do something, fine—he should do it. If he can't, then there's no use fussing about it until he *can* do something.

The day was almost gone. Every move I made was hurting me, and I had to move almighty slow. I wanted to get back to that cave under the stone bridge, but before I'd gone a dozen yards I realized I just didn't have it in me. Like it or not, I was going to have to find somewhere close by, and go without a fire.

The ground was hard and my foot slipped on an icy rock, and I went down. The fall shook me up. It took me a minute or two to get up again. I realized that the cold was growing worse. The river, which had been open water when I'd taken my fall off that lookout point, would be frozen over by now.

Finally, when I was only a hundred yards or so from the ruins of my outfit, I found a place where some slabs of rock had tumbled off the mesa's edge, high above, and in falling had formed a low cave, not over five feet deep and just about large enough for me to curl up inside. There was dead brown grass near the cave, so I tugged on it and pulled enough for ground cover, and I crawled in. And then I just passed out.

In the night, I awakened. My first thought was that of course I knew the names of two of my pursuers. The man who shot me had been called Macon, and then there was Dance, or Dancer. That name had been put to one of the men I'd overheard talking.

I was lying there shivering, when I heard them come back. Only it was not several men, it was only one. The horse came walking along, passing within a few yards of where I lay . . . I could hear the creak of the saddle, and a faint jingle of spurs.

I was too cold and stiff to move, too badly hurt to be of any use to myself. I heard him rousting around in the dark, and once I heard him swear. Then there was a faint glow, and I thought I could detect the crackle of flames. Some little time went by, and finally I must have dozed off again, because when my eyes opened it was daylight.

For a while I just lay still, and then I half-crawled half-rolled out of my hideaway and, using my staff, pushed myself to my feet. It was not until then that I remembered the rider in the nighttime.

Going down to the dim trail, I found his horse's tracks, coming and going. They were sharp, well-defined tracks, made by a horse whose shoes were in good shape. I studied those tracks for a while, and I was not likely to forget them. Then I went back to the wagon.

I saw that he had piled on more brush and lighted it again. Everything was gone now except those black gum hubs for the wheels. They burn mighty hard, and these had only charred over. The fire still smoldered, so I stayed there a few minutes, warming myself.

I didn't need anybody to tell me that I was in bad shape. Somehow I had to get out of that country and get to where I could be cared for, and where I could get a horse and some guns. And then I recalled talk I'd heard of Camp Verde.

Judging by what I'd heard, it could be not much more than thirty miles or so as a crow would fly; but to get there by covering no more than thirty miles a body would surely have to have wings, just like the crow.

None of us Sacketts ever came equipped with wings, and weren't likely to acquire any, judging by the way we lived or the company we kept. The least likely was me, William Tell Sackett, born in the high Cumberland country of Tennessee.

One thing I did know. I wasn't likely to get to Camp Verde by sitting here thinking about it. So I heated that can of beans over what was left of my own wagon's fire, and split the can open with my stone axe. Then I made shift to eat that whole can. After that I took out, walking.

Starved, half-frozen, and sick from the fever of my wounds and lost blood, I made a start. Pa taught us boys there was never to be any quit in us. "You just get goin' an' *try!*" That was what he used to say, and that was all I could do. Somehow or other I had to keep myself alive and cover the forty or more miles it would be to Camp Verde, over the roughest kind of country. I was going as direct as a body could, for I knew the direction, and I didn't have a horse to hunt trails for.

Somehow I got out of Buckhead Canyon, and then I made myself another pair of bark moccasins—I'd already worn through two pair—and crossed over the ridge.

From the top I could see a dim trail going up the hogback leading to the mesa northwest of Buckhead, and that was my direction. It must have been almost a thousand feet from the top of the ridge to the bottom of Pine Canyon, and I did most of it sitting down, sliding or hitching my way along with my hands and one good leg.

The sun was in mid-sky by the time I got down to the bottom of the canyon. And then by crawling up the other ridge I found that trail.

My hands were bleeding again, and I was lightheaded. One side of my brain recognized that fact, just as if it was standing off to one side watching the whole show. But I kept on going, because I hadn't sense enough to lie down and die.

This was an Indian trail, and in this country that meant Apaches, and I knew a good bit about them. Not as much as my brother Tyrel, but I knew a-plenty. I knew if they found me I might as well throw in my hand.

The Apache was a fighting man. He was a warrior, and that was his pride. His reputation was based on how many horses he could steal and how many coups he could count. By the white man's standards this was all wrong, but the Indian had a different way of looking at it. Mercy to your enemy would be evidence of weakness and fear, and the Indian respected only bravery.

He himself had courage, and he had his own viewpoint of honor. I had respect for the Indians. I'd swapped horses with them, fought with them, hunted with them . . . but the last thing I wanted to see now was an Indian.

On top of the mesa, I drank deep and long at Clover Spring, and then I set out again. Time and again I fell down, and each time it was harder to get up, yet each time, somehow, I managed it. Camp Verde, I knew, was off there to the northwest, and it was on the Verde River, or close to it. The only thing I had in mind was to get to the East Verde River—the same one that saved my neck when I fell—and follow it along to the Verde, then follow that north to the Camp.

All my sense of time was gone. Several times I heard myself talking, and once or twice even singing. My feet didn't seem to work the way they should, and walking seemed to mean stumbling and falling and getting up again.

And then all of a sudden I was no longer alone. There was an Apache riding on either side of me.

They rode on past and two more came up. They slowed down, walking their horses. They were lithe, bronzed men, dusty from travel, and some of them carried fresh scalps. They did not speak, they did not make any move toward me, they simply watched me out of their flat black eyes. When I fell down they watched me get up. One Apache laughed when I fell and tried to get up, but that was all.

A mile went behind us. I don't know how many times I fell in that mile, maybe nine or ten times. Each time they waited and let me get up, and I just kept on a-going. The trail finally left the mesa for the East Verde, and the Apaches stayed with me.

When the trail reached the end of Polles Mesa they turned, and one of them rode a horse across in front of me. When I tried to go around him, he backed the horse in front of me again and, sick as I was, delirious as I was, I understood I was a prisoner. One of them pointed with a lance, and I turned north up the gorge.

After maybe a mile we came to a rancheria. All the Apaches came out, women and children, staring at me. I saw them standing there, and then I took another step and my knee just bent over and threw me on my face.

Something in my mind was for an instant clear and sharp, and something said, "Tell, you're through. They will kill you."

And then I passed out. I just faded into a black, pain-filled world that softened around the edges until there was no pain, nothing.

Chapter 4

My eyes had been open for some time before my thoughts fell into place and realization came to me. Over my head was some sort of a brush shelter and I was lying on a couple of deerskins.

Turning my head, I looked down the gentle slope and saw the Apaches. There were six or seven men and twice that many women gathered around a small fire, eating and talking.

It all came back to me then, the Apaches moving up on either side of me, the falling down, the getting up. How long, I wondered, had they followed me?

One of the squaws said something, and a squat, powerfully built Indian got to his feet. He came up the slope, wearing only a headband, breech-clout, and the knee-high moccasins favored by the Apache.

He squatted beside me, gesturing toward my leg, the wound on my skull, and my other injuries. And he made the sign for brave man, holding the left fist in front of the body and striking down past it with the right.

"Friend," I said, "*amigo.*"

He touched the bullet scar on my skull. "Apache?"

"White-eye," I replied, using the term they gave to the white man. And I added, "I will find him."

He nodded, and then said, "You hungry?"

"Yes," I said, and after a moment asked, "How long have I been here?"

He held up three fingers, and added, "We go now."

"To Camp Verde?"

For a minute there I thought he was going to smile. There was a kind of grim humor in his eyes as he shook his head. "No Camp Verde." He waved his hand toward the Mogollons. He studied me carefully. "Soldier at Camp Verde."

He paused while I lay there wondering what was going to happen to me. Would they take me along as a prisoner? Or let me go?

"I need guns," I said, "and a horse. I can get them at Verde."

"You very bad," he said. "You all right now?"

Now that there was a question. To tell the truth, I felt as weak as a cat, but I wasn't telling him that, so I told him I was all right. He stood up suddenly and dropped a buckskin sack beside me and then walked away. What would come now I didn't know, and I was too weak to care. So I closed my eyes for a moment and must have passed right out, because when I opened them again it was cold and dark, and there was no smell of fire, no sound or movement.

Crawling from the deerskin bed where I had been lying, I looked all around. I was alone.

They had cared for me, left me, and gone on about their business. I remembered something Cap Rountree had told me once up in Colorado—that there was no accounting for Indians. Most times, finding a white man alone and helpless as I was, they would have killed him without hesitation, unless he was worth torturing first. It was a good chance that they had followed my trail for miles before they caught up, and they were curious about me. There's nothing an Indian respects more than endurance and courage, and to them that was what I was showing on that trail.

Then I thought of the buckskin sack, and I opened it. My hand, and then a taste, told me it was pinole, so I ate a handful of it and hobbled to the spring to wash it down. When I had eaten another handful or two, I crawled back in my lean-to and went to sleep. When I woke I was ready to go on.

Weak I might be, but I was better off than I had been, and on the fourth day after leaving the Apache rancheria, I made Camp Verde. That day I was on the last of my pinole.

The camp was on the mesa some distance back from the river, and the valley right there was six to seven miles wide. They had a few acres of vegetable garden cultivated, and the place looked almighty good. There was a company of cavalry there, two companies of the Eighth Infantry, and forty Indian scouts under a man named Al Seiber, a powerfully muscled scout who was as much Indian as white man in his thinking.

Well, I was in bad shape, but I made out to walk straight coming up to those soldiers. After all, I'd served through the War Between the States myself, and I didn't figure to shame my service.

Folks came out of tents and stores to look at me as I came in, and I must have looked a sight. I'd thrown away my pine-branch coat, and was wearing those deerskins around my shoulders. What I'd left of my pants wouldn't do to keep a ten-year-old boy from shame.

As I came up, there was a man wearing captain's insignia coming out of the trading post. He was walking with a bull-shouldered man in a buckskin shirt. When the captain saw me he pulled up short.

"Captain," I began, "I—"

"Mr. Seiber," the captain interrupted, and he turned to the man by his side, "see that this man is fed, then bring him to my quarters." After a second glance, he added, "You might find him a shirt and a pair of pants, too."

All of a sudden I felt faint. I half fell against the corner of the building and stayed there a moment. I was like that when a sergeant came out of the store, and I never saw a man look more surprised. *"Tell Sackett!* I'll be damned!"

"Hello, Riley," I said, and then I straightened up and followed off after Al Seiber.

Behind me I heard the captain speak. "Sergeant, do you know that man?"

"Yes, sir. He was in the Sixth Cavalry during the war, and he was a sergeant there at the end, acting in command through several engagements. A sharpshooter, sir, and as fine a horseman as you will be likely to find."

Seiber made me sit down, and he poured a tin cup half full of whiskey. "Drink this, man. You need it."

He rustled around, finding some grub and clothes for me. "Apaches?" he asked.

"White men," I said, and then added, "The only Apaches I saw treated me decent."

"They found you?"

So I told him about it as I ate the food he dished up, and he had me describe the Indian.

"You must be shot with luck," he said. "That sounds like Victorio. He's a coming man among them."

Captain Porter was waiting for me when I walked in, and he waved me to a chair. Beat as I was from the days of travel, my hands just beginning to heal, my head in bad shape, I was still too keyed-up for sleep. The Apaches had treated my wounds, how and with what I had no idea.

Taking as little time as I could, I told him about Ange, the unexpected shot, the burned wagon, and the mules.

"If I can buy a horse," I said, "and maybe a pack mule, I'd like to get myself some guns and go back."

"You must feel that way, I suppose," he said, "but your wife must have been killed . . . murdered, if you will. I understand how you feel; nevertheless, if there are several men against you, as you seem to believe, I am afraid you'll have no success."

He paused. "And that brings me to my problem. I need men. All units here are in need of recruits, and I am allowed six officers. We have only four."

"I was never an officer."

"But you acted in command . . . for how long?"

"It was two or three times. Maybe four or five months in all."

"And the Sixth Cavalry participated in fifty-seven actions during the war, am I right? You must have been in command during some of those actions."

"Yes, sir."

"I could use you, Mr. Sackett. In fact, I need experienced men very badly, particularly those who have done some Indian fighting. You have, I presume?"

"Yes, sir. But I have to go back to the Tonto. My wife is back there, Captain."

We talked for almost an hour, and by then I was beginning to feel everything that had happened to me. The three days in the Apache *rancheria* had helped to bring me out of it, but sitting there listening to the captain talking of old wars and far-off places, I suddenly knew I was a long way from being ready for a fight. And yet there could be no delay. Even now Ange might be somewhere needing help, needing me.

"Are there any new outfits in the country?" I asked him abruptly.

He looked at me sharply, and I thought his face stiffened a little. "Yes, Mr. Sackett, there are. Three or four, I think. All of them big, all of them recently come into the Territory." He paused. "And all of them owned by honorable men."

"That may be, Captain Porter, but one of them saw fit to burn my outfit and try to murder me."

"Perhaps."

"Perhaps? I was there . . . I lived through it."

"Of course. But what can you prove against anyone? You would have to have proof, Mr. Sackett." He hesitated again. "In a court of law—"

"Captain, I'll find the man. I'll find proof before I act, but when I act I'll be my own law." I stopped him before he could interrupt. "Captain, nobody has more respect for the law than I. We boys were raised up to respect it, but there's no law in the Territory that can reach a big cattleman, and you know it. Not even the Army."

"Mr. Sackett, I must warn you not to take the law into your own hands."

"What would you do, sir?"

He shot me a quick, hard look. "You must do as I say, Mr. Sackett, not as I might if I were in your place." And then he asked, "Why do you suppose they tried to kill you? Why do you suppose your outfit was destroyed?"

"That's what puzzles me, Captain. I just don't know."

He walked to the window and stood there with his hands clasped behind his back. "Was your wife a pretty woman, Mr. Sackett?"

There it was, what had been worrying me all the time, but it was the thing I wouldn't let myself face.

"She was beautiful, Captain, and this isn't just what a man in love would say. She was really, genuinely beautiful. All my brothers would tell you the same. Tyrel, he—"

Porter turned around sharply. "*Tyrel Sackett?*" He was startled. "Tyrel Sackett, the Mora gunfighter, is your *brother?*"

"Yes, sir."

"That would mean that Orrin Sackett is your brother too."

"Yes."

"Orrin Sackett," Captain Porter said, "helped us get a bill introduced in the House. He is a very able man, and a good friend of mine."

"And mighty near as good with a gun as Tyrel, when he wants to be."

He returned to Ange. "Mr. Sackett, I do not wish to offend, but how were things between you and Mrs. Sackett?"

"Couldn't be better, sir. We were very much in love." Right there I told him something of how we met, high in the mountains of Colorado. "If you are suggesting she might have left me, you can think again."

He smiled. "Never, Mr. Sackett. The woman who would leave you would certainly not destroy her wagon or those valuable mules, and you have told me of the money . . . she would have taken that. No, what I was thinking of was something else.

"Your wife," he went on, "was an attractive woman, and she was alone. This is a country where there are few women, fewer beautiful women."

"Captain, it just doesn't figure. You know how western folks feel about molesting a woman. Nobody'd be fool enough—"

"Suppose he did not stop to think until too late?" Porter walked over to me. "He would have been wild with panic. He would have been desperate to cover up, to remove any possibility of what he had done ever being discovered."

"What about those men hunting me?"

"When you find them I think you will discover they were looking for you for some other reason. I think one man—someone able to command others—is responsible, and only he or they know the real reason you are to be killed."

Of course, it made sense. Also it meant that Ange was dead, and that her death must have been ugly. Suddenly all the fury that was in me came welling up inside until I was almost blind with it. I stood there, my head down, my whole body shaking with it. Inside me there was only one thing left, a terrible will to destroy, to kill.

After a moment I looked up. "Captain, I got to have some rest."

"Al Seiber will take care of you." Porter paused. "Sackett, this conversation is between us. If it is ever mentioned I shall deny that it ever took place. However, in the morning you will have a horse and a mule at your disposal, and I shall speak to Mr. Seiber about the guns."

"I have money. I can buy them."

He nodded. "Of course. But you will want good weapons, and I am afraid what you would find at the sutler's . . . at the trading post . . . would not be adequate."

When I stepped outside, he stood in the doorway. It was dark now, and he stood there framed against the light. "Remember, my offer holds. If you want to join up, return here. I am sure I can arrange for your old rank, perhaps for a commission."

After the door closed I stood there awhile alone in the darkness. The stars were bright in the desert sky, the night was cold . . . and Ange, my Ange, was dead.

Suddenly I knew she must be dead, and that all Captain Porter had suggested was true. The chances were her body lay somewhere not far from that wagon.

I was going back to look, to give her a decent burial. And then I was going to hunt a man.

It was a long time before I knew what happened inside that building after I left it . . . a long, long time.

Captain Porter went to his table and took out a sheet of paper. He put down the place and the date, and then he wrote out a letter and addressed it, a letter that would be in the mail before I ever left the post.

And that letter was to make all the difference to me. Whether it was to be life or death for me was decided by that cavalry captain putting pen to paper in his quiet quarters that night at Camp Verde . . . but that is another story.

Chapter 5

One thing I'd learned a long time back. When traveling in enemy country, never return by the same trail you used in going out . . . they may be laying for you.

Al Seiber told me of an Indian trail that left the Verde at the big bend below Fossil Creek, so I took it and rode across the top of Hardscrabble Mesa and made camp at Oak Spring.

My hands were only partly healed. I could use a rifle well enough, but would hesitate to draw a Colt against anybody. It was two weeks since I'd taken my fall, and I was still in bad shape, but I could wait no longer. Right now I was no more than two miles from Buckhead Mesa and the canyon where the ruins of my wagon lay.

Two to three miles away to the north there was a Mormon settlement—not a town, just a bunch of folks settled in there who had come down from Utah . . . or so I supposed.

From all I'd heard they were God-fearing folk, and it was there I planned to go when I needed supplies, and it was also where I hoped to get information. For the present what I needed was rest, for I tired easily, and I was still in no condition for what lay ahead.

Oak Spring was a good hide-out. It lay in a canyon, and I'd seen no tracks on the Indian trail leading in here. My good treatment by Victorio, if that was who it was, would mean nothing if I met other Apaches, and the Tontos were some of the worst of the lot.

Over a hatful of fire I made coffee and a good meal, for I had a feeling the meals ahead would be few and far between. At daybreak, back in the saddle, I rode over the mesa, crossed Pine Creek above the canyon and rode back onto Buckhead Mesa.

There were plenty of tracks, most of them at best a week old, all well-shod horses like you'd find on a well-run cow outfit. Nowhere was there the slightest sign there had ever been a wagon on this mesa.

When I reached the site of the burned wagon I got a surprise. Aside from some blackened brush there was no sign there had ever been a wagon here, or a fire. Somebody had done a piece of hard work, doing away with all trace of what had happened. Even the hubs were gone, dragged off somewhere and buried, I figured.

After scouting around and finding nothing, I rode back to where the wagon had been. All the time I was riding with the rifle across my saddle-bows, and keeping a wary eye for riders. I was alone, and how many enemies I had against me I didn't know, but my life wasn't worth a plugged two-bit piece if they found me.

Sitting there by that fire, I was a mighty lonesome man, my heart a-hurting something awful for thoughts of Ange. I'd long been a lonely man before I saw her, and nobody ever had a truer, finer wife.

Being the oldest of the Sacketts, I was first out of the nest when trouble came, and off I'd gone to the war. We were Tennessee folk from the high-up hills, but we had no truck with slavery or looking down the nose at any man. Many a man in my part of the country fought for the South, but while my heart was with her, my head was not, and I rode north to join the Union.

Leaving slavery aside, it was that I was fighting for—the Union. This was my country, and like Sacketts and their kinfolk for many a year, I was ready to take up my rifle and trail it off to the fightin'. Besides, none of us Sacketts were ever much on missing out on a fight. It was just in us to step in and let fly.

So I joined the Sixth Cavalry in Ohio and rode through the war with them, and then when it was over I started west to seek out my fortune, wherever it should take me.

Tyrel and Orrin had already gone, leaving about the time of the war's end, or just after. They'd gone west seeking a home for Ma, and they found it, and meanwhile Tyrel had won him a name with his shooting and had become a lawman. Orrin, he studied law and had been elected to office.

Here I was with nothing. Ange and me, we had us a gold mine in the high-up Colorado mountains, but getting the gold out was not easy, and we'd have only a couple of months each year in which to work. I'd brought some out, but what I really wanted was a ranch of my own. With what gold I had, I bought some stock and my outfit and we headed west for the Tonto Basin. Now Ange was gone, and my outfit was wiped out, and me . . . I was a hunted man, sought after by Lord only knew how many. And not a friend to side me but my Colt and Winchester.

Not that there weren't plenty of Sacketts around the country, and we were a feudin' and a fightin' family, but they were scattered wide and far, and no chance for any help to me. There was Lando, Falcon, Tyrel, Orrin, and many another of our name, and all good men.

After I'd put out my fire, I crawled into the place under the trees close to my horse, and there I stretched out my tired body and closed my eyes in sleep.

The sun was high when I rolled out and led the horse to water. Then I left him on a small patch of grass whilst I made coffee and chewed on some jerky. I had a restless, irritable feeling, and I knew what it was. Being a man slow to anger, and one who can fight his anger back for a while, I knew it was working up to a point where all hell would tear loose . . . and that's no good.

That was the morning I found Ange.

It was only a few rods from where the wagon had been left, and I was scouting around when I saw that crack in the rock. For a moment I stood there, fear climbing up inside me, for all the while my feelings had been fighting against reason, telling me that Ange was still alive, that Ange had somehow gotten away, and that I'd find her.

That crack was no different from others. It was a place where the rocky edge of the mesa had started to break off, and this crack had broken far back into the table rock of the mesa. After a minute I walked over there. Somebody had scooped dirt in there and heaped rock and brush around it. The job had been done in a tearing hurry. Under the brush and the debris, I found Ange.

She had been strangled, but not before she had put up a terrific fight. Her fingernails were stained dark with blood, and there was flesh under them. She had fought, and she had gouged deep.

The bitter cold had left her just as she had been, but I could not bear to look at her face. After what seemed a long time, I got my blanket and wrapped her in it. Then I rode down to where the fire had been; for one thing I'd seen left behind was my shovel. The killer had used it in controlling the fire, and thrown it aside and forgotten it.

Up on the mesa I found a place where the earth was deep and I dug a grave for her, and I buried her there. When it was over I covered the grave with rocks, and then went to work with my new bowie knife and cut a cross for her. Using the heated edge of the shovel, I burned words into this crude cross.

HERE LIES
ANGE SACKETT
MURDERED NEAR THIS SPOT
APRIL 25, 1877

Now whoever had done this would have no doubts. They would know I was alive. But those others, the ones who were hunting me who might not know the truth, they would know it now.

Then I checked my guns again, and mounting up, I rode down off the mesa.

Now the chips were down. They would be hunting me, but I would be hunting them too, and there was no mercy in me. There was only the desire to hunt them down on their bloody trail, and give them a chance to try killing somebody who was not a woman alone.

There wasn't much to Globe in those days, just a few shacks, cabins, and tents scattered along the bank of Pinal Creek. And there were three saloons. I rode up to the first one and swung down, and I saw folks a-looking at me.

Being taller than most, standing six foot three in my socks and somewhat more in boots, I'm accustomed to folks looking at me. But maybe this time there was something else.

In the saloon there were maybe seven or eight men, and I looked around at them. "I'll buy a drink," I said. "I'll buy a drink for the house."

Some of them hesitated, but not for long. A square-jawed man studied me a moment, took up his glass, and looked across it at me. "You aren't celebrating, friend."

"I'm hunting information. I'm looking for a cow outfit that had some hands working the Mogollon country a couple of weeks ago."

Nobody said anything, and finally the man next to me said, "What's the trouble, mister?"

"It's an outfit that has a couple of hands workin' for them named Macon and Dancer."

"You take my advice"—it was a stocky, swarthy-looking man who spoke —"you'll fork that horse of yours and ride out of here."

"I wasn't asking for advice."

The swarthy man grinned at me, but it wasn't friendly. "Why, you damned fool! Macon is the saltiest man with a gun in this country."

"You called me a damned fool."

He put down his glass. "So?"

He was expecting me to reach for my gun, but I couldn't trust my grip, not yet, anyway. So I hit him.

He was almost as tall as me and somewhat heavier—by twenty pounds, maybe. But that first punch counts for a lot, and I meant it to. My left fist smashed him in the teeth, and my right came around and clobbered him on the ear. That ear split and blood started to flow, and he was clawing for a gun, so I reached in and grabbed his belt, jerked him toward me, and then threw him back. He hit the wall with a thud, and when he started to come at me again I gave him a taste of my knuckles in the mouth again, and then both fists in the stomach. He folded up and went down, and I kicked his gun away.

"You talk to me again," I said, "you call me mister."

Then I walked back to the bar and took up my drink.

"That cow outfit," the square-jawed man said, "why are you hunting them?"

The man I'd clobbered was slowly getting off the floor, so I shucked my gun. I couldn't trust myself to draw fast, although I could do all right once it was out. So I just taken it out and held the gun on him and I said, "If you're a friend of Macon's, tell him he didn't kill me the first time. And tell him the next time I'll be looking right at him."

The square-jawed man looked at me from cold, steady eyes. "Are you implying that Sonora Macon shot you in the *back*?"

With my left hand I removed my hat. They could all see the livid bullet scar, still fresh, with the hair shaved back by the Army surgeon. "I wouldn't know him if I saw him, but he knew my back. He shot me off a cliff up on Buckhead Mesa."

"That's hard to believe."

"You can believe it." I tossed off the rest of my drink and stepped back from the bar. "You can tell them, any of them you see, that I'm hunting them.

"They ran me ragged when I was hurt and unarmed, they ran me all over that country. But now I'll be running them. You tell any man of that outfit they can fight or hunt a hole, but I'm coming for them."

"You talk large, stranger."

"Anyone that doubts me," I said, "can come asking."

"That outfit has forty men, forty very tough men. Forty good men."

"Good men? Mister, one or more of those men murdered my wife, killed my mules, burned my wagon."

"Killed your *wife*?"

Now there was quiet in the room. Men looked at me, glasses in their hands, all movement stilled by what I had said.

"I left my wife at my wagon and went scouting a way down off Buckhead. Somebody shot at me an hour or so later, then they hunted for my body. I heard them. I heard the names of Macon and Dancer.

"My wife was a good girl. She was strangled, mister, and whoever did it wears her marks on his face. There was blood and torn flesh under her fingernails.

"Then he killed my mules, burned my wagon and the mules, and tried to wipe out all trace of what he had done. He murdered my wife on the twenty-fifth of last month. Mister, there weren't too many men in that part of the country at that time. So I'll find them."

There was a mutter of anger from the men in the room. The square-jawed man's face was white and stiff, but he did not speak. He turned back to the bar. "I'll have another drink," he said thickly.

The bartender rested his hands on the bar. "Anybody who would murder a woman is a no-good skunk. I'll lend a hand with the rope, mister."

One of them spoke up. "Who might you be, mister? We don't know you."

"I am Tell Sackett," I said, "William Tell Sackett, of Tennessee, Colorado, and a lot of other places."

"You related to the Mora gunfighter?"

"Brother. I taught him to shoot. Although," I added, "he done all right when he taken it up."

The man beside me finished his drink, turned away from the bar, and went outside.

"Who might he be?" somebody asked.

"Cattleman, I guess," another answered. "He's a stranger to me."

Nobody said anything more for a while. Presently the bartender said, "You eaten tonight, mister? You set down over at the table, and I'll fix you up."

Suddenly I was awful tired. My strength was coming back, but that short fight had been too much, too soon. So I leathered my gun and walked over to the table and dropped into a chair.

The bartender brought me food and a pot of coffee, and I thanked him. I ate and drank, but all the while I was thinking of Ange, and away down inside me something burned like a cold fire.

It gnawed away at my insides until there was nothing else in me, nothing to think of, nothing to dream of . . . only the man I wanted to find, the man I wanted to kill.

Man . . . or men . . . There might have been more than one.

Chapter 6

When I'd eaten my fill and drunk my coffee I went outside and stood where the wind came down the draw. It was a wild night, with clouds racing down the long black sky, lighted weirdly by a hiding moon. I stood there alone on what passed for a street, and felt the loneliness and the pain tearing at me.

Angel . . . . Ange had died horribly and alone, attacked while waiting for me, and never a chance at life, for she had spent her years so much alone before I found her high in those Colorado mountains.

Ange, who was beautiful and tender and thoughtful, who could not bear to see nothing suffer, and who was always thinking of what she could do for me to make my life a happier thing. And little enough of happiness had come my way until Ange came.

Now she was gone, and the thought of it was almost too much for me.

Deep down within me an awful rage was burning. I banked the fires of it and waited, knowing my time would come. My horse turned his head and looked at me in a woe-begone manner, for the wind was cold and the night was late, so I went over to him and, taking my Winchester from the scabbard, I stepped into the saddle and walked him down the empty street where dry leaves blew, and the dust.

There was no livery stable in town, only a corral with a few horses standing, tails to the wind. Some boulders and the wall of the mountain made a partial break. So I stripped the leather from him and put it under a little shelter built for the purpose, and then I rubbed him all over with handfuls of grass and turned him into the corral, first standing by while he ate a bit of corn from the sack I carried. It was a small sack, but there was enough to give him the extra something he might need for a long stretch of hard going.

Turning away from the corral, I looked toward the lighted windows. It was late, and this was an early rising town, so it was early to bed. Only a few lights remained, the lights of folks I did not know.

How many such towns had I been in? A lone-riding man is a stranger wherever he goes, and so it had been for me until I met Ange, and so it was again.

There was a bit of a gully where run-off water had cut into the ground, and three times I'd taken care to step over it; but now, so filled I was by my own sorrow, I forgot it. Starting back toward the town I stepped off quickly, put a foot into that ditch, and fell flat on my face . . . and it saved my life.

When I hit the ground there was the roar of a shot in my ears, and then silence. Me, I just never moved. I lay there quiet, waiting and listening. Whoever had shot at me must have figured I was a dead duck, because he just let me lay. After several minutes had passed and I heard no further sound, I eased myself past the corner of the corral and crouched there, waiting. If anybody was going to risk a first move, it was not going to be me.

After some more time I began to feel sure that my unseen attacker had slipped away quietly and was no longer around. But that was a risk I was not prepared to chance. I backed up and got into some brush at the edge of town and circled wide around until I got back to the saloon. No other place in town had a light.

I pushed open the door and stepped in. There were three men inside.

The bartender looked up at me, and then his eyes sort of slipped over to the man at the end of the bar. Not that I mean that bartender was telling me anything, just that he naturally looked toward that man—probably because that man had come in last.

He was a tall man, but on the slender side, with a narrow, tough face.

Walking up to the bar, I held my Winchester in my right hand, and put my left on the bar. "I'll have rye," I said, and then under cover of the bar, I tilted my rifle muzzle past the corner of the bar and within inches of the tall man's heart. And I held it there.

Nobody could see what my gun hand was doing, but when I took up my drink I looked over at this gent and said, "Somebody took a shot at me out by the corral."

Now, I didn't make a thing of it, I just said it mildly, looking at him. But there was another thing I'd noticed. That man had mud on his boot heels, and the only mud I knew of was alongside the corral where the water trough stood.

He looked right at me. "Wasn't me," he said, "or I'd have killed you."

"I think it was you," I said. "You've got mud on your heels."

His fingers had been resting on the edge of the bar and when his hand dropped for his gun, I squeezed the trigger on my rifle.

That .44 slug knocked him back and turned him half around. I jacked another shell into the chamber and stepped around after him.

He was still standing, but he sort of backed up, going to the wall, and I cat-footed it after him. "Were you one of them that killed my wife?"

He stared at me, looking genuinely puzzled. "Wife? Hell, no. I . . . I . . . you tried to kill the boss. Back in the . . . Mogollons." His words came slowly, and his eyes were glazing.

"He lied to you. You're dying for nothing. Who is your boss?"

He just looked at me, but he never answered, nor tried to answer.

When I faced around to the others, the bartender had both hands resting on the bar in plain sight, and the others the same.

"You took advantage," one of them said.

"Mister," I replied, "my wife was murdered. She was strangled trying to defend herself. My wagon was burned, my mules killed, and forty men spent a week or more combing the mountains to kill me. One of them shot me in the back of the head. I'll play this the way they started it. Wherever they are, whoever they are, they got to kill me, light out of the country, or they'll die—wherever and whenever I find them."

The man gave me a cynical look. "I've heard talkers before."

"Mister, the last feud my family taken part in lasted seventy years. The last Higgins died with his gun in his hand, but he died."

Nobody said anything, so I asked, "Who did he work for?"

They just looked at me. My troubles were my own, and they wanted no part of them, nor could I lay blame to them for it. They were family men and townies, and I had come in out of wild country, and was a stranger to them.

"You might take a look at his horse," the bartender said. "There's likely to be only two at the hitch rail, yours and his."

There had been another horse at the rail when I tied mine, so I turned to the door and started through. A rifle bullet smashed splinters from the door jamb within inches of my face, and I threw myself out and down, rolling swiftly into the shadows with a second bullet furrowing the boardwalk right at my side.

In the darkness I rolled back and up to one knee, and I settled myself for a good shot. But nothing happened, nor was there any movement out in the darkness. Two frame buildings and a tent with a floor were just across the street from me; there was also a lot of brush close by, and another corral. I stayed still for several minutes, and then I suddenly thought of that other horse. I went to look, but he was gone.

The horse had been taken away before I came out to the street, but after I had killed the rider in the saloon. And then somebody had waited for me, shooting from the darkness across the street.

Back inside the saloon, the two townsmen were gone . . . through the back door, no doubt. The bartender was wiping off the bar, taking a lot of time at it.

A pot of coffee stood on the stove and a rack of cups was behind the bar. I picked up a cup, and filled it from the pot on the stove. The place I selected to stand was out of line of any doors and windows.

"I got to do some contemplating about you," I said to the bartender.

He straightened up and gave me a slow, careful look. "About me?"

"You mentioned that horse in the corral. When I stepped to the door I nearly got myself killed."

"If you think I'd set you up—" he began.

"I do think you might if you had reason enough. Now I got to decide what stake you have in this."

He came across to me. "Mister, my name is Bob O'Leary, and I've tended bar from Dodge to Deadwood, from Tombstone to San Antone. You ask anybody, and they'll tell you I'm a man of my word. I've done a few things here and there, and I ain't sayin' what they might be, but I never murdered no woman, nor had anything to do with those that would. Like I told you, you find your man, or men, and I'll lend a hand with the rope . . . no matter who they be."

"All right, Mr. Bob O'Leary, for the time being I'll take your word for it. All I'll say is your timing was right."

"Nobody needs timing for you, Sackett. You give it some thought, and you'll see your number is up. You stand to be somebody's favorite target.

"Put yourself in his place. Suppose somebody who can command a lot of men did murder your wife. What's he doin' now? I'll tell you. He's scared . . . he's scared to death. He's not only scared of you, he's scared of what his own men will believe.

"He's told them a story. He's told them, judging by what that puncher said this evening, that you tried to kill him. They accepted that story. They are all trying to kill you, and you'll have to admit it's more exciting than punching cows.

"Only now you're talking. You're telling a different story, and he's got to shut you up fast.

"Look at it this way," he went on. "That man is riding through the rough country alone. He sees your wife waiting in that wagon. She's a young, pretty woman. Maybe he hasn't seen any kind of a woman in weeks . . . maybe months. He talks to her, he makes advances and she turns him down. He gets too brassy about it and they start to fight. Upshot is, he kills her. Chances are he had no mind to do such a thing when it all started, but now where is he?

"Mr. Sackett, you got you a scared man. He knows how western folks feel about women. He knows some of his own men would pull on the rope if they knew what he had done. He's sweating with being scared, so he dumps your wagon off a cliff into a place where he doesn't think it will ever be found.

"He's all scratched up, so he calls in some of his hands and tells them you tried to kill him, and he wants you dead. He probably offers a good price, but he wouldn't need to, for riders are loyal—they ride for the brand."

Well, I was listening to all he said. This O'Leary seemed to have it pegged right.

Now he was saying, "He hurries back, he wipes out all the tracks, he goes down and sets fire to your outfit, making sure the wind will take the smoke away from the hunting party. He not only has to wipe out any trace of your outfit, he has to be able to convince anybody that you were just a drifter."

He refilled my cup. "Sackett, let me tell you something. I don't know who he rides for, but I know this Dancer. He used to come up the trail to Dodge, and he's square. He's a tough man, but he's one to ride the river with."

O'Leary stood there, holding the coffeepot. All the lights in the room were out but one. There was a lamp burning with a reflector behind it, just back of the bar. The light threw dark shadows into the hollows of O'Leary's cheeks.

"I'll tell you something else. He's got Sonora Macon, who is as fast with a gun as any of them, and he's got Al Zabrisky and Rafe Romero . . . and any one of them would just as soon kill you as not, no matter who you are or what you've done or not done."

I got up and taken my rifle from the table beside me. O'Leary, he went over to the light, cupped one hand at the top of the globe, and then blew into it. The light went out, and the room was in darkness.

"All right, Sackett," he said, "you can go when you are ready."

At the door I stopped. "Thanks," I said, and then I asked, "you don't think I've got a chance, do you?"

"I was always a sucker for lost causes," O'Leary said. "But no—to be honest, I don't think you've got a Chinaman's chance . . . not with all that outfit against you."

The wind was making up, and dust skittered down the street. It was long past midnight, and the town was dark and silent. When I stepped to the saddle, my horse turned willingly away.

There was no sound but the clop-clop of my horse's hoofs as I rode past the last building and away from town toward the mountains. Avoiding the trails, I took to the mountain slopes and rode away up under the trees. When I was a few miles out, I unsaddled, picketed my horse, and pulled off my boots. Sitting there on my blanket, I rubbed my tired feet and wondered how a man's life could get him into such a spot.

Three weeks back I had me a lovely wife, a brand-new outfit, and I was driving west to settle. Now I had nothing, and was a hunted man.

With my head against my saddle, I leaned back and looked up at the stars I could make out through the pine tops. Right then I found myself wishing I wasn't alone. I kept thinking back to Tyrel and Orrin, wishing for them to be here with me. With those two brothers to side me, I'd tackle hell with a bucket of water.

Sometime about there I dozed off, and in my dreams I was wandering the Tennessee hills again, just as when a boy I had gone picking pods from the honey-locust trees for the making of metheglin, or hunting the wild hogs that ran free along the ridges. In my dreams, there was Ma in her old rocker, a-watching us boys as we worked in the fields, thinking of Pa, she probably was, who had gone off to the westward many a year before. Gone with the mountain men, with Carson, Bridger, Joe Meek, Isaac Rose, and John Coulter.

The long riding had taken it out of me and left my bones with an ache and my muscles sagging with weariness. I was so tired that I slept sound . . . and then a boot toe took me in the ribs and I was awake, and knew I had awakened too late.

When I looked up, I looked into the blackness of three rifle muzzles, aimed at my head. Three hard men stood over me, no mercy in their eyes.

Chapter 7

Oh, they had me all right! Dead to rights, and not a chance to fight back, for even if I could knock one rifle aside, the others would kill me for sure. Yet there was no give in me, for I'd nothing left to lose.

So I lay there without moving or giving them excuse to shoot, and then when I did move it was to lift my hands slowly and clasp them behind my head.

"Cigar in my vest pocket. I'd like to light it," I said.

"Have at it." The speaker was a square-shouldered, well-set-up man of twenty-four or -five. "I'd give any dog a chance for a last smoke."

"If you didn't have that gun on me you'd not call me that. Courage comes cheap when you've got a man hog-tied."

He started to reply, then shut up, but he was mad, I could see that. So I taken my time with the cigar, thinking hard all the while. They looked to be good, solid men.

"You don't look like men who'd murder a woman," I said.

You would have thought I'd laid across them with a whip. *"What's that?* What d'you mean . . . who murdered a woman?"

"Your outfit," I said, "maybe some of you. You murdered my wife, and burned everything I had. Now you want to kill me so there won't be anybody to ask questions. That wraps it up, all nice and pretty." I looked up at them. "Except you yellow-bellies will have to live with it the rest of your days."

One of them jerked his rifle up to smash the butt into my face, and if he tried that they were going to have to kill me quick. One of the others held up a hand to stop him . . . and me, for he saw what was coming.

From the way the others reacted I knew I'd hit a nerve, and I waited.

"What's all this about a murdered woman?"

"Who you tryin' to buffalo?" I put all the contempt I had into it. "You know damn' well there ain't five men within a hundred miles, leaving your outfit out of it, who wouldn't pull the rope on a woman-killer. And this was my wife, one of the prettiest, finest women alive."

Well, sir, they just looked at me, but I had them. They were learning something they hadn't known, but maybe what I was saying was answering questions they had been asking themselves.

"I'm Tell Sackett," I said, "and there's places where the name carries weight. I drove in here with a wagon and some fine mules. I drove in with a few head of cattle and a herd following after, and I drove with my wife beside me.

"We hadn't been married but a few months. Sort of a honeymoon, it was. I left her a-setting in our wagon atop Buckhead Mesa and rode off to find a way into Tonto Basin.

"When I was standing on the rim of the mesa above the river, somebody shot me off that mesa and I bounced off rocks and brush all the way down.

"You can see where the bullet struck." I touched the scar on my skull. "I was some stove up, and when I finally got back to where I'd left my outfit it was gone . . . and so were all the tracks."

Lying there smoking, I talked as I never talked before. I told them of finding my wagon, finding the mules, and afterwards finding Ange. Of the burning, too, and how when I came back again there had been more burning, and even most of the ashes gone. It hurt, talking of Ange, but I kept on.

"Somebody, the man who started you boys on the hunt for me, he killed my wife. And he carries her marks on him. . . . I saw the blood and flesh under her nails. That somebody is purely scared right now. He's got to have me dead, or folks will find out what happened.

"I don't figure," I added, "that he ever expected you to talk to me. I'm laying five to one you were told to shoot me on sight."

Right then I pushed my luck. I knew I had them off balance and trying to figure it out, so I just naturally got up, put on my hat, and then reached for my gun belt.

"Lay off that!" It was that blocky-built puncher again, but I just paid him no mind.

"Go ahead," I said. "A shot at an unarmed man is just what I'd expect of a woman-killer's outfit."

He was white-mad, but like I figured, these men were decent enough. I'd punched cows with a lot like them—good, hard-working men ready for a wild time in town or a shooting fight, but decent men. He didn't shoot, and I slung that belt around me and stood there an armed man, prepared to take my chances with whatever happened.

I'd pushed my luck right out of a corner and into a place where I had a break, anyway. But I wasn't about to stand back and wait.

"You boys were set on me, and you been hunting me high and low. Up to now I don't hold it against you, because you were told some tale to start you. Now you know the truth, and if you keep on a-chasing me, I'm going to start chasing back."

They weren't even listening to what I was saying. One of them turned right around on me. "Was what you said about your wife true?"

"I raised a marker over her grave, and if we were to hunt long enough we could find pieces of that wagon. And I can take you to folks in Globe and away east who knew us and saw us headed west."

"You were in Globe?"

"My wife and me, we spent two days and nights in that town just three weeks ago come Sunday."

They swapped looks, and I could see that meant something to them, but I wasn't sure what. That tough young puncher, he all of a sudden stood his rifle down and dug into his shirt pocket for the makings. "I don't know about you fellers," he said, "but I've got a feelin' I'd be better off in Texas."

A thought came to me. "About Globe, now. Were you boys in that town three weeks ago?"

"Yeah . . . the whole shootin' outfit. We spent several days there. Fact is, we were supposed to stay longer, but then we got orders to move out, sudden-like, on Monday morning."

That had been the morning we left. . . . Suddenly I was remembering three men who had ridden past our wagon, and one of them had turned to look back at Ange.

The same man had been buying supplies at the same time we were. I tried to place him, but all I could remember was that he was a big man.

Well, I was hungry, and a man isn't going to go far on an empty stomach. Not that I hadn't put miles behind me without food, but right now I had it with me to cook, and I was hungry as a Panhandle coyote. So I put coffee water on the fire and said, "You boys might as well set up. You got something to think about, and this here's as good a place as any."

They moved up to the fire, and I went rousting through my duffle, getting out the bacon and the rest. Then I looked around at them and asked, innocent-like, "Who d'you boys ride for?"

They just looked at me. They might not like what I'd told them, but they weren't going to sell out their boss. They were good men. Only they didn't need to tell me, and maybe they thought of that, too. All I had to do was look past them at the brands on their horses—a capital A lying on its side . . . *Lazy A.*

There had been cattle with that brand in some of the country I'd ridden through, and there had been a horse of that brand at the hitch rail of the saloon when I first rode up to Globe after leaving Camp Verde.

A cattleman or any rider in range country just naturally notices any brand he sees on the stock along the way. He has cattle on his mind, and brands are one of the biggest parts of his job.

Over coffee one of these gents suddenly said, "We got no call to believe what you said, only something about this here has a smell we don't like. You don't size up like any dry-gulching killer. I got a feelin' you been talking truth."

"All I ask," I said, "is not to stand in my way."

"There's some that will."

Evidently they had no news from Globe, so I decided to let them have it, and now. "One tried," I said, "last night down to Globe."

I told them about it, and when I finished they sat still for a moment or two, and then one of them said, "I mind that gully."

"Andersen," another said, "Curly Andersen."

"He was close on to bald."

"I know. That's why we called him Curly. Well, maybe he would try it that way. You beat him to the draw?"

"Mister," I said, "when it comes to fighting, a body makes up his own rules with me. I'll fight him fair as long as he shows himself of a like mind. This Curly Andersen tried to ambush me, so he laid out the rules and I played according."

Reaching for the pot, I filled my cup, then the cups of the others.

"Only maybe he figured *I'd* made the rules. He said I'd tried to ambush his boss back in the Mogollons. Anyway, he drew cards in a tough game."

When they had gone, I saddled up and rode out of there, making it a policy never to stay too long in one place when I knew I had enemies, and especially when they had me located.

All the time I was keeping my thoughts away from Ange. Whenever she came to mind I felt a vast, aching emptiness inside me, and a loneliness such as not even I had ever known.

Three days passed, three days of riding and resting, three days of prowling like a lonely wolf, pushing my horse down old trails and finding new ones through rock and brush and butte. And all the while I was working out the trails of those who hunted me, and of the Lazy A cattle, slowly tracing out the maze they made to find my way to their headquarters.

It was a high and lovely country. I rode through broken land crested and ridged with pines, with beautiful meadows and streams that rushed along over stones with a happy chuckling sound. Cold water it was, from fresh-melted snow.

My strength was building back, and I took good care to give my horses rest and to stake them each night on good grass. Each time I made myself a fire I ate at that spot, and then moved on for a mile or two, camping in some unlikely place, and wiping away all traces of my camp when I left. And every day I varied my way of going, wanting to weave no pattern they could read.

More and more I was finding horse tracks, and I knew I was getting closer. My enemy had men beside him, and I rode alone. My enemy had spare horses, and many eyes with which to seek me out, and I had only two. But there was Indian in my nature if not in my blood, and I hunted my way across country like a ghost, only the butt of that Colt was near my hand, and my rifle ready for use. Sometimes I made dry camp, chewing on jerky or a crust of bread, and always I avoided human beings.

It was a month to the day of the time Ange had been killed when I saw the strange rider.

The weather had turned bad, and I had found a deep hollow under an overhang near the top of the ridge that divided Cibecue Creek from Carrizo Creek. It was wild and lonely here, with only the ghost of an old trail along the ridge that showed no signs of travel, none at all. The trail might have been made a hundred years ago, judging by its vagueness. But in arid country, or even on the lonely ridges in forested country, such trails, used long ago by Indians, seem to last forever.

Thunder rumbled above the rim, dark now with forest and with the impending storm, and a few scattering drops of cold rain fell. The shelter I had was good, although higher on the ridge than I liked, even though the rim towered almost a thousand feet higher three or four miles to the north.

A man riding wild country never stops looking for camping spots. If he doesn't use them at the time, he may next week or next year, or five years later. It is one of those unconscious things a body takes to when riding free of towns and ranches.

The place I'd found was deep under the overhang, masked by some brush, and I'd heaved a couple of rock slabs up to make added shelter. My horse couldn't get into it, but I found him a place under the trees where intersecting branches made cover of a kind.

Before me the ground broke away into the canyon of the Carrizo, and as I looked down the canyon I saw the rider, who drew rein, turned in the saddle, and looked carefully around, like a man who is lost.

I could guess what happened, and it didn't take a lot of figuring. That rider had mistaken the Carrizo for the Cibecue, for back up where the two canyons headed up they weren't more than a couple of miles apart, maybe even less. And there was one branch of the Cibecue that began only a couple of hundred yards from the Carrizo. Somebody not used to the country might easily mistake the one for the other.

That rider was in trouble, for the two canyons ran parallel to each other for only a few miles, and the further down the canyon he rode . . . no, *she* rode, for by that time I was positive the rider was a woman . . . the further down the canyon she rode, the further she would get from where she was going.

Suddenly lightning flashed and thunder crashed, and the rider's horse reared up and bolted. And then the rain came . . . it came hard, and in a real old back-country gully-washer. The rider disappeared below the walls and out of my sight, her horse running wild and crazy in the kind of country where a horse would do well to walk.

The rain drew a gray veil across the landscape, a veil like shimmering steel, that shut out the crags, shut out the darkness of the pines, and started big drops falling over the edge of my overhang.

Here I was snug and dry, but I was unquiet in my mind, for I was thinking of that woman, her horse running away over wet rocks in a wild canyon. If she could stay with the horse and he didn't break his fool leg or her neck, they would be all right. Only I didn't think for a minute she would get through.

I sat there maybe ten minutes, secure in my hideaway, with the rain falling outside. The canyon, I knew, was going to be running belly-deep for a tall horse within the next couple of hours . . . maybe sooner. If anybody was down, but conscious, they might have a chance; unconscious, anybody down there on the ground would be dead.

Finally I got up, cussing myself for being a damned fool to go off a-helping somebody in a country full of enemies.

When I slung a saddle on my horse he gave me a hurt look. He was as tired of it all as I was, and I hadn't my strength back. I had figured to sit right where I was and rest up a couple of days while my enemies worried about where I was.

I found her, and sure enough, she had fallen or been thrown from the saddle. She was lying among the rocks, her face white as all get-out, her black hair spilled around her on the wet sand.

Her horse was fifty yards off, standing three-legged with the saddle under his belly. When I walked over to get the horse and fix the rig up, I saw that he'd gone lame. The leg wasn't broken, but it was hurt, and that horse wasn't going to carry anybody very far, not for a while.

So I led him back to where the lady lay, and I picked her up and slung her over my shoulder and heaved her aboard my own horse. Holding her on the saddle in front of me, I returned to the overhang and my fire.

When I put her down beside the fire she opened a pair of the deepest, blackest eyes I had ever seen, and she said, "Thank you, Mr. Sackett. I was afraid I would never find you."

Chapter 8

Now I was never no hand with womenfolks. Mostly when I went to dances back in the Tennessee hills I went for the fighting that went on between times or after. Orrin, that brother of mine who was a hand to sing and play the fiddle, he could talk to women. Those Trelawney gals back there were always a-taking after him, but he had a way that could charm the prissiest ones into walking out with him. Seemed like he knew every pretty girl from Cumberland Gap to the Highland Rim.

Here was I, a long homely man and no hand to talk, rained into an overhang cave on a Tonto ridge with one of the prettiest little girls you ever did see, and the trails buried stirrup-deep under rushing water. The way she looked up at me, I was almighty sure she was less put out than me.

"What do you mean, ma'am? And how did you know me?"

She was lying there beside the fire, looking as cute as a cub 'coon in a hollow tree, and she seemed in no mind to sit up, although I was fairly a-sweating, wishing she would.

"There's no man anywhere so tall," she said, "or so strong. My! You picked me up as if I was a baby!"

Well, she wasn't any baby. She was little, but she was doing her share where it counted, judging by the way she shaped out her clothes.

"Now see here. I'm not fixed to take care of any woman. I'm a foot-loose, long-riding man, and when this storm is over, you go back to your ma."

"I don't have one."

She gave me a woe-begone look that would have curled my socks, if I'd owned any. I just shoved my bare feet down into my boots.

"And if you keep on I won't have any father, either," she said.

That set me back. So I made up to work over the fire. Only thing wrong with it, that horse of hers wasn't wearing any Lazy A brand. The horse had followed along, limping up the mountain after us, and he was standing under the trees with my two horses.

"How did you expect to find me?"

She sat up and locked her hands around one knee. "By just riding. Only I got lost, somehow."

That didn't make any impression on me. I went about fixing up a bite of something to eat, knowing nobody would smell smoke in all that rain, and probably nobody would be riding until it was over. Nonetheless, I kept an eye on the country around, not really believing this girl was out alone. But the rain was going to wash out any tracks, and anybody hunting me was going to have to wait until I started moving again, or until this girl told it around that she'd seen me.

All the while I fussed over the fire, I was thinking over the business of this girl showing up. Now, this Mogollon country was *wild*. Over here where I was now, over half the country stood on end, and it was crags and boulders, brush and fallen trees. It was really rough, and no place a body would be likely to find a hot-house flower like this girl. She had soft hands and soft skin, and showed little sign of being out much in wind and sun. She could ride, all right, but she was no cow-country girl. Leastways, she hadn't been for some time. If such a girl was in this country at such a time, she was bait for something. And who was everybody fishing for? Me.

The best thing I could do was get shut of this girl as fast as I could, but I surely couldn't drive her out in the rain. Yet the more I thought of it, the uneasier I became. From time to time I sneaked a look at her. She was in no way upset by being caught with a strange man in wild country. She was young, all right, maybe not more than seventeen or eighteen, but there was a kind of wise look about her eyes that made me think that, girl-wise, she'd been up the creek and over the mountain. I began to think that killing me wasn't enough. Now they were fixing to get me hanged.

Making coffee and broiling a couple of venison steaks took little time. Whilst we ate that, and the last of my bread, I figured out what I was a-going to do.

By the time we'd finished eating, the last of the light was going. Maybe I was wrong, but I wasn't going to chance it. I stowed away my eating gear and taken up my saddle. She sat up straight then and looked at me.

"What are you going to do with that?" she asked.

"Put it near my horse," I said, "case I have to light out fast before morning. I always stow my gear where I can lay hand to it."

She couldn't see what I was doing back under the trees, and when I was saddled and packed, I walked back to the overhang. "Ma'am," I said, "you—"

"My name is Lorna," she interrupted.

"All right, ma'am." I stood a good country distance off from her. "I got to look off down the valley. If anything happens I don't get back, you just follow that creek." I indicated the Cibecue. "It will take you down to the flat land."

"Mr. Sackett"—she looked so almighty lonesomelike I almost changed my mind . . . almost—"Mr. Sackett, I am most afraid. Won't you stay with me?"

Well, I swung a leg over my saddle. "Ma'am," I said, "you get scared, 'long about midnight you let out a scream and you'll have all kinds of company. You'll have those boys you got waiting back up there in the trees . . . they'll come a-running."

Then I grinned at her. "Miss Lorna, you scream. I'll bet they'll be mighty surprised when they find you alone."

With that I touched a spur to my horse and went off down the trail toward the Cibecue. Then I doubled back and rode into still rougher country.

It was graying toward light on a wet, still morning when I finally found a place to hole up. It was right under the Tonto Rim, soaring more than a thousand feet above me, near a spring that showed no human, horse, or cow tracks—a sort of natural shelter made by trees falling off the rim and piling up on the rocks. And right there I sat tight for three days.

It was plain enough what they had tried to do. That girl's fall was more than likely the real thing, but the idea was to have her up there with me, and then during the night she would begin to scream and they would come down there and find us together. I'd be hanged right on the spot, and any story I'd told previous would be put down as so many lies. Or they'd claim I got rid of my own wife and tried to lay it to somebody else. I hadn't let her know what I was going to do until I was in the saddle, and if she started screaming then it wasn't going to do much good. I never did hear tell of a man attacking a woman a-horseback.

There was reason to sit still here, for I had some studying to do. It was time to sit and contemplate.

All the while I figured I'd lost them and was riding off scot-free, they had known where I was. They had known right where I stopped and they had that girl ready. For now it wasn't enough just to kill me—they had to scotch that story I'd told of my wife's murder.

But how had they known where I was?

The only way I could figure it, was that they had all the trails watched, and maybe some way of signaling, like the Army heliograph they were using against the Indians. As soon as I'd taken direction, they could begin to concentrate until they had me pegged right to a spot.

And if that was so, they must know where I was now . . . or just about where. They might be closing in on me, surrounding me even now.

When I got to this point in my figuring, I came up off that ground fast. I taken up my rifle and a bag of extra shells and moved out to get my horses . . . but the horses were gone!

Slipping back into my shelter, I picked up what coffee and grub I could carry, took my blanket and poncho, made a quick bundle and a back pack, and then eased out into the open.

What were they fixing to do? They had my horses, what were they waiting for? Maybe for the man who wanted me dead. Maybe he wanted to see me die.

Standing close against a tree, I studied the lay of the ground about me. Right back of me a steep, brush-choked canyon led to the top of the rim. All around there were trees and brush, and the woods were silent . . . too silent for a place where there were squirrels and birds.

Every instinct told me they were out there, that they had me where they wanted me, and this time they did not intend to fail. If I went forward they would be waiting and they would take me, and hang me or shoot me; but what if I moved back, up that brush-filled canyon to the rim?

Then it came to me that that was just what they wanted me to do, that up there, others would be waiting for me.

Cold sweat was on my body, cold fear in my heart. I was downright scared. There was nothing in me that was ready to die . . . at least, not until I found the man or men who murdered Ange.

But it had to be one of the two. There was no other way. To go down the slope into the trees was surely death; to go up the canyon was maybe death. Me, I chose the maybe. Like a ghost I slipped from tree to tree, working my way back and up. Here they had no lookouts, here they could see no further and no better than me, or maybe even less well, for I was like an Indian in the woods . . . I'd spent time with them back in Tennessee.

Once I got into the mouth of the canyon it meant climb, for this was a run-off canyon, cut by water falling from the Mogollon Rim. That rim was up, almost two thousand feet in places.

Thick stands of pine grew along both walls, and among them it was a tangle of brush and fallen trees. The going was a nightmare, and sometimes it was easier to crawl. Down below me I heard a long call, as if somebody down there was signaling to someone up above. And after a while I heard a call from the right, but down below.

It came to me that I didn't have to keep going up—I could go along the face of the canyon wall. Mostly it was covered with thick brush and trees, but in places it was bare rock. A wild, rugged place it was, home for rattlers, cougars, bobcats, and eagles, and no place at all for a man.

Suddenly a branch ripped my shirt. I stopped, sweating and listening, but there was no sound. Yet I knew they were there. I changed direction, easing off toward the left.

The mountain fell away below me and loomed up far above. Each step had to be taken with the greatest care, and each one seemed a dreadful hazard. It seemed almost certain that they were going to get me. I might kill one man, I might kill three or four, but there was an almighty slim chance that I could win out in the end.

Once, skirting a huge rock to which I clung with one hand, the ground gave underfoot, and it was only that I grabbed quick and caught hold of a bush that saved me. The bush started to tear free, but I threw myself forward and got a fresh grip on the rock.

I knew that there were places where I could fall five or six hundred feet, and though in other places I might not fall more than ten, almost everywhere there were jagged rocks or broken-off trees that I would fall on.

I kept on, and sometimes I stopped to rest, panting like a winded horse. My shirt was soaked with perspiration. It was coming on to sundown, and I feared the oncoming night. And I was thinking that by now they either guessed that I was going along the wall or they figured I had stopped somewhere in the canyon.

Presently I saw ahead of me a bare stretch, swept clean by a rock slide. It was a ragged, ugly slope where I would have to work my way across, depending on my hands. If I could get across there, I might find a place to sit down or lie down. Only there for a little space I'd be clean in the open.

My Winchester was hanging by a crude sling from my shoulder, butt up, barrel hanging near my right hand. With infinite care, I put my foot out and down. The rock was solid. It was like crossing a stream on stepping stones, only if these stones gave way, I'd fall a couple of hundred feet.

Me, I was shaking. Twice rocks moved under my feet, and I left them just in time to keep from falling.

Then, when I was almost across, there came the sudden wicked *whap* of a bullet striking near me. Involuntarily I ducked and slipped, catching myself by my hands.

Down there in a clearing, maybe three hundred yards below, I saw the man taking sight on me. He had me dead to rights against that slope, but the light was none too good for him.

One foot braced below me, one knee pressed into a notch of the wall, I grasped my rifle by the barrel and swung it up, my left hand taking the barrel, my right hand going back to the action.

He was standing in the clearing, full in the light. An instant I steadied the rifle, taking up slack on my trigger, and then my rifle jumped in my hands just as he fired. My bullet struck him the instant he shot, because I saw him throw up his rifle, the streak of fire from the muzzle clear in the growing shadows, and then he fell, and the sound of our shots went racketing off against the great crags, and then it was still. The shots had been so close together that they were almost one.

He didn't move. He just lay there, and I held myself still and watched. Score one for me. Now they knew they weren't in this for fun.

When a man takes up guns in fighting, somebody is going to get hurt. Somehow folks mostly think it will be somebody else, but we're all vulnerable, and nobody has a free ride. With guns, you pay to learn, only sometimes you learn too late.

By the time I was on the other side among the trees nobody had come to him, but they would. They would find him there, and they would be able to read the future for some of them.

Just before dark I found a place where deer or other game had walked, a tiny path not over three or four inches wide, hanging above a black gulf. It gave me speed, and I followed it as long as it went straight ahead, but when it turned down slope, I gave it up.

That night I slept behind a log that had fallen along the face of the cliff and lay wedged in the rocks. There was a thin space between the face of the rock and the log, but it wasn't wide enough for a man to fall through. So I just rolled my blanket around me and slept there until daybreak.

When I woke, my first thought was: They had hunted me—now they would see what it meant to be hunted.

Chapter 9

There was a poker game going in Uncle Ben Dowell's saloon in El Paso. The night was quiet and business was slow. The stage had pulled in and gone, and most of the loafers had departed for their beds. From somewhere down the street came the faint sound of a piano.

Nobody in the saloon was a stranger. The drummer who had just walked in and put down his valise could scarcely be called that . . . he had been in El Paso before.

The dark, powerfully built man with the mustache and three scars on his face was not exactly a stranger, either. He had been in El Paso for three days, and the way people were coming and going in this town that practically made him a resident.

That dark man was no kind of a talker, so nobody knew where he was from or where he was going. He had come into town riding a mule, which was strange enough, and riding beside him was the long-jawed, yellow-eyed man with the gold earrings in his ears who was tinkering now with Uncle Ben's clock.

Nobody said anything until the drummer had a drink. "There's hell to pay in the Mogollons," he said when he had put his glass down. "The Lazy A outfit has forty men hunting a man in the wild country under the rim. They'll get him, too."

"Good outfit," Uncle Ben commented. "I know them."

"You *knew* them," the drummer said. "All the old hands have quit, and they've taken on gunmen and man hunters. Only one man against them, and he's running them ragged."

"What started it?"

"Sackett claims his wife was murdered by someone in the Lazy A outfit, and he's sworn to find the murderer. He's—"

The dark man with the scarred face turned his head. "Did you say *Sackett?*"

The drummer looked at him and nodded. "That's right. They say he's Tell Sackett, brother to that Mora gunfighter."

The dark man pushed his chips to the center of the table. "Buy me out," he said. "I'm leaving."

"Look here," a player protested, "you're winning. You can't leave now."

The man stood up. "I'm leaving. You want a chance for your money, you follow me to Arizona."

The tinkering man took up the clock and carried it to the bar. "There you are, Mr. Dowell. It ain't working, but I'll be back this way and do the job right for you."

There was silence in the room when they left, and then somebody said, "Now what started all that?"

Ben Dowell jerked his head to indicate the drummer. "He mentioned a Sackett in trouble. Well, that was Orlando Sackett and his saddle partner, the Tinker."

"What's that mean?"

"It means the Lazy A better hire more men. Forty's not going to be anywhere near enough."

The lone sheepherder paused on the knoll to let the rest of the flock drift past him. He watched his dogs for a minute or two, then his eyes were drawn to the west. The sun was just below the horizon and the red rock cliffs were weirdly lit. Out of the west a tiny puff of dust lifted, grew, and became a fast-running horse.

The rider pulled up, his horse rearing with the sudden stop. "Howdy, Mex! You got any grub to spare? I'm a right hungry man."

"Si, Señor." He pointed toward his camp. "There are frijoles."

The rider wheeled his horse and walked him toward the camp. As they came near the spring the horse tugged toward it, but his rider held him back. "You take it easy, boy. Cool off a mite."

He dropped the reins and walked toward the fire where the blackened coffeepot stood.

The Mexican looked thoughtfully at the horseman. He was a big man, towering well above the Mexican, and he was strongly made. His nose had been broken in more than one fight, and there was a wild, reckless, uncurried look about him.

His black hair hung around his ears, there was a bullet hole in the crown of his hat. He wore two guns, and wore them tied down for action. His buckskin shirt was dark from dust and sweat. His boots were run down at the heel, but he wore jingling spurs with huge rowels, California spurs.

He glanced toward the sheep pens and the corral beyond where several horses stood. "You own those horses?"

"No, Señor. The *patrón*."

"Who's he?"

"Don Manuel Ochoa. He is in Santa Fe, Señor."

"Tell him Nolan Sackett needed a horse. I'm taking the sorrel."

The sheepherder looked again at the shaggy, unkempt rider and the guns. "*Si, Señor*. I will tell him."

When Nolan Sackett went to catch up the sorrel and switch saddles, the sheepherder looked in the bean pot. It was empty. So was the coffee-pot, and the tortillas were gone too.

Nolan Sackett walked the sorrel back to camp to make the change of saddles, and then dug down in his pocket and took out a four-bit piece. He glanced at the half-dollar.

"Mex," he said, "that's all I got, but I owe you for the grub. It was mighty tasty."

"You owe me nothing, Señor. I am honored." The Mexican hesitated, and then said, "You are a brother to Señor Tyrel, perhaps?"

"Cousin, you might say." Nolan glanced quizzically at the sheepherder. "You know Tyrel?"

"No, Señor, but it is known that he is a good man, and a friend to Mexicans." The sheepherder paused. "Señor, the half dollar . . . it is not much." He hesitated again. "Would the señor . . . perhaps a loan?" He extended a gold eagle.

Nolan Sackett, whom not many things could astonish, was astonished now—astonished and touched. He looked at the old Mexican. "You don't know me, old man. And I might never come this way again."

The old man shrugged.

"I can't lay claim to goodness, old man. I'm a Clinch Mountain Sackett, and we've the name of being rough folk. I never paid much mind to where money came from as long as I had it to hand, but nobody ever loaned me any, not as I recall. I'm obliged."

He tightened the cinch, then swung to the saddle. "Thanks, old man. And if somebody comes by, you tell them to ride high-tail to Mora and tell Tyrel and them that a Sackett's in trouble in the Mogollons."

The pound of the horse's hoofs became a lessening sound in the still mountain air. The old Mexican looked after the rider, long after he had disappeared from sight, and then he said, "*Vaya con Dios!*"

In the shadowed coolness of the ranch house on Mora Creek the din-ing-room table was laid for ten, and as the Mexican girls moved swiftly and silently about, making last-minute preparations for dinner, their skirts rustled with excitement. Orrin Sackett was up from Santa Fe after his return from Washington, D.C.

Tyrel Sackett, wearing a black broadcloth suit, sat in a big hide-covered chair listening to Orrin.

The huge living room was two stories high, and was framed by a balcony on three sides with a beautiful staircase leading to the upper floor. The room itself was sparsely furnished and cool.

"Cap should be here any minute, Orrin. He rode out this morning to check the range on the south."

"How is Cap?"

"You know how he is. He's lived all his life on beef, beans, and gun smoke. If somebody doesn't shoot him, he'll live forever."

"Heard from Tell?"

"Never a word since they left for Arizona. I've held back the herd, waiting. But you know Tell . . . he was never any hand to write."

"Look, Tye, I can't tell you how important this meeting is. Ollie Shaddock is coming over, and the men with him want me to run for the United States Senate. It's a big step, and I'd like to try."

"What do they want from me?"

"Tye, the Mexican vote can elect me, and you know as well as I do that most of them do not trust Anglos, and they know very little about them. They do know something about me . . . or you.

"What's important is that they believe in you—they know you, and they like you. What the men back of me want is your assurance that you're supporting me. And they want you to tell some of your Mexican friends."

Tye laughed. "Damn it, Orrin, who else would I support? You're not only my brother, but an honest man. Sure, I'll drop the word, but it isn't necessary. They remember you, and they trust you. Believe me, the only mistake your friends are making is in underrating the political sense of the Mexicans. They aren't easily led, and they certainly aren't easily stampeded."

"I'll need the help, Tye. There's a lot of talk against electing a gunfighter to the Senate—or to any public office."

"You mean they've forgotten about Andy Jackson?" Tyrel said. "Or Thomas Hart Benton? And Cassius Clay, our ambassador to Russia?"

He crossed his legs. "Anyway, Orrin, you weren't the one who got into gunfights. I was the one."

The door opened suddenly, and Drusilla, breathtakingly lovely, stood framed there. "Tye, it's Cap. He's got bad news."

Cap Rountree stepped past her. "Tye, a Mexican boy just rode in.

There's word that Tell's in trouble. The whole Lazy A has taken in after him and they've got him cornered back in the breaks under the Mogollon Rim. They're going to hang him, Tye."

Tyrel Sackett knocked the ash from his Spanish cigar and placed it carefully on the ash tray. "Cap, have them saddle a horse for me."

He turned to Orrin. "Sorry. You can tell them for me that I'm with you . . . all the way . . . when I get back."

"Dru will have to tell them. I'm going along."

"Tye," Cap interrupted, "this here's worse than you think. Somebody killed Ange, and the whole lot of old hands on the Lazy A up an' quit. What they've got now are a passel of border gunmen."

"There's the three of us," Orrin said to his brother, "you, me, and Tell."

"Four," Cap said. "Since when have I missed a Sackett fight?"

It was past midnight when the stage rolled up to Knight's Ranch, and the few passengers got down stiffly. The tall, elegant man who helped his lovely wife from the coach looked unrumpled, showing no evidence of the long, chilling, and dusty ride. Nor did she.

"Better grab a bite to eat, folks," the driver advised. "Doubt if you'll get anything worth eatin' this side of Globe."

The tall man offered his wife his arm and together they went to the door of the thick-walled adobe ranch house that doubled as a stage station. Inside, it was warm and comfortable. The table was freshly laid, with a white cloth and napkins . . . unheard of in western stage stations.

As they stepped through the door, he heard a rattle of hoofs on the hard-packed earth, and turned to look back. Something in the appearance of the two riders arrested his attention.

"Gin, you've been asking me what the mountain people back home look like."

She came back to stand beside him, watching the two tall, long-legged men dismount from their cow ponies. Neither was more than twenty years old, and they were built alike, lean and big-boned. Each carried a rifle as if it were part of him, and they dressed in worn homespun. "Right out of the hills, Gin."

"Falcon, look at them. At their faces."

"Yes, I see what you mean. At least, there's a possibility."

As the two men came through the door, dusty and travel-worn, he turned to them. "Gentlemen? If I may suggest a drink."

They paused, studying him with frank curiosity. Then the older one of the two said, "We'd take that kindly, mister, kindly."

Falcon turned to his wife. "If you will excuse us, Gin?"

The three walked to the bar, and Gin Sackett looked after them, amused.

Tall and lean, the three men stood up to the bar. A girl came from the kitchen and placed a bottle and glasses before them.

"Gentlemen," Falcon said when they had poured, "your health!"

When they had placed their empty glasses back on the bar, he commented, "A fine flavor, gentlemen, although it lacks the taste of the metheglin."

The two exchanged a glance. "I knowed it. Sure enough, I said, a man with a face like that would have to be a Sackett from the Tennessee mountains. Where y'all from?"

"It's been a while," Falcon said. "I'm Falcon Sackett. Tennessee, North Carolina, points west and south."

The taller one, who had a scar on his cheekbone, said, "I'm Flagan Sackett. This here's m'brother, Galloway. We come fresh from the hills, and then last night we heard talk."

"Talk?"

"There's a Sackett ridin' ahead of trouble in the Mogollons. We'uns are Sacketts. So we're ridin' to the Mogollons."

"I hadn't heard."

"Talked about a good bit. Seems he claims some fellers killed his wife when he was off scoutin' trail. He's fetched in after them. Only there's maybe forty of them and one of him, and they've got him treed."

"We'll have to ride hard," Falcon said.

"You comin', mister?" Flagan said.

"I'm with you. But we may be too late."

"He couldn't be so ornery. Not even a Sackett could be so downright ornery. He don't dare let us be late."

"Ornery?"

"He couldn't be so ornery as to kill all forty of 'em before we get there."

Flagan put down his glass, glanced regretfully at the bottle, and moved swiftly from the bar.

Chapter 10

When I opened up my eyes there on the face of that cliff I was a sore and hungry man. There was in me a craving for coffee, and a burning ache to get at those men down below. But first I had to find a way off the cliff where they had me treed.

There was an ugly feeling in me against those men and whoever had killed Ange. It was me or them, with all the advantage on their side. They knew this country better than me, and there was more of them. All the same, I was going to make them pay the price. They'd bought chips in my game, but I was going to spin the wheel.

Slinging my rifle so's my hands would be free, I started along the face of the cliff, and it was getting steeper and steeper. Here and there I hung just by my fingers, and once I had to close my fist and jam it in a crack and hang by it to keep from falling.

And all the while that skittish, scared feeling that they would come upon me while I hung out there against the bare rock. Only they didn't— not right then, at least.

Then, all of a sudden, I saw a ledge about eight feet below me, a ledge not more than a couple of feet wide, and below it the cliff fell sheer away. But it was better than where I was, and I took a chance and let go.

I landed right on the edge on my toes and felt the rock crumble underneath my feet, but I lay hold of a bush and worked myself over to a solid section of the ledge. It was the edge of a strata of sandstone, with limestone over it that had weathered back, and it gave me another chance to make time . . . up to a point.

Crawling around a slight curve, I suddenly found myself facing a full-grown mountain lion that had been coming my way. We stood there, not over ten feet apart, looking each other right in the eye.

He laid his ears back and snarled, but you don't find any bigger coward anywhere than a mountain lion. All the same, if he gets hurt he goes crazy mad. His brain is just one white-hot drive to kill, so what I had to do was bluff that cat, because if I hurt him that would be the end for me right there.

So we stood there a-staring at each other, hating each other, and trying to outprove each other. My rifle was hung by its sling, and the thong was slipped over my .45, so the best I could get at in a hurry was my bowie knife. That old bowie was honed down to shave with, and I could lop off that cat's head with a swipe of it . . . if he didn't get me first.

"Beat it, cat," I said. "I want no truck with you."

He snarled at me, turning his head and avoiding my eyes, and I had no choice but to wait him out. He might go back, but there was no going back for me. At last he did back off and turn, but I didn't move after him. I was perfectly willing to let that lion go.

Then I smelled smoke.

Crouching down on the ledge to make myself small, I gave study to the country below me and around. Away up ahead of me, several miles off, was a projecting point, and if my figuring was right, somewhere between that point and me was the Tonto Trail. And down below in the pines was a campfire—a thin trail of smoke came up from the trees down there.

The face of the rim was less steep where I now was. An agile man could work his way up or down, and there was plenty of cover. So I decided to make them trouble.

I unslung my Winchester and studied that smoke. Men would be gathered around it, and it was likely they were the men hunting me. Only I didn't know that for sure, and any man who shoots at a sound or at any target he cannot see clearly is taking a big chance.

As I squatted there on the ledge I realized that what I needed most of all was some grub and a horse, my own horse if I could find him. The grub I had in my pack, and I dug into the grub sack for a chunk of frying-pan bread and some jerked meat. I ate it, longing for a drink of anything to wash it down. The closest place I could think of to get it was right down there where that smoke was. I put the back of my hand across my mouth to get any stray crumbs, and then I went down the cliff through the trees.

By the time I reached the bottom of the cliff, I was only a hundred yards or so away from the camp. It was in the cool of morning. Dew sparkled on the grass, and the leaves of the low brush dripped with it. Birds were singing and fussing around in the brush, and in one place I saw the tracks of a big cougar . . . maybe the one I'd seen on the trail above. I worked my way along, Injun-like, making a sort of rough half-circle around the camp to see how the land lay.

First off, I located the horses, mine among them. Then I went on, getting closer and closer, and all the while studying how I could get away if the going got rough.

I saw that most of the men were gathered close around the fire. I got within fifty feet of their circle when one of them stood up to fill his cup from the coffeepot and, looking across the circle, saw me. For an instant he just stood there, and then he dropped his cup and grabbed for his gun. I broke his arm with a bullet from my Winchester.

Now, I won't say I was trying for his arm. As a matter of fact, I had that rifle dead-center on his shirt button about two inches above his belt buckle, but his quick move turned him so he wound up with a busted wing, and you never saw such a quiet bunch of men.

"No need for anybody to get theirselves killed," I said conversationally, "although I'm in no way particular."

Nine of them were there, but the man with the broken arm was in no mind to cause further trouble.

"Saw your smoke," I said, "and figured I'd drop in for breakfast. Now just to make sure I'm welcome, you boys sort of unbuckle. I'm not going to give any warnings. If any of you feel like taking a chance, you'll never find a better time to die. It's a right pretty morning."

You never saw so many delicate fingers. Those boys unbuckled so carefully you'd have figured they were picking lint off a polecat's tail.

"You"—I poked one with my rifle muzzle—"move over to the other side."

When he had moved over I told him to rinse out a cup and fill it with coffee. Then I proceeded to eat a chunk of frying-pan bread and most of a frying pan of bacon, and to drink about half a gallon of coffee.

Meanwhile I'd looked this crowd over and had noticed a few things. This was no ordinary bunch of cowhands. They were mounted too well, their saddles were too good, and they were armed too well. I'd seen too many paid warriors in my time not to recognize these for what they were.

"You boys taken the wrong job," I said. "My advice is to light out. You ain't gonna like it here."

"Have your fun," one man said. "You ain't got long."

"None of us have. Only thing a body knows about life is that you're never going to get out of it alive. Only you boys don't want to wait for your time to come, you're asking me to bring it to you.

"Up to now I've been on the dodge. Now I'm going to start pot-hunting. I mean I'm going after scalps. Here and yonder I'm going to lay up and wait for you, and I'm going to shoot you when I see you. This here is all the warning you get."

Well, I backed off a mite and had one of them make a gather of pistol belts and rifles. It was likely some of them had hide-out guns, but I wasn't too worried about that. Then I had one of them saddle up my horse and pack my pack horse.

When I was up in the leather I sat there with my rifle over my saddle-bows and looked at them. "You ain't much," I said. "Why, when us Sacketts fought them Higginses back in the mountains we whopped them good . . . and any one of them would run you boys clean out of the county.

"Case you ain't been told the truth, your boss, or one of your bosses, murdered my wife when I left her alone in our wagon. Then he buried her body and burned my outfit. I figure some of you boys are complete coyote, and some are not. I'll know which is which by the ones who cut out and leave. No decent man would ride for a skunk like that."

"Who did it?" one of them asked.

"That I've got to find out. She scratched him up some when he fought her, but those scratches are likely healed by now. They are healed on the outside, but you can bet they scratched so deep he feels them yet, and somebody saw him while they were still raw."

"You've got the wrong idea," the man said. "The men who own the Lazy A are decent. You'd never find a better pair than Swandle and Allen."

"Maybe . . . but one of that pair is scared enough to pay you boys fighting wages to be rid of me. You figure that out for yourself."

"Why, you damn' fool! You ain't got a chance!"

"Maybe, but how many will I take along when I go? You ask your-selves that." I tapped my Winchester. "I can cut the buttons off your coat with this."

Then I reined my horse around and just rode on out of there, and nobody moved to stop me.

All those men back there were tough men. They had used guns and knew what a gun could do. They weren't taking any more chances than need be. None of them was hunting reputation, and they fought to win. They could sit quiet and listen to me because they felt their time would be coming, and there was no use risking death just to prove how brave they were.

Well, when I rode out of there I didn't waste any time. I headed south and moved right along, and when night fell I camped in Bearhide Canyon about a mile above the spring.

Truth of the matter was, they'd kept me so busy taking care of my hide that I'd had no chance to hunt around to find the man responsible for Ange's death, but every time I tracked Lazy A cattle or riders, they seemed to come from a place over on Cherry Creek.

Could be I was wrong, but as I went along those tracks became many when I worked over in that direction. So, taking my time, I went on, working along the ridges under cover of the trees, easing myself in closer and closer, and all the while I saw more of the cattle wearing that brand.

There was the taste of anger in my mouth, the taste of a deep, abiding hate within me. I didn't like the feeling, but it was there, and these were days when the land where I rode had no law beyond what each man could deliver with his own hand.

Somewhere ahead of me a man waited, a man shaken by a terrible fear, a fear that sweated him at night and knotted his belly. It was not so much fear of me, as fear of what I might say. Already some would be looking askance at him, but not so many would have seen his clawed face . . . what had he done about that?

As long as I lived I would be a threat to him, as long as I lived he would not know when I might not suddenly appear to destroy all that he was or might have been. The man who molests a woman in the West is despised by all, and is hung as fast as ever they can get a rope on him. That man knew it. And all the time he knew deep in his gnawing guts that I was coming for him.

As I rode, I kept thinking of the man who had turned to look at Ange as he rode past us, leaving Globe. That might be the man.

So I rode my horse through the pines, hearing only the soft hoof-falls on the needles that cushioned the trail. Like a shadow we moved along the high ridges with the clouds close above. I rode him through the chill of morning and the damp of gathered fog. I carried my Winchester across my saddle, and the lead in its bullets was meant to find a place in his flesh, in his heart, at the source of his life's blood.

In the cool of a morning I came at last to Apache Ridge, and saw smoke rising from the valley beyond, so I rode down into Salt Lick Canyon and followed down the Tonto, and up through the breaks to Diamond Butte. Hunkered down on top of the butte, I studied what lay below, and within me my heart began to pound.

There were canvas-topped wagons there, and some tents, and a layout like an army camp, and there was a herd of horses watched by two riders.

Slow smoke was rising, and there was the distant clatter of pots, and the friendly movement and sounds of a cattle outfit on the move. Only this one had stopped, and with the fine grass they had found I did not wonder at it. This was a cattleman's heaven, but the man who had brought that herd here had, in one brief moment, turned his life into a hell.

Nobody had to tell me that this was a well-run outfit. A body could see it plain enough. The stock was in good shape, and so was all the gear I could lay eyes on. I studied that place, studied it and every move that was made down there.

There was a cook and his helper, there was a horse wrangler, and there was a man who sat with a rifle over his knees near the biggest of the three tents. He sat some distance away from a smaller tent, but facing it, and it was to that tent that I gave my attention. And all the time my mind was full of its dreadful thoughts.

Swandle and Allen . . . that was the name one of the men back there had said. These were the men who owned the Lazy A brand, and one of them anyway was the man I sought . . . the man who had killed my Ange, who had destroyed all that life meant to me.

We had come to this western country with hopes of our own place, a place where we could build, raise a family, and have the kind of home we'd never had. She had never had a real home at all, and I'd not had one since I was a youngster, and it was little enough I'd seen of my folks. There were Sacketts scattered all over the country, but I'd seen none of them until I came down to Mora to see Ma and the boys. It had been a long spell . . . since before the war.

There was not one chance in a thousand that I would live beyond the death of the man I meant to kill. Not one chance that I could escape after the job was done, and at the moment I did not care.

Swandle and Allen . . . Swandle *or* Allen? I had to know which was the guilty man, and I had no idea how to find out, except that I had the feeling that when I found him I would know him.

I thought it was a wonder they had not posted a man up on this butte, for from here a body could watch the entire layout and see every move that was made. I hunkered down to wait, and I kept my rifle down so it would reflect no sunlight, nor was I wearing anything that would.

Of course, not many cowhands wore such truck on the range. Some of them had town outfits they wore to dances and the like. Most of them wore the best they could afford. I even had a broadcloth suit one time, my-self.

The next thing they measured me for would probably be a wooden overcoat. But before they did that, I was going to get me a man.

Waiting up there on the butte, I got to thinking further on this thing that filled my mind. Up to now I'd been supposing whoever had done it had just happened on Ange there alone, but supposing it was that man we saw down in Globe, and he followed us?

Supposing, even, this wasn't the first woman he'd left dead behind him?

Chapter 11

About mid-morning four riders rode in from the west and dismounted. They stripped their gear from their horses and, leaving them to the wrangler, strolled over to the chuck wagon. One of the four was a man I recognized from Montana, where he had been riding for a cow outfit.

Al Zabrisky was a gunman, a warrior with a gun for hire. He was the sort of man a cow outfit hired when trouble was expected from jayhawkers, homesteaders, or herd-cutters, and he was good at his job.

He was tall, slightly stooped, and sour-looking. Sober, he was a shrewd and calculating enemy, but when drinking he was apt to go completely berserk. At such times he was mean, and a trouble-hunter. The other men were all strangers to me, but they were of much the same sort, the way I figured.

After a bit the wrangler returned with four fresh horses, all saddled up and ready for riding.

Just then the flap of the guarded tent was thrown back and that square-jawed man whom I'd talked to in O'Leary's saloon in Globe came out. He ignored Zabrisky and the others, but crossed over to where the man sat with the rifle across his knees. The guard stood up and they talked together.

All of a sudden, I began to feel uneasy. The two men looked all around, the guard pointed toward the far-off rim, but never once did they look toward Diamond Butte . . . and in another instant, I was moving.

When the notion took me I was squatting on my heels. I did not straighten up, but just turned on the balls of my feet and scooted into the brush behind me. Once hidden, I hesitated, taking time to listen, but there was no sound. Skirting the top of the butte, I came to the trail I'd made coming up. There I crouched among the rocks and waited.

It just didn't stand to reason that two men could look all around and ignore the biggest thing there was nearby. They had been discussing terrain, and if they ignored that butte it was because they had a reason for it. The only reason that came to mind was that they knew I was up there and they were fixing to surround me.

My horse was down below there, and they had found it. Flat out on my belly, I eased up behind a rock, then inched my head over to where I could look past it without outlining myself against the sky.

From where I lay I could see both my horses, but even as I located them a magpie swooped in for a landing in some brush near them. The magpie darted down, then suddenly swung sharply away. Somebody was hiding in that brush.

All right, so they knew where I was. My brain started to figure it out, and I knew they would have the butte surrounded. It was not so large but that a bunch of men could stake out every inch of it. So they had me.

But did they? What about the side where the camp was? It was dollars to doughnuts they never figured I would try that, and the chances were it was unguarded. There were men down there. There were horses, too, and saddles.

So I crawled around, looked the camp over for a minute or two, and then went over the edge. At that point the butte was not so steep, and there was cover here and there. I went down fast, running in short, quick spurts, keeping under cover when possible, crossing gaps as quickly as possible.

At the bottom of the slope I hunkered down behind a clump of brush and gave study to the lay-out before me. The four riders, including Zabrisky, had ridden off. The guard remained at his post, the wrangler was standing alongside the chuck wagon drinking coffee and talking to the cooks. The square-jawed man I'd seen in Globe had gone back into the tent. I now figured him for either Swandle or Allen.

Moving off to the right where my approach was covered by a tent, I came out of the brush, my rifle hung to my hand and easy to use. I crossed behind the big tent and edged up behind the small one. Inside I could hear somebody scratching away with a pen.

Well, I taken a long chance. I wanted that man in there, and I wanted him bad. So I slung my Winchester to my right shoulder and snaked out my Colt. I held the Colt in my right hand, and with my left I held out my bowie knife. Now, that big knife was honed like a razor—I'd shaved with it many a time—and I was counting on surprise. The last thing that man figured would be me right in the middle of his camp, so I stuck my knife into the back of the tent and slashed it wide with one quick sweep, and my Colt had that sitting man as its target. It had him, and it held him right like he was pinned.

"You could call out," I said, "but you don't size up like a man who'd want his last words to be yellin' for help."

He just sat there. At first, he just couldn't believe his eyes, but if he doubted them, he had no doubt at all about either that pistol or my intentions.

"I am not the man you want," he said.

"Maybe," I said. "If you are, I'll take you apart. Right now we're going to settle a little business.

"Some of your boys," I went on, "have my horse and pack outfit staked out over t'other side of the butte. I just naturally was of no mind to go fetch it, so I'll need a saddled horse, and a pack horse with four days' grub on it.

"You call that guard over here," I said, "and you tell him to have a horse saddled and a pack made up. Tell him to do it fast.

"Now, I know there's signals you could give that man, and I could be took . . . taken, I mean. I could be taken right here and now. But when they take me, they would take me with you dead at my feet. If you're the man I want, you know you'll die anyway, but if you ain't, you'd be an awful fool to die for what somebody else did."

"You're a fool, Sackett. Why don't you take the horse and ride out of the country? You haven't a chance."

"You order that horse. The only chance I want is to kill a man, the man who killed my Ange."

"I am sorry for that."

"Order the horse."

Well, he got up, very carefully, and he went to the tent flap. "Dancer? Saddle up that dun gelding, will you? Put Al's spare saddle on it. And a pack horse with a week's grub. I want it right away."

He came back and sat down. "You won't be likely to make it, but you'll get your chance. Take my advice and ride out of here."

"You don't look like a man who would murder a lone woman."

His face went white, and then he colored up. He was mad, clean through. "I know nothing about it . . . if it ever happened."

"It happened." Gesturing toward the tent flap, I said, "Your man Dancer was within a mighty close distance when it happened. He was among those who hunted me after Macon shot me off the cliff."

"You seem to be well informed."

"I overheard talk. They came mighty near me."

We stayed quiet a minute or two, but my ears were busy. The camp was going along just the way it had. No use my trying to watch outside, for I'd have to take my eyes off him. I would have to chance it, and mighty slim chance it was.

I shifted my Colt to my left hand and unslung my Winchester. Covering him with that, I thrust my Colt into my waistband. There was another gun lying there on the cot, so I picked it up.

"Whilst you're idle," I said, "you write out a bill of sale for that outfit I'm taking. Even swap for mine."

"You don't miss much, do you?" He wrote it out. "How can a man as shrewd as you buck such a stacked deck?"

"Mister, that girl of mine was all I had, all I ever had. She was murdered. I don't much care what happens to me as long as I get the man who did it. And I have an idea if a body did some hunting, he might find other dead women on that man's back trail."

His head swung around, his blue eyes hard. "What makes you say that?"

"I've read his sign, and it reads pure lobo. The man's a killer. At first I figured he went panicky, but now I ain't so sure. Maybe he was following a pattern he'd made up long since. There's folks missing out in this country, folks nobody will ever account for.

"This man is no youngster, that's how I read him. A man like that either knows better, or he's laid out his path long before."

We'd kept our voices low, and when the sound of the horses approaching became clear I held up a hand and he was still. The hoof-falls stopped outside the tent, and Dancer spoke.

"You ready, Mr. Swandle? I got the horses."

"Tell him to come in," I said.

"Come in, Dancer."

He came in, a solid, deep-chested cowpuncher with a shock of black hair and a broad, cheerful face. He looked at me, then at his boss. "Well, now. I was wonderin' why the pack hoss. You want I should try him?"

"No, Dancer. As you've probably guessed, this is Sackett."

Me, I put in my words. "Dancer, I've nothing against you. All I want is the name of the man who ordered you to hunt for me."

Dancer grinned right back at me. "Now you don't figure I'd tell you? You try to beat it out of me, and I'll whop you, big as you are. And ever'body for miles would know what was happenin'. Was I you, I'd give up right now."

"And have your boss hang me? He wants to do that, Dancer, and he wants you boys to help him. He wants his skirts clean on this."

"I want him to get out of this tent, Dancer," Swandle said. "I'll not lose a good man when I'm not sure what the stake is."

Me, I stood up, and had to bow my head to do it. "Dancer, I figure you're clear. I figure Swandle here is. I don't see fingernail marks on his face, and there weren't any when I saw him several weeks back. I saw Ange's nails before I buried her. She put up a fight . . . she was a little thing, but she fought, and she had hide and flesh under her nails."

A moment there I paused, listening. It sounded as if somebody was coming. "Dancer, you look like a man to ride the river with," I said, "so don't go to shooting for no man that would murder a lone woman."

His eyes studied my face, and then he stepped back out of the tent and held the flap. Motioning Swandle to go ahead, I followed them out.

It was still out there, a warm, lazy day of early spring. We could hear the voices at the chuck wagon.

"I'm going to ride clear. I'll tell you all just like I told the others . . . stay out of this. I'll kill any man who gets in my way."

"Everything I've got is in this outfit," Swandle said, "every dime. If it's lost, then I'm broke."

"You figure what it's worth, mister. If they get me, there's fifty, maybe a hundred more Sacketts. They'll hear of it, and they will come ridin', as many as needed, and they'll keep comin' as long as they're needed. Maybe it don't make sense, Swandle. I ain't the one to say, but when somebody kills a Sackett he buys grief and death and disaster.

"You get shut of him or you'll go down with him, because I'll wipe him out. When I have to, I'll run; when I can, I'll fight, but whatever I do, I'll not quit. It ain't because I've got more nerve than the next man, it's just that I'm not very smart. Nobody ever taught me when was the time to quit."

I waved a hand around. "Mister, you get twelve dollars out of all you own, and you'll still be alive. You figure it. I never knew of a bullet that had any sense of discrimination. I owe you no trouble, but you'll show up mighty black against a skyline."

"Do you want us to drop our belts?" Swandle asked.

"No . . . if shooting starts I never want it said I killed an unarmed man. You just stay clear."

With that, I taken my Winchester in hand and I led my horses over to the chuck wagon. I balanced the rifle easy-like and I said to the cook, "I'll have a gallon of coffee and that sandwich there. You like whiskey?"

"Hell, yes. What's that to do with it?"

"You fetch me that grub and you stand back, or you'll have so many holes in you, you'll drain whiskey faster'n you can drink it."

So I stood there and ate the beef and bread, swallowed the coffee, and then ate three-quarters of a fresh-baked apple pie, picking it up a quarter at a time and eating each quarter in three juicy bites. When I had wiped off my face with the back of my hand and had drunk the last of the coffee, I swung into the leather and looked around, sizing it all up.

"Mr. Swandle," I said, "Globe is a likely place. Why don't you boys ride off down thataway?"

That wrangler had been standing there, eyes bulging at me, and it was plain that something was worrying him. He was thinking of how when he told of this around the fire somebody might ask what he did, and so instead of being smart, he decided to have something to tell them.

He was wearing a belt gun and it was likely he had been doing some practice out back of the trees. Anyway, as I started to swing my horse, he grabbed iron.

He was a damned fool, for my rifle was gripped in my big right hand, and I'm tall and strong enough to use a rifle like a pistol, almost. So when he grabbed for it I tilted that Winchester and let him have it through the shoulder. It was no hard thing to do . . . he wasn't eighteen feet from me at the time.

He hit ground and stared up at me, hurt and sick-looking, because this was never the way he'd imagined it.

I said to him, "You go to pitchin' hay, son. You got the hands for it." And then I walked my horses away from there, knowing that rifle shot would bring them a-running.

Out of sight of camp, I lit out a-riding hard. Me, I had talked a big show, but I had no liking for forty men all to once. Or even half that many.

Back there I was counting on good sense, and most western men have it. They know that when a man holds a gun he more than likely is willing to use it, so there's no use to provoke him. That wrangler now, he'd live to get some sense. Most youngsters who want to pack a gun always see themselves winning. They never see themselves stretched out in the dirt and blood, with themselves shot open, and maybe crying from hurt and fear.

That night I camped in the cave under the natural bridge on Pine Creek, hard by Buckhead Mesa, and thought of Ange, lying cold in the ground not two miles off. I lay there awake into the small and lonely hours, a-thinking of her, and how little she'd had in her short years.

Nobody deserves to die like that, alone and in terror, hopeless with fear and pain. Had I not left her there, she might be alive now, but a dozen times before I'd gone ahead to scout trail, and a dozen times I'd hurried back to her side.

Tomorrow I was going to lay flowers on her grave. Tomorrow I would ride up Buckhead Mesa, and then I would ride to find my man.

A man named Allen. . . .

Chapter 12

On the ride to the cave I had taken mighty good care to keep under cover of the trees and brush. Studying the rim and the peaks round about, anywhere at all where a watcher might be, I worked to keep myself hidden. It was likely I'd gotten to the cave unseen, but there had been other times when I thought I was safe, and was not. But the way up Pine Creek through the canyon was so hidden that a watcher would have had to ride right on my tail to see me at all.

If Allen was my man he had little time now. He knew as well as I that time was a-pressing.

This much I'll say for Swandle. He had given me a mighty fine horse in trade, and with the bill of sale I had for it and for the pack horse, he would never get me on horse-stealing.

Al Zabrisky I had seen, but where were Romero, Sonora Macon, and the others? It taken me no time at all to find out.

Before daylight I was out of the cave and moving. Along the way I gathered some spring flowers and put them on Ange's grave. Then I turned back to my horse and saw three riders coming up through the trees.

There was no chance to run, nor was I of a mind to. If they wanted it, they could have it. So right there I made my stand, in the open and with my Winchester to hand.

They didn't see me right off. They came riding up, coming out of the trees maybe thirty yards off, all of them riding Lazy A horses.

"You hunting me?" I yelled at them.

They pulled up short. One of them grabbed for his gun and I shot him out of the saddle. Then I dropped to one knee and fired again, jacked another shell into the chamber, and was firing my third shot before the first one came in reply. It was a clean miss. The rider I'd got with my first shot was on the ground. His horse had shied as he fell, disturbing the aim of the others. I fired again and the two remaining riders lit out for the brush on a dead run, one of them hanging to the saddle horn with his left hand, his right dangling useless.

Keeping the fallen man covered, I walked up to him. He was hurt bad, shot through the chest. He was a big, bearded man with a scar on his face, and he stared up at me, fully conscious.

"Am I going to die?"

"You came hunting me. What d'you expect?"

Picking up his guns, I studied him for hide-outs, and then I walked over to where his horse had stopped. I took his Winchester and his saddle-bags, although what they contained I had no idea.

"He'll get you," the wounded man said. "Allen will get you."

When I did not answer, he said, "You ain't got a chance. This time he's got a plan."

"What plan?"

"You're already trapped. You couldn't leave this country if you wanted. They've got you surrounded and now they're going to move in."

"He hasn't got that many men."

His face was white and he was sweating with the pain he was beginning to feel as the shock wore off. "He's got maybe a hundred Apaches. . . . He's promised 'em . . . rifles and whiskey." The words came with difficulty.

Apaches . . .

That would do it, all right. The White Mountain or Tonto Apaches would know this place inside and out. This was their country, and they would know every nook and cranny. The circle would tighten and tighten, with me in the middle. I'd seen wolves hunted on the prairie in just that way.

The man died while I stood there looking down at him.

I mounted up and rode out of there. I headed due west, riding hard and steady. I held to low ground, and saw nobody. Twice I did see signal smokes in the distance, a sure sign that what the man had said about the Apaches was true.

This was rugged, broken country, and what I needed now was speed. At Dead Cow Canyon I turned south and plunged into the lonely wilderness of the Mazatzal Mountains.

It was hot and still. The coolness of the morning was far behind me now, and the climbing had worked my horses hard. On the slope of a cactus-covered ridge I drew up to let them breathe and to contemplate the countryside.

It was good to sit quiet a moment and look upon the land, for the flowers were out and it was carpeted with beauty. Little enough time I had for that, but it came to me through the air I breathed, for the loveliness of this land was always with one who traveled through it.

Far away the mountains were a blue rim. Close by, the canyons clung to their shadows, and setting quiet up there, I just let my eyes roam over the far country and the near, watching, searching.

The Apache of the mountains is a fierce man, given to fighting and raiding, a man who knows his way about, and is always near when he seems far away. The numbers were so against me that there were only two things I could do . . . I could find some place to hole up, leaving no tracks and hoping they would not find me; or I could try to filter through, to work my way into the outside and then ride for an Army post or Globe or Prescott and wait until Allen tired of paying Apaches. But my chances of getting through were slim indeed, and of hiding places there was no chance I could find one that was not already known to the Apaches.

Far away a slim column of smoke lifted, and nearer I could see a small puff of dust, so I walked my horses up the slope and crossed Cactus Ridge on a low saddle and pointed north, toward Knob Mountain.

I thought back to Swandle. He had been stern, but almost friendly. I could believe that he did not approve of what Allen was doing—Allen, the man who remained a mystery to me. And suddenly I remembered the startled look on Swandle's face when I mentioned there might have been other women like Ange. Almost as if he knew something of the sort.

But it was time to face the facts. It was I, not he, who was being hunted by a superior force, and my chance of escape, let alone the chance of facing the guilty man, were almighty small. I was alone, and the forces moving against me were more than I could hope to defeat, and still I had not even seen the man I searched for, nor did I know anything about him beyond the mere name.

Never in my life before had I wished for help, but I found myself wanting it now. I realized that there was almost no chance of my doing the hunting. Somewhere I had to find a place to hide out.

Coming off the shoulder of Knob Mountain, riding toward Midnight Mesa, I saw three riders ahead of me. They came out of the trees and were riding down toward me. Rifle across my saddle, I rode toward them.

They spread out a little when they saw me, but I kept right on, seeming to pay them no mind. My mouth was dry, and I was wary, because no man likes to tackle three tough men head-on, and any man I'd meet riding for Lazy A would be a tough man now. But on the steep slope there was no chance to run. It was bluff or fight, and so I kept right on.

As they drew up, all three were set for trouble, and then I saw one of them glance at the brand on my horse . . . I'd forgotten it was a Lazy A horse.

He chuckled. "Had me worried there for a minute or two," he said. "I thought you was Sackett."

They had all relaxed when they saw my brand, but I kept that rifle on them. "I am Sackett," I said. "You boys unbuckle. And if you want to lose your hair, just have at it."

Oh, they were mad, no question about it, and they dearly wanted to try for their guns, but they had ridden too many trails to want to die easy. They used their fingers mighty careful as they unbuckled.

Then I backed them off about thirty yards and made them dismount. I taken their horses and collected their guns. There was a pack of grub on one of the horses, and I tossed it to them.

"Eat," I said, "and then walk down to the Verde. Sooner or later somebody will come along, or you can high-tail it up to Camp Verde."

Two of them had cartridges I could use, so I stripped the loops of their gun belts. Their six-shooters I hung on a tree where they could be seen, but their rifles I kept. No telling when I might have to fight and no chance to re-load.

And then I rode off and left them cussing me, which I didn't mind, nor did I blame them. It was a sore thing to be set afoot in rough mountain country, with riding boots and a long walk ahead of you.

That night I hid out in the breaks back of Wet Bottom Creek—named for a cowpuncher who fell in—and I cooked myself a batch of bacon and some frying-pan bread. Their horses I had turned loose near sundown, figuring they would head back for the ranch.

Just short of daybreak I rolled out of my blankets and was putting my outfit together for the trail when I heard a quail call. Something about it didn't seem right to me. There were quail all over this country, the blue Mexican quail, but that call sounded a mite odd. So I saddled up and packed up fast.

Meanwhile, another quail answered, and then a third.

My camp had been on an almost level spot under the cottonwoods and sycamores beside the creek. It was a quiet, pleasant place, with the creek chuckling along over the stones, and when the sun was up the ground under the trees was dappled with sunlight and shadow.

Below me the canyon's walls rose almost sheer, and the canyon bottom was rarely touched by sunlight. At the point where I had made camp there was an open space, all of a half-mile long and perhaps a third as wide, with good grass. It was on the edge of this open area that I'd made my camp.

It looked across the stream toward the north and toward a canyon that opened out from that direction. On my right the upper canyon of Wet Bottom led back up toward Bull Spring Canyon and an ancient Indian trail.

It was a likely place, and I'd had hopes of staying awhile, letting my horses rest and getting some rest for myself. After the bad fall I'd had I hadn't yet fully regained my strength although I was much better. Now they had found me—of that I had no doubt. The question was, could I get out and away?

Down canyon might be the safest. Nobody was going to chase me down there, not if they were in their right mind. One man with a rifle could hold off an army there. But once out of the lower canyon I was in the valley of the Verde, and I could lay money there would be Lazy A riders or Indians patrolling along the river.

Those quail calls were likely to be Apaches, and I could expect nothing but trouble from them. The fact that some of them had helped me before meant nothing now, for the chances were slight that they would be the same bunch. Even if they were, they would be ready to earn the rewards offered them.

It was very still. Taking the bridle and lead ropes, I walked to the far side of the clearing, listened, then stepped into the water of the stream. The bottom here was flat rock and coarse gravel, the water clear and cold. It had been a wet spring and this stream, which occasionally almost disappeared, was now running eighteen inches to two feet deep. As the water started to deepen, I stepped into the saddle.

The shoulder of the mesa was close on my right, and I thrust my rifle into its scabbard to give myself greater freedom of movement. Any action now would be pistol action, for a man could see only a few yards in any direction.

Overhead a buzzard swung in lazy, expectant circles. The horses made little sound as they walked through the water, and I could see nothing, wherever I looked. Used as I was to being alone, I found a longing in me for somebody to help me watch out . . . I was up against too much, and unless I had more luck than I could expect, my time was short.

A flash of sunlight on a rifle barrel warned me, and I ducked and jumped my horse with a touch of the spur. I heard the wicked slap of a bullet against the rock wall, and then the echo ringing along the canyon. Almost without willing it, my eyes had turned toward where the shot struck, and I saw a white scar on the face of the rock, not over four feet above the water, so whoever had shot was up on the mountain opposite.

Just as I was searching for the spot from which he'd fired, he raised up to shoot again. It was a far piece for a pistol, so I simply held my fire and pushed my horses toward the shoulder of the rock. As I did so, an Indian suddenly showed on the bank of the stream not twenty feet off.

The soft echoes of my splashing had misled him as to where I was, and he came out of the brush with his eyes pointing about twenty feet behind me, and by the time he could swing them into focus it was too late. I shot across my body at him, and saw the bullet drill his chest. He raised up to his tiptoes, then fell splash into the water. And then I was around the corner and going up Wet Bottom as fast as I could make it.

When I reached the trail crossing at Bull Spring Canyon I turned left and went up the canyon with both horses going all out. About a hundred yards up I slowed down, not wanting to kill the horses, and when I reached the top of the mesa the trail branched. I'd been waiting for that, figuring they might have a man at Bull Spring where the trail split.

They had one there, all right. They had three. I'd been walking my horse, and we made no sound on the deep pine needles along there. Just as I sighted them I gave him a touch of the spur and went into the three of them as if I'd been shot from a gun.

My horse staggered, but he kept his feet, but one of theirs went down, and I shot point-blank into one of the men. I felt a bullet burn my shoulder and almost dropped my gun . . . almost.

We swung right, ducked into the rocks and legged it for the rim of the canyon, which gave me shelter just in time to hear a couple of bullets going overhead. That burn was more than a surface burn, because I could feel blood inside my shirt, and I swore like an Irish gandy-dancer at the knowledge that they'd winged me again.

Then other shots rang out and I felt my horse going under me, and I jumped free just in time. I could hear hoofs pounding the trail from both directions, and I had only time to grab my rifle and hit the rocks before they came sweeping around the bend.

Well, they ran into trouble.

There I was, belly down in the tall grass and rocks, with cactus to left and right of me, and a good Winchester. I poured it to them. They had come asking for it and I shot as fast as I could throw them, and then I grabbed my six-shooter and dusted them off with that.

They broke and ran, with one man down and a horse running free, and another man swearing a blue streak and hanging to his saddle-horn with both hands. His back was bloody. That fellow down on the sand wasn't even twitching.

In the moment I had, I made a dive for that horse. I came out with three rifles and belts. I picked up, and I sprinted for deeper cover among the rocks and felt the whip of a bullet past my face.

Well, those boys wanted me, and they were being paid fighting wages. If they were going to be paid for it, they might as well earn it.

I settled down and studied the land. They could come at me from two ways, and either way was going to be mighty uncomfortable.

Oh, they had me, all right. They had me up the creek without a paddle, but when they salted my hide I'd have plenty of company.

They couldn't come at me very easy, but I had an idea they'd try to get on the canyon wall above me. Come night-time, I was going to have to squeeze out of there, somehow or other.

An hour passed, and then another. The sun was hot and I was glad that soon I was going to be on the shadowed side of that cliff. But when it became dark I wasn't going to be able to see them closing in, so they were in no hurry.

Nobody moved . . . a cicada sang in the brush . . . that buzzard was keeping track of me, for I saw his shadow as he swept overhead. I checked my rifles, reloaded the shells I'd fired, then checked my six-shooter.

The furrow that had been laid in my shoulder was shallow, and it had stopped bleeding. My mouth was dry and I wished for a drink, but my canteen was back there on my horse. The thought came to me of a sudden that I might never get another drink of water. They really had me pinned down now, right back up against Bullfrog Ridge, with the river facing me but a good half-mile or more away.

Suddenly a bullet hit the rock above me, whipping by my head with a nasty whine. And then I was really scared.

This was a trick the soldiers had used on the Apaches in the cave not far from here. They couldn't get at the Indians, so they shot against the back wall . . . ricochets can tear a man up something awful, and I had talked to men who saw what was in that cave afterwards.

I hunted myself a hole, found a narrow crack in the rocks, and squeezed in.

For the next half-hour there was lead and rock chips flying every which way, and if they had come with a rush then they'd have had me sure. I couldn't have gotten out in time to stand them off, but they didn't know that.

Dust got in my eyes, and several times I was stung by chips of flying rock, but no bullet reached me. The way I was squeezed in there, it would have been a miracle if I had been shot, and after a while they gave up. I scrambled out of the hole, and studied the place down there toward the river bank where they'd been shooting from. Seeing nothing of them, I fired a shot to show them I was still around.

Twilight came, and in the desert country there is mighty little of that. Stars started to show up, and I hunted a place to hide. This was going to be the showdown, I could feel it in my bones. They had me treed, and there was just no way out. Judging by the shooting, there'd been a dozen or more men down there. I thought of my horses—the horse I rode was down, and the pack horse had run off a little way, but he might as well have been ten miles off.

The desert air was clear and I could hear the men talking as the night drew on. I could smell the smoke of their fire, and thought I could even smell bacon frying and coffee. It made my stomach growl, for I'd eaten nothing since the night before.

The more I thought of that grub the more I wanted some. They had me, all right, but I might as well die with a full stomach. Maybe I should go down there, Injun up on them and walk in shooting. I'd get a full stomach all right . . . full of lead.

Just after full dark a rider came in. I heard their greetings. Heard him say ". . . one hell of a fight. I don't know where those two came from, but when they were called on they delivered."

"Where was it?"

"Solomonville. Dodie Allen went into this place with Pete Ryland and Collins. They weren't hunting trouble, but you know how Dodie is. Just because his uncle's a big cattleman, he thinks he is too. Or he thought he was."

"Dead?"

"You ain't a-woofin'. Why, he no more'n picked trouble with those two than he was dead."

"What started it?"

"Dodie. He started it. He had two tough men with him, and I guess he figured he was safe. Or maybe he figured he'd been growin' more hair on his chest. Anyway, he said those two looked like they come right out of the hills.

"One of them fellers, he just looked over at him an' said, 'Mebbe.'

"Then Dodie said this here was a rough country on folks from Tennessee—that they had one cornered up in the hills, and they were going to stretch rope with his neck come daylight.

"This here tallest one, he said, 'You-all huntin' a man name of Sackett?' And Dodie, he said he sure was. Collins, he was nudgin' Dodie to shut up, but you know that kid. He's bull-headed as an ornery calf. Dodie said he sure was, and this feller just pulled back an' said, 'You found your-selves two of 'em. You goin' to draw that gun, or suck aigs?'

"Well, sir, Dodie he didn't know what to do. All of a sudden his loud mouth had talked him right into it, and he showed what he was made of. He just stood there swallowin' air and turnin' greener by the minute.

"Ryland, he cut in and said Dodie meant nothin' by it, but they wouldn't let him be.

"'He said you-all was huntin' Sacketts,' the tall one said. 'Well, you found two. I'm Flagan Sackett, and this here's Galloway. You goin' to start shootin', or runnin'?' So they started shootin'."

"Dead?"

"All three of them . . . four shots fired. Four shots killed those boys. Dodie took two of them."

There was silence, and then some murmuring talk I couldn't hear, and then somebody said, "What'll the boss say about that? He set store by Dodie."

"He's fit to be tied. You know how Van is. He's got a temper and he really flew off the handle when he heard it. And Skeeter, too."

"I wouldn't want to be those Sacketts when Skeeter Allen catches up with them."

"I wouldn't want to be Skeeter. You never saw them two work."

It was quiet for a few minutes, and then a voice said, "How about some of that coffee?"

It was time to start moving if I was ever going to try getting out of there. All the shells I had, I loaded in my pockets or the loops of my cartridge belt. Another beltful I slung across my shoulder like a bandolier. Then I taken my own rifle and a spare, and eased down among the rocks.

My mind was a-puzzling over those two Sacketts. There weren't any Sacketts closer than Mora, over in New Mexico, or none that I knew of. It came to mind, though, that there had been a man named Flagan Sackett who lived over at Denney's Gap. This here might be a grandson, or some other relation.

If that tale I'd just heard was true, they sure sounded like Sacketts to me. It was a comfort to feel that maybe I wasn't all alone after all.

Well, I sort of seeped down through those rocks onto the flat land near the river. Those boys had them a big fire, and it threw a lot of light around. If they had been talking around that fire for long they wouldn't be able to see good in the dark, and . . .

All at once an Indian came up off the ground right at my feet. My eyes took the flash of light against a knife blade and I shot my rifle as if it was a pistol, jamming the muzzle against the body and squeezing her off.

As the Indian went down, I lifted the rifle to my shoulder and emptied it into the crowd around the fire, and you never saw such a scattering. A horse dashed near me, and I dropped the empty rifle and grabbed at him.

I laid hold, but he jerked me off my feet and I hit ground, luckily hanging on to my rifle. Bullets were dusting sand all about me and I made a scramble for the rocks. And so there I was, fairly trapped again.

Well, I'd dealt them some misery. They would have that to remember. I crawled back into the rocks, working my way back toward the cliff.

Van Allen . . . for the first time I had the name of the man I wanted, but where was he, and how could I get to him? I laid up there in the rocks, hungry as all get-out, parched for a drink, trying to figure a way out. If it was going to happen, it would have to be at night. When daylight came they were sure as shootin' going to get me. But give me a horse and I'd light out as if the heel flies were after me.

All of a sudden a fire sprang up . . . I could hear the dry branches crackling clear back where I was. The fire was off to my left a little. Then another one came alive off to my right. First thing I knew they had five fires going down there, and it lit up the shore of the Verde all the way along in front of me. Somewhere behind those fires were men with rifles, and beyond them the horses I'd need.

It began to look as if they had me now.

Chapter 13

It was a bitter end that faced me, surrounded by enemies and my back to the wall, but it was not death I was thinking of, but only that I'd let the man live who had killed Ange. She whom life had given so little, to be murdered at the end of it and thrown aside like a used-up thing.

Somewhere out there was Van Allen, always safely out of danger's way, always in the background so that I'd not even know his face if we met. The fires out there were lighting the only way I had of escape, unless I could scale the cliffs behind me. But their light touched upon the cliff too, and I did not wish to pin myself against a wall as a target for their rifles.

Well, if their story was true, there were other Sacketts in the country, and it would not end with me. Where my body lay, others would lie, for Van Allen had no idea when he followed us from Globe that day what hell he was inviting.

A faint stirring in the night warned me, and I moved from where I was. They were creeping up along the cliff, creeping through the rocks to meet me. It would not be a rifle's work when they came close, but work for a pistol.

Then I thought of a long-dead branch I'd seen among the rocks, and I felt for it. Carefully I lifted it up, and stirred the brush eight or ten feet from where I waited. After a moment, I dragged it ever so lightly along the leaves, hoping they would hear it.

Hear they must have, for suddenly they closed in with a rush on the spot just in front of me, and I think it was in their minds to have me alive. I emptied my Colt with one continuous sound like a roll of thunder, then slipped off to one side, grasping my rifle and crouching low. Gun fire stabbed the night, and laced a criss-cross above my head and over to the side where I had been. Putting my rifle down, I thumbed shells into my gun again . . . six of them, and waited.

There was a thrashing around in the brush, and a man cried out in pain. Somebody else was moaning—terrible, shuddering moans. Well, they had asked for it.

Ever so carefully, I eased back from where I was, going around a boulder, and then my boot came down on a dry branch. In an instant the night was whipped by streaking fire. Something slugged me in the wind, and I felt my knees buckle, and I shot and shot again.

Falling, I went down on a man, his face slippery with blood. Gasping for breath and clutching my empty pistol, I ran my hand out along his arm to his hand and twisted the gun free. He was beyond resisting.

In the darkness I crouched there, feeling the slow sickness of a wound coming over me. I put the captured gun down and reloaded the other and leathered it. Rifle in one hand, six-gun in the other, I backed away from the man . . . dead or fatally wounded, I did not know which.

My breath was coming in rasping gasps now. Whether I was shot through the lung or was merely gasping from the effort of movement I had no idea.

From out on the bottom land someone called out, "Well, what happened?"

Somebody moaned, but there was no other reply. Anybody who was alive wasn't about to make a target of himself by speaking.

I dragged myself back further, feeling sick and empty, and my head humming with hurt. I couldn't understand why I felt as I did.

Men appeared between me and the light—three of them. It took a mighty effort to get the rifle around, but I made it. They were coming closer . . . I guess they thought everybody was dead. So I fired, and dropped the one who lagged. I did not think I had killed him, for his leg buckled, but the others ran left and right but not quickly enough that I did not nail another one. I heard him yelp, and he dived away into the darkness.

And then for a time all was still. Maybe I passed out, I do not know. Only when my eyes opened I was looking to the stars and it was quiet all around me. The fires still flared, but nobody moved that I could hear. I lay there in pain, and felt terribly alone. There was no will in me to move . . . only a wishing to hear the wild turkeys calling on the Big South Fork, or to smell the dogwood in April above Crab Orchard.

The night smelled of pine and blood, and there was a wafting of wood smoke from the fires that lighted my way to dying. Only somehow I knew then I was not going to die until I had killed Van Allen. Until I had faced that shadowy figure, that somebody out there whom I had never seen, but who had struck down the girl I loved.

It was a feeling of foolishness that came over me that finally made me move, a realization that no man as tall and tough as I was had a right to die with such melancholy on him.

So I moved, and endured the swift pain that followed, and the sickness. I'd been hit in the side, I thought, when scarce beyond the knock on my skull from Sonora Macon's bullet, and the hurts of my fall.

There was another one I owed . . . Sonora Macon. Where was *he?*

My enemies all seemed beyond me, out of my reach, and even with me running so hard and so long, I could not come upon them.

The fires burned bright out there. No doubt their light was reflected from the face of these rocks where I lay, and a movement here could be seen. Perhaps some of them still lay living among the rocks, waiting for me to move, so they could kill me.

But I knew that somehow I had to live long enough to meet Allen, somehow this must be done. It was the knowledge that other Sacketts might come that helped me then . . . that they might even be close by.

I was a man who had always stood alone, aware of my family though far from it, aware of their instinct for pride of family and their readiness to die for it. No matter that it made little sense to some . . . a man must have something in which to believe, and with us who were Tennessee Sacketts the family came first. Everything—life, food, shelter—all came after.

For a hundred years my family had told stories of Sacketts who came running to help Sacketts, often men they had never known. It was the way of our kind, the way of the hills in which we were bred.

The place where I now crouched among the rocks was only a few miles from where Ange had been killed . . . maybe five or six miles. Buckhead Mesa was almost due north.

There were steep canyons to the right and left of the cliff, canyons that allowed water to fall off the mesa in quick cataracts . . . when there was water to fall. I did not know if I could climb, but I must try, for in the morning they would come at me. If I was going to make a stand I'd have to get well up among the higher rocks, above the bottom land.

Inch by inch, I began to work my way back and up. There were cracks in the rock, and there were clumps of brush, a few small steep slopes, and some ledges. My side hurt me, and my head ached heavily. I could scarce pull up my own weight, but I made it up a few feet, waited a bit, then edged on. Certainly no Apaches were close by, or they'd have heard me.

Once I'd started, there was brush enough on the slope to give me a little cover, but it was steep and I needed special care to keep my rifle from hitting against a rock, for the sound would be heard by any watchers below.

In the reflected light against the wall, I could see a little space beyond a juniper that grew out from the rock. Pushing past it, not without some noise, I found a space not over three feet wide, but it evidently ran along the cliff for some distance. Here was a layer of sandstone that had remained when softer rock had been eroded away—there were many such places in these hills. It gave me a place to rest, and some cover from the men down below.

I had panted and struggled, I had tugged and hauled my way up the side of the mountain, and now that I'd found even this small shelter, I just hadn't anything to go on with. The bitter hard days of riding, my wounds, and the exhaustion suddenly closed in on me. I lay down and the darkness closed around me. The night was fresh and the stars clear, and I slept.

A shout awakened me. I came out of the darkness of sleep . . . I came out a-clawing and a-grabbing, and then I sat up, soaked in cold sweat. It was full daylight, and there were men down below, among the rocks where I'd been.

They were that close, and they were hunting for me. I started to get up, but I couldn't make it. My legs were too weak to hold me, and I just sat down again there where I'd been. By leaning a mite I could see them . . . there were maybe twenty of them down there. I could see their horses back toward the river, in the bottom land. They were held in a rope corral by a wrangler.

Reaching out, I fumbled a grip on my Winchester and drew it to me.

"All right," I said, "you got me. But you're gonna pay to collect." I said it to myself as I eased the Winchester up where I could use it.

And then I heard a rattle among the rocks above me, and a pebble bounced down, struck my shoulder, and fell away among the rocks. A little dust trailed after.

So they were up there too. They were above me as well as below. This time they figured to make it a certain thing.

Chapter 14

Bob O'Leary looked through the glass he was polishing, then added it to the stack on the back bar. He was worried and scared, and he was anxious for the night to end. Nobody was talking, although the saloon was half full.

Al Zabrisky was there, seated at a table in a corner with Burns and Briscoe. O'Leary knew them all, and not favorably, from Mobeetie and Tascosa. He wanted them to leave, but was far too wise a man to order them out. Zabrisky was drinking, and O'Leary knew what that meant, though as yet he had not had much.

Swandle was at the bar, standing alone. He looked thinner, older, and tired. O'Leary knew part of the story and could guess the rest. Swandle had every cent he owned invested in cattle in partnership with Van Allen, and those cattle had just finished a long desert drive a few weeks before. They had lost cattle on that drive and the stock needed time on the lush Tonto grass to recuperate. Swandle wanted no part of the fight Allen had brought on them, but he was unable to get out without losing everything.

O'Leary had just picked up another glass when the door opened. He looked that way and felt something freeze up tight within him. At first glance he thought the newcomer was Tell Sackett, but this man was heavier. He wore his hair down to his shoulders, and there was a scar on his cheekbone.

He wore two tied-down guns and his fringed buckskin jacket was open, showing the butt of a third. He was dusty and unkempt, and he paused momentarily in the door to let his eyes grow accustomed to the light. His nose had been broken in more than one fight, and there was a wild, reckless look about him that made O'Leary's heart miss a beat. He came on to the bar, spurs jingling, a powerful big man with the movements of a stalking lion.

"Rye," he said, then let his eyes drift over the room. They found Zabrisky and rested there, then examined both Burns and Briscoe.

Briscoe, who was the youngest of the three, saw him first, and spoke in an undertone to the others. Zabrisky turned his eyes toward the bar.

Nolan Sackett looked down the room at him and said, "Folks down the trail said somebody up here was huntin' a Sackett."

"So?" It was Zabrisky who spoke.

"I'm Nolan Sackett, of the Clinch Mountain Sacketts, and I've come a fur piece jus' to he'p my kinfolk."

Al Zabrisky had not yet had too much to drink, but what he'd had was working on him. What sanity remained warned him that he was drawing fighting wages to kill *Tell* Sackett. Furthermore, there was nothing about this big, uncurried wolf that appealed to him. The name Nolan Sackett had rung a bell . . . it was a name known wherever outlaws congregated, from Miles City to Durango in Mexico.

The word that came over the grapevine was loud and clear: *Nolan Sackett? Leave him alone.*

"We're not huntin' you," he said.

"Mister, you're huntin' a Sackett, an' the one you're huntin' would, man to man, make you eat that six-gun you're packin'. Howsoever, when you hunt one Sackett, you just naturally make the rest of us feel the urge.

"Now, I don't know if I'll make it up there in time to he'p, so I figured to trim off the edges, like. You look maverick to me, so I figured to put the Sackett brand on you."

There were five other Lazy A gun-handlers in the room. Swandle was at the bar, almost in the line of fire.

For the first time in his life, Al Zabrisky was prepared to talk himself out of a hole. He was a moneyfighter, and there was nothing in this but trouble with a capital T. He started to speak, but his gun holster was in his lap, the butt within easy inches of his hand. Suddenly he thought, *The hell with it!* And he grabbed the bone handle of his six-shooter.

Zabrisky's eye was quick and accurate, but he never saw the draw that killed him. He saw Sackett's hand move and then he was blinded by a stabbing light from the gun muzzle and the wicked blow of a .45 slug taking him in the stomach.

"What . . . ?" He wanted to know what was happening to him, but only the dead could have told him. He started to go down, heard the stabbing roar of guns, and clawed his fingers into the boards of the saloon floor.

Burns was down. In a hurried move backward, his chair had tipped, and when he came up he caught a bullet over the right eye.

At the moment of drawing, Briscoe had thrown himself aside, getting out of the line of fire, but in so doing he lost his grip on his gun. It lay on the floor, inches from his hand. He looked at the gun, then at Nolan Sackett, who stood with his big feet apart, the six-shooter easy in his fist.

"Go ahead, son," Nolan said mildly, "go right ahead an' pick it up. Nobody gets to live forever."

Briscoe was sweating. The gun was close. He could grasp, tilt, and fire. He had a hunch he could do it and kill Nolan Sackett. His ambition told him to go ahead and grab, but his body had better sense, and his muscles refused to respond. Slowly, he sagged back.

Nolan Sackett took a quick step forward. "Here, boy. You might as well have it." He tossed the gun to Briscoe, and the gunman leaped back as if it were redhot, letting the pistol fall to the floor.

Nolan Sackett shook his head reprovingly. "Son, you take it from me. Don't never tie one of those on again. Somebody will feed it to you."

He turned back to the bar and was startled to see a tall elegant young man in a tailored broadcloth suit, a black planter's hat, and Spanish-made boots holding a gun on another table of riders.

The gun was beautifully made, inlaid with gold, and it had pearl grips. Its mate was in its holster, butt forward, on the stranger's left side.

Without averting his eyes from the men at the table, the stranger said, "How are you, Nolan? I am Parmalee Sackett, from under the Highland Rim."

"A flat-land Sackett? I heard tell of 'em. Never did meet up with one before."

"These lads were getting a bit restless," Parmalee Sackett said. "It seemed a good idea to restrain them."

He holstered his pistol. "I'll buy a drink, Nolan, and if these boys gets fractious, we'll share and share alike."

"Only if you let us in," came a voice from the doorway. They turned to face the newcomers.

Orlando Sackett and the Tinker, newly arrived in Globe, walked across to the bar, and were greeted.

Parmalee Sackett turned to Swandle. "I understand you are one of the owners of the Lazy A?"

Swandle straightened up. "I am not wearing a gun."

"This isn't gun trouble," Parmalee replied. "This is business. How much of an outfit do you have?"

"We drove in three thousand head, or a mite over. We lost cattle on the drive."

"You want to sell out?"

"What?" Swandle stared at him. "Sell out to *you?*"

"Why not? You've got everything tied up in that herd, or so they told me. They also told me they doubted if you had anything to do with this trouble."

"I didn't. I'll take an oath. This was Allen's doing."

"All right, I'll buy you out, lock, stock, and barrel."

"You'd become a partner of Allen's?"

"That's right."

"Look," Swandle protested, "the cattle are scattered. Nobody has tried to do a thing with them since this trouble started. The remuda is worn to a frazzle, chasing this kin of yours, and Allen won't listen to anyone. He's obsessed . . . or scared to death."

"The way it looks to me you can stay in and take a gamble on losing it all, or you can sell out now."

"I bought cheap and I'll sell cheap. We picked our cattle up in Chihuahua for little or nothing."

"Name your best price."

Swandle hesitated, but he knew he was going to accept. A few hours before, he had been debating the question of riding out and just leaving it all behind. In fact, he had been thinking that way for several days past. Now he had his chance to ride out with enough to start elsewhere.

What was the real truth of the matter he did not know. He only knew that Tell Sackett's story had sounded convincing, and that Allen had been acting very queer. He also knew that most of the old hands, the hands hired in Texas, had gone. The ones who remained were hired gun hands or no-account drifters.

He had tried reasoning with Allen, but the man would not listen. He had offered to give Allen a note for his, Allen's, share of the cattle and outfit, but Allen had refused to either sell or buy.

Swandle's reputation was good. This he knew, and he knew that in the West even more than elsewhere business was done on reputation.

Now he named his price, and it was low. It was low enough so Parmalee Sackett would not back out, even if he were so inclined. "You've no idea what you're getting into," Swandle warned. "Van Allen is a dangerous man, and he's half-crazy now. All he can think of is killing Tell Sackett."

"If he hasn't killed him by now, he won't."

Parmalee Sackett took a letter from his pocket. "Do you know Fitch and Churchill, the Prescott attorneys?"

"I've done business with them."

"They represent me. Their offices are over the Bank of Arizona, and there is money enough on deposit there to cover this. Take this over to Tom Fitch or Clark Churchill—and you can write me out a bill of sale now."

Swandle stood at the bar and asked for a sheet of paper. When Parmalee Sackett had glanced over the bill of sale, he turned on the Lazy A riders.

"You have heard us make a deal. I am now an equal partner in the Lazy A, and as of now, you are fired. As I understand it, you were hired without the knowledge of Mr. Swandle for a purpose having nothing to do with handling cattle. Therefore, if you are to be paid, you can collect from Mr. Allen . . . or you can go into court and sue me."

Slowly, the men got up. They did not like what they had heard, and liked still less this stranger dude. He had covered them without warning, without their even being aware of his presence, and now he had fired them.

"We got other ways of collecting," one of them said.

Parmalee Sackett nodded. "Of course. You are wearing a gun, so how about now?"

Barney Mifflin, faced with the situation, decided he did not care for it. There was a good chance he would collect nothing for all the riding and shooting he had already done, and only minutes before he had had a demonstration of the brand of shooting at least one Sackett could deliver.

"How about him?" Barney indicated Nolan.

"If it is going to be one at a time, he's out of it. Come on, gentlemen, the line forms on the right. Put up or shut up."

Barney hesitated, then shrugged. "The stakes are too high for what's in the pot. We'll ride out."

Deliberately, Parmalee turned his back to them. But Barney, an observant young man, noticed that he watched them in the mirror.

Outside in the street he said, "I wished I was riding for them. That's an *outfit*."

"Hell!" one of the others said, and he spat into the dust. "They don't need any help. Just the same," he added, "I'd like to be a little bird a-settin' in a tree when the show does come off."

Parmalee turned to the bar. "Nolan, how about that drink?" Then he looked at Orlando and the Tinker. "And you, too, if you will honor me?" His eyes studied Lando's tremendous physique. "You're a Sackett, I take it?"

"Orlando. And this here is the Tinker. He was a pack-peddler and tinker back in the hills."

"Oh, yes, I have heard of you, Tinker." Parmalee indicated the bottle. "Help yourself." And then he added, "You're the tinker who makes the knives . . . the Tinker-made knives that are the finest anywhere."

"We'd better move," Lando said. "Tyrel and them, they left at daybreak."

"Of course. Bartender, the bill please. Also," he said, speaking to O'Leary, "you might pass the word. I am now a full partner, and no gun wages will be paid to anyone."

Nolan emptied his glass. "When that word gets about," he said, "that Allen is goin' to be a mighty lonesome man."

Nolan, Lando, and Parmalee Sackett walked to the door, followed by the Tinker.

When the door had closed behind them, O'Leary turned to a couple of the loafers that were still in the room. "You boys cart those bodies to the stable, and I'll buy the drinks."

When they had gone out, Briscoe got up slowly from his chair and walked over to the bar. "I'll buy one," he said.

"Forget it. This one's on the house."

Briscoe picked up the glass and looked across the bar at the Irishman. "You think I was scared, don't you?"

O'Leary shrugged.

"You want to know something, Bob?" Briscoe said. "I *was* scared. I was scared plumb to death . . . and I never thought I'd admit that to anybody."

"He gave you good advice. You leave those guns off, and you ride out of here."

Briscoe nodded. He tried his drink, put the glass down, and took off his guns and placed them, rolled in their belts, on the bar. "You keep those," he said. "I never want to feel like that again . . . not never."

When he had left, O'Leary took the gun belts and the guns and hung them on a hook back of the bar.

After a few minutes, while rinsing a glass, he looked at them. He could remember the day when he had done the same thing. That was twenty years ago. "And I'm still alive," he said to himself.

The saloon was empty when the door opened and the girl walked in.

"I am Lorna," she said.

"Sorry. We don't serve ladies."

"Oh, come off it! I'm no lady, and you're going to serve me." She put both hands on the bar and looked straight at Bob O'Leary. "Have they caught him yet?"

"No."

"I hope they don't. I hope they never do."

Far down the trail toward the Mogollon country four riders were making dust.

Chapter 15

They called it Wild Rye, and when opportunity offered, it lived up to the name. Ogletree, who owned what passed for a general store and saloon, had first seen the spot when he was a packer with General Crook in the expedition of 1872-73. He returned, put up a crude one-roomed, low-ceilinged log cabin, and went into business with seventy dollars' worth of stock.

Passers-by were few. Occasional Mormons from the settlement at Pine came down looking for drifted cattle or stolen horses, and once in a while there were prospectors or outlaws. Always, of course, there were Indians.

Ogletree was a tough man and a patient one, and he got along well with the Apaches. Usually they traded him fresh meat or skins, but from time to time there was a nugget. He had come into the Tonto prepared to live out his days there. But in less than two years he was setting out to find the source of the Apache gold, for he had learned there was a hidden valley somewhere in the Four Peaks region, only a few miles from his cabin, so one morning he rode away with a pack horse and following a hunch. Several weeks later the horse returned minus the pack and without Ogletree, nor was anything seen of them again.

But at the present time he was finishing his first year in the Tonto, and when the Lazy A riders came into the country Wild Rye had a population of five, including a squaw. From time to time some of the men hunting Tell Sackett stopped by for tobacco, remaining for a drink, and there had been talk.

Ogletree was a bald, stoop-shouldered man, usually seen in undershirt, suspenders, and pants, and carrying a rifle. He was standing in the doorway smoking his pipe when he saw the two riders come up the creek. Both were tall, lean, and young. Each carried a rifle, each wore a gun. Their clothes were shabby, their hair uncut. When they had dismounted they walked up to his store, still carrying their rifles. They appraised him out of cold gray-green eyes and told him they wanted to eat.

"Drink?" he suggested.

"Eat," the taller one replied. And then he added, "I'm Flagan Sackett. This here's Galloway."

Ogletree led the way back into the low room, which was a step down from the level of the ground outside. As he dished up stew for them, he asked, "You any kin to Tell Sackett?"

"I reckon."

"They're huntin' him."

The two men made no response to this, and they ate without comment. When they had finished, Flagan laid two quarters on the counter.

"You tell those fellers they can stop huntin'. We come up to he'p him."

"There's been shootin' over on the East Fork . . . northwest of here, maybe fourteen, fifteen mile."

"Come on, Galloway. That's where we're goin'."

Only a few minutes had passed when Van Allen rode up to the store, accompanied by Sonora Macon and Rafe Romero, and two others whom Ogletree did not know. The storekeeper had seen Allen only once before, shortly after he himself arrived in Tonto. He would not have known him as the same man.

Vancouter Allen was forty years old, a big, strongly built man with thick arms and hands, good-looking in a hard, rough way. There was a tightness around his mouth and eyes that Ogletree had noticed before and had not liked, but now the lines there were sharply defined. Allen's cheeks were gaunt, his eyes hollow.

He carried himself with that impatient arrogance toward others that is often possessed by men who have succeeded by their own efforts, and too easily. A ruthless man, Allen had carried all before him, and had come to believe himself right in whatever he did, simply because he had always been successful. Yet he showed now that he was a frightened man. His own arrogance and an innate brutality had trapped him in the ugliest of situations, and he had been driven wild by fear of discovery. Through a crazy obsession, he found himself faced with ruin, and almost certain death.

He had been striding, hard-heeled, down the boardwalk in Globe when he saw Ange Sackett. He stopped so suddenly he almost staggered, but he recovered himself and walked on slowly. She was sitting quietly on the seat of a covered wagon that was loaded heavily with supplies. At the end of the walk he had turned to watch, and had seen Tell Sackett come out and mount the seat.

He had no idea who they were, and cared less. To him they were "movers," and so to be despised, but Ange was a beautiful girl, and the instant he saw her he wanted her. He had seen no such woman in years, nor any young white woman at all since leaving Texas, almost three months before. He was determined to have her, and never once suspected that he might be unsuccessful. The idea that a mover's woman would refuse him, a rich cattleman, was simply not to be considered.

So he had followed. He had said nothing to anyone, least of all to Swandle. He did make some casual comments about the movers, and so learned they were headed for the Mogollons, where he himself was going.

After leaving his outfit to prospect for the best grass and water, so he said, he followed the trail of the wagon. He saw Tell ride away, and was close enough to hear that he planned to scout around, and that he would be gone for several hours.

He had approached the wagon and had introduced himself, somewhat ostentatiously, as the owner of the Lazy A. When Ange seemed unimpressed, he had mentioned the number of cattle he had, and suggested that as they were neighbors they had better get along together. There was nothing subtle about his approach, and Ange was no fool. She had simply replied that it was a big country and there was small chance they would be neighbors. When he stepped from the saddle and came over to the wagon seat, she had ordered him off.

Vancouter Allen simply didn't believe she meant it. She was playing him along, he was sure, but he was not the sort of man to stand for that. He grabbed her and she slapped him, hard, across the mouth. The mules, startled, surged ahead a few steps and, caught off balance, Ange and Allen fell to the ground together.

Breaking free, Ange scrambled to her feet and ran. He caught up with her within a few steps and took hold of her. This time she had turned and raked him across the face with her nails. Something seemed to burst inside him, and when next he realized what he was doing, Ange Sackett lay on the ground, her clothing ripped and torn, her throat crushed, the skin broken under his powerful hands.

As suddenly as that, she was dead.

He got to his feet, bathed in cold sweat and horror.

There was no remorse in him. There was only fear. He had murdered a white woman . . . murdered the wife of a man who would soon be returning.

It had happened before, but then it was a squaw, and nobody cared about a squaw, at least nobody who was able to do anything about it. Of course, that time he had gotten away from there fast and nobody had ever connected it with him. Once or twice he had imagined that Swandle might have been suspicious, but he had said nothing. Whatever he might have suspected, Swandle kept to himself.

But this was different. This was a white woman.

Panic clutched at his throat. He forced himself to stand still, forced himself not to run. His hands would be coming soon, and they must find neither him nor the wagon.

The solution occurred to him suddenly. Several days before, a rifle bullet had struck near him as he stood near the chuck wagon. It was probably a spent bullet from some hunter higher up in the woods, but now he could use that incident to his advantage. He mounted his horse, after hastily concealing the body, and raced to meet his oncoming riders. Rushing up to them, he told them he had been fired on, and described Sackett and the horse he rode.

"Find him and kill him!" he ordered. "I want him dead, do you hear? Dead!"

Only he was not dead, and he had lived to tell his story in Globe. And not long after that most of the old Lazy A crowd left Allen's outfit.

He had told the gunmen he hired that the rumors were all a pack of lies, but he knew safety lay only in the death of the girl's husband. He did not know the man's name and cared less. To Allen he was still simply a "mover" and of no consequence, one of the little men squatting on land that belonged by the right of rifle possession to the big outfits.

Once the man was dead, Allen felt that he could quiet the story. But when that failed to happen immediately, he had hired Lorna. She was young, unknown west of El Paso, and perfectly willing to earn two hundred dollars by spending the night beside a fire with a stranger and then screaming for help. Allen assured her it was simply a joke. She was not altogether sure of that, but she was sure that two hundred dollars was more money than she had had at one time for three years. Moreover, it was enough to take her to San Francisco and set her up in style.

Now, Allen was thinking, the end of the trail was near. His men had Sackett in a pocket from which he simply could not escape, and Vancouter Allen's fear had turned into a frightful, unreasoning hatred. He wanted to be in at the death.

In front of the store he dismounted stiffly, and walked over to the entrance. He paused there to look around once more. There was little enough to see.

Wild Rye at the time consisted of Ogletree's store, one smaller log cabin, a dugout, and across Rye Creek, two Indian wickiups. There was a pole corral with a water trough, and some distance off a shed where Ogletree made his whiskey.

Inside the store things didn't look much better. There was a counter with a row of shelves behind it, a table, three chairs and a box, and an unmade bed. On the shelves were several empty bottles, a half-dozen gallon cans, some boxes of shells, and assorted odds and ends of cheap gimcracks of the sort that might interest an Indian. There was also a short-legged bench on which stood a barrel with a spigot. At one side of the room was a fireplace.

"What have you got to eat?" Allen demanded.

Ogletree continued washing the dishes left by the two Sacketts for a full minute before he replied. "Stew."

"Any good?" Allen asked. "I mean, is it fit to eat?"

"Those two fellers who just left didn't complain. They ate it right up."

"Some of my men?"

Ogletree turned and looked at Allen with ill-concealed relish. "They said they was huntin' your men. Their name was Sackett."

Allen's head came around sharply. Sonora Macon, just inside the door, had also heard. "Young? Were they young fellers?"

"One maybe eighteen or so . . . the other a year or so older. I'm just guessing, of course. But they're young."

"The same two that killed Dodie, Ryland, and Collins," Macon said. "Let's go get them, boss."

"Wait," Allen said. "They'll keep. I'm hungry."

"They won't run," Ogletree commented, "not them two."

"Nobody asked you," Allen said shortly. "All right, let's have that stew."

He had finished eating and had lighted a cigar when Dancer rode up. Dancer had quit. He had quit the Lazy A and was glad of it, but he could not wait to tell the news he had. He strode into the saloon and ordered a cup of coffee.

He turned to look at Vancouter Allen. "You got you a new partner," he said.

"What's that?"

Dancer shrugged. "First thing he done was fire all those boys you hired. I mean all that were back at the camp. Said he wouldn't pay a dime of fighting wages to anyone."

He had their attention, every bit of it.

"What are you talking about?" Allen demanded, his voice rising.

"Swandle sold out. He got his price and he sold out. By this time he's halfway to Prescott."

"I don't believe it," Allen said contemptuously. "He wouldn't have the guts to sell, and who would he find to buy?"

"Man came to him." Dancer wanted to prolong it, but couldn't wait to see what Allen's expression would be. "Man name of Parmalee Sackett."

Allen sat very still. He could hear his heart pounding with heavy beats. His big hands rested on the table before him and his confused brain tried to absorb the information.

Swandle had sold out . . . sold out. He had a new partner. A partner named Parmalee Sackett. And Sackett had fired his men.

"Are you making this up? By the Lord Harry, Dancer, if you—"

"I ain't makin' it up," Dancer said innocently. "It was right after Al Zabrisky got killed."

He no longer wanted to ask questions, he feared the answers too much. Of course, Al had been killed by a Sackett.

This time it was no use to wait, and Dancer knew it. He leaned his elbow on the bar and looked at his drink. "*Nolan* Sackett done it. You know . . . that Nevada, California outlaw. He's one of them, too, it seems. He's headed this way with that there Parmalee Sackett, and Lando Sackett, and a feller they call the Tinker.

"They're comin' from all over the country, Allen, an' if you'll take my advice you'll hit the saddle and light a shuck out of here. I don't think you'd get away, but you can try. Those feudin', fightin' mountain boys, they surely stick together."

"*Shut up!*"

Nobody said anything. Ogletree took a bottle from under the counter and filled Dancer's glass, waving away the cowboy's protest. "On the house," he said.

Vancouter Allen shoved his chair back, got to his feet, and walked out of the door. The gunmen followed him. Outside, Sonora Macon spoke quietly. "Boss? About that partner, now? Can he really stop our wages?"

"I'm paying you!" Allen said sharply. "I don't need him. I've got the money right here!" He slapped his belt.

Macon exchanged a glance with Romero, who shrugged. "Sure," Macon said. "All right, boss."

Inside the store somebody suddenly began to sing "The Hunters of Kentucky." Ogletree chimed in on the chorus.

Allen, his features ugly with anger, rode away to the north, up Rye Creek.

There was nothing to worry about, he told himself. Tell Sackett was no more than fourteen or fifteen miles away, treed up against the mesa where he could not escape.

They would be there by nightfall.

Chapter 16

So here at last was I, William Tell Sackett, and a far piece I'd come from the Cumberlands, a far piece . . . to die with my back to the wall in the Mogollons.

It left me with no good thought to know I had come so far and done so little with my life. I'd fought for my country in the War Between the States, to save the Union, and I would do it again. I'd fought the redskins, too, and driven cattle north from Texas to Montana, and helped to open up some of the most lovely land under heaven.

At the end, it all came to nothing. Ange murdered, and my death nearing me at the hands of the same man, and no son to leave behind.

Most of all, I hated to leave Allen alive, he who had killed my lovely girl. There's some, I'm told, who frown upon revenge, and perhaps it is better so, but I was a mountain boy, reared in a feudal land, living my life through by the feudal code, and our law was the Mosaic law of an eye for an eye.

They were waiting now, waiting for somebody to come before they moved in for the kill. That somebody had to be Van Allen. He wanted to be here, to be sure I was actually dead. He wanted to look into my dead eyes and know that he was safe. There would be talk, of course, but nobody would push such talk very far in the face of the guns Allen could command. Especially when the only man who could give Allen the lie was dead and buried.

They were waiting for him, then, and that meant that somehow I must stay alive until he got here. I must stay alive and save a bullet for him. Somehow, even in being destroyed, I must destroy him.

I looked about, seeking out a hole into which I might crawl, anywhere to hide. There was no place to run, nor had I the strength for it. It was root hog or die right here. But the place offered me little.

The cliff reared up red and steep behind me, and along the lower reaches it was scattered over with scrub cedar. It was broken, eroded rock, with much stuff fallen from above. The canyons opening to right and left were steep, places where a man might crawl if he could find the cover for it.

Where I was, lay a sort of trough that ran for several yards. Larger slabs of fallen rock had landed out a few feet from the base, and cedar or yucca had grown up among the slabs, so that I could not be seen, even if I moved.

There's seldom a corner so tough a man might not find a way out, if he has the nerve and the strength to try. Nerve enough I had, but I was played out, worn to a frazzle by the exhaustion of weeks of running, piled onto the wounds I'd had.

When I looked down at myself, showing through my torn shirt the way I was, it was a shocking sight. I was a strong-muscled man, but lean. Only now every rib showed. I was ga'nted up like a share-cropper's mule, just a rack of bones and hide.

For a time I lay there watching them. Though I thought they must know where I was, they were avoiding this place, searching out the rocks down below just to make sure I hadn't fooled them, and it was that that gave me the idea.

My strength was slight enough, and going up, if I found a way, would give me nothing but the chance to die on higher ground. So what if, after they'd searched well over the lower ground, I slipped down there and let them move on up, to search up here?

If I could get below, then I'd have them, or some of them, against the hill where they figured to have me. And when Van Allen came, he would be down there, close to me.

Lying quiet, I studied the terrain below, and saw a way it might be done.

There was a sight of Injun in me, though it came of learning and thinking, and not of blood. I'd run the hills with the Cherokees as a boy, them as were called the Overhill Cherokees because they lived west of the mountains. So I laid Injun eyes on the land below me, and saw a slight chance in the way I might go. It was the only chance I had.

They'd not be expecting me to come toward them now. They would watch the likely places, and the one I'd chosen wasn't that . . . it offered little enough place for a man to hide. But the thing I knew was that the best place to hide was in the mind of the searcher, for all men have blind spots in the mind. They rarely see what they do not expect to see, and their minds hold a blindness to what seems unreasonable. Nobody but an Apache would think to choose the way I'd chosen. And if any Apaches were down there, they would not be expecting Apache thinking of a white man.

There was open ground to my left, and it was there I went, edging along, for I had to go slow, and needed to for the quietness my going called for.

There were no big boulders here, no gullies or cracks, and no brush at all. There was just rugged desert ground with a few places here and there, only inches deep, and scattered rocks no bigger than your head. Tufts of bunch grass grew among the yucca, but nothing larger.

First I rubbed my rifle barrel all over with dust to take the shine from it. My clothes, so stained with dust and sweat, were almost of the ground's own color, mingled with blood-stains and the tears where my sunbrowned skin showed through.

Flat on my belly I went. Inch by inch I wormed along, through a space where a few cedars grew. I came to a fairly shallow place and went into it, and there I lay still for a bit. Then on I went, working along, moving so slightly that it scarcely seemed like movement at all.

Apaches had done it . . . I'd known of a case where a man grazed his horse with it tied to a rope and the rope's end in his hand . . . and an Apache slipped up in the bright afternoon sunlight and cut the rope and eased off with the horse. He swung astride him and was gone, leaving the man holding the rope and looking foolish.

My mouth was dry as dust, dry from fear of being seen, and dry from having no drink in many hours. My heart pounded heavily and my head ached from the hunger and tiredness that was in me. But my rifle was in my hand, and when the moment came, if I could only find a rest for it, I'd take a good lot with me down the road to death.

A long, slow hour passed. Once a boot crunched within a few feet above me as I lay still. Another time I heard men talking of a fight there'd been, of men killed with violence, and guns flaring and thundering in O'Leary's place . . . and then I heard the name of Nolan Sackett.

Nolan! He had come, then. Nolan was an outlaw Sackett, a wild and desperate man, and one who had pulled me from a bad hole in California not too far back. Me they might kill, but now I could be sure they'd know the Sackett men before the summer was gone.

There was no doubt in me that I would die, for there was no way out that I could see. For minutes, long minutes, I lay perfectly still, right in the open with those hunting men about me, knowing my only safety lay in their searching minds, for it was up on the higher ground they looked now, and not right there below them.

Suddenly I heard the beat of hoofs on the trail. Riders coming! Then a harsh voice sounded and something within me jolted and my heart seemed to miss a beat, and within me a terrible hatred came up, for I knew that must be the voice.

"We've got him, Mr. Allen," somebody was answering. "He's right up there in those rocks. We've got men along the rim above him, and there's not a chance he can get away."

"All right. Go get him." That voice again . . . how far from me?

They started at once . . . there must have been a dozen men down there, as well as those on the cliffs above. I heard them start, and I reached back and slipped the thong from my six-shooter.

"Put lead on that rock behind him," somebody said. "That will flush him out!"

A half-dozen Winchesters began feeding lead against the hillside, trying to do what the Army had done to the Apaches in the Salt River cave, not more than a whistle and a yell from here. Glancing bullets whined and whipped through the air, and had I been back there I'd have been a lucky man to escape death.

"He's dead or gone," a man called out. "There's no sign of him."

Ahead of me I heard voices. "No, stay here," Allen was saying. "We've got a better view of the mountain from here. If he escapes them, we've got him."

"Boss," another voice spoke up quickly, "there's somebody coming down the trail!"

"Some of the boys, Macon. I told them all to close in."

"They don't look familiar." Macon's voice was doubting.

"I can see our boys up on the hill above him." This voice had a Spanish accent, ever so slight . . . would that be Romero, the Mexican gunfighter? "Which one wears a black coat?"

I lay perfectly still, but my mind felt queer. Somehow I couldn't bring my thoughts to focus, and there was a terrible weakness upon me. I daren't move my head, for I felt sure I was within view of them all, and any movement would be seen. Yet it was now or never.

My left hand pushed the rifle forward, holding it clear of the rocks to make no sound. I turned my head so I could look straight ahead, and I saw a clump of bear grass there, and to my left another.

Suddenly a shout went up behind me. "He's *gone!* Damn it, *he's gone!*"

And then another voice called down, and it was a voice I knew.

"All of you down there . . . back up and drop your guns or we'll cut you to doll rags!"

That was Orrin . . . *Orrin here?*

Allen was standing in his stirrups . . . for the first time I saw my enemy. "What the hell?" he called. "Who's *that?*"

Now I had it to do, so I came up off the ground, rifle in my left hand, my right waiting for the feel of my Colt.

Out of the corner of my eye I could see a row of men along that hill where I'd been lying, just above there where the bullets had gone. They were all moving slowly down the slope.

Orrin was there, all right, and Tyrel. And there were some others that I did not know.

The three men in front of me were staring up the hill. I was somewhat to their left. Close to where I had stood up, there was an ocotillo with its many spines in a stiff clump, flaring out from its base, and just beyond that a yucca. I had stood up so soundlessly that it was a moment before they saw me.

The riders on the road were drawing close. Then I heard Nolan Sackett's voice. "You boys wanted a fight, now you got it."

Sonora Macon, Rafe Romero, and Van Allen . . . all three were looking at me. I lowered the butt of my Winchester to the ground to steady myself. I doubted if I could hold the rifle steady enough without a rest, but I wasn't worried about a six-shooter. I could shoot one of those if I could still breathe.

Allen had been standing in his stirrups, now he lowered himself gently into the saddle. I thought he looked a little gray under the dark stubble of his beard.

"You been huntin' me, Allen. And I been huntin' you."

He looked at me, staring hard. I do not know if he wanted to see the look of the man he'd wronged and tried to kill, or if he was only looking at a man he expected to kill, but I knew deep down within me that no matter what came to me, Van Allen was staring down the black muzzle of death.

"Who are those men?" he demanded.

"Sacketts, mostly," I said. "They're of the Sackett family of Tennessee, or those who stand close to them. I don't know all of them myself."

Cap Rountree was there, and a strange-looking man with gold rings in his ears, the like of which I never did see, but I was a mountain man and had heard tell of the Tinker.

Suddenly a tall man with iron gray at his temples and a coat with a handsome cut was standing beside me. He was a Sackett, all right, although one I'd never seen. "I'm Falcon Sackett, Tell. My son is here also."

"There's going to be shootin'," I said.

"I'll stand with you, William Tell, and a better man I never stood beside."

Overhead the sun was hot, somewhere a horse blew dust from his nostrils and stomped his feet. Allen's gunmen were holding ready for the word, only Allen wasn't giving it. He was looking at me.

Maybe it was the heat waves dancing, maybe it was a blur in my vision. Everything seemed vague and whirly there before me, kind of shimmering, with the shadows of men beyond it.

"She never had much, Mr. Allen," I said. "I'll never forget the first time we met, high up in the Colorado mountains. She said, 'I'm Ange Kerry, and I'm most glad you found me.' It was a heart-tearing thing, the way she spoke, and the littleness and loneliness of her.

"I hoped to make it up to her. I hoped to bring her happiness in this fine new land where the pines stood tall and the water ran cold over the rocks. I wanted to build her a house of her own, and fix it proper, and we'd have our children there. That's what I wanted, Mr. Allen, and you murdered her. You found her alone and you broke the flesh of her throat in your hands. You took the life out of her, Mr. Allen."

Macon shifted his feet. "I didn't know he done that."

"He did it."

"I didn't mean to. I thought . . . well, I figured she was some mover's woman."

"No matter . . . she was a woman. As for movers, you're a mover yourself, Mr. Allen. Where did you move from? And why? Is there blood behind you?"

My knees felt funny and I didn't quite know what I was saying. I could see him up there on his horse, peering at me.

"By God," he shouted suddenly, "I paid you to kill him. Now *kill him!*"

Some fool must have moved . . . and all at once the day was thundering guns and the wicked stab of flame. I could feel my own gun bucking in my grip, and I was stumbling forward toward that man on the horse. I saw his gun up and firing, saw his face twisted in an awful wrench of agony, and saw blood start from his chest. My next bullet ripped the side of his face away, and he fell down, but he came up and threw both hands in front of his face and began to scream. I shot through his hands until my gun was empty, and I was down on my knees and no longer wanted to shoot anybody or anything.

Orrin had me by the shoulders. "Easy, man! Easy, now. It's all over."

When I shook off his hands and staggered up, I saw Macon was down and Romero had fallen off to one side. All around men were standing with their hands up, and nobody wanted to fight any more.

Tyrel walked over to me. It was the first time I had seen him wearing a gun. "Are you all right, Tell?"

Me, I nodded.

"Let's go home," he said.

Behind me I heard Parmalee saying, "Flagan, you and Galloway would please me if you'd stay and help me round up these cattle."

We stopped in Globe and the lot of us lined up in O'Leary's place, all of us together, more Sacketts than I'd ever seen before . . . or anybody else, I guess.

Me, standing there amongst them, I looked around and I knew I was not alone, and I'd never be alone again.

THE LONELY
MEN

*To the people of Schimmert,
in the province of Limburg,
The Netherlands,
who took into their homes
a company of American soldiers,
February 1945.*

Chapter 1

It was hot. The shallow place where I lay atop the desert ridge was like an oven, the rocks like burning coals. Out on the flat below, where the Apaches waited, the heat waves shimmered and danced. Only the far-off mountains looked cool.

When I tried to push out my tongue to touch my cracked lips it was like a dry stick in my mouth, and the dark splashes on the rock were blood . . . my blood.

The round thing lying yonder with a bullet hole in it was my canteen, but there might be a smidgen of water left in the bottom—enough to keep me alive if I could get to it.

Down on the flat lay my sorrel horse, who had run himself to death trying to save my hide, and him with a bullet hole in his belly. In the saddlebags were the few odds and ends that were likely to be as much as I'd ever have of possessions in this life, for I didn't seem to be a fortunate man when it came to getting the riches of the world.

Back in the high-up Tennessee hills they used to tell it that when fighting time came around a body should stand clear of us Sacketts, but those Apaches down yonder had never heard the stories, and wouldn't have paid them no mind if they had.

If you saw an Apache on a parade ground he might not stack up to much, but out in the brush and rocks of his native country, he was a first-class fighting man, and maybe the greatest guerilla fighter the world ever saw.

Squinting my eyes against the glare and the thin trickle of salty sweat in my eyes, I clutched the stock of my rifle right back of the action and searched the terrain for something at which to shoot. My mouth was dry, my fingers stiff, and my rifle action so hot I daren't touch it unless to shoot, and quick.

Down there on the trail Billy Higgins lay gut-shot and dead, killed at the last by my own bullet to save him from torture.

We'd been riding east in the cool of the morning when those Apaches hit us from out of nowhere. Rightly, this wasn't even Apache country. This was Pima or Papago country, and they were Indians who were friendly to us, and who fought the Apaches on every occasion.

When those 'Paches hit us it was every man for himself, and Billy Higgins and me, we taken out a-running, heading for the rocks where we could make a fight of it.

An Apache with a .56 Spencer r'ared up from behind a greasewood and shot Billy right through the belly, opening him up as if it had been done with a saber. It meant he was dying, and he knew it.

Swinging my horse, I came back to him where he had fallen, but he looked up cool as could be and said, "You light out, Tell. I've seen some gut-shot folks in my time, but nobody had it worse than me."

The shock of the bullet was still on him, but in a minute or two he would begin to suffer.

When I got down to lift him up he stopped me. "Before God, Tell, if you try to pick me up everything I've got in me will spill out. You hit the trail, but try to get another one for me, will you? You can he'p more up in the rocks, keepin' them off me."

What he said was gospel true and we both knew it, so I swung my horse and lit a shuck for those rocks as if my sorrel's tail was afire. Only we didn't get far. I heard the shots and felt the sorrel's hoofs break rhythm, and then he started to cave under me, but somehow he fought himself up and kept on for fifty yards more. Then he started to go and I hit the ground running before he was down, with bullets kicking gravel ahead of and around me.

Almost at the top of the ridge a bullet caught me, and it saved my life.

It spun me, knocked me rolling butt over teakettle into the rocks, with two more bullets hitting right where I'd been. Scrambling up, I dove over into that shallow place and lay there, rifle in hand, hugging the ground. When the first Apache showed, I nailed him right between the eyes.

After that things quieted down, but there was no way to get clear. The ground around me hadn't anything in the way of cover, so I had to stay where I was . . . with the morning ebbing away into noontime.

I'd no idea how many Apaches were out there. As they lived off the desert they never traveled in big bunches; there were rarely as many as thirty, more often twelve to eighteen, so far as I'd seen or heard.

Off to the northwest I could hear shooting, time to time, so some of the others must be alive, after all. There'd been six of us, to start, and all strangers who met in Yuma. That was the way it was in those days. More often than not a man might find himself traveling with folks he'd never seen before. None of the six of us had any knowledge of the others before we hit the trail. Traveling alone was a mighty chancy thing in Indian country, so it was lucky that we all shaped up to go east at the same time.

Now Billy was down, but I'd nailed an Apache. Right at the moment my chances didn't look good. If they were settin' a place for me in Tucson they'd best wait, for it began to look like there'd be an empty spot at the table.

I hunkered down a mite and piled a few rocks on the edge of the hollow to give me some more protection, leaving a place here and there to look through or fire through. I took time to replace the shells I'd fired . . . no idea when the chance would come again.

Apaches are great waiters. They could set for hours on end, just waiting a wrong move. A white man, he gets restless, wants to move, and the first thing you know he does, and he dies.

Not me. I grew up in Cherokee country in Tennessee, and my pa had been a mountain man who'd fought Indians from boyhood . . . he'd taught us when he was home, taught us all he could, and I learned from the Indians, too.

This shallow place in which I lay was scarcely three feet deep. It was maybe eight feet each way, and the lowest part was where the run-off water had started a trench that emptied into a draw in back of me.

The sky was a hot yellow, the land pinkish, with outcroppings of dull red or black. There was mighty little growth—just scraggly desert shrubs and prickly pear, and mighty little of that.

The time inched by, with no change in the heat, no change in the sun, no change in the country around. Unless I lifted my head, nothing could be seen and I must trust to my hearing.

On the slope, there was nothing. My horse lay down there, and the body of Billy Higgins.

I hadn't been there long when I heard Billy scream. Taking a chance, I peeked out.

The Apaches were shooting flaming slivers of pitch pine into him with their bows. They were hidden down close to him, and there was no way I could get at them, nor them at me. They were shooting into Billy to torture him, which amused them, but also they were doing it to draw me out.

Three fires were smoldering in him before he screamed. And then he yelled to me: "Tell! For God's sake, Tell! Shoot me!"

He lay out on the white sand in the glare of the awful sun, ripped open by a bullet, and the Apaches kept shooting those little arrows of flaming pitch pine into him.

"Tell!"

There was terrible agony in his voice, and a pleading, too.

All of a sudden, he forced himself up and he put a finger against his skull. "Tell! Right there! For God's sake, Tell!"

So I shot him. He would have done it for me.

You should have heard those Apaches yell. I'd spoiled their fun, and they were mad, real mad.

One of them jumped up, running at me, but just as I was about to shoot he dropped from sight; then another started and another, both disappearing before I could bring my rifle to bear, but each one a few yards closer.

Times like that, a body does some thinking, and right then I was a-wishing I was somewhere else, a-wishing I'd never come to Arizona a-tall, although until then I'd been mighty proud of the Territory, and even though hard times had come upon me I liked the country. Right now all I wanted was a way out . . . any way out. But those Apaches had a mind to keep me there.

All of a sudden one of them came up out of the sand and started for me, but when I swung my gun, another started up.

Now, even a fool boy from the hills is going to learn after a while, and so the next time one started up I didn't swing my gun and try to nail him, I just waited with my eyes on the place where the first one dropped. Not exactly on the place, for no Apache will ever get up from where he drops; he rolls over a few feet to right or left, sometimes quite a few feet.

Another of them started up, but I let him come until he dropped, and I waited for the first one. Sure enough, up he bobbed and I had to move the rifle muzzle only inches, and I nailed him right in the brisket, dusting him on both sides. Before he could fall I worked the lever on my Winchester and got him again.

Then the others were coming and, swinging the gun, I caught another one . . . too low down. He hit the ground in the open and the third one also dropped, not more than twenty feet now from the rim of my hollow.

One lay out there with what looked like a busted leg, and I let him lay until he tried to bring his rifle to bear, and then I eased around for a shot at him. The muzzle of my rifle must have showed a mite beyond the rocks at the edge of my hole, because the third one fired, hitting the rocks and spattering me with stinging rock fragments, one of which took me right in the eye.

Then they came, the two of them. The one with the bloody but unbroken leg, and the third one shooting as he came. I dropped my rifle and, with my eyes full of water from the smart of rock fragments, grabbed my bowie knife.

Now, I'm a pretty big man, standing six foot three in my socks, and although on the lean side what beef I had was packed into my arms and shoulders. That bowie knife was a heavy blade, razor-sharp, and when those two 'Paches jumped into the hollow with me I took a wicked swipe at where they figured to be. Somebody screamed, and I felt a body smash against me. Upping my knee, I threw him off and fell back, just missing a slashing blow that would have taken my head off.

One Apache was down but not out. I could see a little now, and when I started to come up he grabbed at my rifle which was lying there and I threw myself at him, knocking the barrel aside with one hand and ripping up with that blade with the other.

He threw me off and I fell, all sprawled out, and they both came up and at me. One had a wounded leg, one had a slash across the chest and biceps, but they were tigers, believe me. It was like being in a mess of wildcats, and for the next thirty or forty seconds I never knew which end was up, until of a sudden the fight was over and I was lying there on the ground, gasping for breath, with tearing gasps.

Finally I pushed myself up from the sand and turned over into a sitting position.

One Apache was dead, my bowie knife still in his chest. I reached over and pulled it loose, watching the other one. He was lying there on his back and he had a bullet hole in his thigh that was oozing blood and he had at least three knife cuts, one of them low down on his right side that looked mean.

Reaching over, I taken up my rifle and jacked a shell into the chamber.

That 'Pache just kept a-staring at me; he seemed to be paralyzed almost, for he made no move. The other two were dead.

Jerking a cartridge belt from one of the dead ones I looped it around my middle, still keeping an eye on the living one. Then I picked up my bowie knife from the ground and, leaning over the living one I wiped off the blood on him, then stuck the knife into the scabbard.

One by one I collected their rifles and emptied the shells, then threw them wide.

"You're too good a fightin' man to kill," I told him. "You're on your own."

I walked down to where my canteen lay and picked it up. Sure enough, there was maybe a cup of water that had not drained out, and I drank it, watching the rim of the hollow all the while.

By now it was coming on to sundown and there were other Indians about. I took one more look into the hollow and that one was still lying there, although he'd tried to move. I could see a big rock back of his neck that maybe he'd hit across when he fell.

Taking a careful look around, I went down into the shallow gully left by the run-off water and started away.

About that time I found myself going lame. My hip and leg were mighty sore, and when I looked down to size the situation up I saw that a bullet had hit my cartridge belt, fusing two of my .44's together, and a fragment had gone up and hit my side, just a scratch, but it was bloody. That bullet that hit my belt where it crossed the hip had bruised me mighty bad, by the feel of it.

Shadows were creeping out from the rocks, and of a sudden it was cool and dark.

A voice spoke out. "You want to live long in this country you better get shut of them spurs."

It was Spanish Murphy. He came up from behind some brush with Rocca and John J. Battles. Taylor was dead.

Murphy had lost the lobe of his left ear, and Rocca had been burned a couple of times, but no more.

"You get any?" Battles asked.

"Four," I said, knowing that was more Apaches than many an Indian fighter got in a lifetime. "Three, and a possible," I corrected. And then I added, "They got Billy."

"We'd best light out," Spanish suggested, and we walked single file to where their horses were. They had two horses, so we figured to switch off and on.

Spanish was tall as me, but twenty pounds lighter than my one-ninety. He was a reading man, always a-reading. Books, newspapers, even the labels on tin cans . . . anything and everything.

We set out then. After a while I rode Tampico Rocca's horse and he walked. By daybreak both horses were tired out and so were we, but we had sixteen miles behind us and a stage station down on the flat before us.

We were still several hundred yards off when a man walked from the door with a rifle in his hands, and we were almighty sure there was another one behind a window from the way he kept out of line with it.

When we came up to the yard he looked at Murphy, then at the rest of us, and back at Murphy. "Hello, Spanish. What was it? Apaches?"

"Have you got a couple of horses?" I asked him. "I'll buy or borrow."

"Come on inside."

It was cool and still. Me, I dropped into the first chair I saw and put my Winchester on the table.

A second man left the window where he had been keeping watch and, carrying his rifle, he went back toward the kitchen, where he began rattling pots and pans. The first man went over to a table and carried the wooden bucket and the gourd dipper to us. "I'd go easy, there at first," he suggested. And that we did.

The station tender leaned on the bar. "Haven't seen you in years, Spanish. Figured they'd have stretched your neck before now."

"Give 'em time," John J. Battles said.

Setting there in the chair, taking occasional swallows of cool water from the bucket, I began to feel myself getting back to normal.

Spanish, he leaned back in his chair and looked over his cup at the station tender. "Case, how long you been with the Comp'ny?"

"Two . . . maybe two and a half years. My wife lef' me. Said this western country was no place for a woman. She went back to her folks in Boston. I sent her money, time to time. Afraid if I don't she'll come back on me."

"Ain't never married, myself," Spanish said. He looked over at me. "How about you, Tell?"

For a moment there I hadn't anything to say. I kept thinking of Ange, the last times I saw her, and of the first times, high in those Colorado mountains.

"My wife is dead," I told him. "She was a rarely fine girl . . . rarely fine."

"Tough," Spanish said. "You, Rocca?"

"No, señor. I am not a married man. There was a girl . . . but that is far away and long ago, *amigos*. Her father had many cows, many horses . . . me, I had nothing. And I was an Indio . . . my mother was an Apache," he added.

My eyes were on the floor, tracing the cracks in the rough boards, often scrubbed. My hungry flesh was soaking up the lost moisture and I felt sleepy and quiet, liking the square of sunlight that lay inside the door, even the drone of the flies . . . I was alive.

The blood of Apaches was still on my hands. There had been no water in which to wash until now, but soon I would . . . soon.

The room was like many of its kind, differing only in the plank floor. Most floors were of stamped earth. There were several rough board tables, some chairs and benches. The room was low-raftered, the walls were of adobe, the roof of poles and earth. I could smell bacon frying in the kitchen, and coffee.

Spanish Murphy hitched around in his chair. "Tell, we make a team, the four of us, why don't we stick together?"

The man came in from the kitchen with tin plates and a frying pan filled with bacon. He dumped the plates on the table, then forked bacon onto them. He went out and returned with the coffeepot and a plate of *tortillas*. Still another trip and he brought a big bowl of *frijoles*—those big Mexican brown beans—and a dried-apple pie cut into four pieces.

"We'll need a couple of horses," I said, looking around at Case.

"You'll get 'em," Case replied. "I think the Comp'ny would like to get them to a safer place. We've been expectin' an attack also any time."

He gestured toward the bacon. "You got to thank Pete Kitchen for the bacon. He raises hogs down to his place, calls 'em his 'Pache pincushions, they're so shot full of arrows."

John J. Battles, a solid chunk of a man, glanced across the table at me. "Sackett . . . that's a familiar name."

"I'm familiar," I agreed, "once you know me." It wasn't in me to get him comparing notes, figuring out who I was. Once he did, he'd bring up the fight in the Mogollon country, and how Ange was murdered. It was something I was wishful of forgetting.

"I still figure," Spanish said, "that we'd make a team."

"If you want to risk hanging." John J. Battles grinned at us. "You all heard what Case said."

"Me," Rocca said, "I wasn't going nowhere, anyhow."

"Later," I said, "it will have to be later. I've got a trip to take."

They looked at me, all of them. "My brother's kid. I hear tell he's been taken by the Apaches. I've got to go into the Sierra Madre after him."

They thought I was crazy, and I was thinking so myself. Rocca was the first one to speak. "Alone? Señor, an army could not do it. That is the Apache hide-out where no white man goes."

"It's got to be done," I said.

Case, he just looked at me. "You're crazy. You're scrambled in the head."

"He's just a little boy," I said, "and he's alone down yonder. I think he will be expectin' somebody to come for him."

Chapter 2

Laura Sackett was a strikingly pretty young woman, blonde and fragile. Among the dark, sultry beauties of Spanish descent she seemed a pale, delicate flower, aloof, serene, untouchable.

To the young Army officers in the Tucson vicinity, Laura Sackett was utterly fascinating, and this feeling was not dulled by the knowledge that she was a married woman. Her husband, it was known, was Congressman Orrin Sackett, who was in Washington, D.C. Apparently they had separated.

But nobody seemed to know just what the status of the marriage was, and Laura offered no comment, nor did she respond to hints.

Her conduct was irreproachable, her manner ladylike; her voice was soft and pleasant. The more discerning did notice that her mouth was a little too tight, her eyes shadowed with hardness, but these characteristics were usually lost in the quiet smiles that hovered about her lips.

Nobody in Tucson had ever known Jonathan Pritts, Laura's father, and none of them had been present in the vicinity of Mora during the land-grant fighting.

Jonathan Pritts was now dead. A narrow, bigoted man, tight-fisted and arrogant, he had been idolized by his daughter and only child, and with his death her hatred for the Sacketts had become a fierce, burning urge to destroy.

She had seen her father driven from Mora, his dream of empire shattered, his hired gunmen killed or imprisoned. A vain, petty, and self-important man, he had impressed upon his daughter that he was all the things he assumed he was, and to her all other men were but shadows before the reality of her father.

Until he had come west, they had lived together in genteel poverty. His schemes for riches had failed one by one, and with each failure his rancor and bitterness grew. Each failure, he was positive, had come not from any mistake on his part, but always from the envy or hatred of others.

Laura Pritts had married Orrin Sackett with one thought in mind—to further her father's schemes. Orrin, big, handsome, and genial, and fresh from the Tennessee hills, had never seen a girl like Laura. She seemed everything he had ever dreamed of. Tyrel had seen through her at once, and through her father as well, but Orrin would not listen. He was seeing what he wished to see—a great lady, a princess almost—graceful, alluring, a girl of character and refinement. But in the end he saw her, and her father, for what they were, and he had left her. And now Laura Pritts Sackett was returning, without a plan, without anything but the desire to destroy those who had destroyed her father.

As if by magic, on the stage to Tucson, the pieces began to fall into place. At the first stage stop east of Yuma she overheard the driver talking to the station tender.

"Saw him in Yuma," the driver was saying. "I'd have known him anywhere. Those Sackett boys all look alike."

"Sackett? The gunfighter?"

"They're all good with their guns. This one is Tell Sackett. He's been out California way."

The idea came to her that night. She had been trying to think of some way to hurt the Sacketts, to get even with them. Now here was Tell Sackett, the older brother, the one she had never met. It was unlikely that he knew of her difficulties with Orrin. The Sacketts wrote few letters, and from what she remembered Orrin had not seen his brother in years. Of course, he might have seen him since she left; but there was a chance, and she resolved to take it.

The means was supplied to her also by way of a conversation overheard. She had heard many such conversations without thinking of how they might be used. The men were talking of the Apaches, of some children stolen by them, perhaps killed. "Two of them were Dan Creed's boys. I don't know who the other one was."

The young Army lieutenant on the stage had made tentative efforts at a conversation with Laura, all of which she had studiously avoided. At his next attempt she surprised him by turning with a faint, somewhat remote smile.

"Is it true, Lieutenant, that there are Apaches about? Tell me about them."

Lieutenant Jack Davis leaned forward eagerly. He was a very young man, and Laura Sackett was a beautiful young woman. It was true he had himself been on only two scouts into Apache country, but he had served with older, more experienced men who had talked freely, and he had listened well.

"Yes, there are Apaches," he said, "and it is true we might encounter them at any time, but the men on this coach are all armed, and are experienced fighting men. You will not need to worry."

"I was not worried about them, Lieutenant, merely curious. Is it true that when attacked they retreat into Mexico? Into the Sierra Madre?"

"Unfortunately, yes. And the Mexicans are not helpful. They refuse to allow any of our armed forces to cross the border in pursuit, although I believe there are some indications the two governments may work together against the Apaches."

"So it seems likely that if a prisoner were taken over the border into Mexico you would not have much chance of recovering him, would you?"

"Almost none. A few times exchanges have been arranged. In a few cases individuals have traded goods or horses for a prisoner; but if the Apaches are pursued, they usually kill their prisoners."

Laura Pritts Sackett was thoughtful, and at the next stage stop she wrote her note to William Tell Sackett. Unless she was completely mistaken, he would come to Tucson at once; and unless she was equally mistaken, he would start at once for the Sierra Madre. The rest would be up to the Apaches.

What the Apaches failed to do, if they failed, might be done by other means . . . for which the Apaches would receive due credit.

Skillfully, she drew out the young lieutenant, and his comments were added to from time to time by one or another of the coach passengers. By the time the stage arrived in Tucson, Laura was well posted on the activities of the Apaches in Arizona Territory, as well as on the many times they had killed or kidnaped children, from the Oatman Massacre to the moment of her stage trip.

"Supposing one man or several men—not soldiers—were to try to go into the Sierra Madre?" she asked Lieutenant Davis.

"They would never return alive." The lieutenant was positive. "They wouldn't have a chance."

One of the passengers, a bleak, hard-faced man in rough frontier garb, looked around at him briefly. "Depend on the man," he said after a moment, but if he was heard his comment was not acknowledged.

That night, seated before her mirror, Laura Sackett knew she had found what she wanted. To trap his beloved brother would be just as satisfying as to trap Orrin himself, or Tyrel, whom she blamed even more.

She wished only for one thing: to see their faces when they realized how their brother had been duped.

When that man at the stage station in Yuma told me there was a letter for me I thought he was surely mistaken. Why, I couldn't recall getting more than three or four letters in my whole life, and nobody knew I was in Yuma—nobody at all.

None of us folks had been much hand to write. Orrin and Tyrel had learned to write, but with me writing was an almighty slow affair, and not one to be undertaken lightly. And we were never much on just exchanging letters unless there was something all-fired important. But sure enough, this letter was for me, William Tell Sackett. It read:

> *Dear Tell:*
>   *Our son, Orrin's and mine, has been taken by the Apaches.*
> *Orrin is in Washington, D.C. Tyrel is laid up.*
>   *Can you help me?*
>
>   *Laura Sackett*

So old Orrin had him a boy! Now, nobody had seen fit to tell me, but drifting place to place the way I'd been, it was no wonder. And no need for me to know, when it came to that.

None of the family knew where I was, but that need cut no ice now. When I'd needed help the whole lot of them had come a-running, and if the Apaches had Orrin's boy I'd have to move fast before they killed him . . . if they hadn't already.

A body never knew what the Apaches would do. They might kill a child right off, or they might cotton to the youngster and raise him like one of their own sons, and with just as much affection and care. A lot depended on how old the boy was, on how he reacted, and on how fast the Apaches had to move.

The Apaches, I knew, had respect for the brave. They had no use for weakness or cowardice, and you'd get nothing but contempt by asking for mercy.

An Apache admired the virtues he himself needed in the life he led. Bravery, fortitude, endurance, and the skills of the hunter and the hunted —these were important to him, these he understood.

Tucson lay still under a hot noonday sun when we dusted our hocks down the main drag, eyes open for a saloon or an eating house where there'd be shade, something to wet our whistles, and the trail gossip we were eager to hear.

We rode into town with care, for we were all men with enemies. We rode with our guns loose in the holsters, ready to run or fight, as the case might be; but the street was empty, heavy with heat.

The temperature was over a hundred in the shade.

"All this town needs," John J. Battles said, "is more water and a better class of people."

"That's all hell needs," Spanish replied. "Let's get into the shade."

We were hard and lonely men who rode a hard and lonely way. We had known nothing of each other until this ride began in Yuma, and even now we knew scarcely more. But we had sweated and thirsted together, we had hungered and fought, and eaten trail dust together; so now we rode as brothers ride.

We were men with sorrows behind us, and battles too; men with regrets behind us of which we did not speak, nor too often think. With none to share our sorrows or regrets, we kept them to ourselves, and our faces were impassive. Men with no one to share their feelings learn to conceal those feelings. We often spoke lightly of things which we took very seriously indeed.

We were sentimental men, but that was our secret, for an enemy who knows your feelings is an enemy who has a hold on you. Not all poker is played over a card table.

Although we spoke so lightly of Tucson we all liked the town, and were glad to be there.

Me, I was nothing but a tall boy from the high-up Tennessee hills who tried to live the way he'd been taught. Ma hadn't much book learning, but she had straight-out ideas on what was fair and decent, and there was no nonsense about her and pa when it came to dealing with enemies, or those who were evil.

Pa stood by the same principles ma did, but pa taught us other things too: how to stand up for what he believed was right, and to back down for no man when it came to fighting time. He taught us how to fight, how to find our way through rough country, and how to handle cards better than most gamblers, although he didn't hold with gambling.

"If you go among the Philistines," he used to say, "it is better to go armed."

So he taught us how to recognize a bottom deal, and to read marked cards, and how the sharpers operated.

The four of us split up on the street in Tucson. Rocca had some friends in the Mexican town, and Spanish Murphy went with him. John J. Battles had plans of his own, and so had I.

With me there was no choice, and little time. I met an idea head-on, and this time I had to do whatever might be done for that boy of Orrin's. I'd get cleaned up, get a bite to eat, and then I'd find this Laura Sackett.

I'd never met Orrin's wife, but any woman Orrin would cotton to would be all right with me. I'd been away from the other boys and knew little of their affairs. Tyrel had married a girl of Spanish blood, and had done well. Orrin had run for office and been elected, and I did recall some talk of his marrying, but none of the details. Nor had I any idea why she was in Tucson, and him in Washington. Folks' affairs are their own business, and I never was one for asking questions. What folks wanted me to know they would tell me, and I had enough to keep me busy.

The Shoo-Fly Restaurant was a long, narrow room with a white muslin ceiling and a floor of rammed earth. There were a few windows, and a dozen or so tables of pine boards, and some chairs and benches, none of which would set quite even on the floor, but the food was good, and it was a cool, quiet place after the desert.

When I ducked through the door and straightened up inside, it taken me a moment to get my eyes accustomed to the place.

Three Army officers sat at one table, two older men and their wives at another. John Titus and a man named Bashford, both important men in the community, sat nearby. At a table in the corner near the window sat a blonde young woman, pale and pretty, her parasol beside her. When I came in she looked at me quick and puzzled, then glanced away.

Seemed like I was the roughest-dressed man in the place, and the biggest. My boots were down at heel, and my big California-style spurs rattled when I walked. My jeans were 'most wore out, and they carried a blood stain. I'd shaved, all right, but my hair was long and shaggy, and of course I was packing a six-shooter as well as a bowie knife, and carrying a Winchester.

Mrs. Wallen, who ran the place, remembered me from a while back. "How do you do, Mr. Sackett," she said. "Did you just get in?"

"Four of us did," I said dryly. "Two of us didn't."

Titus looked around at me. "Apaches?"

"Uh-huh . . . I'd say about fifteen, twenty of them."

"Get any of them?"

"Some," I said, and took a seat at a table near the wall where I could see the door and could stand my rifle in a corner.

"If you got any," one of the Army officers said, "you were lucky."

"I was lucky," I said.

Mrs. Wallen, who knew hungry men, as any frontier woman would, was already at the table with a cup and a pot of coffee. Then she brought me a slab of beef and some chili and beans, regular fare for that country.

As I ate, my muscles relaxed. A man on the run or fighting can get himself all keyed up with muscle and nerve ready for trouble until he's tighter than a drumhead. This was a pleasant room, and while I was never much hand for mixing in society, I liked folks, and liked to be among them.

Orrin was the mixer of the family. He had him an easy way with folks, he liked to talk and to listen, and he played a guitar and sang like any good Welshman. Give him ten minutes in a room and he'd be friends with everybody there.

Me, I was quiet. I guess I'm friendly enough, but I was never much hand at getting acquainted with folks. I figure I was shaped to be a wallflower, but I don't mind. I sort of like to set back and listen to folks, to drink coffee, and contemplate.

When trouble shaped up, Orrin would try to talk a man out of it, although he was a hand at any kind of fighting when they decided not to listen. Tyrel, he was the mean one. I mean he was a fine man, but you couldn't push him. He just hadn't any give in him at all. If you come to Tyrel a-hunting after trouble he had plenty to offer. Me, I wasn't much of a talker, and no kind of a trouble-hunter. Folks had to bring it to me hard, but when they did that I just naturally reacted.

I'd roped and hogtied many a wild longhorn out on the plains of Texas, and I'd busted some mustangs in my time, and quite a few hard-to-get-along-with men, too. When it came to shooting, well, me and Tyrel could never figure which was best. We had both been shooting since we were big enough to lift a cartridge.

Sitting there in that quiet room, my muscles resting easy and the warmth of food stealing through me, I listened to the talk around and wondered if ever I would have a home of my own. Seemed as if every chance left me with less than before.

My home was wherever I hung my hat, but these here were mostly settled folks out for a bite to eat on a Sunday, which this was. Back in the mountains, some Sunday we used to dress in our go-to-meetin' clothes and drive down to church.

It was a fine old get-together in those days. We'd listen to the preacher expounding of our sins, most of us kind of prideful we'd managed to sin so much, but ashamed before his tongue-lashing, and some were kind of amazed that they were so sinful after all. Seemed like with farming and cussing the mules, a body didn't rightly find much time for sinning.

We'd sing the hymns in fine, rolling, and sometimes out-of-tune voices, and after church we'd set out under the trees with our picnic lunches and some of the womenfolks would swap food back and forth. Emmy Tatum, she made the best watermelon pickles any place around, and old Jeannie Bland from up at the forks of the creek, she could make apple cider that would grow bark on a mushroom.

That was long ago and far away, but sometimes I could set back and close my eyes and still hear those folks a-singing "On Jordan's Stormy Banks" or "Rock of Ages," or maybe the one about the church in the wildwood. Everything was homemade, even the clothes we wore. Why, I'd been nigh to sixteen before I ever saw a pair of store-bought pants, or shoes we hadn't cobbled ourselves out of our own tanned leather.

One of the Army officers was standing beside my table. "Mind if I sit down, sir?" he said.

"Welcome," I said. "My name is Sackett, William Tell Sackett."

He extended his hand. "Captain Lewiston, sir. You mentioned a difficulty with the Apaches. Did you get a good look at any of them?"

"Well, they weren't reservation Indians, if that's what you mean."

"How do you know that?"

Me, I just looked at him. "By the smell of them. They'd come out of the desert after a long ride. The droppings of their horses showed fibers of desert plants they'd eat only if there was nothing else."

"Did you say you got some of them?"

"Three . . . and one I hurt but didn't kill."

He looked at me, and so I told him. "He was too good a fighting man to kill, Captain. I got two of them with my rifle, and then two jumped me in the hollow. One I killed, but the other was a tiger. He seemed to have been paralyzed so I let him lay."

"You weren't alone?"

"Three men along with me, but not right there. I think they might have killed some, too."

"You lost two men?"

"Taylor and Billy Higgins. I never knew Taylor's first name. We didn't get a chance to pick up their bodies. When we could pull out, we did."

"About the dead ones, now. Did one of them have a scar on his cheekbone? That would be just too much to expect, I suppose."

"No . . . not the dead ones. I didn't notice any scars on the dead ones. But that one I left alive, he had a scar on his cheekbone."

Chapter 3

Captain Lewiston sighed. "You may wish you had killed him, Mr. Sackett. That was Kahtenny, one of the most dangerous and elusive Apaches of them all."

"He was in pretty bad shape, Captain, and I'm no man to kill a fighter like that when he's down and helpless."

Lewiston smiled. "I feel the same, but I am afraid there are some who do not. There are those who feel they all should be killed."

That there blonde girl across the room was sure enough listening, although she was making quite a show of doing nothing but sort of idling over her food.

"Captain, I fought those Indians because they attacked me. I don't blame them for that. The Apache has made fighting his way of living for as long as his oldest people can recall. Or as long as the oldest Pimas and Papagos recall.

"The way I figure it, they fight because it's their way, and we fight back because it's our way. Somebody wins, somebody loses. Nobody in this country, or anywhere that I know of, can live in peace unless he's got somebody somewhere, protecting him."

Mrs. Wallen brought the Captain some coffee, and we sat there a few minutes more, discussing the Apache and his ways.

"You've been a soldier, Mr. Sackett?"

"Yes, sir. I served four years during the War Between the States. I was at Shiloh and the Wilderness . . . and a few other places."

"We could use you here. Ever thought of joining up again?"

"No. I did what I had to do when the time came to do it. Now I'll fight when somebody can't be persuaded to leave me alone. Seems to me I've done enough Indian fighting without joining up to hunt for it."

"Are you related to Congressman Sackett?"

"Brother. Fact is, I'm here to talk to his wife."

I glanced across the room at the blonde girl, who was now looking right at me. "I figure to get their son back from the Apaches."

"Their son?" Lewiston looked puzzled, but before he could say more, Laura Sackett interrupted.

"Tell? I am Laura Sackett. Will you join me?"

So I got up. "Excuse me, Captain," I said, and taking my coffee I walked over to her table.

"Howdy, ma'am. Seems strange, not knowing you, but when you and Orrin married I was clean across the country. Never heard much about it."

"Sit down, Tell. We must talk." She put her hand on mine and looked at me with those wide blue eyes. "Let's not talk about trouble now, Tell. I want to know about you. After all, we must get to know each other."

Now, there isn't much that's more likely to make a man talk than a pretty woman who is ready to listen, so I found myself a-talking to her, mostly about Ange and how I found her high up in those far Colorado mountains where nobody lived, and then how she was murdered and how I hunted down the killer and got myself in a tight spot.

She had a pretty smile, and she gave me a lot of it. There were a couple of things about her looks that I didn't really shape up to like, but nobody is perfect. She had a small mouth, and it was kind of tight and hard at times, but she was a pleasure to talk to, and I talked.

Finally, she said would I walk her home, and it came to me suddenly that we'd talked the afternoon away and those Army officers were gone. Once out of the restaurant, she told me about the boy Orry, as she called him.

"He was taken with the Creed boys," she explained, "and the Army can do nothing. I know if Orrin were here he would ride right down into Mexico and bring him back, but by the time Orrin could get here it might be too late. Then I heard you were in Yuma. You were my only chance."

"How old is the boy?"

"He's five . . . going on six." She paused. "I must warn you, Tell, whatever you decide to do, you must not mention it around here. The Army would not allow you to cross the border on any such mission. Right now they are trying to arrange a working agreement with the Mexicans to join forces in stamping out the Apaches. They want to attack them right in their stronghold in the Sierra Madre . . . and that's another reason we must hurry. I have heard that if the Apaches are attacked they will kill all their captives."

Shortening my pace, I walked beside her. There was small chance the boy was alive, but I could not tell her that. Not that I even gave thought to not going to hunt for him. We Sacketts stand by one another, come hell or high water. The boy was a Sackett, and he was my brother's son.

My mind went down that trail into Mexico, and I had a cold feeling along my spine. Every inch of that trail would be trouble, and not only from the Apaches. Water was scarce, and whilst the folks were friendly, the Rurales and the Army were not. They'd likely shoot a man out of hand.

Somewhere along the trail I'd heard about Dan Creed's two boys and another youngster being taken, but I hadn't any details, and they weren't important now.

A body would have to be almighty cautious. If the Army got wind of anyone going into Mexico with any such notion that would be the end of it. They'd surely stop him.

With negotiations going on between the two governments that would be all it would take to end them . . . they'd never believe he'd come into Mexico on his own. My name being Sackett, and all, they might be suspicious. I mean the Army might.

And Laura made me uneasy. I'd no knowledge of womenfolks, and never had been able to talk to any but Ange. Other women left me tongue-tied and restless; and Laura, she was all white lace, blonde hair, and those dainty little lacy gloves with no fingers in them. And that parasol she carried . . . I was a raw country boy from the hills, not used to such fixings.

"You will try, then?" We had stopped at her door, and she rested her hand on my arm. "Tell, you're my only hope. There is no one else."

"I'll do what I can." Standing there on the step, with her a-looking at me from those big blue eyes, it made me wish I was three men, so as I could do more. "Don't you forget, ma'am, there's no accounting for Apaches. They're mighty notional when it comes to prisoners. You mustn't be hoping for much."

"He's such a little boy."

It came on me to wonder if she'd any notion what she was letting me in for, but I pushed the thought away. I had no call to be thinking of myself. How could she know what that trail into Sonora was like? A trail like a walk through hell, with ugly death waiting on every side, at every moment. You had to travel trails like that to know them. In my mind's eye I could see the faint thread of it winding across the hot desert under a brassy sky, with the sand underfoot and all kinds of cactus and thorny bush around, with rattlers and Gila monsters and all . . . to say nothing of outlaws and Indians.

A thought came to me suddenly. "I was wondering how Orrin ever let you get so far from him? You and the boy?"

She smiled quickly, sadly. "It was my father, Tell. He died in California and I had to go there for the funeral. There was no one else. When I found how dangerous it was, I left Orry here . . . I thought he'd be safe here."

That made sense, all right. Still, there was a lot that puzzled me, but a man could waste any amount of time quibbling and fussing over details, which was never my way. If anything was to be done it had to be done fast. With her description of the boy and his clothing, I decided I'd best get together an outfit and pull out.

She stood there, her white dress like a light against the adobe walls. I looked back once as I walked away, and she was still standing there, looking after me.

It worried me some because this whole thing had come on me so sudden that I'd no chance to sort of think things through. Out there on the trail with those Apaches around there'd been no time, and now it seemed there was no time either. Nevertheless, there was some thinking I had to do.

The worst of it was I was almighty short of money, and no matter what a man sets out to do, it seems it costs him something. This here was going to cost money as well as sweat, and maybe blood.

All I had to my name was about two hundred saved-up dollars, the most I'd had in months, and I'd lost my saddle back yonder, and needed a horse. We'd come into Tucson on horses just borrowed from the stage outfit, and they'd be going back soon.

So I needed a horse and an outfit, and a pack horse if I had enough to handle it.

What I wanted was a good used saddle, and there was a reason. I was of no mind to ride into Apache country with a squeaky new saddle. Now, any saddle will squeak a mite, and it's a comforting sort of sound, most times; but when there are Apaches around any sound more than your breathing is liable to get you killed.

I needed not only a saddle, but also, a pair of saddlebags, a canteen, a poncho, a blanket, a spare cartridge belt and a small amount of grub. I'd have to live off the country, on food I could get without shooting. From the time I crossed the border I was going to have to move like a ghost.

Tampico Rocca was in the Quartz Rock Saloon when I came in, and I went to his table and sat down. He leaned across the table. "John J., he rides out tonight. There is trouble, I think."

"Trouble?"

"There was difficulty in Texas. Battles won out. Two of the dead man's brothers are in town, with some friends. Battles wants no more trouble."

"He's broke, isn't he?" Me, I dug down in my jeans. "I'm outfitting for Mexico, but I can let him have twenty dollars."

Rocca shook his head. "This is not what I mean, *amigo*. He will meet us outside of town. He wished me to tell you this so you would not think he rode off alone. We are coming with you, *señor*."

"Now, you see here. This is my affair, and you boys got no call to ride along. It's going to be rough."

Tampico chuckled. "*Amigo*, you talk to Rocca, not to some pilgrim. I am Rocca, who is half Apache and who has lived with them. I know where they go. I know how they live. You will need me, *amigo*."

Well, I just sat there, finding nothing to say. Words just don't come easy to me, and at such times I find myself coming up empty. So I just looked at him and he grinned and waved for another beer.

The place was filling up, and it was a tough place. Nobody ever said the Quartz Rock was gentle. Over at the Congress Hall Saloon you'd find the gentry. You'd find the solid men, the good men, and mixed with them some of the drifters, but the Quartz Rock was rough. At least when Foster ran it.

You drank their liquor and you took your chances at the games, and the men who hung out there were hard cases, men with the bark on, men who had been born with the bark on. There were men came into that place so rough they wore their clothes out from the inside first. When you saw a man walk into the Quartz Rock wearing a six-shooter or a bowie knife he wasn't wearing it for show.

We were finishing our second beer when four men came into the place. Rocca sat up easily and moved on the chair to keep his gun hand free. This was beginning to shape up like grief of some kind, and I was in no mood for it.

They were four of a kind, raw and rugged, just in off the trail and they looked it. Like uncurried wolves they bellied up to the bar, and when they had had a drink, they looked around.

"It is those who seek for John J., *amigo*. I think they know I am his friend."

They crossed the room, the four of them, and every man-jack in the room could smell the trouble they brought with them.

They came to our table and ranged themselves in front of it. All of them were armed, and they wore guns as if they knew how to use them.

Me, I just sort of shifted one foot. The other foot was propped up on a chair's edge, resting easy.

"You!" The one with the handle-bar mustache stabbed a finger at

Rocca. "You, greaser. They tell me you are a friend of the man named Battles."

Rocca was like a coiled snake. He looked at them, and he smiled. Now no Mex likes to be called a greaser. Me, I've been called a gringo many times and couldn't see that it left any scars, but some folks are almighty touchy, and Rocca was that way now. Not that I blamed him. It is all very easy to say trouble can be avoided, but these men were not going to be avoided. They were looking for trouble; they wanted it.

"Si, *señor*," Rocca said gently, "I am honored to call John J. Battles my friend."

"Then I guess we'll just kill you, Mex, seein' as how we can't find him."

Well, I just looked up at the man and I said, "I'm a friend of his, too," and I said it sort of off-hand as if it didn't matter much, but they knew it did.

They turned their eyes on me, and I just sat there, a tall, lonely man in a wore-out buckskin shirt and a beat-up hat.

"You want part of this?" Walrus-mustache was speaking again.

"A man can ride many a long mile in Texas," I said, "and see nothing but grass and sky. There's streams down there, and a man could raise some cows. Here in Arizona there's timber country with fine, beautiful meadows and cold mountain streams—"

"What're you talkin' about?" Handle-bar mustache broke in. "Are you crazy?"

"I was just thinking a man would have to be an awful fool to throw all that away to prove how mean he was. I mean you boys got a choice. You walk back over there and drink your liquor and ride out to those mountain streams where the tall grass grows."

"Or—?"

"Or you stay here, and tomorrow you'll be pushin' grass from the under side."

They stared at me. They were trying to figure whether I was all talk, or whether I was tough. Now, I'm a patient man. Had they been talking to Tyrel, folks would have been laying out the bodies by now. Me, I'm not backward about giving a man a chance. Many a time a man with whiskey in him is apt to talk too much, and suddenly realize he wished he was somewhere else. I was giving them this chance.

They didn't take it.

The long-geared man with the handle-bar mustache looked at me and said, "I'm Arch Hadden," as if he expected me to show scare at the name.

"Glad to meet you, Mr. Hadden," I said gently. "I'll carve the slab myself."

He kind of flushed up, and I could see he was off his step, somehow. He'd come walking up to fight, and my talk had put him off. Also, that name meant nothing to me, and I never was one to put much stock in reputations, anyway.

Rocca had let me talk; he just sat quiet, but I'd come up the trail from Yuma with Tampico Rocca, and knew he was no man to buy trouble with. Arch Hadden had lost step, and he tried to get back again.

"I came to kill this greaser, an' I aim to do it."

Rocca came to his feet in one smooth, easy movement. "Then why not get started?"

The man with the walrus mustache had had more to drink, and he wasn't being bluffed. He went for his gun, and I straightened my leg with a snap. The chair slammed into his legs and he fell against Hadden, and I shot the man on the end while they were falling. I heard another gun boom and then Rocca and me were standing there looking down at Hadden and his brother, one of them in a half-crouch but off balance, the other on one knee.

"You boys brought it to us," I said. "We didn't ask for it. You brought it, and now two of you are dead."

They hadn't looked at their companions until then, and when they did I saw they were suddenly cold sober.

"Arch," I said, "you may be a tough man where you come from, but you're a long way from home. You take my advice and go back."

Rocca was holding a gun on them, as I was. He reached around with his other hand and picked up his beer, and drank it, watching them.

Foster was standing across the room, his back to the bar. "Why don't you boys pack it up before the law gets here?" he suggested. "I don't want any more shooting in here. It's bad for business."

"Sure," I said, and holstered my gun. Deliberately I started for the door.

Tampico Rocca had been called a greaser, so he took his time. He put his glass down gently and he smiled at them. "Keep your guns," he said, "I want to meet you again, *señores.*"

Outside in the street we ducked into an alley and stood listening for footsteps, but hearing none, we walked away.

At the corral we stopped and leaned on the bars, and Rocca built a cigarette. "*Gracias, amigo,*" he said. And then he added, "You are quick, *amigo*. You are very quick."

Chapter 4

Come daybreak, and worry was upon me. It was a real, old-fashioned attack of the dismals.

The shooting of the night before was bad enough, although I never gave much time to worry over those who came asking for trouble. When a man packed a gun he was supposed to give some thought to his actions and his manner of speech, for folks weren't much inclined to set back and let a body run over them.

It was that youngster who was worrying me. There was a small boy, a prisoner of the Apaches, or maybe already killed by them. And he was my blood kin.

Nobody knew better than me the distance I'd have to cover and the way I'd have to live for the next month or more. It was a hard country, almost empty of people, and scarce of food, and rare of water that was fit to drink.

The fact that Tampico Rocca was coming along sort of made it better. Two men can't move as quiet as one, except when one of them is Rocca. But his coming also made it worse, because if anything happened to him it would be because of me.

Now the first thing I needed was a horse, and I could find none for sale. Meantime I sort of sauntered around and let folks know I needed a saddle, and finally bought a beat-up old Spanish single-rig saddle with a *mochila*, or housing, to throw over it, and oxbow stirrups. It was almighty old, but in good shape, and a lot of hard use had worn comfort into it. That saddle set me back eighteen dollars, and I picked up some old saddle-bags for three dollars more. An old Army canteen cost me twenty-five cents. Little by little I put an outfit together, and by the time I'd bought a spare cartridge belt, a bridle, and a few other odds and ends I'd spent more than fifty dollars of what little I had. And still no horse.

Whilst I went around the town of Tucson I kept a careful eye open for Arch and Wolf Hadden. It turned out that one of those boys shot the night before wasn't dead. He'd been hit hard, but he was going to pull through. They planted the other one, wrapped in his blankets, out on Boot Hill.

By noontime I had most of what I would need, but was still shy a horse. Dropping in at the Shoo-Fly I figured to have myself a bite of grub, and maybe I could find somebody with a horse to spare.

So I shaved myself with a broken triangle of glass for a mirror, stuck in the fork of a mesquite tree, while Rocca slept with his head on his saddle close by. We were a mite out of town among some rocks and mesquite, and we'd been there awhile when I heard somebody singing "Oh, Bury Me Not on the Lone Prairie," and Rocca pushed his hat back off his eyes. "Don't shoot," he said, grinning at me. "That's John J."

And it was. Battles came up through the brush and looked us over, and we told him what the score was.

"Where's Spanish?" he wanted to know, and Rocca told him.

"He found himself a gal down yonder. Her name is Conchita, and if she gets mad at him the Apaches will be a relief. But don't you worry none about Spanish. When the time comes he'll fork his saddle and come with us."

When I'd shaved we talked things over a mite and Rocca headed for Mexican town to roust out Spanish Murphy, whilst Battles went back into the brush to keep out of sight. Somehow or other, neither of us thought to tell him about the Hadden outfit.

The Shoo-Fly was crowded when I came in, but I turned some heads. I don't know if it was the gun battle the night before or the whiskey I'd used for shave lotion, but they looked me over some. I'd been sort of side-stepping the marshal, not wanting to be ordered out of town yet, and not wanting trouble, if he was so inclined.

When it came to eating, I was always a good feeder and always ready to set up and partake. Likely this would be the last woman-cooked food I'd have for a while, and even any hot meals I'd cook myself would be al-mighty scarce on that trek down into Sonora and over into Chihuahua. When a man is fighting shy of Apaches he doesn't go around sending up smoke.

Sitting there in the Shoo-Fly, which was not exactly elegant, though the best there was around, a body might have an idea folks would step aside for a body who'd killed his man in a gun battle. No such thing.

Right there in that room there were men like William S. Oury, who had fought through the Texas war for independence, had been a Texas Ranger, and had engaged in many a bloody duel with Apaches and border characters. Most of the men sitting around in their broadcloth suits were men who had engaged in their share of Indian fights, or wars of one kind or another. And they were good citizens—lawyers, mining men, storekeepers and the like.

No sooner had I begun to eat than the door opened and Laura came in. She was in white, and she looked pale and frail. She wore the kind of gloves with no fingers in them that made no sense to me. And she carried a parasol, as most women did.

She stood a moment, letting her eyes grow accustomed to the glare, and then crossed to my table. I got up and seated her, then sat down.

Folks turned to look at her; they were almighty curious, her being such a pretty woman and all, and not many of them knowing we were kin.

"Tell," she said, "I heard you were looking for a horse. Is that true?"

"Yes, ma'am, it is. Mine was killed out yonder. I've got to find a saddle horse and at least one pack horse. Seems Apache raids have cut down the supply, and the Army has been buying saddle stock, too."

"Why didn't you tell me? I can get you some horses. In fact, I have just the horse for you."

"It would help," I admitted. "I've got my outfit together."

She took the coffee Mrs. Wallen brought to the table, and then said, "I hear you had some trouble."

"It wasn't my trouble. They were hunting a man I know, and when they couldn't find him they chose me—that is, me and Rocca, one of the men I rode to town with."

She said no more about it, and I wasn't anxious to talk of it. We talked awhile about the trip, and then she told me where to go to see the horses. "The one I want you to ride," she suggested, "is the big black with the diamond blaze on his hip."

Now, one horse I was not hunting was a big black with a diamond on his hip. Any kind of horse would help, but a black horse was almost as bad as a white one in that country. What I preferred was a roan, a buckskin, or a dun or *grulla*. I wanted a horse whose color would fade into the country, not one that would stand out like a red nose at a teetotal picnic. Of course, there were patches of black rock, shadows, and the like, and a black horse was some better than a white one which would catch the sun and could be seen for miles. However, this was no time to argue.

"All right," I said; and then I added, "If we get the horses I can leave tomorrow."

She talked of Tucson and its discomforts, and how she wished to be back in Santa Fe—or in Washington, she added.

"I like Washington," I said.

She seemed surprised, and said, "You have been there?"

"Yes, ma'am. I was in the Army of the Potomac for a while. I was around Washington quite a bit."

That was a long time ago, and I'd been a boy then, freshly joined up with the Union army.

When she was gone I lingered over coffee, thinking out that trail to the south, trying to foresee the problems that might arise. It wasn't in me to go into things blind, and there was a whole lot about this that made me kind of uneasy, but there was nothing I could pin down.

Mrs. Wallen came over. "Are you related to Laura Sackett?"

"She's my sister-in-law."

"I wondered . . . your names being the same, and all." She still hesitated, then sat down opposite me. "We don't see many women traveling alone in this country."

"Her father died . . . out in Californy," I said. "He was all alone out there, and nobody to see to him. Orrin—he's my brother—had to stay in Washington."

She sat there awhile without saying any more, and then got up and left. I couldn't figure out why she sat down to talk to me. It seemed as if she was going to tell me something—maybe something about the Army or the Apaches.

The black horse was a good one, all right. And that diamond-shaped blaze on his hip and one white stocking was all that kept him from being solid black. He was a whole lot more horse than I expected to find. The two pack horses were nondescript mustangs, but they looked tough.

They were in a barn back of an adobe, and the man who had the care of them squatted on his heels and watched me studying the horses.

"You're takin' a lot of care, mister," he said sourly, "when you got no choice."

He spat out the straw he'd been chewing. "Take 'em or leave 'em. I got no more time to spare. The lady paid for 'em. All you got to do is saddle up and ride."

He didn't like me and I didn't like him, so I taken the horses and got away. I rode them back into the brush where Rocca was waiting and where my gear was cached.

Rocca had rustled a horse from somewhere in Mex town, so we were ready to go.

"You got anything holdin' you?" I asked him.

"Not so's you'd notice. Spanish is out in the brush with John J. They'll meet us south of here."

So we mounted up and rode out of there, paying no mind to anything else. Down country about four miles Spanish rode up to us, and then John J. Battles followed.

"You boys are taking a wild chance," I said. "You got no stake in this."

"Shut up," Spanish said. "You save your breath to cool your porridge."

"I never been to the Sierra Madre," John J. said. "Any place I ain't been I got to see."

We put up some dust and headed south, with me riding up front. The trail was used . . . there was always some riding down toward Kitchen's ranch.

You might think that on a traveled trail you'd be safe, but there was nowhere in this corner of Arizona where a body was safe, one moment to the next. Pete Kitchen had men on watch all hours of the day, and everybody went armed, expecting trouble, so after a while the Apaches kind of fought shy of the Kitchen outfit.

There's been a lot of talk of the rights and wrongs of the Indian wars, and there was wrong on both sides. There were mighty few Indians holding down land in this country when the white man came, and most of them never held to any one spot. They just drifted from place to place, living off the wild game and the plants. The white men came hunting living space, and a place for a home. Instead of roaming as the Indians had done, they settled down to farm the land and build houses.

Some of the white men wanted to live in peace with the red man, and some of the red men wanted to live in peace, too; but some on both sides didn't want anything of the kind. The young bucks wanted to take scalps and steal horses because that made them big men with the squaws, and it was often easier to take them from white men than from other Indians, as they had always done. And whenever the wise old Indians and the wiser and kinder of the white men wanted to make peace, there was always some drunken white man or wild-haired Indian ready to make trouble.

When an Indian made war he made war on women and children as well as on men, and even the friendly white men found it hard to be friendly when they came home and found their cabins burned, their women and children killed. On the other hand, the politically appointed Indian agents and the white men who wanted Indian land or horses would rob, cheat, and murder Indians.

It was no one-sided argument, and I knew it. But now the Apaches had stolen some children and taken them into Mexico, and we were going after them.

We rode through the last of the afternoon and into the cool of the evening. We camped that night in some ruins, half sheltered by adobe walls, and at daybreak we rode out.

On the second night we stayed at Pete Kitchen's ranch.

Chapter 5

We rode south for a few miles after leaving Pete Kitchen's place, then turned off the main trail toward the east. Now, a man who leaves a trail in the desert had best know exactly where he is going, for his life is at stake.

Travel in the desert cannot be haphazard. Every step a man takes in desert country had to be taken with water in mind. He is either heading for water, or figuring how far he will be from it if he gets off the trail. The margin of safety is narrow.

All of us had been south of the border, but it was Tampico Rocca who knew most about it, with me coming second, I suppose. Like everybody else, we had to depend on waterholes, and no matter what route we chose, sooner or later we had to wind up at those watering places. This was just as true for the Apaches.

The desert has known waterholes, but it also has other waterholes not generally known, usually of limited capacity and usually difficult to find. Birds and animals know of those places, and so do the Apaches in most cases. If you did not know of them you had to know how to find them, and that was something that did not come easy.

A man living in wild country has to be aware of everything around him. He has to keep his eyes looking, his ears listening, his every sense alert. And that doesn't mean because of Apaches, but because of the desert itself. You can't fight the desert . . . you have to ride with it.

The desert is not all hot sun and sand; there's the rocks too. Miles of them sometimes, scattered over the desert floor, great heaps of them now and again, or those great broken ridges of dull red or black rock like the broken spines of huge animals. They shove up through the sand, and the sand is trying hard to bury them again.

In much of the southwestern desert there's even a lot of green, although the *playas,* or dry lake beds, are dead white. Some of the desert plants hold back until there's a rain, then they leaf out suddenly and blossom quickly, to take advantage of that water. But much of the greenness of desert plants doesn't mean that rain has fallen, for many of the plants have stored water in their pulpy tissues to save against drought; others have developed hard-surfaced leaves that reflect sunlight and give off no moisture to the sun.

Plants and animals have learned to live with the desert, and so have the Apaches. And we, the four of us, we were like Apaches in that regard.

The desert is the enemy of the careless. Neither time, nor trails, nor equipment will ever change that. A man must stay alert to choose the easiest routes, he travels slow to save himself, he keeps his eyes open to see those signs which indicate where water might be found. The flight of bees or birds, the tracks of small animals, the kind of plants he sees—these things he must notice, for certain plants are indications of ground water, and some birds and animals never live far from water. Others drink little, or rarely, getting the moisture they need from the plants they eat or the animals they kill.

We rode until the sun was two hours in the sky, and then we turned off into a narrow canyon and hunted shade to wait through the hottest hours. We unsaddled, let the horses roll, then watered them at a little seep Rocca knew of. After that, with one man to watch, we stretched out on the sand to catch some rest.

There always had to be a man on watch, because the Apaches were great horse thieves, though not a patch on the Comanches, who could steal a horse from under you whilst you sat in the saddle. You either kept watch or you found yourself afoot; and in the desert, unless you're almighty canny, that means you're dead.

First off, when we rode into that canyon we studied the opening for sign. A man in wild country soon gets so he can read the trail sign as easy as most folks read a newspaper, and often it's even more interesting.

You not only read what sign you see on the ground, but you learn to read dust in the distant air—how many riders there are under that dust, and where they're headed.

The droppings left by horses also have a story to tell; whether that horse has been grain-fed, whether he has been grazing off country grass or desert plants.

And no two horses leave the same track. Each is a mite different, and their gaits are different. Their hoofs do not strike with the same impact, and sometimes there's a difference in the way they are shod.

We could tell that nobody had been in that canyon for weeks. We knew, too, that most of the time during the months of June, July, and August in Sonora you'll get some rain. Sudden showers that may be gone as quick as they come, but enough to settle the dust and to fill some of the "tanks" in the desert mountains.

Among those desert ridges such tanks are frequent, pits hollowed in the rock over the centuries by driving rain, or shaped by run-off water. During heavy rains these tanks collect water and hold it for weeks, or even for months. We'd had some rain, so the better waterholes and tanks were holding water now.

Shortly before sundown, rested by our nap in the shade, we saddled up again. This time I taken the lead.

There were clusters of *cholla* and *ocotillo,* and we took advantage of them as much as possible to shield our movements. The route we used was an ancient one rarely traveled in these days, but from time to time we'd pull up near a clump of brush where the outlines of our horses and ourselves would merge into the growth, and there we'd set, studying the country around us.

You might think that out in such open country, with no good cover anywhere, a body wouldn't have to worry, but knowing Apaches the way we did, we knew that twenty of them could be hidden out there in a matter of yards, and nobody the wiser.

We were taking our time, saving our horses. An Apache, who often rode his horses to death, will make sixty to seventy miles a day if he's in a hurry. On foot he'll cover thirty-five to forty miles a day even in rough country. That was about what we were doing a-horseback.

About an hour after dark we rode down into a little hollow choked with mesquite brush and built ourselves a tiny fire of dried wood and made coffee. The fire was well hidden in the hollow and the brush, and it gave us a chance to get the coffee we dearly needed.

"What you think?" Rocca said suddenly. "One rider?"

"Uh-huh," I said; "a small man or a boy."

"What are you talking about?" Battles asked.

"We've been picking up tracks," I told them. "A shod horse. A small horse, but a good one. Moves well . . . desert bred."

"Injun, on a stolen horse," Spanish said promptly. "No white man would be ridin' alone in this neck of the woods."

Rocca shrugged doubtfully. "Maybe so . . . I don't know."

Those tracks had been worrying my mind for quite a few minutes, for whoever rode that horse was riding with caution, which meant it was no Apache. An Apache would know he was in country where his people were supreme; and although he would keep alert, he would not be pausing to scout the country as this rider was.

In my mind I was sure, and I knew Rocca was sure, that the rider was no Indian. Unless, maybe, an Indian child.

When the desert sun was gone the heat went with it, and a coolness came over the land. The horses, quickened by the cool air, moved forward as eagerly as if they could already smell the pines of the Sierra Madre. From time to time we drew up to listen into the night.

About an hour before daylight we gave our horses a breather. Rocca, squatting on his heels behind a mesquite bush, lit a cigarette cupped in the palm of his hand and glanced at me. "You know the Bavispe?"

"Yes . . . we'll hit at the big bend . . . where she turns south again."

Tampico Rocca knew this country better than I did. After all, he was half Apache, and he had lived in the Sierra Madre. Battles was sleeping, and Spanish he went over to listen to the night sounds, away from our voices. I was hot and tired, and was wishing for a bath in that river up ahead, but it wasn't likely I'd get one.

Rocca was quiet for a spell, and I settled back on the sand and stared up at the stars. They looked lonely up there in the nighttime sky, lonely as we were down here. I was a solitary man, a drifter across the country, with no more home than a tumbleweed, but so were we all. We were men without women, and if all the nights we'd spent under a roof were put together they would scarcely cover four or five weeks.

Men have a way of drifting together without much rhyme or reason; just the circumstances of their living brings them together, just as we had been brought together in Yuma. Now the three of them were chancing their lives to lend me a hand; but that was the way with western men, and chances were I'd have done the same for them.

We started on again when the first streaks of dawn were coloring the eastern sky. The cactus began to be separate from the other shadows, and the rocks stood out, dark and somber. We rode single file, nobody talking until the gray sky was yellowing overhead, and then in a quiet corner we stopped, found a place to hide a fire, and made a small breakfast.

We were careful to build our fire in a hollow and under a mesquite bush, where the rising smoke would be dissipated by the branches overhead . . . though using dry wood there was little smoke. Our time for hot meals was about over. Barring some sort of accident, we should soon come up to the Bavispe. Once we crossed that we would be in the heart of Apache country, with them on every side of us.

The Apache, in a sparse, harsh land where raising any crops was mighty nigh impossible, turned to raiding and robbing.

Generally, the men I'd heard talk of the Indian thought it was taking his land that ruined him. As a matter of fact, it had much to do with it, for an Indian couldn't live on a fixed ten acres or a hundred acres and live as he liked. He needed lots of hunting ground, and country that would support fifty Indians would support ten thousand planting white men.

But the Indian was whipped the first time one of them had a rifle for his own. It was the trader who whipped the Indian by giving or selling him things he couldn't make himself. From that time on, the Indian was dependent on the white man for ammunition, for more guns, for more of the things he was getting a taste for.

It was good sitting there in the cool of early morning, with the faint smell of woodsmoke in the air, the smell of frying bacon, the smell of good coffee. We were taking a chance, but we had scouted the country with care.

"How old's the boy?" Spanish asked suddenly.

"Five . . . I think. About that."

"You think he's still alive, Tamp?" Battles asked.

Rocca shrugged. "Depends on whether he's a nervy kid, maybe. We'll pick up some tracks soon."

"Seen any more of that strange rider?" Battles asked. "I been watching for tracks all morning."

"No," I said, "I haven't seen any."

"What's it like up yonder?" Spanish asked.

"Oaks . . . then pines. Running streams, rocks. All anybody could want but grub. They have to bring it in. They get it from the Mexicans, or they kill them." He gestured. "The Apaches have almost cleared this part of Sonora of the Mexicans. At least the rich ones. And the poor ones can only stay if they'll provide food for the Apaches."

My thoughts went back over the desert to Laura. She was a pretty woman, and she was brave . . . holding herself up, like she did, with her little boy lost, and all. But somehow she left me uneasy. But I was never very comfortable around women . . . except Ange. And the Trelawney girls I'd known back home in the hills.

We sat there quiet a little longer, listening to the horses cropping at the shrubs. Rocca was smoking and squinting at the hills around.

None of us knew what might be waiting for us up yonder. Even if we found the boy alive, we still had to get him from the Apaches and get him back across the border. Our chances were none too good. I looked over at Rocca and said, "Shall we move out?"

He rubbed his cigarette into the sand, and got up.

Me, I just stood there a moment or two thinking. All of a sudden I wished I was somewhere else. We were facing up to a lot of hell, and I looked forward to none of it. Besides, there was something about this whole affair that made me mighty uneasy.

We crossed the Bavispe and took a thin trail that led up through scattered oaks, along steep switchbacks toward the pines. The only sound was the chirping of birds, the grunting of one of the horses over a steep part of the trail, or the clatter of a falling rock.

For an hour we climbed, pausing several times to let the horses catch their breath. Finally we rode out on a bench under the pines where stood the ruins of stone houses built of rough lava blocks with no mortar. There were at least a dozen of them in sight, and maybe more back under the trees. The walls were of a sort of gray felsite, and here and there one appeared to be better built than the others, as though built by different hands, by different thinking.

Rocca indicated a slight depression in the grass near one of the walls. "We're still on the trail."

A crushed pine cone looked as if it had been scarred by a sharp-shod hoof. There were other signs too.

The country here was wild and rugged, and we saw no water. We were now over six thousand feet up, judging by the growth around us, and still we climbed. The trail occasionally wound along a rim with an almost sheer drop falling off on one side or the other. We rode with our rifles in our hands, our boots light in the stirrups, ready to kick free and hit the ground if there was time. Riding that kind of country with Apaches around will put gray in your hair.

We came out presently on a shoulder of the mountain with pines all around us. There was sparse grass, and a thin trickle of snow water ran down the mountain slope. Found the tracks of the rider there . . . plain. The small horse had stood under a tree, tied to a low branch while she scouted ahead.

She?

The word came to me unbidden, without thinking. It came like a voice speaking to me, and I spoke aloud what I had heard in my mind's ear. "It's a woman, Tamp. That's a woman or girl riding that horse."

"A woman?" Battles was incredulous. "It don't stand to reason."

"Did Dan Creed have a wife? Or a daughter?" I asked.

Rocca looked around at me. "I don' know, Tell. I tell you, I don'."

I dropped to the ground. "Sit tight," I said. "I want to see what she went to look at."

A step or two and it was dark and green under the trees. A step or two more and I was lost to them, waiting back there for me. I could see a pressed-down leaf here, and the kicked-over damp, dead leaves, scuffed by a passing boot. The trail was easy, but it took time, for I scouted the trees around me as I moved.

Suddenly—a running man could scarcely have stopped in time—I was on the brink of a cliff. Not sheer, but a steep falling away, something a man could climb down if he could find foothold and used his hands, or if he could slide.

It was maybe a couple of thousand feet down to the bottom, and there was a meadow, the greenest you ever saw, and a pool with trees around it. It was a small hanging valley that opened out over an enormous canyon. There were three cooking fires in sight, and a dozen Apaches.

First I squatted down, easing down so my movement would draw no attention, and then I studied the camp through a manzanita growing on the rim.

Squaws were working, children playing. They felt secure here. Nobody had ever followed them into this country; nobody had ever found them here before. For years, for generations, they had been coming here after their raids, after stealing the cattle, the horses, and the women of the Mexicans. Stealing their food, too, and bringing it here and to other places like this . . . there must be many of them.

Little Orry was in one of them. How long could we look before they caught us?

How long, then, could we expect to live?

But Orry was my brother's son, and I was a Sackett, and in the Sackett veins the blood ran strong and true. It was our nature and our upbringing.

A few minutes longer I squatted there, watching the camp. Not staring, for staring can be felt, and will make an animal or an Indian uneasy. Then I went back through the trees.

"It's a *rancheria*," I said, "but I doubt if it is the one we want."

Chapter 6

Whoever it was who had come up the mountain before us had spent a good bit of time studying that camp. There were a-plenty of tracks, knee impressions, and the like, so we could see whoever it was had stayed there quite some time. And then that person had mounted up and ridden on.

We, too, moved on, and the trail we now followed was a deer trail . . . or maybe one made by big horn sheep, which leave a somewhat similar track. The only other tracks on the trail were those small hoof prints, or sometimes, when the rider got off and walked, were boot tracks.

We entered soon into a wild and broken country, past towering masses of conglomerate and streams of a dull opalescent water, slightly bitter to the taste, but nonetheless good for drinking. Many times we were forced to dismount and lead our mounts, for large limbs or outthrusts of rock projected over the trail.

Among some pines we pulled off and got down from our saddles. Tampico Rocca hunkered down and stared at the ground. Spanish Murphy glanced over at me. "Tell . . . you think we're going to find that boy?"

"Uh-huh."

Well, I knew what he was feeling. The quiet. It was getting us. We were in the heart of Indian country, and we were all jumpy. There wasn't one of us who didn't know what it would mean if we were seen. It would mean a running fight . . . and our only choice would be to try to get away.

Once it was known we were around we'd have no chance to get close to those children. So far we'd had luck, with the skill of Rocca to provide a good part of it—his skill and his knowledge of the country.

Presently we moved on, and now we saw Indian tracks from time to time. Up to now we had been traveling high, lonely country where Indians seldom went, but now we were descending slowly, getting into the areas where there was game, and where at any time we might encounter Indians.

"There's another *rancheria* ahead," Rocca soon said.

This one was also in a hollow, with a towering cliff behind it, and low, rolling pine-clad hills around. The *rancheria* lay in a nest of boulders and trees, with a small stream curving around the encampment. Even as we came up through the pines, several horsemen arrived. They rode into the area accompanied by a small swirl of dust and dropped to the ground. There were six Apaches in the group, four of them armed with bows, two with rifles.

Two of them were carrying chunks of meat, probably from slaughtered cattle. A third was handing down some articles of clothing, evidently stripped from some Mexican or his wife—from our distance we could not determine which.

Suddenly Battles grabbed my arm and pointed. Several children had come up, carrying bundles of sticks. At least one appeared to be a white boy; his face was partly turned from us. He was a tall youngster, perhaps eight or nine years old.

This could be the place. Whatever else we did, we must talk to that boy.

I was conscious of the fresh smell of the pines and of crushed pine needles underfoot. There was a faint smell of smoke from the camp, and I could make out the sound of Indian voices speaking. Inside me, I was still —waiting, thinking.

If there were other white children around, that boy would know about them. But what if he had already become close to being an Apache? Taken young enough, many American or Mexican children had no wish to leave the Apaches. To speak to him was a risk, but it must be done.

Spanish, he looked over at me. "We got us a job, boy," he said.

"I never figured it to be easy." I studied the *rancheria,* and I did not feel happy about the situation.

"We're too close," Rocca said. "We'd better move back. If the wind changed a mite, the dogs could smell us."

So we moved back among the trees and, weaving around a little, we found ourselves a tree-shaded hollow with a lot of boulders around and some big trees. It was a perfect place to hide, and we were out of the wind there.

But I was worried. When I traveled alone, as I most often did, I had nobody to worry about but myself, and if I got into trouble there was only my own scalp to lose. This shape-up was entirely different, for these men had come along only to help me. If anything happened to them I'd have it on my mind.

We were here, though, and we had a job to do. "Rocca," I said, "is it likely that boy yonder would ever be left alone?"

"I doubt it. Depend on how long he's been with them, and how much they've come to trust him. There's a chance maybe."

"He'd be likely to know about other white youngsters, wouldn't he?"

"It's likely. Word gets around, and the Apache children would know, and they'd be apt to speak of it. At least when I was a boy in those Apache camps I knew most of what went on."

For the time being there was nothing much we could do, so the others stretched out to catch a little sleep, and I worked up to the bluff to get a better look than we'd had before.

The camp was quiet. The squaws never stopped working, of course, always busy at something, and a few youngsters played around. One of the Apache braves we had seen ride into camp sat cross-legged in front of his wickiup. He was a stoop-shouldered but strongly made man of about my own age, and he had a new Winchester that was never far from his hand. Even here, in their own hide-out, they never let up.

After a while I returned to camp and Spanish took my place up on the bluff. Under a low tree I settled down for some rest.

When I awoke I fought myself back to reality with an effort. I'd been dog-tired, and whilst I usually was ready to wake up on the slightest sound, this time I had really slept.

The first thing I noticed was the silence. There was no fire, of course, and there was little light. It was late afternoon, and under the trees it was already shading down to dusk.

For a moment I lay quiet, listening. Raising my head, I looked around. Over yonder there was a saddle—I could see the faint shine of it. I could see nothing else, nor could I hear any sound but the soft rustling of the leaves overhead.

My right hand moved for my rifle, closed around the action. A shot fired here would bring Apaches around us like bees from a kicked hive.

Carefully, I eased back the blanket, moved my feet out, and then drew them up and rolled to my knees. Glancing to where John J. Battles was lying, I could see his body under a blanket. He was asleep . . . at least he was not moving.

Rocca was nowhere in sight; his bed was empty. We had purposely scattered out to sleep. It gave us that much more of a chance if the camp was attacked.

A moment longer I waited, then came up swiftly and with one long step was molded into the shadow of a tree. And still nothing stirred.

Nevertheless, I knew it wasn't just a case of worry with me. Somebody or something was prowling our camp, and we were too close to those Apaches for comfort. At the same time I know that the Apache, generally speaking, won't fight after dark. He has the feeling that the soul of a man killed in the night wanders forever in darkness.

Of a sudden, something moved near me.

There was no light but that of the stars. Here and there a tree trunk stood out, or a leaf caught the shine of a reflection.

It was a haunted place, this camp of ours, a corner among the crags, a place where cliffs reared up or fell away, where broken rocks lay among the trees. There were so many shadows that one saw nothing clearly.

Slowly I lowered the butt of my rifle to the ground. At my belt was a bowie knife, sharp enough to shave with—in fact, I often did shave with it. But it was my hands on which I would depend this time; hard work had made them strong, had built muscles into my arms and shoulders. For little softness had come into my life, little but hard riding and harder work. I waited, my hands ready.

The movement was there again, not a sound so much as a suggestion. Then it was the breathing that warned me . . . only breathing, and I reached out with my hands.

Something slipped through my hands like a ghost. My hands touched it, grasped, and the thing wasn't there . . . a faint grasp, and my fingers clutched only hair . . . then it was gone!

Battles sat up. "Tell? What is it?"

"A ghost, I think." I spoke softly. "Whatever it is, I wish it would believe we're not enemies."

But whatever it was, was gone.

A couple of hours later, by the light of day, we found tracks enough. Tip toe tracks of a small foot. I felt a shudder go through me, and Rocca noticed it. "What?" he said. "You are afraid?"

"I was remembering . . . someone who is gone," I said. "But these tracks are not hers. They are small, like hers, and the steps are quick, like hers . . . but she is dead."

Tampico Rocca crossed himself. "She haunts you?"

"No . . . it is only a memory. Her name was Ange, and I found her trail first, like this. I lost her again, like this. But Ange is dead. She was murdered," I said, "up in the Mogollon country."

"Ah!" That was Spanish. "You are *that* Sackett!" He looked at me thoughtfully. "I heard talk of it. I was in Cherry Creek then, but everybody knew the story . . . and how your family came to help."

He looked at me over the tip of his cigarette, and I could guess what he was thinking. In the western lands where all news came by word of mouth, men quickly became legend, they became larger than life. It was so with Ben Thompson, Wild Bill, Mike Fink, or Davy Crockett. The stories grew with telling.

"The boy we're hunting," I said, "is my brother Orrin's boy. Orrin was one of them who rode to the Mogollon."

"I never had a family," Spanish said. "I was always alone."

John J. tamped tobacco into his pipe. "Most men are alone," he said. "We come into life alone, we face our worst troubles alone, and we are alone when we die."

"It was the girl we tracked," I said. I'd been looking around while we talked. "She needed grub. She's taken some bread and some dried apples, and maybe a little jerky."

And then we were quiet again.

We knew what we had to do, and the waiting was hard, for we were men who preferred action. Our way of life had been to act . . . there was rarely need for contemplation. We were men who moved swiftly, surely, and we lived or died by the success of our movement. So to wait now came hard. To wander in the mountains added to our danger, and to wait here was risk, but a man who does not move leaves no tracks.

So we watched and waited, for it was all we could do, and even just watching worried me for men who are being watched become aware of it.

The white boy we had seen appeared again, more than once, but always with Indian boys around him. And then, after another long day of watching, I saw him take a spear and go alone along a trail between some rocks. Like a cat I was off the rock where I watched, nodding to Rocca as I passed him.

Spanish went up to watch from where I had been, and John J. went to the horses—we saddled them each morning—to be ready in case of need.

Tampico Rocca was a ghost on the trail, moving without sound. We snaked down among the rocks, crawled over great boulders, and came down to where we could await the boy.

Was he changed? Had he become an Apache? If so, he would shout when he saw us.

Only he had no chance. Soundlessly Rocca dropped to the trail behind him, put one hand over the boy's mouth, and lifted him into the brush, where we crouched.

He looked wild-eyed with fright, then seeing we were white men he tried to speak. Slowly Rocca took his hand from the boy's mouth.

"Take me away!" he whispered. "My name is Brook. Harry Brook."

"How long have they had you?"

"Two years, I think. Maybe not that long, but a long time."

"Where are the other white children? The Creeds and Orry Sackett."

"The Creeds? I have heard of them. They are in the next *rancheria.*" He pointed. "Over there."

"And the Sackett boy?"

"I do not know. I never heard of another boy. There is a girl with the Creed boys, but she is only five . . . very small."

Well . . . something seemed to drain away inside me. Had they killed him then? Had they killed Orrin's son?

Rocca asked the question.

"Nobody was killed," the boy said. "I was in camp when they brought them in, the Creed boys and the girl."

Squatting down on my heels, I asked, "Can you get to those others? I mean, will you ever see them?"

"You ain't takin' me along with you?" There were tears in his eyes.

"Not right now. Look, if we took you now we'd have to run, wouldn't we? All right, we leave you here. You be ready." I pointed toward a high rock. "Can you see that from camp?"

"Yes."

"All right . . . when you see a black rock atop that, you come to this place, right here. We've got to get those other youngsters."

"You'll get killed. They're in Kahtenny's *rancheria.*"

"Kahtenny? He's alive, then?"

"He sure is. An' all them Apaches yonder take a back seat for him. He's a big man among 'em."

We left him then, worried for fear the Apaches would come scouting to see what he was doing. They trusted no prisoner, even if he seemed to accept their ways. Only thing was, they didn't figure anybody could get away from the Sierra Madre . . . or that anybody would dare come in after them.

The first thing I did was hunt a piece of black lava rock to use when the time came. I placed it handy under a bush, and we went back, mounted up, and followed a trail out of there, skirting a cliff that fell away so sharply you felt as if you rode on a piece of molding along a wall.

That boy back there . . . could he keep them from knowing? That troubled me some.

There was small chance he could get to the other youngsters, but there was some visiting back and forth . . . it could be.

But where was Orry Sackett? Where was my brother's son?

Chapter 7

Through the chill dawn we climbed toward the high peaks, weaving our way among trees that dripped with moisture from the low-hanging clouds. Then we descended several hundred feet into a secluded park ringed with splendid pines. On the far side a cold, clear stream fell over a limestone ledge into a deep pool.

In every sheltered spot there were ruins . . . ancient ruins, half buried in earth or an overgrowth of brush or moss. In one place a gnarled and twisted cedar grew inside a wall, a cedar that itself must have been hundreds of years old.

I questioned Rocca, and he shrugged. "Who knows? They were the People Who Came Before, and they were gone before the Apaches came."

He was only mildly curious. "Many peoples have come and gone. It is the way of the world. The People of the Stone Houses . . . the people who built the cliff dwellings in Arizona and Colorado. They were driven out by the Navajo, who killed many of them.

"The white man has driven out the Indian, but the Indian drove out others before, and those others had driven peoples before them. It is always the same. I think the Indian was defeated by the traders, not by the soldiers."

"How so?" Battles asked.

"The traders made the Indian want things he could not make himself. He came to need the white man, to depend upon him. The Indian had to trade or steal to get the rifles and other things he wanted that the white man had."

It was what I had thought myself.

Rocca shrugged again. "The first white trader who came to the Indians brought their doom in his pack. I think it is so."

We were silent then. We came to a fearful slide and went down it, our horses sliding on their haunches for a good part of the distance to the bottom of a gloomy canyon, through which ran the headwaters of the Bavispe. It was an eerie, haunted spot, and I swung down, standing for a moment with both hands on the saddle, listening. But there was no sound except that of falling water, and the sighing of wind among the pines.

"I don't like it," John J. said. "It looks like the dark edge of hell."

Me, I was thinking of those youngsters among the Apaches, so strange to them, so frightening. They must be scared stiff. Yet I could think of worse things than living out a life in these mountains. The Sierra Madre were beautiful.

We were coming close now, and we could see plenty of Apache sign. In gloomy places like this a body always had the feeling of being watched.

We drank, one at a time, with the others watching and in the saddle. We crossed the river then and went up a switchback trail for a thousand feet toward a tremendous promontory.

Storm clouds hung over the nearby peaks, and there was electricity in the air. Kahtenny's *rancheria* was somewhere below us, hidden in the low clouds. We started down through the trees, but had gone only a short distance when the rain began to fall in sheets, swept by a violent wind.

The forest offered slight cover, and there was nothing to do but hole up and wait it out. We found a place where a great pine had fallen almost to the ground, part of it resting among the rocks. We cut away the branches on the under side and took shelter there, leading our horses under cover with us. There was barely room for us, and the pommel of my saddle brushed the bark of the pine.

We took a chance, with the rain to keep down the smoke and keep the Apaches under shelter, and built a small fire where we made soup and coffee.

After a bit, with the rain still falling, I took up my rifle and went out on a scout. Keeping to the trees, I worked my way along the cliff. The rocks glistened with wet, and the raindrops pelted my slicker like thrown stones, but the trees offered some shelter.

Suddenly I was looking down into Kahtenny's *rancheria*. There were a few smokes from wickiups, but nobody was visible.

I felt a movement behind me, and I turned sharply. It was Tampico Rocca.

He indicated the *rancheria* below us. "I could not fool them now," he said. "They would smell the difference in me. I have been eating the white man's food."

"How many would you guess there are?" I asked. "Twenty, maybe?"

"Twenty, or twenty-five."

Two dozen human wolves . . . and I mean nothing against them. My enemies for the time, yes . . . but I respected them. At trailing or fighting they were fierce and relentless as wolves; and we had done the impossible and followed them into their almost impregnable Sierra Madre.

"I'm going down," I said. "I shall get close and listen."

Rocca stared at me. "You crazy. They will hear you. Their dogs will smell you."

"Maybe, but the rain will help."

"All right," he said, "we both go."

It would be a daring thing, but there was enough of the Apache in him to be cautious. And it would be a chance to count coups against the Apaches.

We crawled and slid down the mountain. From time to time we paused to listen, then moved on. We were fools, I told myself. What we did was insanity, no less. But I had to find Orry, and every hour in these mountains was an hour of danger for us . . . and for him.

Together we crept to the edge of the encampment in the driving rain. Rocca darted to the wall of one of the wickiups, and I went to another. Crouching in the rain, I listened, but heard nothing except the low mutter of Indian voices and the crackle of a fire. As I was moving to another, I was stopped for a moment by Rocca's uplifted finger. Hesitating, I watched him, holding my rifle, muzzle down under my slicker. He shook his head, and moved on. We had listened at five wickiups and were about ready to give up. . . . Suppose the children were not talking? Suppose they were not there at all?

Rocca gestured suddenly, and I went to him. We heard a mutter of talk within, and then, sure enough, a boy speaking plainly in English.

I caught Rocca's arm. "Cover me," I said, and lifting the flap, I stepped in.

For a moment I could see nothing, although I had taken the precaution of closing my eyes for a moment before stepping inside. Then in the red glow of the coals I saw a startled buck staring at me, and beginning to rise. On a pile of skins near one wall were three white children . . . I could just make them out.

A squaw was there, holding a child at her breast. She stared at me, no anger or hatred in her eyes, just a calm acceptance. "Do not cry out," I said in Apache. Then in the event she did not understand my poor use of the Apache tongue, I repeated it in Spanish.

The buck was past his astonishment, and he came at me with a lunge. I met him halfway with the butt of my rifle, and he went down in a heap, out cold.

"All right," I said to the children, "we're all going home. Wrap those skins around you and come on."

Turning to the young Indian woman, who had not stirred, I spoke quietly in Spanish. "I do not wish to hurt anybody. I want only to take these children home."

She merely looked at me as the three children ran toward me. I saw that one of them was a girl. I waved them past, toward the wickiup entrance, and they went out quickly into the rain. With another glance at the squaw, I followed.

Tampico Rocca was already hurrying the youngsters toward the brush-clad hill where we had come down, and he was backing away, covering the wickiups with his rifle. I ran toward him, and was almost in to the hillside when a man with a bloody head sprang from the wickiup from which we had taken the children.

He leaped out, staggered, then glared wildly around. His first yell failed him, but he shouted again and his voice came full and strong. As he yelled he lifted his rifle, and Rocca shot him.

The children were in the brush and climbing the steep slope, faster than I would have believed possible.

Backing after them, I let the Apaches come boiling out into the rain, and then fired rapidly.

One Indian spun and dropped his rifle; another yelled and started for me. I let him come, and shot past him at another who was lifting a rifle to fire. That Indian staggered and fell, then started up again.

The running Indian had a knife, and he was almost on me. Shortening my grip on my rifle, I took a long swing that caught the running Indian in the belly. He caved in with a choking cry, and I scrambled up the muddy slope, grabbing at branches.

From above there was a sudden cannonade of fire as our friends up there, who had heard the shooting, opened up on the Indians to cover our retreat.

Scrambling, falling, and scrambling on, we made the crest, and when the little girl fell I caught her up and ran after Rocca, with the others covering us as best they could.

We made our camp, swung into our saddles, and with three of us each carrying a child, we raced off along the ridge, rain whipping our faces.

We ran our horses when we could, then slowed for the steep, dangerous trail down. Falling rain masked the depths below; the great peaks were shrouded in cloud. Thunder rumbled around us, tremendous sounds as if we were inside an enormous drum. We dashed into a pine forest, ran our horses for a hundred yards, then slowed for a steep slide and a muddy scramble.

Battles' horse slipped and fell, spilling him from the saddle, but the horse was game and scrambled up. By the time it was on its feet, Battles was in the saddle again.

There was no chance now for the black rock atop the boulder. Anyway, because of the rain Harry could not see it.

Me, I kept looking back over my shoulder, wondering when the Indians would catch up. The rain might have muffled the shots enough so that the other *rancherias* would not be alerted to our coming. We drew up briefly under the trees and I eased the girl into a better position on the saddle before me.

"Were there any other children back there?" I asked her. "White ones, I mean?"

"No," she said. Her eyes were bright, but she looked excited rather than scared.

"Which one is Orry Sackett?" I asked.

She just looked at me. "Neither one. Those two are the Creed boys. I never heard of any boy called Orry."

Something turned over inside me. "Tamp," I yelled, "my nephew isn't here!"

"I know it," he said. "He ain't here at all. These were the youngsters the 'Paches took. The only ones."

"That's not possible!"

"You better get goin'," Spanish said. "This here is no time to talk."

We started on, knowing there could be no hesitating, no turning back. The hills would be alive with Apaches now, and if we got out of here alive we'd have to have uncommon luck, which we had come into the mountains knowing.

Slipping and running, scrambling up and down muddy slopes, slapped by wet branches, racing through the forest . . . first and last, it was a nightmare.

We came finally to the place above the first Indian encampment, and I passed the girl over to Battles.

"I've got to get that boy Harry!" I told him.

"Don't be a fool! There's no chance!"

"Keep going," I said. "I promised him."

They all looked at me, each of them holding a youngster—three tough, hard-bitten men with no families, no homes, nothing to call their own but a set of guns and saddles. They sat there in the rain, and not one of them could come with me because now they had the children to think of.

"Run for it," I said. "This here's my scalp."

"Good luck," Spanish said, and they were gone.

Me, I watched them go, then swung my horse toward that boulder. Far back up the mountains, I thought I heard a shout and a shot. But I went down that trail to the place where I'd met the boy.

Rounding the boulder, rifle ready, I stared toward the *rancheria*, and suddenly out of the wet brush came the boy, Harry Brook. He was soaked to the skin and he was scared, but he came toward me. "Mister," he said, and he was crying. "Mister, I was scared you wouldn't make it."

Reaching down, I caught his hand and swung him up to the saddle.

"They know you're gone?" I asked.

"I think so . . . by now. Somebody came in and said he'd heard shootin', but the old bucks wouldn't believe him. No chance in this rain, they said, not in these mountains. I figured it was you, so first chance I had, I cut and run."

We started up the trail. Up there on the ridge I could see the muddy tracks of the other horses, and I swung into the trail after them, but then pulled up sharp. Their trail was almost wiped out by the track of other horses, unshod horses.

" 'Paches," I said. "Is there another trail?"

"Down there." The boy pointed toward the canyon. "The Old Ones' trail. An Apache boy showed it to me. It goes out across Sonora to the big water." Harry looked up at me, his face glistening with rain. "Anyway, that's what he said."

The black was fidgeting. He liked the situation no more than I did, so I pointed his nose where the boy said. He shied at the trail, then took it gingerly.

It was no kind of a place to ride even in good weather, let alone in a rain like this. Thunder crashed, and there was a vivid streak of lightning that lit up everything around. The trail was only a glistening thread along the face of a cliff.

But the black was game. He went as if stepping on eggs, but he went; and I held my breath for the three of us. Far down below my right stirrup I could see the tops of pine trees, maybe five hundred feet down there. We edged along, taking one careful step at a time, until we were almost at the bottom, when the trail widened out.

It took no time at all to see that this was no traveled trail. Rocks had fallen into it ages back, trees had grown up right in the middle, and we had to skirt around them. Me, I kept looking back. Sure as shootin' we were going to get ourselves trapped. Still, all a body could do was push on, so we pushed.

Night was a-coming, and with all those clouds and rain it was going to come soon, but there was no place to stop.

We had come down about a thousand feet, and were moving along a watercourse that wound through poplars and maples, gigantic agaves and clumps of maidenhair fern. Everything was wet.

Suddenly, off to our left, I saw one of those ruins—an ancient wall, half broken by a huge maple that had grown through it. There was a stream running that way, and it was only inches deep. Turning the black, I walked him along the stream until we could turn behind the wall where the maple grew.

There was a sort of clearing there, sheltered on one side by the wall, and falling away on the other toward a bigger stream; trees were all around. The maple had huge limbs that stretched out over the wall and made a shelter. I swung down under it and lifted the boy to the ground. "Stay up close to the tree," I said, "until I can rig something for us."

Now, a body doesn't spend his years wandering around the country without learning how to make do. I'd made wet camp a good many times before this, and I had been keeping my eyes open for a likely spot, one that had what we'd need.

First off, I saw how the ground slanted away toward the big creek, and I figured that wall offered fair protection. The maple was alive, but in some storm the wind had broken off a big limb, with a lot of branches on it, and it lay there on the ground. Maple burns mighty well, and makes a hot fire.

That big tree would give some shelter, and the wall would make a reflector for my fire. One branch of the tree extended across a corner of the wall, and I ducked under it and rolled away a couple of fallen stones that lay there. The big fallen limb and its branches offered partial cover for the corner, so I cut some pine branches and wove them in among the branches of the maple until I had a fair shelter.

Tying the black horse under the maple, but on a rope long enough so he could graze, I carried the saddle and gear to the shelter. The boy was already seated in the corner.

From under a couple of fallen trees I peeled some dry bark, gathered twigs from the fallen maple limb, and in a few minutes I had a fire going. It looked good, and felt better.

I had built the fire close against the wall so the heat would be reflected, and there we huddled in reasonable comfort. The wall, the sheltering trees, and our improvised shelter kept off most of the rain. After a few minutes, the boy fell asleep.

I checked my guns, made sure my rifle was fully loaded, and trusting to the black to warn me, I huddled against the wall on the opposite side of the fire from the boy, and slept too.

Chapter 8

The night wind moaned in the passes, and the small fire sputtered. The fuel burned down to coals, and the coals were a dull red except when touched briefly by the wind. The rain had come to an end, but big drops fell now and again from the leaves of the maple.

From time to time I opened my eyes, looked around, and slept again. It was always so with me . . . I can remember few nights when I slept the hours through without awakening, usually to lie awake listening for a while, sometimes to get up and prowl restlessly.

The black horse, now that the rain had stopped, moved away from the tree to crop the thick grass. Up on the ridges the grass had been sparse and had little nourishment, but the grass that grew around the fallen stones was rich and green.

You know how it is when you hear something a long time before you are really aware of it? It was like that now with riders coming down the trail. Most likely I didn't hear much . . . maybe only a whisper of sound . . . maybe some hidden sense felt the difference in the night; for they came like ghosts in the darkness, or like wolves, soft-footed and sure of their prey.

They must have been puzzled, and worried too, for I'd come down the trail of the Old Ones, where no one ever rode.

It was a spirit trail, and they would not have liked it, especially in the night. Their horses would be mountain-bred and sure-footed, and more than likely they had known this valley of the ruins when they ran wild, for there was grass here, good grass and water.

These riders must have been slow in getting away from their *rancheria*, coming after my tracks had crossed the trail of the Apaches that pursued my compadres. Seeing the tracks of my lone horse, they had followed, sure of a kill.

My small fire gave off so little smoke as to remain undetected, and its slight red glow would be hidden by the tree and the wall. Yet they found me. I suppose they heard my horse cropping grass.

All was still in my camp. A drop fell hissing into the coals, and my horse stopped cropping grass and lifted his head, blowing softly through his nostrils. I came clean awake.

An instant I lay there, listening, and then I rolled over and left the blanket in a long smooth dive into the darkness, and heard the whip of an arrow as I went. When I looked back, I saw that the arrow had gone through my blanket into the ground.

They came in fast, and my butt stroke missed the head of the nearest attacker, and hit his shoulder, staggering him. Then my rifle was knocked from my hands.

Now, back yonder in the mountains where I hail from, the boys and men do a sight of knuckle and skull thumping. The girls go to the dances for the dancing and the boys; and the boys go for the fighting and the girls.

Me being such a tall kind of homely boy, I had more time for fighting. Then in the Army, and on the river boats, and all—well, I'd done my share. So when I lost my rifle it just sort of freed me for fighting.

A body lunged against mine and I butted at the face, used my knee in his crotch, lifting him clean off the ground, so as I could lay hands on him. I fairly picked him up and threw him, and then I took a roundhouse swing at something coming at me. I saw a knife flash, and my fist landed and I felt bone crunch.

It was bang with both hands, swing, grab, butt. Apaches were fair hands at wrestling, but they had no experience at fist-fighting, and that was what I was doing. One short, powerful Apache grabbed me by the arm and the waist to throw me, but I brought my boot heel down on his instep and he let go and I could swing my elbow against his ear.

It was kind of lively there for a few minutes. There was three of them, but I was bigger and stronger. One of them jumped on my back with his forearm across my throat, but I grabbed his hand and elbow and flung him over my shoulder and smack down across the stone wall. He hit hard, and I heard him scream. And just then there was a shot.

Coming from outside of camp, it caught us unawares, but I saw an Apache fall and then the others ghosted into the night, one of them dragging the one I'd thrown across the wall. Then they disappeared like drops of water into a pool. They were there, and they were gone.

The one who had been shot was lying there near the fire, and Harry, his skins clutched around him, was sitting up, huddled and scared, in the corner of the wall.

And then a low voice said, "Hello, the camp!"

I said, "Come in, if you're of a mind to," and the next thing there walks into camp the cutest button of a girl you ever laid eyes on.

She was scarcely more than five feet tall and wore a buckskin hunting shirt that looked better than any such shirt I'd ever seen before. She was quick and pert, and she was leading her pony, but the Winchester in her hands wasn't for fun—that Apache would have realized it had he lived past her bullet.

She held out her hand. "I am Dorset Binny," she said, "and I hope you will forgive me for not looking as much like a lady as I should."

"Ma'am," I assured her, honestly enough, "when you come up like that and shoot that straight, I couldn't care how you're dressed."

And I added, "I am William Tell Sackett, and the boy yonder is Harry Brook, recently taken back from the Apaches."

We had both moved back into the shadows, and with that much said we took to listening. It was my idea those Apaches had them a bellyful, but they weren't alone, and this was no place to dally.

"Some other children got away, didn't they?"

"Yes—a couple of boys and a small girl."

"The girl was my sister. That is why I am here."

Well, she was talking to a shadow, for I was already saddling up. Right then, what I wanted between me and those Apaches was distance, for within a matter of hours the mountain would be alive with them, like a kicked anthill with ants.

She came along with me and the boy, and for an hour we followed the old trail north, then we turned west, taking a trail on which I found no tracks. Once in a while through the parted clouds I could see the sky, and sometimes a star was right above us. Black walls crowded closer, and we were skirting some almighty big boulders. Me, I kept thinking what a nasty place we were in, with the weather what it was. A body didn't need to look at the walls for a high-water mark. You just knew that the water must run through here thirty feet deep for an hour or two after a heavy storm. But the water had already passed on . . . and I wished for no more rain now.

The folks that had made this trail had no horses; it was a moccasin trail. After a while we had to get down and lead, for there was just no riding, but I let Harry stay on the black.

What I wanted most just now was to get out of these mountains and head off across the flatland, and maybe get to a ranch. But I had a time keeping my thoughts on my business with that girl along.

She was only a bit of a thing, but she must be packing a lot of nerve to come into this country after her sister. There was no chance to talk, for we were going single file, and I wasn't stopping. This was a strange trail, and we'd no idea where it might lead. Mayhap right into a bunch of Apaches —in which case some brave might have my scalp in his wickiup, if he bothered to take it. The Apaches were very strong on scalping.

At the top of a long slope we paused for a breather, and I looked around at Dorset. She was right behind me, leading her pony, and taking two steps to my one. Harry Brook, up there on the horse, had not said a word.

We stood there for a mite, and she said, "The sky's turning."

There was gray in it, all right, and day would come quickly now. We stood quiet then, saying nothing nor needing to, but there was communication in the night; we felt each other, felt the darkness and the danger around us, and felt the cool dampness of the canyon after the rain. We could smell the pines . . . and we smelled something else.

We smelled smoke.

It was enough to curl your hair. In this layout we couldn't expect friends. My partners had lit out to the north, I was sure, and if there was anybody here it had to be Apaches. And that smoke was right ahead of us.

We daren't go back, and we couldn't climb out. Me, I slipped the Winchester out of its scabbard, and so did she.

"We'll go ahead quiet," I whispered, "and if we can get by 'em, we will. Otherwise, we got to mount up and run for it. You and the boy get on the same horse, and if trouble shows, run."

"What about you?"

Me, I smiled. "Lady, you're not looking at no hero. I'll get off a few shots and I'll be dusting the trail right behind you, so don't slow up or I'll run right up your shirt tail."

We started on. Dawn was streaking the sky when we saw the canyon was starting to widen out. Then I saw moccasin tracks, some shreds of bark, and a few sticks—somebody collecting firewood. And then we heard yelling ahead of us, and I knew that kind of yelling.

"Might be," I said, "we can get by. They're mighty concerned, right now."

She looked at me. She said, "What concerns an Apache so much that we might slip by his camp?"

A man couldn't look into those honest gray eyes and lie. She would guess, anyway. "They got them a prisoner," I said, "and they're tryin' to find out how much of a man they caught. If he stands up to torture and dies well, they will figure they're big men, because they caught a big man."

We moved ahead, each of us warning our horse against noise; and those horses could be warned, they were that smart. Aside from their own instincts, they had caught some of our wariness for danger; for a horse, like a dog, can become extremely sensitive to the moods of his rider.

The western man trusted to his horse's ears, its eyes, its senses. He shared with it his water, and if need be, his food.

We moved forward quietly but steadily, and soon we saw their camp on a bench near the stream, partly hidden by brush and trees. The stream was not over four feet wide and no more than four or five inches deep, and the canyon through which we had come evidently caught the overflow.

Rifle ready, I led the way, watching the camp from the corner of my eye.

Here the dry stream-bed was perhaps fifty feet wide, most of it white sand dotted with rocks, many of them half buried. The brush was mostly willow, and thick.

It was a cool morning but I could feel sweat trickling down my back between my shoulder blades, and I worried for fear a hoof would strike stone. We went steadily on, drawing close to the camp, then abreast of it.

The Indians were almighty concerned with their prisoner, and they were shooting at him with arrows, missing him as close as they could, pinning the sides of his shirt to the tree, parting his hair with arrows. There was a trickle of blood down his forehead which I glimpsed when he lifted his head, and for the first time above their yells I heard his voice, and he was singing.

It was Spanish Murphy.

Yes, sir. Spanish was tied to a cottonwood in the clearing and the Apaches were shooting arrows at him and working themselves up to more serious ways of hurting . . . and he was singing!

Oh, they hated him for it, but they loved him for it, too, if I knew Indians. For their prisoner was a man with nerve, singing his defiance right into their faces . . . and it was also a means of keeping up his courage.

They would kill him, all right. They were devils when it came to inflicting pain, and they would try to make him last as long as possible, devising new tricks to give him the tortures of hell, and loving him for his strength and his guts.

Spanish was a singing man who loved the sound of the old songs, the western songs, the songs from the high-up hills. He was singing "Zebra

Dun" when we caught sight of him, and raising his head, he looked right through an open space in the brush, looked right at us, and he changed his tune to "John Hardy."

> "John Hardy was a desperate man, he carried his
> two guns every day.
> He killed a man on the West Virginny line, but you ought
> to *see Tell Sackett gettin' away,*
> *I want to see Tell Sackett gettin' away!"*

There he was, a-warning me. Him in all that trouble, but thinking most of us getting out of there. And me, I daren't stop, for I had a girl and a small boy depending on me. But this I did see. There weren't more than nine or ten Indians there, so far as I could see; they were all warriors.

We went on, our skins crawling with fear for Spanish Murphy, and also with fear for ourselves. We were beyond their camp now, but were expecting any moment to hear a yell behind us and to see the Apaches come streaming after us.

The thing that played into our hand was that the Indians probably had no idea there was anybody else about. They had either killed the others, or they'd taken out running.

Fifty yards beyond their camp the canyon took a bend, and when we had it behind us we felt some better.

I decided we didn't have much time before those 'Paches got down to serious business with Spanish. I knew I had to get him out of there, and I had to do it before he was hurt too bad to travel.

When we had gone a little way I pulled up. "You'll have to go on alone from here," I said to Dorset Binny. "Do you know Sonora?"

"No."

"The Apaches have run most of the folks off their ranches north of here, and the few who are still there won't fight back. I'd say ride due west and watch for a trail. If you can find a ranch, ask them to take you in and hide you."

She lingered, and I said, "Whatever made you try this, anyway?"

"There was nobody else to come. I didn't want my sister growing up an Apache." She hesitated. "Not that what we had was so much better. Since Pa died I've been trying to ranch, but we haven't done very well."

"You ride west," I repeated. "I don't need to tell you to be careful. You didn't get this far riding it blind."

I swung my horse, lifting a finger to my hatbrim. " 'Bye, Dorset."

"Good-bye, William Tell," she said, and they rode away up the canyon and I turned back.

I had no idea in my mind at all about what I was going to do. How does a body go about taking a prisoner away from blood-hungry Apaches? I couldn't just open fire. In the first place, they'd scatter out, pin me down, and surround me in no time. Also, they might just up and kill Spanish right off.

All the time there was a-nagging at me a thing I knew about Indians. Ninety-nine times out of a hundred a man who rides into an Indian camp is safe as long as he stays there—that is, if he rides in of his own notion, and not forced.

It was a long chance, for we were already shooting-enemies. They most likely knew me by sight by this time. Yet try as I might, I just couldn't come up with any other idea. But what to do when I got into their camp? How to get Spanish out of there?

I could get along in the language. Not that I was an easy talker like Tampico Rocca, but I could make out.

Spanish Murphy was in this fix because he had chosen to ride with me to Mexico, and it was up to me to take him from those Apaches, or to die with him.

I was packing plenty of iron. My Winchester was loaded, and I carried a six-shooter in my holster, with which I'd always been considered uncommonly swift. There was another six-shooter tucked into my belt.

So I swung my black horse up that bank and rode in amongst them.

For a minute there, you never saw anybody more surprised. These were Netdahee Apaches—killer warriors—dedicated to wiping out their enemies.

Now, as I've said, the Indian is a curious sort of man. They were bred to battle, and among the Apaches the Netdahee were the fiercest, a warrior society of chosen men. They appreciated nerve, but they were curious, and maybe they wanted to see what I was going to do. Maybe it was because I was inside their camp, but nobody lifted a hand.

My eyes took in the lot of them, methodically picking the ones at whom I would shoot first. If trouble started I'd have small time to pick targets, but if I could nail a few of them . . .

"Greetings!" I spoke to them in Apache. "I have come for my friend!"

Chapter 9

They turned like tigers at bay, cornered, their black eyes staring. Of the nine of them, one was wearing an old Army coat, another a faded red shirt, and the others were naked except for breech-clouts and knee-high, Apache-style moccasins.

One held a rifle, two had pistols, and one held a bow and a handful of arrows. The others were armed only with their knives. Their rifles and bows lay near the fire.

The Apache with the bow and the one with the rifle, those I'd take first. An Apache can shoot his arrows just as fast as a man can work the lever on a Winchester . . . and they made a nastier wound.

"The man you have tied is my friend. We have come far together, and we have fought well together. He is a good man in the desert or in the mountains."

My sudden appearance had startled them, and they were unsure. Was I alone? I saw their eyes go to the rocks around their camp.

They could not believe I would ride into their camp alone. There was brush along both sides of the stream from where I had come, and the hills at this point were lower and covered with boulders.

They were all in front of me now, and I dared not ride among them. Taking my time, and lifting one hand to hold them as they were, I then lifted my rifle and pointed it at Spanish, then lowered the muzzle a trifle and fired.

My bullet cut the rope where it passed around the tree to which Spanish was tied. He tugged, the rope loosened, and he tugged again.

Suddenly one of the Apaches moved. "Kill him!" he shrieked.

And I shot the man with the bow, then spurred the black and he leaped among them. I fired again, missed, and swung the stock of my rifle against an Apache skull. My horse went through them, turned swiftly, and started back.

A shot came from the rocks, then another. Spanish was loose and running toward the Apache horses.

A lean, fierce-looking Indian started for him and I held my sight an instant on his spine, then squeezed off the shot. The Apache kept running straight into a large boulder, hit it and seemed to rebound, then fell.

One Apache warrior made a running dive and sprang at me, grasping my saddle and swinging up to my horse, striving to get behind me.

I struck out savagely, guiding my horse with my knees, and for an instant we fought desperately. But I had both feet in my stirrups and a better purchase than he, so I threw him loose.

Spanish came charging from the horses, riding his own mount, and we went into the stream-bed side by side at a dead run, while the Apaches vanished into the rocks, shooting at the surrounding hills.

As we hit the sand of the stream-bed there was a rattle of rocks and, swinging around ready to fire, we saw Tampico Rocca and Battles riding neck and neck down the slope in a cascade of gravel.

We raced our horses for half a mile, then slowed to save them, and almost at once saw a fairly wide trail run off to the north from the stream. We took it, and crossed over a low hill into what must have been another part of the same stream-bed.

Then we held our horses to a good steady pace, keeping a sharp lookout behind. Nobody was talking. Me, I was watching the trail for some sign of Dorset and the boy, but we saw no tracks.

We were riding in the lower foothills of the Sierra Madre now, and while the ridges were covered with pines, the lower slopes were a lush growth of maple, juniper, oak, and willow, with a thick underbrush of rose and hackberry. Small streams were frequent.

Somehow, more by chance than by skill, we had thrown them off our trail, but we knew better than to think it meant anything more than a breather. Surprise had worked for us, but the Apaches would find our trail, and they would catch up.

We lifted our horses into a trot, frequently glancing back over our shoulders, yet always watching the ridges around. We were now traversing a broken but relatively open country with trees along the streams or growing here and there in small clumps. After the heavy rains our passage raised no dust, and the hoofs of our horses made little sound in the grass.

Twice we forded streams, three times we rode upstream or downstream in the water to lose whatever trail we might leave.

Once in the shade of the great arching trees, while giving our horses a breather and a chance to drink at a small stream, I told them about Dorset Binny and the boy. "If anything happens to me," I said, "find them and get them out of here."

The other youngsters had been riding quiet, scared and hungry, no doubt. Had it been us alone we'd never have chanced stopping to fix grub, but the children needed it, and we found ourselves a likely spot. While Rocca stood watch and Spanish fixed some food, Battles and me turned in under a tree for some sleep. It seemed like years since I'd caught more than a few catnaps.

When I woke up my mouth was dry, and I sat up, staring around, just taking stock. It was almighty quiet, a beautiful quiet such as you only find in the forest. Far off, we could hear the stir of wind in the pines, a wonderful sound. Closer to, there was only the murmur of water around the stones of the creek, and a faint chirping of birds. It was a natural, friendly quiet.

Tampico Rocca and Spanish came over to me. Battles was on lookout, perched up among the rocks where he could keep out of sight and still look the country over. The youngsters were sleeping.

"Got any idea where we are?" I asked Rocca.

"I been thinking on it." With his finger he drew a wavy line in the sand. "This here is the Bavispe," he said, and he pointed west. "She lies right yonder. If we cross the river there's some ranches. I wouldn't count on there being folks about, but it could be. Mostly the Apaches have wiped 'em out, burned 'em out, or stole them out. But it would be a good place to stop. There'll be old walls, water, and grass.

"Next we head for the Santa Margaritas . . . I know an old mining camp where we can hole up. Then we can head for Chinapa, on the Sonora River."

"Sounds good."

Spanish was chewing on a blade of grass. "Fact remains," he said, "that we didn't get what we come for. We didn't find your nephew."

Rocca was looking at me, watching me. "The little ones," he said, "they know nothing of such a boy . . . and they would know if the Indians had him."

"I put no faith in women," Spanish said, "meanin' no offense, but did you ever . . . I mean, you and your sister-in-law . . ."

I looked right at him. "I'll take no offense, Spanish—you've stood by me. I never saw her before we met in Tucson. I haven't seen my brother in some time . . . never did talk to him about his affairs. Little time we had together we mostly talked about the old days and what become of folks we knew." I looked around at them. "I ain't been home much. I've been drifting."

Nobody said anything for a while, and then Battles, who had come out of the brush, said, "I figure you've been lied to, Sackett."

"It don't make sense."

"Any reason she'd want you dead? You got to realize . . . not many come back from here. We ain't even sure we're gettin' back."

"The children never heard of any other boy," Rocca repeated, "and they'd know. And, Harry Brook would. He speaks the language pretty good, and there's talk around the Indian villages."

Well, there was no use studying on it now. We had miles to travel. I said as much as we saddled up and moved down the creek.

Rocca rode with his head over his shoulder. I mean he was a worried man. When you see Apaches you're worried, but when you don't see them you're maybe really in trouble. They could be all around you.

When the shadows were beginning to reach out from the hills we came up to a ranch, four tired men with some tired children. As we neared it we spread out and I rode with my Winchester up in my hands, my eyes moving under the low brim of my hat, searching each shadow, each doubtful place.

No smoke . . . no movement. Somewhere a blue jay fussed, somewhere a quail called into the stillness and another made reply. Otherwise it was still.

Nobody spoke, and we rode into the yard. Battles rode through the gate, and I went through a gap in the ruined wall. Spanish circled to the right, Rocca to the left.

The ranch was deserted . . . a ruin. Fire had gutted it, and some of the stone walls had toppled. The windows gapped like great, hollow eyes that stared upon nothing. The barns were a tumbled mass of burned timbers and the fallen stones of foundation walls. Mesquite trees choked up the corrals.

But trees still shaded the ranch yard. Water ran from an iron pipe into a tank. An oak limb had grown through an open window. In the patio the blocks of stone that paved it had been thrust by a growing sycamore, which was now several inches through.

Once this ranch had been a splendid place, once the fields had been green and men had worked here, lived here, and loved here.

We rode into the thick grass where the ranch yard had been and we drew up. We heard only the wind . . . only the trickle of water into the tank.

John J. Battles looked slowly around and said nothing, and Spanish Murphy sat silent for a long moment. Then he said, "This is the sort of place you dream about, when you're on a long, dusty trail, or you're in the desert and short of water."

"We'd better have a look around," I said. "Tamp, you scout to the wall yonder. Spanish can stay with the children."

We moved out. A rabbit sprang from under my feet and went bounding away. We searched the place, but we found nothing, nothing at all.

There was a watch tower on one corner of the place, shrewdly built to observe the country around, but now partly masked by the tops of trees. While I took the first watch, Battles put some grub together for a meal.

The sun was warm and pleasant, but it bothered me for I could see too little in the open country to the west. Our enemies should come from the east, but trust an Apache to use the sun's glare if he figured on an attack. But the sun sank behind the mountains to westward and I studied the country all around with great care, and saw nothing.

Where were Dorset Binny and the boy? If they had ridden the way we planned they should be not too far away, for our course had veered around and we, too, had come west.

From the watch tower I could study the terrain and my eyes searched out all possible hiding places. The position of the ranch had been well chosen. The place had a good field of fire in every direction and must have been easy to defend back in the old days, yet the Indians had taken it, burned it out, and more than likely killed everybody on the ranch.

It seemed to me at least fifteen to twenty men would have been needed to defend the ranch. Maybe they were shorthanded when the attack came.

In the last minutes of daylight, I saw them coming—two riders, not over half a mile off.

I called softly to Murphy, who was closest, and knelt by one of the openings left in the wall for a firing position. But I was sure right from the start. As they drew nearer I could see them clear enough.

Standing up on the tower I called out, "Dorset! Dorset Binny! Come on in!"

Chapter 10

Laura Pritts Sackett was immaculate. She was cool, aloof, yet she managed to convey the idea that beneath that still surface there was turmoil, waiting to be exploited. A cold, emotionless young woman, she had learned very early that the appearance of deep emotion and passion beneath the quiet exterior was a tool and a weapon to be used, and so she had used it.

Her adoration for her father had resulted in hatred for all who in any way thwarted or opposed him.

As the days passed into weeks and she heard nothing from Mexico, she grew worried. Suppose, after all, Tell Sackett was not killed by the Apaches? Suppose he did return, and her falsehood was exposed? She was less worried, however, about being exposed—she had no intention of remaining in Tucson anyway—than about Sackett not being killed.

She knew enough about the Sacketts to know they had a way of getting out of corners. Suddenly, she made up her mind.

She would leave Tucson. She would go back east without waiting any longer. She might never hear what happened in Sonora, and there was no sense in staying on here, in this heat, and merely waiting. Her father had a little property in the East, and it was time she returned to settle the estate. But first she would make one final effort.

She was seated in the Shoo-Fly when she reached that decision. She knew, as did everyone, about the gun battle in the Quartz Rock Saloon, and she had seen the Hadden boys around town. She knew also that the Haddens had been doing some talking about what would happen when they met Tell Sackett and Tampico Rocca again.

Suddenly the door opened and Captain Lewiston came in, accompanied by Lieutenant Jack Davis, whom she remembered from the stage ride to Tucson.

They came to her table. "Mrs. Sackett," Davis said, "I want to present Captain Lewiston."

She turned her wide blue eyes on the Captain and sensed a coolness, a reserve. This one would not be so easy as Davis to wind around her finger. "How do you do, Captain," she said. "Won't you sit down?"

The men seated themselves and ordered coffee. "I hope you will forgive the intrusion, Mrs. Sackett," Captain Lewiston said, "but we were wondering if you could tell us anything about the present location of Tell Sackett. I believe he is a relative of yours."

"He is my brother-in-law," she said, "although I had never met him until a few weeks ago. Right here in this room, in fact. He was with some other men. I don't know where they went. Is he in trouble?"

Lewiston hesitated. "Yes and no," he said finally. "If he rode into Apache country, as we have heard that he did, he may be in very serious trouble indeed."

She allowed her lip to tremble. "He . . . he hasn't been killed, has he? The Sacketts are reckless, daring men, and . . ." She let her words trail away.

"We have heard nothing," Lewiston said. "We are planning a strike against the Apaches that will take us deep into Mexico. We would not want them stirred up by some unauthorized foray into their country."

"I . . . I did not know. If anything should happen to Mr. Sackett my husband would be very upset. They are very close."

"Mrs. Sackett, I understand you provided Mr. Sackett with a horse? Is that true?"

"Of course. His own had been killed and he was unable to purchase one. I merely helped." She smiled. "What else could I do?"

Lewiston was not satisfied, yet there was certainly nothing wrong with her story, nor had he any reason to suspect she knew Tell Sackett's whereabouts, except the fact that they were relatives, and had talked together. He could not have given any reason for his dissatisfaction, but he felt it. Moreover, he had liked Tell, and he was worried about him.

Later he said as much to Davis. "Oh, come now, Captain!" Davis said. "If Laura Sackett knew anything about Sackett she would tell you. What possible reason would she have for lying?"

"I don't know. But why is she staying on in Tucson? She has no relatives here, no friends, and this is no time of year to be here if you can be anywhere else. I mean, I like the place, but not many eastern women such as Laura Sackett are inclined to want to stay here."

Davis had done some wondering about that himself. Tucson was a hot, dusty little desert town, and not a likely place for a lady of aristocratic background such as Laura had implied in a few carefully casual references. A stopover to recover from the rigors of a stage trip from California would be natural, but the days had stretched on, and still she remained.

Had she been known in the area or had friends there, her presence would have been no cause for comment, but she kept very much to herself and indicated no desire to make acquaintances.

Laura was unconcerned as to what anyone thought. She detested Tucson and its people, and wanted nothing so much as to go on to El Paso and thence to New Orleans and the East. If she could only be sure Tell Sackett was dead she would leave.

She knew what she must do. Tell Sackett had now been gone for three weeks, and while it seemed likely that he was dead, he might even now be coming north over the trails through Sonora. So she had one more thing to do. She had to make sure that, if he had lived through the journey into the Apache stronghold, he would die before getting back to Tucson. Somehow she must manage to talk with Arch or Wolf Hadden.

They came rarely to the Shoo-Fly. There were other places to eat among their own kind, and she had seen them on the streets with other toughs of ugly reputation. By listening to talk she heard around her, she learned that the Haddens were, among other things, bronc riders and wild-horse hunters. They had come into town with several horses for sale or trade.

She spoke to Mrs. Wallen quite casually. "There is a man about town," she said, "a rough-looking man named Hadden, who has a sorrel gelding for sale. I would like to talk to him."

Mrs. Wallen hesitated, putting her hands on her hips. "Ma'am, those Haddens are not fit men for a lady to know. I will have Mr. Wallen talk to them."

"If you please," Laura Sackett answered coolly, "I would prefer to talk to them myself. I have dealt with many rough men whom my father employed. I have also had some experience in buying horses."

"Very well," Mrs. Wallen replied stiffly, "have it your own way."

Laura was amused. Mrs. Wallen did not like her, she knew, and Laura cared not at all, but it made her feel good to put her in her place, if ever so gently.

She finished her tea and, getting to her feet, she gathered her skirt in one dainty gloved hand and went out on the boardwalk. The heat struck her face like heat from the open door of a furnace. She stood an instant, looking up and down the street, and then she went on to her rooming house.

Arch Hadden was seated on the steps. He got to his feet as she approached. "Wallen said you wanted to see me about a horse."

She studied him for a moment. "About a horse," she said, "and some other matters. If you will saddle that sorrel you have and bring him around in the morning I shall ride out with you. If the horse is satisfactory, I will buy him."

The next morning in the early coolness they rode out beyond the mission. The little sorrel moved well, but Laura was not interested in the horse. In a thick grove of cactus and brush, she drew up and Arch Hadden rode up close beside her.

He looked at her with a knowing leer. "Ma'am, I reckon you come to the right man. Now I'll just get down an' he'p you off that horse. . . ."

In her hand she held a two-barreled derringer. "Stay right where you are, Hadden," she said. "I brought you out here to talk to you. Do you know what my name is?"

He stared at her, puzzled but wary. "Can't say as I do. At the livery stable Wallen just told me to come and see the blonde lady at that roomin' house. I reckon ever'body in town has seen you, ma'am."

"I am Laura Pritts Sackett."

His face sharpened suddenly as if the skin had drawn tight. He was very still and with amusement she could see what was happening in his mind. She was a woman, and she had a gun on him. She could kill him and say he had attacked her, and she would not be blamed; but if he drew on her and killed her, he would be hung for murder.

"Don't be frightened, Hadden. I am not going to kill you. In fact, I want you to kill somebody for me—for both of us."

"What's that mean?"

"There is a man who has gone down into Mexico and I think the Apaches may have killed him, but if he should be coming back I want him killed before he reaches Tucson."

Hadden shook his head. "I've killed a few men," he said, "but only in fights. I ain't no paid killer, ma'am."

"Not even if the man is Tell Sackett?"

He was still wary, but interested. "You askin' me that? And you a Sackett?"

"I am not a Sackett, Hadden. I had the misfortune to marry one. I married him to help my father, but they turned on him anyway. Tell Sackett is my brother-in-law, and I want him killed, Hadden.

"There are men in this town, Hadden, who would kill a man for fifty dollars, and there are others all along the border. I will give you two hundred dollars if you will bring me evidence that Tell Sackett is dead. I don't care whether you kill him or somebody else does. All I want is proof."

Hadden rested his palms on the saddle horn and chewed on his mustache. He had heard that Sackett had ridden south, but he also knew that Spanish Murphy, who had ridden with him, had told some friends in Mex town that he would be back in a few weeks.

Arch Hadden was a hard, tough man, and a bitter one. He had ridden into Tucson hunting John J. Battles, an old enemy. He had decided to kill Tampico Rocca, knowing nothing about him, because Rocca was Battles' friend and it would bring Battles out of hiding. Tell Sackett had simply been a stranger of whom he had known nothing. Since the gun battle in which Arch Hadden had been so roughly treated and one of his men had been killed, another seriously wounded, he had heard a lot about the Sacketts. He wanted to kill Tell Sackett, but he was no longer at all sure he could kill him in a stand-up gun fight. On the other hand, here was an offer of two hundred dollars, representing six months' hard work on the cattle ranges, for killing him, money it would be a pleasure to earn.

Slowly, he dug out the makings and rolled a smoke. Laura Sackett seemed in no hurry, and Arch wanted to think this thing through.

"There would be no trouble for you, Hadden," she persisted. "You have already had a fight with him. If there is another fight and you kill him, nobody would be surprised."

"Why'd you pick on me?"

"You're the obvious one. He bested you. You want him beaten or dead. You are the one who can do it and no questions asked."

"How you figure to pay me?"

"I will give you one hundred dollars now, and the other hundred will be left at the Wells-Fargo office to be delivered to you by my order."

"Won't folks wonder why you're payin' me money?"

"No. You will be rounding up and breaking four horses for me, to be delivered in El Paso. The money would be in payment for that."

Grimly, he stared at her. The derringer was still in her hand, and now he knew she would shoot if need be. Not that there would be any cause for it, but this was a dangerous woman.

"Supposin' I was to take your hundred dollars an' ride off?" he suggested.

She smiled. "Hadden, my father and I were in the land grant wars in New Mexico. We had occasion to hire men who could use their guns. I have told you there are plenty of men along the border who would kill for fifty dollars. If you took my money without trying to make good on it, I would hire four separate killers and send them out with good rifles to get you—and they would, Hadden."

He chuckled. "I just wondered. All right, ma'am, I'll take the hundred. I been figurin' on killin' Sackett, an' this here will pay expenses while I do it."

She rode back to town with Hadden trailing behind, and at the livery stable, before witnesses, she said, "I do not like the sorrel, Hadden, but I do want four horses delivered to me in El Paso. I will pay you one hundred dollars now, the other hundred to be paid by Wells Fargo on my authorization when the horses are delivered."

Arch Hadden stabled his horses and went outside. He rolled another smoke, lit the cigarette, and drew deeply. This was money he was going to enjoy earning. He looked around and saw Wolf approaching. "Wolf, we got us a job," he said. "We got us a good job."

Chapter 11

We passed a quiet night. Until the last of the twilight was gone I could still hear the quail. These were the Mexican blue quail that run along the ground more than they fly, ofttimes thirty or forty of them in a covey.

Around a small fire, we talked it over. We had invaded Apache country and taken prisoners from them, so they would be on our trail, they would never let up.

The horses needed rest. The deserted ranch had water and plenty of good grass, and there was a good field of fire. We decided to stay put, and that was all right with me. I'd seen no such beautiful place in all my life, and I said as much to Dorset.

"It *is* beautiful," she agreed, "and peaceful. I wonder they ever left . . . the people who lived here."

"Apaches. They devastated this whole stretch of country. Folks tried again and again to build homes here, but they couldn't make it.

"When we leave here," I went on, "we're going to have to run. It is going to be pure hell betwixt here and the border towns."

"Why did she do it, Tell?" Dorset asked suddenly. "Why did she want you killed?"

"I don't know that she did."

"There was no Orry Sackett, Tell. Can't you see that? She lied to you. All the children are accounted for. There were the Creed youngsters and my sister. Harry had been taken long before, and there simply were no others."

This idea about Orry worried me. It was something that needed contemplating, but there was another worry in what Dorset said; for if there was no child, why send me skyhootin' into such dangerous country? Unless she did want me dead? And if she wanted me dead, would she stop with this? Suppose she tried again to kill me when I showed up alive . . . if I did?

I never was much good at thinking complicated things out. Mostly I studied on situations and then went ahead and did what I would have done, anyway. When it comes to work and travel or a fighting situation, I can come up with answers, but I never was any good at figuring out why folks turned to evil.

"Dorset," I said, "I can't think of a reason why anybody should want me killed like that. Why, she might be the death of these men with me, too."

"Maybe she wants to get back at your brother. Maybe she hates the name of Sackett."

It made no kind of sense, but I had one thought a body couldn't get around. And that was that she had sent me off to Mexico after a child who I now felt sure never existed.

You might figure I could have looked around more, but not if you knew Apaches. If any Apaches had a white prisoner it would be known to all of them. They had few secrets among themselves. So I was left with the almost certain knowledge that I'd been sent down here on a wild-goose chase that would be almost sure to get me killed.

Nor was there much I could do about it if I got back. She would simply say that I lied, that she had told me no such thing—if she was even around to be accused.

And she would know I wasn't going to beat up a woman or shoot her. We Sacketts treated womenfolk gentle, even when they didn't deserve it.

Had it been only me, I'd have figured I'd been played for a sucker and I'd have let it go at that, though it wouldn't have been a pretty thought. But she had risked the lives of my friends.

We laid up at that deserted ranch for three days. It wasn't only that we needed the rest, or that our horses did. It was because a man who doesn't travel doesn't leave any trail. And those Apaches would be looking for a trail. They would figure that we would naturally hightail it for the border, and when the trail was lost they'd head for the border by several trails, exchanging smokes to talk across the country. So by laying low at this ranch we left them with no trail to see, and the feeling that we had taken some other, unknown route.

On the morning of the fourth day we moved out. Tampico Rocca knew of a ranch twenty-odd miles west, and we headed for that, keeping off the ridges and using every trick we knew to cover our sign.

But we weren't trusting to that. We rode with our eyes looking all around all the time, and our rifles across our saddles. We rode loose and we made pretty good time all this first day, wanting distance behind us.

It was rough country. You've got to see some of that country to believe it. Water was growing scarcer, there were fewer trees except along the river bottoms, and there was more cactus. We saw antelope now and again, and once, passing through a rugged stretch of bare rock mountains, we saw some desert bighorns. They're pretty near the finest meat the country offered, but we weren't about to shoot a rifle.

When we reached the ranch we found that it was a big one, and it lay right out in the open country, with a small stream winding past. There was a dam across the stream and a fair sized pond had backed up behind it. Cottonwoods and other trees grew around, and a big Spanish-style ranch house was set amongst them. And it was occupied.

We drew up on the crest of a low ridge among some ocotillo and other growth and studied the layout. We weren't going to ride up to any place without giving thought to what lay before us.

Slow smoke was rising from the chimney, and we could hear the squeak of a windlass as somebody pulled water at a well. We could see a couple of vaqueros riding out of the back gate, heading for the hills to the south-east of us. They were riding relaxed and easy, sitting lazy in the saddle as if neither of them had ever known a care or the name of trouble.

We came down off the slope, riding scattered out a little until we were channeled by a lane through wide fields of planting.

"Somebody watches us." Rocca indicated a low tower, and we could see sunlight gleam on a fieldglass or telescope.

Whoever it was must have seen the children and decided we could be trusted, because the big wooden gates opened, although nobody was in sight. But as we drew closer we could see the black muzzles of the rifles that covered our approach.

We rode in through the gates and they closed behind us. At least six vaqueros were now in sight, and standing on the wide veranda, a thin Cuban cigar in his teeth, was a tall old man with white hair and an erect, proud figure.

He came down two steps to greet us, his sharp eyes taking us in with quick intelligence. I think he knew our story before I spoke, for the hard-ridden horses, and the children, one of them dressed like an Apache boy, told it.

"*Buenos dias, señores*," he said, and then added in English, "My house is yours."

"You may not wish us to stay, *señor*," I said. "We have taken these children from the Apaches, and they will be looking for us."

"They have visited us before, and with less reason. You are my guests, gentlemen. I am Don Luis Cisneros."

"I am Tell Sackett," I said, and introduced the others.

He greeted them and then turned his eyes to me. "Yours is a familiar name," he said. "There was a Sackett who married the granddaughter of an old friend."

"That would be my younger brother, Tyrel. He married into the Alvarado family."

"Come in," he said, and as we walked into the dim coolness of the interior, he added, "We are old friends, my family and the Alvarados. I have heard much of your family, *amigo.* Your brother stood between Alvarado and his enemies."

Hours later, when we had bathed and eaten a good dinner at his table, we sat about smoking the Don's Cuban cigars. I was never much of a hand to smoke, but did from time to time, and this was one time I joined in.

Dorset and the children had gone off with the Don's daughters, and the boys and me we stayed with our host.

"You have a dangerous road before you. I can let you have a dozen riders," he said.

"No. You may need them. We've come this far, and we'll ride on." Sitting back in the big cowhide chair, I told him the whole story, and he listened without comment. At the end he said nothing for several minutes.

"I have news of your family. I wish you could have known it sooner. The woman you speak of was married to your brother Orrin, but they have separated. She was the daughter of Jonathan Pritts, the man who led the men who tried to seize the Alvarado Grant. It was your brother Tyrel who led the fight that defeated him, and when Orrin found his wife was involved, he left her. She has hatred for all who bear the name of Sackett. You were to be killed, *amigo.*"

It seemed unreasonable that a woman would go to such lengths to get a man killed, a man who had done her no harm, but it all tied up into a neat package. And there wasn't much I could do about it. Maybe the best way to get even would be just to get back alive, so all her plotting would come to nothing.

In the quiet of the lovely old hacienda, all that lay outside seemed far away, not something that lurked just beyond the adobe walls. But deep in our hearts not one of us thought himself free of what was to come. The miles of the desert that lay between us and the relative safety of Tucson could be nightmare miles. They were ever-present in our minds, but they were a fact of our lives to be taken in stride.

Old Don Luis talked quietly and easily of the problems of living among the Apaches. As Pete Kitchen had survived north of the border, so had he survived south of it. He had his own small army of tough, seasoned vaqueros, fighters every one of them.

As he talked he glanced over at Rocca. "If you ever want a job, *señor*," he said, "come to me here. There is a place for you. I have two vaqueros here who grew up with the Apaches."

"It is a good place," Rocca said. "It may be that one day I shall come riding here."

Long after the others had turned in, I sat in the quiet of the old Don's study and talked with him. The walls of the room were lined with shelves and leatherbound books, more than I had ever seen, and he talked of them and of what they had told him, and of what they meant to him.

"These are my world," he said. "Had I been born in another time or to another way of life I should have been a scholar. My father had this place and he needed sons to carry on, so I came back from Spain to this place. It has been good to me. I have seen my crops grow and my herds increase, and if I have not written words upon paper as I should like to have done, I have written large upon the page of life that was left open for me.

"There is tonic in this." He gestured toward the out-of-doors. "I have used the plow and the Winchester instead of the pen and the inkstand. There is tonic in the riding, in the living dangerously, in the building of something.

"I know how the Apache feels. He loves his land as I do, and now he sees another way of life supplanting his. The wise ones know they can neither win nor last, but it is not we who destroy them, but the times.

"All things change. One species gives way to another better equipped to survive. Their world is going, but they brought destruction to another when they came, and just so will we one day be forced out by others who will come. It is the way of the world; the one thing we know is that all things change.

"Each of us in his own way wars against change. Even those who fancy themselves the most progressive will fight against other kinds of progress, for each of us is convinced that our way is the best way.

"I have lived well here. I should like to see this last because I have built it strong and made it good, but I know it will not. Even my books may not last, but the ideas will endure. It is easy to destroy a book, but an idea once implanted has roots no man can utterly destroy."

He paused and looked at me. "You are bored with an old man talking."

"No, sir. I am learning. We are a people who have hungered after learning, Don Luis, and who have had too little of it. I mean we Sacketts. Our mountain lands had thin soil, and they gave us nothing more than just a living until we came west."

I looked at him and felt ashamed. "I can barely read, sir. It is a struggle to make out the words, and what they mean. Some I hunt down like a coyote after a rabbit. I look at those books with longing, sir, and think of all the things they might say to me."

I got up, for of a sudden there was a heavy weariness upon me. "My books have been the mountains," I said. "The desert, the forest, and the wide places where the grass grows. I must learn what I can from the reading I can do."

Don Luis got up also, holding out his hand. "Each of us must find wisdom in his own way. Mine is one way, yours another. Perhaps we each need more of what the other knows. . . . Good night, *señor*."

When I went outside I walked through the gate to smell the wind, to test the night. By the wall near me a cigarette glowed, cupped in a hand.

"How goes the watch?" I asked in Spanish.

"Well, *señor*." He held the cigarette behind the wall in the darkness. He bowed his head and drew deep; the small red fire glowed and faded again. "We are not alone, *señor*. Your friends and ours, they are out there . . . waiting."

So they had caught up with us. Now there would be hell to pay in Sonora.

Turning on my heel, I went back into the house. The old Don was just leaving his study.

"You have many horses?" I asked.

"All you need," he assured me.

"Can you give us three apiece? I can't pay you now, but—"

"Do not speak of pay," he interrupted. "Your brother is the husband of my old friend's granddaughter. You may have the horses." He looked closely at me. "What will you do?"

"Your vaquero says they are waiting out there now. I think he is right. And so I think we will take our chances and run for it. We'll switch horses without stopping . . . maybe we can outdistance them."

Don Luis Cisneros shrugged. "You might," he said. "I will have the horses ready at daybreak."

"An hour before," I said. "And *gracias*."

Chapter 12

The horses were ready and we were mounted, the children with us. The Don's men were posted on the walls to cover our going. My horse was restive, eager to be away, but I glanced around at Dorset. In the vague light her face seemed pale, her eyes unusually large. I suspected mine were the same.

"The tall pine yonder," I said, and pointed in the direction. "Ride for it, ride hard. They will be close around, with their horses well back from where they wait. With luck, we can ride through them and be away before they can get off more than a shot or two."

Sixteen men were on the walls, rifles ready for firing. Other men stood by the gates, prepared to swing them open.

Don Luis walked over to me and held up his hand, and I took it. "Vaya con dios, amigo," he said gravely, and then he lifted a hand to the men at the gates and they swung them wide.

We went through the gates with a rush at the same instant as all sixteen men fired. Some had targets chosen, having spotted lurking Apaches, others fired at bits of likely cover.

We hit the trail running, with Spanish Murphy and myself in the lead. I saw the dark form of an Apache rise up almost directly before me and chopped down to fire with my pistol, but the horse struck him and knocked him rolling. A hoof spurned his body, and then we were past and running, with the vaqueros on the wall picking targets from those we drove from hiding.

The tall pine was a mile off, and we rode directly for it through the half-light of the early dawn. We covered that mile at a dead run, slowing to a trot as we neared the tree. I glanced around swiftly.

"How is it? Are we all here?" I asked.

"I was the last one," Battles said. "We all made it."

"Anybody hurt?"

"They burned my shoulder," Rocca said. "It is nothing."

So I led them away at a fast trot for a little way, then I ran the horses again for a good half-mile, slowed to a trot and then a walk, then ran them again.

At noon we drew up at a small seep that came from the base of a grass-covered dune. We watered our horses, exchanged saddles to fresh horses, and pushed on.

We kept a good pace, riding wide of any places of ambush, and watching for dust clouds. There were bandits as well as Indians to be feared, and there were soldiers, too, who might resent our being here. All this while the children did not cry, they did not once call out. The Apaches had taught them that, if nothing more.

At midafternoon we rode into a deserted village. The ruins of a large adobe still stood, and a half-completed church. There was water running in an irrigation ditch.

In a corner of one of the houses was a skeleton, still half-clothed, of a Mexican who had died fighting. The left arm of the skeleton showed a break that had mended badly, leaving the arm shorter and crooked.

Tampico looked at it then at the dried leather of the holster on which an initial had been carved. It was a large B.

"So this is where it happened, Benito," he said, and then glancing around at me, he said, "I knew him. He was a bad one, but brave."

We made coffee there, and a hot soup from the jerked beef, and some corn, potatoes, and onions found in the deserted fields, now gone to weeds. We ate quickly, but we ate well.

Spanish wiped his hands on his chaps and looked at me. "Let's be gettin' on," he said. "There's a smell of death about this place."

John J. Battles was already in his saddle, waiting. We mounted up and moved out, riding fresh horses again, so as to use none of them too hard.

It was hot and still in those late hours of the day, and the dust did not rise. Suddenly Murphy indicated a place on the horizon where a blue-gray finger of smoke made a question mark against the mountains. It was ahead of us off to the east. We knew what it meant, and we pressed on, picking up the north star for guiding, following it as best we could, with what the terrain offered.

After midnight we stopped among some willows and made dry camp in an arroyo.

Short of daybreak we were in the saddle again, and pushing on. We passed a village off to our right.

"Tres Alamos," Rocca said. Three Cottonwoods . . . it was the name of many villages. Later we passed near another village, but avoided it, for there was no time for answering questions, and they would not like us bringing the Apaches on them. This was Senokipe—hollow tree.

I loved the names the country gave, the sound of them made music to the ear. Santa Rosalia . . . Soledad . . . Remedios . . . Soyopa . . . Nacori . . . Chimala . . . Kiburi. Okitoa, a sparrow hawk's nest; Batuco, a waterhole; Cumuripa, a rathole . . . Matape, the red cliff; and Bacadeguatzi, meaning "at the white mountain." The men who came first to this land used the names descriptive of it, the names that grew as naturally from the land as the cottonwood, the willow, or the ocotillo.

Dawn came up in crimson light over the eastern mountains; it flushed the mountainsides with a kind of dull flame.

"I don't like it," Rocca muttered gloomily. "It looks like blood."

In the next hour we counted three smokes . . . three and an answering smoke.

We stopped at a small creek, watered the horses, and shifted saddles.

"If anything goes wrong," I said to Dorset, "you take the children and ride for the border. Harry can handle his own horse and one of the youngsters."

Rocca turned in his saddle. "I can smell Apaches. They have been by this way, and not long since."

Murphy chuckled. "You're dreamin', boy. Nobody can smell that good."

"They have been here," Rocca insisted. "And they will come again."

Now that we were further north, the grass was sparser, there were bare sandhills, and the bare brown-red rock of the mountains was streaked with the white of quartz. The sun was hot two hours before noon. The air was still; nothing stirred anywhere. Dancing heat waves emphasized the dead quiet.

My skin crawled. Again and again I shifted my rifle to wipe the sweat from my hands. Sweat streaked the dust on the faces of my companions, and the sweat trickling down my spine was cold and clammy under the slight stir of wind. I tried to assay our chances and came up empty.

John J. Battles suddenly spoke. "I'd like to see the leaves turning red and gold again, and hear the wild geese honk."

"You're thinking of a northern land," Spanish Murphy said. "I remember a time like that in Wyomin'. I drove a herd east from Oregon."

Dorset edged close to me. "Tell," she said softly, "do you think we'll make it?"

I did not want to talk; it was a time for listening. "We've had luck so far," I answered.

We switched horses again and pushed on through the nooning time—four bold but lonely men, a girl scarcely become a woman, and the youngsters, four of them. With the spare horses, three per rider, and our pack horse, we made a solid bunch. Our other pack horse had long since been lost.

Somewhere, still far off to the north of us, lay the border, a thin line drawn on maps, and a thin line in our consciousness, but a strong one across our lives. North of it there might be help. And further north still there was sanctuary.

We slowed the horses to a walk. It was very hot. The sun was lost in a brassy sky.

I think we all knew that the Apaches would come. We could elude a few, but we could not elude them all. The Apache had no regard for horse flesh. He would ride a horse to death and then eat him, so he rode often at a killing pace. And there were the talking smokes, speaking across the distance.

I did not hate the Apache. He was my enemy as I was his because of the time and the circumstances; but he was a fighting man, and a strong man who endured much to live in this country. If they captured us they would kill us. There would be torture for the men, worse perhaps for the girl, but it was their way of life, and you judge each man by his time and his way of life.

We walked our horses while the saddles creaked, and we blinked our eyes to see past the sting of the salty sweat trickling into them. Dark stains showed on our shirts. We drank water from our canteens, and kept on.

We knew there was a waterhole ahead. Rocca knew where it lay, Spanish knew, and I knew. We thinned out as we rode nearer, and we cut for sign, but found none. We could see a cottonwood up ahead, and a small clump of willows. Off to the east, fifty yards or more from the waterhole, rose a bare upthrust of rocks perhaps half a mile long, and not more than a hundred yards wide for most of its length.

Pulling up, I studied those rocks. "That waterhole now," I said. "If somebody was up in those rocks anybody at the waterhole would be a sitting duck."

"We got to have water," Murphy said.

Glancing around, I saw a separate small island of rocks rising perhaps from a buried spur of the ridge. "You folks hole up over yonder," I said, "and I'll take three horses and the canteens and ride over there for water. You cover me. If any shooting starts, you open up on the ridge over there. I'll water the horses, and fill the canteens."

Leading the horses, I rode to the waterhole. There was a desert wren singing in the willows, and the cottonwood leaves were rustling, as they do in the slightest breeze. Some quail sifted away through the low brush as I approached, the horses quickening their pace as they neared the water.

If there were Apaches near they would surely have seen my friends take their rifles and get down among the rocks, and they would be almighty sure to know that meant trouble if they opened fire. But it was a shaky business, a-setting out there on a horse, letting the other ones take the time to drink, and just a-waiting for a bullet.

After a bit I got down, went around the waterhole, and began filling canteens. First off, on coming up to the waterhole I'd taken notice of the ground, and saw a coyote, bighorn, and wild horse tracks, and the track of a desert fox, too, but no tracks of anything human. That didn't mean a whole lot. An Apache, if he figured there were white men around, would never go near a waterhole unless he was dying of thirst. He would just hole up some place close by and wait.

One by one I filled the canteens, getting a drink myself in the meantime, and then I mounted up and rode back and took the rest of the horses.

It was an eerie sort of thing, watching the horses dip their muzzles into the water and drink, and listening to that wren in the brush. I could see a place where some javelinas, the wild pig of the desert, had been bedded down.

When the last horse had drunk his fill, I gathered the reins on the black and put a boot into the stirrup. I started to swing up, but something glanced sharp across my eyes and I let go the pommel and dropped.

The bullet, timed for my swing into the saddle, clipped a twig where my head would have been, had I not been warned by that flash of sunlight on a rifle barrel.

On one knee I aimed and fired, my shot echoing those fired by my friends among the rocks, and they all hit within inches of where the Apache had been. Then I was in the saddle and racing the horses back to the rocks. In an instant we were all riding, and another shot hit the sand behind us.

"Only one," Rocca said, "but he'll send up a smoke."

"Maybe we got him," Spanish said.

"We'd have to have luck. We worried him, but I don't think we got him."

We glanced back, and in another minute saw a thin column of smoke rising. We looked at it, but nobody made any comment. The horses were slowed to a walk—they might need to run later. We traveled down an arroyo that left no tracks to speak of, the deep sand obliterating all but indefinite hollows.

We went down across a desert flat and into several parallel ranges of bare ridges, their slopes partly covered with the drift sand. The ridges gave us a little cover, and we stepped up the pace.

The children were very tired now. The endless motion of the horses had lulled them into a state where nothing mattered but a longed-for end of it. As for the rest of us, we lived by the moment, counting on nothing more, knowing that the worst might still lay before us.

Dorset came close to me, and for some time we rode side by side without speaking. Suddenly, about half a mile off to our right, we saw a rider. It was an Apache, but he made no effort to close the distance, simply holding a course parallel to our own. A few minutes later another appeared, to our left.

"They're closing in." Battles lit a cigar, squinting his eyes through the smoke. "I think they've got some place in mind, somewhere up ahead."

Tampico stood in his stirrups, scanning the country around. "We'll turn west," he said.

We wheeled quickly and charged in that direction, spurring our horses for speed, and drove right at the man on that flank.

For a startled instant I think the Apache had no idea what to do, and then he fled off to the northwest as far as his pony could carry him.

We kept on west at top speed, wanting to cover ground before they could adjust to our change of direction and pace. We dipped into a hollow dotted with clumps of ocotillo and prickly pear, and charged down it, out of sight of the Apaches for at least a mile. Then we rode up a shallow wash and out on the flat above.

There were at least a dozen Apaches off to the east, riding on a course that would join with ours somewhere ahead. Others were coming up behind, and to the west we could see another party coming along fast to head us off.

Me, my eyes were taking in the country around. We were being boxed. "All right," I said, "we'll run!"

And we ran.

I figure we all knew we were up against it then. They knew we had been swapping saddles, but now they weren't going to give us a chance to do that. They were going to run us the way they'd run wild horses, in relays. If we stopped they'd move in and surround us, so we had to run. And they knew where we were running to.

Oh, they were sly, all right, cunning as wolves. Ahead of us a canyon mouth suddenly opened, a wide, shallow canyon like some of those in western Texas, with sides sloping steeply up to a sheer rock wall about thirty or forty feet high. The Apaches closed in on the sides, driving us into that canyon like into a trap. And we knew it would be a box canyon, with a dead end somewhere up ahead.

"Slow down," I said. "Rocca, we got to find us a place up on the slope, somewhere open to the top."

A shot rang out and one of our horses stumbled, and fell. I swore. Nobody ever likes to see a good horse die, but this one would be eaten by the Apaches.

They had fallen behind now, but they were in the canyon top, which was over four hundred yards wide at this point. There was a thin trickle of water in the bottom, at the east side.

We were almost abreast of what looked like a means of escape before we saw it—hollow up near the rim, a sort of half-basin scooped out by some fall of rock, followed by erosion. Pulling up, I pointed. "We're going up there."

"It's a trap," Rocca said. "We'll never get out of it."

"It's a place to stand and fight from," Battles answered, looking up. He wheeled his horse and started up the slope.

He rode left for about fifty paces, leading the pack horse, then back right, riding a switchback trail he was making himself.

Tampico Rocca was already down behind some rocks, and I dropped beside him. "Go on up," I told Dorset. "At the top you'll have to lead your horse, but keep going."

She was not one to ask unnecessary questions. She knew what Rocca and I were set to do, and she wasted no time. John J. Battles was already halfway up, and he was on his feet, leading his struggling horses. Harry Brook, with one of the Creed boys, was right behind him, but being lighter they could stay on the horses.

Spanish Murphy was waiting, Winchester in his hand, and when Dorset passed him he followed, leading the other horses. They strung out on the trail, making quite a cavalcade.

"Tamp," I said, "there's a steep fall of rock, a sort of watercourse, to the left of where they are going up. It will be steeper but faster."

"*Bueno,*" he said, and looked around at me. "It has been a good race. A very good one, I think."

The Apaches were coming closer—there must have been at least thirty of them. Again I glanced at the slope, checking out the route, the possible cover, the quickest way to the hollow up under the rim. It was farther up there than it looked, and already the others were looking a lot smaller, but they still had a way to go.

One of the Apaches was trying to climb the slope behind us. Rocca tucked the butt of his Winchester against his shoulder, held his aim for an instant, and fired. We saw the Apache slip, half fall, then catch himself and turn his horse away from us.

We waited. The other Indians were scattering out now. We fired, choosing our targets, but we could not see whether we scored or not. But all the Apaches in sight went to the ground.

Rocca ducked back, running swiftly from rock to rock. He was an Apache again himself, swift and daring, yet sure. He paused once, shot quickly, then ran on.

I balanced my Winchester in my hands, took a quick glance toward a bunch of brush and rocks about thirty feet away, and ran for it. A bullet kicked dust just ahead of me . . . another ricocheted off a rock with an angry snarl, a nasty sound; the flattened bullet could have made an ugly wound.

Crawling a dozen feet, and scrambling through the brush, I got up again, rounded a boulder, and was in plain sight of them. I brought my rifle up swiftly. An Apache was running straight toward me when I stepped out, but before he could stop or hunt cover, I squeezed off my shot.

He was not seventy yards away and was facing full toward me, and there was no way I could miss. The bullet caught him running, and he took two steps before he pitched on his face in the gravel of the slope.

Up the watercourse I could hear scrambling feet, and I ran that way. I was taking long strides, leaping from rock to rock like a mountain goat, with lead spattering around me. Once I lost my footing, my heel skidded off a water-worn boulder, and I was pitched into the sand. I came up fast and felt a bullet snatch at my hat as I fired . . . and missed.

The Apache I'd seen was gone. The one I had killed was still lying back there on the gravel.

My breath was tearing at my lungs but I scrambled on up, crawling over boulders, pulling myself from rock to rock. From time to time I was out of their sight.

Suddenly Rocca was right ahead of me. He turned to speak and I saw the bullet catch him. It dusted him on both sides, and he squatted suddenly on his haunches with blood coming from his side, staining his shirt.

He let go of his rifle and started to fall forward, but I caught him.

Ahead of us was about sixty yards of talus slope, and then the hollow toward which we'd headed.

When I caught Rocca I just naturally let him fall across my shoulders, catching hold of his collar with my right hand. My Winchester was in my left, and I reached down and got a finger through the lever on his rifle and lunged up straight. Then I started up the slope.

That struggle up, with Rocca across my shoulders, my breath most gone, and those bullets coming toward us from behind . . . I never want to do that again.

Somehow I made it, and then stumbled and sort of fell into the hollow. Somebody lifted Rocca off my back, and I saw he'd been hit at least one more time.

Gasping for breath, I stared around me. They were all there, Dorset, the children, Murphy, and Battles, and the horses. And now there was us two.

"The trouble is," John J. Battles said, "we're trapped. There's no way out."

Chapter 13

The hollow was nowhere more than seventy or eighty feet across, and the side up which we had come spilled over in a slope of broken rock and gravel. Elsewhere the sides sloped up steeply in banks of blown sand and gravel, littered with broken rock from the escarpment above, and dotted with sparse brush. The sheer wall above varied from eight feet in height to twice that.

Our rifles could command the slope down to the canyon where the Apaches now were. With no trouble, one or two men could prevent them from reaching us. On the other hand, if they reached the top of the mesa above us, we could be picked off at their leisure.

My eyes searched the rim. It was cracked and broken, and there were places where a man might be able to reach the top, but no place where a horse could go up.

Dorset was working over Rocca; she had him resting as easy as he could, and she was stopping the blood. Harry Brook, needing nobody to tell him, had bunched our horses at the back of the hollow, out of rifle shot from below. The children were huddled together, watching with wide eyes. Nobody was saying anything, but our situation looked bad. We had water enough for a day, perhaps two.

Slowly, I got to my feet. I said, pointing to the rim, "I'm going to find a way out of this hole."

"Wings." Rocca spoke around the cigarette Dorset had lighted for him. "You would need wings."

"Spanish," I said, "you an' Battles stand 'em off. I'm going up yonder."

They studied the wall. "That's more of a climb than it looks," Spanish said. "But we'd better have somebody up there to hold them back."

I started up the slope, angling across it for easier going. It took all of ten minutes to get to the foot of the escarpment.

On the rock wall I came to one of the cracks I'd seen from below. It was a foot wide at the bottom, widening above to maybe three feet. Here and there a few broken slabs of rock had fallen into it and become wedged. A man could climb out of it all right, but he surely couldn't take a wounded man up that way, so I worked my way along the face.

First thing I saw was a lion track, or maybe it was a jaguar's. There were a lot of those big spotted cats in Sonora; you even saw one in Arizona or California time to time.

The tracks, which were several days old, led right along the face and I followed them, studying every break in the rock that I came to. When I'd gone almost around the basin, the tracks suddenly disappeared.

Now, even a cat, tricky as they may be, cannot vanish into thin air, so I contemplated the problem.

That cat had come up from the canyon below, and he surely wasn't going back down. The last set of tracks showed the hind feet dug in a mite, and it looked as if the cat had taken a jump. Then I saw a rock where he might have landed. From where I stood the rock's face was sheer, but the edge, about six feet above my head, was broken, and the cracks were filled with talus.

I realized I couldn't, even by jumping, reach the edge, but when I climbed up on a small rock I could see scratches on the big one I wanted to reach, and there were so many scratches that it looked as if that cat had used this trail a good many times.

Hunting for foot-holds, I found a couple and managed to scramble onto the big rock. There was a crack in the rock that led to the rim in a steep slide, filled with broken rock. In a few minutes I was up on top of the mesa, which stretched away for miles. Here there was thin grass, a few clumps of prickly pear, and the cat tracks, fading away to the northwest.

From where I now stood I could not see the hollow, but only the further rim of the canyon and some of the bottom. There were no Apaches in view, and it was likely none of them could see me.

I went back down into the crack and studied it. It would be a steep scramble, but I'd taken horses up worse places. If I could just get them over that first rock. . . .

As I was easing down bit by bit so as to keep out of sight of the Apaches, I heard a rifle shot from below. That worried me none at all. No Apache was going to climb up that slope with a rifle up there; no Apache was fool enough to try. Chances were some Indian showed himself to test us out and Spanish or Battles let him have one to know we weren't asleep.

What I needed now was to be able to figure out a way to get the folks out of that hole. And it was surely up to me. Dorset and the children aside, the boys with me had come just because they were my friends and knew I needed some help.

That big rock was the thing. There were cracks in it, but none very deep that I'd noticed, so I worked my way back for a closer look. On one side it was cracked and broken, and I began digging at it, hoping to dig out enough so that a couple of horses might scramble up or be hauled up.

First, I pulled out several chunks of rock that were in the crack, big pieces of fifty or sixty pounds. With a call to look out below, I tumbled them over. For almost an hour I worked at it.

The Apaches had taken no action against us, and that gave me hope. None of them had taken off to ride around and get up above us; and as they knew the country, maybe they knew it was miles before there was a way out of that barranca.

Down below me occasional shots sounded, and the Apaches fired a time or two. The way I was fixed they couldn't see me, nor what I was doing. They knew better than anybody that there was no help I could call on, and no matter what I did they'd have my scalp sooner or later. But I planned to make them work for it. If they wanted my hair they'd have to get it the hard way.

So I kept on at the rock, and unloaded a good many chunks of it.

A long, thin slab formed one side of the crack I was digging into. It was all of six or eight feet long, and must have weighed a ton or more, but as I dug down around it I could see it was a free slab, broken clean off the main rock.

There were a few loose rocks at the base, and I climbed down and pulled them free. I had me an idea now, and I didn't figure to give up on it. In a time and place like that, you gamble on any wild-haired chance. We were boxed in, the Apaches were down below, and they were willing to wait. We had water enough for a while, and ammunition enough for quite a fight, but that wasn't going to get us out of here.

The sun beat down on my back and my shirt was wet with sweat, but I'd never done anything much in my life but work hard, and didn't know any different. Besides, we Sacketts were a right stubborn folk. We just didn't have much give-up in us. We always kept plugging away, and that's what I was doing this time.

Finally, when I'd done what I could in the hole, I climbed up and did what I'd been figuring on. I got into the top of that crack, put my back against one side, and my feet against the other, which bowed up my knees. Then with my hands braced against the rock behind me, I began to push.

The sweat broke out on my face and rolled down me in streams. Nothing happened—nothing at all. I rested a mite and then I tried again. It was on the third try that I felt her give a mite. So I buckled down and tried still another time, and she gave a bit more.

Rocks and gravel trickled down into the hollow below, and then Battles climbed up there to help.

He studied the layout and shook his head. "I don't believe it. Even if you can do it, what then?"

"I figure our number's up," I said. "Not that I don't figure to make them earn it with blood, but that girl now—she's got to have a running chance. She's got to get out, and those children."

He squatted on his heels and looked at me. "So?"

"That little buckskin, now. That's a mountain horse, a mountain mustang, and I figure she could climb a tree if need be. The girl's horse is another. Both of them are small, both are quick and smart. I think we might, if we can make any sort of a way to, get the girl and those youngsters out of here. Might even be a chance for us."

He studied the layout again. If that slab toppled over, it would leave a steep slide of gravel and broken rock. With a couple of husky men pulling and a horse scrambling, it might work. With one horse on top and a rope around the pommel, we might get another out.

Battles got down into the crack and scraped some good footing for himself, and then put his shoulder against the slab. Together we pushed, we strained. Of a sudden she gave. I slid lower to get a better purchase, and we tried it again. She tilted a bit, then stuck. Try as we might, we couldn't push that slab any further.

We backed off and studied the situation, and John J. kept looking at that crack. It was a whole lot wider than it had been, and slanted steeply down to the gravel slope below.

He looked at the crack, and then he looked at me again. "Shall we try it?" he asked.

Well, now. It was almighty steep, but it was all we had. I'd seen wild horses scramble up some steep slopes, but none as bad as this—but with a little help . . .

We went back down into the hollow below where the others waited, and I took a long pull at a canteen. When I looked up to where we'd been it fairly turned my stomach. What we needed was a set of wings.

I saw that they had rigged a little shade for Rocca—a poncho over a couple of rocks, propped up with a stick. I went over and squatted down beside him. "I'm hit pretty hard, *amigo*," he said.

"You'll make it."

He looked up to the rock where I'd been. "What you got in mind?"

"That's the only way out for the two little horses, the girl and the youngsters. That girl's got savvy. Get them out of here, and she's a good bet to make the border."

"I keep thinkin' of that ranch back yonder," Rocca said; "of those trees, an' the grass."

"It was quite a place."

"If a man had to die, that would be the best he'd be likely to find. I figure heaven must be like that. Not that I'm likely to make it."

He looked at me. "When you going to try it?"

"It's coming on for evenin'. I think we'll try then."

He closed his eyes. "Wish I could help."

Dorset came over and I laid it out for her. We were going to try to get them out, and she was to light a shuck for the border, hiding out by day, riding in the evening or early morning. But she already knew what she needed to do.

She didn't ask any foolish questions, either. She knew what was likely to happen here, and she knew what we needed was a miracle.

"When you get back," I told her, "you might write a letter to Tyrel Sackett, up in Mora. You tell him about it. Tell him about Laura, too— how she sent me down here on a wild-goose chase."

"I'll do that," Dorset said quietly. "When it comes to that, I may go to see her myself."

"Leave her be. She's poison."

It was no trouble for Dorset, Harry Brook, and the other youngsters to get to the top. Children are good at scrambling in rough places, and they took it as a lark. While Battles stood guard after, it was up to Spanish and me to get the horses up.

The little buckskin was quick and nimble. She climbed the gravel slope with me leading on the bridle, and though she went to her knees once, she made it. But when I looked up at that crack in the rock, I had my doubts.

Knowing the route, I went ahead, leading the buckskin. Spanish came along behind, but when I climbed into the crack the mustang pulled back and just wasn't having any part of it.

Spanish, he was right behind her, and he took off his sombrero and hit her a lick across the behind. She was almighty startled and gave a big jump, and before she knew what had happened she had her front feet on the crack and her hind feet scrambling for a grip on the slope.

Me, I tugged at the bridle. Spanish hit her another lick with his hat and she scrambled into the crack. There we held up for a mite, to catch our wind.

It was the cool of evening now, with the sky still pale blue in the far-off place where the sun had gone down, but overhead there were a few stars. Sitting back there on a rock, holding the bridle, I took long, deep breaths of that cool air.

All of a sudden the mare decided she wasn't too almighty comfortable standing spread out on the steep side of a hill, so of her own notion she scrambled a few steps higher, then stopped, and we let her be. It was still a far piece to the top.

After we'd all caught our breath we started on, and it was a struggle. But little by little we scrambled up until at last we got on top. By that time it was full dark and we still had the other horse to bring up.

Battles was down there alone, or as good as. Rocca was in no shape to lend a hand, and might be asleep. The Apaches didn't attack at night as a rule, for they had the notion that if a man was killed in the darkness his soul would wander forever in darkness. But if they did try coming up that slope in the dark, Battles could never hold them.

Leaving Dorset with the mare and the youngsters, Spanish and me made our way back into the basin. By the time we reached the bottom we were so almighty tired we were staggering, and we just naturally caved in.

John J. reported no movement as far as he knew of. Rocca was sleeping. He had lost a lot of blood, and we had no way of treating a wound. Up on the mesa we might find one of the herbs the Indians used, but down here there was nothing.

Spanish worked a hollow for his hip in the sand and went to sleep. After I took John J.'s place, he did the same.

It was still, and overhead the stars were bright as they can only be in a desert sky. A coolness came up from the barranca below, and I listened for any whisper of sound, struggling against my own weariness and the need for sleep. But a few minutes of sleep might mean death for all of us. Only my wariness stood guard, and the thought of them trusting me.

A long while later, Spanish came to me. "You better get a little sleep," he said; "but if we're figuring on getting that horse up the mountain, it won't be much."

There was no need for me to move. I just let go and closed my eyes; and when I woke up it was with a hand on my shoulder.

"They're stirrin' around down there," Spanish said, "and it's gettin' on toward dawn."

"You two hold 'em," I said, getting up. "I'll take that other horse up the mountain."

"Alone? It can't be done."

"It's got to be," I said. "The Apaches will figure it out if we wait. Maybe they already have."

John J. was on his feet, his gun belted on and his Winchester in his hand, a spare cartridge belt draped over his shoulder.

"If it gets bad, pull back to Rocca here, and make a stand," I said. "I'll get back as soon as I can."

He indicated the horses. "Do you think we could make a break for it? Down the slope and right into them, shooting all the while?"

It was a thought, and I said so, but I told him no, not yet. Then I went and caught up the other mustang and headed for the slope. Oddly enough, Dorset's horse took to it as if it was home country. More than likely she could smell the other horse, and knew it had gone this way. Maybe she could also smell Dorset. Wild horses can follow a trail as good as any wolf—I've seen them do it many a time. And the other horse, with us working to help, had maybe made the trail a little better.

The horse had to struggle, and I tugged and braced myself and pulled, and that game little horse stayed right with it. With daybreak tinting the sky, we made it to the rim.

And then we heard the shots. Somebody down there was using a Winchester.

We heard the chatter of the rifle, then a few slower, paced shots. There was silence, then another shot.

The children were wide-eyed and scared, but they were pioneer youngsters, and no telling the trouble they'd seen before this. Dorset stepped into the saddle and I taken her hand.

"Ride," I said, "and stay with it. Hide out by day, ride by night," I told her again. "Don't shoot unless they get close, and then shoot to kill. I figure you're going to make it. We can hold them a day or two."

She put her hand on mine. "Tell, thank them for me, will you? All of them?"

"Sure."

The shooting down there was steady now. They needed me down there. I knew how Apaches could come up a slope. Nothing to shoot at but a few bobbing, flashing figures, you scarce saw them when they vanished, appeared again elsewhere, and came on.

Dorset knew it, too. She turned her horse, lifted a hand, and they rode off into the coming morning. I taken one look and then I hit the slope a-sliding. Far below I could see the Indians.

Battles was on the rim, bellied down behind rock slabs. Far off, near the stream, I could see the Apache ponies, but nothing was moving on the slope. Behind Battles I could see Spanish, and he was rolling some rocks into place, lifting others, making a sort of rough wall from where John J. was firing to where Rocca was lying. He was getting set for a last-ditch fight, and the lay of the land sort of favored our position by being a mite lower than the rest of the hollow.

Of a sudden an Apache came up from behind a rock and started to move forward, and my Winchester came up as if it moved of its own will, and I taken a quick sight and let go.

High on the slope the way I was, right under the rim, I had a good view of what lay below. That Apache was a good three hundred yards off and lower down, but I held low a-purpose and that bullet caught him full in the chest.

He stopped in his tracks and Battles shot into him, getting off two fast shots before he could drop, but when he did drop he just rolled over and lay sprawled out, face up to the sun.

A number of shots were fired at me, but all of them hit the slope a good fifty feet below me, and I decided right then I was going to stay where I was.

It stayed quiet then, and slowly the afternoon drew on. Our horses had been bunched by Spanish so that they were close to Rocca, and the position seemed pretty good unless the Apaches decided to attack by night. But I kept on thinking about what we might do. There had to be a way out.

Now, my pappy was always one for figuring things. He told me time and again that when in difficulty a body should always take time to contemplate. "The only way folks got to where they are," he'd say, "was by thinkin' things out. No man ever had the claws of a grizzly nor the speed of a deer—what he had was a brain."

Right now we had here a stalemate, but it worked in favor of the Apache. It worked for him because he had access to plenty of water and grass, which we did not have.

And I knew the Apache would no longer wait. He'd be scaling that rimrock himself, and without horses he could get up there all right, although it would take some doing. We could figure on having them above us by the next daybreak, and then that hollow would be nothing but a place to die in.

We had to make it out of there, and right now. Nobody expects to live forever, but nobody wishes to shorten his time. Of course, a body never knows which turn will shorten it. Like when a bunch of us boys went off to the war we left a friend behind who paid a substitute. We all came back, safe and sound, but the one who stayed home was dead—thrown from a horse he'd ridden for three years . . . scared by a rabbit, it jumped, and he lit on his head. So a man never knows.

Only if we didn't get out of this place we weren't going to be laying many plans.

Up there where I was, I began to give study to the country around.

I knew that getting the rest of those horses up to the top was an unlikely chance. In the first place, most of them were larger and heavier, and altogether harder to handle than the two we had got out. We might just possibly get one horse up, or even two. We would never make three or four.

So I cut that out of my thinking. Somehow we had to get out by going downhill, and that meant riding right through that bunch of Apaches. . . .

Now, wait a minute, I told myself. There to the right . . . there's a slide of sand, but there's a mixed lot of growth in it. There don't seem to be so many large rocks. I studied it as carefully as the light would allow.

If we could just . . . I began to see how we, or some of us, might make it. If we stayed here none of us would make it through tomorrow.

I was going down there right now and face them with it. Only first there was that Apache off to the left. He had been coming up the hill for the last half-hour, creeping, crawling, out of sight more than two-thirds of the time, but always getting closer. Now when he moved again . . .

Settling myself into the sand, I braced my elbow and taken a careful sight. Then I waited. His foot moved. . . . I waited. . . . Then he lunged into view and I squeezed off my shot. He never even twitched.

Chapter 14

When I came sliding into the hollow Spanish looked at me. "Was I you, I'd still be travelin'," he said. "It don't look like we're goin' no place down here."

"I've got an idea," I said.

He searched my face. "Well, you Sacketts have come up with some good ones. I hear tell whenever one of you boys are in trouble, the rest come a-runnin'. I'd like to see that now. I surely would."

"They don't know where I'm at."

John J. was stuffing a pipe. He looked haggard and honed down. I hadn't the heart to look at Rocca yet. "What's this idea?" John J. asked. "Right about now I'll buy anything."

"Yonder," I said, "there's a corner of slope that's mostly free of big rocks. There's some grass and some brush, but it's low stuff, and the sand looks as if it's packed."

"So?"

"Come nightfall we mount up. We stampede the horses down that slope into the Apache camp and we go with them. Only we keep on riding."

Battles gave study to it. Spanish, he just looked at me. "How many do you think would make it?" he asked.

"Maybe none . . . maybe one."

Battles shrugged. "Well, it's no worse than here. At least we'd be trying."

"What about Tamp?" Spanish asked.

"He isn't getting any better, is he? How much chance has he got here?"

"None at all."

"All right. So we get him into a saddle. You put that Mex on a horse and he'll ride it to hell and gone. I know him. If we get him up in a saddle he'll stay there as long as any of us, dead or alive."

"All right," Battles said, "I'll buy it. What do we do?"

"Pick your best horse. We'll load the pack horse. Maybe he can stay with us, maybe he can't. Maybe he'll follow and catch up. You know how horses like to stay together."

We sat about there, chewing on jerked beef and trying to see all the angles, but there wasn't much we could do but trust to luck. We could hold to the far side of the bunch away from the Apache camp, although that might be the worst thing, for there'd likely be Apaches sleeping around, or watching from everywhere.

Time was a-passing, but we daren't do anything to let those Indians know what we were planning. Saddling up had to be done after dark, and all we could do would be to pray none of them got up on the rimrock before night came on.

Tampico Rocca was lying there with his eyes open when I sat down beside him. "You don't have to tell me," he said. "I heard you talking."

"You reckon you can set up there like I said?"

"You get me into the saddle, that's all I ask. That and a couple of short-guns."

"You'll have them."

We sat quiet then for quite a spell. It was almighty hot, and even sitting still the sweat trickled down my body. We drank and drank again, and we all ate a little more . . . no telling when we'd get to eat or drink again, if ever.

Finally I taken my rifle and climbed up on the rim. We had to make those Apaches think they had us, and after my helping in two kills from up there, they'd be sure I'd stay there.

Up on the rim I could see no cover for an Apache up there, no way one could come on a man except by night, and if anybody rode from their camp, I could see him.

The camp was too far for a rifle shot, but I could see their cook fires, and see them moving around. Our horses, if we could start them slow, might get within easy distance of their camp before we had to stampede them. And we might be lucky enough to stampede their pony herd, but I wasn't betting on anything.

When it was fairly dark I came down off the rim and we lighted a small fire to make coffee. They knew where we were, and we wanted them to think of us as staying put, although the idea of us trying to break out probably never came to their minds. They knew we were boxed in.

Over coffee we just sat around, keeping an ear tuned for movement. Rocca was propped up by his saddle atop a couple of rocks.

John J. Battles was quiet, saying nothing much until suddenly he started to talk of home. It seemed he'd come from New England, of a good, solid family. He had made a place for himself in the town and was a respected young businessman, and then he got involved with a girl, and another young man from a respected but high-riding family had come for him with a gun. This fellow had been drinking, and threatened to kill Battles on sight. When they met again Battles was armed, and in the exchange of shots, he killed the man.

There had been a trial, and Battles was cleared of the shooting, but he found himself no longer welcome at the girl's house, or anywhere else in town. So he sold his business, went west, and had drifted. He had driven stage, ridden shotgun for Wells Fargo, during which time he killed a holdup man and wounded his partner. He had been a deputy marshal for a time, had driven north with a cattle drive, and scouted against the Cheyenne.

"What happened to the girl?" Spanish wanted to know.

Battles glanced up. "What you'd expect. She married somebody else, not as well off as I'd been, and he got to hitting the bottle. A couple of years later his horse ran away with his rig and he was killed.

"She wrote, wanted me to come back. Offered to come west to me, and you know something? Try as I might, I couldn't even remember exactly what she looked like."

"You didn't have a picture?"

"Had one. Lost it when the Cheyennes ambushed a stage I was traveling on." He paused for a moment. "I'd like to have seen the leaves change color back in the Vermont hills again. I'd like to have seen my family again."

"I thought you had no family," I said.

"I've got a sister and two brothers." He sipped some coffee. "One brother is a banker in Boston. The other one is a teacher. I'd gone into business, but a teacher was what I really wanted to be; only when the moment came I was steadier with a gun than I should have been."

Nobody talked there for a time, and then Battles looked around at me. "Any of your family ever in New England? There was a man named Sackett made quite a name for himself up in Maine during the Revolution. Seems he was wounded or hurt or something, and he spent the winter on the farm with my great-grandparents, helped them through a bad time."

"Uh-huh. My great-grandfather fought in the Revolution. He was with Dearborn at Saratoga, and he was in Dearborn's command when they marched with General Sullivan to destroy the towns of the Iroquois."

"Likely it's the same man." Battles put down his coffee cup and began to stoke his pipe.

Spanish walked in from the lookout. "All quiet," he said. "There's still one fire goin'."

Quiet as could be, we saddled our horses, and loaded what grub was left on our pack horse. Overhead the stars were very bright, and the night was still. Whilst the others got Rocca ready for traveling, binding his wounds tighter, I crept over to the place where we were going to try to ride down.

The ground was packed pretty good, and there was no slide sand.

The place was narrow, just a strip that might ordinarily have gone unnoticed, except that in our desperation we had looked for any possibility at all. Of course the Apaches might have seen it, too, and might be waiting for us down there, for it was the only place where we could come off the mountain with any speed. But we had not seen it from below, only from the view on the rimrock.

We gathered near the edge, the loose horses before us, held by me and Spanish. Tampico Rocca was in the saddle, John J. Battles beside him, holding our two horses.

It was near the middle of the night when we released our hold on the horses and went back to step into our saddles. "All right," I said, "let's go."

We started the horses forward. We made almost no sound in the night; there was a whisper of hoofs in the sand, a slight creak of saddle leather. I could feel a tightness in my chest, and I gripped hard on the pistol butt in my hand. This would be close, fast work—no chance for a rifle here.

The lead horses disappeared over the edge before us and started down, and as they reached a point about a third of the way down we let out a whoop and each of us fired a shot.

Startled, the half-broken horses lunged into a run. They went down the slope in a scattered band and hit the flat below running all out. A rifle flashed, somebody shouted, and a fire flared up. The Apaches had prepared fires for light, and they lit the wild scene with a dancing glare.

Low down on the black horse, I charged into the night, gun held low and ready. The wind whipped my face, and the horses thundered into the Apache camp.

Off to my left Rocca's gun was blazing. I saw a wild Apache face spring at him out of the dark, saw the flash of the pistol, and the face vanished into the darkness. Somewhere a horse screamed, and I heard a shout from Battles as his horse spilled head over heels, and John J. hit the sand running. I saw him slide to a stop and slam two fast shots at the running Apaches. Then he wheeled and, holstering his pistol as he moved, he made a wild grab at the streaming mane of one of our horses, somehow turned aside from the first rush. He was almost swept from his feet, but he went astride the horse, clinging to his hold on its mane.

Flames stabbed from every side, and then we were through the camp and racing away down the bottom of the barranca.

My black was running all out, and I turned a little in my saddle. Rocca was still coming, riding loose in the saddle, his hat on the back of his neck, held by the string of his chin-strap which had slipped to his throat.

Spanish was off to my right—or so I thought—and we charged on into the night, some of the horses running wild ahead of us, others scattered to left and right.

We raced on, and somehow the horses found a winding trail to the cap rock and slowed to climb it. I called out, but there was no reply. Finally the black struggled over the rim onto the mesa. There was more light there, under the high stars.

I drew up. Here and there I glimpsed a horse, but none that carried a rider.

Slowly I rode on, talking to the horses and hoping the others would follow. Daylight was still far away, but none of us would dare to stop. If they were alive they, too, would keep on.

There was no use to try to find anybody. In the darkness a body could be missed, and any one of us would shy from any other rider for fear he was facing an Indian.

Through the night I rode, once lifting my horse to a trot for a few miles, then slowing again to walk. I reloaded my gun, checked my rifle. Once, worn out as I was, I dozed in the saddle.

Finally, in the gray light of day, I stopped. Carefully standing in my stirrups, I looked in every direction. I could see for a good distance on all sides, but there was nothing but desert and sky. Wearily, I started the black horse on again, heading north.

By noontime, with nothing in sight, I got down and stumbled on, leading the horse. There was no telling when I might need all that horse had to make a run for it.

There were no tracks. There was only silence. Overhead a buzzard swept down the sky, returned and circled widely above me. After that he stayed with me, and I figured a buzzard had pretty good judgment about where he might get a meal.

The sun was hot, and no breeze stirred. My canteen had been holed by a bullet and was empty. I stumbled along like a sleepwalker, dead on my feet, yet not daring to stop. Finally I gave up and climbed into the saddle again.

Ahead of me, almost lost in the blue of distance, the cap rock seemed to break off. There were mountains beyond; behind me to the east was nothing.

Water . . . I had to have water, and so did my horse. Under a desert sun a man cannot live long without water.

The mesa ended abruptly, but there was no trail to the rough, rolling land below. Here there was another stretch of the rimrock, nowhere less than thirty feet of sheer wall, then a steep, rock-strewn slope.

Far off I thought I could see a patch of green in a fold of the earth. Skirting the cliff, I rode on. Suddenly I saw the tracks of shod hoofs.

The tracks were familiar. They were the tracks of a horse that Spanish Murphy had ridden, a tough, mountain-bred horse, larger than the average mustang, and weighing almost a thousand pounds. Turning into the trail, I followed it along the rim. We came abruptly to a cleft where the rock wall had broken away and there was an easy though steep descent to the valley below. We made it.

We rode on, the black and me, with the black quickening his pace so as to come up with his friend. Sure enough, we'd gone not over five miles when we saw the bay mustang ahead of us. He had stopped, and was looking ahead, ears pricked.

Well, I shucked that Winchester before you could say aye, yes, or no, and I eared back the hammer and walked the black right up alongside that mustang. I spoke easy to him, and he didn't do more than side-step a mite, knowing my voice. Then I looked where he was looking.

There was a thick clump of ironwood beside the way we were taking, and a horse was standing head down there, just waiting, and sitting up on its back was a man. He was sitting there, hands on the pommel, head hanging like the horse's, and when we started forward, he paid us no mind.

Good reason why. It was Tampico Rocca, and he was dead.

Even before I got to him I could see by the blood on his vest that he'd been shot at least twice, but he'd lived long enough to lash one hand to the saddlehorn and tangle the fingers of the other hand in the turns of the rope.

Rocca had said that if he got into the saddle he would stay there, and he meant it.

Chapter 15

There was no need to stay close to him, and I was wary. Had the Apaches seen me coming, it would have been like them to leave Rocca there, and I wanted no traps.

An arroyo offered some shelter, and after a quick glance I rode into it and waited there, listening.

For several minutes I watched Rocca, the horse, and the rocks around. Mostly, it was the horse I watched, for the actions of the horse would warn me if there was anyone close by.

Following the arroyo a little further, I saw a clump of brush and low trees near the lip of the draw, so I rode up the bank in their shelter. After a while, reasonably sure that it was safe, I went back to the horse and its burden.

The trailing bridle had caught in the brush, and I let it stay there while I lifted Rocca from the saddle after freeing his hands. There was nothing with which to prepare a grave, so I found a shallow watercourse, placed him in it, and covered the body with brush and rocks.

But first, I had taken his guns and ammunition, to leave nothing for the Apaches if they found him. There was a full belt of ammunition as well as some loose cartridges. And there was a swallow of water in the canteen.

In his pocket I found a stub of pencil and some old papers on which he had been learning to write his name. He had gotten somebody to write it for him, or had taken it from something addressed to him, and had practiced, over and over again, on many different surfaces. I had never seen him do so, nor likely had anyone else, for he was a proud man, ashamed to let us know he could not write, and that he cared.

There was no address, nothing to show that there was anyone to whom he belonged. But there had been a girl he had talked of, so I took what money he had, only a few dollars and some pesos, to give to her.

Scarcely twenty minutes was used in burying the body. Then, leading the spare horse, I went back to the arroyo and followed it for perhaps a mile, the soft sand leaving no tracks that could be recognized. When I came out I started across country.

The sun had gone down by now and the desert was cool. Off in the distance I could hear a quail call . . . I hoped it was a real quail.

I felt stiff and cold now, and I worked my fingers to keep them easy for my gun. Shifting to Rocca's horse, I rode on into the night. There was no trail, but I went ahead, all the time looking for water. The green place I'd seen from afar should be near.

The black horse pulled up alongside me, and Rocca's horse quickened its pace. They smelled it.

An arroyo opened on my right and I found my way into it, listened, then walked the horses on, knowing the arroyo would end where the water was. The arroyo gaped, and I looked into a small oasis darkening with the cool of evening.

There were a dozen cottonwoods, some mesquite and willows, and slopes green with grass, and through the trees a glimmer of water. I could hear birds twittering. The horses tugged at their bits, wanting to go forward. Winchester in hand, I walked them slowly, ready with a spur if need be.

Suddenly my way was blocked by a low stone wall that looked to be a part of one of those *trincheras* the ancient people built to terrace and till their land, or sometimes for dams. I'd seen a lot of them in Mexico.

Dismounting, I led the horses around it and down to a broken place in the wall, and saw something dark and shadowy through the trees. There was no sound but the water, and the rustle of the cottonwood leaves. I walked ahead to an opening among the trees, and came to an ancient ruin. It had once been a considerable structure, built right from the edge of the pool back to the cliffs where it joined the native rock.

Only the floor remained, and a corner of a wall that reached up to six feet, slanting down to no more than three feet near the water. There was green grass all around, and a stillness that came from utter isolation.

First off, I let the horses drink sparingly, and drank myself, and then filled Rocca's canteen. All the while I kept my ears tuned for any sound. But there were no tracks around that I could see, no signs of campfires, nothing to show anybody had been here at all in years.

Picketing the horses, I found a corner of the wall that protected me on two sides. A pile of fallen adobe bricks mingled with chunks of rock that had been used in the walls formed a partial breastwork on the other sides.

Tired as I was, there was no sleep in me. Places like this made a man sort of sad. Somebody had lived here, and judging by the look of the place, different people at different times. There had once been a building of native stone. It had fallen in and been rebuilt with adobe and rock; and it looked as if the last time was no more than thirty, forty years back. Indians had perhaps built the place first, and rebuilt it, too. Later white people had settled in here until driven out.

It was a quiet place. A small garden patch had been worked at one time, and there was a meadow where hay might have been cut, but nobody could live long in such a place with the Apaches on the rampage.

I settled down, and after a while I slept. I awoke when the morning sun began to filter through the leaves. Everything was as quiet as before. I watered the horses, saddled them, and prepared to move out, but first I had scouting to do.

There were crude steps cut from the rocks at one side, taking advantage of natural steps left by the erosion of rock layers. Climbing these, I found a natural hollow that had been shaped by hand into a lookout of some comfort, with a view in all directions.

For several minutes I studied the desert, but saw nothing. Back down below again, I dug into my saddlebags for the small packet of coffee I always carried for emergencies. Often I carried some jerky and flour, but now there was only the coffee.

I built a small fire, and rinsed out an old clay jar I found. When I'd made coffee I filled a cup and prowled around, and finding some chia, I gathered a handful of the seeds and ate them. Then I went up for another look.

Off to the north I glimpsed a buzzard. There might be a dead steer, or it might be one of my friends, and buzzards do not always wait for a man to die.

Due north I rode, then I swung wide to the east, cutting for a sign. Whatever was up ahead must have left tracks getting there, and I wished to find out what I was up against.

"Tell," I told myself, "you better ride easy in the saddle. I think you're headin' into trouble."

That black flicked an ear at me as if to show he agreed. A lonely man a-horseback in wild country gets to carryin' on conversations with his horse, and some horses become right knowledgeable and understanding.

No tracks. I rode up on the east of where the buzzard circled, and swung in closer. Standing in my stirrups I looked the country over, and at first I saw only a lot of prickly pear around, and some clumps of cholla, all white thorns on top, brown underneath.

Then I saw the horse—a horse down, a saddled horse.

Circling around it, rifle in hand, I taken a chance and called out: "Spanish? Is that you?"

A couple of buzzards roosting in a palo verde tree nearby looked mighty upset with me, and one of them flopped his wings as if to scare me off or stampede my horses.

No answer came back. So I cut a little closer, then drew up and looked around. It was all just as it should be, sunlit and still.

My black was curious, too. He could sense something I could not, and though it made him curious, it was something he shied from. Probably it was the dead horse.

I walked him slowly forward, the hammer of my Winchester eared back for trouble.

The shirt was what I saw first, then the boots, and the Mexican spurs with the big rowels. It was Spanish.

I swung down and, having tied the black to a mesquite, I walked up to him.

He was lying face down in the sand, but he had pulled his saddlebags across his kidneys; so he'd been alive and conscious when he hit the ground. He knew that buzzards went for the eyes and the kidneys first, so he'd rolled on his face and pulled those saddlebags over him. They might not help much, but getting them off him might bring him to enough to fight the buzzards off.

Lifting the saddlebags free, I rolled him over.

There was blood all over the front of him, dried blood that seemed to come from a shoulder wound. And there was blood lower down that came from some place in his middle. But he was breathing.

We were right out in the open, and those buzzards could attract more than me; so, good for him or not, we had to move.

He muttered something, so I tried to let him know who was with him. "It's all right, Spanish," I said. "You'll see that girl in Tucson yet."

There was no time for fixing him up at all. Gathering him into my arms, I went with him to the spare horse and put him in the saddle; then I lashed his wrists to the pommel and his boots into the stirrups. I taken his saddlebags, although what was in them I didn't know. Then I checked his horse, but the animal was dead. There was a rifle in the saddle scabbard, so I took it along. There was no canteen.

We rode out of there at a good clip. The country ahead promised nothing. We had two, three days to cross the border, but we'd not be safe until we got to Pete Kitchen's or to the settlement on the border.

Taking advantage of every chance to mask my trail, and trying to keep down the dust, I rode north, leading Spanish on Rocca's horse. The wind was picking up a mite, which might drift enough sand to cover my tracks, but there was small chance it would be in time. Several times I slowed down, checking animal tracks, and watching for any sign that might indicate water.

The trail behind was empty, and the trail ahead looked clear. I rode in my own small world of sunlight, the movement of horses, and the smell of dust and sweat. Ahead of me, on the right, a sawtooth range showed itself above the flatter country around us.

I slowed my horse to a walk, for there were dark streaks of sweat along his flanks. An arroyo opened ahead of me, and I rode into it and found a way up the opposite bank. A towering butte was ahead for destination.

The bullet smashed against the pommel of my saddle, then ricocheted away with a nasty whine, and the heavy report of the rifle followed. Slapping spurs to my horse, I started to run him as three Apaches broke from cover to my right. They had waited in ambush, but my dip into the arroyo had fooled them and now they came running.

Turning in the saddle, I taken aim as best I might and fired . . . once, twice . . . three times. I saw a horse stagger and go down, spilling head over heels in the sand.

Ahead of me three more Apaches had come from right out of the desert, it seemed. I turned my mount a little away from them and raced on, holding my fire. Behind me Spanish rode like a sack of grain in the saddle, his body lurching with every jump, yet somehow he remained upright.

They came at me, and suddenly I wheeled the black and charged into them, firing my Winchester with one hand as if it was a pistol.

The sudden switch surprised them and one of them turned so sharply his horse spilled into the sand. Another was right ahead of my rifle barrel and not thirty feet away when I shot into his chest, dusting him on both sides. He went down, and then we were through and riding for that butte.

Behind me there was a shot and something tugged at my shoulder, but we were off and away. Sliding my Winchester into its scabbard, I drew a six-gun and fired, slowly and deliberately, trying for a score. The first shot missed; so did the second. Then an Apache elected to swing his horse around a small cedar just as I thumbed back the hammer. He was broadside to me and I let go, heard the slam of the shot, and saw the Apache lurch in the saddle, then swing off to one side, barely clinging to his horse.

Suddenly, from ahead there was the hard bark of a rifle, and glancing back, I saw another Indian falling. I raced forward, scarcely daring to believe it could be help, but the Apaches, wily fighters always, were swinging away. And Spanish was still riding behind me.

The desert fell away in a long slope ahead of us, and on the rim stood John J. Battles, dusty, bloody, his hat gone, his shirt torn. He got up from the ground as we approached and swung into the saddle . . . and he had the pack horse.

"She found me," he said. "Came trailing along the desert, part of her pack gone, the rest hanging under her belly."

"Did you see anything of the youngsters?" I asked.

"No, not a sign." He looked back at Spanish. "He hurt bad?"

"I haven't had time to look. I think so."

We pushed on, praying for the night to hurry, and finally it came. Our horses slowed to a walk, and Battles and me, we swung down to save them as much as we might.

"How far d'you think to the border?" Battles asked.

"Maybe sixty miles," I said. "Might be less."

He stopped to work his toes around in his boots. I knew the signs, for I was doing the same thing. We were both almighty tired. I figured I was stronger than him, and I'd been running on nerve. I seemed to have been hot, tired, and sore as long as I could remember. My muscles ached, my eyes hurt from the glare, and felt all the time as if they had sand in them. I was wanting to stop with every step, and I knew the horses didn't feel any better.

But we kept on, because neither of us was smart enough to quit. Finally Battles stumbled and went to his knees, and he was slow getting up.

"You better get on your horse and ride for it," he said. "Ride that horse to death if need be, but get to safety. We just ain't a-going to make it like this."

I didn't answer, but kept on going. Every time I put one foot ahead of the other I figured I'd gained just that much. Then when I had stumbled a couple of times myself, I realized the black horse was tugging at the bridle. He wanted to go off to the east.

"Mount up, John J.," I said. "Maybe we've found something, but you hold ready to shoot, because we may find trouble." I was so dry I had to try twice before I could make the words come.

Once in the saddle, I just let the black have his head, and that horse started off at a good clip, considering the shape he was in. And the others came on behind, Spanish Murphy still a-setting up there like a preacher pronouncing sentence on Satan, his head bowed but his shoulders hunched as if he figured maybe Satan was aimed to get in one more blow.

It wasn't long before we felt a coolness, and the horses lurched down into an arroyo and all of a sudden we came up to a small fire where there were four or five Apaches gathered around, eating a fresh-killed horse.

No telling who was the most surprised, but Battles got off the first shot and he drilled one of those Injuns with meat in his teeth, and the rest of them fell away into the shadows like so many ghosts. I slammed spurs to my black and jumped him across the fire in time to see one Apache snaking into the brush, and I cut down on him. Something slammed alongside my head and I felt myself hit ground, bounce, and fall free, losing a boot in the stirrup.

I rolled over, my Winchester gone in the brush, and I clawed for a six-shooter. And then I froze right where I lay, because an Apache was standing astride of me and he had the razor edge of his blade right across my throat. He was looking me right in the eyes, and I could see the firelight on his scarred face, and we knew one another at the first glance. It was Kahtenny, the Indian I hadn't been willing to kill, way back there in my fight with the Apaches.

"You better hold back on that edge," I said. "You're liable to cut somebody."

Chapter 16

He still stood astride of me, that knife edge against my throat, and he never moved it one mite. He kept looking right into my eyes and I looked right back at him, and I knew all he had to do was make one quick slash to end my days.

Then easylike, to give no false notions, I lifted my hand to his wrist and pushed the blade away, very gently.

"That's a good knife. Got quite an edge to it," I said.

"You are brave man. You are warrior."

"We are warriors together," I said. "It is enough for you and for me that we know each other."

The other Apaches were filtering back out of the darkness, and their black eyes were reaching to me in anticipation, I expect, for the torture of a strong prisoner was a pleasure not to be missed.

Right off I recognized Toclani among them. He had served in the army under Emmet Crawford as one of his company of Apache scouts. Toclani and me, we had ridden together, shared our grub, and fought side by side against other Apaches. Now I had no idea whether that would help me any at all, for Toclani might have returned to the wild ones, the broncho Apaches who fought whoever stood in their way.

They had me dead to rights. What lay ahead I knew full well, as any man along the border would know, but what worried me now was what had become of Spanish and Battles. Had they got clean away? Spanish was more dead than alive, anyway, and Battles was neither as good as Spanish or me when it came to desert travel.

Nobody had made a move to tie me, but they had taken my knife and my guns, and there was not much of a chance to run for it. Moreover, I was in mighty bad shape. I needed a drink, and my stomach was growling at the smell of the meat on the fire.

We had accounted for a couple of the Apaches, but there'd been at least a dozen out under the brush before the shooting started, and now they came up to the fire, and kindled another one close by.

I could see my Winchester lying over yonder beside my Colt, but they were thirty feet away and I'd have no chance to go after them. Kahtenny was off to one side, beyond the fire, and he was talking to the others, but I couldn't make out a thing they were saying. All I could gather was that some kind of an argument was going on, and I had an idea it concerned my hide.

While the Apaches ate, at least three of them kept a watch on me all the time, but seeing I wasn't going anywhere anyway, I stretched out and, using my hat for a pillow, I went to sleep.

When I woke up it was maybe two hours later and the fire was down. Most of the Apaches lay around sleeping, and I still wasn't tied, which made no sense at all unless they figured on having some fun when I made a break for it.

Thirst was about to strangle me and the waterhole was right beyond the edge of camp, so I got up, making no special try at keeping quiet, and I walked over to the waterhole, lay down and drank. Then I went back and stretched out again.

I knew as well as anything that at least four or five pairs of eyes had been on me all the while, and had I jumped for a gun or a horse they'd have had me. So I just stretched out quiet, feeling a whole lot better for the drink.

Presently Kahtenny got up and walked over to me and sat down. He rolled himself a smoke as easy as any cowpoke you ever did see, and he sat there smoking until half of it was gone before he spoke.

"Somebody want to kill you."

"Me?" I chuckled. "Maybe a lot of folks." I sized him up as having something puzzling on his mind. "You mean your boys?"

"Other man. White man."

"A white man wants me dead? What makes you think so?"

"He have my squaw. He say, you dead he give her to me. I bring your body, he gives squaw."

"So why haven't you done it?"

Kahtenny looked puzzled. "Why he wants you dead? I think somehow it is a trick."

"How'd you get the news? Did Toclani bring it?"

He showed no surprise that I knew Toclani. "Yes . . . he bring it. My squaw . . . she talk to sister at San Carlo. She go quickly in the night, but when she leave these men take her."

"Did they hurt her?"

"No. Toclani say no." He looked at me. "Me fight Toclani, but Toclani good man. My squaw good woman. Toclani puts Apaches to watch out for my squaw."

"Who are these white men?"

"Their name is Hadden. There are several. Toclani sees them. Why they want you dead?"

"I shot them up. Rocca . . . you know Tampico Rocca? They called him greaser and were going to kill him. We fought. Rocca and me, we kill one . . . maybe two of them."

He still was not satisfied. "Toclani says you good man. Great warrior."

There wasn't much I could say to that, so I kept my mouth shut and waited, but my mind was working as fast as I could make it. I lay no claims to being a thinker or a planner. I'm just a mountain boy who grew up to be a free drifting man, but it didn't take much figuring to see I had a way out of this if I could come up with the right ideas.

Trouble was, I had to play my cards almighty careful, because I surely didn't have any hole card. One thing working for me was that Kahtenny was suspicious, and feared a trap.

To kill me of his own idea would be simple enough, and likely that's what he would have done, after some torture to see what kind of a man I was. But now somebody else wanted me dead, and he was puzzled.

From what I gathered, Kahtenny's squaw had slipped back into the reservation to see her sister and that was when the Hadden boys caught her . . . waiting until she started to leave.

It was nothing unusual for a wild Apache to return to the reservation, stay awhile, and then leave. The Army was always trying to get them to return, and often the squaws would come back first to look over the situation.

Now they had Kahtenny's squaw and he wanted her back, but he was like a wild thing that sniffs trouble at every change, and there was a lot about this offer that he did not like.

He sat smoking and waiting, and finally I said, "I think you can not trust them."

He looked at me. "They will kill her?"

"They are bad men. They would have killed Rocca for nothing. I think if you take my body to them they will kill her and you also . . . if they can."

He waited awhile, and I poked sticks into the fire. Then I said, "Give me my guns, I will get your squaw for you."

For a long time he said nothing, then abruptly he got up and went to the other fire, where he remained, occasionally in low-voiced conversation.

After a while he came back and sat down on the sand. "You can get my squaw?"

"Kahtenny is a warrior. He knows the ways of war. Much can happen, but this I promise. I shall get her safely if it can be done."

After a pause, I added, more quietly, "The Haddens are not Apaches. They are fierce men, but they are not Apaches. I can get your squaw."

"She is a good woman. She has been with me for many moons."

"Do you know where they are?"

"We take you there. It is near the border."

Nobody needed to warn me that my troubles were only beginning. Kahtenny might use me to get his squaw back, and then shoot me down in my tracks. It wasn't that an Apache wasn't grateful, he just had different ideas than we folks had. If you were not of the tribe you were a potential enemy, and killing you was in the cards.

There had been no sign of Spanish or of John J. Nor in the little I could overhear was there mention of them. It seemed likely that they had gotten clean off. Well, luck to them.

At daybreak they led my black horse to me and I saddled up, taking my time; but when I started for my guns, they stopped me and Toclani took my Winchester and hung my gun belt over his shoulder. They let me fill a canteen, and then we started out.

All the time we were riding I kept thinking about Neiss, who was one of five men on a stage near Stein's Peak when it was hit by Cochise and his band. The driver and a man named Elder were killed right off, the stage capsized, and the men were preparing for a fight when Neiss talked them out of it. Cochise, he said, was an old friend; just let Neiss talk to Cochise and all would be well, so they tried it. Cochise roped Neiss and dragged him up the canyon over the rocks, cactus, and brush, while two other warriors did the same for the others. Then they were tortured to death. That happened in April of 1861.

Thinking of this, I was placing no great faith in my chances with them, and although they watched me like hawks, I kept a wary eye out for any chance of escape.

There wasn't any.

My black horse was gaunt and worn by hard travel. To break and run, even if the chance came, would get me nowhere. I had no weapon and there was no place to go . . . no place I could reach in time.

The sun glared down on us as we walked our horses across the parched, rocky hills, weaving amongst the cactus and the greasewood. It was rolling land, broken by short sawtooth ranges of dull red or brown rock, and occasional flows of lava marked by the white streaks of dry washes. Indians rode on all four sides of me, always alert, always ready.

Nobody talked.

Each step my horse took seemed to be carrying me closer to death . . . escape would be too much luck.

I could expect no help from the Haddens. I had no idea how I was going to get the squaw away from them, and I felt sure they had no intention of letting her go free. Even among good men the depredations carried on by the Apaches had created the desire to exterminate them, one and all . . . and the Haddens were not good men.

Me, I always had great respect for the Apache. He had learned to live off a mighty bleak and hard country, and he had none of the white man's ways of thinking, and you had to reach out to try to understand how he felt and what he wanted to do.

After a while we began to see more cholla, great stretches of it, all pale yellow under the bright sun, with the dark browns and blacks of the old branches down below. Jumping cactus, we called it, because if a body passed too close it seemed to jump out to stick you. The Apaches thinned out to single file as we went through it.

All of a sudden we drew up. Kahtenny turned and pointed out a low mountain ahead of us, off to the east. "It is there they are," he said, "at Dead Man's Tank. They are six men, and my squaw, and they want you."

They wanted me dead.

Though Kahtenny would have killed me without waiting if he figured that would be enough, he was no more trusting of the Haddens than I was. They would get my body, but that didn't mean he would get his squaw.

"You're going to have to give me my guns," I said. "If I ride in there without them, they'll kill the both of us if they can. I figure to handle the Haddens. Without them, the others aren't likely to cut up no fuss."

The funny thing about it was, all day my mind had been miles from that hot desert and back in the hill country of the Cumberland. They say a man's whole life passes before him when he's about to die. I can't say that mine did . . . only those times back in the mountains, so long ago.

All day my mind kept going back to turnip greens, and to wild-hog hunting in the hills on those foggy mornings when the forest dripped and a body prowled through it like a red Indian, scouting for wild hogs to give us bacon to cook with turnip greens in an iron pot.

Me and Orrin used to go out, or sometimes Tyrel, though he was younger. Never knew Tyrel to miss, though on occasion I did.

I'd never seen that country since. Never seen it . . . but I hankered for it. Many a time on the desert I looked up to the stars and wished I was back there, seein' the kitchen door open with its light shining out and me coming up from the milking with my pails full to overflow.

You wouldn't hardly think my mind would be on that now, with the trouble I was in right this minute, but that's the way it was . . . as if I had to give my mind some ease with good rememberin'. So all the time, as we rode along, my thoughts kept going back to that green and lovely country.

I thought of the time I floated down the Big South Fork on a flat-boat to New Orleans, taking what we had to trade—corn, sorghum molasses, and maybe some tobacco. We Sacketts never had much to trade except muscle, because our poor ridge-land didn't raise more than enough to feed us, even if we hunted the forest too. But folks liked to have a Sackett along going downriver through some country where unruly folks were liable to be.

My thoughts came back to where I was, and I saw that Kahtenny was pointing out the land. "You go," he said, "you go get my squaw."

He handed me my gun belt and Winchester, and I checked them for loads. My mouth felt as dry as one of those empty creek beds.

"You keep an eye out," I said. "Maybe I won't be comin' back with her."

We sat there a moment, and then I held out a hand. "Loan me a spare," I said. "I may need it bad."

Well, sir, he looked at me, and then he taken out his six-gun and passed it over. It was a Navy .44, and a likely piece. I shoved it down in my waistband back of my vest.

Toclani rode up. "I will go with you," he said.

"No, thanks. You stay here. If they see me comin' alone maybe they'll let me get close enough to talk. If they see two of us comin' they might just shoot."

So I spoke to that ga'nted-up black horse and we started down, and back behind me Kahtenny said, "You bring back my squaw."

I'd be lucky to do it. I'd be a whole sight luckier if I rode out with a whole hide.

"All right, horse," I said to the black, "let's go talk to them."

And we rode through the cholla toward Dead Man's Tank.

Chapter 17

The vague blue feather of smoke lifted faintly above the rocks of an old lava flow. I could hear my horse's hoofs strike stone, or his muffled hoof-falls in the sand. I sat tall in the saddle, Winchester in the scabbard, my mind open and alert.

There can be no planning in such a situation. Until a man is in the midst of it, he has no idea of the lay of the land, no idea of how the ones he's going to meet will be strung out. You just have to ride in and handle it by main strength and awkwardness, with maybe the salt of a little luck.

The men up ahead wanted me dead. No doubt they had me in their sights right now. No doubt they were holding off to crow over me a mite, or to see what I had to say. As to that Apache squaw, they didn't care one whit. But the Haddens were new in Apache country, and they had no idea what they were up against. If Kahtenny didn't get his squaw, nobody was riding out of there with a whole skin . . . not if Kahtenny could help it.

There was a little thorny, scraggly brush growing amongst the rocks, but the land around was mostly slabs of broken rock, falls of talus off the slopes, or ridges shoved up through the sand.

Glancing back, I could see two Apaches back there, and only two. That meant the others had scattered out and even now were moving in, getting in position for the kill.

Now, I'm a peace-loving man, inclined to easy riding and talking around a fire, and the more Apaches I get around me the more peace-loving I become. Riding up there to those rocks around Dead Man's Tank, I could feel my scalp a-prickling as if it guessed it was going to be lifted.

I taken the thong off the hammer of my Colt, and I rode up a narrow trail through the rocks and looked over into a shallow basin.

Dead Man's Tank lay before me, a pool of water maybe ten feet across, each way. Beyond it was a mite of fire, with the thin line of smoke losing itself in the sky. I could see half a dozen horses, and what might be the ears of a couple more beyond the rocks.

The Haddens were standing wide-legged facing me, and there was a man higher up in the rocks with a Winchester across his knees. Two more were by the fire, and likely another might be somewhere about.

Right beyond the fire was Kahtenny's squaw, and even at this distance I could see she was both young and pretty. She looked straight at me, and I was betting she was counting on Kahtenny to get her loose from this setup.

And then I saw Dorset.

Dorset, and one of the youngsters. I gave a quick look around, but saw neither hide nor hair of the others. Maybe they were dead now, or else were crossing the border to safety.

Arch Hadden was looking right at me, and he was smiling, but there was nothing you'd call friendly in that smile. "Well, look who's here," he said. "That would-be tough Sackett."

"Got a message for you, Arch," I said, resting my hands on the pommel, left hand on top. "Kahtenny is out there, and he wants his squaw."

"We told him to send you dead."

"Must have been some mistake there," I said. "I'm still alive."

"Not for long," the other Hadden said, sounding mighty savage.

"I take it you boys haven't had much doings with the Apaches," I said, "so listen to some reason. No matter what's between you boys and me, you'd better listen real good.

"That Kahtenny is poison mean, and he's a fighter from way back. You see him out there almost alone, but he isn't alone. He's got a dozen Indians in these rocks, and more a-coming. If you want to get out of here alive you'd better turn loose his squaw."

The one in the rocks, he ups and says, "We've fit Injuns afore. We ain't turnin' her loose. That there's a right tasty bit of Injun."

Now I knew the chips were down and their cards were on the table. I was sort of watching everything, thinking about how long it had been since I practiced a left-hand draw, and thinking how they were probably counting on that right hand, far from the gun and resting on the pommel, under the left one. I had done that a-purpose, and was hoping it was going to give me the margin I needed. There was this thing of reaction time . . . it takes an instant to see what's happening and for it to register on the mind and dictate a move.

"If you boys are as smart as I think you are," I said, "you'll let that squaw loose, and the same for the young lady over yonder. You know what will happen if you bother a white girl out here."

"Nothin'." That was the man with the rifle up in the rocks. "Ain't nobody goin' to tell."

"You're forgetting about my boys," I said. "They'll know and they'll be telling the story about now."

"Not Spanish Murphy," Arch Hadden said. "He won't tell nobody nothin'. We found him tied on his horse and he didn't look like he was going to make it, so we shot him. We just naturally finished him off."

Dorset was right behind the squaw now, and I never had any doubts about her doing what was best. That little lady had a head on her shoulders and the chances were that right now she was unloosing the squaw.

I knew I had to stall. I had to play for time. "No use you boys building up for trouble," I said. "Turn that squaw loose, and the lot of us have got a fighting chance. We can make it out of here if we move fast, before Kahtenny gets fifty, sixty Injuns out yonder."

"You ain't got the message," Wolf Hadden said. "We're goin' to kill you, boy."

Me, I smiled at him. Somehow I had to keep those boys talking, get their mind off the moment to give myself an edge. If I was going to do anything at all against the lot of them, I'd need all I could get.

"Most men who try to fight Apaches only learn by losing . . . and when you lose a fight to an Apache you never get no chance to use what you learned. You boys take my advice and turn loose that squaw, and Kahtenny might just ride off and leave you be."

"You scared?" That was that one up on the rocks. He was beginning to get kind of irritating, like a mosquito around the ear.

"You bet I'm scared. I've seen these boys work. Now, I—"

All of a sudden one of those boys yelled, "Arch! That damn squaw—"

She was loose and she was moving, and she was moving almighty fast. The man up in the rocks swung his rifle and when he did I forked out that waistband gun with my left hand and my shot was a hair faster than his.

He fired at the squaw and I shot him right through the brisket, and then swung the gun to Wolf, who was coming up with a Remington Navy.

Dorset, she suddenly threw herself at the man nearest her and she hit him right behind the knees. He was standing on a bit of a slope, and when she hit him he buckled at the knees and fell forward on the gravelly hillside.

The man who'd been alongside the fire, instead of grabbing his gun, turned to lay hold of Dorset, and at the same time that I cut loose at Wolf I jumped my horse at Arch.

He made a quick step back to get out of the way, and a rock rolled under his feet. He fell as he drew, jolting the gun from his hand.

I swung my horse and got in another shot at Wolf, who burned me with one alongside the shoulder. He was just setting up to take a dead shot when my second bullet caught him, and he backed up a full step. My black was on him, and he rolled aside, and I felt bullets whipping around me.

Somehow Dorset had a gun. She fired at one of those boys and then taken out running, the child in her arms, for the pony string.

About that time I saw an Apache up on the slope, and he was shooting down at us. I swung my horse again and went after Dorset.

She wasn't wasting any time, and fortunately they had left a couple of horses saddled. She pulled the drawstring on one of them and swung the child to the saddle, then she went into the saddle herself with a flying leap and we were off, running our horses across that desert like crazy folks.

Maybe we *were* a mite crazy. I had an idea we weren't going to make it, but every jump we took gave us a better chance. Behind us I could hear a fight taking place, and somebody else was running a horse off to the right.

Suddenly the desert split right open ahead of us, a deep cut maybe eight or ten feet across. I saw Dorset jump her horse, and I slapped spurs to mine and that black took to flying as if it was second nature. We both landed safe and swung down into a hollow, raced across it and up the other side, and into a forest of cholla where our horses swung right and left and about through that prickly stuff.

We leveled out in the open and put them to a run; and when we finally got them slowed down we had made it away . . . for now.

Looking back, I could see nothing behind us. We had come several miles, and now we walked the horses under some cedars whilst I unlimbered my Winchester, checked it again, and returned it to the scabbard. Then I reloaded both my six-shooters. I could remember shooting four to five times, but eight shots had been fired, showing I'd been doubling up. I had no recollection of having drawn the second gun, but I surely had.

When I'd reloaded, I moved alongside Dorset. She was holding the youngster on the saddle in front of her.

"What happened to the others?" I asked.

"They got away. Harry is like a little Apache himself. When those men came up he just disappeared into the brush with the others."

"Let's hope he made it."

The country was changing now. It was much more broken, but there was also more growth. There had been a desert shower, one of those sudden rains that sometimes deluge only a small area and then vanish. This one had left water standing in the bottoms of the washes and in hollows atop the rocks. It had filled the desert tanks, so we watered the horses.

My eyes felt like hot lumps in my skull, and they seemed to move with incredible slowness when I turned to look around. My fingers felt stiff, and I worked them and tried to loosen them up. My mouth was dry, and after I'd drunk it was dry again in a few minutes.

All of a sudden I was dead tired again. All the days of driving ahead, running, fighting, and worrying a way out were beginning to catch up with me. But we started on.

The horses plodded ahead, dazed with weariness. Several times I found myself dozing in the saddle; each time I'd wake up with a start of fear, and look all around. My mind seemed to be in a state of despair. Spanish was dead . . . Tampico Rocca was dead . . . where was John J.?

It would soon be dark, and if we expected to make the border we had to find a place to stop for rest. If it had to be, we ourselves could keep going, but not the horses, and without them our chances were gone.

"Do you think they're following us?" Dorset asked.

"I don't know," I answered, and said no more.

The sun disappeared and shadows gathered in the folded hills. The sahuaro lifted questioning fingers, stark against the yellow sky. The quail began to talk across the silences, the wind stirred, rustling the dry leaves on the parched brush. Our horses' hoofs whispered in the sand.

A lone coyote showed for an instant, then like a shadow was gone, leaving no more sign than an Apache. A few stars began to appear . . . one bright one was low in the sky, and held steady. Time to time I looked at it, and finally I said, "That there's a light. A fire, maybe."

Dorset turned her head to look. "It's not an Indian fire," she said.

We drew up, and I turned, standing in my stirrups to look back.

"It might be the Haddens," I said.

She glanced at me. "After you finished with them? What you didn't get, the Apaches got. You took two of them, I'd swear. Maybe three."

Well, maybe. I wasn't making any claims. I never was one to file notches on a gun . . . a tinhorn trick.

"Shall we try for it?" I said. "It's closer than the border. And the border never meant anything to an Apache except that south of it he was free of the American troops."

"We can scout it," Dorset answered. She swung her pony and headed toward the fire.

The yellow sky faded into gray and velvety dark. Even before we came up to it, I could see it was an Army fire . . . it looked big because there were three of them in line. It was a Cavalry troop of maybe forty men. We pulled up and I hailed the camp.

"Howdy, there. Is it all right to come in? There's a woman and a child with me."

Silence. . . .

It was a long moment, and I guess somebody was trying to make us out with field glasses, though now there was not much light.

"All right," came the answer. "Ride in. Ride carefully."

I knew that voice. It was Captain Lewiston. Lieutenant Jack Davis stood beside him.

Lewiston looked from me to Dorset Binny. He tipped his hat. "How do you do, ma'am. We have been worried for you."

"I'm all right. Thanks to Mr. Sackett."

"Did you come upon any other youngsters, Cap'n?" I asked. "Harry Brook and the Creed youngsters?"

"They're here, and they're safe. That's why we waited for you."

We walked our horses into camp and swung down. I staggered when I hit ground, and Lewiston was beside me. "Here, man, you'd better sit down."

"Got to care for my horse. You take the lady and the child, Cap'n, I—"

"No." Lewiston's tone was suddenly stern. He turned. "Corporal, take this man's horse. See that it is cared for just as mine is. The others also."

He turned back to me. "Sackett, I regret to inform you that you are under arrest."

Me, I just looked at him. "For crossing the border? Cap'n, Laura Sackett told me her son had been taken by the Apaches."

"She has no son!" Davis spoke sharply. "Sackett, that's a damned—"

Lewiston's voice cracked like a whip. "*Lieutenant!*"

Davis stopped, his face flushed. "I tell you, Captain, this man is—"

"Silence! Lieutenant Davis, I suggest you inspect the guard. Whatever needs to be said to Mr. Sackett, I will say."

Davis turned on his heel and stalked away. "Forgive him, Sackett. He's young and I'm afraid he's smitten by Laura Sackett. He is very proud, and he feels he must defend her honor."

"Let him defend it, Cap'n, but keep him away from me. Him being new to the country I might not shoot him, but I am afraid if he said what he started to say he'd be shy a good many teeth."

"There will be no fighting. You seem to have forgotten, Sackett. You are under arrest."

Well, I just walked over to the fire and sat down. Then I dug into my gear which had been dropped there and got out my cup. Reaching for the pot, I poured coffee.

"All right, Cap'n," I said, "you tell me about it. Why are you arresting me?"

"You are under arrest for murder. You are under arrest for the murder of Billy Higgins."

"Higgins?"

"We found his body out on the Yuma road. He had been shot in the head."

"Among other things," I said, "the Apaches wounded him, and then they shot him full of splinters."

"But you killed him."

"That's right, I did." Carefully, with several men standing about, I told him what had happened that day. Some of it I'd told him before, back in the Shoo-Fly when he told me about Kahtenny.

"He begged me to shoot him. Under the same situation I'd have done the same, more than likely."

"Perhaps." Lewiston looked hard at me. "Sackett, is it not true that your family feuded for years with a family named Higgins? That you hunted each other and killed each other on sight?"

"That was over years ago," I said. "Anyway, I ain't been back in that country since the war. As for this Higgins, I never gave it no thought. It's been a good while since I've had any cause to think of it."

"Nevertheless, Billy Higgins is dead, killed by your bullet. I have to warn you, Sackett, the story is out, and there's considerable feeling in Tucson. Higgins had friends there."

"But I tell you, I—"

"Don't tell me. Tell the jury."

He walked away from me, and I sat there by the fire, a-staring into it. I'd run a long way. I'd fought some hard fights. I'd stood off the Apaches and the Haddens, and now here I was, arrested for a crime that was no crime, but a crime they could hang me for.

And there was only one person in Tucson likely to know about that old Higgins-Sackett feud.

Laura Sackett. . . .

Chapter 18

You can take it from me that no jail cell is a place for a mountain boy. I was raised up where folks looked to the hills, only up where we came from you hadn't a chance to look much higher, we were that near the top of the ridge.

This cell they put me into had one small window, too small for me to crawl out of, and a door that was as barred as could be. When I heard the door clang shut I wasn't at all happy. Only thing I knew, I was going to catch up on my sleep, and at least I could eat. And right about that time I was hungry enough to eat an old saddle, stirrups and all.

Captain Lewiston was my first visitor. He came early in the morning, and brought a chair into the cell with him. He also brought the company clerk.

"Sackett," he began, "I want you to give me the whole story, in your own words. I want to help you if I can. Right now the people are divided. Some want to hang you for killing Billy Higgins, and some want to give you a medal for saving those youngsters."

So I gave it to him. How the bunch of us, unknown to each other until then, had banded together to ride to Tucson.

The story of our fight with Kahtenny's Apaches I repeated for him, as I'd told him the whole story before, except the part about me killing Billy Higgins, which I didn't like to think on. Then I told him about my meeting with Laura Sackett, and her story of the lost boy.

"This much I have learned since your departure," Lewiston said. "Laura Sackett was divorced from your brother, and your brothers and her father had been deadly enemies."

"If I ever heard of that, I'd forgotten. We Sacketts were never much on talking of troubles when we were together. It never does any good to go worrying your thoughts about things gone by."

"I approached her last night about your story," Captain Lewiston said. "She denies ever mentioning a child to you, or giving you any cause to ride into Mexico."

I just looked at him. It was no use to say she was lying, although she surely was.

"As a matter of fact, she says you ran away to Mexico for fear somebody would discover you had taken advantage of an Apache attack to kill Higgins."

"Those boys I was with knew better. Why else would they come with me?"

"I am afraid that won't help you at all. I believe you told me that they are dead."

"I buried Rocca with my own hands. Spanish Murphy was finished off by the Haddens. By their own say-so. John J. . . . well, I guess he never made it that far."

"You have no witnesses then?"

"No, sir. Nary a one. You see, Cap'n, none of those men saw it anyway. When I shot Billy Higgins there was just him and me. Nobody was close enough to hear what was said."

Well, we talked awhile, and he asked a sight of questions, but after that neither of us had much hope. That feud was ten years out of my mind when I met those men in Yuma, and the name Higgins meant nothing at all to me.

So here I was in jail, and Laura Sackett, who'd been the cause of the deaths of at least three good men, was walking free.

After the captain left I sat on my cot and stared at the blank wall, trying to see my way clear, but nothing came to me; so finally, tired as I still was, I rolled over on the cot and went to sleep.

When I opened my eyes again it was nigh on to sundown and the jailer was at the door.

"Lady to see you," he said.

"All right." I got up, staggering with sleep and trying to get my bearings. This would be Dorset, I figured.

Only it wasn't. It was the last person in the world I expected—Laura Sackett.

She turned to the jailer. "May I talk with my brother-in-law alone?"

When the jailer had gone, she turned those big blue eyes on me.

"I never expected you to get back," she told me coolly, "but I am glad you did. Now I can see you hang, with my own eyes."

"Now that isn't what you'd call neighborly," I said, determined not to let her get any more satisfaction than I could help.

"I only wish Orrin could be here to see you hang," she said, staring at me. "And Tyrel . . . I hated him the most."

"Maybe that's because you couldn't fool him," I said. "But ma'am, do you really want to see me hang that much? I never did you any harm. Never even saw you until I came up the trail from Yuma."

"I want to see you hang, and I will. I only wish I could see Orrin's face when he gets the news."

"Maybe you will see him," I said. "Orrin's a right good lawyer. If he can be free of his duties that long, I'll maybe get him to defend me in court."

She did not like that. Orrin was a mighty impressive figure of a man, and he could talk. He had the Welsh gift for talking, and she knew how persuasive he could be.

"He'll never get here. If you send for him I'll get Arch Hadden to kill him."

"Arch? So that's why he was in Mexico, a-hunting me? I wondered how he knew we'd be there, when we were so all-fired careful that nobody knew."

"Yes, I sent them after you. And I'll send Arch after Orrin, if he comes here."

"So Arch is in town, is he?" That was something to consider, and of a sudden those prison walls began to seem as if they were crowding in on me. Arch Hadden would know I was in jail, and he would come for me. I glanced at that high-up window, and was suddenly glad it was so small and so high up.

"Send for Orrin. I would like that. I will have him killed." As she spoke it seemed to me there was something in those blue eyes that looked mighty like insanity.

"You mistake Orrin. He won't kill easy, and Arch Hadden never saw the day he could draw with Orrin."

I was talking to the wind. She didn't hear me and would have paid it no mind if she had, for I knew she had no such idea as them drawing against each other. She meant a rifle from a hilltop at some stage stop, or something of that kind.

After she had gone I studied about it a mite, and then called the jailer.

"You get word to Cap'n Lewiston, will you? I got to see him."

"Sure." The jailer eyed me thoughtfully. "Did you really shoot that Higgins feller?"

"If you were lying out in the glare of the sun, and you were gut-shot and dying and the Apaches were shooting flaming slivers of pitch into your hide, wouldn't you ask to be shot?"

"That the way it was? I heered he was an enemy of yourn."

So I explained about the old Higgins-Sackett feud. And I said again, "But I haven't given thought to that fight in ten years. Besides, when a man's hunkered down on a ridge alone, and the Apaches are around him, do you think he'd waste a shot to kill a man the Indians were sure to get?"

"No, sir, I surely don't," he said.

He went away then, and I was alone until the door opened and Dorset came in. She was carrying a plate all covered over. "The lady over at the Shoo-Fly sent this," she said. She lifted her chin defensively. "I didn't have any money or I'd have brought something for you."

"You've done enough. How about you and your sister? Have you got a place to stay?"

"With the Creeds. They'll be coming to thank you. Dan Creed said he'd bust you out of here if you wanted."

"I'll stay. Maybe I'm a fool, but no Sackett aside from Nolan ever rode in flight from the law."

We talked for a spell, and then she left. The jailer returned, but he'd not seen hide nor hair of Captain Lewiston. Lieutenant Davis had been walking out with Laura Sackett, so he had avoided them.

Alone again, I did some right serious thinking. Tampico Rocca and Spanish Murphy were dead. Battles probably was, but even had they been alive there was nothing any of them could tell that would speak for me, because when I shot Higgins I was alone. I'd been a fool to mention it to Laura, but it lay heavy on my mind, and at the time I figured her for family.

What really stood against me was that I'd shot a man who carried a name of a family against which my family had feuded. The man had been wounded several times before, but there was only my say-so that the Indians had done it. The pitch-pine slivers was Apache work, nobody denied that. But the way the talk was going made it seem as if I'd taken advantage of Apache trouble to kill an old enemy, and a thing like that is hard to down.

Billy Higgins had a sight of friends around Tucson, and nobody there knew me except by name. A good part of the talk going around was carried on by Lieutenant Davis, who believed whatever Laura told him.

Two days passed slowly, and I just sat on my cot, and played checkers with the jailer. One thing had changed. That jailer never went off and left me alone any more, and he kept the door to the street locked.

The sheriff was out of town, and wasn't due back for a week, and I began to get the feeling that the quicker they tried me the better. If they didn't hurry, some of those boys outside might be figuring on a necktie party. I began to wish for the high-up country away out yonder, where nobody goes but eagles and mountain sheep. By the wall outside the cell I could see my own outfit—my saddle, bridle, and saddlebags, my rifle and pistol belt. I wanted a horse between my knees, and a Winchester.

Dan Creed came to see me. The jailer knew him and admitted him without hesitation. "You'd better let me get you a gun," Creed said when the jailer had gone back to the office. "They're surely figuring on stringing you up. I've talked until I'm blue in the face, but they pay me no mind. They say, 'sure, he brought your youngsters out of Mexico. You'd speak for him no matter what kind of coyote he is.' "

"What else are they saying?"

"Well, they say they've only your word for it that the Apaches were still there when you shot Higgins. They say when the Injuns pulled out you just figured to be rid of another Higgins."

Lewiston, who seemed to have been my friend, was gone. Even if I could get word to Orrin and Tyrel, they were too far away to do much good. It began to look to me as if my number was really up.

In matters such as lynching there's always toughs who are ready for it, and there are always people who don't want to be involved. There are men who would attempt such things, but it takes a strong man who will make the attempt. I'd never expected to be on the end of the rope myself, although anybody who packs a gun runs that risk.

Again night came, and outside I could hear the mutter of voices, and angry talk. There was no telling if it would come to more than talk, but lying on that prison cot in the darkness I wasn't willing to bet on it.

Suddenly, from out of the darkness outside my window, a voice spoke. "We're going to get you, Sackett. We're going to see you hang!"

My feet swung to the floor, and I was mad clear through. "Come an' get me, Yellow Belly," I said. "I'll know your voice when I hear it. You just come asking, and you'll get it!"

There was a grate of boots on gravel, and a sound of retreating footsteps.

Suddenly I realized that I was no longer tired. I'd come to this place physically exhausted, but now I'd had three good days of rest, and I was ready. I got up and went to the bars.

"Jim!" I hailed the jailer. "Come running! I got to see you!"

There was no answer, and I yelled again.

There was still no reply. But I heard a mutter of voices.

The jailer was gone, and they had come for me.

Chapter 19

Tucson was for the most part a town of law-abiding citizens. I knew that, and so did that crowd out there. The trouble was, would those citizens get here in time to help me? I knew what those men outside wanted most was quiet, but I aimed to see they didn't get it.

Getting up from my cot, I gave a look around. There was nothing there that would make a weapon except the frame of the cot, which was a half-inch pipe. So I just wrenched the cot clear of the wall, breaking it enough to unscrew two sections of it, one about seven feet long, the other an end piece that was about three feet in length, with an elbow on it.

Standing both pieces close by, I waited. Outside I could hear somebody by the window; then the door from the outer office opened into the prison section. Men came crowding through, and I could see others in the office.

I stood up then. "You boys huntin' something?" I spoke careless-like. "If you are, you've come to the wrong place."

"We're a-goin' to hang you for killin' Billy Higgins."

"I killed him—he asked me to. In his place or mine, you'd have done the same."

I could smell the whiskey on them. This bunch had been drinking to get up the nerve to come after me, but they were tough men nonetheless. I heard somebody fumbling with keys, and knew there was no time to lose.

"I'm going to tell you once, and that's all," I said. "You boys get out of here, an' get fast."

They'd come without a light, and it was dark as a pit in there. They hadn't figured they'd need a light to take me out of the cell, and they didn't want to draw any more attention than need be. I was only one man and they were twenty.

"Look who's givin' orders!" somebody said. "Get that lock open and let's get him out of here!"

Now, there's a time for talk and a time for action, and I never was much gifted with oratory. I picked up the long pipe, and when I heard them trying to get the key into the lock I gripped that pipe with both hands shoulder high and, holding it tight, I jammed it between the bars. At close quarters and in the dark it was a terrible weapon. The passage outside the cells was narrow and they were packed in tight.

With all the power that was in me, I jammed that pipe into the crowd beyond the bars. I heard the crunch, then a horrible, choking scream.

"What was it? What happened?" somebody yelled, and there was panic in the voice.

Drawing back on the pipe, I held it waist high and jammed it through again, further into them.

Another scream, then a cry, "Back! For God's sake, let us out of here!"

Somebody else yelled, "What's the matter? You gone crazy? Let's get him!"

Jerking the pipe back, I smashed hard at the voice and heard a scream. Then came a shout, "Get out! Get out!"

Men were fighting and struggling to get out of the narrow passageway. Thrusting my pipe through the bars this time at ankle height, I heard several of them go sprawling. Somebody jerked a gun and fired blindly through the bars, the shot missing me by several feet. I drove my bar at the flash and heard a grunt, then anguished cries of pain, and stampeding feet. Suddenly the passage was empty except for somebody who lay groaning on the floor.

"Serves you right," I said calmly. "Whoever you are, you got what you had coming."

"Help! For God's sake, help me!"

"How am I going to do that?" I said. "I'm behind bars. You just crawl outside and get some of those murdering friends of yours to help."

There was another shuddering groan and I heard the sound of dragging. I stood my pipe against the cell wall, and waited. If they came again it would be to shoot, but I had a hunch they wouldn't come.

Now I heard angry questions outside in the street, and then the outer door opened. A match scratched and somebody lit the lamp. Men appeared in the passageway. One of them was Oury, whom I knew to be a reputable man.

"What's happened? What's going on here?" he said.

A man was lying on the floor, and a trail of blood showed where another had dragged himself. A loose coil of rope and a six-shooter lay just outside the cell.

"Seems I had visitors," I said, leaning on the bars. "They wanted me for a necktie party. Only I didn't think it ought to go on without some sort of official plannin', so those folks, they taken off."

Oury's face was grim. "I am sorry, young man. Those were a bunch of drunken teamsters and drifters, not citizens of Tucson."

"I figured as much," I said. "Mr. Oury, do you reckon you could get somebody to bring me a pot of coffee from the Shoo-Fly, and something to eat? I'm getting almighty hungry."

"I will do more than that. Jim"—he turned to one of the others—"get me the keys. I am taking this young man to dinner."

He looked around again. The man lying on the floor was being examined. The doctor looked up. "This man has three broken ribs and a punctured lung," he said quietly.

"That's his problem," I said harshly. "Anybody who fools around with the bandwagon is likely to get hit with a horn."

"Those are my sentiments," Oury said crisply.

The keys jangled, the door swung wide. "Come, Mr. Sackett, you are my guest."

"I don't mind if I do," I said, "but I warn you, I'm an eating man, just getting my appetite back."

The Shoo-Fly was almost empty when we went in, but a few minutes afterward it was crowded to the doors.

When I'd eaten, I sat back in my chair. One of the Tucson citizens came in with my Winchester and gun belt. "If you're staying in town," he said, "you'd better go armed."

"I am staying," I replied, "until this matter is cleared up. I did nothing wrong out there. I killed a good man, a tough man. He might have lived for hours in that boiling hot sun with those slivers burning into him. He was not a man to die easy."

"I might have asked for the same thing," somebody said.

I was quiet after that. I'd eaten well, and I had my guns on again, and all I wanted was to get this affair cleared up and pull out for Tyrel's outfit in New Mexico. As for this town, it was no place for me until my enemies had drifted, and being drifters, I knew they'd soon be gone.

The doctor came in and gave me a hard look. "I'll say this for you," he said, "you're a bad man to corner. You've put four men in bed. One of them has a smashed cheekbone, his face is ripped open, and he's lost nine teeth. One has a torn shoulder muscle, another has a dent in his skull and his scalp is ripped right across the top, laid open for five inches. The one with the punctured lung will live if he's lucky. All said and done, you put four men out of action, and injured six or seven more."

"They came after me," I said.

The outer door opened then and two men came in. One was Captain Lewiston, the other was Toclani, the Apache scout. They looked around until their eyes spotted me, and they came over to my table.

"Sackett," Lewiston said, "Toclani has talked to Kahtenny. They verify your story. Kahtenny told us in detail, as did several other Apaches, what was happening out there during the attack when you shot Higgins."

"You talked to Kahtenny?" I asked Toclani.

"He, too." He indicated Lewiston. "We ride together to Apache camp."

I looked at Lewiston. "You taken a long chance, man."

"It was simple justice. I knew that the people who would surely know what happened were the Apaches. I did not know they would talk, but Toclani came with me, and Kahtenny had much to say of you, Sackett. He said you were a brave man, a strong man, and a warrior."

"Did he get his squaw back?"

"Yes, and he thanks you." Lewiston looked at me. "He may come in. All because of that, he may come in."

"I hope he does," I said. "He's a good Indian."

And so it was over. Nobody wanted me back in jail any longer, but I figured to stay around until the sheriff came back so as there'd be no argument. Around town folks stopped to speak to me on the street, and several thanked me for bringing the youngsters back.

But I saw nothing of Laura . . . had she left town? Or was she still there, waiting, planning?

My mind kept turning to Dorset. Although it was in my thoughts, I'd no right to go a-courting, for I'd no money and no prospects worth counting on. Mr. Rockfellow, who had a herd he wanted pushed over into the Sulphur Springs Valley, hired me and some other hands, but it was a short job, and left me with nothing more than eating money.

The sheriff came back to town, and after hearing what had happened he gave me a clean bill on the charges against me, so I figured to saddle up and show some dust, only I hadn't enough cash to lay in supplies to take me anywhere.

Then at the Shoo-Fly I heard that Pete Kitchen had located himself a mining claim down in the Pajaritos, so I rode down. When he found out I was a hand with a pick and shovel, as well as with a cutting horse and a rope, he hired me for the job.

When he was laying out the grub for me to take along he put in a couple of hundred rounds of .44's. "With your kind of luck, and that being Injun country, you're liable to need them."

Well, I almost backed out. I'd had my fill of 'Pache fighting, and wanted nothing so much as a spell of setting and contemplating.

The Pajaritos are not much when it comes to mountains. They are named for an odd birdlike formation on the butte. I rode down there, leading a jack mule, and I found the mining claim.

There was a wash where run-off water had cut down among the rocks and laid bare some ore. It wasn't of much account, but gave promise of growing richer as it went deeper.

On the back side of a knoll, partly screened by brush and boulders, I made me a camp. On some rough grass nearby I picketed my stock. Then I sat down to contemplate what lay before me.

Now, I'm no mining man, but you don't prospect around, work in mines, or even loaf around mining towns without picking up some of the lingo as well as a scraping of information.

This whole place was faulted. Movements of the earth in bygone times had tilted and fractured the crust until you had a good idea of what lay under you as well as in front of you. The gold, what there was of it, occurred in quartz veins. It looked to me like what they call a cretaceous bed that had rested on diorite, but some of the dikes that intruded offered a chance of some likely ore.

My job was to cut into that, do enough work to establish a right to the claim for Kitchen, and maybe explore enough so as he'd have an idea what lay below. Doing the work I was going to do wasn't going to help much, but I wanted to do the best job for him I could. I never did figure a man hired to do a job should just do it the easiest way. I figure a man should do the best he knows how. So I taken up my pick and went to work on that bank.

While I had a little blasting powder and some fuse, I had no notion of using it. Blasting makes an awful lot of noise, enough to bring every Apache in the country around, and I hoped to do my work quietlike, by main strength and awkwardness, and then pack up and light a shuck for Kitchen's ranch.

After working a couple of hours I sat down to take some rest, and began to notice the bees. Some had gone past while I was working, and now I noticed more of them. I left my pick and shovel and, taking up my Winchester, which I kept ready to hand, I went off up the mountain. Just over the shoulder of it I picked up tracks of a desert fox, just enough to indicate direction.

Between occasional tracks and the bees, I located a rock tank, nigh full of water. Two streams of run-off water coming down off the butte had worn places in the rocks. With a branch from an ocotillo, a dead branch I found nearby, I tried to measure the depth of water in the tank. I touched no bottom, but it was anyway more than six feet deep . . . water enough for my stock and me. It was half hidden under an overhang, and the water was icy cold and clean.

Next morning, after a quick breakfast, I got at my work again. Here and there I found a good piece of ore which I put aside. Now I was doing the same thing most prospectors do. I was putting aside the best pieces, an easy way to lead others to invest, and to lead yourself into believing you've got more than you have. Using water from the tank, I washed out a couple of pans from the dry wash below the claim and picked up a few small colors, nothing worth getting excited about. Unless that vein widened out below where I'd been digging, it was going to cost Pete more to get the gold than it was worth.

By nightfall the cut I'd made was beginning to look like something. I'd sacked up three sacks of samples and had crushed a few of them and panned out the fragments, getting a little color.

The next two days I worked from can-see to can't-see, and had enough done to count this as a working claim. One more day for good measure, and I would saddle up for Tucson.

This spell had given me some time to think, and it showed me there was no sense in saddle-tramping around, riding the grub line or picking up a day of work hither and yon. It was time I settled in for a lifetime at some kind of job, or on a place of my own.

It meant hard work, and lots of it. Living a life is much like climbing mountains—the summits are always further off than you think, but when a man has a goal, he always feels he's working toward something.

The next morning, when I'd been working an hour by sun, I hit the pocket.

It was a crumbling ledge of decomposed quartz, seemingly unrelated to what was on either side, and the piece that I found was no bigger than an upright piano, but it seemed to be only the top of a larger ledge. Anyway, in the next three hours I brought up enough of that quartz to get out maybe two thousand dollars' worth of gold.

Pete Kitchen was going to be almighty pleased. I dumped one of my other sacks back in the hole and filled the sack with the rich stuff. I was just loading the last of it and was too busy to be rightly paying mind to anything else when I heard a voice saying, "Looks like this trip is going to pay off mighty handsome."

Laura Sackett was there, and three men were with her—Arch Hadden,

Johnny Wheeler, sometime gunman for a smuggling outfit, and one of the gents who had been with Hadden in the fight at Dead Man's Tank.

They had come down here for only one reason, and that was to kill me, and they wanted to tell me about it. There was no call for conversation, not having to stall like before, so I just peeled back my forty-five and wasted no time.

I turned and saw and drew and fired, all kind of in one breath. My first shot took Johnny Wheeler, whose hand was lingering around the butt of his six-gun as if he was minded to use it.

That shot hit right where the ribs spread apart. My second shot was for Arch Hadden, but it missed. Arch had suddenly whipped his horse around and was running like all get-out.

Laura's horse reared up and she toppled from the saddle, and of a sudden the other gunman was shooting past me. I turned to see the Apaches coming down and recognized one of them as Kahtenny.

Me, I dove into that hole I'd been digging and had sense enough to grab the picket ropes of my horses, which I'd had up, loading for the homeward trip.

The Apaches swept by and I saw that third gunman go down. I heard the bark of Apache guns and saw the dust jump from his vest. He came up shooting, only another bullet nailed him.

They caught Arch Hadden.

I saw them catch him. It was Kahtenny and two others, and I saw him turn to fight as they rode up, but a rope sailed out, and then another, and the Apaches had themselves a prisoner.

Well, I'd told him. He had stolen Kahtenny's squaw, and he had been warned. With Apaches, nothing much was doubtful from here on—only how long Hadden had the guts to stick it out.

This was a hard land, and the rules were written plain in the way we lived. If you overstepped the rules you had bought yourself trouble, and from now on it was going to be settled between Hadden and Kahtenny.

Me, I got up and went to my horses. I fed shells into my six-shooters again, and then I walked over to the man I'd shot to see if he was alive. He wasn't. Johnny Wheeler was buzzard meat.

I taken his guns off, and what he had on him for identification. Might be somebody, somewhere, who'd be wishful to know what happened.

And then Laura Sackett got up off the ground and we just looked at each other. I never did see such hatred in anybody's eyes.

"Downright mis'rable, ain't we?" I said calmly. "You'd think one of us

Sacketts would be considerate enough to die so's you could get some of that bile out of your system."

"I suppose you're going to kill me?" she said.

"No, I ain't. It would be a kindness to the world, but I never shot a woman yet, and don't figure to now. Now, I'm just goin' to leave you. I'm just goin' to mount up and ride right out of here."

"You'd leave me here?" She was incredulous.

"There's a horse yonder. You get on that horse and ride."

Putting my foot in the stirrup, I swung into the saddle, and you can just bet that before I swung a-straddle of that horse I swung the animal around so I could keep an eye on her whilst I was doing it.

I taken a turn around the saddlehorn with the lead rope of the pack horse, and she said, "What if those Indians come back?"

"It's their tough luck, ma'am," I said, "but I hope not, for their sakes. Apaches aren't bad folks. They have trouble enough without wishin' you on them. Only it might work out for the best. A session with some of those Apache squaws might teach you some manners."

I touched my hat. "I hope I won't be seein' you, ma'am. Good-bye!"

That black of mine went down into the arroyo as if he knew what was behind him, and when he topped out on the rise beyond we were out of rifle shot. I pulled up then and looked back.

She had caught one of the horses and was trying to mount. The horse was worried by her skirt, and was sidling around.

That was the last I saw of her, of Laura, who had been Orrin's wife.

I rode east, with the sun going down behind me, the feel of a good saddle under me, and a horse between my legs. The trail dipped into a wide hollow, shadowy with evening, and somewhere a quail called. Across yonder hills, miles away, was Pete Kitchen's. I'd make camp before I got there, because nobody in his right mind rode up to Pete's in the nighttime.

He was paying me twenty dollars for the job, and might cut me in for some of the profits. Anyway, it was a road stake, and maybe before lining out for somewhere across the country I'd just ride around and call on Dorset.

I liked that little girl. She was pert and she was pretty, and she had nerve.

A star came out, the desert night was soft, and a coolness came over it.

It came on me to sing, but my horse was carrying me along nicely, and I was not wishful for trouble.

TREASURE
MOUNTAIN

Chapter 1

"To kill a man, my dear, is not always to make an end of him." The statement was made by Andre Baston.

"But after twenty years? *Twenty years?*" said the woman.

"A lifetime to you, Fanny, but only yesterday to a man like your Uncle Philip."

"But how could anyone *know?* It all happened so long ago, and so far away!"

"Nevertheless, a man is here in New Orleans and he is asking questions. His name is Sackett."

"What?"

"Orrin Sackett. He is an attorney, a lawyer. He has the same name as the man who went to the western mountains with Pierre."

Fanny Baston was small, slender, voluptuous, and beautiful. Her shoulders were soft and amazingly white, her lips were warm and a little full, and her eyes were large.

She shrugged. "What different can it make? Let him ask his questions. We simply know nothing. Who is left who could possibly know anything?"

Andre scowled. "I do not know. Nobody, perhaps. But I do not like him asking questions. If Philip ever found out . . ."

"It would be the end," Paul said. "The end. He would cut us off, leave us nothing."

"You, perhaps," Fanny said to Andre. "But I was a baby. Not five years old. And Paul, you were not even in your teens. We had nothing to do with it."

"Do you think that would matter?" said Paul. "Uncle Philip only needs an excuse to cut us all off. You too. You aren't exactly his pride and joy, you know."

"Then," she leaned forward, dusting the ash of her small cigar into a saucer, "kill him. Kill this Orrin Sackett and drop him in the bayou before he can even be connected to us. Kill him at once."

Andre was no longer surprised at anything his niece said. "You have an idea?"

"Do it yourself, Andre. He would not be the first." She looked up at him and smiled. "Why not? Find an excuse, challenge him. There is not a better shot in New Orleans, and as for a rapier . . . how many men have you killed, Andre? In duels, I mean?"

"Twelve," he replied. "You have a point. It might be the answer."

"You are too bloody," Paul objected. "If you want him killed, there are other ways. We might get him into one of the concert-saloons—the Buffalo Bill House, for example. Williams would take care of him for us."

"No." Fanny spoke sharply. "No, Paul. If there is killing to be done, the fewer who know the better. And nobody outside the family."

"She's right," Andre said, "but this is all so premature. This Orrin Sackett cannot know anything. Pierre was obviously French, obviously from Louisiana. He brought Sackett back here to outfit before we started west, but Sackett never left the river front. I don't know what stirred this up, but all we have to do is sit quietly and allow it to pass. If he gets close then we can act." He shrugged, looking down at the tip of his cigar. "After all, New Orleans may take care of him without our help. He would not be the first."

"Have you seen him?" Fanny asked.

"Yes. He's a big man, nearly as big as I am. Perhaps even as big. He's a good-looking fellow, dresses well, seems to know his way around."

Paul looked up. "Andre, wasn't there some disturbance down on the waterfront a few years back? Some trouble involving some Sacketts?"

"I believe you are right, Paul. I do recall something of the kind. An attempt was made to rob one of them and there was a fight—quite a bloody one."

"That could be the answer, Uncle Andre," Fanny suggested. "A Sackett returns . . . a revenge killing."

She was right, of course. It was a simple, logical method if it became necessary. He would make a few inquiries. If any of the old crowd were around he might just drop a word here and there. Anyway, this was all over nothing. This Sackett knew nothing, could know nothing.

A thought suddenly occurred to him. He still had the map. He had kept it, believing it held a clue to the treasure.

None of them knew he had it, for he had never mentioned it to anyone. After all, when one holds the only clue to the location of thirty million in gold one does not talk about it. The stuff was there. He had taken the time to look up the old reports turned into the government those many years ago, and of course, there was mention of the gold the French army had mined—*thirty millions!*

He had been thinking of going back to look for that gold, and this was probably the time. He was forty years old now, stronger and more able than ever. He must think about the future, and he had little faith in what Philip might leave them. Philip liked none of them too well, and with good reason.

What did Sackett *know?*

Orrin Sackett, standing before his mirror in the Saint Charles Hotel, combed his hair carefully, set his cravat in place, and left his room. At the head of the stairs he paused momentarily and touched his left side lightly. The Smith and Wesson Russian he carried was resting easily. No trouble was expected, but habit remains with a man.

So far the trip had netted him exactly nothing. He had doubted from the first that they would uncover anything. New Orleans was a big city. Twenty years had passed, and the clues he had were slight. Still, if it would please ma there was no effort he would not make.

After all, what information did he have? Twenty years ago a man of strong French accent wanted to make a trip to a certain place in the western mountains. That implied that he had made a previous trip or that he had knowledge of someone who had made such a trip.

Pa had been asked to guide this Frenchman, and the trip was expected to last but a few months—time to get there and return.

What would take a man to lonely mountains at the risk of being killed by Indians? Furs? To trap furs a man had to remain the winter through. A mine? Perhaps. He might wish to ascertain if the mine was worth development. Yet . . . wasn't it more likely that he knew of gold already mined?

Or thought he did?

When Orrin added up all the information he had, he was looking for a Frenchman, probably from Louisiana, who had some previous connection, direct or indirect, with someone who had been to the western mountains.

Flimsy as that was, it did much to clear the field, for not many Frenchmen had gone west from Louisiana. From Canada . . . yes. Of course, France had controlled all of Louisiana for a time, and, during the period of the Mississippi Bubble and John Law, great efforts had been made to find gold and silver. Law had promised his investors wealth, and he made every effort to discover it—or indications of it.

This Frenchman had not wanted a large party. Yet, it was unlikely that they had actually gone alone.

Hence one of the party might have returned, or there might be a relative who knew something about the affair. The trouble was he had no starting point. Yet, the simplest way was often the best, and that meant checking the obvious sources—in this case, government records of mines, claims, and exploring expeditions in the back country.

Another way, equally simple, was to meet some of the older citizens and start them recalling their youth. It sometimes required patience, but he had an interest in such things and could afford a few days. Or he could get some discussion started of the John Law period—the most likely time for any mineral exploration.

Bienville, during his governorship, had wasted little time searching for nonexistent minerals. His had been a more practical, down-to-earth approach, and, had he been let alone to proceed as he wished, the colony might have been successful long before it was.

At dinner Orrin sat quietly and alone, listening to the idle talk around him and enjoying the lights and music. He had always enjoyed dining alone, for it gave him time to think as well as to absorb the atmosphere around him. And tonight the dining room was filled with attractive, beautifully gowned women and handsomely dressed men.

The two tables closest to his were occupied: one of them by a group of people of his own age or younger, the other by a very handsome older couple, a distinguished-looking man with a beautiful woman, her hair almost white, her eyes remarkably youthful.

He ordered his meal when the waiter appeared. "And the wine, sir?"

"Châteauneuf-du-Pape," he said quietly.

The older gentleman turned his head and glanced at him. Their eyes met, and Orrin smiled. "An excellent wine, sir," the man said.

"Thank you. Anything less would not fit the surroundings."

"You are a stranger here?"

"I have been here more than once. But this is the first opportunity I have had to relax in a long while." Orrin watched the waiter open his wine, tasted it, then said to the old man, "I am interested in some mining claims in the San Juan Mountains in Colorado. I have heard rumors to the effect that people from New Orleans located mines in that area."

The old man smiled. "I doubt that, sir. There was much talk of gold, of course, and stories of discoveries in the Far West, but nothing came of it, nothing at all."

"Men did go out there, however?"

"A few. Adventurers or fools. Oh, yes! I believe the French government did send a military detachment to the West at one time, but that was very long ago."

"Did you know any of those who went west?"

"No . . . no, I think not. We were planting sugar then and were much too busy to think of such things. And I believe very few did go."

"What of Pierre?" his wife suggested.

"Pierre?" he frowned. "Oh, yes! But that was later. He never came back, so we never did know what he went after, exactly. Some wild-goose chase, I expect. The Bastons were a mixed lot. Not very steady, you know. Chopping about from one thing to another. They still are, for that matter."

"Charles!"

"Well, it's true, and you know it. That Andre, for example, he is nothing but a—"

Suddenly a man was standing by the table. "You were saying, La-Croix?"

Orrin glanced up. The man was tall and broad, strongly built with a face that might have been carved from granite. The eyes were cold and blue, the face clean-shaven but for a waxed mustache.

"You were speaking of me, LaCroix?"

Orrin was shocked when he glanced at the old man for his face had gone white and stiff. He was frightened, but even as Orrin looked, the man's pride asserted itself and he started to rise.

Instantly, Orrin was on his feet. "I am afraid you have the advantage of me, sir. We were talking of my old neighbors, Andy and Bert Masters. Do you know them, then?"

"Who?"

Andre Baston faced sharply around.

"If you know them," Orrin said, smiling, "you'll understand. Andy, he was a moonshiner. Came from Tennessee and settled down here in the bayous and took to makin' whiskey—by the way, what did you say your name was? Mine is Sackett. Orrin Sackett."

"I'm Andre Baston. I do not understand you, sir." Andre's tone was cold. "I understood this man to say—"

"Sure you did. The Masters were a no-good lot. I never did figure that was even their name. Even the 'shine they made wasn't much, but one thing I'll give ol' Andy. He had him a couple of the best coonhounds—"

"I am afraid there is some mistake," Andre said coldly. He stared into Orrin's eyes. "You, sir, I do not like."

Orrin chuckled. "Now, isn't that a coincidence? I was just about to say the same thing. I don't like you, either, but while we're on the subject, what did happen to Pierre?"

Andre's face went pale with shock, then reddened. Before he could speak, Orrin said, "Not that I care, but folks ask questions when a man disappears. Especially a man like Pierre. He wasn't alone, was he? Man should never go into wild country alone. Of course, that always raises the question of what happened to those who were with him? Did any of them get back?"

Orrin thrust out his hand. "Nice talking to you, Mr. Baston, maybe we can sit down for a real confidential talk one of these times."

Abruptly, Orrin sat down, and Andre Baston walked away.

The old man was sunken in his chair, his face gray. His wife looked across at Orrin. "Thank you, oh, thank you! You saved his life, you know. They have never liked us, and Andre Baston is a duelist."

"He is?" Orrin glanced at Andre. He was seating himself at the adjoining table. "Was he with Pierre on that trip west?"

For a moment there was no reply, and then the woman spoke softly. "We must go now, monsieur. It is late and my husband is tired."

LaCroix got to his feet slowly. For a moment Orrin thought he was about to fall, but he stiffened his shoulders. Then he looked down at Orrin. "I am not sure. I believe he was."

Orrin got to his feet. "I have enjoyed the conversation. If I can be of any assistance—"

"Thank you."

He sat down again, watching them walk slowly away, two fine, proud people.

Suddenly, a voice spoke. "Mr. Sackett? I am Fanny Baston, and my uncle is very sorry for the way he acted. He believed it was his name he heard."

Orrin Sackett looked up into the eyes of one of the most beautiful girls he had ever seen. Quickly, he got to his feet. "It was a natural mistake," he said.

"We must make amends. We would not wish you to leave New Orleans thinking us inhospitable." She put her hand on his. "Mr. Sackett, would you come to dinner at our home? Thursday night?"

"Of course," he said. "I'd be glad to come."

When she seated herself at her own table, she looked at her brother and uncle. "There!" she said. "Now it is up to you! What did we come here for, anyway?"

Chapter 2

We Sacketts been going down to New Orleans ever since there was a town yonder. This time I wasn't going to see the lights or dance the fandango, but to help Orrin work out a trail.

The trail along which we had to read sign was twenty years cold, and it was the trail of our own father.

Pa was what you'd call a wandering man, a mountain man in his later years, who understood the trapping of fur and how to get along with the red man.

He had been to the shining mountains a time or two, but the last time he never come home. That wasn't so unusual as to raise sweat on a man, for those were parlous times, and many a man went west and nobody saw anything of him after that but maybe his hair at some Indian's belt.

We boys knew the country ways, and we figured pa was thrown from his horse somewhere on the high plains, got caught without water, or run short of powder and lead with the Indians closing in. There was a sight of things could happen to a body in western lands, and betwixt us we'd come up against most of them. The trouble was with ma.

She was growing old now, and with the passing of years her memories turned more and more to pa, and to wondering what had become of him. She was fearful he might be stove up and helpless somewhere back in the hills, or maybe held hostage by some Indians. Of a night ma didn't sleep very well, and she'd set up in her old rocker and worry about pa.

Now pa was a knowing kind of a man. He could make do with mighty little, and, given time, he could edge himself out of any kind of a fix. We boys figured that if pa was alive he'd come home, one way or t'other.

We were living in New Mexico now. Tyrel was trying to sell his holdings near Mora, figuring on moving west to the new town of Shalako. Orrin was busy with his law practice, but he said he could take some time, and I guess I was actually free to roam. Anyway, no woman, except ma, would worry for me.

"I'll go to New Orleans, Tell," Orrin told me, "and I'll check what rec-

ords I can find. When you come along down I'll try to have a starting
place."

The three of us set down with ma to talk over pa's last days at home to
find some clue to just where he was going. The Rockies are a wide and
wonderful bunch of mountains, but they aren't just one range. There are
hundreds of them, so where in the high-up hills do you begin to hunt for
a man?

Do you start hunting sign in the Black Hills or the Big Belts? The Ab-
sarokas, Sawatch, or Sangre de Cristos? Do you search the Greenhorns,
the Big Horns, Wind Rivers, San Juans, La Platas, the Needles, Mogollons, Uintas, Crazy Mountains, or Salish? The Abajos, Henrys, Pelon-
cillos, the Chiricahuas, or the Snake Range? Do you cross the Black Rock
Desert or the Painted? Do you search down in Hell's Canyon? On the
Green or the Popo Agie?

Where do you hunt for one man where armies might be lost?

New Orleans was a far piece from the fur-trapped streams where the
beaver build, but it was there the trail should begin, for it was there pa
headed when he rode away from the Cumberland Hills of Tennessee.

Cities made me uneasy. A body couldn't blaze a trail in a city, and folks
weren't out and out what they seemed. Usually, they made it a point to
show one face while hiding another.

Orrin was city-wise. He could read city-sign the way I'd track a mustang
horse across a flat-rock mesa. Of course, Orrin was also a fair hand at
tracking and nigh as good in a shoot-out as me or Tyrel. Orrin had started
early to reading law, packing a copy of Blackstone in his saddlebags and
reading whenever there was time. He was also an upstanding, handsome
man, and when he started to talk even the rocks and trees had to listen.
We Sacketts were English and Welsh mostly, but Orrin must have taken
after the Welsh, who have the gift of speaking with a song in their words.

New Orleans wasn't no new place to me, like I said. We Sacketts, along
with other hill folks from Kentucky or Tennessee, been floating rafts of
logs downstream for a coon's age, but the places I knew best weren't likely
to be on Orrin's callin' list. Come to think of it most of those places were
joints where I'd gone to roust out our shanty boys to get them started
home. Places like Billy Phillip's 101 Ranch, Lulu White's Mahogany
Hall, the Five Dollar House, and the Frenchman's. Or maybe Murphy's
Dance House on Gallatin Street.

You had to be a man with the bark on to even go into those places. I
never paid 'em much mind, but when you went down-river with a shanty-
boat crew you wound up in some mighty rough places. I usually had to

lead the fight that got them out, and those fights aren't for the delicate. It was fist, skull, an' batter 'em down, and you stayed on your feet or you got tromped.

The Saint Charles Hotel was a mighty fine place, the like of which I'd not seen before. In my dusty black suit and boots I didn't shape up to the kind of folks they quartered there.

The clerk had his hair slicked down like he'd been licked to be swallered, and he looked at me like I was something a dog dragged up on the porch. "Yes?" he said.

"I am hunting Orrin Sackett," I said. "He's bedded down here."

The clerk took down a big register and checked the list. "Oh, yes! Mr. Sackett. But he is no longer with us. He's been gone—let's see—he left on the twentieth, sir. He's been gone two days."

Now that just didn't set right. Orrin had said positive that he would meet me at the Saint Charles today. So if he was gone, he'd be back.

"You sure? He was to meet me here."

"I am sorry, sir. Mr. Sackett checked out and left no forwarding address."

"He took his duffle, his bags, an' like that?"

"Of course, he—" This gent held up suddenly like he'd thought of something. "When I think of it, he did leave his saddle here and a rifle, I believe."

Now I was worried. No Sackett goes off anywhere without a saddle and a Winchester. It just didn't stand to reason Orrin would.

"I guess you better let me have a room," I said. "The same room he had if it's available."

He hesitated, evidently not sure if I could stand the traffic, but I took out my poke and shook him out a couple of double eagles. "You set that by," I said, "an' when she's et up, you give me a whistle.

"Whilst you're about it, send up a tailor. I got to order some Sunday-go-to-meetin' clothes."

That room was most elegant. Had a big flowered bowl and pitcher, and there was a bathroom right down the hall. I set my gear down and took a quick look around. The room had been cleaned so there'd be nothing of Orrin's left, but I knew Orrin real well and had an idea where to look.

Under a corner of the rug, pasted there neat as could be, were two gold pieces. That was a trait of Orrin's—it was getaway money in case he got robbed or whatever. Now I knew for sure something was wrong, wrong as all get-out. If he had reason to leave his saddle and rifle, Orrin would never leave without his getaway money.

Right then I set down and went to figuring. Gettin' yourself robbed, knocked on the head, or killed in New Orleans in these 1870s was about the easiest thing a body could do, but Orrin was no pilgrim. He'd been where the bear walks an' the buzzard roosts, and he was uncommon shrewd in the ways of men.

About then I pulled up and set my saddle. Orrin was knowing in the ways of men, but his record was no good when it come to reading sign on women. Tyrel or me, we were more suspicious, maybe because women hadn't paid us so much mind as they had Orrin. He had takin' ways, and kind of expected women to like him, which they usually did. More than that, he was a downright friendly man, and if Orrin was in trouble you can bet there was a woman somewhere around. Of course, you can say that of most men.

After the tailor had come to measure me for a couple of suits, I talked to the boy who showed him up to the room. "This here room," I said, "was occupied until a couple of days ago by a handsome big man with a nice smile. You recall him?"

"I do."

"Now, I am his brother, so you can talk free. Did he have him a woman around?"

"He did not. He was in his room very little. I remember him, suh. He was most thoughtful, suh."

"Did you see him with anyone else? I've got to find him." I put a silver dollar in his hand. "You ask around. Come to me as soon as you hear tell of him and I'll have another of those for you."

Disappearing is one of the least easy things to do if a body has any recognizable way of living. We all set patterns, and if we break them somebody is sure to notice, although it may be somebody we don't even know.

Orrin was a man easy to notice and easy to remember. He never made it a point to be nice to folks . . . he just was. It was him. He was polite to everyone, a man folks talked to mighty easy, a man with a pleasant way about him who would sooner avoid trouble than have it. He could put you off guard and turn a conversation from trouble into casual talk better than anybody I ever knew.

At the same time he was strong, as strong as me, I expect, and I never took hold of anything that it didn't move. He was a fine boxer, a better than average Cornish-style wrestler, and a dead shot with either hand. Peaceful man though he was, I never knew anybody to take more pleasure in a plain or fancy knockdown and drag-out brawl. In spite of his easy-go-

ing ways, if you shaped up to tear down his meathouse you'd bought yourself a packet of trouble.

So I just idled about, listening and talking to a few folks about my
brother, but nobody recalled anything helpful. People around the Saint
Charles remembered him and so did a boy at the corner who sold newspapers, a man down the street at a secondhand book store, and a girl who
served him coffee a couple of times in a restaurant down the street a few
blocks. An old Negro who drove a carriage for hire told me about him
going there.

It was a small place under a wrought-iron balcony. There was a table
near a wide window looking out on the street.

Now I'm a coffee-drinking man and always kind of had an urge for the
coffee they brew down Louisiana way, so I took a table by the window
and a right pretty girl with dark hair and dark eyes brought me coffee.
Right off I asked about Orrin.

"Oh, yes! I remember him very well, but he has not been in lately.
Not for two or three days."

"Did he come here often?"

"He surely did. And he always sat right where you're sitting. He said
he liked to watch people walking along the street."

"Was he always alone?"

"Yes—always. I never even saw him speak to anyone until the last time
he was in. He spoke to a lady who comes in sometimes."

"Young?"

"Oh, no. Mrs. LaCroix is—well, she's past sixty, I'd say."

"Did they have coffee?"

"Oh, no. They just spoke. Well, she did talk to him a little. She was
thanking him for something. I—I didn't listen, you know, but I couldn't
help but hear. It was something that happened in the dining room at the
Saint Charles. I have no idea what it was about except that Mr. Sackett
avoided trouble for them, somehow."

Well, that was something.

Orrin never was much inclined to just sit around and drink coffee, so if
he came here more than once he had him a reason. Orrin liked to watch
the people pass, did he?

What people? There was a lot of folks yonder, and somebody was
passin' every minute, but I had an idea he wouldn't sit here just on the
chance somebody would pass . . . he must have known somebody would
go by there, or maybe there was somebody he could watch from where
he sat.

I sat there about half an hour when the waitress returned to my table. The other folks who had been drinking coffee were gone.

"Sit down," I suggested. "My front name is Tell, short for William Tell, a man my pa favored for his arrow shooting and his way of thinking. It's mighty nice, just to set and watch the folks go by. I've seen more people in the last half hour than I see in two months out yonder where I've been, and I've never seen so many people afoot."

She was amused. "Do you ride everywhere?"

"A man wouldn't be caught dead without a horse, ma'am. Why, when Eb Farley was to be buried out yonder they laid him out in the hearse nice an' proper, an' d'you know what the corpse done? He got right up out of the coffin, straddled a horse, an' rode all the way to the bone yard; then he crawled back into the coffin and they buried him peaceful."

At that moment a man walked out of the saloon across the street. He was a huge man with heavy shoulders, the biggest hands and feet I ever did see, and a wide, flat face. He wore boots, a red sash about his waist, and a nondescript gray coat and pants.

"Who's *that?*"

She looked quickly, then away. "Don't let him see you looking at him. That's Hippo Swan. He's a notorious bully. He used to be overseer at the Baston plantation before they lost their slaves. Now he just hangs around the dance-saloons."

When I returned to the hotel I went to the desk. "Did my brother leave no message at all when he left?" I asked.

"As a matter of fact, Mr. Sackett, I did not see your brother that day. He sent a messenger for his valise."

"Just that? No written message?"

"Of course. We would never give a guest's baggage to anyone without an order. In fact, we have it on file." He got out the message. It was written on ordinary tablet paper, and the handwriting was nothing like my brother's excellent script.

Opening the register to my brother's entry I laid the two signatures side by side. There was no resemblance.

The clerk's face grew flushed. "I am sorry, sir. I think I had better call the manager."

Chapter 3

Up in my room, I sat down to do some figuring. Orrin was surely in trouble, and it was serious trouble by the look of it. He was not a man to seek difficulties, and he had a smooth tongue for them when they came, so what could have happened?

He had not returned to his room. Somebody else had picked up his luggage, using a forged note to do it. Whoever came for the valise hadn't dreamed there'd be a rifle and saddle locked up at the hotel. Folks visiting in New Orleans rarely came equipped like that.

Looked to me like the only lead I had was that woman he'd spoken to in the coffee shop—Mrs. LaCroix—the name was not uncommon.

She had been in the dining room of the Saint Charles, and Orrin had helped her with some difficulty. Now that would be like Orrin. No Sackett ever stood by with a woman needing help. Looked to me like the dining room was the place to start inquiries.

Missing two days . . . I was scared.

Orrin could be just one of many to be robbed or killed. The only lead I had was what took place in the dining room and that might be nothing at all. Of course, there was that time, years back, when we came downriver with a raft of logs and had that shindig on the river front, but more than likely nobody remembered that. Still, a look along the dance-saloon route might turn up something.

Come to think of it, I had a friend down yonder. There was a woman down there, a mighty notorious woman now, from what I heard. She'd been a hard case even as a youngster when I helped her out a couple of times. Brick-top Jackson was now figured to be as tough as they come, a mighty handsome woman with a figure like nothing you ever saw, but a woman who could, and would, fight like the dirtiest waterfront brawler you ever did see. Brick-top was a thief, a murderer, and a lot of other things, but she would know what was happening along the mean streets, and maybe she would tell me.

There was a tap on the door. I took up my Colt and shoved it down behind my waistband, then opened the door.

It was that Negro bell man that I'd given the dollar to.

"Mr. Sackett?" He stepped in and closed the door behind him. "I have some information, suh."

Well, I went down into my pocket for a dollar, but he wasn't hungry. He said, "Your brother had an altercation, suh. He exchanged a few words with Mr. Baston, suh."

"Baston?" Where had I heard that name?

"Andre Baston, suh."

He said it like it was a name I should know. When I looked puzzled he said, "Andre Baston is thought by some to be the most dangerous man in New Orleans, suh. He has killed twelve men . . . in duels, suh; with pistol, knife, or rapier he is considered the best."

In some places that might not have meant so much, but New Orleans was no ordinary town.

"What happened?"

Briefly, he explained what had happened in the dining room, but it did not come to much. There had been some words, but it was purely a small matter, and, had anybody but this here Baston been involved, nobody would have paid it much mind.

"Those people he was talking to? Was their name LaCroix?"

"Yes, suh. It was. They are fine people, very fine people, suh."

"And the Bastons?"

This Negro was a fine-looking man of fifty or so, with an inborn dignity and obviously some education. His distaste for gossip was evident, but there was something more here, too. Now I ain't given to second sight, but feelings show through, and it was right plain that this man liked the LaCroix people, but not the Bastons.

"There are many Bastons, suh. Some of them fine people. Most of them, in fact. Old Mr. Philip, suh . . . before the war, suh, I was one of his people. He was a fine man, a fine man."

"What about Andre?"

He hesitated. "Mr. Sackett, I would have no dealings with him, suh."

"You did say he had killed twelve men."

"I said he had killed twelve men in duels, suh. There have been others, suh, when the arrangements were less formal."

Well, that didn't get me anywhere. Orrin had exchanged a few words with Baston and they had parted. If I could talk to the LaCroix people they could tell me what was said, but the lead did not look promising. It looked to me like Orrin had just dropped off the world.

Two days more of hunting and inquiring left me exactly where I was when I arrived. Now Orrin had been missing four days. And then I located the LaCroix family.

When I was shown into the library where they were sitting they seemed surprised. Mr. LaCroix got up quickly, but he was a mite stiff, I could see. He was a fine-looking man, well up in years. "Mr. Sackett? I am sorry. I was expecting—"

"My brother, I guess. Orrin's a sight better looking than me."

"You are—"

"William Tell Sackett, ma'am. Fact is, I came to see if you had seen my brother?"

"Seen him? Of course. He sat beside us at dinner one night, and I believe Mrs. LaCroix saw him at the coffee shop one day."

"Yes, I did. It was a chance meeting but a fortunate one as I wished to thank him again."

"Sir? What happened that night? I mean, if you don't mind. You see, Orrin's been missing for four days."

Well, they exchanged a look, and it was a scared look.

"If you could tell me just what happened, it might help," I suggested. "I've heard a good deal as far as Baston is concerned, but what happened there in the dining room?"

Betwixt them, they laid it out for me, and all of it made sense except that last question about what happened to Pierre. When I brought that up they told me Orrin said he was interested in some mining claims out in the San Juans, which is about what Orrin would say to cover his reasons for asking questions. It might give him a lead on somebody who left New Orleans for the wild lands to the west, as it seemed likely to have done.

It began to look like Orrin had thrown that Pierre question in there on chance. It was one of his lawyer's tricks, and it had taken Andre Baston off guard . . . but it might have gotten Orrin killed, too. A body just didn't play games with a man like Baston.

"This Andre Baston now? Was he alone?"

"He was joining his niece, Fanny, and nephew at a table near your brother."

"And this Pierre they spoke of?"

"Pierre Bontemps. He was Andre's brother-in-law. He went west on some wild venture. Pierre was that way, always going off somewhere at the least excuse. He was killed out there, by Indians, it was said. Andre got back."

It still didn't shape up to much. Orrin had exchanged a few words with a man with a reputation as a duelist, and he had said something to which I gathered Baston's reaction was mighty strong.

A few more questions, and it began to look like when pa went west it was with Pierre Bontemps, Andre Baston, and some others. I had no idea how many others and who they were.

After a little more talk I got into a carriage and returned to the Saint Charles. When I stepped down from the carriage, Hippo Swan was standing on the curb opposite the hotel. And when I saw him I remembered where I'd heard the name Baston before. The girl in the coffee shop had said he had once worked for someone named Baston.

When I reached the door, I glanced back. Hippo Swan was lighting a cigar, but he was holding the match up higher than necessary, or so it seemed to me.

A signal? If so, to whom?

Well, now. Chances were I was just seeing shadows where none existed, but it costs nothing to play it safe. Nobody had left any messages at the desk for me so I started on up to my room.

The window, I recalled, looked over the street out front. A body standing in that window could easily see a match struck down there on the street.

Turning around on the stairs I went back down to the desk. The clerk was gone, but the Negro I'd talked to earlier was standing there.

"Is there anyone in the room adjoining mine? The one with the door opening into mine?"

He consulted the register. "Not at present, suh."

I put a silver dollar on the desk. "Could you let me have it for a few minutes?"

He looked straight into my eyes. "What seems to be the trouble, Mr. Sackett?"

"Well, now. I'm kind of a cautious man. It seems to me that one Sackett disappearing is enough, and if somebody was inside my room now, somebody who was waiting for me, he'd be likely to be waiting beside the hall door."

"It is likely, suh." He pushed the key toward me and my dollar as well. "Would you like me to call the hotel officer, suh?"

"Thank you . . . no."

Turning away I started for the steps. He spoke after me. "Good hunting, suh."

I walked softly down the carpeted hall and opened the room next to mine, then ever so gently I put the key into the lock, careful to make no sound. I ran quickly around to my own door, fumbled with the knob, then swore softly, muttering something about the key.

I ran back to the door in the adjoining room and opened it suddenly.

There was a little light from the window, and the bulk of a man waiting by the door. A shadow moved as the door swung wide . . . there was *another man!*

They came for me, both of them. They were big men and were probably considered quite tough. They came for me, one from each direction. I had my knife and I had my Colt, but the Colt seemed an unfair advantage, and no doubt there was folks asleep upstairs or around me. I stepped in to meet them as they came at me from two sides, but I hooked a toe behind a chair and kicked it in front of the one coming from the right, and, as he fell over it, I lowered the boom on the second one with a good right fist.

He was ambitious, that gent was, and he was coming in fast, so when he met my right fist halfway he was driving right into it with all the thrust of his legs.

There was a *splat*, then a crunch, as his nose folded like an accordion under my fist. As he hit the floor I kicked him in the side of the head.

The first man was starting to get up, but I was through fooling around. I put the point of my knife against his throat right over the jugular vein, and I said, "I don't care if I do or I don't. What d' you think?"

He was sure of one thing, and he didn't need to be sure of anything else. One twist of that blade and tomorrow morning they'd be throwing dirt over him.

He held right still. "For God's sake, mister! Don't kill me! I didn't mean nothin'!"

"Who set you up to this?"

"I don't—"

That knife point dug a mite deeper. A tiny push now and he'd be bleeding on the carpet. "You tell me. You tell me who sent you and what you were to do with me."

"Swan sent me. The Hippo. We was to lay you out and pack you out the back way and down to the swamp."

"Get up, then." I took a step back and let him up, and I didn't much care if he wanted to open the ball or not, but he'd had all he wanted. There was a trickle of blood down his neck and it scared him. He was only scratched, but he didn't know how much and he was so scared he was ready to cry.

"Take that," I pointed my foot at the other man, "and clear out of here. Next time you tackle a Sackett, you be sure his hands are tied."

He backed away from me. "I had nothin' to do with that. It was him," he gestured to the man on the floor, "an' Hippo. They done it."

For a moment I looked at him, then, the edge of my blade up, I stepped toward him. "Where did they take him?"

His voice was a whisper. "To the swamp. To a houseboat on the bayou. I don't know which one."

"Get out!"

He stooped, lifting the other man with an effort, and staggered out. Closing the door after him I lit the light, then I closed and locked the door to the adjoining room. There was a spot of blood on the point of my knife and I wiped it clean.

There was a light tap on the door. It was the Negro again. "The key, suh? I supposed you might be through with it."

"Thanks—I am. But I believe I've broken a chair."

He glanced at it. "I hope that wasn't all," he said quietly. He gathered the pieces. "A chair can be replaced."

"What's your name?" I asked him, suddenly aware that I wanted to know.

He did not smile. "Judas, suh. Judas Priest."

"Thank you, Judas."

The Negro turned at the door. "Two of them, suh? That's doing very well, suh."

"You saw them?"

"Oh, yes, suh! Of course." He slipped his hand into his pocket, and it came out wearing a very formidable set of brass knuckles. "We couldn't allow anything to happen to a guest! Not at the Saint Charles, suh!"

"Much obliged. That's what I'd call service. I'd better put in a good word for you to the management."

"If you don't mind, suh, my participation would have been entirely my own responsibility."

"Thank you, Judas."

He drew the door shut after him, and I dropped down on the bed. Orrin was in a houseboat on a bayou. That was mighty little to know, for there were dozens of bayous and probably hundreds of houseboats.

Orrin might be dead, or dying. Right now he might be needing all the help he could get.

And I could not help him . . .

Chapter 4

Settin' on the side of the bed I gave thought to my problem. I had to find Orrin and almighty quick. They had no reason I could think of for keepin' him alive, but Orrin was a glib-tongued man and if anybody could find them a reason, he could.

There seemed no rhyme or reason to it. Most killings these days started from nothing, some measly argument that suddenly becomes all-fired important. But even allowing for that there still seemed to be more to it.

When it came right down to it, I had little to go on, and nobody ever accused me of being brighter than average. I can handle any kind of a fightin' weapon as good or better than most, and I'm rawhide tough and bull-strong, but when it comes to connivin' I ain't up to it. Straight out an' straight forward, that's me.

Orrin had come to town lookin' for some sign of that Frenchman who had gone off with pa to the western mountains, and a small chance of finding it, yet somehow he had evidently come up with something. Then, settin' at table he had struck up conversation with those LaCroix people and a name had been dropped. Out of the words that followed, Orrin, always good at keeping a witness off balance, asked what had become of Pierre? And he struck a nerve.

Pierre had not returned from a trip to the western lands. Andre Baston had been on that trip. Andre had not liked that question about Pierre, so what could a body figure from that? Maybe he had run out and left Pierre in a fight. Maybe he had taken something that belonged to Pierre . . . and maybe he had killed Pierre.

All that was speculation, and a man can get carried away by a reasonable theory. Often a man finds a theory that explains things and he builds atop that theory, finding all the right answers . . . only the basic theory is wrong. But that's the last thing he will want to admit.

Pa had left New Orleans for the western lands at about that time. The name Sackett had jolted Andre when Orrin spoke it. And right after

Orrin had introduced himself as a Sackett and prodded Andre Baston with the name of Pierre, Orrin disappeared.

What I had to do now was find one houseboat where there might be four or five hundred, and the only way I knew to look was to head for Gallatin Street, and after that the swamp. I spoke reasonable Spanish of a Mexican sort, and a few odd words of French, picked up in Louisiana or up along the Canadian border. I'd need them words. New Orleans had been a French and Spanish city for nearly a hundred years before it became American, and a lot of folks along the bayous spoke only French, like along the Bayou Teche, where the Cajuns lived.

First off, I needed somebody who knew the bayous, so I'd start down yonder where folks have all manner of secret knowledge. Time was I knowed a few folks. Somebody had told me Brick-top was gone.

Brick-top Jackson was meaner than a grizzly bear with a sore tooth and apt to be on the prod most of the time. There toward the end she hung out with a man named Miller who had an iron ball where his hand had been. One time he come home with a whip and tried to take it to her. She took the whip from him and beat him half to death, so he tried a knife, and she took that and fed it to him five or six times. Miller got tired of it then and up and died on her. They'd fit many a time before, but he spited her this time, and when the law came and found him they carted the Brick-top off to prison.

At one time I'd helped her a mite, not even knowing who she was, and I don't know whether that surprised her more than me going on about my business. Only she told folks I was one man she'd go to hell for. I think she went to hell for a lot of men.

But along the river a man meets a sight of strange people, and I never had no preaching in mind. I'd made a friend hither and yon, and it seemed likely there were a few down on the mean streets, so I went there.

The folks who decided what sin was never walked Gallatin Street in its wild days. Had they done so, their catalogue of evil would have stretched out a good bit, and we'd have a hundred commandments rather than ten. It was thieving, brawling, and murderous. There was the Blue Anchor, the Baltimore, the Amsterdam, and Mother Burke's Den. (The Canton House was closed after Canton kicked a sailor to death.) Nobody needed to hunt for a place in which to get drunk or robbed, and nine times out of ten if it was one it was surely the other.

Tarantula juice was the cheapest drink, two gallons of raw alcohol, a shaved plug of tobacco and half a dozen burnt peaches mixed in a five-gallon keg of water. If they stinted on anything it was the alcohol, but in the meaner dives they were inclined to add almost anything to make up the volume.

From joint to joint I went, keeping a weather eye open for a face I knew. All were familiar. I guess you could find them on any waterfront in the world, swaggering, tough, ready with fist or knife, and in Murphy's dance-saloon I struck it rich. I'd ordered a beer—his beer was usually safe— and was looking around when a tall, slim man with a gold ring in his ear came up alongside me.

He was a long-jawed man with yellow eyes, and he was wearing a planter's hat with a bandana tied beneath it and a brown coat with a scarf about his neck. He was thin, but with a whipcord look of strength about him.

"You can trust the beer, Sackett, and Murphy too, up to a point."

"Thanks," I said, "but can I trust a stranger with a ring in his ear?"

"I'm the Tinker," he said, and that explained everything to a man from our hills.

The Tinker was a tinker, he was also a pack-peddler who roamed the back mountain trails to sell or trade whatever he could. He was a man from foreign places who seemed always to have been amongst us, and although he looked thirty he might have been ninety. He had wandered the lonely roads through the Cumberlands and the Smokies and the Blue Ridge. They knew him on the Highland Rim, and from the breaks of the Sandy to the Choccoloco. Among other things, he made knives of a kind like you've never seen, knives sold to few, given to none.

"I'm glad to see you, then, for I need someone who knows the bayous."

"I know them a little," he said, "and I know those who know them better. I have people here."

The Tinker was a gypsy, and among that society he was held in vast respect. Whether he was a king among them, or a worker of magic, or simply a better man with steel, I never knew.

"They've got Orrin," I said. "A man named Andre Baston's behind it, and Hippo Swan."

"When a Sackett breeds enemies," the Tinker said, "he never looks among the weak for them. They are a wicked lot, Tell Sackett."

"You know me then?"

"I was among them who rode to the Mogollon when trouble was upon you there. I rode with your cousin Lando, who is my friend. Where will you be if I have anything to tell you?"

"The Saint Charles. If I am not in, there is a man of color there, Judas Priest, you may speak to him."

"I know the man, and who does not?"

"You know him, too?"

"He is a friend to have."

The Tinker stood away from the bar and motioned to a man who loafed not far away. He put his hand on my arm. "This is Tell Sackett, a friend of mine."

"Of course," he said.

The Tinker looked around at me. "Now you will not be bothered," he said. "Go where you will in New Orleans but I cannot answer for the swamp or the bayous."

All around us was a sweaty, pushing, swearing, pocket-picking, poke-slitting lot, but now as I turned to leave they rolled away from me, and the way was easy. Among the crowd I saw the Tinker's friend and some others with him, and usually one of them was close to me.

The gypsies had their own way of doing things in New Orleans, and there were always more of them about than one believed.

I was tired from my search through the dives. I turned back toward the hotel when suddenly Hippo Swan was before me. "Bring him to the Saint Charles, Hippo," I said. "If I have to come after him, you will deal with me."

He laughed, and glanced around for his men, but they had disappeared and there was an open space around us. He did not like it. He was afraid of no man, but something had happened here that he could not judge, for he had come with a half dozen men and now he was alone.

He had white skin, thick lips, and small, cruel eyes almost hidden under thick flesh. He was even larger than I had at first believed, with great, heavy shoulders and arms, and hands both broad and thick.

"I will deal with you, will I? I shall like that, me bucko, oh, I shall like that!" he said.

I did not like the man. There is that in me that bristles at the bully, and this man was such a one. Yet he was not to be taken lightly. This man was cruel because he liked being cruel!

"If he's harmed, Hippo, I'll let the fish have what's left of you."

He laughed again. Oh, he was not worried by me. I always thought a threat an empty thing, but in this case I had a brother to help, and if a threat might hold them off even a little, I'd use it.

"What's one Sackett more or less?" he scoffed.

"Nothing to you, but a lot to the rest of us."

"Us? I see only one."

I smiled at him. "Hippo," I said quietly, "there are as many of us as there need to be. I've never seen more than a dozen at one time except when great-grandpa and great-grandma had their wedding anniversary. There were more than a hundred men. I did not count them all."

He didn't believe me. Neither did he like the way his men disappeared from around him, nor the look of some of the dark, strange faces in the crowd. Perhaps they were the same he had always seen, but suddenly they must have seemed different.

"I'll choose my time," he muttered, "and I'll break you—like *that!*" He made a snapping motion with hands that looked big enough to break anything, and then he walked away from me, and I went back to the Saint Charles and changed my clothes for dinner.

My new suit had come, and it fit exceedingly well. All the clothes I'd had since the time ma wove and stitched them with her own hands I'd either made myself from buckskin or they were hand-me-downs from the shelves of cattle-town stores.

It seemed to me that I looked very fine, and I looked away from the mirror, suddenly embarrassed. After all, why get big ideas? I was nothing but a country boy, a hill boy if you wish, who'd put in a few years and a few calluses on his hands from work and on his behind from saddles.

What was I doing here in this fine suit? How many times would I wear it? And what was I doing in this fine hotel? I was a man of campfires, line camps, and bunkhouses, a drifter with a rope and a saddle and very little else. And I'd better never forget it.

Yet sometimes things can make a man forget. Orrin had a right to trust women. He was easy to look at, and he had a foot for the dancing and an ear for the music and a voice to charm the beaver out of their ponds.

None of that was true of me. I was a big, homely man—with wide shoulders, big hands, and a face like a wedge: hard cheekbones, and a few scars picked up from places where I shouldn't have been, maybe. I had scars on my heart, too, from the few times I'd won, only to lose again.

Soft carpets and white linen and the gleam of expensive glass and silver, they weren't for the likes of me. I was a man born to the smell of pine knots burning, to sleeping under the stars or under a chuck wagon, maybe, or to the smell of branding fires or powder-smoke.

Yet I polished my boots some, and slicked back my hair as best I could, and, with a twist at my mustache, I went down the stairs to the dining room.

The traps that life lays for a man are not always of steel, nor is the bait what he'd expect.

When I came through the door she was setting there alone, and when she looked up at me her eyes seemed to widen and a sort of half-smile trembled on her lips.

She was beautiful, so beautiful I felt my heart ache with the sight of her. Suddenly scared, I made a start to turn away, but she got to her feet quickly but gracefully, and she said, "Mr. Sackett? William Tell Sackett?"

"Yes, ma'am." I twisted my hat in my hands. "Yes, ma'am. I was just aimin' to set for supper. Have you had yours yet?"

"I was waiting for you," she said, and dropped her eyes. "I am afraid you'll think me very bold, but I . . ."

"No such thing," I said. I drew back a chair for her. "I surely dread eatin' supper alone. Seems to me I'm the only one alone, most of the time."

"Have you been alone a lot, Mr. Sackett?"

She looked up at me out of those big, soft eyes and I couldn't swallow. Not hardly.

"Yes, ma'am. I've traveled wild country a sight, and away out in the mountains and upon the far plains a body sets alone . . . although there's camp-robber jays or sometimes coyotes around."

"You must be awfully brave."

"No, ma'am. I just don't know no better. It comes natural when you've growed—grown—up with it."

My collar felt tight, but then I never did like them stiff collars. They chafed my neck. My gun had twisted over on my belly and was gouging me. I could feel the sweat on my forehead and I desperately wanted to wipe it away.

"Your face looks so—so hard! I mean the skin! Like mahogany."

"It ain't much," I said, "although it cuts less than most. Why, I mind the time—"

Well, I caught myself in time. That there was no story for a genteel girl like this here. She suddenly put her hand up to my face.

"Do you mind? I just have to see if it's as hard as it looks!" Her hand was soft, like the feathers on a dove. I could feel my heart pounding, and I was afraid she'd hear it. It had been a long time since any woman made up to me like that.

Suddenly somebody was beside the table. "Mr. Sackett, suh? A message for you, suh." And then in a slightly different tone, he said, and it was Judas talkin', "How do you do, Miss Baston?"

Chapter 5

That name did just what Judas figured it would do and brought me right down out of the clouds. He shot down my balloon with one word, and it was well he did so, because it was only filled with hot air, anyway. No girl like this one would set her cap for a man like me unless there was double-dealing in it.

She smiled just as brightly, but it seemed to me there was a mean kind of anger in her eyes. Right then she could have shot Judas Priest.

For a moment there I forgot the message I had in my hand, but it was Fanny Baston who brought my attention back to it.

Judas had disappeared without even getting a reply from her, but I reckon he wasn't expecting one. Miss Baston glanced at the note in my hand. "Something always interrupts whenever I start talkin' to a good-looking man, Mr. Sackett. You can attend to that later, if you don't mind."

I just smiled at her. I had my good sense back now, or part of it. "It might be important."

Unfolding the note, I read: *Absinthe House. 11 o'clock tonight.* And it was signed with a profile of the Tinker. One quick, but amazingly lifelike line.

I folded the note and put it in my shirt pocket and buttoned down the flap. I had a feeling she was itching to put her dainty white hands on it. She'd get it only over my dead body. I had a feeling she'd thought of that, too.

"I was lookin' forward to meetin' you, ma'am," I said, and then I lied to her. "Orrin, he said he'd met you and was plannin' to see you soon."

Her eyelids flickered with annoyance. She had not expected that, but folks who deal in crime should recall that folks like to talk, and will tell most everything, given a chance. She had no way of knowing that I hadn't seen or heard from Orrin.

"I am afraid you have gathered the wrong impression," she said. "I only met your brother briefly, but I found him most attractive. As a matter of fact, that was why I came here tonight. He was to have called on us and did not, and then they told me you were here. Where is your brother?"

"I was just goin' to ask you that question, ma'am. He's a man never fails to keep an appointment, so something serious must have happened. We had some business here in town."

"If we could help, Mr. Sackett, you have only to ask. We have many friends here. Our people have lived in New Orleans since shortly after it was founded."

"Must have been mighty hard on the menfolks back in those times," I said. "There weren't many women around. Not until they sent in the correction girls."

Bienville, when he was governor down here and had girls sent in from France to make wives for his men, got a shipload of eighty-eight or -nine girls from a prison or "house of correction" in Paris. They were a bad lot, causing no end of trouble, so after that they shipped in some girls from the better classes, each of which was given a small chest of clothing and what not. These were a good lot of girls, serious and skilled at making a home, and they were called *filles à la cassette*—the casket girls.

Now as New Orleans folks have told me, nobody wanted to claim a correction girl as an ancestor, so the way it sounds all those girls died without issue, as the saying goes. And everybody who claims ancestry from those days claims a casket girl. This I knew from talk I'd heard, but I played it like I never heard of casket girls.

"No reason why some of those correction girls shouldn't have turned out all right," I said. "You've no reason to be shamed by it."

Her face flushed angrily and she said sharply, "We had nothing to do with correction girls, Mr. Sackett! The Bastons descended from a very fine family—"

"I've no doubt," I agreed. "Anyway, a mill doesn't turn on water that's past, and no doubt your folks are contributing a great deal to the welfare of Louisiana right now. Why, I'd say there's probably a number of upstanding citizens among them."

From all I'd heard I knew the family had pretty much gone to seed. Philip was the only one folks seemed to respect. The others had pride, an old home, and a willingness to do anything as long as it wasn't work. One branch of the family had turned out honorable men, planters, public servants, soldiers, and the like; the other, and that was the line Andre and Fanny belonged to, had turned to gambling, spending, slave trading in the days when they could, and a lot of questionable activities.

Fanny Baston did not like me. I could see that plain, and she was very rapidly beginning to wish she'd never come here on what was, I suspected, a kind of fishing expedition.

Yet she stuck to the job, I'll give her that. "If you have business we would be glad to help. Would you mind telling me what it is?"

Now I'd been giving thought to all of this, and it seemed to me there could be only two reasons for the Bastons getting all heated up. They were afraid we were trying to discover something or uncover something.

They'd likely not be interested unless there was money in it. Pa had taken off to the western mountains with Pierre . . . for what?

It looked to me like Pierre knew, or thought he knew, where there was gold. From the fact that the trip was supposed to be a quick one, the gold must have been dug already, which meant hidden treasure.

"As a matter of fact," I said, "Orrin an' me were trying to trace down our pa. He disappeared down thisaway some years back."

"Isn't it possible that he's dead?"

"Surely is, ma'am, only we want to *know*. Ma's getting on in years, and she worries about it. I suspect pa went west guiding some hunters, if he didn't get himself killed right here in town. Anyway, soon's we find out we're going home."

"To Tennessee?"

"No, ma'am. We live in New Mexico now, but we're fixing to move to Colorado and settle in the La Plata mountain country. Some of the boys are already there. Tyrel's in Santa Fe . . . unless he's on his way down here."

"*Here?*" Seemed to me there was anxiety in her voice, and I guess she was wondering how many she'd have to deal with.

"Yes, ma'am. Tyrel may come, too. He's the best of the lot at uncovering things. He's been a marshal in several towns out yonder. He's used to investigations."

We ordered some grub and talked of this and that for a while. It was early yet, and I had time to waste until that meeting with the Tinker. If he'd sent for me it meant he'd uncovered something, and it had to be something pretty positive or he wouldn't call me.

Fanny seemed anxious to leave Orrin out of it, and she chatted away, telling stories about the French Quarter, the old homes, and the plantations. "I'd love to show you ours," she told me. "It is a lovely old place, magnificent oaks with long Spanish moss trailing from them, flowers, green lawns . . . it is lovely!"

"I'll bet it is," I said, and meant it. There were some beautiful places around, and as for me, if I had to be in a city, there was no place I'd rather be in than New Orleans . . . if I had time on my hands. It had beauty and it had atmosphere, and as for the mean streets, well, they added color and excitement to the town.

"You mentioned Colorado," Fanny said. "Where do you plan to live?"

"Like I said, some of the boys have settled on the La Plata. That's pretty much down in the southwestern corner, just beyond the San Juans."

Well, I'm too old a fisherman not to know when I'd had a nibble, and I had one. Just what it was about her expression I don't know, but I knew she was interested when I mentioned the San Juans.

Now that's no little string of hills. There are fourteen peaks that go up fourteen thousand feet or more, and that's some of the most rugged country in the world. When it starts to snow back in there you either light a shuck and get out fast or you dig in for the winter.

"What is it like? I have never seen a mountain."

Well, I just looked at her, but I wasn't seeing her. I was seeing the La Plata River where it comes down from the mountain country, picking up little streams as it comes along, tumbling over the rocks, shaded by trees, chilled by the snow water, catching the color of the sky and the shadows of clouds. The stillness of beaver ponds, broken only by the widening V of a beaver swimming, mirroring the trunks of the aspen, catching the gold of the sun. Canyons quiet as the day after the earth was born, heights where the air was so clear the miles vanished and the faraway mountains of New Mexico showed themselves through the purple haze.

"Ma'am," I said, "I don't know what it is you are wishful for in this life, but you set down of a night and you pray to God that he'll let you walk alone across a mountain meadow when the wild flowers are blooming.

"You pray he'll let you set by a mountain stream with sunlight falling through the aspens, or that he'll let you ride across an above-timberline plateau with the strong bare peaks around you and the black thunderheads gathering around them—great, swelling rain clouds ready to turn the meadows into swamp in a minute or two . . . you let him show you those things, ma'am, and you'll never miss heaven if you don't make it.

"There's majesty in those peaks, ma'am, and grandeur in the clouds, and there's a far and wonderful beauty in the distance.

"Have you never looked upon distance, ma'am? Have you never pulled up your horse where your trail drops off into a black, deep canyon? Brimful with darkness and shadow? Or seen a deer pause on the edge of a meadow and lift its head to look at you? Standing there still as the trees around you to watch it? Have you never seen the trout leaping in a still mountain lake? Ma'am, I have, and before God . . . that's *country!*"

For a moment she sat still, looking at me. "You are a strange man, Tell Sackett, and I don't believe I should know you long."

She got up suddenly. "You would ruin me for what I want, and I'd ruin you because of what I am."

"No, ma'am, I would not ruin you for what you want because all those things you want don't amount to anything. They are just little bits of fluff and window dressing that you think will make you look better in the eyes of folks.

"You think maybe having a mite more money will build a wall around you to keep you from what's creeping up on you, but it won't. Out there where I come from, there's folks that want the same things you do and will go just as far to get them, but all of them wind up on the short end of the stick.

"As for me, ma'am, I wouldn't ruin as easy as you might think. There's nothing you could offer me that I'd swap for one afternoon ride through the hills, and I mean it. Once a man has lived with mountains you can't offer him a home with a prairie dog."

She walked away from me then and I stood and watched her go, a beautiful woman, beautifully gowned. Never did I see a woman walk away from me but I regretted it. I had no woman now. Ange was gone. We'd had something fine there, for a little while. As for Dorset—she'd gone off and I did not know if ever we'd meet again.

Sitting alone, I had another glass of wine and thought about what was to come.

I knew the Absinthe House. It was a popular place in New Orleans, and a lot of the young bloods did their drinking there, and their meeting of each other. It was on a busy corner where two people meeting would not be noticed much.

I paid my bill and went out into the quiet warmth of the street. There were many people there, strolling, talking, laughing. From the cafés and the dance-saloons there was music, but I walked down along the avenue, hearing little of the talk, pausing from time to time to check my back trail.

At the corner where the Absinthe House stood there were many people walking back and forth. I went into the café, glanced around at the crowd there and saw no familiar face. As I turned, a short, thickset man appeared close to my side. "This way, m'sieu." When we stepped around the corner, the Tinker was standing by a covered carriage.

We got in, the thickset man climbed to the driver's seat, and we rolled away.

"We have found him, I think. And there will be trouble."

"All right," I replied, "just let's get to him in time."

We turned into darker and darker streets. I recognized a sign here and there, and then at last we drew to a stop. I heard somebody singing from a shack close by, a lonely, sad-sounding song.

Leaving our cab we started down a dark alleyway. A cat sprang away from beneath our feet. Somebody threw a bottle from a window and it broke upon other bottles. We went up a few wooden steps to a small dock by the river.

All was still. No lights shone from this dock. From the neighboring dock, an open window cast a gleam of light upon the dark, swirling waters of the river.

A boat was tied there, bumping against the underpinning of the dock, and on the shore a man waited. A dark man in a striped shirt that fit tightly over powerful muscles.

By the sound of his French he was a Cajun. He led the way down to the boat, and then we pushed off. There were three other men in the boat. I balanced myself on a thwart amidships and watched them hoist the small brown sail. There was little wind, but we caught what there was and moved out on the dark water.

We were off to find Orrin. Please God, he'd be alive.

"Quietly," the Tinker said, "it must be done quietly. They have more friends close by than we."

"You have a blade?" the man in the striped shirt asked.

"I do," I said, and no further words were spoken as we moved out along the river.

The night was still and warm. My mouth felt dry, and I was uneasy in the boat. I was at home in a saddle, but not here. My hand went again to the knife.

Chapter 6

The wind died, lost in the surrounding trees and brush. The only sound was the chunk of the oar at the stern. The water shone a dull black. Overhead a few stars showed themselves faintly in the ribbon of sky the trees permitted us to see.

We passed several boats tied up along shore, all dark and still. Twice we passed cabins where lights still showed, and from one came drunken arguing and shouting. We moved on, ghostlike, along the bayou.

I wondered if Orrin would be alive. There was small chance of it, although the Tinker, who had access to much information, believed he was.

I shucked my coat, wishing I had left it behind, but there had been nowhere to leave it. A man did not appear coatless in the evening at the Saint Charles.

"Not much further," someone said, and I touched the haft of my knife.

Orrin lay bound in the darkness. Now and then a spider or a daddy longlegs crept over his face. His shirt was soaked with perspiration, even where it had been stiff with blood. He needed a drink desperately, but the men who held him prisoner could not care less about his comfort.

They believed he knew something, believed he was after gold. Not for one minute had they bought the idea that he was only looking for information about his father. Somehow, something he had said had blown the lid off. He had frightened them. He didn't doubt that they intended to kill him when they had their information, so he had stalled, watching for a break.

They did not know his strength or agility. They had no idea of his skill with weapons and he had done nothing to lead them to believe he was anything more than a lawyer, a deskman.

He hadn't been taken in by Fanny Baston. She was beautiful, but there was something else about her, some unhealthy air that disturbed him. He had been careful.

Every step of the way he had been sure that no one was behind him, that he was always ready. He had not suspected his drink . . . not so soon.

Actually, although wary of trouble, he had not expected it. They were fishing to see what he knew, of that he was sure, and he suspected that when they decided he knew nothing they would bid him good night and that would be the end of it.

From the first, he had known that his mention of Pierre frightened them. Obviously, something had happened on that western expedition that they did not wish known. That in itself was peculiar because jurisdiction would be hard if not impossible to establish, witnesses impossible to obtain.

From the idle talk over dinner, before things became serious, he had heard Philip mentioned several times. And Philip, he gathered, was well-off. Philip had also been close to Pierre. Whether they were blood brothers he had not grasped, but it was clear that there was a bond of affection between them.

The knockout drops were unexpected. All had been casual. Andre was at the table . . . so were Paul and Fanny.

The drug was in the coffee, which was strong enough to cover the taste, and within a few minutes after he drank the coffee he realized he was in trouble. But by that time his movements were slowed, his coordination affected. He tried to get up, but Andre contemptuously shoved him back into his chair. The last thing he remembered was their faces as they sat around watching him with casual disinterest, almost boredom, as he faded out.

Something was happening. A boat bumped against the side of the houseboat and men came aboard. There was low argument, orders, men running. Suddenly the door to the hatchway descending into the hold where he lay was opened. A lantern held high found him with eyes closed. The hatch closed again, and he heard the bar drop.

He could only guess what was happening. Either they were leaving here or they were expecting someone, and it appeared to be the latter.

In the bilge there was a little black, dirty water slopping about. Several hours before, Orrin had worked loose one of the boards, then another. He had been soaking the rawhide that bound his wrists in this water, and the rawhide was slowly stretching. Already he could detect some looseness . . . just a little more.

Now he hooked a slightly loosened cord over a nail projecting from where he had removed the board, and he began to tug.

Sweat broke out on his forehead and his body. The rawhide cut deeply into his wrists, but he continued to work and strain. Nothing happened, but the rawhide did seem a little looser. Again he lay listening, his bound wrists in the water.

He could hear rats rustling somewhere forward. So far they had not come near him. Given time, they would.

Above, all was still. How many men were aboard? There had been two, but now there must be at least four, and they were waiting . . . waiting in the darkness, armed and ready.

It had to be Tell, of course.

If anybody was coming to help it had to be his brother, for there was no one else. Tyrel was far away in New Mexico, and none of the others were anywhere around as far as he knew.

Rousing himself, he strained against the rawhide. Then he hooked it over the nail again and chafed it against the nailhead.

The minutes passed. He worked, strained, tugged against the nail, and soaked the rawhide. He tried to turn his wrists inside the thongs, and they turned, ever so slightly.

Something furry brushed near him and he made a violent movement of repulsion. The rat went scurrying. He hooked the thong over the nail again and jerked and tugged. Suddenly, something gave. The strain on his wrists slackened. He shook his wrists, twisted them, and the thongs came free.

He brought his hands around in front of him. His wrists were raw and bloody, the cuffs on his shirt were blood-stained. He opened and closed his hands—they worked.

Swiftly, he went to work on his ankles. Topside all was still . . . he must remember that. In this quiet they could hear any unusual movement. He had no weapon, but he stood up slowly, making a noose of the rawhide. The piece from his ankles was all of five feet long. He tucked it into his belt and picked up one of the loose boards.

Not heavy. About six feet long and one by four inches. Not what he would like, but useful.

He stretched his muscles and moved closer to the hatch. There was a door, then four steps to the deck. He moaned . . . then again.

There was a stir topside. He grunted, thumped the deck, and then he heard soft footsteps. He heard fumbling with the hasp on the outside of the door, then a low call. "Hurry, Jake! Here they come!"

The door opened and the man with the lantern leaned forward and extended the lantern, peering into the dark hold.

With all the force he could muster, Orrin smashed him in the face with the end of the board, driving it with two hands, like a lance.

The man screamed and toppled over backward, his lantern falling, breaking, and spilling kerosene all over the steps. Flames sprang up, but Orrin leaped over them and lunged up the steps.

Somebody out on the water yelled, "Back off! Back off!" There was the roar of a shotgun. Orrin lifted the fallen man from the deck, slammed him against the bulkhead, and ripped a gun and a knife from his belt. He knocked the man sprawling and ran for the rail.

A huge man rushed around the corner and Orrin struck out with his fist, the fist that gripped the knife. The blow was wild, but it connected solidly, and he cut back and down with the blade. He felt cloth tear, heard a grunt of pain. A teeth-rattling blow caught him on the side of the head.

Orrin staggered, swung again, and then, knife still in hand, went over the rail into the water. Meanwhile, he was conscious of several gunshots, and a second bellow of the shotgun.

He came up in the dark water, felt the smack of a bullet on the water near him, then went under, turning at right angles. But he had seen the boat, and he struck out for it, swimming strongly.

His head came above water, and he said, "Tell!" in a low but carrying voice.

Instantly, the boat turned toward him. He dove, coming up on the far side. He grasped the gunwale of the boat. He saw the mast, several men, and light reflected on gun barrels. In the houseboat beyond, flames were leaping from the hatch and they could see men running with buckets, trying to put out the fire.

"Tell?" he whispered again.

"Orrin, damn you, when you get in be careful where you set. I got a new suit-coat folded on that seat, yonder."

Hands helped him in, and then the oar began, sculling the boat further away on the dark water.

Orrin's head still buzzed with the blow he had received, and the raw flesh on his wrists was stinging with salt from the water.

"Anybody got anything to drink? I haven't had a swallow since morning time."

Somebody handed him a bottle. He drank. "Burgundy," he said, "but a poor year."

"What happened to you?" I said. "You've been missing for days."

Orrin chuckled, drank again, and said, "Well, you see there was this girl—"

"I met her."

"I'll bet. But did you ever see that house she lives in? All white, with pillars yet, and great big oaks all around, and lawns, and—"

"What happened?" I repeated.

"We had a nice drink, and then dinner. By that time I wanted to return to the hotel. We had coffee and when I came out of it I was on that houseboat yonder and they were asking me questions about Colorado—about something hidden there.

"What could I tell them? All we're looking for is pa, but they wouldn't believe that. They beat me around a little, but not near as much as you did a few times back home when we were tussling. They figured on using some red-hot irons next time, so I decided it was time I left."

He drank again. "I've heard of southern hospitality, but this is going too far."

A little breeze came in from the sea and we hoisted our sail. I picked up my coat and held it in my lap.

Setting there in the boat, I listened to the low rumble of talk between the men. Somebody had warned the men on the houseboat and they had been waiting for us. Only the scream of the man Orrin hit had warned us. As it was, they had shot too soon when we were still only a shadow on the water, and their old-fashioned guns had scattered shot too quickly.

Despite our precautions, we had been followed. Somebody had seen us leave, and they had brought word to the houseboat by some shorter route through the bayous. Had Orrin made his break an instant later we'd have been within sight and range, and some of us, perhaps all, would be feeding the fish and the 'gators.

"Tell," Orrin edged closer in the boat. "We've stirred up more than we know. There's been something lying quiet down here ever since pa disappeared, and we've upset the applecart."

"We'd better leave," I suggested. "It ain't worth getting killed over. Not just to find out what happened twenty years ago."

"Before we leave we'll make a call on Philip Baston. I think he could tell us something."

Well, we could do that, but I wanted to leave. New Orleans had always been a favorite town for me, but this time we just weren't likely to have much fun.

Yet what had happened those long years ago? And what did it have to do with us, and with pa? Somebody wanted to keep us from stirring muddy waters, but they also suspected we were here for some other purpose than hunting for pa.

Nobody was around when we tied our boat to the old dark wharf and came ashore. The Tinker and Tomas, the man in the striped shirt, walked along with us to the Saint Charles.

It was almost daybreak and there was nobody about, and I was just as pleased. Neither me nor Orrin looked like anybody you would expect to see at such an elegant hotel, but nobody saw us as we came in.

We'd slept maybe an hour when there was a discreet tapping on the door. It was Judas Priest.

"I've drawn a bath," he said, "and if you will, gentlemen, take no more time than you need. Meanwhile, I will brush and press your clothing."

"What's up?"

"The law," he said gently. "The law will wish to talk to you. I suggest you look and talk as innocently as possible. It is easier to get into prison here than to get out, and Andre Baston still has friends in town."

He took out his watch. "At best you have an hour. Probably less."

An hour later we were seated in the dining room, bathed, shaved, and combed. Our clothing was pressed, our manner calm. Each of us was reading a newspaper when the law came in.

Chapter 7

The man who approached our table was short, thickset, and dapper, but there was about him an air of competence, as Orrin said. He looked to me like a tough man to handle in a brawl.

He glanced at a paper in his hand. "Orrin and William T. Sackett?"

"That is correct, sir," Orrin said, folding his paper. "What can I do for you?"

"My name is Barres. I am a police officer."

Orrin smiled. "It is always a pleasure to meet another officer of the law."

Barres was surprised. "You're an officer?"

"An attorney, if you will. However, both my brother and myself have been marshals or deputy sheriffs out west."

"I was not aware of that. You are in town on business?"

"Legal business, actually." Orrin took a coffee cup from the next table and filled it from our coffeepot. "We are looking into the question of our father's death. It was some years ago, but there is an estate involved and we are doing our best to ascertain the facts."

"I see." Barres seemed to be searching for an approach. He looked at the cuts and bruises on Orrin's face. "What happened to you?"

"Let us put it this way, Mr. Barres, we do not intend to prefer charges unless charges are preferred against us."

Barres sipped some coffee. "There was some sort of a shooting on the river last night. Can you tell me anything about it?"

"Off the record, Mr. Barres, I was kidnapped, held in a houseboat on a bayou for several days, threatened often, and beaten several times. I escaped, and while I was escaping shots were fired."

"Could you identify any of those involved?"

"Certainly. I can identify almost all of them. And, if it comes to a matter of a trial, I can produce evidence as well as witnesses."

Barres was disturbed. He had come here under orders to make an inquiry and probably an arrest. Certain powers in the parish would prefer to have both Sacketts behind bars, and at once. They would also prefer to keep them there. Barres was not in favor of such tactics, but in the New Orleans of the seventies such things had been known to occur.

Furthermore, he had been told the Sacketts were a pair of thugs from Tennessee. For years most of the trouble along the river front had been caused by Kentucky or Tennessee boatmen, so arresting such men was quite in the usual order of business.

That they stayed at the Saint Charles was the first surprise, the second was their opulent appearance, the third that one of them was an attorney. Under the conditions, Barres being no fool, he chose to proceed cautiously.

"Might I ask where you make your home?"

"Santa Fe. Until recently I was a member of the legislature from New Mexico."

Worse and worse. Such men were not apt to be bluffing if they said they had evidence.

"Mr. Barres," Orrin suggested, "I came here to discover, if I could, who went west with my father. Almost at once I found difficulties arising that suggested to me that much more might be involved than simply locating the place of his death and burial.

"Now if this case goes to court it is going to create a scandal. It is going to cause considerable embarrassment to many people. We have one more call to make in New Orleans and then we expect to leave. To avoid trouble I suggest we be allowed to do just that.

"I have been in politics and I know that no political figure likes to be embarrassed or found supporting the wrong side. If such a thing occurs, he would have no kind thoughts about the officer who opened the whole Pandora's box."

"You're suggesting I drop the whole affair?"

"Yes. Within forty-eight hours we will be gone, and it is unlikely we will return to New Orleans for some time."

"Off the record, will you tell me about it?"

"Off the record, yes." Refilling his own cup, Orrin proceeded to outline the events of the past few days, beginning with his arrival in the city.

He named names, and he pulled no punches. "I suspect, Mr. Barres, that you are aware of the situation. These people are criminal of mind and intent; they are extremely dangerous because they believe themselves untouchable, but they are also amateurs.

"We wanted only information. We suspected nothing criminal. We wished to involve no one. All we wanted was the time of departure from

New Orleans and the probable destination. I suspect that information could have been given to us by any of the Baston family."

"And suppose I were to arrest you now? This minute?"

Orrin smiled pleasantly. "Mr. Barres, I am sure you have no such intention. I believe you to be an honest man and a capable one. You are also intelligent enough to know that I am prepared for that eventuality.

"Two letters have been mailed. One before the arrival of my brother, another since the events of last night. If we do not contact my brother Tyrel in Mora within the next few days, he will initiate an investigation at the highest state level."

Barres chuckled. "Well, you don't forget much, do you? Also, off the record, Mr. Sackett, Andre Baston is a scalp-hunter. He's got a bloody record. Dueling is an old custom here. Usually, a little blood is drawn and that's the end of it . . . but not with Andre. He kills. I think he likes to kill."

"I've met the kind."

"What I am saying is, be careful. He may try to pick a quarrel now."

Orrin smiled. "Mr. Barres, my folks were feudal stock. We youngsters cut our teeth on gun butts. Tyrel and me, we crossed the plains in '66 and '67. If Andre Baston wants a fight, he has come to the right place to get it."

Barres shrugged. As I set there watching and listening, I knew that he, like many another man, was fooled by Orrin's easy-going manner. Orrin was an agreeable man, hard to annoy or offend, but hell on wheels in action.

"And the one man you wish to see?"

"Philip Baston. You may come with us, if you like."

"Me?" Barres was startled. "Mr. Sackett, you just don't understand. The only way I could get into Philip Baston's house is through the servants' entrance. If we had to arrest him for murder it would have to be done by the chief himself, along with the chief prosecuting officer. Philip Baston owns half a dozen sugar plantations, at least four ships sailing out of New Orleans, and a lot of buildings here in town. He's worth millions, but he's a gentleman, sir, a gentleman.

"He rarely leaves his home except to visit with an old friend or two or to supervise his properties. He contributes to charity, and he's ready to help with anything for the betterment of the city." Barres paused. "You may have trouble getting to see him."

After Barres took his leave, we finished our breakfast. It was nearly midday, and I couldn't recall a time in my life when I was still setting about the table at such an hour. Orrin, he done a part of his work that way, and usually had a book propped alongside him. Me, I was out yonder with a rope and a saddle and a bronc.

"Speaking of duels," Orrin said, "as the challenged party I would have the choice of weapons. A few years ago there was a member of the legislature down here who was seven feet tall—he'd been a blacksmith or something. He was challenged by a famous duelist who was much shorter. The big man did not want to fight, thought it useless, so he accepted the challenge and suggested sledgehammers, in six feet of water."

"What happened?"

"It amused the duelist so much he withdrew his challenge and the two became friends."

A carriage took us up the circular drive to the door. The house was a story and a half in height with six Doric columns across the front, the windows barred with wrought iron. Stretching out in front of the house as far as the bayou was a lawn scattered with huge old oaks trailing Spanish moss.

There were azaleas and camellias wherever we looked. It was a right fine place, and old.

Orrin sent in his card and we waited, seated in highbacked chairs the like of which I'd never seen. For my taste, there was kind of too much furniture in the room, me being used to Spanish ranch-house styles which were spacious, cool.

We waited a few moments and then Philip Baston came in. He was a tall man, although not as tall as Orrin or me, and slender. He glanced at both of us. "I am Philip Baston. You wished to see me?"

"Sir," Orrin spoke quietly, "we do not wish to take more of your time than need be, although I confess there's a restfulness in this house that makes me wish to prolong my stay.

"My brother, William Tell Sackett, and I are trying to locate our father's grave. We understand he left here with your brother-in-law, Pierre Bontemps, and we thought you might be able to provide us with the date and destination."

Philip Baston considered that, and then said briefly, "Your father was known to Pierre through an acquaintance who was killed. It was known that your father was familiar with the San Juan Mountains in Colorado, and Pierre asked him to act as a guide and to share in the results, if any.

"They left here twenty years ago, almost to the day. My brother-in-law and I were very close, gentlemen, closer I might add, than I and my brother. He wrote to me from Natchez, and another letter came from the mouth of the Arkansas.

"I believe they went up the Arkansas from there to Webber's Falls, but that is pure guesswork. From there it was overland, but at that point they were together."

"Pierre Bontemps, my father, and—"

Philip Baston hesitated, and then said, "There were four more at the time. My brother Andre, then a very young man, a man named Pettigrew, and another named Swan."

"*Hippo* Swan?" I asked.

Baston glanced at me. "Do you know the man?"

"He was pointed out to me."

He seemed about to say something further, then turned back to Orrin. "There was one other . . . a slave."

"His name?"

Again there was a moment of hesitation. "Priest. Angus Priest."

Orrin got to his feet. "One thing more, sir, and then we shall be on our way. What were they after?"

Baston looked disgusted. "They were hunting gold buried by a French army detachment that mined it earlier. Supposedly this detachment was sent in there around 1790, and I believe there is some record of it.

"The reports vary, of course, but the consensus is that they dug some five million dollars in gold. The figure increases with each retelling of the story. I think Pierre and Andre believed the figure was closer to thirty million. In any event, from one cause or another the strength of the detachment was cut until a final Indian attack left only five of them to escape.

"Pierre had a map. Your father told him he could take him to the location. So they started out."

"Thanks very much." Orrin thrust out his hand, and Philip took it. If he knew anything of our difficulties with his brother, he said nothing about it.

In the carriage we set quiet for a time, and then I said, "The gold could be there. There was many a place, them years, where a party of men could mine that much."

"Do you know the country?"

"Uh-huh. No city man's goin' to find anything up there, Orrin. That's almighty rough country, and she's high up. You've got a few months each year when a body can work, and then you have to hightail it out of there or get snowed in.

"Landmarks don't last in that high country, Orrin. There's heavy snow, wind, lightnin', an' rain. There's snowslides, landslides, and the passage of men and animals. Only the rocks last . . . for a while."

"What do you think about pa?"

"I think he took 'em to the hills. I think he took 'em high up yonder, and I think there was blood, Orrin. Andre and them, they're runnin' scared. Something happened only Andre knows of and the rest suspect."

"What could they be afraid of now? Us?"

"No, sir. Of Philip yonder. That's a fine, proud old man, and he has money. I think the rest of them hope to inherit, but likely he doesn't approve of them, and if he found some cause to suspect what happened to Pierre, well, they'd have nothing."

"I think they have some notion of going for the gold."

"Likely."

"What do you think we should do?"

"I think we should catch ourselves a steamer, Orrin, and go back upriver hunting folks with long memories. There's always one, a-settin' by somewheres who'll recall. We want a man who can recall."

"Tomorrow?"

"I reckon. First, though, I've got a little something to do. I'm going to have a little quiet talk with a priest."

Chapter 8

We packed our gear in the morning, and we booked our passage north, and as much as I liked that wonderful, colorful town, I was ready to hit for the high country again. I wanted to see the wide plains with the mountains in the purple haze yonder, and I wanted to feel a good horse under me and ride out where the long wind bends the grass.

First I had to talk to a priest—a Judas Priest. And he was nowhere in sight, nor to be found wherever I looked. He'd quit his hotel job. They spoke well of him, although they looked at me strangely when I asked after him, and they commented that he was an odd one.

"What do you mean—odd?" Orrin asked.

The man just shrugged and would say nothing, but I wasn't going to leave it at that, so I caught up with another porter I'd seen around and I took out a couple of silver dollars, tossed them and ketched them.

When I asked my question he looked at me and at those dollars. "He took to you, mister. He done tol' me so. He thought there was a charm on you. He thought you walked well with the spirits, mister. He said you follered the right, and the evil would never come to you."

"Where will I find him?"

"If'n he wishes to be found, he'll find you. Don't you look, mister. He's voodoo, he is. Pow'ful strong voodoo."

Well, no matter what he was, I wanted to talk with him. The slave who had gone west with Pierre Bontemps had been named Angus Priest, and I had a hunch there was more than one reason behind the help Judas had provided.

We saw nothing of Andre Baston, nor of the others. I had an urge to go hunting Hippo Swan, but I fought it down. We'd promised Barres we'd leave and take the ache from his thoughts, so we done it, but I left not thinking kindly of Hippo.

The river was a busy place them days. We took a stateroom called the Texas, the highest point on a riverboat except the pilothouse. It was said along the river that Shreve, for whom Shreveport was named, had named cabins for the various states, and ever after they were called staterooms.

Now I've no knowledge of the language or anything. I'm a fair hand with a rope and a horse, with some know-how about cattle and reading sign, but words kind of interest me, and many a time I've covered miles out yonder where there's nothing but grass and sky, just figuring on how words came to be. Like Dixie Land. For a time they issued a ten-dollar note down there in New Orleans that had a *ten* on one side and a *dix*— French for ten—on the other. Folks began calling them *dixies*, and the word somehow got to mean the place they were used—Dixie Land.

At the last minute the Tinker showed up and wanted to go along with us, so the three of us headed north for the Arkansas. The Tinker showed for dinner in a perfectly tailored black suit, looking almighty elegant like some foreign prince, which among his own folks he probably was.

We set up to table, hungry as all get-out. We were giving study to the card on which they'd printed what grub was available when a soft voice said, "Something from the bar, gentlemen?" It was Judas Priest.

"I have been wanting to talk to you," I said.

He smiled with sly amusement. "Ah? Of course. I shall be available later." He paused a moment. "If you gentlemen do not object, and could use some good cooking on your way west, I would be pleased to accompany you."

"Can you ride?"

He smiled again. "Yes, suh. I can ride. And to answer your question, suh," he looked at me, "I look for a grave as well as you. I also look for the reason why there needs to be a grave."

"Come along, then," Orrin replied. "And we'll take you up on the cooking."

It was midnight, a few days later, when we transferred from our upriver steamer to the smaller steamer that would take us up the Arkansas. Judas, in his mysterious way, had transferred too, refusing any assistance from us.

Orrin went to his cabin, and I loitered on deck, watching the lights of the big steamer as it pulled away, churning the water to foam as it made the turn. In the waves thrown up by the paddle wheels there was a boat, a small boat that seemed to have appeared from the other side of the steamer. I watched it idly, but it was dark after the steamer's lights and I could make out nothing. A little later I heard the dip and splash of oars. The boat was pulling in alongside a keelboat moored below us.

It seemed to me that two men, perhaps three, left the boat. I was tired now, and walked slowly forward to our cabin.

The Tinker moved from the shadow of some barrels. "Did you see that boat?"

"Yes."

"Somebody could have gotten off on the river side."

"You're a suspicious man, Tinker."

"I am a living man, my friend."

We stood together in the darkness watching the water as our small steamer got underway. If we did not get aground too often we'd soon be riding out for Colorado. Yet river travel was a chancy thing, subject to sudden lows or highs along the river, unexpected sand bars, snags, and all drifting matter. A pilot had to be a bit of a magician to do it well, and navigating these branches of the Big River was doubly difficult. Nor did they dare to go too far upstream for they might suddenly be left high and dry as a sudden flood played out.

"Your pa, now. You never heard anything after New Orleans?" said the Tinker.

"We never heard from him from there that I recall, but my memory is hazy, and it wasn't long after that before I took off to make my way in the world. Then the war came along and blotted a lot of memories for us who fought."

We were silent for a while, listening to the river whispering along the hull. There was a light on that keelboat downstream now.

"When somebody is around home there's talk, and the talk awakens memories, so a body has many a thing fresh in mind that otherwise might fade out.

"There are sons and daughters of the same folks who have altogether different memories, and each one thinks he remembers better. The last one at home, of course, has had his memories renewed by talk. I suspect Orrin or Tyrel would recall better than me. Especially Tyrel. He never forgets anything."

"Your pa may have been murdered."

"Maybe."

"I don't like the feel of it, Tell. There's something that doesn't feel right about it," he said.

"Could be Andre took off and left them in a bind—pulled out—and he's shamed Philip may find out and cut them off. From all I could gather, Andre, Paul, and Fanny have gone through everything they have. They're in a tight for cash, and they've got to set right with Philip or go to work."

"There's more to it," said Tinker and went in to the cabin.

There was some stirring around on the keelboat aft of us. I didn't pay it much mind, only to notice.

The river rustled by our hull. The deck below was piled high with cargo. I'd seen these riverboats so piled with bales of cotton that folks in the cabins had to live by candlelight even at midday. That water down there had melted from high-mountain snows not long since. It had trickled down, pure and cold from up where the glaciers still live, where the rivers are born.

Soon I'd be riding where that water came from. Here it was muddy with earth, with death and plants and bugs, and with whatever man left in it. Far up there where the snows were the water was pure and cold.

No getting away from it, I was wilderness born and bred and never was I wishful to be far from it. I like to bed down where a man can look up at the stars, where he can taste the wind to test the weather, and where he can watch the wild things about their business.

When a man lives with the wilderness he comes to an acceptance of death as a part of living, he sees the leaves fall and rot away to build the soil for other trees and plants to be born. The leaves gather strength from sun and rain, gathering the capital on which they live to return it to the soil when they die. Only for a time have they borrowed their life from the sum of things, using their small portion of sun, earth, and rain, some of the chemicals that go into their being—all to be paid back when death comes. All to be used again and again.

Feet rustled on the deck behind me, a swift movement, and on instinct I squatted quickly, turned and lifted with all the thrust of my legs into an upward drive. I felt legs across my back and shoulders, then the weight slid off me and over the rail into the water.

He'd been wet before he fell, which meant that he probably swam over, crawled up on the deck, and came at me from behind with a knife or a club. He'd jumped at me, and when I dropped he just carried right on over, helped a mite by my boost.

He went down a long way because we were a far piece above the water, and when he came up I called down, "How's the water there, son?"

He made reply, but it sounded almighty unpleasant, so I just turned about and went to our cabin. Orrin was asleep, and so was the Tinker.

I shucked my coat and boots, took my gun close to hand, and peeled to my long-johns. I stretched out on the bunk and looked up into the blackness. It was going to be all right. I was headed back for the mountains . . .

When the little steamer tied up at Webber's Falls, we were the first ones down the gangplank. "They're in town," I told Orrin and the Tinker. "Walk easy and keep your eyes open. You boys get us some grub and supplies at the store. I'll wait for Judas and then try to find some horses."

When Judas came off the boat I told him to meet us at the store later and to watch himself.

There was a livery stable and a corral down the street. Strolling along, I stopped and leaned on the rails. A man with a straw hat and bib overalls came over to me. "Nice stock," he commented.

There were a dozen horses in the corral; all but two would be useless to us. Two were farm animals, the rest Indian ponies. The other horses, the two I fancied above the rest, were still not what I wanted.

"Not for me," I shook my head. "Isn't there anything better around?"

"Well," he said, "there's a man with a ranch the other side of town. His name is Halloran, Doc Halloran. He buys cattle, sells them, buys horses, races them. He's got fine stock but he ain't in the trading business."

He hired me a rig and I stopped by the store. When I explained what I was about, the Tinker said, "Doc Halloran, you say? I'll go along."

Orrin was still buying, so we drove off.

It was an interesting place. A log house of five or six rooms, a handsome big barn, corrals, a well, some hay meadows, and a green lawn in front of the house.

A tall, lean man came from the house as we drove up. A couple of Indian cowhands were at the corral.

I started to speak, but the tall man was looking past me at the Tinker. A broad smile broke over his face. "Tinker! Well, I'll be forever damned!"

"I hope not, Doc. Good to see you. This is Tell Sackett."

"Where's Lando? Is he still fighting?" He turned to me. "Are you kin to Lando? He won me more money than I ever won anywhere else. Fight? That's the fightin'est man who ever walked."

"He's my cousin," I said. "We Sacketts run to boys and fighting."

"Come in! Come in! By the lord harry, this is great! Tinker, I've often wondered what became of you. Figured you must have gone back to pack-peddling in the mountains. What brings you to the Falls?"

"Headed west," I said, "and we heard you had some horses that weren't for sale. We also heard they were the best stock anywhere around."

"How many d'you need?"

"Three packhorses, four head of riding stock, and we want stayers."

"I've got what you need. A few years back, just after I moved up here from Oakville where I met Lando an' the Tinker, I swapped for an appaloosa stallion. A half-breed Injun from up Idaho way rode him into town. On the dodge, I reckon.

"Well, I bred that appaloosa to some Morgan mares I had here, and wait until you see 'em!" He stopped suddenly, looking from one to the other. "You boys ain't runnin' from something, are you?"

"No. Kind of scouting my father's trail," I explained. "Is there anybody around who was here twenty years ago? Somebody who might have outfitted another party with horses?"

"More than likely they outfitted at Fort Gibson, right up the line. Those days nobody stopped here very much. This place was started by a part-blood Creek who came in here a good many years back. He took over the saltworks up the stream. Did right well. But anybody outfitting for the western ride would go to Fort Gibson."

We finished our coffee and got up. "Let's see those horses," I suggested. "We've got to get back to town. Orrin will be waiting."

There were three of them, sixteen hands, beautifully built, and in fine shape. One was a gray with a splash of white with black spots on the right shoulder, and a few spots freckled over the hips, black amidst the gray. The other horses were both black with splashes of white on the hips and the usual spots of the appaloosa.

"We'll take them. How about packhorses?"

"There," he indicated a dun, a pinto, and a buckskin. "They're good stock themselves, mustang cross."

"How much?"

He laughed. "Take 'em and forget it. Look, when Lando Sackett whupped Dunc Caffrey down to Oakville I went down for all I had, and with my winnings I bought this place and my stock. I built it up and I still have money in the bank.

"Take 'em along, an' welcome. Only thing is, if Lando fights again, you write me. I'll come a-runnin'."

"Thanks," I said, "but—"

"No buts." Doc Halloran shook his head at me. "Forget it.

"Reason I asked was you on the dodge," he said, "because three hard cases drifted in a few days ago. They've been sort of hangin' around as if on the lookout for somebody."

The Tinker looked at me, and me at him. Then we sprinted for the buckboard.

Chapter 9

Orrin didn't make it sound like much when he told us of it after. He was in that there store, and it was like most country stores, smelling of everything that was in it—good, rich, wonderful smells of new leather, fresh-ground coffee, cured hams and bacon, spices, and the like.

He knew where we were going and how we'd have to live. We'd have fresh meat from the country around us, and we'd have what we could gather in the way of roots and such, only that wouldn't amount to much unless we happened on it.

A man traveling doesn't have much time for stopping off to look or pick, so Orrin was buying sides of bacon, flour, meal, coffee, dried fruit, and whatever figured to be handy.

He also was buying some .44's for our Winchesters and pistols, and the man who owned the store took down a spanking new Smith and Wesson .44 and was showing it to Orrin.

Orrin had just put it down when those hard cases walked in. Now they weren't from the western lands, they were river men, mean as all get-out, but they didn't know Orrin. They'd been told they were to kill a lawyer . . . now there's lawyers and there's lawyers.

Just like there was a dentist named Doc Holiday.

They came in the store at the front, and Orrin was back yonder at the counter. He must have turned to look, as he would, but likely he was expecting the Tinker an' me.

Now those three spread out a little after they got through the door, and they were all looking at him. It was three to one, and Orrin spoke to the storekeeper out of the corner of his mouth. "You better get out. This appears to be a shooting matter."

"You know those men?"

"No, but they look like they're hunting."

One of them, who wore a tall beaver hat, noticed the gun on the counter. He had his in his hand. He smiled past some broken, yellowed teeth and a straggly mustache.

"There it is, mister lawyer. You better try for it."

Now that gun was brand new and empty. Orrin knew that, even if they didn't. He could also see these were river men, and while there'd been a sight of shooting and killing along the Mississippi, very little of it was based on fast drawing.

"If I reached for that gun, you'd kill me."

The man with the beaver hat gave him a wolfish grin. "I reckon."

"But if I don't reach for it, you'll kill me anyway?"

"I reckon we'll do that, too." He was enjoying himself.

"Then I haven't much choice, have I?"

"Nope. You sure ain't."

The other two men were shifting, one to get far over on his left side. One of them was momentarily behind some bib overalls hung from a rafter.

"But if I don't want to reach for that gun, how about this?"

As Orrin spoke, he drew and fired.

Reaction time was important. The three would-be killers were sure that he was frightened, that being a lawyer he would not be a gunfighter, and that if he reached it would be for the gun on the counter.

Orrin had always been quick. And he was a dead shot. He fired and turned sharply to bring the second man in line, when there was the bellow of a shotgun behind him. The man farthest right cried out and ran for the door. He blundered into the doorpost and then almost fell through the screen door in getting out, a growing circle of blood on his back and shoulder.

The third man, who had been moving toward the left, dropped his gun and lifted his hands. "Don't shoot! For God's sake, *don't shoot!*"

Orrin held his gun ready. "All right," he said quietly, "move toward the door. Your friend out there may need some help."

The man gestured toward the one with the beaver hat, who had a blue hole between his eyes. "What about him?"

"Take him out and bury him. Then if you want to kill somebody, go get the man who set you up for this."

"They said you was a lawyer!"

"I am. But out where I come from every butcher, baker, and candlestick maker has used a gun. Besides, haven't you ever heard of Temple Houston? He is old Sam Houston's boy, and a lawyer, too, but a dead shot. It doesn't pay to take anything for granted."

The man left, and Orrin turned to the storekeeper. "Thanks, friend. Thanks, indeed."

The old man was brusque. "Don't thank me, young man. I can't have folks comin' in here shootin' at my customers. It's bad for business."

That was the way it set when our buckboard came a-hellin' down the street from Doc Halloran's place. We saw a man lyin' bloody on the boardwalk and another kneelin' by him.

The Tinker and me unlimbered from that buckboard and the kneeling man looked up. "Don't go in there, fellers. That lawyer in there's hell on wheels."

"It'll be all right," I said. "I'm his brother."

"Who put you up to it?" the Tinker asked.

"A couple of dudes. We was to get fifty dollars a piece for you two. That's a sight of money, mister."

Orrin came through the door. "How much is it to your dead friend in-side?" he asked.

The man stared from him to me.

"What about those dudes who hired you?" I said. "Two young men?"

"No, sir. A young man and a woman. Looked to be brother and sister."

"In New Orleans?"

"No, sir. In Natchez-under-the-Hill."

Orrin looked at me. "They are following us, then."

The man looked up. "Mister, would you help me get this man to a doctor?"

A bystander said, "We've no doctor here. The storekeeper usually fixes folks up when they're hurt."

"Him?" The man on his knees looked bleak. "He already done fixed him once."

Orrin spoke more quietly. "My friend, I am sorry for you. You were just in the wrong line of work, but if you'll take a closer look, your friend has just run out of time."

And it was so. The man on the ground was dead.

Slowly, the man got up. He wiped his palms on his pants. He was young, not more than twenty-two, but at the moment he was drawn and old. "What happens now? Does the law want me?"

Someone standing there said, "You just leave town, mister. We don't have any law here. Just a graveyard."

Judas came along when the shooting was all over, and we stayed the night at Halloran's. In the morning, once more in the saddle, we started west.

Four of us riding west, two from Tennessee, a gypsy, and a black man, under the same sun, feeling the same wind. We rode through Indian territory, avoiding villages, avoiding the occasional cattle herds, wanting only to move west toward the mountains.

We cut over the Rabbit Ear Creek country toward Fort Arbuckle. This was Creek Indian country. The land was mostly grass with some patches of timber here and there, mostly blackjack of white oak with redbud growing in thick clumps along the creeks.

We had grub enough, so we fought shy of folks, watched our back trail, and moved along about thirty miles or so each day. Arbuckle had been deserted by the army, but there were a few Indians camped there, trading horses and such. They were a mixed lot, Seminoles, Choctaws, and Creeks mostly, with a few Pottawattomies. We bought some coffee from them, and I traded for a beaded hunting shirt tanned almost white, a beautiful job.

"Be careful," a Creek warned us, "the Comanches have been raiding south and west of here. They ran off some horses only a few miles west."

Glancing around at Judas, I asked, "Can you shoot?"

"I can, suh."

Well, that was enough for me. He was no spring chicken but the first time I seen him top off a bronc I knew he'd been there before. He told me he could ride and he could, so when he told me he could shoot, I believed him.

As we rode out of Arbuckle and headed west up the Washita, I dropped back beside him. "Do you know any more about what happened than we do?"

"I doubt it, suh. Angus was slave to Mr. Pierre. Angus liked him, and Mr. Pierre was both a gentleman and a kind man. Angus was of an adventurous spirit, suh. He was a fine hunter and a man who liked the wilderness."

"Did you talk to him after plans were made to go west?"

"Once, only. He had met Mr. Sackett, your father, and liked him. Your father had very kindly advised him as to what he might encounter, the best clothing, and as to caution in all things.

"May I also say, suh, that he did not like Mr. Swan, and none of us cared for Andre Baston. Do not mistake it, suh, Mr. Baston is a very dangerous man."

We saw occasional antelope, and twice we encountered small herds of buffalo, but we did not hunt. This was Indian country and for the moment we did not need meat. We neither wanted to shoot their game, for this was on land allotted to them, nor to attract attention to us from wild Indians.

Several times we cut their sign. Comanches . . . at least a dozen riding together.

"Raiders," Orrin said, and I agreed. Only warriors, no women, no travois.

This was all Indian country, about half wild and half friendly, and the friendly Indians suffered as much from the wild ones as the white men would. It was the old story of nomadic peoples raiding the settlements, and it has happened the world over.

Our camps at night were hidden, meals hastily prepared, and the fires kept to coals or to nothing at all. Judas proved an excellent camp cook, which pleased me. I could cook but didn't favor it much, and Orrin was no better than me. As for the Tinker, he kept silent on the subject.

We were coming up to the site of old Fort Cobb when Orrin, who was riding point, suddenly pulled up. A horse nickered, and then a dozen Indians rode over the crest of the hill.

Sighting us they pulled up sharp, but I held my hand up, palm out, as a signal we were peaceful, and they rode up.

They were Cheyennes, and they had been hunting along Cache Creek. By the look of things they had been successful, for they were loaded down with meat.

They warned us of a war party of Kiowas over west and south and swapped some meat with us for some sugar. We sat our horses and watched them go, and I suggested we swing north.

For the next few days we switched directions four or five times, riding north to Pond Creek, following it for a day or so, then a little south to confuse anybody following us, and finally north toward the Antelope Hills and the Texas Panhandle.

This was open grass country with a few trees along the water courses, but little enough timber even there. We picked up fuel where we could find it during the day, and at night gathered buffalo chips. We were heading into empty country where there would be almost no water.

We came suddenly upon a group of some twenty horses, all unshod, traveling northwest by north. I pulled rein.

"Indians," I said.

The Tinker glanced at me. "Might they not be wild horses?"

"Uh-uh. If they were wild horses, you'd find a pile of dung, but you see it's scattered along and that means the Indians kept their horses in motion.

"The tracks are two days old," I added, "and were made early in the morning."

The Tinker was amused, but curious too. "How do you figure that?"

"Look," I said, "there's sand stuck to those blades of grass that were packed down by the horses' hooves—over there, too. See? There hasn't been any dew for the past two mornings, but three days ago there was a heavy dew. That's when they passed by here."

"Then we don't have to worry," he suggested.

I chuckled. "Suppose we meet them coming back?"

We rode on, holding to shallow ground when we could find it. We were now coming into an area that undoubtedly has some of the flattest land on earth—land cut by several major canyons. However, those canyons were, I believed, much to the south of us.

I was pretty sure we were following much the same route pa would have taken in coming west. We'd switched around here and there, but nonetheless I believed our general route to be the one he would have followed twenty years before.

Their needs for water and fuel would have been the same as ours, and their fears of Indians even greater since this had been entirely Indian country in their time. The times when I'd traveled wilderness country with pa had been few, mostly in the mountains, when I was a very young boy. Yet I knew how his thinking went, for he had given us much of our early education, either by the fireside or out in the hills. He was a thinking man, and he had little enough to leave us aside from the almost uncanny knowledge of wilderness living that he had picked up over the years.

No man likes to think of all he has learned going up like the smoke of a fire, to be lost in the vastness of sky and cloud. Pa wanted to share it with us, to give us what he learned, and I listened well, them days, and I learned a sight more than I guessed.

So when we saw that knoll with the flat rocks atop it and the creek with trees growing along it, I said to Orrin, "About there, Orrin. I'd say about there."

"I'll bet," he agreed.

"What is it?" Judas inquired.

"That's the sort of place pa would camp, an' if I ain't mistaken, that there's McClellan Creek."

Chapter 10

We spurred our horses and loped on up to the edge of a valley maybe a mile wide. There were large cottonwoods along the banks of a mighty pretty stream that was about twenty feet wide but no more than six inches deep.

The water was clear and pure, coming down from the Staked Plain that loomed above and to the west of us. None of us relished that ride, but we had it to do.

"Marcy named this stream after McClellan," Orrin said. "He believed McClellan was the first white man to see it. Marcy was exploring the headwaters of the Red and the Canadian rivers on that trip."

"We'll camp," I said.

We scouted the stream for the best location for a camp and found it at a place where a huge old cottonwood had toppled to the ground. The upper branches and some leaves that still clung to them were in the water, but the trunk of the tree made a good break from the wind, and the other cottonwoods shaded the place. There was a kind of natural corral where we could bunch the horses.

First we staked them out to graze. The Tinker set watch over them whilst Judas whipped up the grub.

Orrin and me, we nosed around.

The way we figured, we were right on pa's old trail, and we were wishful of looking about to see if he left sign. Now all men have their patterns of using tools, making camp, and the like. Time had swept away most things a man might leave behind, and this was a country of cold and heat with hard winds and strong rains coming along all too often.

This was likely a camp where they'd spend time. A long trek was behind them, the Staked Plain before them, and they knew what that meant.

It was a snug camp. When the horses had grazed enough on the bottom grass, the Tinker brought them in and we settled them down in the corral.

A man riding wild country keeps his eyes open for camping places. He may not need one at that spot on the way out, but it might be just what the doctor ordered on the way back. Camps, fuel, defensive positions, water, landmarks, travel-sign . . . a man never stops looking.

We'd traveled steady, if not fast, and we'd lost time here and there trying to leave nothing an Indian would care to follow, yet I was uneasy. Too many attempts had been made to do away with us, and it wasn't likely we'd gotten off scot-free.

Leaving camp, I wandered off upstream toward where the creek came down from under the cap rock. It was good sweet water and there wasn't much of that hereabouts, for most of the streams were carrying gypsum, or salts, or something of the kind.

Andre Baston had evidently been with the party when it reached here, so he would know of this water and would come to it. How many he would have with him I wouldn't be able to guess, but he would pick up some hard cases along the way and he'd be prepared for trouble.

The feel of the country isn't right, and something inside tells me, warns me. What is it? Instinct? But what is instinct? Is it the accumulation of everything I've ever seen or smelled tickling a little place in my memory?

This is the kind of place I like. It is one of those lonely, lovely places you have to go through hell to reach. Many a man's home is just that, I expect.

Thin water running over sand—water so clear the whole bottom is revealed to you, and even a track left an hour ago may still be there . . . like *that* one.

The track of a horse, and beyond it another. I waded the stream, following them.

A slight smudge of a hoof on the grassy bank, tracks going away toward the cliffs. I was careful not to let my eyes look that way, but turned and strolled casually along the stream bank for thirty or forty yards, and then I walked back to camp.

I stopped twice on the way back. Once to pick up some sticks for fuel, another time to look at a place where a rabbit had been sleeping. At camp I dropped the fuel.

Orrin had gone off downstream, and I had to get him back.

"Tracks," I told them. "Get your rifles and keep a careful eye open all around. That was a shod horse, so they're here—or somebody is."

"How old was that track?" the Tinker wondered.

"Hour—maybe more. That water's not running so fast. It isn't carrying much silt, so it's hard to say. A track like that will lose its shape pretty fast, so I'd surmise not over an hour, and we've been here about half that time—maybe more.

"My guess would be they've seen us coming and they figured we wouldn't pass up a good camp spot like this. I think they are out there now . . . waiting."

I took my Winchester, and I shoved two handfuls of shells into my pockets. I was already wearing a cartridge belt, every loop loaded.

"Take nothing for granted. They may wait until night and they may come just any time." Thinking about it, I said, "Make out to be collecting fuel, but sort of pick up around. Get everything packed except grub and the frying pan. We may move suddenlike."

The brush was thicker downstream, and there were more cottonwoods and willows. A few paths ran away through the brush—deer, buffalo, and whatnot. Moving out, I hung my Winchester over my shoulder by its sling, just hanging muzzle down from my left shoulder, my left hand holding the barrel. A lift of the left hand, the muzzle goes up, the butt comes down, and the right hand grabs the trigger guard. With practice, a man can get a rifle into action as quickly as a six-gun.

Thick blackberry brush, some willows, and some really big cottonwoods. Orrin's tracks were there, and then Orrin.

He turned when he saw me coming. "Whatever happened, must have happened *there*—in the mountains, I mean, or on the way back."

"You think they found the gold?"

"Found it, or sign of it," he said. "Maybe it was late in the season before they located anything, and all of a sudden Andre or Pierre or somebody suddenly got the idea they should have it all."

"Andre got back, and Hippo Swan. They must have been the youngsters of the group."

Quietly then, I told him of the horse tracks and my feeling about them. We started back toward camp, taking our time and returning by a somewhat different route. We were only a few hundred yards downstream, but I'd caught no pattern to Andre's thinking, so I'd no way of knowing how he might choose to attack.

He was a fighting man, that much I knew, and I gathered that he'd not step back from murder. He didn't strike me as a man of honor, and from what I'd heard of his dueling and of his approach to LaCroix, I figured him to be a man to take any advantage.

"Orrin, there's no use in setting by an' lettin' him choose his time. Besides, we're lookin' to find what happened to pa, not to have a shootout with Andre Baston."

"What are you suggesting?"

"That come nightfall we Injun out of here, back south for the Red, follow it right up the canyon as far as we can go, then take off across the Staked Plains for Tucumcari or somewhere yonder."

We left our fire burning where the grass wouldn't catch, and we Injuned out of there, holding to the brush until it was fairly dark, then heading off to the south. For four mounted men with packhorses we moved fast and light and made mighty little sound.

By sunup we were twenty miles off, following along the route McClellan had taken in 1852. We camped, rested an hour or two, then turned west across the plains toward the canyon of the Red.

Finally the sandy bottom of the stream played out and the water was sweet where it ran over rock. The last tributaries must have been bringing the gypsum into the water.

We found a trail where a steep climb and a scramble would get us out of the canyon and we took off across country. I knew about where Tucumcari Mountain lay, a good landmark for old Fort Bascom. Twice we made dry camp, and once we found a spring. We stopped again when we met a sheepman who provided us with tortillas and frijoles. Our horses were taking a beating, so when we spotted a herd of horses and some smoke, we came down off the mesa and cut across the desert toward them.

Orrin eased his horse closer to mine. "I don't like the look of it," he said. "That's no ordinary bunch of stock."

We slowed down to come up to the herd at a walk. We saw four men: three hard-looking white men and a Mexican with twin bandoliers loaded with rifle cartridges. They were set up as if for a fight.

"Howdy!" I said affably. "You got any water?"

The sandy-haired white man jerked his head toward some brush. "There's a seep." He was looking at our horses. Hard-ridden as they were, they still showed their quality. "Want to swap horses?"

"No," Orrin said, "just a drink and we'll drift."

As we rode by I glanced at the brands, something any stockman will do as naturally as clearing his throat. At the seep I swung my horse, facing them, "Orrin, you an' the Tinker drink. I don't like this outfit."

"See those brands?" he said. "That's all full-grown stock, but there isn't a healed brand in the lot."

"They've just worked them over," I agreed. "They'll hold them here until they're healed, then drift them out of the country."

"There's some good stock there," the Tinker said. "Some of the best."

When Orrin and the Tinker were in the saddle, I stepped down with

Judas Priest. He drank, and then me, and as I got up from the water, Orrin said, "Watch it, boy," to me.

They were coming toward us.

I waited for them. They didn't know who we were, but they had an eye for our horses, all fine stock although ganted down from hard riding over rough country.

"Where you from?" asked the sandy-haired man.

"Passin' through," I replied mildly, "just passin' through."

"We'd like to swap horses," he said. "You've good stock. We'll swap two for one."

"With a bill of sale?" I suggested.

He turned sharp on me. He had a long neck, and when he turned like that he reminded me of a turkey buzzard. "What's that mean?"

"Nothin'," I replied mildly. "On'y my brother here, he's a lawyer. Likes to see things done proper."

He glanced at Orrin, wearing several days' growth of beard, his clothes dusty. "I'll bet!" he sneered.

"Better fill your canteens," I told Judas. "We may make a dry camp tonight."

"All right, Mr. Sackett," he said.

The sandy-haired man jerked as if slapped. "What was that? *What* did you call him?"

"Sackett," Judas said.

The other men backed off now, spreading out a little. The sandy-haired man's face was pale. "Now, see here," he said. "I'm just drivin' these horses across country. Hired by a man," he said nervously. "We were hired to drive these horses."

"Where's the man who hired you?"

"He's comin' along. There's a bunch of them. They'll be along directly."

"What's his name?" Orrin demanded suddenly.

The man hesitated. "Charley McCaire," he said finally.

Orrin glanced at me. McCaire was a gunfighter, a man with a reputation as a troublemaker, but one who so far had always kept on the good side of the law. He ranched in Arizona now, but he had several brothers who still lived in New Mexico and Texas.

"Orrin," I said, "keep an eye on these boys. I'm going to ride over and have a better look at those horses."

"Like hell you are!" the man said harshly. "You leave that herd alone!"

"Sit quiet," Orrin advised. "We're just wondering why the name Sackett upset you so."

Well, I trotted my appaloosa over to those horses and skirted around them a couple of times, then I bunched them a mite and rode back.

"Blotted," I said, "and a poor job. They read *888* and they should read *Slash SS.*"

"Tyrel's road brand," Orrin said. "Well, I'll be damned!"

Chapter 11

The man's face was tight. "Now, you see here!" he said. "I—"

"Shut up," Orrin said sternly. His eyes went from one face to the other. "As of this moment you are all under arrest. I am making a citizen's arrest. Under the circumstances, if you do not offer resistance, I may be able to save you from hanging."

"We'll see about that!" the sandy-haired man yelled angrily. "You talk to Charley McCaire! And there he comes!"

Judas and the Tinker had spread out a little, facing the cattle drivers. Orrin an' me, we just naturally turned around to face the riders coming up to us. There were seven in the group, and a salty-looking bunch they were.

McCaire was a big man, rawboned and strong. Once you had a look at him you had no doubt who was in command. A weathered face, high cheekbones, and a great beak of a nose above a tight, hard mouth and a strong jaw.

"What the hell's goin' on here?" he demanded.

"Mr. McCaire? I am Orrin Sackett. I have just made an arrest of these men, found with stolen horses."

"*Stolen* horses?" McCaire's voice was harsh. "Those horses carry my brand."

"Every brand is blotted," I said calmly. "Three Eights over a Slash SS. That's Tyrel Sackett's road brand."

Now a man expecting trouble had better not miss anything. To the right of McCaire, there was a younger man with lean, flashy good looks about him—one of those men you sometimes see who just doesn't seem to hang together, and he was acting a mite itchy and tight around the mouth.

As I looked, his horse sort of fidgeted around, and I saw that gent's hand drop to his gun.

"*McCaire!* You tell that man to get his hand off his gun! There needn't be any shooting here, but if he wants it, he can have it."

McCaire's head swiveled around and his voice rapped like a gavel. "Get your hand off that gun, Boley!" He turned to the rest of his men. "Nobody starts shooting here until I do! *Get that?*"

Then he turned his eyes back to me, and, brother, those eyes of his, cold gray against his dark, windburned features, looked into me like a couple of gun muzzles. "Who're you?"

"William Tell Sackett's the name. Brother to Orrin here, and to Tyrel, whose horses these are."

"Those ain't nobody's horses but Charley's," Boley said.

Orrin ignored him. "Mr. McCaire, you're known as a hard man but a fair one. You can read brands as well as any man . . . and those are raw brands, Mr. McCaire, and there isn't a horse in that lot under four years old, nor are they mustangs. Such horses would have been branded long since."

McCaire turned in the saddle to an older man near him. "Tom, let's go have a look." He said to the others, "You boys just sit your saddles and don't start anything."

Orrin started to ride off with them and glanced at me. I grinned at him. "I'll just sort of sit here, too, Orrin. No reason these boys should get lonesome."

Boley looked past me at Judas, then at the Tinker. "Who are them?" he demanded. "What kinda people are you, anyhow?"

The Tinker smiled, flashing his white teeth, his eyes faintly ironic. "I'm a gypsy, if you'd enjoy knowing, and they call me the Tinker. I fix things," he added. "I put things together to make them work, but I can take them apart, too." He took his knife from its scabbard. "Sometimes I take things apart so they never work again." He dropped the knife back to its sheath.

Judas said nothing, merely looking at them, his eyes steady, his hands still.

Charley McCaire was at the horses now, him and that segundo of his. He would be able to see those were blotted brands, but a whole lot depended on whether he wanted to see them or not. We could always shoot one of the horses and skin him to look at the back of the hide—they read right that way. Trouble was, I didn't want to shoot no horse and wanted nobody else to. Moreover, there was no reason. The brands had been blotted, all right. They hadn't taken the trouble to burn over the old brand, just added to it. So a blind man could see what had been done. But supposin' he didn't want to see? To recognize the fact would incriminate several of his own men and would also mean a respectable loss of the cash money such horses would bring.

Charley McCaire was a strong-tempered man, and what happened depended on how that temper veered. Me, I meant to be ready. Horse stealing was a hanging matter anywhere west of the Mississippi and some places east of it. It was also a shooting matter, and I had an idea this Boley gent knew aplenty about how those brands were burned.

Suddenly, McCaire reined around and came back on a lope.

Orrin followed just behind Tom. When we were all together again, Charley turned to face us. "Ride off," he said. "We're through talkin'."

"Charley," Tom said, "look here, man, I—"

"Are you ridin' for the brand or agin it?" Charley's face was flushed and angry. "If you ain't with us, ride out of here."

"Charley! *Think!* You've always been an honest man, and by the lord harry, you know those brands are—"

Boley's hand dropped for his gun . . . mine was covering him. "You draw that," I said, "and when she clears leather you'll be belly up to the sky."

Nobody moved. "All right, Charley," Tom said, "I've rode for your brand for nigh onto twelve year now, but I'm quittin'. You just keep what you owe me because a man cheap enough to read those brands wrong is nobody whose money I want."

"Tom!" It was a protest.

"No."

"Go to hell, then!"

"That's your route, Charley, not mine."

Tom turned his horse and rode slowly away over the bunch grass.

My gun was still in my hand. Boley was pale around the gills. He fancied himself with a six-gun, I could see that, but he wasn't up to it.

"That's a mighty rough trail you're choosin' for yourself," I said casually. "This is a flat-out steal, McCaire, if you can bring it off."

"Don't be a fool! We outnumber you three to one!"

"You better look at your hole card, mister," I told him. "I'm already holding a gun. Now I don't know how the rest of your boys will make out, but I'll lay you five to one you an' Boley are dead."

"Take 'em, Uncle Charley," Boley said. "There's only two of 'em. That nigger won't stand. Neither will the other one."

"If you think I won't stand, suh," Judas said politely, "why don't you just step out to one side an' let just the two of us try it?"

Boley started to move, then stopped, his eyes on Judas Priest's gun. It was a Colt revolving shotgun.

"Finally got around to looking, did you? This here weapon holds four ca'tridges . . . an' if I can hit a duck on the wing I believe I can hit a man in a saddle."

Well, this Boley sort of backed off and flattened his hair down. A shotgun has that effect on a lot of folks. It seems somehow dampening to the spirits.

"Mr. McCaire," Orrin suggested, "why not give this further thought? We've no desire for trouble. As a matter of fact, this man here and those with him have already been notified of their arrest for possession of stolen property and an apparent theft of horses."

"You're no officer!"

"I made a citizen's arrest, but even so, every lawyer is an officer of the court."

Charley McCaire was simmering down a mite, but I had my doubts whether he'd changed his mind. My gun was one thing he could not sidestep. After Boley's move I had drawn without starting anything, and fast enough so that nobody had a chance to do much about it. A man could see that somebody was going to get shot, and Charley was smart enough to see he was first man up on the list.

"How do I know you ain't bluffin'? I don't know what your brother's road brand is, or even that he's fixin' to move stock."

"Unless I am mistaken about my brother, Mr. McCaire, he's on the trail of this missing stock right now, and unless I am again mistaken I would say you're a lot better off with us than with him.

"Tyrel," he added, "doesn't have the patience that Tell and I have, and I think he's every bit as good with a gun as Tell, here. Back home we always figured him to be the mean one of the family."

We didn't want any shooting. The incident had happened unexpectedly, and now a wrong word could turn that meadow into a bloodbath.

The next thing we heard was a pound of hooves, and into the valley came Tyrel, riding straight up in the saddle, young and tall in a fitted buckskin jacket of the Spanish style.

Behind him were half a dozen riders, all Mexicans, sporting big sombreros, bandoliers, and six-shooters as well as rifles. I knew those vaqueros of Tyrel's and they were a salty lot. He wouldn't have a man on the place who wasn't a fighter as well as a stockman.

Believe me, they were a pretty sight to see. He always mounted his men well, and those vaqueros rode like nothing you ever saw. They were a bold, reckless lot of men, and they'd have followed Tyrel through the bottom layer of hell.

"Looks like you boys found my horses," he said. He glanced over at Charley McCaire, then at the others. Tyrel looked better than I'd ever seen him. He was six feet two in his sock feet; he must've weighed a good one-ninety, and not an ounce of it was excess weight. "You'll find the brands altered," said Orrin.

Tyrel glanced at him. Orrin said, "This is Charley McCaire, of the Three Eights. Some of his hands got a little ambitious, but it's all straight now."

The vaqueros bunched the horses and started them toward the trail, then held up. The Tinker turned his horse and waited for Priest to come alongside. Then Tyrel turned to his men.

"We're taking our horses back," he said, "and, at the request of my brother we're making no further move, but if any of you ever see one of these men near any of my stock, shoot him."

The vaqueros sat their horses, rifles ready, while the rest of us bunched our stock and started moving. Then they rode to join us.

Glancing back, I saw McCaire jerk his hat from his head and throw it to the ground, but that was all I saw, and I was too far away to hear what he said.

Tyrel and Orrin rode point, and I guess Orrin was filling in the blank spaces on the horse stealing and then on pa. I trailed off to one side, away from the dust of the horses and riders. I needed to think, and a riding man is always better thinking off by himself. Leastways, that's the way I think best, if I think at all.

Sometimes I wonder how much thinking anybody does, and if their life hasn't shaped every decision for them before they make it. But now I had to consider pa. I had to put myself in his place.

The gold Pierre and the others were hunting seemed to be in the San Juans, and certainly, the last I heard, there was a lot of it. Also, that was a mighty bunch of mountains, some thundering deep canyons, and a lot of high, rough country no white man had ever ridden over.

Galloway and Flagan Sackett had moved some stock there near the town of Shalako and set up camp. They'd established no proper ranch yet, as they were still kind of looking around, but from all they'd said in their letters it was our kind of country.

I'd been to the San Juans before. It was in the mountains above Vallecitos where I'd found out Ange and Tyrel as well as pa had been through

Baker Park and the country around Durango. Pa had known that country pretty well—probably as well as anybody could know it without a good many years up there.

The way I figured it, we'd take the same route north Cap Rountree an' me had taken when we went back up the Vallecitos to stake our claims. We'd ride north from Mora, go up through the Eagle's Nest country and E-town, then to the San Luis Valley and west on the trail into the San Juans.

Suppose pa was still alive, like ma thought? Suppose he was busted up and back in a corner of the mountains he couldn't get out of? Or held by Indians? I hadn't a moment's thought that such could be true, but pa was a tough man, a hang-in-there-an'-fight sort of man, and a body would have to go all the way to salt him down.

We camped that night by a spring of cold, clear water where there was grass for the horses.

When everybody was around the fire, I took my Winchester and climbed to the rim of the mesa. There was an almighty fine view up there. The sun was gone, but she'd left gold in the sky and streaks of red, as well as a few pink puffballs of cloud.

Up there on the rimrock I sat down and let my legs hang over and looked to the west.

Tyrel had Drusilla, and Orrin had the law, at least, and most women-folks catered to him, but what did I have? What would I ever have? Seemed like I just wasn't the kind to make out with womenfolks, and I was a lonesome man who was wishful of a home and a woman of my own.

Folks had it down that I was a wanderin' man, but most wanderin' men I've known only wandered because of the home they expected to find . . . *hoped* to find, I mean.

Looking westward the way we were to ride, I wondered if I'd find what I was hunting.

Flagan had said there were some other Sacketts out there. No kind of kin to us that we knowed of, but good folks by all accounts, and we'd fight shy of them and try to make them no trouble.

Glancing back, as I stood up to go back down the cliff trail, I glimpsed a far-off campfire, a single red eye, winking, but with evil in it.

Somebody back yonder the way we had come, somebody trailing us, maybe.

Charley McCaire? Or Andre Baston?

Or both?

Chapter 12

About noontime a few days later, we rode up to San Luis, and the first man I saw was Esteban Mendoza. He'd married Tina, a girl Tyrel had helped out of a bad situation some years back during the settlement fight.

"Ah, señor! When I see you far away I say to Tina it is you! No man sits a saddle as do you! What can I do for you?"

"We want to get under cover, and we want a good bait for our stock."

When he had shown us where to put our horses, he stopped to talk while I stripped the gear from my appaloosa. "Is it trouble, amigo?"

I warned him about the kind of people who might be riding our trail, and then I asked him, "Esteban, you've been here awhile now. Who is the oldest man in town? I mean, somebody with a good memory that can reach back twenty years?"

"Twenty years? It is a long time. A man remembers a woman, a fight, perhaps a very good horse for twenty years, but not much else."

"This is a man—several men—who came through here headed for the San Juans and Wolf Creek Pass."

He shrugged. "It is a long time, amigo."

"One of them was my father, Esteban. He did not come back from that ride."

"I see."

Esteban started away, and I spoke after him. "These men who follow me. One of them was with my father then. You be careful, and warn your people. Start nothing, but be wary. They are hard men, Esteban, and they have killed before."

He smiled, his teeth flashing under his mustache. "We have hard men, too, amigo, but I will pass the word. They will know. It is always better to know."

We ate, but I was restless, and, good as the food was, I was uneasy. It seemed every time I came to San Luis there was trouble, not for the town or from the town, but for me. It was a pleasant little village, settled in 1851, some said.

Stepping outside I stood for a moment, enjoying the stars and the cool air. Looming on the skyline to the west was the towering bulk of Mount Blanca.

My father had been here, in this village. San Luis was a natural stop if you came from the south or the east.

The wind was cool from off the mountains and I stood there, leaning against the bars of the old corral, smelling the good smells of the barnyard, the freshly mown hay, and the horses.

Tyrel and his vaqueros came out. The men rounded up all their horses, and Tyrel said good-bye to me. They were headed back to Mora for the time being, and I told Tyrel that he would hear from us as soon as we knew anything.

Esteban came up from the town walking with an old man—looked like a Mexican. "You must sit down, amigo," he said to me. "This man is very old, and he is much shorter than you."

There was a bench under an old tree and I sat down beside the old man. "Viejo," Esteban said, "this is the man I told you about, Tell Sackett."

"Sackett," he mumbled crossly, "of course there was a Sackett! A good man—good man. Strong—very—strong! He had been to the mountains for fur but now he was going back—for gold."

"Did he say that, viejo?"

"Of course he did not! But I do not need to know what he say. He speaks of the mountains, of Wolf Creek Pass, and I tell him not to go. He is wasting his time. Others have looked and found nothing."

"Were they here long?"

"Two, three days. They wanted horses, and Huerta sent to the mountains for them. They were impatient to be off, and of course . . . well, two of them did not want to go. I did not think Sackett wanted to go. I think he did not like these people. Neither did the other man . . . Petgrew."

Now I just sat quiet. Petgrew? Was it a new name? Or had I heard it before and not remembered? There had been another man, but what happened to him, anyway?

Was Petgrew the name of the man Philip Baston had told us about? More than likely. I remembered finally. It was Pettigrew.

"It is cold in the mountains when the snow falls," I said. "They would not be able to last through the winter."

"They were not there after the snow fell. They came out in time. At least, three of them did. The big young man whom I did not like—he came out. So did the handsome one, who was cruel."

"And the other?"

His thoughts had wandered off. "Cold, yes it is cold. Men have lived. If they know how to live sometimes they can, but food . . . most of them starve.

"It is not only the cold. We were worried for them and thought of going out for them. Twenty years ago—I was a young man then—scarcely sixty years I had. And until I was seventy I could ride as well as any man in the valley . . . better. Better.

"Two of them came down, and I was over near the pass then and saw them coming.

"I hid. I do not know why—I was not afraid of them, but I hid. They rode right past me. One of their horses caught my scent. Oh, he smelled me, all right! But they were stupid. They do not live with horses so they do not know.

"They rode past, but they did not stop in San Luis. They went to Fort Garland."

"You followed them?"

"No, I did not follow. Later, I heard of it. This is not a big country for people. What one does here is heard of, you know? Somebody sees. It is something to tell when we have so little to tell.

"No, I did not follow. I went up the mountain. I was curious, you see. Like the bear or the wolf I am curious.

"Only two tracks—two horses. No more. I find elk tracks. Ah! That is something! We need meat, so I trailed the elk and killed it, and when I had the meat it was late, and it was cold, and my horse, it was frighten— very frighten.

"To go down the mountain? The wind was rising. It is colder when the wind blows, and home lay far out across the plains . . . those plains can be terrible, terrible when the wind blows.

"High up the mountain there was a cave. Several times I had sheltered there. So had we all. I mean, men from this village and the Fort. We knew of the cave.

"So I went higher up the mountain in the snow, and I reached the trail up there. It was a mistake—or it was the good God speaking to me. On the trail were the tracks of *three* horses . . . three? Yes.

"Now I had to take cover and build a fire to warm me. It was very cold. I rode down the trail to the cave and I took my horse inside. I put him behind me. And then I went with my axe to cut a tree. One must be very careful to cut a tree when it is frozen. It is easy to cut a leg. I was careful.

"There was a good tree close by and some dead branches. I pull them in, and I tug on another, and I hear something.

"There was a sound, a small sound. Not the sound of a tree, not a branch breaking . . . an animal sound. I pull the branch again, and then I see it, lying over the bank . . . a branch of the tree is there, too, but it is a horse."

"A horse?"

"With a saddle. The horse try to get up. He cannot get up because he lies with his legs uphill. If his legs were downhill he could get up, I think.

"So I get his bridle. It is frozen stiff. I take the bridle and pull him over, pull his head over and hope he will keep it there. I get a rope on him, go back for my horse, and with my horse I get him up.

"When he is on his feet I look around. Where the horse was is a hollow in the snow. He must have struggled and worked himself down into the snow. He would have frozen there. But a horse, amigo? A horse with a saddle? I explain to myself that a horse with a saddle and no rider is not reasonable, you see?

"I look. Further down in the snow, I see him. A man lying there almost covered with snow. Near him are some tracks.

"It seems to me somebody has made the horse jump. He is frighten, this horse. And when he jumps he falls, and the man is thrown and hurt, you see? Then I think somebody walks down to where he lies and hits him again, then leaves him in the cold.

"It will look an accident, you see? A man thrown, frozen to death. I think they did not want to trust to shooting . . . people wonder, you know."

The old man's voice was slowing, and he was growing tired. I sat there in the darkness thinking back. A man must have returned with Baston and Swan, and for some reason they had decided to kill him. A man left unconscious in the snow at such a time would have small chance of survival, yet the human creature is amazing. Nobody knew that better than me. I had seen men survive from impossible wounds, seen them walk out of the desert or mountains. I'd had a few bad times myself.

"You saved him?"

"It was cold. It was starting to snow, and the man was not big, but heavy, very heavy, señor. I could not get him up the slope. It was steep . . . steep. Many trees and rocks.

"The man was cold—he was freeze, I think. I could not carry him up the slope."

I waited, knowing he had to tell it in his own way, in his own time, yet

I could see him there at the body of the unconscious man. Up above was a cave, shelter for the horses and himself, a good place for a fire, and fuel for it. And down below there an old man standing in the falling snow.

A time or two I'd had to carry unconscious men. It was far from easy. Up a slope like that? Not many men could manage it. Probably not one in a hundred.

What to do? The wind was rising, snow was falling, and with the rising wind the cold would grow more penetrating. Maybe the man would die, anyway. Perhaps he was almost dead. Why risk his life to save a stranger who was dying, anyway?

"To climb alone would be all. I left the man, and I climbed up. It was only a little way—a hundred feet, I think, perhaps a little more, you know?

"I got my blanket roll and I slid back down. Then into the snow I dug a hole. I built high the walls of snow around us, and I gathered sticks and laid some down and built upon them a fire.

"I rolled the man upon my bed, and the night long I kept the fire going, and I was alone so I talked to him. I talked to this man. I told him he was a lot of trouble to me. I told him there was a nice warm cave above and because of him I had to sit in the cold. I told him the only decent thing to do was to live.

"It was very cold . . . *mucho frío*, señor. I shivered, swung my arms, danced in the snow, but most of the time I collected wood. There were fallen trees on that slope. And just a little way from there was a tangle of branches.

"I tried to climb up again, but it was too slippery from other climbs, so I went into the tangle and pulled myself up from tree to tree. Then I made a fire in the cave. I must think of my horses, señor. They were good horses, mine and the hurt man's horse, and it was not their fault they were in this cold place. I built a fire up there, and then I climbed down, and my fire down below was almost gone. Again I put fuel on the coals, and it burned up.

"I looked at the man. I felt his arms and his legs. I moved them. Nothing seemed broken, so only the head was hurt. I knew the man's face."

"Who was he, viejo? Who was the man?"

"It was Pet-grew. And he did not die. He did not waste my time. He lived, señor. By morning he was a little *rojo*. His face, señor, was flushed, and his breath was better."

"You saved him, then?"

"Ah? It was the good Lord who saved him, señor. I sat by him and kept the fire warm. I kept the fire for the horses, too. Up and down, up and down . . . it was the longest night, the coldest night, and I was afraid all would die. The man, the horses, me.

"We were high up, señor. Perhaps ten thousand feet. You know what it is . . . the cold."

"And the man? Where is he?" I paused. "What became of him, viejo?"

He put a trembling hand on my sleeve. "He did not leave us. He is here."

Chapter 13

Morning lay bright upon the town when we rode out of the streets of San Luis. The sky was a magnificent San Juan mountain blue, with puffs of white cloud scattered about.

Sunlight touched the snow upon the distant peaks, and as we rode there were no sounds but the beat of our horses' hooves and the creak of saddle leather.

We four rode out with Esteban, rode west to the little ranch on the Rio Grande del Norte.

It was an adobe house with projecting roof beams—a comfortable house of several spacious rooms, a long barn, corrals, and a few fruit trees.

As we rode into the yard a man limped to the door, using a cane. He wore a six-shooter rigged for a crossdraw.

He was a stocky man with a round, pleasant face, red cheeks, and a tuft of gray hair sticking up from the crown of his head. His eyes went to Esteban and he waved. "*Buenos dias,* amigo!" he said cheerfully.

"'Light an' set!"

There was a measure of caution in the glance he gave us, and I thought his eyes lingered on Orrin's face, then mine.

It was cool inside the house. "Set," he said. "I am Nativity Pettigrew, Connecticut born, Missouri bred. Who might you be?"

"I am Orrin Sackett," Orrin said, "and this here is my brother, William T. Sackett." He introduced the Tinker and Judas, then sat down.

"Mr. Pettigrew, you were with my father in the mountains?"

Pettigrew got out his pipe and loaded it with tobacco. He turned his head toward an inner door, "Juana? Bring us some coffee, will you?"

He glanced around apologetically. "Don't like to be waited on, but with this game leg I don't get around so well no more." He tamped the tobacco firmly. "So you're Sackett's boys, are you? I heard tell of you a time or two, figured soon or late we'd come to meet."

A pretty Mexican woman entered with a tray of cups and a coffeepot. "This here's Juana. We been married nigh onto nineteen year."

We all arose hurriedly, acknowledging the introduction. She smiled—a soft, pretty woman, and very shy.

"We're tryin' to find out what become of pa," I explained. "Ma's gettin' on in years, and she's wishful to know."

He smoked in silence for a moment. "It ain't as easy as you think. I took a rap on the skull up yonder and my memory gets kind of hazy. I do remember that Baston, though, and Swan. Must've been one of them hit me.

"My horse spooked. Maybe they hit him, burned him, I don't know what. Anyway, he was always a nervous one and he just jumped right out there an' fell. Last thing I recalled, until several days later when I come to in the snow with that old Mexican—he's Juana's grandpa—a-settin' by the fire, tendin' me like.

"Good man. Saved my life, so I just figured I'd never find better folks than these, an' I settled down right here. Bought this place off kinfolk of hers."

"You had some money, then?"

Pettigrew smiled. It was a careful smile, and he looked down at his pipe, puffed a couple of times, and said, "I had a mite. They knowed nothing of it or they'd surely have taken it."

"What was the last you saw of pa?"

Pettigrew shifted a little in his hide-bottomed chair. "He took us there, right up Wolf Creek Pass to the mountain, but there was trouble making up. Your pa, he was a quiet man, minded his own affairs, but he didn't miss much. He got along fine with Pierre Bontemps. The Frenchman was a fine man, a flighty one, but strong, always ready to carry his share and more. Trouble didn't develop until we got up in the mountains along Wolf Creek.

"Bontemps had a map, but you know the wild country—unless a map's laid out with care she ain't worth the match to burn it with.

"Whoever made that map made it quick, and either he made it with no ken of how things are in the mountains or he was figuring on coming right back.

"We located some of the landmarks. One tree, all important to locating the gold, was gone. One rock wasn't shaped like it was supposed to be. Sackett found the other half of it down in a canyon where it had weathered and fallen off. Upshot of it was, we never found no gold.

"I had trouble with Baston, an' I up an' quit. I took off down the mountain. A couple of days later, Swan an' Baston caught up with me. They said they'd quit, too."

Orrin sat staring into the fire, listening. Finally he put down his cup. "And you know nothing of what happened to pa?"

"No, sir. I don't."

I didn't believe him. He was telling the truth up to a point, but he was holding back on quite a lot.

So I figured to shake him up a little. "It's ma we want to know for," I said. "She's an old woman, close on to her deathtime, an' we are wishful that she rest easy, content that pa's gone on ahead of her to blaze the trail.

"We can't let it lay, and we ain't about to. We're goin' to worry at this until we find out what happened."

"After so long a time you won't find anything," he muttered. He stared into his empty cup. "Nothing lasts much, on them mountains."

"Can't tell about that. I once found a wolf carcass in a cave that must have been there years an' years. My brother an' me, we're readers of sign. We'll find the answer.

"Fact is, I spent some time a few years ago over on the Vallecitos. I still have some claims over there."

He looked up, surprised. "Are you that Sackett? I heard of some shooting over there."

"I done my share. I came in first, and I was the last to go."

He seemed restless, and I had a feeling he wanted us to go. A couple of times I heard rustling around in the kitchen and I wondered how much Juana knew of all this.

Finally, I got up. Orrin followed suit, and Judas and the Tinker wandered over to the door. "One thing, Mr. Pettigrew," I said, "if you had trouble with Baston and Swan, you'd best keep a gun handy."

He looked up sharply. "Why's that?"

"Because they're comin' along right behind us. I don't know why they want to come back, but they do. They may figure they missed something up yonder, and they'll be asking questions around."

"What?" He got up, struggling to his feet, weaving a little, and if ever I saw fear in a man's eyes, it was in his.

"They're coming here?"

"Not more than two days behind us, probably less. Yes, they are coming, and if I were you I'd get myself out of sight, and your wife, too. Better not leave anything they can get hold of."

We started back to San Luis where we scouted the town for Andre Baston and Swan, but there was nothing to be seen of them. I was coming out of the cantina, however, when I saw a man down by the corral. He turned sharp away when I glimpsed him, so I took notice. He looked an almighty lot like one of the hands who had ridden with Charley McCaire.

That set me to pondering. McCaire was a hard-as-nails man, used to riding roughshod over anything got in his way. He'd lost the game with us, but would he take it?

I wasn't worried about him tangling with Tyrel. Nobody worried about Tyrel. Tyrel wasn't the kind you expected would be taken advantage of. He was a fair man, and not a trouble-hunting man, but I never knew anybody as ready to take up trouble if it came his way.

If Charley McCaire hunted trouble with Tyrel he just had my sympathy . . . him or his boys. As for Tyrel's vaqueros, they liked him, and if he told them to they'd damp down the fires of hell.

Of course, that puncher, if it was him I saw, he might just have quit and drifted.

Still, I was going to keep my eyes open and give thought to my back trail.

We would be pulling out with daybreak, riding west into the mountains, and everyone turned in early against the riding to come.

One more time I went out to the corral to take a look around. All was quiet. The house was dark, the horses nickered a little when I came close because I was always packing little odds and ends of grub for them. This time I had a carrot for each, and I stood there by the rail listening to them crunch, when I heard a faint drum of hooves.

Now I was wearing a shootin' iron. So I just sort of faded back against the corral bars and scrunched down by one of the poles to get sight of whoever it was before they saw me.

The rider slowed down, walked the horse into the yard, hesitated, then slid down and trailed the reins. It was a woman.

I stood up and said, "Ma'am?"

She turned sharp, but stood her ground. "Who is it?"

I knew the voice, and it was Juana Pettigrew. "Tell Sackett, ma'am. I was just checking my horses."

"Here." She came at me and thrust something into my hand. "Take that, and say nothing." She looked up at me. "You are good people, you Sacketts. Tina has told me of you, and my cousin once worked for your brother at Mora. I want to help, and it is wrong for my husband not to give you this."

Then she was in the saddle once more and headed back. It was a long, hard ride she had ahead of her.

Inside the house I squatted by the light from the fire. In my hand was a large brown envelope like I'd seen them use for deeds and the like. It was fastened with a twist of string, and I opened it.

What I saw stopped me cold. It was pa's handwriting.

For a moment there I just held those papers in my hand, my heart beating heavy. Pa's handwriting . . . and pa had been dead for twenty years . . . or had he?

Juana had brought this to me, which meant that Nativity Pettigrew had it in his possession. He knew pa had a family, so why had he made no effort to get it to us?

> *April 20:* Weather bad. Hard wind, rain turning to snow. Snow still on the mountains but Bontemps is wishful to proceed. He's got enthusazm enough for two. Don't like this. Trouble has a smell to it, and Baston's a hard man. I've had words with Swan twict over the way he treats Angus.
>
> *April 23:* Clearing. Trail muddy, grass very wet. Horses about stove up. Nobody knows mountains but me. They've no idea how miserable it can be up yonder this time of year. They won't show me the map. If it's like most it just is no good.

I read on. The paper was old and rotting and some of the words were blurred.

> *April 26:* In camp. Third day. Trail belly-deep in snow, drifts very deep. Only the fact they couldn't find anything in the snow is keeping them in camp. Situation growing touchy. Pierre straightened Andre out today. Thought there'd be . . . Angus steady. Pettigrew talks a lot, does his work. No idea where he stands.
>
> *April 29:* Moved on today. Ground soggy with snow-melt. Occasional sleet.
>
> *April 30:* Showed me map. No good. Hadn't been for ma and boys I'd not be here. Chance to get enough to settle down, education, home for ma. Landmarks poorly chosen, same from several points, important tree gone.
>
> *May 4:* In camp on mountain. Three days scouting, digging. Nothing. Utes scouting us. Pierre won't . . . Utes or lack of treasure. Swan sullen, Andre furious. Pettigrew quiet, secretive.

Orrin raised up from bed. "What is it?"

"Kind of a daybook. Pa's. Juana Pettigrew brought it to us. I ain't read it all yet."

"Better get some sleep. I think we're riding up to trouble. Whatever's there won't have changed by tomorrow."

"You're right." I was dead tired. We'd covered a lot of country and tomorrow there'd be more. Pa wasn't tellin' much, but a body could see how touchy things had become. Swan an' Andre sore, Pettigrew kind of bidin' his time, and Pierre still unwillin' to believe he'd lost the pot. Only maybe they hadn't. Pettigrew come out of it with enough to buy a ranch and stock it. Now that mightn't take so much, but it surely cost something.

Stretched out in bed I pondered the daybook. Pa wasn't much hand to write. He'd had some schoolin' and he'd read a lot, although his grammar was only a mite better'n mine.

Why would he write that stuff? Was there more to it than met the eye? Was he tryin' to leave us a message, feelin' he might not get back? But pa wasn't apt to think that way. He was a tough, capable man—but careful, too. Maybe the daybook was in case—just in case something went wrong.

Why had Juana brought it to me? Because it was pa's? Because it was intended for us? Or because she didn't want Pettigrew going off to the mountains again?

Now why had I thought that? Did the book have a clue to where pa was? Or where the gold might be?

Pettigrew came back with something, but Andre did not know it or he'd have robbed him. Or Swan would have.

Yet Andre may have come back with something, too. Suppose they had found some of the gold and not all of it?

Chapter 14

Since reaching San Luis we had used Esteban's horses, but now we saddled our own mounts and were gone with the sun's rising. Clear and cool the morning was, and I breathed deeply of the fresh air from off the mountains.

Westward we rode, seeing the peaks loom up before us, the twin peaks of Blanca and Baldy looking from some angles like one gigantic mountain. The old Indian traditions speak of them as one—long, long ago.

We rode and we camped and rode again. At night I read to them from pa's daybook, and passed it at times to Orrin.

There had been growing animosity in the camp on the mountain.

Nat Pettigrew is a prying man, forever peering, listening and poking about. He is able, does his share and more. He's a good man on a horse and handy with a rifle, but I do not trust him. Yet he is all for himself, and not for them.

May 20: This morning there was trouble. Swan struck Angus, knocking him down. Pierre was on his feet at once and for a moment I was sure they would come to blows. I noticed also that Andre stood to one side making no effort to stop Swan, who is his man. Andre just stood there with a little smile on his face. I believe Andre hates his brother-in-law, and I wish I was free of them, and far away.

Angus, the black slave, is a powerful man loyal to Pierre, and a fair woodsman. I believe he'd do even better in the swamps of Louisiana than here, yet I doubt if he has long to live.

There was a gap here, looked like a couple of lost pages, then some words were smeared.

. . . suddenly there was an outburst of firing. Somebody yelled "Indians!" and we all fell into defensive positions. For awhile there was no sound, then a single shot. For some time there was no sound and when we took stock, Angus was dead—shot in the back of the head. When I talked with Pettigrew later, he admitted to having seen no Indians, nor had Pierre. Swan had seen one, Andre thought he had seen them. Andre showed a scar on the bark of a tree made by a bullet, and of course, Angus was dead.

Well, now Judas knew what happened to his brother. I looked at him in the firelight and thought I saw tears in his eyes. There seemed nothing to say to him. He stood and walked away from the fire.

"What do you think?" I asked Orrin. We were on the banks of the Rio Grande with Del Norte Peak looming to the southwest. Orrin shook his head.

The Rio Grande headed up in those mountains in the direction we were riding, and it gave me an odd feeling to think this water I looked at was headed down toward El Paso and then Laredo, and finally to enter the Gulf below Brownsville. It was a far, far stretch.

"Orrin," I said, "I wished pa had just up and rode off. He guided them there, and he owed them nothing."

"He was in for a piece of it," said Orrin. "He wanted it for ma, and for an education for us boys."

"I wished he'd pulled out."

"You know what I think?" Orrin held up the papers and the book to me. "I think somebody in that outfit's found gold."

"You mean somebody knows where the stuff is and is holding it for himself?"

"Look at it, Tell. It needn't have been the big caches. There were supposed to be three, weren't there? All right. You know what soldiers are. Some individual soldiers may have had their own pokes stuffed with gold, and they may have hid them. I think somebody found some gold, and I think Angus was killed to take help from Pierre. I think he's next."

"Or pa," I said.

Setting late by the fire, I pondered it. Pa was up there in May. Unless it was unusually warm for the year, there'd still be snow up there where he was, and it would be almighty cold. But there couldn't have been too much snow left, or they'd have found no landmarks at all.

Of course, there were some slopes where the wind could sweep away the snow, but there was risk of a bad storm at any time.

Judas suddenly came in out of the darkness. "Suh? We are followed, suh."

"You're surely right. How far back are they?"

"They are gaining, suh. And there are more than we believed."

"More?" the Tinker said.

"They have two fires," Judas said. "I would imagine there are at least ten men, perhaps twice as many."

At daybreak our camp was an hour behind us, and we were climbing steadily. There'd been no chance to get back to pa's daybook. Me an' Orrin . . . well, it had felt almost like we were talkin' to pa, yet he was shorter of word than usual in this writin' of his. Mostly pa was a man with a dry humor, a quick man to see things, and he always had a comment. He knew most tricks a body could play, was slick with cards when he needed to be, and had seen a lot of the world, time to time.

We came up to the forks of the Rio Grande and it was the South Fork pointed the way up Wolf Creek Pass. Pa had come this way, and the fact that he was keepin' a daybook showed he had something to tell us—who else but us? Pa was a considering man, and I'd no doubt he figured somehow to get that daybook to us. Maybe he'd trusted Nativity Pettigrew to bring it to us, or mail it. If so, his gamble failed.

If he had planned to get it to us, he must have been wishful to get some particular word to us. We'd likely have to read careful so we'd miss nothing.

Orrin dropped back from the point. "Tell, is there any other way to that mountain? I mean other than right up the pass?"

"Well, I reckon." I pointed. "That there's Cattle Mountain, with Demijohn right behind it. I never followed that trail, but Cap Rountree told me of it one time."

"Let's worry them a little," Orrin suggested, so I went up to ride point. Watching carefully, I turned off and took a dim trail leading up the east side of Grouse Mountain. We followed that up a switchback trail and over the saddle on Cattle Mountain then down the trail west of the Demijohn and onto the Ribbon Mesa trail.

It was narrow, twisty, and rough. Several times we heard the warning whistles of marmots looking like balls of brown fur as they scattered into the rocks. We skirted a meadow where mountain lupine, Indian paintbrush, and heartleaf arnica added their blue, red, and gold to the scene. It was very quiet except for the murmur of the waters of the creek. We twisted, doubled, rode back over our tracks, and did everything possible to confuse our trail. The way was rocky, torn by slides. Leaving Park Creek, I cut over the pass back of Fox Mountain down Middle Creek about a mile and then took a dimmer trail that led us right over the mountain.

We rode through aspens, skirted groves of them, and then we rode across high mountain meadows, leaving as little sign as we could. If Andre Baston had a dozen men with him he probably had some mountain-riding men, but if he caught up with us I was figuring to make him earn it.

Of course, they might have taken the easy way right up Wolf Creek Pass. Indians and mountain men had used it for years, along with occasional prospectors. More than likely the French soldiers who'd buried that gold had come down Wolf Creek.

We had come down the slope into the canyon of Silver Creek with the San Juan just ahead and below. On our west was the mountain of the treasure, and a whole lot of mountain it was, too.

Orrin pointed out a cove in the mountainside, and we skirted a tight grove of aspen and moved into a small meadow with a plunging stream alongside it. We pulled up under the trees and stepped down, and, believe me, I was tired.

We stripped the gear from our horses, and, after I'd rubbed my horse and one of the packhorses a mite, I wandered off down to the stream, hunting wood. I picked up some good dead branches, heavy stuff, and then tasted the water. It was fresh, cold, and clear. As I started to rise I heard a faint *chink* of metal. It sounded from upstream. Well, I shucked my gun and kind of eased back under the bank.

After finding the wood, I'd kind of explored along the riverbank, so camp was a good hundred yards back of me now.

Crouching near some cottonwood roots that ran down into the earth under the water, I waited, listening. The stream chuckled along over the stones, and upstream I could hear a bird singing. After that I heard only the stream.

Ahead of me, the stream took a little bend, curving around some rocks and thick brush—dogwood, willow, and the like. Searching the ground between me and that brush, I saw nothing to worry me, so I started forward, walking mighty easy to make no sound.

Reaching the little bend, I eased up on the bank to look through the brush. From behind the brush and rocks I had a clear view of fifty yards or more of the stream.

Up yonder about as far as my eyes could take me was a woman. It looked to be a girl—a chancy judgment at that distance—and she was panning gravel, handling that pan like she'd done it before, a lot of times before.

I looked up the bank as far as I could, but there was no camp, nor was there anything like it that I could see.

Seemed to me the situation called for study, and if a body aims to study women it's better done at close range, so I came down from my perch and started around that bend. When I cleared it and had a view of the stream again, she was gone!

Yes, sir. She was vanished out of there. Now I was a puzzled man. Surely my eyes hadn't played games with me. Of course, when a man is long enough without a woman he begins to see them, or imagine them, everywhere.

I walked across that creek, which was shallow at that point, and I went upstream, stepping careful. I'd kept my gun in my hand without really thinking, except it seemed logical that where there'd be a pretty woman there'd likely be a man.

When I got up to where she'd been, sure enough there were tracks in the sand. I started to look around when a voice spoke from right behind me. I'd knowed I should have looked into that tangle right up the slope, but I hadn't done it.

"You stand where you be, mister," a girl's voice said, "and if you're wishful of savoring your supper, don't fool around. Now you stick that piece back in the leather, and you do it right quick or I'll run a lead tunnel through your brisket!"

"I'm a peaceful man, ma'am, plumb peaceful. I seen what looked like a woman up here, an'—"

Her tone was scornful. "*Looked* like a woman? Why, you two-by-twice foreigner, I'm more woman than you ever did see! Turn around, damn you, and take a good look!"

Well, I turned, and from what I seen I was in no position to argue. She was about three inches over five feet, I'd guess, and must have weighed what it needed to fill that space out proper, with maybe a mite extry here an' yonder.

"Yes, ma'am." She had a cute nose, freckles, and rusty hair, and taking all in all, the way a woman should be taken, she was pretty as a button.

She was also holding a Spencer .56 that wasn't no way cute at all, and from the way she held it a body could see she was no stranger to its use.

She was kind of staring at me like she couldn't believe it, and, knowing my ownself, I knew it wasn't good looks she was staring at.

"Well!" she said, gesturing with the gun muzzle a mite. "You jest back up an' set on that log, yonder. And don't you go to stretching for that gun because by tomorrow mornin' your body would have drawn so many flies I'd have to find a new place to pan."

"I'm peaceful, ma'am, but if I have to be shot it couldn't be by a prettier girl."

"Don't give me that, Sackett! Sweet talk will get you no place with me!"

Sackett? Now, how in—

"Oh, don't look so surprised! Up where I come from ever'body knows the Sackett boys. How could they help it with the country overrun with them? Best thing ever happened to Tennessee was when they opened up the west and found some way to shuck some of you Sacketts."

"You're from the Cumberland?"

Her disgust was plain. "Where else? Do you conceited mountain boys think you're known everywhere? Who would know you were a Sackett but somebody from yonder? You all have those same weatherbeaten, homely faces and those big hands!"

"Wasn't for your hair I'd say you was a Trelawney girl," I said, "but the only ones of them I ever met up with had black hair. Fact is, I run into one of them down on the Colorado one time, and she gave me no end of trouble."

"Served you right. Which Sackett are you, anyway?"

"William Tell. And you?"

"I'm Nell—Jack Ben's daughter."

Well, now. That made me back up for another look. The Sacketts ran long on boys, the Trelawneys on girls, but when the Trelawneys number a boy in their get, he was usually quite somebody. Ol' Jack Ben was no exception. He was saltier than that creek which runs into Coon Hollow an' meaner than a tied-up wolf.

We Sacketts carried on a fightin'-shootin' feud with the Higgins outfit for many a year, but ol' Jack Ben, he handled his own fightin'. I also recall that he was most tender about what boys come a-courtin' his girls.

You could always tell a boy who'd been tryin' to court one of Jack Ben's girls because he walked kind of straight up an' bent back, and he never set down nowhere. That was because of the rock salt ol' Jack Ben kep' in his shotgun.

"You ain't alone up here, are you?"

"S'posin' I am? I can take care of myself."

"Now, you see here, Nell Trelawney, there's some folks a-comin' along behind us that are meaner than all get-out an' no respecters of womanfolk, so—"

"You runnin' scared?" she scoffed. "First time I ever heard of a Sackett runnin' . . . unless pa was a-shootin' at him."

Darkness had kind of shut down on us. "You better get back to your camp," I said. "They'll be expectin' me back yonder."

"You mean you ain't goin' to see me home? If you're scared, I'll tell you now. Ol' Jack Ben ain't there. I am surely alone. And I ain't scared—much of the time."

Chapter 15

"Where's your pa?"

"He's down to Shalako. That new town over west. He's down there a-waitin' for me to come bail him out."

"He's in jail?"

"No such thing! He's—he's laid up, that's all. We come west without—well, we didn't have much to do with, an' pa figured he could mine for gold.

"Well, he tried it, and it brought on his rheumatism again and he's laid up. On'y things about him ain't ailin' is his trigger finger and his jaw.

"A man down yonder panned gold out of this stream, and he told us of it, so I done left a note to tell pa where I'd gone, an' then I hightailed it up here."

"You come all the way by yourself?"

"No, sir. I got a mule down yonder. A fast-walkin' mule and just like me he'll take nothing from nobody. I've also got a dog that's half bear."

"You're funnin'—half bear? It won't work."

"You should of told his ma that. Anyway, I reckon that ol' he-bear wasn't askin' any questions. I tell you I got a dog that's half bear."

She glanced up at me as we walked along. "You said you took up with a Trelawney girl out west. Which one was it?"

"You mean there's more than the two of you come west? How much can this country stand, all to one time? Her name was Dorinda."

"Oh-oh-oh! Maybe I got to look at you in daylight, mister. If Dorinda took up with you there must be more to you than I figured. She was a beautiful one, Dorinda was."

"Yes, ma'am, but not to be trusted. Back in the mountains we could always count on a Trelawney girl to do her best, but that one! That Dorinda usually done her worst. She nigh got me killed."

We'd come up to a shelving shore where she'd put together a lean-to under some trees. Sure enough, there was a mule, a big, rawboned no-nonsense Missouri mule that must have weighed fifteen hundred pounds and every bit of it meanness.

I heard a low growl. Mister, if that dog wasn't half bear he was half of something that was big, and he was mean and ugly. He must have weighed two hundred and fifty pounds. He had a head like a bull mastiff and teeth that would give one of them dinnysouers a scare.

"It's all right, Neb," Nell said. "He's friendly."

"If I wasn't," I said, "I'd start being. That's the biggest durned dog I ever did see."

"He's big, all right."

"What do you feed him? A calf a day?"

"He rustles his own grub. Maybe he eats people. I wouldn't know. He goes off in the woods now and again, and when he comes back he's licking his chops."

"Where'd you latch onto him?"

"He took up with me. I was huntin' elk up top and this here dog came up out of the bottoms. There's a place where the rim drops off about twelve hundred feet, and I had just killed me an elk, when this dog showed up.

"He stretched out with his head on his paws, like, and I figured him for a bear, so I slung him a chunk of meat. After that he sort of stayed with me."

"In Shalako, too? Why he'd stampede every horse in the valley!"

"He don't stampede Jacob. Jacob an' him, they get along."

Jacob, I took it, was the mule.

"Well," I got up. "Those boys yonder will think I went to get a drink and the hogs et me. I'd better start back, but you come down and see us. We'll be around for a day or two . . . and you keep an eye open for those men I spoke of. They ain't pleasant folks. Nobody you'd invite to a quiltin' or a box social, like."

By the time I got back to the fire everybody was settin' about. They'd eaten and were drinking coffee and listening for trouble. I made no effort to be quiet, and, when I was within distance, I hailed the fire, as a gentleman should. The ungentlemanly often ended up with a bellyful of buckshot.

A man who shoots when you don't call out doesn't have too many friends, but his enemies are surely all dead.

"What took you so long?" Orrin asked.

The Tinker was looking at me kind of wise and so was Judas Priest.

"I was keepin' comp'ny," I said. "I was settin' out with a gal."

"Up here?" Orrin scoffed.

"I think he's telling the truth," the Tinker said. "He doesn't act like he'd been out among the bears."

So I explained to them about Nell Trelawney and about old Jack Ben Trelawney down at Shalako waiting for his daughter to pan out enough gold to get them out of hock.

Orrin shook his head. "That's hard work for a man," he grumbled, "and no woman should be doing it."

"Jack Ben's all crippled up," I said. "What would you have her do? Set still while they starve?"

"All the Trelawney girls could cook," he suggested, "and the food isn't all that good in these mining towns."

"That needs cash money to lay out for flour and the like. You got to have a place."

"I agree with Mr. Orrin," Judas said positively. "It is no task for a woman."

We had our own problems, and that night I got out the daybook again. I gave it to Orrin to read to us.

> I have been writing in secret, but it is far from easy. I think Pettigrew suspects what I am doing, but he is a secretive man and merely smiles that sly smile and says nothing.
>
> Somebody has found gold! This morning Pierre found a small hole, dug near a tree and hastily filled in. The marks near the tree were of Pettigrew's boots.
>
> Later, alone with Pierre, I told him the tracks were faked to implicate Pettigrew. He scoffed at me and didn't believe it. I told him they wanted to eliminate anyone who might be on his side and they would probably try to raise suspicion about me next, and if that didn't work, there would be another Indian attack. He was angry and demanded to know what I meant by that. I told him there had been no Indians, I had found no tracks. Had there been Indians, they would have returned to destroy us.
>
> He was listening by then, and he asked who would fake such an attack and why. I told him I thought it was Andre and Swan. He was annoyed because I accused his brother-in-law. I said it seemed clear that Andre didn't mind killing and neither did he seem to mind Swan's brutality to Angus.
>
> Pierre did not like it, but he listened. "You think gold has

been found and held out?" he said. I told him that was exactly what I believed.

I took to sleeping away from the others, on a pretense of watching for Indians, and I made my bed among leaves and branches that could not be walked over without noise. Moreover I watched my back.

We read on. Pa had apparently been doing some scouting around and he had come up with a camp location—two locations, in fact. He argued with Pierre Bontemps that there had been friction within the detachment. The story was that the Utes had attacked them, killed many, and that some had died of starvation later. Only a few men were supposed to have escaped. For several reasons, the story did not make a lot of sense, for this hadn't been a patrol, but a large body of men—perhaps as many as three hundred. Pa believed there were less.

He figured there had been difficulties in the camp and they had separated. Under such primitive conditions animosities could develop, and something had obviously happened there. Pa found two camps, both with stone walls roughly put together, and he found postholes—the posts were rotted away but the holes could be cleaned out. Rough shelters—he found a button or two, and a broken knife.

Pa was shot at twice in the woods, but merely commented it must be Indians. Meanwhile he stopped telling anyone his conclusions. From bones he dug up and other signs, he decided one camp was doing a lot better than the other. The men in that part of the French military detachment were eating better, living better.

. . . must be an Indian or a mountain man in that outfit.
May 24: On the run. Wounded. We found the gold, or some of it. Andre and Swan acted at once. Luckily I'd spread my bed as usual, then being uneasy I moved back into the aspen. Had a devil of a time finding a place to stretch out, so close they were. Suddenly I awakened and heard movement, then a roar of rifles. They'd slipped up and shot into my bedding. Unable to get close, they stood back and fired. They must have poured a dozen rounds into the place where my bedding was.

I heard Andre say, "Now for Pettigrew. Move quickly, man. Tell him it's Indians and when you get close . . ." Swan asked

him what to do about Pierre, and Baston said, "Leave 'im to
me."

I couldn't get to both of them in time, but I ran toward
Pierre, moving silently as could be.

We didn't need no pictures to tell us what was happening there atop
the mountain. Baston and Swan had turned to murder as soon as night
came, wanting the gold for themselves. They'd tried to kill pa first, and
they believed the job was done. Only it didn't work out the way they
planned. When Swan got to Nativity Pettigrew's bed, the man was gone.
It wasn't until later that they discovered a horse was also gone.

Getting out of the aspen was a job, and pa had to find his way back to
the camp in the darkness, expecting a shot any minute, having only a sin-
gle-shot rifle and a pistol.

He was coming up on them when he heard Baston.

"... no use reaching for that gun. I took the powder from it
last evening, Pierre. Sackett is dead, and soon you will be."
There was a shot, then Baston laughed, a mean laugh it was,
too. "That was one leg, Pierre." Another shot. "The other leg. I
never liked you, you know. I knew someday I'd do this,
planned it, thought about it. I just wish I could stay and watch
you die."

Swan ran up, and there was talk. I guess they'd found Pettigrew was gone. I heard swearing, and I moved in for a shot.

Eager to get a shot, and unable to see in the dark I lifted my
rifle, stepped forward for a better shot, and stepped into an unexpected hole. My body crashed into a bush. My rifle went off,
and bullets cut leaves near my head. Another shot was fired,
and I felt the shock of a bullet. I went down, falling on my pistol. If I moved they'd hear me. I drew my knife and waited.

They did not find me, and neither was of a mind to come
hunting me in the dark. I heard Baston talking to Pierre, saying, "You're dead. I will leave you here to die. You've lost
blood, both knees are broken, and you'll never be found. We
didn't find as much gold as I'd hoped, but we can always come
back. We'll be the only ones who know where it is now."

"Pettigrew got away. He'll tell them," Pierre said.

And Andre answered, "Him? We'll catch him before he
gets off the mountain. And when we do, we'll kill him."

Chapter 16

When Orrin put down the daybook, too sleepy to read further, I was of no mind to take it up. Mayhap I was fearful of what I'd find, or just too tired, but the thought was with us all that Andre Baston, Hippo Swan, and whoever was riding with them were comin' up behind us.

No doubt, after shooting Pierre Bontemps and killing Angus and maybe pa, they had taken off, carrying gold with them. However, they had unfinished business. If Pettigrew got away, they had to run him down and kill him, or try. And that was what they'd done.

We were lyin' in our blankets when Orrin said, "They daren't leave pa alive. Philip Baston seemed a kindly man, but Andre fears him or fears what he can do, and Andre is his own brother and knows him better than we do."

"I'm wonderin' where Pettigrew got that daybook. Did he steal it off pa? Or did he come back and find it later?"

Tomorrow we had to go up the mountain with a lot of questions unanswered. Facing us was a showdown with Baston, and there was no low-rating the man. Some of the things we'd been reading about him in pa's daybook were clumsy, you might say, but Andre had twenty years to grow handier with his killing, and by all accounts he'd not wasted his time. All of them seemed to have low-rated Nativity Pettigrew, including Andre, and they never guessed that Pettigrew had come by some gold.

Lying there, before I dropped off to sleep, I worried some about Nell Trelawney. Of course, she had that dog . . . if it was a dog.

Anybody going around there at night would be apt to lose a leg or an arm before he knew what he was tangling with. One time I met a man told me about the mastiffs they have in Tibet. They're as big as the mastiffs we have only they have much longer hair. This Neb dog might be one of them.

Morning found nobody wishful of using language. We set around glumlike, roasting our meat over the fire and drinking coffee.

Orrin got up and took his Winchester. "Judas, stay by the camp, if you will. We can't afford to lose the stock or whatever else we've got. And

Tinker, if you'll go see to Miss Trelawney we'd be pleased. Tell and I will scout around up top."

It was no easy climb. Heavy timber, with game trails here and there, and we made it up to the top. We Injuned around, looking for sign. It was there, all right, but from down those forgotten years. Marks of axes where men had chopped wood for fires long since burned up, branches cut to make a lean-to or to hang kettles from. There was evidence enough that men had lived around about at some time far gone.

We split up and worked back and forth across the top of the mountain, comparing notes now and again. We wanted to find some sign of pa, but we kind of hoped we wouldn't. When you don't see a body laid away, that person is never quite dead for you, just sort of gone away, or not around right then.

We were playing against time. Whatever we were going to find we'd have to find now, for Andre, Swan, and them would be coming up the slope. And I wondered a little about Pettigrew. He was a sly man, maybe not as crippled up as he let on.

Orrin crouched beside me under a tree. "The story has it there were three separate caches of gold," he said. "Now, even if there was only five million, it is still a lot of gold to carry, and none of them took more away than could be carried on the horses they rode.

"It is my thought, and I believe it to be yours, that some soldiers kept some gold for themselves. Perhaps they were permitted to. Perhaps they simply highgraded it, but I believe that is what Pettigrew found, and what Andre himself found.

"I think two things are at work here. They fear what we might discover and reveal to Philip, but also they fear we may find the gold they failed to find."

Sunlight fell through the trees, and a camp-robber jay hopped from branch to branch above us. I looked off through the trees, thinking of pa and what his thoughts must have been when he had played out his deadly hand, knowing the fall of any card might mean death to him.

At the end there, lying wounded in the brush with Pierre crippled and perhaps beyond help, the rest of them riding away, what would pa have been thinking?

We had to find that place, but how, after so many years? Had Pierre Bontemps died there?

My eyes wandered over the slope. The human eye has a readiness for patterns. Much is not seen simply because the mind is blind, not the eyes. The eyes see in lines, curves, and patterns. Man himself works in patterns simple or complex, and such things are often evidence of man's previous presence.

Twenty years ago some evidence of the old camps had remained, even after half a century that had fallen between. "Orrin, there's got to be some sign of those camps. Stone walled, they said."

"Yes, there should be something of them left." He got up, and, skirmisher fashion, we moved off through the scattered trees, walking on pine needles, eyes alert for everything.

High up in the mountains you don't have to think of rattlers. They stay down lower where it is warmer, and they thin out mighty fast above sixty-five hundred feet.

As we moved along under the trees the camp-robber jay followed us, never more than twenty feet off. They are the greatest companions in the high mountains, but also the worst thieves. Anything left where they can get at it is eaten or gone, and they'll do things mighty nigh unbelievable to get at what they want.

"Tell?" Orrin pointed with his rifle. Under the trees up ahead we could see a dug-out hole, and when we got there we could see it was old. Somebody had dug down four feet or so, but the edges had caved in, and plants were growing into it. There was a patch of snow in the bottom where no sun reached.

It might be a hole dug by the folks we knew of, or it might have been dug by some other treasure hunter. There was nothing up here an animal would dig for.

We studied around but found no sign to identify anything. We went west along the slope. Right above us we could see the trees flagging as they do when the strong winds work on them, and here and there were brown tops on the green trees where the tops had stuck out of the snow and frozen.

My belly was asking questions of me before we spotted the first fort. It was lined-up rocks, tumbled this way and that, but it was clear to see that somebody had forted up here long ago. Not many yards west, we found the other camp, and right away I saw what pa meant.

Whoever built the second camp knew what he was about. He had shaped it for comfort and a good field of fire in all directions. A place had been found where boulders and stunted trees made a partial wall against the prevailing winds, which were indicated by the way the trees flagged. On mountain tops the branches are apt to be all or mostly on one side of a tree, streaming out the way the wind blows.

More time had been taken with this second fort, the rocks had been fitted better, so some of them still sat fixed as they'd been left. It was obvious that, although there'd been a split in the camp, each wanted to have support from the other in case of Indians.

And from all reports, the Indians had come.

We poked around inside the second circle of rocks. We found a button and a broken tinderbox and nothing else that spoke of human habitation.

"The three big caches were probably sunk deep by order of the officer in command, and my guess is they were done damned well," said Orrin. "The army expected to return for them, and they would be buried to be excavated by the army. Those little caches Baston found and the one Pettigrew probably found were buried shallow or hidden in hollows of rocks or trees, somewhere the men who hid them could grab them quick.

"Are you thinking what I am? That Indian or mountain man pa mentioned might have taken that second outfit toward the west."

"Uh-huh," I said. "Two camps like this mean there was trouble, as pa figured, and if they did go west they could have gone south from Pagosa Springs to Santa Fe, or even further west."

We sat silent, considering that. Our thoughts were strangely captured by that mysterious mountain man who was with them.

Had the military chosen him as guide? Had he come from New Orleans with them or joined them en route? Or could he have come upon them in the mountains?

There was a route from Shalako to Santa Fe, certainly traveled by Rivera in 1765, and by Escalante about 1776. There could have been others before them—perhaps a hundred or more years before them—and any man who knew the country would know the old Spanish Trail.

We were on a sort of mesa above the San Juan River. From the timber cut down and the way things looked the French army had a permanent camp here, with quite a few horses. Another party of Frenchmen had come in afterwards, and they must have arrived and departed only a few years before pa and his party came there.

When I mentioned that, Orrin said, "Departed? Maybe."

Off to one side we found evidence of quite a battle. Old shells were lying about, and they had to be from a later crowd. When the first bunch was here there were only muzzle-loaders, and there were signs of some quick defensive positions thrown up—they might have been wiped out by the Utes.

"Pa was keepin' that daybook," I said to Orrin. "He figured somehow to get it to us, so he must've left his mark around here. Maybe some mark only a Sackett would know."

"What would that be?" Orrin asked, and he had me there. Nonetheless, I was looking.

It had to be something that would last. We were mere boys then, so we'd not be hunting for him or coming west until years later. Yet pa was a man given to considering, and he'd talked about the western lands, had prepared us for what was to come. He had wandered the west, and he was wishful we would do the same.

We found nothing a man could tie to. There had been holes dug, some of them by folks who came later, but none of them looked ambitious. Whether all that gold was buried in one hole or three, it must have been well dug and well lined. Whoever was in command had the man power and the will, I was sure of that. Judging by what I knew of such affairs, it seemed to me they had started to break up toward the end when one crowd wanted to leave and another wanted to stay or go by another route. It takes a mighty fine discipline to hold men together when trouble is creeping up on you. Yet without discipline there is surely disaster. The best discipline comes from within a man, but you'll never get a party of men together where all have it.

This bunch had split, and most of the discipline was in the camp that had the mountain man. I don't mean one of those trappers, like pa and Kit Carson or Bridger—they came later. I mean a man who had lived in the mountains before and knew how to get along.

"Orrin," I said, "we'd better be lookin' down that trail. We're about to run out of time."

"We'll do it together," he said. "I wish Tyrel was with us."

"'If wishes were horses, then beggars would ride,'" I quoted at him. "A body shouldn't heed what might be. He's got to do with what is.

"There's a whole lot of mountain here, and you and me packed a rifle over mountains before either of us was knee-high to a possum. Anyway, it does no good to pack up an' run. A body has to stay in there and fight. No matter how many times you get knocked down you got to keep gettin' up until the other man quits."

"Easier said," Orrin commented.

"Well, I knew of a man who was defeated by just about everything. He failed in business back in 1831. He was defeated for the legislature in 1832, failed in business again in 1833, was elected to the legislature in 1834. His sweetheart died in 1835. He had a nervous breakdown in 1836, was defeated for speaker in 1838, defeated for land officer in 1843, defeated for Congress in 1843, elected to Congress in 1846, defeated for reelection in 1848, defeated for the Senate in 1855, defeated for vice-president in 1856, and defeated for the Senate in 1858."

"I'd of quit," Orrin said.

"No you wouldn't. I know you too well. This man didn't quit either. He was elected president in 1860."

"What?"

"Sure. His name was Abraham Lincoln."

Chapter 17

Our camp was about a mile from Nell's. She had located not far from Silver Falls, and we were down creek from her just beyond the beaver ponds.

Tinker was back at camp when Orrin and me dropped down off Treasure Mountain. "She's all right," he told us. "Anybody who'd take after her with that animal about would be crazy. All the time I was there he watched every move I made and growled if I got too close to her."

"She pannin' today?"

"Some—showing some color, too. Not much, but if she can stay with it in that cold water she'll come out with a stake."

"It's better than huntin' that gold. Why, this here mountain must cover thirty square miles! There's no tellin' where they hid the stuff, and a man could work his life away and come up empty."

Orrin filled his cup. "Tell? What do you think we should do? We've found no clue to pa. If you're right and that other party went west, he might have done the same, if he got out."

"He must've lived. There's still a few pages of the daybook covered with writin'. But what he was wishful of us knowing he'd guard somehow. We've got to read carefully. I say we read what he says, and then we should work that mountain one time more. You know, pa knew the country west of here. He told us about time spent on the Dolores River."

We ate, and then we brewed some fresh coffee. Just as I'd gotten out the daybook we heard an animal coming and eased back from the firelight.

A voice called out of the darkness, "Hello, the fire! I'm coming in!"

It was Nell Trelawney astride that mule Jacob, with Neb trailing alongside. "I got lonesome," she said, "seeing your fire. I decided to come along down."

"Set down. We're about to read from pa's daybook. We've got to listen sharp for a clue."

> . . . drew my knife and waited. Nobody come. After awhile I
> crawled out of the brush, and then I was shamed. That bullet

done me no harm. It must have hit something before me. Anyway, it hit my belt and tomahawk handle, nigh cutting the belt in two, gouging the handle, and bruising my hipbone.

Nobody was around. I crawled to Pierre and he was still alive. Working in the dark I got his wounds stopped up with moss and eased him where he lay.

Two days have passed. At daybreak I set both of Pierre's legs in splints. Doubt if he will ever walk—if he lives. Made a travois with two poles, two buffalo coats. Put bottoms of coats together, ran the poles through the arms of each coat, then buttoned the coats and managed to get Pierre on it.

The horses had disappeared, whether taken or driven off I didn't know. Andre and Swan had taken all the food but the little I had in my gear, and I'd little to do with.

Taking up the ends of the two poles, I started out. It was a slow business. Pierre was hurting and the trail narrow. By nightfall I'd reached the spring near Windy Pass. I figured to hit the valley of the West Fork of the San Juan and follow the San Juan.

I am writing this beside the spring at Windy Pass. We have had a little to eat. Pierre says Andre fears Philip, but shot Pierre not only because of hate, but because he wished to inherit. "He will be fooled," Pierre said. "I left all to Philip."

We are somewhat sheltered here, but the wind is cold. It has the feel of snow from the high peaks.

"Is it not late for snow?" Judas asked.

"Not in these mountains. He's nigh the end of May, but he's ten thousand feet up. I've seen bad snow storms in the Rockies later than that."

"We get only a part," the Tinker said. "He does not say how bad it is. He has drawn that travois, with a heavy man and all they have, more than six miles in one day."

Pa was never one for carryin' on about his hurts, but he had him a badly bruised hipbone, and haulin' the travois must have been a trial for a man of his years, even one as bull-strong as he was.

Just why pa chose the western route I wasn't sure—the first of it was easier, and also Andre and Swan had gone the other way and pa might have thought they'd be lyin' in wait to see if they were followed.

Right below the spring where pa stopped with Pierre, only about two miles away, was the valley of the West Fork of the San Juan, and a lovely valley it was.

I could picture them, Pierre lyin' there suffering in his pain, pa tired as all get-out what with pullin' a load at a high altitude and his hip bothering him and all. I'd had a few badly bruised bones, once from a bullet, another time when a bronc pitched me into some rocks, and the last time when a steer flung his head around and hit me with a horn.

The fire would be flickerin' on their faces, drawn and tired as they were, and right behind them the shadows of rocks and trees.

Orrin took up reading again. He had a better voice than me, and he made a better thing of it.

Pierre is at last asleep, which gives him relief. I have gathered wood for the night and the morning fire. My hip is bothering me, and I'm afraid it will stiffen during the night. I have been thinking much of ma and the boys, wondering if ever they will see these words, if ever they will know what has become of me. They are good boys, and will grow strong and tall. I wish I could be there to see them, but tonight I feel no confidence. A growing thing is in me, not a fear of Andre or of Utes, not even a fear of death, only a fear I shall not see them again.

I was awakened by muttering from Pierre. The man was delirious, and I worried. I looked at him in the fire's red light, and he looked wildly at me and muttered about Philip. I made hot broth and managed to get some of it into him, but he talked wildly of poison, of the death of his father, of some thin red line that ran through the Baston line, and a lot that made no sense to me.

June 2: Camp on the West Fork. Pierre in bad shape. His legs in splints, but nothing more I can do. They are in frightful shape. Several times he has thanked me for staying by him.

June 3: Same place. No more than 15 miles from where we started. Ute tracks, some unshod horses, nothing fresh. I must have fires to heat water. Hot water on his legs seems to ease him somewhat. The coffee is almost gone.

June 4: Pierre is dead! Went to the river for water and returning found him dead, stabbed three times in the heart. It was no Indian, for nothing was taken, not the coffee or the sugar, nor powder or lead.

Andre or Swan? I dare have no fire now. I shall bury Pierre, gather my few things, and take to the woods.

I have just seen three of our horses grazing a little way

downstream! I believe they will come to me for I always had something for them. I shall go now, and try.

That was the end of it. No more. Pa had gone to try for those horses.

"Nativity Pettigrew," I said. "He had the daybook. How did he come by it?"

"Maybe he was the one who murdered Pierre," the Tinker suggested. "Maybe when your pa went after the horses he came back, stole the book, and took off. You recall what your pa said? Pettigrew suspected him of writing things down? That daybook must have worried him."

"We've got to find that camp. That may be the last lead we get."

We sat around the fire talking it over, drinking coffee, keeping our ears in tune with the night. I was restless, ready to move on. A lot of men had looked for gold here and not found it, and I did not wish to become another of them. Nor did Orrin.

In the morning we would take the route to Windy Pass.

At first Nell would have none of it, but we argued there was gold closer to where her pa was.

I think we all turned in figuring that tomorrow would tell us the end of the story of pa's disappearance.

None of us wanted a fight with Andre and them. Well, I'll have to back up on that. Fact was, I'd not mind so much, only that it would profit nobody. I had an itch to tangle—especially with Swan. There's something gets up in my craw when I come up against a bully, and Hippo Swan was that.

There was nothing to be gained by fighting them, and I was ready to ride off and leave them be. Just the same, I felt one of the true pleasures of life would be to plant a fist in Hippo's face. But I was prepared to deny myself that pleasure.

Some things just don't shape up the way a man hopes for.

Come morning we packed our gear, and we helped Nell get straightened around, and then we headed for Windy Pass as our first stop on the way west to Shalako.

Looking back with regret, I saw that little mountain valley disappear behind us. It was a place we'd stopped at for only a few days, but I'd come to love it—the beaver ponds, the distant sound of Silver Falls, the cold, sparkling waters of the East Fork.

There was an easier trail down the East Fork to the main valley, but we were wishful of scouting around the pass, so we went up the mountain. It was just a mite over two miles to Windy Pass.

We found signs of several old fires up yonder, but nothing more to tell us anything about pa. He'd been there, but so had others.

Orrin pulled up quick, just as we started out. "I thought I heard a shot," he said.

I'd heard nothing, but Judas believed he had, too.

We rode out on the trail to the valley and turned south. To really appreciate the valley of the West Fork of the San Juan you've got to see it from north of where we were, up yonder where the Wolf Creek Pass trail takes a big swing and starts down the mountain. There's a place there that's a thousand feet above the valley floor. You can see right down the length of the valley and there isn't a prettier sight under heaven.

We turned into the trail and started along, moving at a good pace. We had Nell with us, and, like I've said, we weren't shaping up for no fight. None of us liked Andre. We figured him for a murdering so-and-so, but we weren't elected by the good Lord to put out his light . . . not so far as we knew.

I surely wasn't going to hunt him, but if he happened to come up in my sights, it would be a mighty temptation.

It was a beautiful morning, a morning to ride and feel, and we all felt the same about that. None of us were much given to talk, although Orrin could sing. He sang while we rode—"Tenting Tonight on the Old Camp-Ground," "Black, Black, Black," and "Barbry Allen." I was wishful of joining him when he sang "Brennan on the Moor," but there was no use to wake the coyotes or disturb the peace of Jacob, the mule. Only time I sing is when I am alone on a sleepy horse. There's limits to everything.

Meanwhile, we rode wary for pa's camp. A lot of time had gone by, but there was a chance we could find something.

The way we figured it now, somebody had returned to murder Pierre and pa.

Andre and Swan? Or Pettigrew?

I couldn't get Nativity Pettigrew out of my mind. He was a sly man, a murderous man possibly, but he'd had the daybook, and the only way he could have gotten that daybook would have been to follow pa and Pierre.

Pettigrew had gold on his mind, and mayhap he had found it, and was wishful of keeping it. He would have to be mighty shy of how he brought it down off that mountain. A lot of people wish to find treasure, but few of them realize how hard it is to handle after you've got it.

How do you bring a million dollars in gold down off a mountain? Mules, you say? You've got to get mules or horses, and that starts people wondering what you want them for. And you may need help, but help can be greedy, often as murderous as you.

I tell you, gold is easier found than kept.

Chapter 18

Neb scouted ahead for us, and that was a canny dog. He was big enough to be kin to a grizzly and had a nose like an Arkansas coonhound.

We rode scattered out, not talking, wary for traps because this was Indian country, but wary for those coming down behind us, too.

Pa's travois would have made an easy trail to follow, and I wondered if he, too, had feared what was behind him. When we came up to his camp we saw why he'd chosen it. That camp was well out in the open, among just a few trees and some brush, and there was a good field of fire wherever a body looked.

Of course, at first we weren't sure it was pa's camp. It was a likely spot, and there were stones blackened by fires in a clearing among the trees. We got down from our horses and, while the Tinker kept a lookout, we stood around and sized up the situation.

Nell found the grave. She had walked to the other side of the small clearing among the trees. It was there, south of the patch of woods and a small knoll. Only one grave. Above it was a cross and the name, *Pierre Bontemps*.

Pa had walked away from here when he saw the horses, and that might be any place to the south, but he saw them from here. He'd made no mention of burying Pierre, so he must have come back . . . but Pierre's killer could have buried him. And suppose pa lay in the same grave?

Neither Orrin nor me figured such would be the case, but scattered out around that little nest of trees to see what we could find. Others had been here since, and there would be nothing left unless pa had left some sign intentionally, or unless there was some item time had not destroyed.

We found nothing.

"Tell," Orrin said, "you were a mite older than any of us, and you knew pa a little better. What do you think he would have done at this point?"

"Whoever killed Pierre may have killed him," the Tinker suggested. "He may have laid by those horses waiting for your father."

Judas objected. "That is a possibility, of course. But it seems to me that whoever killed Mr. Bontemps was not one to take chances. He stabbed a wounded, helpless man three times. I believe he would prefer to wait, to catch Mr. Sackett asleep or somehow helpless."

"The way I see it, Orrin," I said, "knowin' the kind of man pa was, why he came west and all, I think, once he had the horses and no longer had to worry about Pierre, he'd go back after some of that gold."

"I think he did go back," Nell said.

"Well, maybe," I said doubtfully. "I think he *would*, but we don't know if he did."

"I know," Nell repeated. "I am sure he went back."

"Why?" Orrin asked.

"I think when he left the second time, having some gold and all, and remembering what happened to Mr. Bontemps, I think he would take another route," she said.

"These mountains offer very few roads," Judas objected, "and this is the best way, obviously."

"And the most dangerous. Best routes never meant much to a mountain-born Sackett, anyway," she insisted. "I want to tell you something.

"Just east of Silver Falls I found an old Indian trail. It heads off south along the shoulder above Quartz Creek. When I first settled in there to pan that creek I studied the country in case I had to run. I scouted that trail across the high-up mountains until I could see where it led.

"It goes right to Pagosa Springs, although there's a branch, looks like, that swings south. I've got a feeling it joins up with a trail I saw coming in from the south at Haystack Mountain."

It surely made sense. Pa was never one to set himself up for somebody, and if he now had some gold he would be doubly in danger. He'd keep off the main trails, use routes where he could find cover from which to study his back trail, and he'd head west.

If anybody was lying in wait it would be along the trail east. Folks at San Luis might have talked, and there were always bad men around who'd lie up for a man and try to gather in what he had.

Pa had wintered out west and he liked that country. If he had taken his gold that way he could come by an unexpected way and likely would avoid trouble. Still, any man packing gold was sure to be an uneasy man.

Seemed to me the only thing to do now was to cut out for Shalako, scout around there and talk to some of the Utes who might know something. Mighty few people travel through Indian country without being seen, and it was likely the Utes knew all that had taken place around Treasure Mountain—if they'd talk.

We headed west, rattling our hocks down the trail for Shalako. We knew that our cousins Flagan and Galloway had settled in that neighborhood a short time back, and we figured to meet up with them, then get our bearings. Galloway was a great hand to make friends, and chances were that he had Indian friends among them.

We Sacketts have fought Indians, camped with them, hunted with them, told stories with them, slept in their tipis and wickiups, and fought with them again. Sometimes all was friendly, depending on the tribe and how they felt at the moment. Pa had lived with Indians, too, and favored their way of life, and, of course, back there in the high-up hills of Tennessee and North Carolina, we'd had many a friend among the Cherokee, Shawnee, or Chickasaws.

They had their way of life and we had ours, and when the white man moved in he did just what the Indians had done before him. He took what land he needed. There were mighty few Indians for the size of the country, and we crowded them like they crowded others.

Life had been that way from the beginning of time, and I could see no end to it.

Over there in Europe the Celts crowded the Picts, and the Saxons crowded the Celts, and then the Normans moved in and took over the country, and it was the same story all across the world.

Five days later we rode into Animas City which they were building into quite a town. Must have been twenty or twenty-five buildings there, most of them dwellings of one sort or another.

We rode up to Schwenk and Will's saloon, which was also a store. By the look of it, this place had just been opened, but business wasn't suffering. There were half a dozen men at the bar and this was just after midday.

The Tinker and Judas took the horses down to the river for water, Nell went with them, and Orrin and me decided to listen to what was being said and try to find out what we could.

A couple of men nodded as we came in, and one of them spoke. The rest just glanced around and paid us no mind.

Nobody was talking very much. There was some talk of a railroad coming in, but it looked to me like that was nothing that was going to happen very soon.

The bartender came down our way and we both ordered rye. He glanced at us real sharp, then again. "Travelin' through?"

"Maybe."

"Pretty country," Orrin commented, "right pretty country. Much going on around?"

"Mining. Cattle. You a cattleman?"

"Lawyer," Orrin said. "But I've worked with cattle. Much ranching around here?"

"West of here, and south. Some good outfits. There's a new bunch over on the La Plata. Name of Sackett."

"Heard of them," Orrin said.

"There's other Sacketts around here. One of the first men in this country was Seth Sackett. He came in with the Baker outfit."

"Good folks, no doubt," I said.

"The best," said the bartender. He was a shrewd competent-looking man. "You boys could do worse than to settle here yourselves."

"Maybe we'll ride over and see those Sacketts. The ones over on the La Plata."

"If you go," the bartender advised, "better go friendly. They're good boys but they don't take kindly to folks pushing them.

"They've got them a ranch over just beyond that new town—Shalako, or some such name. They've brought in some cattle, but from all I hear they're still sort of camping out. Haven't started to build, yet."

We drank our rye, then ordered coffee. We could see the Tinker had come back and was loafing near the corral, honing the blade of that Tinker-made knife of his. Perhaps the finest knife ever made.

"You been around here long?" Orrin asked.

"We just opened up. Nobody's been here very long, some folks came in in '73, but the town didn't sort of begin to settle up until '76. If you ride around much, keep your eyes open and a gun handy. The Utes haven't decided what to do about us yet."

One of the other men—a short, barrel-chested man with a broad, friendly face—was looking at me. Suddenly he said, "Speaking of Sacketts, there was one come into this country some years back. Had him a claim up on the Vallecitos. He was hell-on-wheels with a pistol."

"You don't say?" I said, innocently. "Well, I figure if you leave those folks alone they'll leave you alone."

"There's something else, though," I added. "If any of you know anybody who was around here about twenty years back, I'd like to talk to him . . . or them."

"Ask Flagan or Galloway Sackett. They're new in the country but they've got an old Indian working for them who has been in this country since those mountains were holes in the ground—goes by the name of Powder-Face."

We finished our coffee and drifted outside. It was a warm, pleasant morning with a blue sky overhead and a scattering of white clouds here and there, a real picture-book sky, typical of that country.

"I've got an uneasy feelin'," I told Orrin.

He nodded. "Reason I wanted to get out of there. No use mixing innocent people in our troubles."

"That one man knew me, or figured he did."

We stood there looking up and down the street. Animas City wasn't much of a town, but it was growing, and it looked like there would be business enough with the mining, ranching, and all.

The Tinker strolled over and joined us. "Man just rode in," he said. "Tied his horse over yonder by the drugstore."

The Newman, Chestnut, and Stevens Drugstore was right along the street. We walked out and went down to the blacksmith shop run by the Naegelin Brothers, and we glanced across at the horse.

The brand was visible from there, and it was 888.

"Charley McCaire's brand," I said. "What do you make of that?"

Orrin shrugged. "Let's ride out."

We walked back to the Tinker and then the three of us went to where Nell and Judas Priest were setting on the bank by the river. We all mounted up and rode out. As we glanced back we saw a man come out of the drugstore and look after us.

A short time later we stopped near the Twin Buttes and waited, studying our back trail, but nobody showed so we rode on, walking our horses as it was mostly uphill, although the grade was not too steep.

The town of Shalako lay on a flat bench with a looming backdrop of the La Plata Mountains behind it. On past the town a trail went on up La Plata Canyon, following the La Plata River. There were very few buildings in the town—one of them was a saloon.

The man behind the bar was a big Swede. He sized me up as I came through the door. Orrin and the others were following me.

He grinned and came around the bar. "Tell! Tell Sackett! Well, I'll be damned! The boys said you'd be coming up sooner or later, but this is great! Have a drink on the house!"

"We'd rather eat," I said. "We've just come in from Animas City." I drew back a chair and sat down.

"Orrin, this here is Swede Berglund, a good man anywhere you find him."

They shook hands, and then he greeted Judas, Nell, and the Tinker and went to the kitchen to stir up the grub. I wiped the sweat from my hatband and squinted out the open door. Across the street was a supply outfit—general store, miners' supplies, and whatever, and next to that was a livery stable.

When I looked across the street again two men were getting down in front of the store. They looked like they'd come a far piece, and one of them stayed beside the horses while the other went into the store.

The flank of one horse was turned toward me and I could read the brand.

Three Eights . . .

"Orrin," I said, "looks like we've got comp'ny."

Chapter 19

"Could be chance," he said, glancing out the window. "I doubt if Charley McCaire's mad enough to follow us here."

"Suppose he tied up with Baston an' them?"

He shrugged. "Unlikely, but it could be."

There was no use asking for trouble. We'd had a mite of difficulty with McCaire back yonder in New Mexico, and he was truly a hard, stubborn man. Of course, this was good cattle country, with water aplenty and grass. A desert or dry-plains country rancher will ride a far piece for range country like there was hereabouts.

Berglund was putting some bowls of stew on the table, and slabs of bread made from stone-ground wheat. "Eat up, the coffee's gettin' hot."

"That peak yonder," I said, indicating a smooth-domed mountain that seemed to be covered with green growth right over the top, "what peak is that?"

"Baldy," Berglund said. "That's Parrott Peak on the other side of the canyon."

"That's La Plata Canyon?"

"Sure is. The river comes right down from the top. That's rough country up yonder, rough and beautiful."

"Heard about it," I said. "The river heads up a big glacial basin?"

"What they call a cirque. Yeah, that's right. She picks up some other little streams on the way down. I've only been part way up. Lots of elk and deer up there, and bear, too.

"Last time I was up there I stopped to pick wild strawberries and saw a grizzly doing the same thing. I just backed off and left him alone. It was a good hundred yards off, but that wasn't far enough for me. It's wonderful how cramped a country can get when it's you and a grizzly in the same neighborhood."

Pa had taken off from Treasure Mountain and come down. Chances were he came this far, for he knew the La Plata country as well as that west of here. He might have stopped in the Animas Valley, but, knowing him, I doubted it.

"Orrin, tomorrow you ought to scout around for a place, something ma would like to pass her days in, where we could raise up some cattle."

"What about you?"

"I'm going to find old Powder-Face and make talk with him. If pa came into this country you can bet those Indians knew about it."

The stew was good, and, as I ate, my mind went a-wandering into those far-up hills, seeking out the way pa might have taken. The minds of men are not so different, and the mountains do not allow for much changing of direction.

If a body takes out to follow a made trail down over the hills, he'd best hold to that trail, for there are not too many ways to go. Most of the trouble a man finds in the mountains is when he tries shortcuts or leaves a known way.

Trails are usually made by game or by Indians, then used by late-comers, but the trails are there because somebody has found—through trial and error—the best way to get somewhere. If you see an easier looking way in the mountains, don't take it. You may walk two or three miles and find yourself standing on the edge of a cliff with no way down.

When a body sets out to find another man's trail, he has to sort of ease his way into that man's thoughts and try to reason out what he might have done.

Now pa was a man knew wild country. We had to look at it two ways. He had gold or he didn't, and first off I was going to figure it the hard way: he had him some gold, and he had the problem of getting it out of there.

First off, he'd head for some place he knew, and that was here. He would have extra horses, no need to worry about that, but he would have heavy packs, and folks can be almighty curious. And a man has to sleep.

He'd be tired, and he'd want to get out of this country and back home. Had he been followed? The chances were he had. Baston and Swan had left Pettigrew for dead . . . but had they left Treasure Mountain right after that, or weeks later? We had little information on that score and what little we had came from Pettigrew himself.

Somebody had followed and killed Pierre Bontemps, and most likely that same somebody had followed pa, waiting for a chance. That somebody knew, or thought he knew, where all the gold was, and he didn't want anybody around to dig it up before he had a chance.

Suddenly, I got up. "Orrin, I got a sight of travelin' to do, and I want to do it without having to watch my back trail too much. I just think I'll walk yonder to the store and buy something. If any of those riders are wishful of talking to me they can have at it."

"Want company?" Orrin asked.

"No, sir. I surely don't. If the two of us went they might think we were hunting. I'll just mosey over and give them a chance."

I strolled out and walked across the street. I opened the door and stepped into the store.

You could find its like in almost any western town. Bales of jeans, barrels of flour, a coffee grinder and the smell of fresh-ground coffee, prunes, dried apples, apricots, a barrel of crackers, and rows of canned goods.

Behind the counter there was a rack of rifles and shotguns; there were boots, hats, saddles, bridles, spurs, bandanas, vests, gloves, and just about all a man could want. It was my kind of store. In Saint Louis or New Orleans I could walk into a store full of things I just didn't want, but this was no city, and there wasn't a thing here a man wouldn't have use for.

Except maybe those two cowhands standing up by the counter. So I walked along up there, paying them no mind, and they turned to look.

There were things I truly needed, so I shuffled through the jeans, finding a pair long enough for a man six foot three and lean in the hips and waist. I stacked those jeans and a few things I needed whilst those gents dickered over some buying of their own. They were trying to decide about a .44 Smith and Wesson.

"But will it shoot straight?" one of them asked. "I used a Colt some, but this here gun—"

Reaching over I took it from his hand, picked up a box of shells, and thumbed some into the chambers, sayin' meanwhile, very pleasantlike, "May I settle the question for you gents? If you'll come to the door—"

One of them had started to get mad, but, by the time he was makin' up his mind, I already had two shells in the gun and he sort of decided against arguing. Nonetheless, they didn't like it. I just turned and ambled off to the door, and they traipsed after me, the storekeeper following along.

When I rode into town I'd noticed somebody had left a board standing against a rock, kind of leaning there. Maybe somebody had figured on putting up a sign and then got called away, but the board, which was about three by two, still sat there. I'd also noticed there was a knot in the board, of slightly darker color.

I hefted that Smith and Wesson in my mitt, knowing they'd always made a straight-shooting gun and knowing that I could rely on it to do what I asked. That board was a good seventy yards off and the knot was not visible.

"Now you take that board yonder? See the knothole in it?"

"I don't see no knothole," the short one said, kind of irritatedlike.

Well, I let 'er drive, right from where I held it. "Now you just go look," I said. "If that's not a hole, what is it?

"Fact is—" I let her bang a couple more times, so fast it sounded like one shot, "you go look and you'll find three holes, yonder. If you don't find one hole atop with two on each side below it, you come back and I'll buy the drinks."

Then I turned around and went back into the store. The storekeeper went behind the counter and picked up some field glasses. "Saves walking," he said, grinning. He was a young man with a nice smile. He walked outside again.

I was shoving some shells into those empty cylinders. I do hate an empty gun. Seems almost everybody who gets shot accidentally gets it with an empty gun. When I pull the trigger on a gun it's no accident, and I never pulled one whilst foolin' around.

That storekeeper came back. "My name's Johnny Kyme," he said, "and you surely put those bullets where you said. Was there really a knot there?"

"Uh-huh. There surely was, but you'll not find it now, unless you look near the edges."

"You must have good eyesight."

The two gents were coming back inside, growling a little and looking sour but more respectful.

"No," I said seriously, keeping a very straight face, "I shot it from memory. That's the way I do. I make a mental note of where the first shirt button above a man's belt is. Then I always know where to put the bullet."

"That's shootin'," the short man grumbled. "I figure we should buy the drinks."

"Thanks, gentlemen," I said, "but the day is young. One of these days, if we all live long enough, I'll belly up to the bar and collect that drink—and buy one."

I paid Kyme for the gun and the other things and turned to go. When I reached the door, I turned and said, "When you boys see Charley McCaire, tell him Tell Sackett sends his regards."

I went across the street for more coffee. Later on, Johnny Kyme told me what was said. That short one said, "Tell Sackett? Hell, that's the man—"

"I never saw *him* before," Kyme told them, "but he's got two cousins here that can shoot just about as good, maybe better. They just wound up a little go-around with Curly Dunn's outfit."

"Dunn? I remember them. What happened?" they asked.

Kyme said, "Oh, the few that were left dragged their tails out of here, they seemed to have the notion there were easier places to bulldoze."

When they left, Kyme said they looked mighty sober like they had aplenty to think about.

I was never much for showin' off, but if a bullet through a board can prevent a shoot-out, why not do it? I hold nothing against any man unless he comes at me, and I usually put that down to ignorance.

Now these here Three Eight hands would never have that excuse. If they came they'd know what was waiting for them.

Orrin was lounging in the door when I walked back. "Did you read them from the book?" he asked.

"Nope," I said, "I just showed 'em the pictures."

Chapter 20

That night, a couple of hundred yards from town, we bedded down about a dozen feet back from the La Plata, unrolling our blankets on the green grass near some cottonwoods. We were cut off from sight of the town by a wall of cottonwood, aspen, and pine trees.

We picketed our horses on the grass and settled down to sleep. Nell had gone to stay with the family who had been caring for her pa. He was feeling better now and figuring on a place of his own.

The four of us were asleep, eased to our comfort by the rustling leaves and the water running a few yards off. I don't know what it was made me wake up, but suddenlike in the middle of the night I was wide awake.

Our fire was down to red coals glowing, and beside it sat a man.

It took me a minute to adjust my mind to it, but sure enough, there he sat, cross-legged by the fire and still as death. My fingers took hold of the butt of my gun, but he seemed peaceful enough so I just lay and watched him for a moment.

It was an Indian, and he was old. His hair hung in two braids, and even at a distance I could see it was part gray. Indians have their ways and we have ours, but a guest at my fire is always welcome to coffee, so I threw back the covers, shoved my feet into the moccasins I keep handy for nightwork or for the woods, and went over to the fire.

He didn't look up or say anything. His hands were brown and old, with large veins, and his nails were cut flat across. He wore a knife and there was a Winchester alongside of him.

Poking some sticks into the coals, I edged the coffeepot a mite closer and got some biscuits we'd bought in the store a few hours earlier.

He had his own cup and I filled it, then filled mine. The wind guttered the fire a little and I added more fuel. The wind down that canyon could be right chill on occasion.

His eyes were old, but their gaze was sharp and level when he looked at me. "I am Tell Sackett," I said. "You are Powder-Face?"

"You look for your papa?"

The word sounded strange on his lips, and I said, "It has been twenty years. He is dead, I believe."

He tasted his coffee. "Good!" he said. "Good!"

"I want to know what happened to him, and to find where he lies, if that is possible."

"He was a good man—two times. I knew him two times. The first time we shot at him ourselves."

"Did you kill him?"

He looked up. "No! He was a good man—good! The first time—long ago —I did not know him, or him me. We shot—we missed.

"I thought he dead. I waited—long time. I went for his hair—he was gone.

"I went back—my horse was gone. Tied where my horse had been was a tomahawk and some red cloth. This is strange man—we shoot, we miss, he goes *poof!* Then my horse goes *poof.* But if he can take my horse, it is his. If I can get it back, it is mine.

"He takes it. The tomahawk is good, sharp edge. The cloth is good for squaw—maybe he needs horse.

"Seven suns. Day comes, the sun rises on my horse, tied near my head. How? I do not know. Why is horse quiet? I do not know. It is magic? Perhaps."

"My father brought him back?"

"It is so. Many suns, and one day when the people of our village are hungry, I see an elk. I stalk. I am lifting the bow and arrow ready to fly when from close under the bush where I am, another elk leaps up—all run. I miss.

"Suddenly there is a shot, the elk falls. I wait, nobody comes. I wait— nobody comes. I go to the elk. Then he stands up, this man who is your father. He lifts his hand to me, and then he turns his back and walks away. He has given us meat. It is a good thing he has done, and my people are no longer hungry.

"At night I tell them of this man, and we wonder about him. Who has sent him? What does he do here?

"His tracks are near our village. I think sometimes he watches us. We are not many braves, and there are too many young ones, too many women. I must hunt always, but the bow does not shoot far—hunting is hard.

"One morning when I leave my lodge there is a rifle there, lying upon a skin. Beside it are powder and ball. Only he could have left it. Only he could come into our village and leave without being seen. But then we see him no more."

"No more?"

"Many moons, the snows come and they go—more than two times. Three? Four? We do not know. After a long time we are in village on back side of Beaver Mountain.

"In the night the dogs bark, we see nothing. In the morning we find a haunch of elk meat hanging from a tree. Our friend is back.

"We owe him much, for when the hunting was bad the rifle he left us kept our lodges with meat. This time we do not need the meat he has left us and he knows this. He has left it to tell us he is back.

"Often we see him then, but we do not like all we see, and he faces toward us one time and makes the signs not to come near, and the sign for bad heart."

We drank our coffee slowly. The old man was tired.

"Now we have young braves. They know of the white man who gave us meat. They are like small deer—very curious. They watch. They come back to village to tell what they have seen."

The firelight played upon the seamed brown face, and the old man lifted his cup in two hands and emptied it. Once more I filled the cup. This man had known my father.

This man had watched him upon his last trail, had known how he thought, at least about some things. The white man of the mountains often fought the Indian, but there was understanding between them— rarely hatred. They fought as strong men fight, for the love of battle and because fighting is a part of the life they live.

The Indian lived a life that demanded courage, demanded strength, stamina, and the will to survive; and the white men who came first to the mountains had such qualities—or they would not have come in the first place, and they could not have lasted in the second.

Most mountain men were affiliated with one tribe or another, all had respect for Indians. Some found the only life they loved among the Indians. My father was a man of two worlds. Whether he walked among savages or among the civilized he was equally at home.

"I must know where my father died. I would like to know how he died, but to know where is enough. My mother grows old. She worries that the bones of her husband lie exposed to the wind and have been picked by coyotes. They must be buried, as is our custom."

He sat a long time. "I do not know where he died. I know he went away. He went to walk upon the mountains and he did not return. I can show you the trail he took."

"He went alone?"

"Alone—but others followed."

There was a knot lying near, and I added it to the fire, for the night was cold. Wind stirred the leaves, ruffled the flames. I gathered sticks and broke them with my hands and built more warmth for the old man, then I filled his cup with coffee and sat beside the fire again, waiting for whatever else he would say.

"A trail lies there, high upon the mountain, some call it the Ute Trail, but the trail was old before the Utes came to these mountains. I do not know where the trail leads, nor does any man, but there are harsh, cold winds and sudden, terrible storms. There are days with blue skies and tufts of cloud—but these days are few among the high peaks."

"Do you know the trail?"

"It lies there." He pointed toward the mountains. "I know where it is, not where it leads. I am an old man. I have no strength to follow such a trail, and when I was a young man, I was afraid."

"If my father went there, then I must go."

"He died there."

"We shall see." Again I added a chunk of wood to the fire. "Be warm, Old One. There is fuel. Now I shall sleep. In the morning I will take the way you show me."

"I will go with you."

"No. I shall go alone. Rest here, Old One. My cousins have given your people a place. Stay with them, guide them."

"I think soon the Indian will walk no more upon the land. When I look into the fire, I think this."

"Some will," I said, "some will not. Civilization is a trap for some men, a place of glory for others. The mountains change with years, so must the Indian change. The old way is finished, for my father as well as for you, for the man of the wilderness whether he be Indian or white."

"I think it will come again. All things change. But if the Indian would live he must go the white man's way. There are too many white men and they will not be denied."

Powder-Face shrugged. "I know," he said simply. "We killed them and killed them and killed them, and still they came. It was not the horse soldiers that whipped us, it was not the death of the buffalo, nor the white man's cows. It was the people. It was the families.

"The rest we might conquer, but the people kept coming and they built their lodges where no Indian could live. They brought children and women, they brought the knife that cuts the earth. They built their lodges of trees, of sod cut from the earth, of boards, of whatever they could find.

"We burned them out, we killed them, we drove off their horses, and we rode away. When we came back others were there as if grown from the ground—and others, and others, and others.

"They were too many for us. We killed them, but our young men died, too, and we had not enough young men to father our children, so we must stop fighting."

"Remember this, Old One. The white man respects success. For the poor, the weak, and the inefficient, he has pity or contempt. Whatever the color of your skin, whatever country you come from, he will respect you if you do well what it is you do."

"You may be right. I am an old man, and I am confused. The trail is no longer clear."

"You brought your people to my cousins. You work for them now, so you are our people as well. You came to them when they needed you, and you will always have a home where they are."

The flames burned low, flickered, and went out. Red coals remained. The chill wind stirred the leaves again. Powder-Face sat silently, and I went to my blankets.

Nativity Pettigrew had led us to believe he had come right down the mountain and the others after him, but that had not happened. Somebody —maybe several of them—had followed pa. Somebody had come back, discovered Pierre's body gone and no sign of pa, so they'd followed, found Pierre's grave, and knew pa was alive.

Pa might return to New Orleans and tell Philip what happened in the mountains. Or he might come back and get more gold. It must have been obvious from the tracks that pa's horses were carrying heavy. What they carried had to be gold.

Pa knew this country, and he knew old Powder-Face. He knew he could stay with him until he was rested and strong again, and he could hide the gold close by and Powder-Face would not disturb it. So he had come west, and he had been followed.

Lying there looking up at the clouds, I considered. I'd take my appaloosa, I'd take that buckskin packhorse, and enough grub for two weeks, and I'd plan to stay in the mountains until I found what I was hunting or ran out of grub.

It began to spatter rain so I tugged my tarp over my head and just let her spatter. It was a good sound, that rain.

Tyrel would be coming along from New Mexico soon and he would be bringing ma. They would bring cattle and take up land at the foot of the mountains somewhere. We were mountain folk, and we cottoned to the high-up hills.

There'd be Tyrel and me, Flagan and Galloway, and maybe Orrin would hang out his shingle down in Animas City or even in Shalako, although there was mighty little for a lawyer to do there. But just give folks time. You can't get two people together without soon or late they're lawin' at each other.

Far up there on the cold, gray rocks of the peaks where the last streaks of snow were melting off, up there would be strong, fierce winds blowing, weeping over the high plateaus, trimming the spruce to one level, driving the freezing rain into every crevice in the rock.

How could I find anything up there? If pa had died, what would be left of him now? Some scattered bones, his boot heels, maybe, and part of his holster and belt, chewed by wolves or other varmints.

It would be a lonely place to die, but maybe such a place as he'd want, for he was no stay-a-bed man. He'd always been up and doing, and when it came to that, what better way to go than on the trail somewhere, packing a gun and riding the high country?

The spattering rain made me think of Powder-Face. I raised up my head to look, but the old one was gone, vanished into the night and the rain as if he had never been.

For a moment he held in my thoughts, and I wondered how many times he or his kind has sat staring into the flames and feeling the rain fall and the wind blow?

Man had enemies, that was in the nature of things, but when it comes right down to it his battle to live is with that world out there, the cold, the rain, the wind—the heat, the drought, and the sun-parched pools where water had been.

Hunger, thirst, and cold—man's first enemies, and no doubt his last.

Chapter 21

That appaloosa and me had reached a kind of understanding. On a chilly morning he liked to buck the frost out of his system, so whenever I put a foot in the stirrup around daybreak I knew he was going to unwind.

Naturally, I wasted no time getting into the saddle. If I put a foot in the stirrup and swung my leg over real fast, me and the saddle would come together on the rise.

Of course, I always managed to mount a little away from camp so's I wouldn't buck right through breakfast. That's the sort of thing can make a man right unpopular in any kind of outfit.

This morning that appaloosa really unwound. He was feelin' good and it done me no harm to just sit up there and let him have at it. Ridin' easy in the saddle all the time can make a man downright lazy, so when they feel like buckin', I say let 'em buck. I don't care which nor whether.

When Ap had bucked himself into good nature and an appetite, I took him back to the fire and lit down from the saddle.

Judas had put together some grub and like always when he done the cookin' it tasted mighty fine. He was spoilin' me for my own cookin', and soon I'd be out yonder on the trail with nobody but myself to cook.

I told them all about the visit from Powder-Face and about my plan.

"You sure you don't want me to ride along?" Orrin asked.

"I would prefer to ride with you, suh," Judas said. "It might be that I could be of service."

The Tinker said nothing. He was ready to go if I wanted him, and well he knew it and I knew it.

"It would be pleasurable," I said. "I could do with the comp'ny and the cookin', but a man listens better when he's alone, and he hears better."

When we'd finished breakfast, and I'd lingered as long as I could afford over my coffee, I went to my horses. "You ride loose, Tell," Orrin advised. "This isn't any western outfit. They're a murderin' lot."

I stepped into the saddle. Ap had finished with bucking during our little set-to of the morning, and he made no fuss. Besides, he knew I was now in no mood for catywampusing around.

"The way I'm riding is round about," I said, "but I want to come into the mountains the way pa did. If I see the country the way he saw it maybe I can catch his frame of mind.

"By the time he started up that trail, June must have been pretty well gone, and we know the snow was light that year and had mostly gone off. He wouldn't find much snow except where the shadows gathered and in deep hollows. The trail Powder-Face speaks of might be the one he took."

"I was talking to one of the young braves," said Orrin. "Some call it the Ghost Trail. They say it was made by The People Who Went Before . . ."

"Well," I gathered the reins, "you know me, Orrin. I'm going to ride easy into the hills and sort of let it come to me."

When I rode down what you could call the street of Shalako, Nell was standing out before a new-built house. I drew up and took off my hat. "Howdy, ma'am," I said, "I'm off for a ride."

She looked at me, seriouslike and tender. It kind of worried me, that look did, but then I figured it was just that we'd known each other awhile, not that she was thinking gentle thoughts of me. I'd gotten used to womenfolks speaking to me and passin' by toward handsome gents who had some flash and flare to 'em. Not that I blamed 'em any. I'm just a big ol' homely man who's kind of handy with horses, guns, and cattle, which doesn't fit me very much for cuttin' didoes with the female sex.

"Now you be careful, Tell Sackett!" she said. "I wish you'd not go."

"Somewhere my pa lies dead, unburied, perhaps, and ma's growing on in her years and it frets her to think of it. I'm going to ride yonder and try to find what remains of him so ma can go her way in comfort."

Her eyes were big and serious. "It is a fine thing," she said, "but it will do your ma no good to have your own bones unburied on some fool mountain! I wish I could talk to your ma! I'd speak to her! I'd tell her what she's doing!"

"It was not her idea that we ride out and look," I said. "It was ours. But it is a small thing we can do to comfort her."

She put her hand up to me and touched me gentle on the sleeves. "Tell? Do ride careful, now, and when you're back, will you come calling?"

"I will," I said. "I'll ride by and halloo the house."

"You'll get down and come in!" she flared.

"Dast I? Seems to me I recall ol' Jack Ben was some hand with the rock salt when the boys come a-courtin' around."

She flushed. "He never shot at you, did he? You don't look like you caught much salt, the way you set that saddle! If pa'd shot you, you'd still be ridin' high in your stirrups!"

"I never came around," I said simply. "I didn't reckon there was much point in it." I blushed my ownself. "I never was much hand to court, Nell Trelawney, I never quite got the feel of it. Now if it was somethin' I could catch with a rope, I'd—"

"Oh, go along with you!" She stepped back, looking up at me, disgusted maybe. I never was much hand at readin' the faces of womenfolks, nor understandin' their ways. I go at 'em too gentlelike, I suspect. Sometimes it's better to use the rawhide manner.

Anyway, when I turned in the saddle she lifted a hand at me, and I got to thinking maybe I should fetch up to her door when my way led down the mountain again.

The trail I wanted was best found riding out of Animas City, but I figured there was no point in showin' everybody what was on my mind, so instead of taking off up Junction Creek I went up Lightner Creek and found my way by game trails over to where Ruby Gulch opens into Junction.

It was mighty pretty country, forest and mountain and a trickle of water here and there, some of them good-sized streams. I scrambled my horses up a slope onto a point of the mountain that gave me a sight of country to see over. It was open a mite, there on the point, backed up with scattered aspen and then a thick stand that climbed up the point behind.

There was a place just back of the point where a big old spruce had been torn up by the wind. Where its roots pulled free of the soil there was a kind of hollow where the grass had begun to grow. In the grass where no trees grew, I picketed the horses, stripped the gear from them, and went about putting together a mite of fire. The wood I chose was dry, and it burned with almost no smoke, and after I'd eaten I set on the point between two trees where the branches hung low and shadowed me.

For over an hour I just set there, a-listening to the evening. There was sunlight on the mountain across from me, but it was high up, toward the crest of the ridge. There was stillness in the canyon below, and a marvelous coolness coming up.

Somewhere an owl spoke his question to the evening, and the aspen leaves hung as still as you'll ever see them, for they move most of the time.

It was a mighty fine thing setting there getting the feel of the night, a kind of stillness like you never felt anywhere else but in the far-off wilderness. There was no vanity here, nor greed, there was only a kind of quietness, and the thought came upon me that maybe this was how pa wanted to go, out on some rocky ledge with the whole world falling away before him, a gun in his hand, or a knife—the love of the world in his guts and the going out of it like an old wolf goes, teeth bared to his enemies.

I never was much to mind where my bones would lie once the good Lord had taken my soul. I had a feeling maybe I'd like to leave myself upon the mountains, my spirit free to lean against the wind.

Death never spent time in my thoughts, for where a man is there is no death, and when death is there a man is gone, or the image of him. Sometimes I think a man walks many lives like he does trails. I recall a man in a cow camp who was a-reading to us about some old battle the Greeks had fought a time long ago, and suddenly I was all asweat and my breath was coming hard, and I could feel a knife turning in my guts.

The man looked at me and lowered the book and said, "I did not know I read so well, Sackett."

"You read mighty well," I said. "It's like I was there."

"Maybe you were, Tell, maybe you were."

Well, I don't know about that, but the shadows came down the canyon and the trees lost themselves in it, crowding all together until they were like one big darkness.

And then I heard in the darkness a faint *chink* of metal on stone.

So . . . after all, I was not alone. Something, somebody was out there.

The butt of my gun felt cool in my fist. I did not draw my piece; I just sat there, listening. There was no further sound, and, softly as a cat walks, I went from there and back to my camp.

My fire was down to coals.

I brought the horses in closer, picketing one on either side of me, and then I went to sleep. Nothing, man or beast, would come near without a warning from them, and I was a light sleeper.

Once, in the night, awakened by some small sound, I lay for a time. Overhead I saw a great horned owl go sweeping down some mysterious channel of the night, piloted by I know not what lust, what urge, what hidden drive. Was it simply that, like me, he loved the forest night and liked to curve his velvety paths among the dark columns of the spruce?

I am one with these creatures of the night and of the high places. Like them I love the coolness, the nearness of the stars, the sudden outthrusts of rock that fall off into the unbelievable vastness below.

Like them, sometimes I think I have no sense of time, no knowledge of years, only the changing of seasons but not the counting of them.

And then I was asleep again and awake with the faint grayness of the morning.

Out of the blankets, I glanced at the dead coals. No fire this morning, no smell of smoke for them if they hadn't got the smell last night. Hat on first, like any good cowhand, then boots, and then the easy, practiced flip of the gun belt about my waist. Stamping to settle feet into boots, saddling up, loading the gear without sound, spreading the fire. It had left no coals, burning down to the softest of gray ashes.

A few minutes to smooth out the earth where my boots left tracks, a scuffing up of trampled grass. A good tracker would know there'd been a camp, but time would be needed to tell who was there or how many. In the saddle then, and riding between the trees to the north.

Where Heffernan Gulch came into Junction Creek there was a bend in the canyon of Junction that shielded me from downstream observation, so I took advantage to find my way across Junction and up the trail along Heffernan Gulch.

Almost at once I saw it. A deep cut in an aspen, a notch cut with an axe—not a blaze—pa never liked the glaring white of a new blaze. "If you want to follow my trail, boy," he used to tell me, "you've got to look sharp."

It was his notch, and to make it sure, another one fifty feet along, "All right, Ap," I said, "this is the trail. This is the one we've been looking for."

Ap's ears flickered around, then ahead, pricked, interested. We walked on. Occasionally I glanced back. As far as I could see there was nothing. Yet what might be sheltered under those trees?

There was one more notch on that trail, and I came near to missing it. The tree was big and old, a spruce, and it was tumbled on its side at the trail's edge. A casual glance caught the old notch there . . . and after that there were no more trees.

The trail showed no recent signs of use. Rocks had tumbled down from the face of the mountain, but there had been no big slides. The appaloosa picked his way delicately over the fallen rock, the buckskin following.

The trail grew steeper. Far above I could see the outer rim of the cirque that was Cumberland Basin. Above me loomed Snowstorm Peak, more than twelve thousand feet high, and before me and on my left was Cumberland Mountain, nearly as high. Both mountains were bare and cold, towering a thousand feet above timberline, their flanks still flecked with patches of snow or long streamers of it that lay in crevices or cracks.

Turning up the collar of my jacket, I hunched my shoulders against the cold wind. The trail was narrow, a drop of hundreds of feet if a hoof should slip. Here and there were patches of ice—dark, old ice, and old snow as well.

In places, my knee rubbed the inner wall of rocks. Further along, the mountain slanted steeply away, but here it fell sheer from the trail to a long, steep talus slope that ended finally in the tree line, a ragged rank of stiff and noble trees making a bold stand against the destruction that hung over them.

Glancing back, I caught a movement. A rider came out of the trees far below me, and then another and another.

They didn't look familiar, and neither did their horses. With my field glasses I could have recognized them, but what was the point? When they caught up, if they did, they would make themselves known, and they'd have a chance to get acquainted with me, too.

Seems to me folks waste a sight of time crossing bridges before they get to them. They clutter their minds with odds and ends that interfere with clear thinking.

Those folks were certainly following me, and it was equally certain they were none of my people. When they caught up there'd likely be trouble, but I wasn't going out hunting it. I was looking for signs of pa.

Far and away on my right lay a vast and tumbled mass of distant peaks and forest, bare rock shoved up here and there, high mountain parks and meadows . . . magnificent country. Overhead, the sky was impossibly blue and dotted with those white fluffs of cloud that seemed always to float over the La Platas and the San Juans. Trouble coming or not, this was great country, a man's country.

The trail took a turn and I lost sight of them below. Alongside the trail there was a beautiful little patch of blue, like a chunk of the sky had floated down to rest on that frost-shattered rock and gravel beside the trail —it was some alpine forget-me-not. Down the steep slope where a fallen man or horse would roll and tumble for seven or eight hundred feet, I could see the bright gold of avalanche lilies here and there.

The last few yards was a scramble, but Ap was a mountain horse and the buckskin seemed content to follow any place Ap would go.

When we topped out on the rim there was a view you wouldn't believe. Down below us was a huge basin, one side opening and spilling down into La Plata Canyon. There was another vast glacial gouge on my left, and ahead of me I could see the thread of that high, ancient trail winding its way across the country, a thin thread through the green of the high grass that was flecked with wild flowers of every description.

All around were vast and tumbled mountains. I was twelve thousand feet above sea level. Far off to the north I could see the great shaft of the Lizard Head and get a glimpse of Engineer Mountain, and off to the east were the Needles, White Dome, Storm King, and what might be the Rio Grande Pyramid, near which the Rio Grande rises. It was the kind of view that leaves a man with a feeling of magnificence, but there just ain't words to cover it.

Old Ap, he seemed happy on that high place, too, but he snorted a little when I started him down the thread of trail that led through the gravel and the frost-shattered rocks on the inside of the cirque.

It was like going down the inside of a volcanic crater, only there was a meadow at the bottom and no fires.

The man lying under the spruce had been there since shortly after daylight. He had a Sharps rifle, one of the best long-range weapons there is, and he had a natural rest across the top of a fallen tree. His view of the trail down the inside of the rim was clear and perfect, and when he saw Tell Sackett top the rim he was pleased. This was going to be the easiest hundred dollars he had ever earned—and it surely beat punching cows.

He was a dead shot, a painstaking man with a natural affinity for weapons and a particular ease with rifles. He let Sackett come on, shortening the distance for him.

He picked his spot, a place where the steepness of the trail seemed to level off for a few feet. When Sackett reached there, he would take him. The range was roughly four hundred yards—possibly a bit over. He had killed elk at that distance, and kills had been scored with a Sharps at upwards of a thousand yards.

He sighted, waited a little, then sighted again. About twenty yards now . . . he settled himself into the dirt, firmed his position. Sackett was a salty customer, it was said. Well, soon he'd be a salted customer.

He looked again, sighted on a spot below the shoulder and in a mite toward the chest, took a long breath, eased it out, and squeezed off his shot.

The best laid plans of mice and men often seem to be the toys of fate. The marksman had figured on everything that could be figured. His distance, the timing, the fact that the rider was at least a hundred and fifty feet higher than himself. He was a good shot and he had thought of it all.

He had the rider dead in his sights, and a moment after the squeeze of the trigger William Tell Sackett should have been bloody and dead on the trail.

The trouble was in the trail itself.

At some time in the not too distant past, nature had taken a hand in the game, and in a playful moment had trickled a small avalanche off the rim, down the slope, and across the trail. In so doing it left a gouge in the trail that was about a foot deep.

As the marksman squeezed off his shot, the appaloosa stepped down into that gully. The drop—as well as the lurch in the saddle that followed —was just enough. The bullet intended for Tell's chest nicked the top of his ear.

The sting on my ear, the flash of the rifle, and the boom that followed seemed to come all at once, and whatever else pa taught us boys he taught us not to set up there and make a target of yourself.

Now it was a good hundred and fifty yards to the foot of the trail and every yard of it was bare slope where I'd stand out like a whiskey nose at a teetotalers' picnic. So I just never gave it a thought, there wasn't time for it. I just flung myself out of that saddle, latching onto my Winchester as I kicked loose and let go. I hit that slope on my shoulder, like I'd planned, rolled over and over, and came up at the base of the slope with my rifle still in my hands and a mad coming up in me.

Nobody needed to tell me that anybody shooting at me now had been posted and waiting for me. This was some sure-thing killer out scalp hunting, and I have a kind of feeling against being shot at by strangers. Least a man can do is introduce himself.

When I reached the bottom of that slope I had a second boom ringing in my ears, but that shot—it sounded like a Sharps buffalo gun so he must have reloaded fast—had missed complete. Nonetheless the thing to do at such a time is be someplace else, so I rolled over in the grass, hit a low spot, and scrambled on knees and elbows, rifle across my forearms, to put some distance from where I fell.

Chances were nine out of ten he figured he'd got me with the first shot, because I fell right then. Chances also were he'd wait a bit and if I didn't get up he'd come scouting for the body, and I meant to be damned sure he found one . . . his.

Ap had stopped only a moment. That was a right sensible horse and he knew he had no business up there on that bare slope, so he trotted along to the bottom. The buckskin stayed right with him, the lead rope still snubbed to the saddle horn. I was going to need those horses so I kept an eye on them. Pretty soon they began to feed on the meadow.

When I'd scrambled fifty yards or so, I was behind a kind of low dome, maybe some dirt pushed up by the last small glacier when it slid off the walls and pushed along the bottom of the cirque.

My ear was bleeding and it stung like crazy, and that kind of riled me, too. That man over yonder sure had a lot to answer for.

Careful to keep my rifle down so the sun wouldn't gleam on it, I edged along that earth dome until I was on the far shoulder of it. Then I chanced a look toward those spruce trees where the shot had come from.

Nothing.

Minutes passed. About that time a thought occurred to me that had me sweating.

Those folks coming up the trail back of the mountain would be topping out on the crest and looking down into that basin. Now while that sport over yonder with the Sharps couldn't see me—at least I hoped he couldn't —I'd be wide open and in the clear for those people when they topped out on the rim.

They'd have me from both sides and I'd be a dead coon.

I've been shot at now and again, and I've taken some lead here and there, but I never cared for it much. To tell you the truth, I'd as leave let it lay. There's something mighty disconcerting about a bullet in the brisket . . . lead sets heavy on the stomach.

The trouble was I'd about run out of places to go. From here on, I was in the open unless I could squeeze right into the ground. Nowhere could I see more than two or three inches of cover, and I was going to want more —a whole lot more.

One thing I did know. If those people topped out on that rise and raised a gun at me, they were going to find it was an uncomfortable place to be. Because I was going to start shooting, and their horses would come down off that rim one way or the other, probably running and buck-jumping.

Of a sudden I heard a faint stir, and I turned very carefully.

A man, rifle held in his hands ready for use, was standing just in front of the spruce trees. He was standing stock-still and he was listening.

I eased my rifle forward and waited. The man stood there, took a couple of steps forward, and stopped again. From where I'd fallen when he fired he would be merged against that spruce background and not easily seen; from where I now lay he was outlined stark and clear. He took another step forward, and then one of the riders topping the ridge evidently got a glimpse of me. He up with his rifle and let drive, and I shot at the man by the spruce trees.

I left the ground in a diving run. I had no hopes of scoring a good hit, but the bullet turned him. As I had run to his right, which meant he had to swing toward the hard side, he missed his shot at me. I went into some hummocks of grass and rubble, rolled over three times, and took another diving run into the woods.

Turning, I shot three times at the bunch on the ridge as fast as I could work the lever on the Winchester. I was shooting at a target seven or eight hundred feet higher and some distance off, but the bullets lit among them.

Like I figured, it blew things all to bloody hell. One of those horses jumped right straight out ahead of him, hit that slope on all fours, went to his knees, throwing his rider, and, still sliding, scrambled up and made it to the bottom.

Another of the horses came down the slope on that narrow path hell-bent for election with the rider hanging on with both hands. The horse hit the bottom of the trail and stopped short, and the rider went right on over his head. He hit hard, got up, and fell over.

The other two who had been up there disappeared down the other side. I kept on moving. Somewhere in this same patch of woods was that killer who had come close to notching my skull a few minutes back.

If I'd put a bullet in him, I'd be lucky, but I might just have burned him or his rifle or hit near him. Any one of those things can make a man jump.

I lit out at a run along the slope, keeping into the trees. Mostly I went downhill because that was the easiest way to go. Then I slowed down and worked my way along the slope to get to where Ap was feeding.

There were dips and hollows in the land, brush and trees here and there, but mostly just grass and flowers. The rim of the cirque was just over yonder, so I went that way, doing the Injun in the grass, snaking along when necessary, running when I could.

At that altitude, even if you're used to it as I was, you just don't do much running. Finally I hunkered down between three thick-boled old spruce and waited, catching my breath and trying to see where they were located.

My horses were grazing about a hundred yards off, and one of theirs, his saddle under his belly, stood spraddle-legged about that same distance away but closer to where they must be.

Having a moment to spare, I fed some shells into my rifle and held my place. At least two of them had reached the bottom, and one was in no shape for action, judging by the tumble taken. One of them was out in front of me somewhere and so was the one who first shot at me.

Time dragged by slowly. Shadows began to gather in the basin. On the rim there was golden sunlight, and there was a pinkish tinge to the clouds. Out over the basin, somebody called . . . it sounded like a woman, but that couldn't be.

Looking toward my horses, I decided to try for them. I went forward, keeping to the deepest grass and wild flowers, some of which were almost waist-high.

No telling who they were out there. Andre Baston and Hippo Swan? Probably. But they had started one bunch of killers after me a good while back, and they'd surely not hesitate to try again. Killing was something you could buy cheap, these days. The chances of being charged with a killing out here were slight. Many men went west, many never came back, and few questions were asked.

It took me some stretch of time before I reached my horses, even though they weren't far off. I moved along, keeping out of sight as best I could, and heard nothing. And then, just as dark was coming on the rim up yonder, I saw a rider top out there, hold fast for a minute, and start down the trail. All he could see from up there was a great black bowl of darkness.

As I edged closer, old Ap pricked his ears and took a step toward me, curious as to why I was down there on the ground. "Easy, boy!" I whispered. "Easy, now!"

He stood fast and my hand went out to gather up the reins. I drew the horse nearer to me, then, carefully, I got to my feet.

Suddenly, at my elbow, a voice spoke—a woman's voice. The shock of it sent a chill right up my spine.

"I believe I have been hurt. Can you help me?"

Chapter 22

It was Fanny Baston.

She had a voice that was one in ten thousand—low, soft, inviting. Even in the darkness I could see there was blood on her face, her blouse and coat were torn, and she was favoring one leg.

"Your friends are close by." I wanted no part of her, just none at all. She was hurt, all right, but she had a brother and an uncle within call, and mayhap others as well.

"I think I am . . ." she just let go everything and slumped to the ground, passed out.

I swore. Yessir, I swore. The last thing I needed right now was to be saddled with a hurt woman, especially this one. She hadn't seemed to know me. Maybe that rap on the skull had done it, but there wasn't much a body could do.

If I called for them, I'd get shot. If I left her there, she might die. I'd no idea how bad off she was, and I couldn't see any way but to take her along. So I picked her up and put her in the saddle. Holding her with one hand I started forward. I hadn't gone that way more than a few minutes when Ap stopped. I tried to urge him on, but he wouldn't budge a step. Leaving Fanny Baston slumped over the saddle horn, I went forward and almost stepped off of the world.

My foot went off the edge, and it was lucky I had hold of the bridle. Pulling back, I knocked a small rock off into space, and it fell what seemed like a long time. I backed up and turned the horse, and we worked back into the scattered trees and into the grass.

What I needed now was a hideout. Wandering around in the dark at the edge of a cliff was no way to find one, yet find one I did. It was fool's luck, nothing else.

I came to another place where the horse stopped, but that time I could see trees ahead of me. I dropped a rock and it fell only a few feet and lit soft.

I worked along the edge until I found a place that sort of slanted off and I went down. I was on a lower level, maybe six or eight feet lower than where I'd been, and there was thick grass underfoot.

I had tied Fanny's hands to the pommel, and now I led the horses down and along under the trees. When I got behind a small shoulder of that ledge, I pulled up, knelt close to the ground, and took the chance to strike a match.

Some tall spruce, boles eight to ten inches through, were close around me. I was on level, grassy ground.

I untied Fanny's hands and lifted her down. She was unconscious, or seemed to be. If she was shamming, she was doing an almighty good job of it. I put her on the grass, stripped the gear from my horses, and led them over on the grass and picketed them.

Coming back to the trees, I stood there for a moment, getting the feel of the place. All around me was darkness, overhead a starlit sky except where the limbs of spruce intervened.

We seemed to be in a sort of pocket. One edge of it, I was quite sure, was the lip of that drop-off over which I'd almost stepped—the outer edge of the mountain itself.

Down here, and under the spruce, there seemed a good chance a fire would not be seen. In the dark I surely could do nothing for that girl, and I was hungry and wanting coffee.

Breaking a few of the dried suckers from the trees and gathering wood by the feel, I put together enough for a fire, then lit a small blaze.

Fanny Baston was out cold, all right, and she was pale as anybody I'd seen who was also alive. She'd had a nasty blow on the skull and her head was cut to the bone. One arm was scraped, taking a lot of the hide off. Her leg wasn't broken, but there was a swelling and a bruised bone. I heated water, started coffee, and bathed some of the blood off her face and head. I also bathed the arm a little, getting some of the grass and gravel out of the skinned place.

I took the thong off my six-shooter. If I needed a gun I was going to need it fast. My Winchester I kept to hand, but across the fire from that woman.

By the time I'd made coffee her breathing was less ragged and she was settling down into what seemed to be a natural sleep. She was a beautiful woman, no denying it, but here I was, so weary I scarce could stand, and I dasn't sleep for fear she'd wake up in the middle of the night and put a blade into me.

And she had one. She had it strapped to her leg under her dress, a neat little knife, scarcely wider than her little finger but two-edged as well as pointed. I'd come onto it whilst I was checking that bad leg, but I left it right where it was.

After a bit I walked off into the dark and went back up on the level. There was no sign of that place from above, and the little fire I had was well hidden. I listened for a spell, then strolled back. Fanny Baston had not moved. At least not so's I could see.

Taking my blankets I moved back among those trees. Three spruces grew together, their trunks starting almost from the same spot. I settled down amongst them with my pistol hitched around between my legs and my Winchester handy. Wrapped in a blanket, I settled down for the night.

The trees formed a V and I put a couple of small branches across the wide part of it. To reach me they'd have to step one foot there, and I had a notion I'd hear them first. And there was always the horses to warn me of folks a-coming.

There for a time I slept, dozed, slept again, and dozed. Then I was awake for a spell. Easing out of my place I added a few small sticks to the fire, checked Fanny, covering her better with the blanket, then went back to my corner.

It was not yet daybreak when I finally awakened, and I sat there for a bit, thinking about pa and about this place and wondering what had become of him.

Wherever he'd come to the end could not be far from here unless he taken that ghost trail clean out of the country. Knowing pa, he might have done just that. I was wishing I had ol' Powder-Face with me. That was a canny Injun, and he'd be a help to a man in sorting out a twenty-year-old trail.

When the sky was gray I eased out of my corner and stretched to get the stiffness out of me. I was still tired, but I knew that this day I had it to do.

First off I strolled over to the rim. There was a drop of around a thousand feet, and, at the point where I'd almost stepped off, a sheer drop. Far off I could see a red cliff showing above the green, and still further the endless mountains rolling away like the waves of the sea to the horizon.

There was no easy way into that vast hollow, but on a point some distance off there was the thin line of a game trail, probably made by elk. It might lead into the basin.

I started back to camp.

Nobody needed to tell me the showdown was here. It was now; it was today.

Andre Baston had followed me from New Orleans, and with him Hippo Swan. They knew what happened here twenty years ago. That Fanny Baston had come with them was a measure of their desperation.

They'd lived mighty easy most of their days. They'd built themselves a style of life they preferred, and then they discovered that money did not last forever. Ahead of them was loss of face and poverty, and all that would go with it, and they had no courage to face what many face with dignity their life long.

They had staked everything on what would happen today. Not only to prevent the discovery of what had gone before, but if possible to find the treasure—or a part of it—for themselves.

When daylight came I could see that I was on a sort of ledge that sat like a step below the rim. It was covered with grass and scattered with trees and it seemed to curve on around until it lined out along a great bare-backed ridge.

The ledge varied in width, maybe a hundred feet at its widest point, narrowing down here and there to no more than a third of that. It was a place that no one would suspect until they were right on it, and I couldn't have found anything better.

From anywhere on that ledge a body could see most of it, and I could see no movement yonder where Fanny Baston was lying. I went to my horses and moved them further along. This was good grass and they were having a time of it; and they deserved it.

Nevertheless, being a man who placed no trust in any future I had not shaped myself, I packed my saddle yonder and slapped it on the appaloosa. Then I put together most of my gear and took it down behind a shoulder of rock near the buckskin.

Right above the ledge was a high, rocky knoll that overlooked everything around. From the ledge I could crawl out and climb that knoll and have a good view of the whole basin.

First I walked back to camp. Fanny Baston was sitting up, her arms around her knees. She looked up at me, her eyes blank.

"Where is this place?" she asked.

"On top of a mountain," I said. I did not know what to think of her, and I was careful. My right hand held my rifle by the action, thumb on the hammer in case of unexpected company. "You had a fall. Your horse jumped off the trail."

She looked at me. "Are you taking care of me? I mean . . . why are we here?"

She seemed genuinely puzzled, but I was of no mind to play games. I knew the showdown was close to hand. "You followed me to kill me," I said. "You and your uncle and them."

"Why should we want to kill you?" She looked mystified. "I can't imagine wanting to kill you, or hurt you—you're—you're nice."

She said it in a little girl's voice. "And you're so tall, so strong looking." She got up. "Are you strong? Could you hold me?"

She took a step toward me. Her dress was torn and her shoulder was bare above that scraped-up arm.

"Your brother and your uncle are right over yonder," I said, "and if you start walking that way, they'll find you."

"But—but I don't *want* to go! I want to stay with you."

"You must have taken more of a rap on the skull than I figured," I told her. "You're a right fine lookin' figure of a woman, but I wouldn't touch you with a hayfork, ma'am. I don't think you've got an honest bone in you."

She smiled. "I *do* like you!"

She came toward me, moving in close. "Tell, please! Let's forget all this! Let's take the horses and go back down the way we came! We could keep right on—to California! Anywhere!"

"Yes, ma'am. We could, but—"

Suddenly, she jumped at me, grabbing at my rifle with both hands. She latched on to it and then she grabbed my wrist. "*Now*, Paul! *Now!*"

Scared, I threw her off me, sending her tumbling on the grass. She cried out as she hit, and I lost balance and went to one knee.

Paul was standing there, a rifle in his hands, and, even as I looked, its muzzle stabbed flame.

Chapter 23

Paul was no such killer as his uncle. He shot too quickly and at a moving target, and his bullet missed. Mine did not.

Yet it was an almost miss. The bullet I had intended for his body was high. It struck the action of the rifle, ripping into his hand, cutting a furrow along his cheek, and taking the lobe from his ear.

He screamed, dropped the rifle, and ran.

Fanny, crying hoarsely with anger, scrambled to her feet and ran for the rifle. I struck her aside, knocking her into the grass once more. I picked up the rifle and threw it.

It cleared the edge and fell, disappearing from sight.

Someone shouted, "They've found him! Come on!"

I turned and ran swiftly back toward my horses, keeping trees between me and them. I heard a shot, and a bullet scattered twigs and bark over my head, so I swung behind a tree, gasping for breath, but ready to shoot.

There was no target.

Then I heard Fanny shouting, her voice hoarse and angry. "Paul had him! He shot right at him and missed! And then he ran like a rabbit!"

It was easy to cast blame. Chances were Paul had never faced gunfire before. Like a lot of others he was ready to hurt or kill, but not to be hurt or killed.

Many men avoid battle not from cowardice but from fear of cowardice, fear when the moment of truth comes they will not have the courage to face up to it. Paul had no such nerve, and he had been hurt—perhaps not badly, and certainly not fatally, but he had seen his own blood flowing, a profound shock to some.

"It is no problem," I heard Andre's voice, calm and easy. "No problem. I know the place where he is, and there's no way out. It worked before and it will again."

Before?

I looked around me.

Here? Had this been where pa died? I looked toward the corner where the horses were. There?

I had seen no bones, no grave. Wild animals might have scattered the bones, or the body might have been thrown over the edge into the hollow below.

Here . . . had pa come to an end here? And was I to follow him?

The situation was different, I told myself. I had a good Winchester, plenty of food, ammunition . . . I could stand a siege. Unless there was something else, some unknown factor.

Some time back Judas had said that Andre Baston had ten men with him. It might be an exaggeration, but there were several. I could hear their voices.

After a moment, seeing all clear, I retreated to where the horses were. Here the cul-de-sac narrowed down, and the drop into the basin below was steep. Even had a man been able to get down there, until he could reach the trees, he would be wide open for a shot from the rim. And Andre wasn't likely to miss, as Paul had.

It looked like there might be a narrow way along the rim, a way that might be used by man or horse, but it showed no tracks, no trail, no sign of use. There was also a good chance that a rifleman would be waiting at the other end, with a certain target. There'd be no chance of missing if the target was approaching over a way not three feet wide.

Some rocks had been heaped up here, one slab on another, and some had fallen from a higher barricade. Now there was a fallen tree, the needles still clinging to the dead branches.

When I reached the horses I broke open a box of cartridges and filled my coat pockets. My Winchester '73 was fully loaded, and I was ready as a man could be.

Right over beyond that bare knoll that towered above me was the basin, and from the lower side of the basin a trail went down La Plata Canyon to Shalako.

At Shalako were at least three Sacketts and some friends, but that was six or seven miles away, maybe further, and they might as well be in China for all the good they'd do.

What happened here was up to me. And only me.

I just had a thought that worried me. It passed through my mind while I was considering other things. Something was suddenly nagging me . . . what could it have been?

There was some factor in my setup here . . .

I had a good field of fire down the ledge from where I'd chosen my hiding place. There were a few dips and hollows, some fallen logs, some of them almost rotted through.

Getting the horses into as safe a spot as could be, I settled down and gave study to the situation. Over my shoulder I could see the almost bare flank of that ridge where the ghost trail led. Now if I could get over there. . . .

Nobody was coming. Evidently they were sure they had me and would let me worry a mite. I smelled smoke . . . they were fixing some breakfast. Well, why not me?

I gathered some sticks and put together a bit of a blaze and set some coffee to boiling. Then I got out my skillet and fried up some bacon. Meanwhile I kept an eye open for those gents who were hunting me.

If this was where they had cornered pa, where were his bones? And what became of his outfit? And the gold?

Pa was a canny man, and he'd not be wishful of them profiting by his death. If this was where it happened, then he would have made some show of hiding things.

Yet, how had it happened? True, pa only had a muzzle-loader, and, fast as he was, he'd not be able to fight off a bunch of them for long. But he had a pistol—or should have had.

Thing that disturbed me was the fact that Baston and them were so sure they had me. Now if I could just see what they were about . . .

Suddenly a cold chill went through me, like they say happens when somebody steps on your grave.

All of a sudden I knew why they were so sure of themselves.

They had a man atop that knoll who could shoot into this place where I was.

He was probably up there now, and, when the attack began and my attention was directed down along the ledge, he'd shoot me from the top of that hill. Actually, it was a peak, standing higher than anything close by. Looking up at it, I could see where a man up there, if willing to expose himself a little, could fire at almost every corner of this ledge—*almost* every corner.

Well, cross that bridge when it came. Now for the bacon. I ate it there, liking the smell of it and the smell of the fire. What would I miss most, I wondered, if I should be killed here? The sight of those clouds gathering over the mountains yonder? The smell of woodsmoke and coffee and bacon? The feel of a good horse under me? Or the sunlight through the aspen leaves?

I hadn't a lot to remember, I guess. I'd been to none of the great places, nor walked among people of fame. I'd never eaten very fancy, nor been to many drama-shows. I'd set over many a campfire and slept out under the stars so much I knew all their shapes and formations from looking up at them time after time.

There'd been some good horses here and there, and some long trails and wide deserts I'd traveled. I had those memories, and I guess they stacked up to quite a lot when a fellow thought of it. But pa was away head of me when he settled down here to make his stand. He had a wife back home, and some boys growing, boys to carry on his name and carry on his living for him. I hadn't a son nor a daughter. If I went out now there'd be nobody to mourn me. My brothers, yes. But a man needs a woman to cry for him when he goes out.

Still, I'd want to be the last to go. I'd want to see her safely to bed before I cashed in my checks. Maybe it is easier for a man to be alone than a woman. I wouldn't know much about such things.

They are gettin' busy over yonder. Voices are closer. I reckon the fussin' and the feudin' are shapin' up to start. I reckon this is how some of those old Trojans felt when they put on their armor for the last fight, when the Greeks were closing in and they knew they weren't going to make it.

But I am going to make it. No man should go down the long way without leaving something behind him, and all I've got to leave will disappear when the dust settles.

A man can carve from stone, he can write fine words, or he can do something to hold himself in the hearts of people. I hadn't done any of those things, not yet.

Maybe I never would.

The wind was dying. Leaves hanging still. There was the coolness of the mountains around me. This here place must be close onto twelve thousand feet up. A shade less, because there were trees around me. But the trees stopped not fifty yards off, and even here there weren't very many.

Looked like something moved atop that knoll. I'd like to burn him a mite, like to singe his scalp so's he'll know it ain't all going to be fun.

They were comin' now. Some movement down the ledge. I ate the last strip of bacon and refilled my cup with coffee.

A bullet nudged at the rock over my head, spilling fragments into my coffee. I swore. Now they shouldn't ought to have done that. A body can take just so much, and I set store by a good cup of coffee.

If I stayed back close to the rocks nobody was going to get a real good shot at me, so I just set there. When shootin' time come, I'd do my share. No use to take the fun away from those anxious folks down there. A couple of more shots from down the ledge, but they done nobody any harm. I took another gulp of coffee and looked out yonder at the mountain peaks. Some of them were fifty, sixty miles off.

I wished I could see the one called the Sleeping Ute, but that mountain was hidden behind the rim yonder. When I leaned forward to take up the pot, that gent atop the knoll shot right into my fire. I slapped around, putting out sparks. He was going to get almighty annoying if he kept that up.

There were several more shots, but I finished my coffee before I took up my rifle.

Thing about fightin' with folks unused to fightin' is that a body should give them time. They get eager to get on with it and haven't the patience to set and wait. Me, I was in no hurry. I wasn't going no place.

First thing you know they were shootin'—scatterin' lead every which way—but I just set back in my corner enjoying my coffee and let them have at it.

They were wishful that I'd move out where I could shoot back so that gent atop the knoll could settle my hash. I'd no mind to let him do it.

Finally, I just got tired of the racket.

The horses were in the best spot of all. They hadn't picked no fight. I had them in a place where bullets couldn't reach, and they had sense enough to stand there and switch flies off one another.

After a mite I decided that gent on the knoll might be gettin' eager enough to make a fool of himself, so I took my rifle and edged around to where I could peek up yonder without showing too much. Sure enough, I saw his rifle barrel. Then I saw something against the sky—a shoulder in a blue shirt, maybe. It disappeared, but folks being what they are, I just waited, knowing he'd be apt to do the same thing again, and he did.

Me, I just up with that '73 and shot him, right in the whatever it was he was showin'. I heard a yelp, then a rifle fell loose on the grassy slope of that knoll, and I edged out to where I could see down the ledge.

I caught a glimpse of a plaid shirt down thataway. I triggered the '73, and whatever I'd shot at disappeared.

After that there was a kind of letup in the shootin'.

Those shots hadn't stopped them, just made them a mite more cautious. They knew now it wasn't going to be all downhill, but I'm tellin' the world I was a mighty lonesome man, a-settin' there, waitin' for them to come. And only a few miles off I had family tough enough to whip an army. Looked to me like I had it to do all by myself.

Well, that was the way I'd done most things in my life long.

I fed a couple of cartridges into my rifle and took a look at the horses. They were standing, half-asleep, undisturbed by the doings of us humans. I went down among them and talked to 'em a little and then eased myself back up to where I'd been.

There was no easy way out of this, but one thing I knew: come night-time I wasn't going to set waitin'. I was going out among 'em. And I was going shootin'.

Come hell or high water, I was going out yonder. If they wanted to land this fish, they were going to find out they had something on the hook.

Chapter 24

It was a long day. From time to time a shot came into the hollow, but they made no frontal attack. The failure of the shots from the top of the knoll had apparently left them at a loss, and they hadn't figured out what to do.

Nobody ever won a fight by setting back and waiting, at least, not in my circumstances. In any case, my only way of fighting was to attack, and I believe in it, anyway. Attack, always attack.

They had me bottled up where I couldn't move by day, but night was something else, and I intended to move out and hunt them down. No doubt they planned to come and get me as soon as darkness fell.

Lying there I studied the possible routes out of my cul-de-sac, and getting out was no problem for a man on foot. In my saddlebags I carried my moccasins. I'd been a woodsman before I was ever a rider, and it come natural to me to move quiet.

Many a time as a boy I had either to ease up on game or not get a shot. A kill meant that I'd eat, and often it was only me and the family when pa was gone and the other boys still too young to hunt.

Judging by what Andre had said pa had come here. Probably he had died here. And he must have had the gold when he reached this place.

What had become of it? Was it still hidden close by?

I set back and took a careful look around. Supposin' I had gold to hide, quite a bit of it. Where would I hide it where it would be unlikely to be found? Supposin' I was here, figured I still had a fightin' chance, but knew I might have to slip out and travel light, just like I was going to do when darkness came?

Where would I hide the gold?

There was a level place of green grass, partly protected from rifle fire by a shoulder of the rock that walled the ledge. There was a sort of cove in the wall, scarcely more than enough to hide the two horses.

A tree that must have fallen five or six years ago lay close by, its trunk breaking up to pay its debt to the soil it came from. Lying near to it was the fallen tree with the brown needles still in place. It must have been broken off this past winter. Those trees hadn't been there when pa made his stand—if he did.

I had another thing to go by. Pa had known all the Indian ways of marking a trail, and he had taught them to us boys. One way was to place one rock atop another as a trail marker and a rock alongside the marker to show the direction of travel. Often when we were youngsters he'd lay out a trail for us to follow. He'd gather a tuft of grass and tie it around with more grass, or he'd break a branch and stick it in the ground to show the way he'd gone.

Often the Indians would bend a living tree to mark the way. From time to time in wandering the woods one will wonder about a tree that grows parallel to the ground for a ways. Chances are it was some marker used by Indians in the long ago.

Pa taught us boys as best he could. He'd find a spot in the deep woods and he'd clear the ground of all leaves, branches, stones, and whatever. Then he'd smooth out the dust, leaving some food, both meat and seeds, in the center. We'd surround it with a circle of branches or stones, and we'd come back each morning to see who'd been there.

It wasn't long until we boys could tell the track of any animal or bird or reptile that crossed the smooth dust.

Pa was forever pointing at some tracks or tree or bunch of rocks and asking us what we thought happened there, or what was happening. It's an amazing thing how much a boy can learn in a short time.

You found where animals had fought, mated, and died. You learned which animals moved about at night, which would come for meat, and which for seeds or other food.

We got so we just saw things without having to look for them. It was natural to us to know what was happening in the mountains and in the forest. Just as people differ one from another, so do the trees, even the trees of one species.

After a while I put my fire together again and fixed a little food, made fresh coffee, and took time to study the situation. Pa had been in this spot twenty years ago, and things would have looked very different. The older of the fallen trees would have been growing then, and several others within the range of my eyes would have been fair-sized trees. Others, larger and older, might now be gone.

The high winds, snows, and ice of the alpine heights are hard on trees. The bristlecone pine, which seems to survive anything, outlasts the others. This shelf where I had taken refuge would be deep under snow much of the year, and when pa was here some snow might have still been left. To understand his situation I had to bring back the shelf the way it must have been when he saw it.

Surely there'd have been snow where I sat, snow in this pocket and along the side where the shadows stayed almost all day long. He'd have made his notch somewhere here, but the tree might have fallen. It might be this very tree that was rotting away before me, or it might have been burned in campfires or fallen clear over the rim. There were scattered carcasses of trees along the steep slope below the cliff.

Pa respected his boys, respected our knowledge of things, and if he'd had the chance he'd have left us a clue, some hint as to where the gold was, and maybe as to what had become of him.

Had the journal ended with the loss of that daybook? Or had he some other means of writing? I'd better consider that.

I needed Orrin here. He had a contemplative mind and he was a lawyer, a man accustomed to dealing with the trickiness of the human mind. Tyrel would have been a help, too, for Tyrel took nothing for granted. He was a right suspicious man. He liked folks, but never expected much of them. If his best friend betrayed him he'd not be surprised. He figured we were all human, all weak at times, and mostly selfish. And we all, he figured, had traits of nobility, self-sacrifice, and courage. In short, we were folks, people.

Tyrel never held it against any man for what he did. He trusted nobody too much, liked most people, and he was wary. But at a time like this he would have been a help. He had a reasoning, logical brain unhampered by much sentiment.

One thing was a help. We Sacketts bred true. I mean, we bred to type. Like the Morgan horse. Pa used to say he'd known a sight of Sacketts one time and another, and they varied in size, but most of them ran to dark, kind of Indian-like features and to willingness to fight. Even those Clinch Mountain Sacketts, who were a cattle-rustling, moonshining lot, would stand fast in a showdown, and they'd never go back on their word or fail a friend.

They might steal his horse, if it was a good one and chance offered, but they were just as like to stand over his wounded body and fight off the redskins or give him one of their own horses, even their only horse, to get away on.

Logan and Nolan, for example. They were Clinch Mountain Sacketts, and their pa was meaner than a rattlesnake in the blind, but they never walked away from a friend in trouble, or anybody else, for that matter.

Nolan was forted up down in the Panhandle country with some Comanches yonder a-shootin' at him. One of them got lead into him. He nailed that one right through the ears as he turned his head to speak to the other one, and then he wounded the last one. Nolan walked in on him, kicked the gun out of his hand, and stood there looking down at him, gun in his fist, and that Comanche glared right back at him, dared him to shoot, and tried to spit at him.

Nolan laughed, picked that Injun up by the hair and dragged him to his horse. He loaded that Indian on, tied him in place, then mounted his own horse and rode right to that Comanche village.

He walked his horse right in among the lodges and stopped.

The Comanches were fighters. No braver men ever lived, and they wanted Nolan's hair, but they came out and gathered around to see what he had on his mind.

Nolan sat up there in the middle of his mustang, and he told them what a brave man this warrior was, how he had fought him until he was wounded, his gun empty, and then had cussed him and tried to fight him with his hands.

"I did not kill him. He is a brave man. You should be proud to have such a warrior. I brought him back to you to get well from his wounds. Maybe some day we can fight again."

And then he dropped the lead rope and rode right out of that village, walking his horse and never looking back.

Any one of them could have shot him. He knew that. But Indians, of any persuasion, have always respected bravery, and he had given them back one of their own and had promised to fight him again when he had his strength.

So they let Nolan ride away, and to this day in Comanche villages they tell the story. And the Indian he brought back tells it best.

I didn't really have time to contemplate the past. I had mighty little time left and I wanted to find out what happened to pa.

Clouds were making up. Nearly every afternoon there was a brief thundershower high up in the mountains, and now the clouds were gathering. I guess I was feeling kind of pleased about that. I had an idea those folks were new to the high-up hills and if so they were in for a shock.

Rain can fall pretty hard, and of course you're right in the clouds. Right amongst them. Lightning gets to flashing around, and—even without it flashing—the electricity in the air makes your hair prickle like a scared dog's.

I didn't much relish running around atop that mountain with a rifle in my hands, but it looked like I had it to do.

The bulging dark clouds moved down and began to spatter rain, and I came off that log where I was settin' like a chipmunk headin' for a tree. I went around the tree holding my rifle in one hand, scrambled up the rocks, took a quick look, and ran on the double for that knoll.

If they broke and ran for shelter, I would make it. I started up the knoll knowing that in just about a minute it was going to be all wet grass, slippery as ice. Just as I was topping out on the rise a man raised up, rifle in hand.

He'd no idea there was anybody even close. He was getting set to run for shelter from the rain, I figure, and was taking a quick look before he left; and there I was, coming up out of that drifting cloud right at him.

Neither of us had time to think. My Winchester was in my right hand in the trail position, and when he hove up in front of me I just drove the muzzle at him. It was hanging at my side at arm's length. When that man came up off the ground I swang it forward and there was power behind it.

The muzzle caught him right under the nose, smashing up hard. It knocked him right over backwards, and he let a scream out of him like you never heard. It must've hurt real bad.

He tumbled head over heels down the side of that steep knoll and wound up at the bottom, his face all bloody. I stood there looking down at him.

The knoll was kind of like a pyramid too narrow for its height, covered with grass and scattered rocks. That cloud was drifting over, and he could see me up there, rifle in hand.

He figured I was going to kill him, and for a moment there I gave it thought.

"You get off down the mountain, boy," I told him, "and you keep goin'. You folks are about to get me upset."

Still looking at me, he began to back himself off, still lying on the grass, the rain pelting him.

I looked around and there was nobody in sight. I turned and went back down the knoll to my hideout.

When I got to the horses I pulled the picket pins and coiled the ropes. I stowed them away and gathered the reins and was just about to stick a toe in a stirrup when I realized how wet my feet were going to get in those moccasins.

My boots were handy so I got into my slicker and set down to haul on my boots—when my eyes leveled on that crack in the rocks.

It wasn't no kind of a place, just a layered rock where one layer had fallen or been pulled out—leaving a kind of gap not over two inches wide. It was deeper than it looked at first, and there was something in there.

I slipped my hand in and found myself touching some kind of a book. I took it out and it was another daybook, almost like the first, but it was in worse shape.

When I scrambled up that rock wall I must have stepped on a piece of the rock that had been shoved in there to keep the wet off and the animals from gettin' at it.

It was a daybook, and I knew it had been pa's. I shifted it to my left hand and started to slip it into my coat pocket when a voice said, "I'll take that!"

It was Andre Baston, and he was right on the bank with a gun on me.

Chapter 25

There's times when a man might talk himself out of trouble, but this wasn't one of those times.

Andre Baston was a killing man and he had a gun on me. I've known men who would have shot me and taken the book out of my dead hand, but Baston was not only a killer, he was cruel. He liked somebody to know he was going to kill 'em.

Moreover he'd been used to those set-tos where there's a challenge, seconds meet, a duel is arranged, and two men walk out on the greensward—whatever that is—and, after a certain number of paces, they turn around and shoot at each other most politely.

Me, I'd grown up to a different manner of doing. You drew and you shot, and no fancy didoes were cut. Nobody needed to tell me what Andre had in mind. I had the same thing in mind for him only I wasn't wastin' around about it.

He'd said, "I'll take that!" And he had a gun on me.

A man who doesn't want to get shot hadn't better pack a gun in the first place. I knew when I laid my hand on that gun that I was going to get shot, but I also had it in mind to shoot back.

I figured, *all right, he's going to nail me, but if he kills me I'll take him with me, and if he doesn't kill me I'll surely get him.*

He didn't expect it—I had that going for me, but it wasn't enough. My hand went to the gun and she came up fast and smooth. When she came level I was going to let drive, and I kind of braced myself for the shock of a bullet.

My .44 bucked in my hands, and, an instant before it went off, his gun stabbed flame. I just stood there and thumbed back that hammer. *No matter how many times he shoots, you got to kill him,* I told myself. I just eared her back and let 'er bang, and Andre Baston kind of stood up on his toes. I let her go again, and his gun went off into the grass at his feet and he fell off the ledge sidewise and lit right at my feet.

"You!" There was an ugly hatred in his eyes. "You aren't even a *gentle-man!*"

"No, sir," I said politely, "but I'm a damned good shot."

Andre Baston, of New Orleans, died on the rim of Cumberland Basin with the rain falling into his wide-open eyes, trickling down his freshly shaved jaws.

"Well, pa," I said, "if this was the one, he's signed the bill for it. You rest easy, wherever you lie."

With a sweep of my palm I swept the water from my saddle and stepped up there on old Ap and pointed his nose down the basin, the buckskin right behind us. We just climbed out of that shelf and rounded a clump of spruce, and I looked back yonder at the knoll, half-hidden in clouds now.

It came to me then, ridin' away, that Andre had missed me. I'd been so almighty sure I was going to get shot, I was ready to take the lead and send it back. But he missed. Maybe when he saw me reaching he hurried too much, maybe the panic came up in him like it does in a lot of men when they know they're going to be shot at—a kind of uncomfortable feeling.

But like I said, when you pick up a weapon you can expect a weapon to be used against you.

They had them a sort of camp on the slope, a mighty poor shelter, I'd say. I rode right up to them, two men I didn't know, and Paul, looking like something blown up against a fence by a wet wind. Of course, Fanny was there, startled to see me, the softness gone from her features, her mouth drawn hard.

"You better go get your uncle," I said. "He's up there lyin' in the rain."

They did not believe me. I had my rifle across my saddlebows, its black muzzle looking one-eyed at them, so they stood quiet.

"Was I in your place," I suggested, "I'd light a shuck for Bourbon Street or places around, and when I got there I'd start burning a few candles at the altar of your Uncle Philip. There's nothing left for you here."

The trail was muddy, full of doubles and switchbacks, with little streams crossing it here and there. That was a day when it kept right on raining, and through the rain dripping off my hat I saw the fresh green of the forest and the grass.

It was a narrow trail, no question of hurrying. All I wanted was to get to the bottom, back down to Shalako where I could wrap myself around a few steaks and some hot coffee. This was a day when I'd rather set by an inside fire and watch the raindrops fall.

Every once in a while when I'd duck under a tree, a few raindrops, always the coldest ones, would shake loose and trickle down the back of my neck.

Alongside the trail, sometimes close by, sometimes down in a rocky gorge below me, was the La Plata. Waterfalls along the trail added to the river's volume. The trail was washed out in places.

Nobody used this trail but the Utes, or occasional hunters and prospectors.

Yet all of a sudden I saw something else. In the bank where the trail passed there was a fresh, scuffed place. My hand went under my slicker to my six-shooter.

Somebody had stepped off this trail minutes before, stepping quickly up into the trees that lined the trail. One boot had crushed the grass on the low bank that edged the trail.

Ap turned quickly around a corner of the trail and I glanced up, seeing nothing. The man had gone into the woods, hearing me on the trail, and he hadn't the time to do more than disappear somewhere just within the edge of the trees.

Who would be coming up here on a day like this? No Indian, for it had been a boot track, a wide boot, not far from new.

Nothing happened. I rode on, switching back and around on the narrow trail, and when I reached a straight stretch I stepped up the pace and let Ap trot for a while.

Safely away, I began now to look for more tracks. Occasionally I saw them, shapeless, not to be identified, but tracks nonetheless, and the tracks of somebody who did not wish to be seen. Wherever he could, he walked off the trail.

There were places when the sides were too steep, or the gorge beside the trail too deep for him to avoid the trail. The man had a good stride. He was a heavy man, too, but possibly not a tall one despite the good steps he took.

Might be a smaller man carrying a heavy pack. Had the tracks not been so sloppy I might have been able to tell if the man carried a heavy pack or was himself heavy. Of course, it might be both.

It worried me. Who was he? And why was he going up the mountain today?

Well, if he was a friend to the Bastons it did not matter, and if he was their enemy, it might be they'd shoot each other.

I was going for a hot meal, a night's rest, and a chance to put down my gun.

There's something about gold that nags at a man. I've seen it at work a time or two. I think we Sacketts have less of it than most—with us it's land. We like the ownership of land, large pieces of mountain country, that's for us.

Nonetheless, pa labored hard for that gold. He found it, brought it off down the mountain, and now it was cached up yonder . . . sure as shootin' it was there. It puzzled a man to guess where.

By the time I rode up to Shalako the sun was out and sparkling on the rain-wet leaves. Orrin came out of the store and stood waiting.

He gave me a long look. "You all right?"

"I been through it." I stepped down and stood, hands resting on the saddle, and then I turned my head toward him. "I left Andre up yonder. Right where pa was cornered, I think."

"The rest of them?"

"Up there. Paul's there with Fanny and a couple of others."

"Leave your horses," Orrin said. "Judas said to tell you he'd care for them. You come in and have some grub."

Judas came out to take Ap and the buckskin, and I walked across to the saloon with Orrin.

"There was a man came into town. Had his face all torn up and couldn't talk much, or didn't want to. He went off down the road mumbling to himself."

"He ran into a rifle muzzle, I guess. Orrin, did you see anybody else? Did anybody go up the canyon?"

"Not by daylight. We've been watching. I mean we've been watching that road every minute."

I told him about the tracks in the trail, but he shook his head, having no more explanation than I did.

"Somebody followed pa to that place. Somebody cornered him up there, and he may have been hurt. Pa taught us boys so much, and we've lived about the same. I figured I'd just let myself go the likely way. He left notches here and there, the deep, gashlike blazes, you know." I took the other daybook out of my pocket. "And I found this."

Orrin took it in his hands. "I wonder what pa was thinking, Tell. Why he took to keeping these on that last trip? Do you suppose he had a premonition?"

I'd been thinking of it, too. "Either that, or something was turning wrong with him. He never was much to complain, you know, and we always just took it for granted he was about the strongest man around. Maybe he was feeling poorly and wasn't wishful that we know."

The words were no sooner out than I was sure I'd hit on it. This trip had been pa's last chance to do something for his family. He'd cared for us, but suddenly he might have felt he wouldn't be able to, and he began to worry.

Neither of us wanted to open the book. This would be our last word from pa, and these last few weeks we'd felt close to him again, walking in his footsteps and all. After this we both felt there would be nothing left to the story, nothing but what must have happened when he stopped writing.

Berglund brought some hot soup and bread and I made a meal of it. The book lay there on the table, and from time to time I looked up to see it there.

Tired as I was, my thoughts kept returning to the mountain trail, and I wanted to go back. I wanted to walk there again, to stand on that shelf again looking out over the mountains and sky.

The feeling stayed with me that there was something I had not found. "Where's Nell Trelawney?" I asked suddenly. "I haven't seen her."

"You will," Orrin chuckled as he said it. "She's been around every day wanting us to go up the canyon and find you. She was sure you were in trouble."

He grinned. "I told her you'd been in trouble all your born days."

"Any more of those Three Eight hands around?"

"Boley McCaire—the young one who was so itchy. He rode into town, but he's been holed up somewhere down the creek. I've a hunch that Baston made some kind of a deal with them."

Something kept worrying me at the back of my mind, and it was not only those tracks along the way. I did not like things left hanging. Nobody went up that mountain trail in the rain without reason. The folks at Shalako had seen nobody pass, and the road was right yonder. Nobody could pass along without being seen, so if somebody had gone up the creek he had taken pains not to be seen.

Who? And why? And what was he doing now?

Judas came in, and then the Tinker. The Tinker sat down near a window where he could watch the street and the trail to the mountains.

"Judas," I said suddenly, "have you known the Bastons long?"

He hesitated and seemed to be considering. "Fifty years," he said quietly. "Possibly even longer."

"Would Andre have followed Pierre and stabbed him?"

Judas thought for a moment. "Of course. But I do not believe he did. It was someone else."

"Who?"

He shrugged, and then he said, "Andre would not have dared let Pierre live, not after attacking him. The very idea would have been frightening. Had Andre any thought that Pierre lived after he shot him, he'd have killed him or fled—to Africa or South America."

"Why, in God's name?"

"Andre was afraid. He was a brave man, although a murderer, but he feared one man. He was afraid of Philip."

"*Afraid* of him?"

Judas looked at me, then at the rest of us. "Yes, you see Philip was the worst of them, by far the worst."

Chapter 26

We looked at him, wondering if he was joking, but he was very serious.

"I knew him, you see, and he was good to us. I mean to his slaves, but we had no choice but to obey him, and, being wise, we did obey.

"He liked Pierre Bontemps. He was also amused by him. Pierre was a romantic, an adventurer. Both men had been buccaneers, and this was known of Pierre, but not of Philip.

"Philip surrounded himself with calm, dignity, and reserve. He liked me because I had some education and because he knew I did not talk of what I knew or had seen.

"He was not a vindictive man, not a hater. He was simply a man without scruple. He had contempt for others, whom he considered less than himself. He did nothing to exhibit himself except in that quiet, dignified manner.

"He removed anyone who got in his way. Had you not killed Andre, he would have had it done, or done it himself, for Andre had become notorious.

"Each of us has in his mind an image of what he believes himself to be, and Philip Baston saw himself as a prince of the old school. He had read Machiavelli, studied the careers of Orsini, Sforza, and Sigismondo Malatesta, and in his small way he lived accordingly.

"The Bastons had money, and, from time to time, power, but not enough of either to please any of them. Philip served briefly at sea in a French ship, then became a pirate.

"Lafitte was notorious. Baston was more cunning. He slipped into New Orleans and bought property, always small pieces, nothing to attract attention. He bought land in other parts of Louisiana, and when it became no longer safe to carry on as a pirate he simply came ashore, moved into the old Baston home and carried on as if he had never been gone. It wasn't realized for several years that he was enormously wealthy.

"He aspired to be governor. He lived in the grand manner, and anyone who got in his way was removed. Now he thinks of his family, his name.

At first he looked on Andre's duels with favor. They had a certain style, and it was good to be feared. There came a time however when it became obvious that Andre *killed*. He was not content to win. This was looked upon with distaste, and I believe that for some time Philip has intended to be rid of Andre."

"But you said Andre was afraid of him. Is Philip such a fighter?"

"He is a superb swordsman and a dead shot, but Philip would not have done it himself unless forced into the position. He would have made other arrangements."

It was interesting, but nothing that meant much to us now. Philip Baston was in New Orleans.

What interested me more was the identity of the unknown man who left the footprints on the trail.

If he had a horse, where had it been?

Orrin got up. "You better get some rest. I am going to ride over and see Flagan."

The Swede had a back room with a spare bunk in it, and he showed me to the place. I shucked my boots, hat, and gun belt and stretched out on that bunk with a deep sigh. I'd no recollection of ever feeling so tired before.

I'd been on the trail for a long while, and a man tires faster when his nerves are on edge. When you're hunting and being hunted, every fiber of your being is poised and ready.

I felt the tenseness go out of me slow, and I dozed off. I woke briefly and watched the aspens beyond the window. It was fifty or sixty feet to the edge of the woods. The curtain stirred in the breeze, and I watched it lazily, then drifted off into a sound sleep.

Under the aspens the man waited. He had a shotgun in his hands, and he knew what he wanted to do. Inside the room near the opposite wall was a chair. Over the back of the chair hung a gun belt.

He heard the boots hit the floor and thought he heard a creak of a bed when the man lay down.

Just a few minutes now . . . a few minutes.

The big, good-looking brother had ridden off on his horse. The Negro was in the barn, working on some of their saddlegear. The Tinker had taken a pole and headed for the La Plata, and Swede Berglund was tending that garden he was trying. So William Tell Sackett was there alone, and soon he would be asleep.

The hunter had patience. He had seen the young Sackett with another daybook in his hands, but the daybook could not have been with the body. He had gone over it thoroughly those twenty years ago.

Was it with the gold? No . . . for gold hadn't been brought off the mountain today.

The book would certainly tell where old man Sackett had hidden the gold. They had all been so sure Sackett was dead, and Pierre, too. Well, Pierre was dead now, that was sure, and so was Sackett.

The trouble was Sackett had gone back and gotten the gold after they were all gone. Not all the gold on Treasure Mountain, but a good lot of it, anyway.

This William Tell Sackett worried him. The man was a tracker, and a good one. He could read sign like an Apache, and there was no safety with him about.

Sackett had killed Andre. The man had not seen it but he heard the girl and the others talking of it. That must have taken some doing, for Andre was dangerous, good with a gun, and ready to use it.

So much the better. With Andre gone, the rest of them were nothing. Paul was a weakling. That girl was murderous enough, but she was a woman, and she was too impulsive.

Well inside the curtain of aspens, crouched low among the tall grass, wild flowers, and oak brush, he was well hidden. He would give Sackett plenty of time to get to sleep, really to sleep.

Crouched in the bushes, the man waited. The shotgun had two barrels, and he wore a long-barreled six-shooter for insurance and had a rifle on his horse. As he waited he once more studied the ground. He knew just where each foot would touch ground, where he would go into the trees, where he would turn after entering the woods. He had chosen two alternative routes. He was a careful man.

Ten to fifteen seconds to the window, lean in, fire his shot. Then, instead of running directly away, he would run along the wall of the saloon, go around the outhouse, and crouch along the corral into the scrub oaks.

On the other side of the oak brush a trail dipped into the river bottom where his horse waited. He would ride south, away from the canyon, where there was more room to lose himself.

He waited a moment longer, got to his feet, glanced left and right, and stepped out of the brush, walking swiftly to the window.

Glancing left and right, he saw no one. The shotgun came up in his hands, and he was almost running when he reached the window. He started to thrust the shotgun into the open window when suddenly a voice on his left said, "You lookin' for something, mister?"

It was that Trelawney girl, and she had a rifle in her hands, not aimed at him, but in a position where only an instant would be needed to aim it. He hesitated, kept his head tilted downward. He muttered under his breath, then turned sharply away and walked toward the outhouse.

"Mister? *Mister!*"

He ducked around the small building and ran along the corral into the woods. Another ten seconds! He swore, bitterly. Another ten seconds and he would have killed Tell Sackett and be on the run . . . well away to his horse.

Nell walked to the window, glancing in. Taking one more quick look after the fleeing man, gone now, she went around to the front. The Tinker was standing in front of the store. She explained quickly.

The Tinker glanced toward the woods beyond the corral. "He's gone. You scared him off."

"But who *was* he? I never saw him before!"

The Tinker shrugged. "It will not happen again." He walked around the building, glanced toward the woods, then sat down. "I'll stay right here until he wakes up. Don't you worry now."

Morning light was laying across the windowsill before my eyes opened, and for a time I just lay still, letting myself get wide awake. That there was the soundest sleep I'd had in a long, long time. Finally, I swung my feet to the floor and reached for my boots.

Something stirred outside the window, and Tinker said, "Tell? Better come out and have a look."

When I was dressed and out there beside him, he showed me the tracks. There were only parts of two foot tracks, the rest were on grass and left no mark that remained to show size.

It was the same track I'd seen on the trail.

"He was out to get you, Tell. There's a place where he waited in the aspens over there. He must've waited an hour or more."

In the earth back of the outhouse we found another track, smudged and shapeless because he had been running. We found where his horse had stood, tied and waiting.

I studied the tracks, knowing I had seen them before, but without remembering where. To a tracker a track is like a signature, and as easy to identify, but this was not one I had remembered, hence it was no one I had ever followed. It was simply a track I had noted casually without paying it any mind, but one thing I knew. If I saw that track again, I would remember it.

Orrin came in from the ranch. "Good place," he said, "and I've found a spot for us."

When I told him what had happened, he looked grim, "I should have come back. I knew I should have come back."

"Nothing gets by that girl," Tinker commented. "She had that man dead to rights."

We drank coffee, ate breakfast, and watched the cloud shadows change on Baldy. "I'm going up there again," I said. "I've got to settle it in my mind. I've got to find what remains of him."

"He's lost," Berglund said. "Coyotes or bears carried off the bones . . . or the buzzards dropped them. Nothing lasts long up there that isn't stone."

"There's evidence of that," the Tinker said quietly, "coming down the trail."

Four horses, four riders—a rain-wet, beat-up looking crew—and one of them was Fanny Baston. Paul was there, one hand all tied up with a bandage, and those two riders they'd picked up from somewhere.

They came down the trail, and we stepped outside to see them pass, but they looked neither to the right nor the left, they just rode on through. They carried nothing, nor did they stop for grub.

"She's a beautiful woman," Orrin said. "You should have seen her the night we met."

"Mountains are hard upon evil," I said. "They don't hold with it."

Back inside we drank coffee whilst Judas saddled up for us. He came across the road, a neat black man in a neat black coat. "I would like to ride along with you, suh," he suggested.

"Why not? You're a man to ride with, Priest. But ride ready for war. It may come upon us."

We packed the buckskin again, for we'd be gone one night, anyway.

We rode out into the street and started for the trail, and two more riders came up from the other end of town. It was Nell Trelawney and old Jack Ben.

"See here," I said, pulling rein, "this is a rough ride, and you've been ailin'."

"I ain't ailin' now," old Jack Ben said irritably, "and as for rough rides, I was ridin' rough country before your head was as high as a stirrup! You just ride along now, and pay us no mind."

"No use to argue," Orrin said. "He was always a hard-headed, unreasonable old coot."

Jack Ben snorted, but when we started off they were right behind us, and there they stayed, all the way up the mountain, and we rode with our rifles ready to hand. Yet no trouble came to us, and we rode easy in our saddles, the wind cool and pleasant in our faces, winding around and doubling back, the wild waters of the La Plata tumbling over the rocks or slowing down where the canyon widened out.

Midday was long gone when we rode into the basin. The grass was a glorious green, wild flowers were everywhere.

When we went down on the shelf Andre's body was gone. I showed them where the daybook had been. We had brought it along to read on the spot.

It was getting on for sundown, so we unsaddled and staked out our horses. When the fire was lit and the coffee on, I took out the daybook.

Chapter 27

Judas was fixing supper. The Tinker sat a little away from us in the dark where he could listen better to the night sounds.

With firelight flickering on the faces around, I tilted the book to catch the glow and settled down to read. There was a smudge on the first page.

. . . wind blowing, hard to write. Played out. A man trailin' me got a bullet into me when I went to move the picket pin. Low down on my left side. Hurts like hell. Lost blood. Worst is, he's in a place where I can't get a shot at him. Dasn't have no fire.

Later: shot twice. Missed. I shot at sound, figured to make him carefuller. Gold hid. Got to hide this book—the other one's been stolen. If the boys come a-huntin', soon or late they'll find it. I trust if somebody else does he'll call the boys and share up. I don't expect no man to find gold and give it all up. Figured that was Andre, yonder. It ain't. Andre ain't that good in the brush. This'ns like Injun.

Later: ain't et for two days. Canteen empty. Licked dew off the grass. Caught a swallow of rain in my coffeepot. Wounds in bad shape.

Writing time to time. Boys will find that gold. They'll remember when it comes right down to it. That Orrin, he should recall, him always wantin' the cream of things. No further than from the house to the old well. Ma could find it. How many times she scolded that boy!

Comin'. Been backed up here five days now. Grub's gone. Coffee's gone. No water but dew and rain. Whoever it is out there won't take a chance. Got a funny walk. Hear him. Got another bullet into me. Boys, I ain't goin' to make it. Be good boys. Be good. Take care—got to put this away.

He was cornered like the old bear driven to the wall, wounded and dying, but his last thoughts were of us. He'd have handled everything all right if he could have moved around, but he was bad hurt. That bullet in the side, now. That must have been worse than he said . . . and no water. He must have caught some rain in his coffeepot, but that wouldn't have been much. He would have been slower in his movements with that bruised hipbone.

When I finished reading, we just sat there thinking of pa, remembering the way he walked, the lessons he taught us, his humor, his handiness with tools.

"That gold's somewheres about," Jack Ben said, "an' he left you clues. 'No further than from the house to the old well.' That there should mean somethin'. I recall that old well. She always had good water. Cold water, too. On'y it was too far from the house on a winter's mornin' so your grandpa dug one closer."

"It ain't the gold, Jack Ben. It's pa. We want to find what remains of him."

"You know what I think?" The Tinker turned his head toward us, firelight glinting on the gold rings in his ears. "I think that's the same man after you. The one who killed your pa. I think he's out there right now."

We set quiet, contemplating on that. It could be . . . but who?

"A Higgins," Jack Ben said, remembering the old feud in Tennessee. "It must be a Higgins you've paid no mind to. He got your pa, now he's after the rest of the Sacketts."

That might be, but something worried me. Couldn't put a finger on it, but something about this whole setup bothered me to fits. Nell set over there kind of watching me and that upset my considering. Hard to keep a mind on business with her setting over there breathing. Every time she took a deep breath my forehead broke out with sweat.

"Go back over it," Judas suggested. "Cover every step. Possibly there is a thing that does not fit, something that will explain it all."

"It might be the McCaire outfit," Orrin said. "Charley McCaire didn't take kindly to losing those horses even if he had no hand in stealing them."

"You don't think he did?" I asked.

"I doubt it. I think it was somebody in his outfit. But once he had them he didn't want to give them up or to have it believed that anyone in his outfit was a thief. If Tyrel hadn't ridden up when he did we'd have had to shoot our way out."

"I don't think it's any of them," I said. "There's something odd about this man."

"What became of Swan?" Judas asked.

I shrugged. I'd been wondering that myself. We'd seen nothing of him, yet surely he was around. He was not with Paul and Fanny when they left . . . if they had.

Finishing my coffee, I threw the grounds into the fire and rinsed out my cup. We would find the gold. I was sure of that, but I had never been a money-hungry man. We'd started out to find pa, or what remained of him, and we'd come a long way. We had to find out what happened in those last hours or minutes.

I put my cup away and went into the darkness near the trees, stood there a moment, and worked my way over to where the Tinker was.

He spoke as I neared him. "Tell? There's somebody or something out there."

His whisper was very soft, only for my ears. I squatted near him. "Nothing definite . . . just something moving . . . scarcely no sound."

I noticed that he held his knife in his hand. The Tinker was always a careful man.

"I'm going out there."

"No." The Tinker put his hand on my arm. "I will go."

"This here's my job. Just tell them I am out there. And be careful, there's no telling what he will do."

It was very dark. There were a few stars among scattered clouds. I made no attempt to keep to the brush. I moved through the knee-high grass and wild flowers.

When I was thirty yards out from camp, I stopped to listen. What was he doing? Trying for a shot? Or merely listening?

I moved on among the scattered spruce, keeping low to the ground. I stopped, and a voice spoke, very low.

"Have you found the gold?"

There was a chill along my back. "No," I said after a moment.

"It is mine. It is all mine. You will not find it."

That voice! There was something . . . some thread of sound . . .

"We can find it," I said calmly, "and no one else can. The message my father left is one only we could understand."

There was a long silence. "I do not believe it. How could that be?"

"It has to do with our home in Tennessee."

What manner of man was this who would so coolly talk to me in the darkness? And where was he? The direction was obvious, but if I leaped, and missed, I'd be dead in the next moment.

"It is *my* gold." He spoke softly. "Go away and I'll not kill you."

"You're through killing. If anybody does it now, it will be us."

He did not speak, and I wondered if he were gone. I listened . . . the man was a ghost in the woods. I was good, but this man, I believed, was better.

"You killed my father," I said.

"He was a good man. I did not wish to do it, but he had my gold."

"The Frenchmen mined the gold. They buried it. They sold their claim to it with Louisiana. It was anybody's gold."

"You will not have it. I will kill you all."

After a moment of listening, I said, "Where is my father's body?"

If I could keep him talking, just a little longer. I shifted my position slightly, making no sound.

"It is beyond there, beyond your camp. I buried him in a crack. It is at the edge, near the roots of a tree."

The faintest sound. I moved swiftly, felt the sudden rush of a body in the darkness, saw the gleam of a knife in a short, wicked sidewise swing at my ribs. He swung with his right arm, and I pulled back and dropped to my right. His knife went past me, and I rolled up on the small of my back and kicked out viciously with both feet, kicking where his body had to be.

The double kick caught him on the side and knocked him rolling. Coming up like a cat, knife in hand, I went for him. I saw the black bulk of him roll up and come at me, felt the edge of the knife and the point take my sleeve, and then I came up on his right side and brought my knife up from below.

His elbow caught my wrist and I almost lost my grip on the knife. He twisted away, turned, and threw his weight into me. He was heavy and bull-strong. The charge threw me back, but I caught my left forearm under his chin and brought him over with me. He landed on his back just above me and then we both came up, panting fiercely, gasping for breath at that altitude.

He circled . . . I could barely see him. I could hear his breath and see the cold light gleam along his blade. Suddenly I stopped, poised, yet still. Instantly he threw himself into me and I sidestepped off to my left, leaving my extended right leg for him to trip over. As his toe hooked over my leg, I swung back and down with my blade.

It caught him—too high—it ripped his coat and must have nicked his neck, for I heard a gasp of pain and then he wheeled into me again. This time his head was up and I jabbed him in the face with my fist. He did not expect it; my fist smashed him back on his heels, and I stepped in, stabbing low and hard.

At the last instant he tried to evade my thrust, throwing himself backward down a small declivity. For an instant he vanished, and then I was down and after him.

He was gone.

Stopping, poised for battle, I listened. Not a sound except a soft wind in the trees. A cloud drifted over the stars and it was darker. Every sense alert, I listened.

Nothing. . . nothing at all.

A brief, utterly futile battle. A moment of desperate struggle, and then nothing.

Yet I should have known. He was a sure-thing killer, who could stab the wounded and helpless Pierre, who could shoot my father from ambush and then lurk, waiting for days for a final shot.

He had thought to kill me there in the darkness, coming at me suddenly, yet I had been ready. And I had nicked him. Of that I was sure.

After a moment I walked back. "I believe I scratched him," I said and explained.

At the edge of the cliff where he had said my father's body was hidden, I hesitated. It was the very edge, and there looked to have been some crumbling. Probably the result of the tree roots.

There was a crack, all right, and some dirt had been filled in. Orrin came closer, holding a burning branch in his left hand. I leaned over to look closer, put my foot on the outer edge of the crack and leaned still further, astride the crack.

Suddenly there was a grating sound, the outer edge fell away under my foot and I felt myself falling. Half-turning I made a futile grab at anything, the rock crumbling from under my feet.

A hand caught mine, the branch dropped, another hand grabbed my sleeve, and I was hauled up on the ledge.

There was a moment when I said nothing. I looked over into the terrible void of blackness behind me, listening to the last particles of rock fall, strike, and rattle away on the last slope.

"Thanks," I said.

"It was a trap," Orrin said dryly. "There's more than one way to kill a man."

Chapter 28

We still had no idea who the killer was. He was somebody who fancied he'd a claim on all that gold, and he was bound and determined to keep everybody else away and to have it all for himself.

At daylight we took a look at the place where I'd almost gone over. There was no evidence to show that a body had ever been there. I reckon the killer had seen the place, figured it was ready to collapse, and just used it on chance.

A woodsman is forever noticing small things like that. He'll have in his mind many possible camps that he'll never have time to use, and he'll notice tangles to avoid, things a man might trip over, and bad footing generally. After a time a man takes all these things in without really thinking about it. But if something is out of place he will see it instantly.

Judas fixed us bacon and eggs from the outfit he'd brought up the trail. It wasn't often we had eggs unless setting down at table, but Judas was a planning man, and he'd packed for good cooking. When we finished I took my Winchester, shifted into moccasins, and walked out to where we'd had our scuffle the night before.

There were tracks aplenty, but might few of them a body could read, for we'd fought mostly on crushed-down grass and flowers, and some of them were already springing back into place.

After a while I found a couple of fair prints. It was the same boot I'd seen on the trail, and I worked around, trying to pick up sign that would take me where he was going.

Trailing a man like that would be like trailing an old silvertip grizzly. He'd be watching his back trail and would be apt to see me before I saw him, and that wasn't pleasant to contemplate.

Not that I had anybody to mourn much for me but brothers. Ange was dead, the other girls I'd known were scattered and gone, but I could do some mourning for myself. It seemed to me I had a lot of living to do and no particular desire to cash in my chips up here in Cumberland Basin.

Nevertheless, I poked around. He'd taken off in an almighty hurry, not scared, mind you, but lacking that extra percentage he always had to have. When he took those first steps he'd be getting away, not thinking of hiding a trail. By his third or fourth step he'd be thinking of that, if I knew my man.

Sure enough, I found a toe print, gouged deep. I followed a few bruised blades of grass, the edge of a heel print, a crushed pine cone, and a slip in a muddy place, and I came through a patch of scattered spruce and into the open beyond.

I had to pull up short. Chances were nine out of ten he'd changed direction right there. So I scouted around and after a few minutes worked out a trail down into the hollow that lay on the east side of the basin. He had gone down into it, then switched on a fallen log, walked its length, and started back up to the ridge.

By night he couldn't see what he'd done, but crushed grass or leaves had left a greenish smudge atop that log in two places. He had stepped on the log and grass from his boots had stuck to it, just as a body will track dirt and the like into a house.

Four or five places in the next hundred yards or so took me along a diagonal route to the high-line trail. That Ghost Trail, as some called it.

A pebble kicked from its place on the muddy path and a couple of partial tracks showed me he was following along the trail.

This here was rifle country, most of it wide open, for the trees give out in the high-up country. Trees were scattered hither and yon, singly or in bunches, among some brush. Higher up the only trees had been barbered by the wind until they looked like upturned brushes. Then there was grass and bare rock, the far-away mountains on every hand, and over all the sky, always scattered with white clouds.

If that hidin' man was in a swivet to get himself killed he'd have to bring it to me. Generally speaking I'm not a techous man, taking most things calm. When a man is about to get shot at he'd better be calm. As much as he can be, at least. Nobody looks favorably on the idea of being shot at.

Trouble was, it was such all-fired pretty country, a man had trouble keeping his mind to it. And quiet? No sound but maybe an eagle, some distance off.

You'd think that in a bald out country like that there'd be no place to hide, but there were places, and any one of them might hide that man.

He'd held to the path—a wise man holds to what trails he can find in the mountains. I picked up sign here and there. He'd slowed down, and a couple of times he'd stopped to catch breath or to ponder.

He knew come daybreak I'd be seekin' his sign. I never minced about shootin' when it had come to that. Back in the Tennessee hills nobody did. Many a girl back yonder bloused her waist to carry a pistol, and we Sackett boys had been toting shootin' irons since we were as tall as pa's belt.

A man walked wary facin' up to a man like this one, so I held my rifle in two hands and kept it right up there where I could shoot without wasting time.

The trail led past a couple of small pools of water, then took a sharp right-hand switch to go out along the ridge toward the north. Spread out before me was a sight of beautiful country that I knowed nothing about but tell-of.

Folks around had talked of it. I'd heard some talk from Cap Rountree when we were up on the Vallecitos that time, and from others here and there. I was looking down Magnetic Gulch toward Bear Creek, and the bear-toothed mountains opposite were Sharkstooth Peak, Banded Mountain, and beyond it the peak of Hesperus.

From where I stood she dropped off some two thousand feet to the bottoms along Bear Creek. I was twelve thousand feet up. I hunkered down behind some rocks, sort of sizing things up before I moved out.

An eagle soared yonder toward the Sharkstooth, and as I looked, some elk came out of the trees into open country and moved across a bench toward the north of the gulch. Now something had moved those elk . . . they weren't just a-playin' "Skip to My Lou." They hied themselves across the clearin' and into the trees.

Might be a bear or a lion, they grow them big in these hills, especially the grizzlies. The grizzly was big, and, when riled, he was mean, but he wouldn't last—because he was fearless. Until the white man came along with his rifle-guns the grizzly was king of the world. He walked where he had a mind to, and nobody trifled with his temper. He couldn't get used to man, although lately he'd become cautious. Maybe too late.

The ridge trail led along the west side of the mountain along here. A man with a rifle would have to be a good shot, used to mountain country.

I stood up and went down into the trees just north of the gulch. When I got into the trees I hunkered down and listened.

There was only the wind, the eternal wind, moving along the high-up peaks, liking them as much as we did.

The grass smelled good. I looked at the rough, gray bark of an old tree, peeling a mite here and there. I saw where a pika had been feeding, and I looked off down the sunlit slope and saw nothing. Then I turned toward the dark clump of spruce further down the slope. I felt suddenly hungry and I stood up and put my left hand into my pocket for some jerky.

I put my rifle down against a limb and boosted the bottom of the pocket a little to get at the jerky. And then from behind me I heard that voice. "Got you, Sackett! Turn around and die!"

Well, I didn't figure he meant to sing me no lullabies, nor the words to "Darlin' Cory," so when I turned around my hand was movin' and I hauled out that ol' .44, eared her back and let 'er bang.

He had a rifle and when I turned I was lookin' right down the barrel. I just said to myself, Tell Sackett, you'll die like your pa done, lonesomelike and hunted down. But that .44 was a pretty good gun. She knew her piece and she spoke it, clear and sharp. I felt the *whiff* of his bullet.

He'd missed. The best of us do it, but a body hadn't better do so when the chips are down and you've laid out your hand on the table with no way but to win or die.

My bullet took him. It took him right where he lives, and the second one done the same like it wanted company.

He couldn't believe he could miss. Maybe he was too sure of it. I stood there, a long, tall man from the Tennessee hills with my pistol in my fist, and I watched him go.

He wanted to shoot again, but that first shot had done something to him, cut his spinal cord, maybe, for his hands kind of opened up and the rifle slid into the grass.

"Nativity Pettigrew," I said, "where did you bury pa?"

His voice was hoarse. "There's a green hillside where a creek runs down at the base of Banded Mountain. You'll find him there at the foot of a rock, a finger that points at the sky, and if you look sharp you'll find his grave and the marker I carved with my hands.

"He had my gold and he had to die, but there's no gainsaying he tried . . . I liked him, lad, but I shot him dead and buried him there where he fell.

"Beat as he was, and wounded bad, he crawled over the mountain to get me. It was him or me, there at the last, and I carry the lead he gave me."

He lay there dying, his eyes open wide to the sun, and I hated him not. He'd played a rough game and, when the last cards were laid down, he lost. But it might have been me.

"When we get the gold out, I'll give some to your wife. She's a good woman," I told him.

"Please," he said.

He died there, and I'd bury him where he fell.

When I came up to the campfire, they were sitting around and waiting. Flagan was there, who'd come up from Shalako, riding a mouse-colored horse.

"You'll have to forget Hippo Swan," Orrin said. "He came hunting you to Shalako, and Flagan said you weren't the only Sackett, and they fought."

"Sorry, Tell," Flagan said, "but he'd come wanting and I'd not see him go the same way. He fought well but his skin cut too easy, and now he's gone down the road feelin' bad."

"We found the gold, too," Orrin said. "Remember what pa said about me always wanting the cream of things and about the distance to the old well and how many times ma scolded me for it.

"Well, I got to thinking. That word *cream* did it. Remember how we used the well to keep our milk cold? When I was a youngster I used to go out and skim the cream off. Ma was always after me about it. Well, this was the same kind of place—a hole in the rocks—about the same distance away as the well.

"He'd laid rocks back into the hole, threw dirt and such at it, I guess. Anyway, we pulled out the stones and there she was. More than enough to buy us land and cattle to match Tyrel's."

I sat there, saying nothing, and they all looked at me. Then Orrin said, "What happened to you?"

"It was Nativity Pettigrew," I said. "Not so crippled up as he made out. Pa followed him—maybe a mile out there, or more. He crawled up on him and they swapped shots. Pa got lead into him but pa was killed, and Nativity buried him yonder on the slope of Banded Mountain."

"Kind of him," Orrin said, and I agreed.

"We'll do the same for him," I said. "Where he lies we'll put him down. What was it pa used to say? 'Where the chips fall, there let them lie.'"

Nell Trelawney stood up. "Are you going home now, Tell? It's time."

"I reckon," I said, and we went to our horses together.

MUSTANG
MAN

Author's Note

Borregos Plaza was on the south bank of the Canadian River, only a short distance from the river crossing that was to become Tascosa. Tascosa went from a booming and untamed cow town to a ghost town, and is presently the site of Boys' Ranch, founded by Panhandle businessmen.

Romero, a small town in ranching country, has a long memory of buffalo hunting and Indian fighting days. The country around is little changed from the period of my story.

The Rabbit Ears, known to many travelers along the Old Santa Fe Trail, is only a little way from the town of Clayton, New Mexico. The box canyon featured in the story is there, so is the pool, which is usually covered with a green scum, and there is also an open hole some three to four feet in diameter. Around it the walls and rocks are blackened by fire, likely the result of some explosion of oil or gas.

Loma Parda on the Mora River is now a ghost town, some eight miles northwest of Watrous, New Mexico. When Fort Union was abandoned the town began to die, but in the 1870's it had a rough and bloody reputation.

At the time of my story the buffalo hunters still had two or three good years ahead of them, and they would be replaced by cattlemen. Practically the only settlers in the Panhandle country then were Mexicans from Taos or Mora with their sheep.

The Sostenes l'Archeveque mentioned early in the story was a notorious outlaw and killer of the period, often credited with twenty-three killings. He was killed by his own people when his conduct became too unruly.

Chapter 1

When I came down off the cap rock riding a wind-broken bronc, half of New Mexico must have been trailin' behind me, all ready to shake out a loop for a hanging.

Nobody told me I should wait around and get my neck stretched, so when I'd seen them coming my way I just wrapped myself around the nearest horse and taken off down country. Seemed likely those boys would run out of ambition before long, but they must have been mighty shy of entertainment in that gyp-rock country, because they kept a-coming.

Me, I high-tailed it out of there as fast as that bronc would take me, and for a spell that was pretty fast. Only the bronc had run himself out trying to save my bacon and now I needed myself a fresh horse, or else I'd never need another.

About that time I sighted a clump of cottonwoods down on the flat, and cottonwoods spell water in any man's country. Water usually meant there was stock close by, and probably folks. Where there was either there might be a horse.

So right then I began building myself a fresh dust cloud behind me, and when I rode up to those trees I was just a-fogging it. Sure enough, there were horses there, and some mighty fine stock, too. So I shook out a loop and dabbed it on a handsome line-back dun with a black mane and tail.

Snubbing him to a post, I stepped down and unlatched my saddle and threw it on the dun. I cinched up tight, and was about to climb into the leather when I heard the click of a cocked hammer and froze right where I was. That gun was behind me, but judging by the sound the range was no more than twenty feet; and my ma never raised no foolish papooses. Back there in the Clinch Mountains of Tennessee we boys learned to use guns mighty early, but we also learned to hold them in respect. When a man puts a gun on you, you've no cause to believe he won't use it.

"Mister"—the voice was dry and cold—"you sure ain't pa'tic'lar where you put your saddle."

"Figured I was mighty pa'tic'lar. If that ain't the best horse in the lot, you show me a better and I'll switch my saddle."

He chuckled, but I knew that rifle hadn't moved any. This was a hard man there behind me.

"What you figure gives you title to that horse?"

"You keep an eye on the rim of the cap rock yonder, and when you see dust a-fetching up over the rim you'll know what gives me title. Those boys back yonder got themselves a rope, and they figure on making me the belle of the ball."

"What did you do?"

Well, I taken a chance and turned around. That old man held a Sharps .50 buffalo gun on me, a gun that would open a hole in a man as big as your fist. He was slight built, but he had a pair of the coldest eyes you ever did see.

"I fetched my gun a mite faster'n another man; only I was a stranger, and that other man, he owned himself a big outfit and a lot of good friends."

"You got a name? Something folks call you by?"

"Nolan Sackett."

"Heard of you. Outlaw, the way folks tell it."

"Look at that rim, mister. There's your dust. Now this here ain't no time to start discussin' a man's moral outlook. There's no time to talk about my past, not if I am to have a future."

He stepped around me so's he could look at the rim, and then he said, "What d'you figure to do now, Sackett?"

"Seems to me I've got a choice between a rope and a bullet, or a rope and a chance. Folks consider me a right fast hand with a six-shooter, so I'm likely to take the chance and see if I could beat you to a killing."

"You wouldn't beat me, Sackett, but I like your sand. You get up on that horse and light out. Hold to the bottom yonder and you'll be out of sight. The canyon cuts back toward the Yellow House, and you'll have a fair run down the valley. Give that horse a spell now and again and he'll take you clear of them."

Well, I taken out. But not before I had one long look at that old man. "Thanks," I said; "and you need a friend, you call on Nolan Sackett. Or any Sackett, for that matter, for we run long on kinfolk."

That line-back dun taken out of there like he had a fire under his tail and was tryin' to outrun it. Sure enough, the canyon forked, and I went up the branch called Yellow House. An hour later, when I topped out on the cap rock again, there was no sign of pursuit. So I slowed the dun to a canter, and then to a walk.

That was wide-open country, and vast plain cut by occasional ravines, the rare streams flowing into the Arkansas or the Canadian River, although both rivers lay north of where I was riding, the Arkansas far to the north.

This was buffalo country and Indian country, and a man could lose his hair in one unwary moment anywhere within a thousand square miles. Buffalo hunters had come into it, coming out of Dodge, and here and there a few cattlemen had the idea of moving in, only mostly it was just an idea.

The outlaws had come early. Up north of the Canadian was the stretch of country they called No Man's Land, and east of there was Indian Territory. No man in his right mind rode into that country without a gun ready to hand, and the will to use it. There were canyons like the Palo Duro and the Yellow House, but mostly it was cap-rock country, and water a rare thing unless you knew where to find it.

The buffalo knew. They knew not only the few permanent springs and creeks, but rain-water lakes that sometimes lasted several weeks or even months if the rains had been heavy. Often enough, though, they vanished within a few days, so following buffalo tracks to hunt water was a chancy thing.

Nothing had ever led me to believe that anything would be easy for me. The only trails I knew were long and dusty, blazing hot or freezing cold. The nights I'd slept under a roof these past years were mighty few.

A body can get the name of outlaw sometimes without half trying, and I hadn't tried. I guess I never cared much, either. We Clinch Mountain Sacketts were good enough folk, I guess, but a mite poorer and rougher than those over in the Cumberlands or down on the flatlands.

We sprung from thin soil, and raised more kin than crops, but we were proud folk, too, and in those days a man's pride was defended by a gun. I ain't saying it was right, only that was the way it was, and gun battles were not only a matter of us feuding folks from Tennessee, nor in the West. It was the way things were done all over the country, and in Europe too, they say.

Andrew Jackson himself, him who was president of the United States, engaged in several gun battles, and killed Charles Dickinson in a duel. He got his shoulders shot up in the fight with the Bentons; and it was claimed that he had a hand in a hundred and three duels, as a fighter, a second, or a member of the party.

He was only one of many. Few prominent men avoided duels if they entered public life, where somebody might speak slander of them. Nor could a man continue to live in any community where it was known he had been called a liar and had failed to fight, or, in fact, if he had failed to fight whenever honor demanded it.

But I could lay no claim to dueling or fighting in the way of defending my honor or anybody else's. Soon as I was old enough, I drifted west, living as best I could. There was little enough at home, and when I was gone there was one less to feed. What fights I had, after the Higgins feud, were mostly with rough men who lived in the same way I did.

Now as I rode, the plains stretched wide around me, flat as a floor as far as a man could ride. Not a tree, not a bush, just the low, dusty grass, and the wide milky-blue sky above.

I took off my beat-up old hat and wiped the sweat-band. That hat had never been much account, and the bullet hole left there by a Kiowa brave before he died had done it no good.

Looking at the hat made me feel glum. A man ought to have a few worthwhile things in his life. All my years I'd honed for a store-bought suit, but I'd never managed it yet, nor even a good saddle. It was little enough a man could have unless he got lucky with cards or went west to the goldfields. Some folks had the turn for making money. Seemed to me I never did.

But that was a good horse I rode now. Maybe the best I'd ever had, and I owed that old man a debt. There was something about him I cottoned to, anyway. He was a hard old man, and he would have torn my guts out with that buffalo gun if I'd made a move for my gun; but when the chips were down and I'd been holding no more than a couple of deuces, he had come through.

Of a sudden, I saw the wagon.

For several minutes I'd been watching what looked to be a low white cloud lying off on the horizon, and hoping it was no thunderhead. Thunder storms can roll up almighty fast out there on the plains, and such lightning as you never saw. A man standing out on the level lands is a natural attraction for lightning, to say nothing of a man on horseback carrying a pistol and a rifle.

Now as I rode on I began to see it was no cloud, but a wagon top, and beside the wagon a woman was standing.

She was a mile or more off, but it was a woman, all right. What set me to fretting was that she was alone—nobody else in sight, and no stock of any kind—no horses, or mules, or oxen. And that worried me. Folks caught up with trouble out on the grasslands would do almost anything for a horse, and I was riding a good one. So I didn't just fetch up to that wagon, I veered wide around it.

That woman, she started to wave at me, but I just waved back and rode wide around her, keeping an eye on her and a hand on my rifle. Only I took time out to glance at the ground from time to time, for I wanted to know where the wagon came from, and what had happened to the horses or oxen that had hauled it there.

Horses . . . six head of horses heavy enough to pull that wagon, and two head of saddle horses, led off by a man afoot.

Circling on around, I came on the tracks of the wagon as it went along to the place where it now stood. The tracks had cut into the turf . . . that wagon was loaded, really loaded.

Right then he made a mistake, and moved. A man lying still is hard to see if his clothes blend into the background, but movement draws the eye. He was bellied down in a slight depression on the cap rock, just a-fixing to take my scalp and my horse when I came riding up.

So I pulled up a good three hundred yards off and shucked my own Winchester. Then I started circling again, and he had to keep moving to keep me in sight. By the time I'd made a complete circle he could see I'd outfoxed him, and he quit on me.

He was smart enough not to risk a bullet unless he could score a kill with the first shot, but with me moving like I was, he couldn't be sure. Even if he got a bullet into me at that distance I might ride away; or if I fell, my horse might be frightened off. Circling as I was, I could bring my rifle to bear at any moment, and I was able to make him move as I wanted.

He spoke to the woman, saying something I could not make out at that distance, and then he stood up, his hands empty. I moved in closer then, keeping them lined up ahead of me. He was surely carrying a hand-gun, and I did not like the way she was keeping one hand hidden in the folds of her skirt. Either or both of them might try a sneak shot at me. Looked to me like I'd ridden into a nest of rattlers.

At fifty yards I drew up once more, taking my time in looking them over. My rifle was held pistol-fashion in my right hand, and I was a fair shot from that position. "You shed that small gun," I told him, "and tell your woman that if she doesn't drop that pistol I'll shoot both of you."

"You'd shoot a woman?"

"If she's holding iron on me," I said, "I'd shoot her as quick as you. You tell her to drop it, mister, if you figure to watch the sunset tonight."

He unlatched his gun belt and let it fall, and that girl, she walked over to a blanket near the fire and dropped her gun. Then I rode up to them, watching like a cougar watches a rattler.

He was a slim, wiry young man, scarcely more than a boy, and he wore city clothes, but they were dusty now. He had a square, pleasant-looking, young boy's face, only when you got close enough you could see his eyes were not pleasant now.

The girl was not more than eighteen, I'd guess, and she was pretty as a white-tailed pony. And the two of them were alike as two could be.

As for me, I knew what they saw, looking at me, and it wasn't much. My jaw was blunt and my nose had been broken, and I carried most of my two hundred and fifteen pounds in my chest and shoulders. I had a fifty-inch chest above a rider's small waist, and biceps and neck that measured seventeen inches around. My fists were big and hard, the kind a man can get from wrestling big steers, wild mustangs, and wilder, rougher men.

The wool shirt I wore had been red at one time, but had faded, and my vest was made from the hide of a black and white cow. Nothing I wore or owned was new, and my outfit was beat-up, rained-on, and sand-weathered, and that included me too. Along with it I had a stubble of beard on a face deep-browned by the sun, and green eyes that showed up lighter than they were, against my dark skin.

I had me a fine-working Winchester and a pair of bone-handled six-shooters, only one of which was carried in sight. In my belt there was a bowie knife, and down the back of my neck a throwing knife, both of them Tinker-made.

This outfit I'd come upon was no rawhide bunch. The wagon showed travel signs, but it had been new not long ago, and both of these folks were dressed mighty well.

I hooked a knee around the pommel of the saddle, rested the muzzle of the Winchester in their general direction across my knee, and started to build myself a smoke.

"You all going somewhere," I said, "or do you like it here?"

"I'm sorry," the man said, "I am afraid we made the wrong impression."

"And you've been keeping the wrong comp'ny. Like the man who drove off your stock."

"What do you know about that?"

"Well, it's fair to surmise you didn't haul that wagon here by yourselves, and now you've got no stock."

"Indians might have taken them."

"It ain't likely. They'd have had your scalps too. No, it was somebody in your own outfit, somebody who figured to leave you high and dry out here on the cap rock; so you reckoned to kill me and ride out of here on my horse."

"We thought you were an Indian," the girl said.

Now, anybody could see a mile off that I was no Injun; but it wasn't just the lie that bothered me, it was the casual way they had set themselves out to kill a stranger. They didn't plan to ask me to ride for help, they just simply planned murder. That man had been bedded down for an ambush. Had I gone riding right up to the wagon at that girl's wave, I'd be dead by now and they would be riding out of here on my horse.

Wary as I was, I was also curious. What had brought them to this place? Who were they? Where had they come from? Where were they going? And why had their man left them and taken all their stock?

That last question provided its own answer. Either he was afraid of them, or he wanted what was in that wagon. If the last was true, the easiest way to get it was simply to drive off their stock and stay out of the way until they died or were killed. The fact that they were in this place at all gave some weight to this last theory, for they were right in the middle of nowhere, on the road to nowhere. Nobody in his right mind would have come this way with a wagon.

"Get down and join us," the man said. "We were just about to have coffee."

"Don't mind if I do," I said, swinging down, the horse between me and them. "This is mighty dry country."

My comment brought no reaction from them, which improved my hunch that they had no idea of the fix they were in. For there was no water anywhere around. They had two barrels slung to the side of the wagon, but I figured they weren't anywheres near full, and the nearest water—if there was any there—was a good forty miles away.

"You folks got yourselves in a peck of trouble," I commented. "You'll be lucky to get out of here alive."

They both looked at me, just looked, as if trying to understand me. "What do you mean by that?" the girl asked.

"Nearest water I know of is forty miles from here . . . if the creek ain't dry, which it sometimes is. If it's dry, you got twenty miles further to go. Even if you could haul the wagon—which you can't—it would mean days from here. You're way off the trail."

"It's a short cut."

"Whoever told you that had no love for you. The only place this will short-cut you to is the dry side of hell."

They both were looking hard at me.

"Your best chance is to try walking out," I said. "At best you got a fifty-fifty chance."

"But there's your horse." He gave me a cool look. "My sister and I could share it."

Now, I've come up against some mean folks in my time, but nobody quite as cool about it as these. They were in trouble, but they either had no realization of how much trouble, or they were almighty sure of themselves.

"You ain't got my horse, *amigo*," I said, "and you ain't about to get him. And if you had him, you'd not know which way to go. If you knew where to go, you wouldn't have come here in the first place."

They exchanged a glance. They did not believe me, and they still wanted that horse of mine.

"You've got a chance," I added, "if I ride out of here and send somebody back with a team to haul the wagon out. That's if I can find somebody who's willing to come out here.

"This here is Comanche country," I went on. "Kiowas to the north, and Apaches west and south. Nobody wants to come into this country at all."

All of a sudden I had a feeling. They were not worried, because they were waiting for something, or somebody. Something they *knew* would happen. Nothing I had said had impressed them in the least. They were simply waiting.

The afternoon was almost gone, and it lacked only a few hours until darkness. Was there somebody else out there? Somebody I had not seen or heard?

Suddenly the itchy feet of fear were crawling right up my back. Somebody was out there, somewhere, watching me.

"The closest place for you is Borregos Plaza," I said, "or maybe Fort Bascom, over west of here." All the time I was trying to figure which way trouble would come from.

They were eastern folk, but I wouldn't think of them as tenderfeet. There was much they didn't know of the West, if they knew anything at all about it, but they had a quality about them . . . they were ice-hard and without mercy. I had me a hunch that when in doubt they would kill, without rhyme or reason.

The company I'd known since leaving the mountains, and much of it before that, had been hard company. Feuding and fighting men, hard-working and hard-drinking men often enough, but they had fought from anger or for pay; and when they killed it was from anger or for pay, or perhaps, by blunder, but not as these two would kill.

The girl had poured a cup of coffee for me. I'd been making believe to loosen the cinch on the saddle, but had not done so. I had an idea that when I left out of there it would be of a sudden with no time to tighten a cinch.

Turning my horse, I walked toward her, keeping the horse between me and where I suspected their man to be, if man there was. Close to the fire I stopped and squatted on my heels, and glanced quickly over to where I thought he was at, and just as my eyes shifted I saw that girl shove something back in the pocket of her skirt.

Now, nothing in my life led me to be what you'd call a trusting man. Back in the Tennessee hills we did a sight of swapping, and a boy soon learned that when it came to swapping he couldn't trust even his own kin. It was a game, sort of, and we all swapped back and forth and the best stories told around the cracker barrel in the store at the crossroads or around a cabin fire were about swaps and swapping, and about who got taken. This just naturally made you grow up sort of skeptical.

So when that dewy-eyed girl handed me that coffee I took it, longing for a swallow, but just a mite afraid it might be my last. So I held it, wondering how a man could keep from drinking it without arousing suspicions.

Back on Clinch Mountain there was an old-timer who could set and talk by the hour and not say a word a body could recall; he would just ramble on spreading words around like a man forking hay on a stack. Right then I decided to talk.

" 'Bout the time I sighted you folks I was gettin' fed to the teeth with my own company, and there's just so much you can say to a horse. You never talked to a horse? Ma'am, you just ain't ridden far in lonesome country. Why, I'd reach out to say the horses of this man's territory know more about what's going on than anybody else. Everybody out here talks to his horse. I've seen the time I hadn't nobody else to talk to, weeks on end.

"You take this here country now. A man can ride for days and not see even a hump in the ground, let alone a man or a horse. Maybe you'd sight some antelope, or a herd of buffalo, although they are coming up scarce about now. A body can just ride on and on across the country, watching far-off rain squalls or maybe buzzards. Not much else to see.

"And traveling in this area ain't just what you're expecting. Now you folks, for instance. You head west from here, and what do you find? A canyon maybe three, four hundred feet deep. It's cap-rock country, so usually where the land breaks off there's a drop of four to fourteen feet of sheer rock, then a steep slope off to the bottom, and you may go miles before you can find a spot to go down into the canyon, or a place to climb out.

"You never see those canyons until you're right on top of them. Comanches used to hole up in them and wait for the Comancheros coming out from Santa Fe to trade with 'em. I come upon an Indian camp one time when there must have been seven or eight thousand head of horses there—fine stock, some of them."

Both of them were watching me. I was holding the cup in my hand, gesturing with it once in a while, just running off at the mouth like that old coot back in the hills.

"You take Indians now, they're all around you before you know they're in the country. And women folks—if they know you got a woman along, they'll hunt you for miles.

"You people here, you're ripe for the picking. Any Comanche youngster could shoot you both before you even knew he were near. I'd say without help you ain't got a chance of getting out of here.

"You figure on my horse? Why, he couldn't carry the both of you even half the distance you got to go. And your wagon would have to be left where it is. Take a six-ox team to move that out of here, heavy like it is."

"What makes you think our wagon is heavy?"

Me, I grinned at him, and shoved my hat back a mite with the lip of the cup. "Why, your tracks. The deep bite they take into the prairie tells a body that. Moreover, I'd lay a bet the Indians know where you are, and are closing in about now."

"Don't be silly," the girl said. "If they knew where we were and wanted to attack they would have done it long since."

I chuckled. "That's your thinkin', but it ain't Injun thinkin'. You take those Indians now, to speak proper of them—they know you ain't going no place. They know where that canyon is up ahead, and they know what you'll have to do when you get there. Meanwhile you're getting closer and closer to where they want you. They probably have a camp some place up ahead, and when you get close enough so they won't have to pack all they take from you for any distance, why, they'll move in."

Of a sudden I glanced at my coffee. "Well, what d' you know? I been settin' here talkin' until my coffee's gone cold."

And as I said it I splashed the coffee on the ground, set down the cup, and picked up the coffee pot with my left hand. My right still held my

Winchester. I filled the cup about a third full, sloshed it about and dumped it again. "Warms the cup," I said. "I do shy from coffee in a cold cup." Then I refilled it and sat back on my heels. "Now, where was I?"

Well, their faces were a study. They didn't know whether I was smart to them, or just dumb. He was exasperated, but she was so mad she turned a little pale. I gulped down some of the hot coffee and it tasted good— kind of a chicory taste to it, like some of that New Orleans make.

Setting there a-drinking my coffee, seeming to pay them no mind, nor nothing else, I wasn't much worried. I could see over east toward where that canyon was from the tail of my eye, one of the quickest ways to detect movement, and I was keeping my horse within my range of vision. Shadows were growing on the lee side of that wagon, when of a sudden my mustang's ears pricked and I put my cup down.

That mustang, like all wild stock, was quick to see anything that moved. Most horses are quick enough to see anything that moved. Most horses are quick enough to see and hear, but there's nothing like a wild one for letting you know when trouble's about. His ears warned me that whoever was out there had begun to move.

Any sudden move of mine to get away would bring on the fight I wanted to avoid. I didn't cater to these folks' way of figuring things, and I didn't aim to let them take my scalp.

There was little cover out on those grasslands, and even the grass was skimpy, so if I tried to ride for it I would have two or maybe three of them shooting at me. Unless I waited until dark . . . though every minute I waited increased my own risk, for darkness gave them freedom of movement.

So I just shifted my Winchester forward in my hands and looked at that young man standing over there beside his sister, and I said, "If you two figure to get where you're going all in one piece, you better tell your friend out there to stand up and come in with his hands up."

That set them back a notch. They just looked at me, and I eased back the hammer on the Winchester.

He turned a shade paler and said, "I don't know what you mean."

"You just speak up and tell him. You got a full thirty seconds to do it in, or I'll spread you wide open for the buzzards and the ants."

He didn't want to believe it, and when he decided he'd better he still didn't want to.

"It'll be you first," I said, "and then the girl and the other one. You got ten seconds now, and I'm takin' up slack."

My finger tightened on the trigger.

Chapter 2

"Andrew," the girl spoke out loud and clear, "come in with your hands up."

"Sylvie," her brother protested, "he wouldn't shoot. He wouldn't dare."

"He'll shoot, all right!" Sylvie said. "He would kill you very quickly, Ralph, and I believe he would kill me too."

There was a stir out in the darkness, and then a fat, stupid-looking boy came in toward us. He might have been only seventeen, but the rifle he carried was grown up.

"Put it down," I said to him, but I was prepared for him to try a shot. He looked at me, then shifted his eyes toward Sylvie . . . toward her, not toward her brother.

"Do what he says, Andrew."

Reluctantly, he put down the rifle, then sat down abruptly and crossed his legs.

"Like I said, I don't want any trouble, but I've grown up with it. My advice to you folks is to go slow. You'll find things are different out here, and there's a lot of folks who will shoot first and ask questions later, if they have any to ask.

"Now, if you'll lay off trying to shoot me, I'll see if I can get you out of here."

"Why should you?" Ralph asked.

On that one I hedged. After all, why not ride out and leave them to get what they deserved? "You've got guns," I said. "I wouldn't want them in the hands of the Indians."

They didn't believe me. I doubt if they could believe any reason that was not entirely selfish.

"No matter which way you go, you ain't likely to find anybody inside of a hundred miles. I hear Jim Cator has a buffalo camp on the North Palo Duro, and the settlements west are nearer to two hundred miles than one."

They sat watching me, taking in every word.

"Whoever brought you in here trapped you for fair . . . but there's a chance I might catch up to him and bring the horses back."

"If you could bring those horses back," Ralph said, "and kill the thief who stole them, I would give you fifty dollars."

"There's some who would do it for that," I commented, "but I am not one. However, it would be easier to get your horses back than to ride out and send somebody in for you." I stood up suddenly. "I'll ride after him."

They all stood up at that, their eyes on me, ready to take any advantage. "Why not stay and try in the morning?" Sylvie suggested. "You can't track horses at night."

Stepping up, I took the bridle and turned my horse to watch them across the saddle, and then I mounted quickly, my rifle ready, covering them casually. "I don't need to track them," I replied. "He'll take them to water. I'll follow."

Swinging the horse, I rode a widening half-circle around the camp, keeping them under my gun until I was well into the darkness, then quickly I switched direction and walked my horse until I had put a good distance behind me. When I was a mile off I drew up and took off my hat and wiped the sweat-band. For a while there they had me treed.

Then I set off through the night, taking my course from the stars. I had a fair idea where those horses would be, and if they were there, I'd look the situation over before making a move. I had no use for that lot back there, but I couldn't leave a woman to die out on the plains, nor did I want those guns in the hands of Indians, who had enough guns as it was.

The night was cool, and despite the fact my horse was tired, I kept him moving, and he was game enough. I don't think he'd liked that bunch any more than I had.

At times I got down and walked to save the horse. The dun had come far that day, for I had pushed him hard since early morning, but I had a hunch. There was a place in the cap rock that I knew of . . . I'd been told of it by a Comanchero who had watered there at times when driving from Santa Fe over to a rendezvous with the Comanches.

It was a mere gap in the rock forty or fifty yards wide, and scarcely longer, but there was water in the bottom, a little grass, and a cottonwood tree or two. There was a chance that the man I followed knew of it too, although few did. If he could water there, he could drive the stock north, and after another fifteen miles or so would come upon a series of small hollows fringed with cottonwoods and willows where there were fresh water lakes, or sloughs. From that time on he could move toward Tule Creek, with water to be found at intervals all along the way.

The last bright stars were hanging low in the sky when I came up to the water hole. There was the low, questioning nicker from a horse, and a sudden movement, then silence.

My move was just as quick. Leaving the dun standing, reins trailing, I ducked off to the left where a cottonwood made a shadow on the land, and I crouched there, waiting.

Slowly, the moments passed. The dun, weary of waiting when water was so close, walked a few steps toward the hollow, holding his head off to one side to keep from stepping on the reins. This was what I had expected would happen, and what I wanted to happen. Whoever was waiting would be likely to think it was a stray horse. Or so I hoped.

The dun was all mustang, however, and not one to go right down into the hollow. He pricked his ears and whinnied a bit, and from the hollow there was an answering whinny. After a moment the dun walked on, then stopped again. Only this time he stopped because he was close to somebody.

Not moving a muscle, I waited. And then I heard a low, coaxing voice. He was trying to call my horse close enough to lay hand to the reins. The dun, knowing I was out and about, was not likely to let a strange hand reach him. Had he been a stray, lost and wandering, he might have let himself be caught . . . at least as long as he had that saddle on him.

Suddenly the dun shied away . . . evidently the man had tried to reach for him, which meant he was growing impatient.

The dun backed off a step and stood there, and I just waited. Five, maybe ten minutes went by, and then the man stepped from the darkness and reached for the reins. The horse backed off a couple of steps, and I could have kissed him, for the man went after him.

"Hold it!" I spoke loud enough for him to hear, but not too loud, and as I spoke I cocked my rifle.

He made a move as if to dive for shelter, but I spoke again, quickly. "Don't try! You ain't got a chance."

"Who are you?"

"A driftin' man. That there's my horse."

"Thought he was strayed." I had gotten to my feet and started toward him as he spoke. "Didn't see anybody around."

"Hadn't planned on it. Don't get nervous now . . . I'm holding a light trigger."

He had turned and was facing me, a stocky, barrel-chested man with his face in shadow. Suddenly he spoke. "Hell, you're Nolan Sackett!"

"Unbuckle your belt."

"Now, see here—"

I was getting impatient. "Mister, if you figure on eatin' breakfast, you'd better drop that gun belt."

He reached for the buckle, protesting. "Now look, Sackett. I'm Steve Hooker. We met one time over in the Nation, an' you got no call to stand me up."

"Maybe, maybe not."

When he'd unbuckled his gun belt and dropped it, I had him back off while I moved in and took up the belt and slung it over my shoulder.

Gathering the dun's reins, I followed my prisoner back down into the hollow. The horses were there, a fine team of six head, and two saddle horses. Down among the willows he had a fire going that had not been visible from the cap rock. I could smell coffee, and realized I'd not had a mouthful of food all day.

Once we got into the firelight I had him face around, and I knew him all right. He had been a teamster for a freight outfit, fired for selling stock feed that belonged to the company. He had killed a tame Indian over at Fort Griffin one time. Nobody did anything about it, but nobody had any use for him after that.

I turned him around and lashed his hands together behind his back, then tied his ankles and his knees. After setting him where I could keep an eye on him, I stripped the rig from my dun and let him roll, then rubbed him down carefully with a few handfuls of dried grass. Then I put him on a picket line where he could graze, and let him go to water as he wished.

Getting a slab of bacon from my pack, I shaved slices into a pan and ᴅroke out a half a loaf of bakery bread, brought from town. Whilst I was frying it, I poured myself a cup of coffee and made idle talk about the Indian Territory.

"Where'd you get the team?" I asked suddenly.

"They're mine. Drivin' em west to sell in New Mexico."

I just looked at him, disgusted. "That's a mighty pretty story to tell a pilgrim," I said, "but nobody in his right mind comes alone into this country, especially with horses." And then I added, "I rode in from the south."

He made no comment about that, although he was doing some thinking, wondering whether I'd seen the wagon or not. "How did you find me?" he said, after a bit.

"You left tracks, and I followed them." And then I added, "You also left a woman back there, where she could be taken by Indians."

"That ain't no woman! She's a blasted devil! She's a witch right out of hell."

"Looked young an' pretty to me. Didn't seem any place to leave a couple of tenderfeet." I paused, turned the bacon over with a fork, then added, "You could get lynched for that."

"They'd of killed me. They were fixing to. I heard 'em talk of it."

"Where did you pick them up?"

He hesitated. "I seen 'em first in Fort Worth. They were dressed elegant and seemed to have money. I sort of listened around and heard him making inquiries about the country west of Griffin."

"So?"

He peered at me. "Now look, Sackett. You ain't no fool. Why would a couple of well-dressed tenderfeet like them be interested in this country? This is buffalo country, Indian country. It's also cattle country, or so some think; but there's no fancy hotels and nothing to attract folks of that kind."

"What's your idea?"

"Gold, that's what. Gold, and lots of it. You think they'd come looking for range land, them folks? Not on your bottom dollar. Whatever they're huntin' is something they can carry away, and I think the answer to it is in that wagon."

"What's in it?"

"Now that's an odd thing. They never did let me see, and I tried. Maybe that's why they figured to kill me."

"Where were they headed?"

Steve Hooker was silent, probably deciding how much he should tell and how much he should hold back. Meanwhile, I started eating the bacon and fried bread right out of the frying pan. I was hungry enough to eat pan and all, but had to settle for about a dozen slices of thick bacon and the half-loaf of bread fried in bacon grease. And I drank most of Hooker's coffee.

"You better tell me," I went on, refilling my cup for the last time, "I ain't made up my mind whether to take you back to them, or let you waste away right here. You talk fast an' right and maybe you'll get a chance."

"What kind of talk is that? There's a good thing in this . . . for both of us."

Well, now. I felt a sight better. I set back against the bank and watched my horse pulling at the green grass, feeling almighty pleased with the

world. Still, I had this man tied up and I was of no mind to trust him untied, especially as I was sleepy.

"What questions did they ask you?"

"Oh, they knew something, all right. I think they had read something or
heard something, but they had special knowledge too. I mean they knew
where they wanted to go."

He gave it to me, a little at a time. He had followed them when they
went from Fort Worth to Fort Griffin by stage. Actually, he had ridden
the stage with them, keeping his mouth shut and listening to the questions they asked. The girl had been very good at getting a couple of western men to talking; above all, she seemed interested in place names . . .
thought they were so colorful, she said.

"Like what?" I asked.

"Cross Timbers . . . the Llano Estacado . . . Boggy Depot . . . the
Rabbit Ears."

Hooker hitched himself around a little, but I paid him no mind. He was
hinting that I should loosen him up a little, which I wasn't about to do.

"She got them to talk about those places."

"Ask any questions?"

"Full of 'em. She asked questions half the night. Her brother finally
went to sleep, but not her. She kept prying away at what those men knew,
but what she kept coming back to was the Rabbit Ears."

I went to the edge of the willows and broke up some sticks and twisted
some dead limbs off a fallen cottonwood. When I came back I started
feeding the fire again and made another pot of coffee. I knew a thing or
two about the Rabbit Ears country, and I'd heard some stories. More than
likely, bunkhouse talk being what it was, Steve Hooker had heard the
same tales. And like he said, there was no good reason for anybody like
those folks to want to go into such country.

"You sure took them far off the route," I commented dryly, "where
they'd meet nobody who could tell them different."

"When we got to Griffin," Hooker said, "I approached her, told her as
how I'd heard she wanted a wagon man, and I was a man who knew the
country to the west. Upshot of it was, she bought the horses and wagon,
outfitted us complete."

He looked around at me. "She had me spooked, that girl did. And he
was almost as bad. I don't know what it was, nothing they did or said, but
she kept a-watching me and it kind of got me.

"Then one night I heard them talking. They thought I'd taken the
stock off to water, and so I had, but I snuck back to listen. First thing

I heard her say was 'Of course. Why waste our money on him? When we get to the Rabbit Ears we'll know our way back, so we'll kill him.' Thing that got me was she was so matter of fact about it, like she'd ask the time of day.

"Next morning I began to pull off south. I figured to get them lost so they'd never find their way back by themselves, and would need me. Then I got to thinkin'."

"I know," I said, "you got to thinking about that outfit. You got to figuring what it would bring you at Cherry Creek, or even Santa Fe. Six head of fine horses, a brand new wagon, and whatever they had inside."

"Well, what of it? They were fixin' to kill me."

"How'd you manage? Weren't they suspicious?"

"You're darn tootin' they were! They watched me all the time. On'y I told them we would make camp half a mile from water . . . too many mosquitoes."

"Then you came to this place?"

"Sure. Them tenderfeet would never find it. I on'y had to wait. Just set still an' wait."

"What about Rabbit Ears?"

"Who knows anything? She worried around that subject, but nobody had anything to offer except me, and I kept my mouth shut, on'y just saying enough to make 'em ready to talk to me when the time came."

"What did you say?"

"That Rabbit Ears was named for an old Injun chief. That was every bit I said."

There was no logical reason for anybody to come out from the East just to visit Rabbit Ears Mountain. As mountains went, it was nothing very much. Not too far west there were real mountains covered with timber, and much of the year with snow. Rabbit Ears Mountain lay just off the Santa Fe Trail, and was no more striking than many another hill or mountain. Of course, her questions might have masked some other interest in the country nearby.

After a bit Hooker interrupted my thoughts. "What do you figure to do?"

"I'm taking their horses back. After that, it's up to them."

"What about me?"

"You get out of here the best way you can. You're no pilgrim. You got yourself into this."

"You'd set me afoot out here?"

"No." I grinned at him. "You can go back to work for them, if you're of a mind to. When a man starts out on something like you started he takes his own chances."

The firelight danced weirdly against the dark, fragile arms of the willows. Walking over to my saddle, I got my blanket and poncho and brought it back to a place near the fire, but in the shadows. I added fuel to the fire, pulled off my boots, and prepared to settle down for the night. From my pack I took a pair of moccasins and pulled them on . . . in the night I might have to make a quick move, with no chance to get my boots on.

Then I went over and released Hooker and let him move around a little before I tied him for the night. He was a wily one, and I stood back away from him and kept my rifle in hand.

After he was tied up again and covered with his blanket, I went back and rolled up to sleep. When I fell asleep I was still giving thought to the Rabbit Ears, and what those folks might want out there. Oddly enough, I'd never even heard the name those folks used . . . and it might make a difference.

Although in the West we set no store on names.

Chapter 3

At daybreak I walked Hooker out on the cap rock with a canteen, a pack of grub, and his guns. His gun belts I took with me and rode off maybe three hundred yards, where I dropped them for him to pick up. Then I gathered the horses and started back.

Now, I was in no way anxious to be riding back to that outfit. In a way I had no blame for Hooker, although I'd leave no woman out there a prey to Indians, nor did I aim to give them a chance at me.

In my time I'd known a few killers, but I'd never known anybody quite as anxious to kill as these folks. Even when it was of no particular use to them. Whatever it was they were after, they didn't want anybody interfering with them, or even knowing what they were about.

Well, I wasn't going to play nurse to them. I liked my sleep too well. They would have the team, and if they got out of there they would do it under their own power and by their own skill.

The girl came out to meet me. She was bait, I had no doubt, and believe me, that Sylvie was tasty bait for any man's trap, and she knew it. She walked out when she saw me coming, skirting the clumps of prickly pear or the prairie-dog holes. And then she stopped until I rode up to her.

Only my rifle was laid across my saddle bows, just sort of casual-like, but the muzzle kind of followed her when she moved. But she brought her hands into the open where I could see them, and kept them there.

"Here's your horses," I told her, "and the rest is up to you. You take my advice and you'll turn back to Fort Griffin. You don't fit into this country."

She smiled at me. "Why, Mr. Sackett! I thought you liked me?"

"You're a mighty pretty girl, Sylvie, and just about as safe as a nest of rattlers. But you take it from me and cut out of this country. Go east, where you belong."

She came closer, looking up at me with those big, dark eyes. "Come with us. Please do. We need you, Mr. Sackett, we're all alone out here, and neither of the boys has ever driven a team." She reached up and touched my hand with her fingers. "Mr. Sackett, come with us. Believe me, you'd never be sorry . . . and I'd be very grateful."

Well, now. She wasn't promising me anything, but in a way she was promising me everything, and she was quite a woman, that one. Only I wasn't having any.

"Sorry," I said. "Maybe if you were alone; but I'd trust none of you. You've got the horses. Hitch up and pull out right away, and follow my tracks. You'll come to water, and you'd better fill your barrels. They should help you over the dry stretch, and after that there's water most of the way north. Only you're going to run into the Palo Duro Canyon . . . maybe a thousand feet deep in places."

"Are there no ranchers? No towns?"

"Lady, this here is Indian country. You won't even find any buffalo hunters until you get farther north. There's said to be some folks at Borregos Plaza on the south bank of the Canadian. They're good folks, Mexicans from Mora and Taos, and they run sheep. If you act right, they'll sell you a little food and tell you how to get on to the north.

"I say they're good people, and they are, but there's one hombre from Santa Fe named Sostenes l'Archeveque . . . he'd kill you as soon as look at you. He idles around there from time to time . . . leave him alone."

All the time I'd been talking to her I'd been holding her right hand. A time or two she gave it a tug to get free, but I decided it was safer that way and, holding her right hand, I kept my eyes watching the other two. Finally I dropped her hand.

"*Adios!*" I said suddenly, and wheeled and rode off.

I gave my horse about three jumps north before I turned him sharply east, then west. Glancing back, I caught the gleam of light on a rifle barrel, but by that time I was another hundred yards off and a poor risk for a shot at the distance, and moving the way I was. So I rode away, and was glad to be gone.

About that time I began to give thought to myself. Here I was, riding away from trouble, no more than eight or nine dollars in my pocket, and nothing more in sight. For a man with the name of outlaw, I was doing mighty poor at it. When it came to that, I never did see any rich outlaws. All I ever saw were living on the dodge, out on the plains, in the mountains, or in outlaw hide-outs, ragged, dirty, and miserable.

Buffalo hunting was about over. In no time at all the hunters would have wiped out the buffalo in this country, and would pull out. What I should do was to get myself a few head of cattle and start myself a ranch right here in the Panhandle of Texas. It would be no time at all until cat-

tle were streaming into this country. The buffalo hunters would be telling
of the good grass and the water holes, and no cattleman would ask for
more.

I had the name of being a rough man, and that came of the troubles I'd
seen, and the fact that I'd come out of them winning instead of losing.
This was a time of bitter war and struggle, for the Indian gave up his
hunting grounds reluctantly, and even those of us in sympathy with him
were compelled to fight, because they could not always distinguish between friends and enemies. Of course, it wasn't only the white man
fighting the Indian, for the Indians were constantly at war with each
other.

Now I drifted north, holding to the high ridges, where I rode just
below the crest, out of sight yet high enough to ride easy and keep a wide
view of the country. When I saw dust, I drew up and got down and
waited until it had gone out of sight, for though it might be white men
raising the dust, I'd no reason to think they would be friendly.

All the time, my mind was being busy trying to remember all I'd heard
of the Rabbit Ears, and the one thing I kept coming back to was a story I'd
heard trail-side down on the Neuces seven or eight years back.

The story was already old, and the man who told it to me was a Mexican from across the Rio Grande. He had hailed my camp from out of the
night, and I told him to come in. That was brush country, and rougher
than a cob; every other man an outlaw or a renegade hiding out from the
Davis police.

John Wesley Hardin was on the dodge then, and Bill Longley, just to
name two. Up in northeast Texas Cullen Baker was dead, or at least they
said they had killed him, and he never showed up around after that. All
these men were refugees from the Davis police.

I had stepped back in the shadows to let that Mex come in, and he
came politely, with his hands up. He was an oldish man, but dapper and
mighty elegant still. His boots were dusty, and although he had tried to
brush himself off there was trail-dust on him.

"Señor?"

Well, I stepped out of the brush. By and large I'd found Mexicans the
salt of the earth, and many a time when on the dodge the only thing that
kept me alive was a bait of frijoles and tortillas at some Mexican sheep
camp.

"Come in and set," I said. "There's coffee ready and beans in the pot."

So we ate, and then he rolled him a smoke and we yarned the night
away. He was afoot . . . he didn't say how or why, and in those days a

body didn't ask questions. It happened I had an extra horse, a paint pony, pretty as a picture. A few days before that pony had been ridden by a mighty handsome young Comanche with bad judgment. He was riding loose, hunting for some action, and when he saw me he exercised that bad judgment . . . he decided I was easy pickings and fell in on my trail. Only I was keeping an eye on my back trail and when I saw I was followed I circled around and hunched down close to the trail to see who it was.

When I saw it was a Comanche with two fresh scalps, I stepped out and spoke to him. He turned as if he was shot and started to lift his rifle, which was his second case of bad judgment, for I only figured to set him afoot so he couldn't follow me any longer.

He put hand to that rifle and I shot him through the brisket, emptying the paint pony's saddle like there'd never been anything there. The Comanche was game; he came up fighting, so I let him have another one, caught up the pony, and left out of the country.

"You need a horse," I said to the Mexican; "you take that one. The Comanche who owned him won't be hunting him."

"*Gracias, señor.*" He spoke simply, yet with feeling, and he had a right. In that country at that time the only folks he was apt to meet would more than likely finish him off for his guns or whatever else he might have.

We drank more coffee and talked, and then at the last he said, "*Amigo,* I have no money. I cannot pay for the horse."

"He is yours, think nothing of it."

"My grandfather," he said, "used to drive mules on the Santa Fe Trail."

Well, now. That was an interesting bit of information if I'd been interested in his grandfather, which I wasn't, or in the Santa Fe Trail, which I'd seen my ownself.

"It was there he nearly lost his life. He was *jefe* of a pack train for Nathan Hume."

It all came back to me now, and I recalled as if it had been last night, us sitting by the fire and him telling me about that pack train. They had come from Santa Fe, and were crossing the plains, bound for Independence, Missouri, or some such place, and they had been making good time until they were hit by a war party of Kiowas.

They were strung out too far, and they didn't have much chance. A few of them gathering around Nathan Hume himself, among them my Mexican friend's grandfather, bunched up and made a retreating fight of it back to the Rabbit Ears Mountain, where they dug in for a stand.

They were wiped out . . . all but that Mexican, who found a hole and crawled into it. The Kiowas scalped and mutilated the bodies after robbing them of everything worth having, and then rode off a-running. After a bit that Mex came out and hoofed it back to Santa Fe.

When he got back he was warned to lie low, that the governor had sent a detachment of soldiers after Hume, and that if he were found he would be arrested. Nathan Hume had been smuggling gold secretly mined in the San Juans. So this Mexican smuggled himself out of town on a borrowed mule and then joined a train headed for Mexico City. He had friends there, and he planned to get some help and return, for he was sure he knew where the gold was . . . and was sure the Indians had not found it.

The trouble was, shortly after arriving in Mexico he was thrown from his horse. His back was broken and he never walked again.

He knew where three hundred pounds of gold was hidden, and he couldn't do a thing about it.

This was the story that was told to me by the Mex to whom I'd given a horse.

"Did you ever give thought to hunting that gold?" I'd asked him.

"Of course, señor, but"—he shrugged—"I had a difficulty in Taos . . . a matter of a señorita . . . and I was followed to Las Vegas. I killed a man, señor, a man with many brothers and cousins and uncles."

He put his cigarette in the fire and smiled. "I like life, señor, and I am a man who is content with a little now and another time. If I went north I *might* find the gold. I might also find a grave, and the odds for the latter are best. If you want the gold it is yours, señor."

"Any idea where it is?"

"There's a box canyon back of Rabbit Ears. It was there they made their stand . . . the bones of the mules might still be there.

"There was a pool of water there, covered with a green moss or scum, and beyond the pool a hole under a boulder. The gold was hidden in the hole, rocks tumbled over it, and with a broken gun Nathan Hume chipped a cross on the boulder. You should find it."

The next morning we parted, and once in the saddle he held out his hand to me and we shook hands. "Be careful, señor, and ask no questions. The Mexicans who mined the gold had sons and grandsons and they know that Nathan Hume's mule train did not get to Missouri . . . they might even have spoken to the Indians."

It was not the first trail-side story I'd heard of buried gold or lost mines. Such stories were told and retold all up and down the country, although this was the first time I'd heard this one. But I kept it in mind, and planned to take a look for myself sometime. Only things kept happening.

In Serbin, a town of Wendish folk in Texas where I'd had friends, I killed a carpetbagger and was thrown in jail for it. But my Wendish friends found a way to help me escape and left my horse where I could find it. I joined up with a trailherd headed for the Kansas towns, but I was a man wanted by the law.

In Abilene, which was new, raw and wild, I found my name was known. There'd been a cousin of mine there named Tyrel and he'd killed a man in the streets, somebody said; but then I got the straight of it. He had faced down Reed Carney, walked up to him, and made him drop his gun belt in the street.

Tyrel and Orrin Sackett—I'd heard tell of them although they came from the Cumberland Gap country; but it gave me a rarely good feeling to know the Sackett blood ran true.

That was long ago, and now I was here, riding north in the Panhandle of Texas, riding over the Staked Plains and heading north toward Borregos Plaza, Adobe Walls, and the buffalo camps. I was riding a line-back dun across the plains where a man could stand in his stirrups and look straight away for three days, it was that level.

So I shoved my rifle down in the boot, I canted my hat back on my head, and I looked off across the country and opened my mouth in song. At least, I felt it was song, and tried to make it that way, although the dun wasn't sure. The sky was blue and the plains were wide, and there was land around to stretch in. Maybe I'd only a few dollars in my jeans and a hanging party left behind, but the wind smelled good and the sun was warm, and it was a great time to be alive.

The country around me began to break up again into softly rolling hills, with a few ridges and some hollows where there were trees.

"Oh, I left my girl in San Antone,
Away down near the border,
I—"

A tuft of feathers showed over the crest of a low hill, and a dozen yards away an Indian appeared, and then another and another. A broken line of Kiowas stretched out for two hundred yards. They were riding slowly toward me, their lances pointed skyward. I glanced around quickly, and across the valley there were half a dozen more riding toward me, walking their horses.

At least a dozen of them had rifles, and they seemed in no hurry. Down the valley the way lay open, but several of the Indians were further along than I was, and they had only to cut over and head me off. There were at least thirty Indians in the whole party, and they had me boxed.

Sweat broke out on my forehead, but my mouth was dry. I had seen what Kiowas could do to a prisoner, for I had come upon what was left when they had finished, and it was no sight for a man with a weak stomach.

If I tried to make a run for it I would be dead within a minute.

Turning my horse at right angles, I rode straight for them, still singing.

Chapter 4

My rifle was in the boot, and to reach for it would mean death. My pistol, in its holster, was held down by the thong hooked over the hammer, a necessity when riding rough country.

So I rode straight for them, pointing the dun to ride right between two of them who rode some thirty yards apart, and singing as I rode.

Nobody ever figured a way to account for the thinking of an Indian. They were curious as any wild animal, and at times as temperamental, but the thing they admired most was courage, because you needed courage to be a good Indian. I knew I wouldn't get anywhere now trying to run; and when it comes to that, I am not a man who cares to run, unless it's *toward* something.

That dun pricked up his ears. He knew we were in trouble, and he didn't like the smell of Indians; I could feel every muscle in him poised with eagerness to take out and run.

These braves weren't hunting me. They were a war party all right, and they were out for bigger game. But if they were fixing for trouble with me they were going to get it. As I walked my horse toward them I made up my mind what to do. The big Indian on the right was my meat. If they made a hostile move I'd jump my horse into him, and grab for my pistol. I went through the motions in my mind, and all the while I was singing about that girl I left in San Antone.

Behind me I could hear the riders closing in, and in front of me they had slowed their horses a little, but I kept right on riding. My right hand was on my thigh, where it had been all along, only inches from the butt of my gun. I knew that if I got my gun out before they killed me I wouldn't go alone. If there was one thing I could do well in this world it was shoot a pistol.

Back in the Clinch Mountains in the fifties and sixties a boy just naturally cut his teeth on guns, and before I was twelve years old I'd been out in the woods feeding the family with a rifle, and with little time for anything else.

My eyes held straight ahead, yet I was watching the Indian on either side of me. There were a-plenty of others there, but it was those two who would bring on the trouble and they were coming closer and closer. My spur was just caressing that bronc's flank, ready to nudge him into action.

Those Indians came right on and I rode right toward them. Of a sudden the one on my left brought his lance down slowly, pointing it at me, but I never flinched. Had I showed one sign of the scare that was in me, he'd have run me through, or tried it.

He put the point of that lance right against my chest, and I looked over it and right into his eyes. I put my left hand up, still holding the reins, and pushed the point aside, just nice and easy, and then I walked my horse right on past.

Believe me, the skin was crawling up my back and the hair on the back of my neck was prickling, but I didn't dare take a look back. Suddenly there was a rustle of hoofs in the grass, but a sharp command stopped them. One of those Indians, probably an old chief, had saved my bacon. I kept right on, walking my horse, the sweat dripping off my face as if I'd dipped my head under a pump.

I went right on until I had the low ridge behind me, and then I touched the dun with the spur and we lit out of there like the fires of hell were behind us.

Then I slowed, turned at right angles to my route and rode down into the bed of a small stream and followed it west for a couple of miles.

Riding in water is far from a full-proof way to hide a trail. My horse's tracks would remain in the bottom for maybe an hour or more with the stream running at that slow rate, and the water being clear as it was, so when I got upstream I caved dirt into the water at several points to muddy the stream so the tracks couldn't be seen, and also to give the stream more silt to fill in the tracks. It would take some time for the water to become clear again.

They'd let me go on, more than likely, because they respected me, or because they were hunting bigger game, but some of the young braves might change their minds and trail off after me, liking the looks of my horse or my guns.

Alternately walking or trotting my horse, I worked my way across country, keeping an eye out for any movement, and all the time wary of my back trail. Antelope were nearly always in sight, and from time to time I saw buffalo, scattered bunches of them, growing more frequent as I moved north. But I saw no more Indians.

Once I found wheel tracks, but they were months old. I took in after them and followed their trail, camping near water every night, occasionally laying over until noontime to give the dun a rest and a chance to graze.

The country grew rougher as I went on. The stubble on my face grew thicker, and my bones and muscles grew weary of riding. Sometimes it seemed as if there must be dust and sand all through me, and half the water I drank was gyp water. But every night I checked my guns, keeping them clean and ready for trouble.

Somewhere to the north, I knew, was the Mexican town of Romero. It was a little place, and had been there quite a spell. The folks there were friendly to the Indians, and some said had been Comancheros, who traded with the Indians, selling them guns in exchange for whatever the Indians had taken from the white men moving west. Nobody liked the Comancheros much, not even their own people. But I never put my stock in that story about the folks at Romero being Comancheros.

But Borregos Plaza was the first place I would come to, and I was drawing close to it—at least, the way distances go in that country.

At daybreak I dipped into the Palo Duro, feeling uneasy because this was the heart of the Comanche country; but I rested in a clump of willows until nigh on to sundown, letting the dun eat that rich green bottom grass, and drink the water there. When the shadows started reaching out, I saddled up and scouted a way out of the canyon I was in, and I breathed easier when I was back on the plains.

The tiny cantina at Borregos Plaza was bright with lights when I walked my horse up the trail to the settlement. Dogs barked, and here and there I glimpsed movement in a darkened doorway. Strangers were welcome at Borregos Plaza, but the Mexicans who lived there had learned to be wary of them, too. It was a wild, rough land, and the few men who rode there were often wild, rough men.

Swinging down in front of the cantina I tied the dun and, ducking my head, went through the door. There was a bar about twenty feet long, and four tables with chairs around them. A fat Mexican in a white shirt stood behind the bar, his forearms on the bar. Two leather-chapped vaqueros stood near him, drinking. At one of the tables sat two older men, one with white hair.

The room was small, immaculate, and cool, with that sense of spaciousness one gets from Mexican buildings. All eyes turned on me, a big, dusty, travel-stained man. I went up to the bar, and ordered a drink.

"You have come far, señor?"

"Too far . . . ran into a war party of Kiowas."

"You were fortunate. You are still alive."

"No figuring on Indians. I rode right through them. Nobody lifted a hand."

They exchanged glances. It took nerve to ride through a bunch of Kiowas, and they knew that if I'd shown any weakness I would be dead now. But nobody knew how scared I'd been, and I wasn't planning on telling them.

"You will be hungry, señor? If you will sit down my wife will bring food to you."

"*Gracias.*" I walked over to a table and dropped wearily into a chair, then I removed my hat and ran my fingers through my hair. I could have fallen asleep right there.

The señora brought a plate of beans, beef, and tortillas to the table, and a pot of coffee. It was late, and the others drifted out to go home. The Mexican came out from behind the bar and sat down and filled a cup with fresh coffee.

"I am called Pio. . . . You want a place to stay?"

"No . . . I've slept out so long I'd never be able to sleep inside. I'll go out under the trees."

"You won't have trouble. Those who live here are good people."

"Are there any other strangers around?"

"There was a man . . . he rode through here yesterday but he wasn't around long. He acted as if somebody was following him."

He looked up into my eyes but I grinned at him. "You got me wrong. I ain't after anybody. I'm just riding north, going up to Romero, and then if things look good, maybe over to the Colorado mines."

He was skeptical, I could see that, but he was a good man, and he was willing to wait for any further information.

Me, I knew better than to start anything in these quiet little places. They were quiet because they were left alone. The men here, each man in each house, had a buffalo gun and he could shoot. Each man in this town had fought Indians, renegades, and whoever wanted a fight. If a man started trouble in one of these little western towns he was setting himself up at the end of a shooting gallery. Moreover, it was an even-money bet that Pio knew about the shooting down country. News like that travels fast.

After I'd eaten and had drunk a quart of coffee, I went outside and led my horse into the trees and beyond them to the meadow. Then, stripping off the saddle, I gave him a careful rubdown while he fed on a bait of corn I'd gotten from Pio. Western horses got mighty little corn, but that dun had it coming; and thinking of him made me think kindly of that old man back there who had given him to me.

Before this, I hadn't dared to strip the saddle from him for fear I might have to light out again, to light a shuck, as the saying was.

It was a quiet night. I could hear the rustle of the cottonwood leaves, and sometimes heard subdued sounds from the plaza. There was a coyote out on the knoll making music at the stars. Rolled up in my blankets, two of them, atop my poncho, I slept like a baby . . . a baby who'd never known a night in his life when there mightn't be trouble.

Sunup was a rare fine thing. Washing my face in the water that poured into the horse trough, I glanced over at the buckboard standing in front of the cantina. A Mexican was hitching a fresh team to the buckboard, and the rattle of the trace chains was the only sound in the little street, shaded by the huge old cottonwoods.

My fingers had to do for a comb, something I'd not owned in more than a year, but I saddled up before I went into my saddlebags for my razor, which I stropped on my belt. Then I shaved, using the still end of the horse trough for a mirror. It made me look some better, although I'd never win no prizes for looks, not with that broken nose of mine.

When I'd finished shaving, I dabbed whiskey on my jaws for a shaving lotion and then led my dun across to the hitch rail. A man living my kind of life never would let himself get caught without a gun or a saddle horse.

I went inside, where Pio was standing over a table at which three people were sitting, but the first one I saw was the girl.

She was young . . . maybe seventeen. Most girls were married at her age, or soon after. She had kind of dark red hair and brown eyes. . . . She was beautiful . . . taller than most girls . . . and shaped like music.

The old man with her was rail-thin and waspish, with hard gray eyes and a gray mustache mixed with red. You could see at a glance that he was a man with no give to him, and a man that no man in his right mind would try to cross. The third man was a breed . . . I'd say half Indian, anyway. A slight-built man, he was, and past middle age.

When I sat down at a table Pio's wife came in with a plate of food, a heaping plate, for she had noticed the night before that I was a good feeder. She was one of those women who liked nothing better than to see a man sit up to table and put away the food.

A couple of times the old man glanced my way, and once the girl did. I heard Pio say something about "Romero . . ." but his voice trailed off.

Pretty soon he came over to my table and dropped into a chair. He motioned to his wife for a fresh pot of coffee and we started in on it, Pio being as good a hand at putting it away as I was myself.

"Those people," Pio said, "they go north."

"Yeah?"

"I fear for them. She is young, the señorita. And the men . . . good men, but not plainsmen."

"What are they doin' out here then? No man in his right mind brings a woman like that into this country."

Pio shrugged. "I brought mine. What must be done must be done. Perhaps there was no other place."

There were questions I could have asked, but it was none of my business. I was lighting out of here right soon, and more than likely I wouldn't be back this way again.

Only that pack train of Nathan Hume's kept sticking in my mind. If all that gold was up there in those mountains, maybe I should just look around. I wanted no part of that outfit I'd left behind, but it was likely I'd be there before them.

"It is said you are an outlaw, señor?"

I looked up at him but I did not speak. It was said, but I didn't much like it.

"I think, myself, you are an honest man, and a caballero. I think you are one to be trusted."

"You think whatever you like."

"Those three . . . they need help."

My hand was reaching for the bean pot, but it stopped halfway. "No, you don't," I said. "Not me. I'm not being saddled with no pilgrims. Not crossing that country."

"It was a thought."

"You better give it another think. I'm a fast-travelin' man in Injun country. I want it so's I can run or hide, and you'd play hell hidin' a buckboard or its tracks. It's a far stretch from here to wherever they're headed, and I've got business up country."

"She is a pretty girl. The Comanches . . ."

"Too bad."

Pio was silent. Maybe he knew more about me than I wanted to admit to myself, but he just sat there and waited, and like a damned fool I looked over at that girl setting there with her pa, if that was what he was, and that breed.

She was so fresh and young and pretty that I had to look away fast or soon I'd be doing just what Pio wanted, and making a fool of myself. Yet a body couldn't see her setting there looking so young and lovely without thinking what would happen to her if the Comanches got her.

Now, back east where the Indians are tame and mighty few, a lot of folks have started talking about the poor red man, but believe me, when you saw an Indian out on the plains settin' up on a pony with a Winchester in his hand or a lance, there was nothing poor about him. He was a fighting man from way back, and he was a savage . . . a stranger was an enemy, and an enemy was to be killed or, if captured, tortured to see how brave he was.

In my time I'd had my share of troubles with Comanches, Kiowas, Arapahos, Utes, Cheyennes, Sioux, and about every kind of redskin there was. With some I got along fine; but when he's fighting no Indian needs take a back seat for any man. They'd been called, by one of Europe's greatest generals, "the finest light cavalry under the sun."

When a man traveled in Indian country he sort of sifted through, gentle-like and taking up no more room than need be. He kept out of sight, and slept without a fire at night unless he could hide it well. And on top of that he prayed, if he was a praying man, and the deeper you got into Indian country the more of a praying man you got to be. You just couldn't afford to miss any bets.

Pio talked about the sheep. He talked about cattle. It would be no time at all, he was saying, until the Texas cattlemen started bringing their herds into the Panhandle. The buffalo was going, the Indian would be driven out, and the cattle would come.

"And then the farmers," I said, with disgust. My own folks had farmed, if you could call it that, on the thin soil of the Clinch Mountain slopes, but I wanted no farmers cutting up this country.

"No, this country is no good for farm," Pio said. "We try it. The wind blows too much. Only the grass ties it down."

"I know," I agreed, finishing off the last of the food on my plate. "That last dust storm we had, I could taste some Kansas dust in it. I knew a man one time in the Brazos country who could tell what county he was in by the taste of the dust."

Well, right then I made a big mistake. I looked over at that girl again. Of course, you've got to realize that I hadn't seen a white woman for a good long time, and this one was kind of special.

"All right, Pio," I said, "pick up the chips. You go tell them I'll try to get them through to Romero, anyway."

"*Bueno!*" Pio smiled at me. "I knew this was what you would do. I tell them so. I tell them just to wait, that you're a good man."

Me? It was the first time in a long while anybody had said that about Nolan Sackett. Oh, they say "He's a good man with a gun," or "He's a fair hand with a rope," or "He can ride anything wears hair," but nobody just out and said I was a good man.

A man had to avoid that sort of thing. First thing a man knows he's tryin' to live up to it. And then what kind of an outlaw is he?

So I glanced over there again and the girl smiled at me. Well, that was all right. And as for the breed, I always got along with breeds all right. Only that old man had too stiff a neck to suit me. He would be bull-headed as an old mossy-horn range cow.

Anyway, I was in for it. Least I could do was have another cup of coffee.

Chapter 5

Sitting at the table, I could look out the open door and into the street. The sun was bright on the street, but the doorway of the cantina was shadowed by huge old trees that stood nearby. Across the street were the cottonwoods and willows beyond which I had slept the night before.

It was pleasant, sitting there and looking out on that sunlit street, and I wished I had such a place of my own, a little cantina somewhere along a trail where folks would stop off from time to time. You never saw anything more peaceful.

On the other side of the street and down a bit, just where I could see just one window and a corner of a building, stood an adobe that was partly fallen to ruin. It was small, and was likely among the first houses built here.

Pio came back to my table with those three people, and they all sat down around the table, leaving me only a partial view out of the door.

"Señor Nolan Sackett," Pio said, "I wish you to meet Señor Jacob Loomis, and Señorita Penelope Hume, and this here is Flinch."

Now, when I heard that name Hume I kept a straight face. My muscles never even twitched, me being a poker player of some experience. It seemed to me, all of a sudden, that the Llano Estacado was being invaded by folks all with the same idea.

"Howdy," I said, and just let it lay there. From now on until I got the lay of the land they could do the talking.

The man called Loomis spoke. "We understand you are riding toward Romero, and that you might guide us there. We would pay, of course."

Nobody had said anything about paying me until now, but for a man with no more money in his jeans than I was packing that was welcome news.

"It's risky," I said, knowing that committed me to nothing at all. "It's almighty risky. The Comanches and Kiowas are riding, and they're upset by the buffalo hunters coming south. You'd be better off to stay right where you are."

"In the middle of nowhere?" Loomis responded in a tone of disgust. "Young man, we'll give you fifty dollars to guide us, and to fight for us if there's trouble."

"For fifty dollars," I said, honestly enough, "I'd fight the whole Comanche tribe."

A flicker of shadow caught my eye, something in the background. Looking past Loomis, I could see nothing but the sunlight on the road and a lone hen pecking at something in the dust.

"Were you figuring on stopping in Romero?"

Now, I needn't have asked that question, because nobody stopped in Romero except the Mexicans who lived there. Romero was a nice, pleasant little place at the end of several trails, none of them traveled very much.

"We will decide about that when the time comes," he replied, and his voice was testy, as if he didn't care much for questions.

"All right," I said, "you be ready to pull out come daybreak . . . and I mean first light, not a mite later."

"I will decide about that." Loomis was brusque. "You will get your orders from me."

"No," I said, "not if I am to take you through. If you want me for a guide, you'll go when I say, stop when I say, and make as little noise as ever you can." I got up. That shadow movement I'd seen was itching at me. "You make up your mind, Mr. Loomis. I am leaving out of here when there's a streak of gray in the sky. You want to go along, you all be ready, because that's when I'm going."

Oh, he didn't like it. He wasn't even one bit happy with me, and I didn't care. Fifty dollars was a lot of money, but a whole hide counted pretty high with me. Besides, I had a few dollars when I rode in, and I'd have most of it riding out.

Now, I hadn't missed the girl's name . . . Hume. And the man who supposedly hid that treasure in the Rabbit Ears was Nathan Hume. Some folks might consider that was just a coincidence, but not me.

Loomis pushed back from the table and was about to get up, so I put my coffee cup down and said, "Seen some folks headed that way. City folks . . . young fellow and a girl."

You'd of thought I'd slapped him. "Didn't get their name," I said, "but the girl was called Sylvie. Matter of fact, there were three of them. I didn't cotton to 'em very much."

Penelope's eyes just got bigger and darker, it seemed like, but that old man went white as death. He sat down again, sat down hard, and for a minute or two he didn't say anything.

"You *saw* them?"

"Uh-huh . . . unpleasant folks, I'd say." I looked up at Loomis from under my eyebrows. "You know them?"

He said nothing for a moment, then shrugged. "Not with favor, sir, not with favor. A most untrustworthy lot."

He got up again. "Come, Penelope. Daybreak will come all too soon."

After they had gone I saw Pio watching me. "What is it, señor? Who are those people you spoke of? He was afraid of them, I think."

So I told him a little about Sylvie and her brother, enough to put him on his guard against them. "I'd say they were touched . . . off the trail somewhere in their heads, but what makes them dangerous is that they don't look it."

Whether he believed me I could not guess, but I left him to think about it and wandered outside. It was cool and pleasant under the old cottonwoods. The dun was living it up on that fresh green grass, with plenty of water close at hand. But I wasn't looking forward to playing shepherd to that buckboard.

With my back to a tree where I could look down the street, I considered what lay ahead . . . and kept an eye on that empty building across the street from the cantina. Had the flicker of movement come from there?

Time dragged slowly by, and I watched, half-dozing, yet my eyes were ready to catch any movement. Shadows fell around me, and I didn't think anybody could see me clearly—not to be sure, anyway. The dun was feeding right behind me, so nobody was going to come up on my blind side.

While I waited there I thought of tomorrow. Leaving town, we would go northwest along Punta de Aguas Creek, which emptied into the Canadian only a few miles off. Holding south of the creek, we could make Romero in three to four days, depending on how game they were to travel and how much trouble we had. With luck we could make ten, twelve miles in a day.

After a while I shifted the dun's picket pin to fresh grass, then, spurs jingling, strolled back to the cantina and sat down inside. Pio was gone, but the señora came out and brought me a meal of buffalo steak, eggs and beans. I sat where I could keep an eye on the adobe on the other side of the street. When I'd been there only a few minutes, Penelope Hume came in.

Now, I'm no hand with womenfolks. I'm a rough, hardhanded man, doing most any kind of work or getting into any kind of a fighting shindig. Womenfolks, especially the young, pretty kind, put a loop on my tongue to where it can scarce wiggle. And this Penelope, she was fresh and lovely, and kind of sparkly when she laughed. Like I've said, she was a tall girl and well made. She was put together so that when she moved it had a way of making a man mighty restless.

"Mr. Sackett, may I sit down?"

Now there's things we don't know back in the Clinch Mountains, but a man knows enough to stand when a lady comes up to him, so I got up quick, almost spilling my coffee, and sat down only after she had been helped into her chair.

She looked across the table at me. "Mr. Sackett, I am glad you are going to show us the way to Romero, but I thought you should be warned. There's going to be trouble."

"I was born to it."

"I know. But you weren't born around Sylvie, Ralph, and Andrew."

"So you know them. Do they have another name?"

"Their name is Karnes. They are kinfolk, in a way . . . there's no blood relation between us. But they knew . . . well, they pried. They learned something only I was supposed to know; and now they are trying to get where we are going before we do."

I didn't ask any questions about that. The trouble was, these folks probably believed the secret of Nathan Hume's treasure was something only they knew. As far as the hiding place was concerned, if they knew that, it *was* something nobody else knew. But I was pretty sure I wasn't the only one who knew about that gold. Only most of the others didn't know as much as I did.

"What started you folks out here all to once?"

"My grandmother died, and when she died she mentioned a packet of letters in her will, and they were to come to me, as my father and mother were both dead. Sylvie and Ralph were there, although they had no right to be. There was little enough to leave and, as I said, they were no blood relation. But they heard the reading of the will, and in it grandmother mentioned that in the packet of letters was an account of where Nathan Hume's gold was buried."

"Somebody must've got away and told about it. I mean, when Nathan Hume was killed."

"You knew about that?"

"He was a known man. He'd been taking pack trains from Missouri to Santa Fe for years."

"Grandfather drew a picture, wrote a few lines, and gave it to an Indian boy. He thought the boy might get away, and if he did he was to mail this to grandmother. The letter was all addressed, everything. Well, the Indian boy did get away, and he sent the message."

"How about Sylvie?"

"After the reading of the will she was just too nice, and so was Ralph. Sylvie made some tea—. What's the matter?"

"Sylvie offered me some coffee, one time."

"It may have been the same sort of thing. She made some tea, and I took it to my room, only I got busy writing letters and forgot to drink it. In the middle of the night I woke up and Sylvie was standing there reading the letters by candlelight.

"I got them away from her, but she was furious—she threatened me, laughed at me, said there was no gold, and even if there was I could never get it."

The sun had moved beyond the cottonwoods, throwing a shadow across the street and across our door. A dog trotted up the street and paused outside, and I watched him, for something worried him. He sniffed, trying to catch some scent that kept getting away from him.

It was a nice thing, setting here in this cool, pleasant room talking to Penelope Hume.

"You said your folks were dead. What about Loomis—who is he?"

"He was a friend of my father, and of my grandfather too. He offered to help. Flinch found us, or we found him, at Fort Griffin. He has been very loyal."

That answered one question for me. If I could answer the one about the adobe across the street I'd be happier, but I had a good idea about that, too. And I was watching the dog. He was a big dog, and part wolf by the look of him, with all a wolf's suspicion.

We talked of other things, Penelope and me. She told me of her home back in New York State, and I talked a bit about Tennessee, but more about the country we were in.

"Folks out here are a rough lot, ma'am. There's the good and the bad, and there's many a man who has come west to get away from something, some trouble he's had. You'll find men from the oldest families and with the best education working right alongside a cowhand who can't read or write.

"The trouble is, too many folks come just to get rich and then get out. They don't care what they leave behind as long as they can take riches with them."

All the time I talked I thought of how it seemed to set across the table from such a girl, me who owned nothing but a pistol, a Winchester, a beat-up blanket or two, and a borrowed horse. And likely would never have anything more.

"I'd better go," she said. "Mr. Loomis wouldn't like it at all if he knew where I was."

"You're all right with me," I said; "but ma'am, I'd not be trusting folks. There are some would murder you for what you know about Nathan Hume."

"My dear cousins? I know."

"Not only them," I said. "When it comes to money or a pretty woman, there's not many who can be trusted."

"Not you, Mr. Sackett?"

"I've the name of being an outlaw," I said.

Chapter 6

A spatter of rain was falling when Flinch led out the horses in the morning. It was dark, with only a faint suggestion of light showing beyond the cottonwoods. Underneath them it was still like night. I tethered the dun near the buckboard and, rifle in hand, went across to Pio's.

The room was lighted by candles. It was warm and pleasant, with the smell of breakfast cooking. Loomis was already at the table, his face stiff with sleep; only the eyes seemed awake. Drawing up a chair, I sat down opposite him, and was scarcely seated when Penelope came in, hurrying to her chair. I rose and seated her, and Loomis gave me a dark, angry look.

Whether he was irritated with me because he believed I was making up to her, I don't know, and cared less. Flinch came in, walking quiet as a ghost, and sat down at the end of the table.

The señora came from the kitchen with a platter of food, and then brought a steaming pot of coffee. We ate in silence, all of us heavy with sleep. As for me, I knew I should be thinking of the trail ahead, and the day before us. But I could not keep my thoughts from going back to yesterday, and the dog.

Whoever had been in the adobe house across the way had gone before the dog could find him. I remembered how the dog, hackles stiff, had walked toward the adobe, growling. Nobody else had seemed to be watching him.

He went inside the open doorway, and I got up and strolled across the street and followed him. He knew me, had been smelling around when I picketed my horse the night before, and had seen me that day around Pio's house. He looked up at me, then smelled around the empty room.

The lean-to behind the adobe showed where a man had slept and smoked cigarettes, a lot of them. The big dog sniffed curiously, then wandered out to the low back wall where the man had evidently gone . . .

Steve Hooker? I wondered.

It was still dark when we went outside. The air was cool and the spatter of raindrops had begun again. The old buckboard creaked when they climbed into it. Flinch gathered the reins, and they moved off.

Pio came out as I stepped into the saddle. "I do not like it, *amigo*," he said. "The señorita will have trouble, I think. We like her very much, my wife and I."

"Her worst enemies are behind us. The ones of whom I spoke. Tell them nothing."

"*Adios*," he said, and I left him there, and moved out after the buckboard.

We crossed the Canadian, which was mostly a wide bed of sand, and then went west on the farther side, keeping well back from the bank to avoid the numerous creeks. But occasionally we traveled in the dry river bed itself, the narrow stream of the river shifting from one side to the other as we moved along. By daylight we were well on our way.

Riding ahead, I scouted the country for Indians or for anybody else who might be around. As it grew light, I swung right and left now and again to cut for sign. Most of the tracks I found were those of sheep from Borregos Plaza, or of buffalo.

The light rain increased, and I led the way out of the river bed. It never took long in this country for a flash flood to come, and I didn't know how much it had been raining up the country.

When we were maybe a mile back from the river, I caught movement in the willows ahead and below us, and two riders came in sight from the direction of the river. At that distance I couldn't make them out, but they never so much as glimpsed us, but rode on ahead.

It took only a few minutes for me to ride down the hill and pick up their sign. They had been bedded down under a rough shelter on the bank of the river overlooking the trail, and they had been waiting there for some time. Crouching, I looked back the way we had come. They must have seen us leave the river bed.

Who were those two who had been tricked out of their ambush by sheer luck? If there had not been those heavy clouds in the distance and that rain to worry me about the river bed, we would have walked into the ambush and they would have had us cold turkey.

Where they had waited they had a thick screen of boughs for concealment, and yet a perfect field of fire through neatly prepared openings in the brush where they had broken away leaves and twigs. They could have taken me and one of the others with the first two shots, and the ones who were left would never have gotten away.

Those two men were western men; I knew that by the way they rode, and they were experienced at their work. Right then I began casting around in my memory for some clue as to who they might be.

Men hired for the job, surely. I could bet on that. So who was there around Griffin or Fort Phantom Hill who might be hired?

The names I came up with weren't happy ones to think about. I knew of several around this part of the country, and any one of them would be a package of trouble. The two who had laid for us were good at their job, too good for comfort.

I walked the dun up out of the brush and across the green slope through the rain, and was thinking about what would happen when all of these treasure-seekers reached the Rabbit Ears at the same time . . . Or could we get there first?

"Who were those men?" Loomis asked as I came back to the buckboard.

He had had his eyes open then. "Hunters . . . big-game hunters, Mr. Loomis, and we're the game."

"They were waiting for us?" He was incredulous. "Who could they be?"

"Somebody hired for cash to do a job. Good at the work, too. We were lucky this time, but we can't count on luck next time. Mr. Loomis, I didn't figure on this when I signed up with you, but it looks like I've got to go hunting for them. Either I take those men, or they'll take us."

He didn't come up with any objection, and from his remarks he seemed more worried about who was doing the hiring than about the killers themselves. There was nothing I could tell him about that, but I knew we were in trouble a-plenty. The best way I knew to keep those two from doing their job was to find them first.

The rain continued to fall—a light, gentle rain. Although there was no flash flood in the river, the water widened and deepened, and we went on, keeping some distance back from the bank.

It was close to noontime before we turned off up Punta de Agua Creek. We had to pick our way along, avoiding obvious places of ambush and trying to keep in the open without becoming too good a target. It wasn't easy.

My dun covered twice the distance of that buckboard, just checking back and forth. We held north on the right of the creek and when we made camp on Los Redos Creek we were about half a mile back of its junction with Punta de Agua.

Nobody had much to say. All of us were beat from the rough country we'd crossed, and Loomis was glum and mean looking. We watered the horses, then picketed them in close. I put together a bed for Penelope, and then went out a ways from camp and bedded down near a rock wall where nobody could come up on me sudden, and where I had a lookout over the camp.

The trend of Punta de Agua was a little westward, then north, but when we started out again we held due north. About four miles out the creek turned westward, but I kept the buckboard headed north. I had a hunch that would worry those men who were packing guns for us, for if we were headed for the Rabbit Ears and Romero it would seem more than likely that we would follow the creek. However, Punta de Agua Creek took another bend north, and I figured to cut west and pick up the creek at that bend.

I rode ahead and scouted the country and we made good time. The rain had stopped, but the slopes were wet and slippery. Meanwhile, I was doing some contemplating. Those ambushers would be somewhere ahead . . . but where? If I could figure that out, I might sort of roust around and get the best of them.

We turned suddenly and headed due west for Rita Blanca Creek, and when we reached it we stopped to eat. Loomis was giving me angry looks and he stalked off to the crest of a rise.

"He'll get himself killed if he isn't careful," I said to Penelope, who was standing near me.

But I wasn't watching Loomis, I was watching Flinch. The breed had me puzzled. He was a canny man, and a quiet one who did no talking at all, but he didn't seem to miss much. A couple of times I'd seen him casting about for sign. Now he was gathering sticks for a fire.

There was a good bit of broken brush and dead stuff lying near the creek. Flinch moved like a wild animal. A wild creature will move through the forest and never step on a fallen twig or branch. A horse might, or a cow, but never a deer or other wild animal, and Flinch was like that. You just never heard him as he moved, and scarcely saw him.

Was it entirely coincidence that he had been around when Loomis was looking for somebody to join them? He had not said he was familiar with this country, but I was sure he knew it as well if not better than I did myself.

As Penelope and I were talking, Loomis came back, and he looked at her sharply. "Penelope! You come here!"

She turned, her chin up. "Mr. Loomis, I will not have you speaking to me like that! You're not my father, and you're not my guardian!"

A moment there he was mad enough to strike her had she been close enough. He glared at her, then said stiffly, "I gave up my business to come and help you. Is this the thanks I get?"

Well, I had to hand it to her, the way she stood up to him. "Mr. Loomis, I am very grateful for your coming, and I thank you for it, but that gives you no right to direct my life. If we find the gold, you will be paid."

At that, his face flushed. "You talk too much!" he flared.

"If you mean she talks too much about Nathan Hume's gold," I said casually, "you're wrong. She's never mentioned it until now, and as far as that goes, nearly everybody in this here country knows that story. I'd bet a pretty penny Flinch knows it, too." I looked at Flinch.

He looked back at me and said nothing, but he knew all right.

"Her name was enough, even if it hadn't been for other things."

Now, I'd lied a little bit there, saying she'd said nothing about the gold, but she was in trouble enough and I wanted to leave Loomis without a leg to stand on. And I was beginning to be suspicious of his motives. He didn't strike me as the sort to pull up stakes and take a young girl west on a wild gold chase.

"This ain't exactly a traveled country," I added, "and the route you're takin' ain't the one I'd have picked for you. But I'll take you through to Romero if that's where you want to go. Or if it suits you better, I'll take you right to the Rabbit Ears."

Penelope looked thoughtful. "Which is the shortest?"

"Right up Rita Blanca Creek, I'd say. The difference is slight, but it *is* a difference, and the travel is a whole lot easier."

"We have to go to Romero," Loomis said stubbornly. "I planned on buying supplies there."

"If you know where the gold is," I suggested, "you'd be better off to get there as fast as you can and get it before the whole country moves in on you.

"Somebody paid those gents who were laying out for you. Maybe it was that Karnes outfit, maybe somebody else. I'd suggest you move fast and get there first . . . if you can."

Well, that slowed him down. He wanted that gold, and he wanted it almighty bad. After a moment he said, "All right, you take us the quickest way."

We headed off the way we'd been traveling. This was a wide-open and barren country, but there were long swells you'd scarcely call hills that would offer some concealment. I knew how to cross country unseen, for I was a man who'd lived that way.

Riding warily, I studied the country around, and suddenly came upon a stretch of rock swept clean by the wind. It was a place where there was a little firewood from dead brush on the creek banks, so we pulled up and made camp. It was early, but I had an idea of what I wanted to do.

We made a small fire and boiled some coffee and ate supper. I cleared a space around the fire so it wouldn't spread. Then I added some sticks that would burn slowly and would add more fuel to the fire kind of gradual. I even built a small rack of sticks above the fire, with the stick ends right in the flames. This would in time drop down, and help to keep the fire going.

When it was full dark I pulled my people back into the darkness. I wrapped the trace chains so they wouldn't jangle, and then we took off into the night, leaving the fire burning behind us. I knew that fire, rigged the way it was, would keep burning or smoking until well after daylight, and by that time I figured to be well away. We pulled out across the rock, and then into the scattered dunes. Those dunes by day were always feathered with a little wind-blown sand, and whatever tracks we made wouldn't last long.

This was bunch-grass country with ridges or dunes or sand breaking through from time to time. We headed north, keeping away from the creek but riding parallel to it. We traveled well into the night, and it was after midnight when we came to the place I was hunting, a sort of slough, with cattails around it, in a hollow among the low hills. We pulled up there, to spend the rest of the night there without a fire.

I slipped on my moccasins, and went out and dusted over our last tracks a mite. Then I taken my own horse and went down into the cattails to a place I knew where there was a piece of solid ground among them, and there I staked out my horse and bedded down, maybe a hundred feet or so off from the others. Nobody could get to me without splashing into water, and the dun would let me know anyway. Then I slept, not worrying about a knife in the ribs or a knock on the skull.

There was a time there before I slept when I lay thinking back over the past few days, but thinking ahead. It was in my mind to try to foresee what might happen, and so be prepared for it. There's no way I know of that a body can foresee the future, but sometimes he can read it pretty well if he knows the way folks think.

Now, there's something about gold and the finding of it that changes a man's viewpoint. When it came to gold, I trusted nobody, not even myself. I'd never had much, and the sight of all that gold might turn me into a worse man than I figured to be.

Moreover, it might affect the others, and I'd no amount of respect for any of them, unless it was the girl. A young girl alone in the world without money is in for a hard time. She's prey to all sorts of advances and misfortunes, and hers can be a hard-bought life. Whatever happened, I wanted to see that the girl got her share of it.

I was thinking of myself too. Where there was gold I figured to get my share of it; but I have an idea that when that gold was found it would be every man for himself and the devil take the hindmost.

Morning came too soon and I was scarce awake, it being something short of daylight, when I heard a faint rustle in the water. I opened my eyes and looked up at the dun and his ears were pricked, so I just naturally reached down beside me and laid hand to my old Tinker.

Now, a Tinker-made knife was a handsome thing with a cutting edge like a razor—I often shaved with mine—but a strong blade that would cut through bone as well as flesh. They were made by a traveling peddler and tinker from back in the mountains, a gypsy man who traveled through, selling other things too, but from time to time with a Tinker-made knife to sell.

The water rustled, just faintly, and I thought of how a body approached this island in the reeds, and how much could be seen before he got right on it. Suddenly I heard the squish of a wet boot and looked up to see Loomis standing there with an axe in his hand.

He was within reach of me, and he had that axe ready, but when our eyes met he stopped. His eyes were as mean-looking as I've ever seen. Now, I've lived a good part of my life in difficulties, and my mind thinks in terms of fighting. The way he was holding that axe told me he was going to cut down and to the left with it. A man swinging an axe from the right-shoulder side can't cut much to the right. Not with accuracy.

Loomis, if he tried to hit me, would cut down and left, so I was all braced to roll right and come up. His knuckles were white with gripping the axe, and I could see the hate in his face. Of a sudden it came to me that, old as he was, Loomis didn't only want that gold, he wanted the girl.

A moment there I thought he was stopped, then he suddenly took a deep, rasping breath and swung. The breath warned me, but he swung faster than I'd thought and I just skinned by, the axe missing by inches.

But then I was on my feet, like a cat, and had my Tinker pointed tight against his wishbone. He didn't have a chance to lift that axe again; my knife was right where I could open him up, and he knew it. I looked right down into his eyes and said, "Loomis, you're a murdering skunk. I got me a notion to kill you."

All the same I was in a fix, and I knew it. If he killed me, nobody would question it much. Penelope might, but she would have nobody to argue with, and I was a known outlaw. Flinch would say nothing of it, or think nothing of it. On the other hand, if I killed him, nobody would believe me at all.

So I just looked into his eyes . . . we stood chest to chest, not eighteen inches between us, and I reached up with my knife and flicked a button from his coat . . . and then another, and another, until I was right under his chin. Then I touched the point under his chin and just pricked him a mite.

"Mr. Loomis," I said, "you hadn't ought to done that. You make a body right mistrustful of folks. Now you just turn your tail around and hike back to camp . . . And, Mr. Loomis, don't you ever try that again or I'll part your brisket with this blade."

Well, he was sweating like nothing you ever saw, he was that scared. He backed off, and then turned and ran back through the water.

I saddled up and loaded up and, taking my Winchester, walked the dun along the edge of the slough for a ways, then came out and skirted the camp. I wanted to scout the country anyway, but I also wanted to come into camp so's I could see everybody. It wasn't in my mind to ride up and have somebody a-laying for me.

When I rode in Penelope gave me an odd look, but nothing was said. I had an idea Flinch knew what was going on, for that breed missed very little. He was the sort that remains on the sidelines and then picks up the pieces after the fighting is over.

We took out across the prairie. They would be hunting us by now, and no doubt would be following along streams where there was water. But from now on there were a good many scattered sloughs or pools, and water would not be so hard to come by.

That night we made camp in a depression north of Carrizo Creek, a place unlikely to be seen until a man was within a few yards of it.

Loomis was restless and on edge. He avoided me, and I was just as glad. Squatting near the fire, I drank hot black coffee and talked to Penelope. It had been a while since I'd had a chance to talk to any girl.

"You be careful," I warned her there at the last; "you trust nobody. You're a mighty pretty girl, and where gold and women are concerned not many can be trusted."

"How about you, Nolan?" This was the first time she had called me by my given name.

"Me neither. I'm as hungry for gold as the next man."

"And women?"

"Well, up to a point. My ma raised me to respect womenfolks."

She was quiet for a minute or two and then she spoke very quietly. "I don't trust people altogether, Nolan."

"You must trust Loomis, to come clear out here with him."

"He's old enough to be my father. Or my grandfather, almost. Besides, how else could I get out here? Would you tell someone how to find a buried treasure and just let them go, hoping you'd get a share?"

"Nope."

"Neither would I."

We moved out from camp before the first light. There were clumps of mesquite about, and more prickly pear than we had been seeing before. I shucked my Winchester and rode with it to hand. We angled northwest across the country, headed for a crossing of Perico Creek almost due south of the Rabbit Ears.

The dun and me, we stayed off to one side, either in front of the buckboard or behind it, always keeping it within sight; but I was careful to offer no target for my back.

Where, I wondered, was Sylvie Karnes and her brothers? And what had become of Steve Hooker?

Topping out on a low rise I saw the Rabbit Ears off to the north, showing just above the horizon and a good ways off. They were two nubbins of mountain, scarcely big enough to be called a mountain in this country. But even from this distance you could see why it got its name of Rabbit Ears.

It was near noontime, and we were a mile or so short of the ford. Down off the rise you couldn't see the Rabbit Ears, and I said nothing about them to the others.

The thought in my mind was that we were now within a few miles of more gold than most people had ever seen, and unless I missed my guess half a dozen people were ready to kill for it.

A moment there I thought, why not just light out? Why walk into something that was none of my business? Let the murdering Karnes outfit and the rest of them fight it out . . . was any amount of gold worth that much risk? I doubted it.

It would be mighty easy to turn my horse and ride away. A few days' ride to the west was Mora, where I had kinfolk. To the north there were the hell-for-leather mining towns where a man could make do one way or another. A twitch of the bridle and I would be off and free-riding with nothing to worry about but Comanches.

The trouble was, there was a girl back there; and mean though I might be, I couldn't leave that girl to a pack of wolves. It just wasn't in me.

Every ounce of horse sense I had told me to cut and run, but I swung my horse and rode on toward the ford on the Perico.

And right into a bellyful of trouble.

Chapter 7

Steve Hooker, Tex Parker, and Charlie Hurst were sitting their horses just across the ford, blocking the trail. They all had rifles, and they were just sitting there, and Hooker was grinning. The thing was, they expected me to stop.

"You boys want something?" I called out.

"You turn around and git out'n here!" Hurst yelled. By that time I was at the water's edge.

That water was no more than eight inches deep and there was good hard bottom, so I let the dun have the spurs and went through the water and up the bank and into them before they realized I wasn't going to stop and parley.

They sure enough expected me to pull up and talk about it, but when trouble faces me I never was much on the talk. So I rode right into them, and then I dropped the reins and slammed right and left with the rifle.

Hurst tried to duck, but the rifle barrel caught him behind the ear and knocked him from the saddle. Parker was reaching for me when I swung the rifle across and drove the barrel into the side of his head. It struck him with a *tunk* like the butt of an axe against a log, and he went out. Grabbing the reins as my horse turned, I put the muzzle of the gun on Steve Hooker. His own rifle was coming up and I shot him, holding high a-purpose so he'd take it through the shoulder. He jerked, but stayed in the saddle, losing his grip on his rifle.

He started to swear, and I said, "You still got a left hand. You want to try for none?"

"You played hell!" he shouted at me. "Do you know who those boys are?"

"Sure. They ride with Bill Coe. I know all that outfit, and you can tell Coe he knows where I am if he ever wants to come hunting."

"You think he won't?"

"That's right. I know Coe, and he knows me. You'd have to weigh a lot of gold in the other side of the scales before he'd make a move toward me."

The buckboard came down to the water and drew up sharply. "What's going on here?" Loomis called.

"No trouble," I said, and swinging down I caught Parker by the scruff of the neck and dragged him clear of the trail. Both of their horses had been frightened into running off a ways. "Drive right on through. These boys figured to stop us, but they had a change of mind."

Penelope's face was white and shocked. "Are . . . are those men dead?"

"No, ma'am. They'll both have headaches tomorrow, that's all."

"Was this necessary?" Loomis demanded.

"If you want to cross the ford it was necessary. You wanted me to take you where you're going and I'm doing it."

Wheeling the dun, I rode off up the trail, and the buckboard rattled on after me. It didn't make a mite of difference what Loomis thought, but the expression on Penelope's face bothered me. A lot of people hear about violence but never come face to face with it, and they've no experience with men of violence. One thing I'd learned a long time back: you just can't waste time talking. If there's talking to do, do it afterwards.

All the time we'd been traveling I'd been looking for wagon tracks. I didn't see how the Karnes outfit—Sylvie, Ralph, and Andrew—could make it faster than we had, but it never pays to weigh an opponent too light.

It was a far-stretching open land through which we rode. It was a country with lava outcroppings here and there, with the yellow-brown grass and the green showing through. It was the bright green of mesquite, and the oddly jointed clumps of prickly pear. A man could hear the cicadas singing, endlessly in the brush, and from time to time he'd see a rattler curled in the shade of a bush.

It was bunch-grass country where buffalo ran, and it was mustang country, wild and free. Maybe I would never have very much in the way of money, but I'd have the memories of this land when it was fresh and open, the memories of one of the grandest pieces of country a man could ever see.

The dun liked it, too. Whenever we topped out on a rise his nostrils would widen to test the wind, and he'd toss his head a little, ears pricked, looking straight away into the far distance.

Well, we were a part of this country, that dun mustang and me. Our natures bred us for it, and our way of living was the way the country demanded.

Back there I'd mentioned William Coe. Now, I would never hold him as a small-calibered man. Coe had a gang of men and a stone fortress not far north of here on the Cimarron, a regular Robbers' Roost. His men were tough, and wild and uncurried. He was a steady man, if an outlaw, not one to be stampeded into doing anything foolish. I wasn't hunting trouble with Coe, and he wouldn't be hunting any with me . . . unless the price was right.

But if we got that gold out of the ground—three hundred pounds of it—the price would be right and all bets off. But Coe wasn't going to come hunting my kind of trouble because I'd rough-handled some of his men. He'd figure they were big boys now, big enough to saddle their own broncs.

Coe knew me maybe as well as I knew myself, for we'd been acquainted back yonder. He knew that trouble had become blood-kin to me, and that something in me wouldn't let me back up or back down, no matter what happened. When trouble showed, when I was faced with it, I just naturally stiffened my neck and went ahead. There was a streak of wildness in me, a streak of recklessness that I disliked. The cool way was the best way, that I knew, but at times I just naturally went hog-wild and started throwing lead or punches at whatever was in the way. It was going to get me killed some day.

The Rabbit Ears were standing up there plain now. I could see them clear, and so could Loomis and the others, so I dropped back alongside the buckboard.

"There they are, Loomis," I said, "and whatever happens will happen soon now. If we can get in there first and get that gold out, and high-tail it out of here, we may get away without a fight. But we won't have much time."

"How much time do we have?"

"Maybe a day . . . maybe a day and a night. No longer."

"Do you think Hooker rounded up those men himself? Or were they acting for somebody else?"

"I think it was his show, but from here on it may not be. Those other men were outlaws of the Coe gang . . . their Roost isn't far from here. If Coe gets wind of that gold, and we get it out of the ground, we'll have us a running fight."

"Does he have many men?"

"Anywhere from three to thirty, depending on who is hanging out up there. He will have enough."

Now I dropped behind them and stayed off to one side. As we rode I studied the country, cutting for sign. There had been some movement around, and it worried me. Rabbit Ears Mountain wasn't far off the Santa Fe Trail, but as a usual thing there wasn't too much movement off the trail. But now there had been.

I was a fool to go riding over there for a treasure of which I'd been offered no part, guiding them there, and then having to choose whether or not to leave Penelope to her friends and her enemies, or to stay on and fight and perhaps get no thanks in the end.

But she was a fair lady, a girl's bright eyes have won the day more than once, and I was the fool ever to look into them. For I am an unhandsome man, and the romance in my heart does not show past the bend in my nose, or at least the girls don't seem to look beyond that.

Back in our Tennessee hills we had few books to read, and I'd never learned beyond the spelling out of words; but we had copies of Sir Walter Scott there in the mountains, and a teacher or a preacher to read them to us in passing. It was always as Ivanhoe that I saw myself, and always as the Norman knight that I was being seen by others.

Yet being the fool I was, I was forever riding into trouble because of a pair of pretty lips or a soft expression in the eyes of a girl. Nor was this time to be different. Even as I thought of riding off into the night, I knew it was not in me to go, and I'd risk a bullet in the back from that cold chill of a man up yonder in the buckboard. Or maybe from that quiet one who sat saying nothing, but seeing and hearing everything, that Flinch, who was one to fear and be careful of.

The Rabbit Ears were close now, so I closed in on the buckboard. My foolishness for the eyes of Penelope did not lead me to foolishness with Loomis. There was no nonsense in me where men were concerned, and if he wanted my kind of trouble I'd serve it up hot and well done for him, and he'd get indigestion from it, too, or I'd know the reason why.

"There are the Rabbit Ears," I said. "No doubt you know where to find the gold of Nathan Hume."

Loomis drew up, for he was driving then, and he reached in his pocket and paid me fifty dollars.

"Your money," he said. "You've been paid, and we have no more use for you."

Penelope was keeping her eyes straight front, so I said to her, "And you, ma'am? If you want me to stay and see you clear with your gold, I'll do it, and no pay asked or wanted."

"No," she said, not looking at me at all. "No, I want nothing more from you. Mr. Loomis is here. He will take care of things."

"I've no doubt," I said, and turned my horse away, but not my eyes, for I knew Loomis was one to shoot a man in the back if chance offered. At the moment, I almost wished he would take the chance, so that I might lay him dead across the buckboard seat.

I skirted a low hill and drew up in the shade of a clump of mesquite to contemplate.

This was another time when the maiden fair saw me only as the Norman knight.

Chapter 8

So I'd been given my walking papers, and now there was nothing to keep me here. Penelope Hume had said not a word to keep me, and I was no longer responsible. Moreover, this was not the kind of country I cottoned to, wishing more for the sight of trees and real mountains right now, although I'll say no word against the far-reaching plains, wherever they lie.

The Rabbit Ears were basaltic rock—or lava, if that comes easier. There were ancient volcanoes to the north, and much of this country had been torn and ruptured by volcanic fires long ago. Where the wind had swept the flat country clear it was sandstone.

The Rabbit Ears could scarcely be called a mountain, as I've said. They were more like big mounds, falling away on all sides. At their highest they stood about a thousand feet above the surrounding country.

Circling wide, I drifted on across country to the north, and watered at Rabbit Ears Creek, then followed the creek toward the west. On the northwest side of the mountain I found myself a notch in the rocks screened by brush and low trees, where there was a patch of grass sub-irrigated by flow from the mountain.

I staked the dun out on the grass and, swapping boots for moccasins, I climbed up the mountain. It was sundown, with the last rays of the sun slanting across the land and showing all the hollows.

There was a thin line of smoke rising from the brush along Rabbit Ears Creek; more than likely this was the camp of Loomis, Penelope, and Flinch.

Over east, maybe seven or eight miles from there, I caught a suggestion of smoke, and near it a white spot. It was so far off that had the sun not picked up that white I might never have noticed it. Even the smoke might be something my expectation had put there after I glimpsed that spot of white. For that white could be nothing but a wagon top . . . the Karnes outfit, or somebody else.

What about Hooker? He had a bad shoulder. Tex and Charlie Hurst would have aching heads. Would they quit now? I decided it was unlikely.

William Coe would be at his Roost over on the Cimarron, not nearly as far away as I wished, for his was a tough, salty outfit, and Coe was game. He'd fight anything at the drop of a hat; he'd even drop it himself.

His outfit had raided Trinidad, had even raided as far east as Dodge, and had stolen stock from Fort Union, government stock. They had nerve. If one of those boys rode for Coe, I'd be in trouble.

On the north side of Rabbit Ears all the ravines ran down toward Cienequilla Creek. The location of the box canyon was unknown to me, and it might be anywhere between the mountain and the creek, or even over on the other side.

After I'd walked and slid back down the mountain I shifted the dun's picket-pin to fresh grazing and made myself a pot of coffee from dry, relatively smokeless wood. In the corner where I was the fire couldn't be seen fifteen feet away.

A man on the dodge, or in Indian country, soon learns to watch for such a place as this. His life depends on it. And if he travels very much his memory is soon filled with such places. As mine was.

Sitting beside the fire, I cleaned my pistol, my Winchester lying at hand, just in case. Then I checked both of my knives. The one I wore down the back of my neck inside my shirt collar slid easy and nice from its scabbard. A time or two in passing through brush or under low trees I'd gotten leaves or bits of them into the scabbard, and I knew that in the next few days I might need that knife almighty bad.

Later, lying on my blankets, I looked up at the stars through the leaves. My fire was down to red coals and my pot was still full of coffee. Tired as I was, I was in no mind to sleep.

My ears began making a check on all the little sounds around me. They were sounds of birds, of insects, or of night-prowling animals, and were familiar to me. But in every place some of the sounds are different. Dead branches make a rattle of their own; grass or leaves rustle in a certain way, yet in no two places are the sounds exactly the same. Always before I slept I checked the sounds in my mind. It was a trick I'd learned from an old Mexican sheepherder and mountain man.

Of course the dun was there, and as I've said, there's nothing like a mustang to warn a man if he hears something strange. For that matter, I was of the same breed. I was a mustang man—a man riding the long prairie, the high mesa, the lonely ridges.

That Penelope now . . .

This was no time to think of her. Forcing my thoughts away from her, I considered the situation. Sylvie Karnes and her brothers wanted that gold, and they would stop at nothing to get it. I'd never come across anybody quite like them, and they worried me. I'd known plenty of folks who would kill for money, for hatred, or for a lot of reasons, but I'd met nobody so willing to kill just to be killing as they were, or appeared to be.

Sure as shootin', that coffee she fixed for me had been poisoned. No telling how many dead lay behind them, or lay ahead, for that matter.

Loomis would be after that gold, but he wanted the girl too. He would need her until they got the gold and after that? That was when Penelope Hume would come face to face with a showdown, and all alone.

Had she really wanted to go on without me? Or had they forced her to get rid of me? She had not looked my way even once, there at the end. Maybe they had talked her into it, but it might be that Loomis had threatened her.

Law and order were made for women. They are hedged around by protection. But out in the wilderness they are only as safe as men will let them be. Penelope Hume was a long way from any law, and it was likely that nobody even knew where she was, or where she was going. Loomis would have seen to that. If she never appeared again, nobody would be asking questions; and if anyone did ask, no one would answer. Many a man and many a woman disappeared in the western lands, left in an unmarked grave, or in no grave at all.

Whatever law there might be would be local law, administered only in the towns. Few officers ever rode out into the unsettled country unless they were Federal officers, and most of those were active only in the Indian Territory.

These were my thoughts as I mounted up and worked my way on down the mountain, keeping to whatever cover I could find. That box canyon would not be easy to find, but should be simpler for me, who knew this kind of country, than for either Loomis or the Karnes outfit.

Suppose I could get there first and get that gold out? Finders was keepers, wasn't that so? That was how I felt, and yet the idea made me uneasy. There would be nothing for that girl, for Penelope. I wasn't worried about Sylvie . . . her kind could always get along. Penelope was something else, and I couldn't leave her without a two-bit piece to her name.

She was pretty, and she was a city girl. Both qualities put her in a bad spot. She was pretty enough to attract trouble, and had too much of the city in her to know how to cope with this kind of country.

Right beyond me was a place where the canyon down which I was riding sort of opened out. There were trees along the creek ahead, and trees and brush along the mountainside. Slowing down, I peered ahead, searching for any sign of movement. I'd slip down there, I thought, find that box canyon, find the gold if I could, and then round up Penelope and the others and get the girl out of trouble.

It seemed to me she was safe until they either found or failed to find the gold; after that she would be fair game. Only I was uneasy, leaving her at all. She needed somebody at hand to care for her.

Ahead of me was some low brush; on the side of the mountain a few piñon. I started to swing around a big boulder when the corner of my eye caught a flash of light and I ducked. Something hit me a wicked blow on the skull, and the dun shied violently, a report went racketing off down the canyon, followed closely by another, and then I was laying on the ground among some rocks, looking at a pool of red on the sand.

Instinct told me I must move from where I lay, and yet I couldn't move a muscle. My brain told me to get up and get going, but nothing happened; and then I heard a voice call out.

"Ralph! You stop right there! I always was a better shot than you, and if you take one step nearer I'll break your leg!"

"Pen! Now, don't be foolish! We just came to help you. If you knew what we know about Loomis—"

"I don't need any help. You just turn back and leave that man alone."

"But he's after the gold, too! We've got to be rid of him, Pen!"

"You back up, Ralph! You and Sylvie and Andrew might just as well go home. You don't know where the gold is, and you'll never find it unless you know."

Ralph laughed, and it was an unpleasant laugh. "We don't have to find it, Pen. We'll just let you and Loomis do that for us!"

"You heard me, Ralph. Back up and let him alone."

"I'm going to kill him, Pen. If he isn't dead already, I'm going to kill him."

"Ralph"—Pen spoke matter-of-factly—"you make the slightest move this way and I'll not stop with breaking one leg—I'll break them both and just let you lie there. Nobody would ever find you except the buzzards."

Ralph must have believed her. I didn't see how he could, but maybe he knew her better than I did.

All that time, I simply couldn't move. I was all sprawled out among the rocks, and I seemed to be paralyzed. I could hear, all right, and I could see, but I couldn't move. But all the while I knew that if that girl had not stood there with a rifle, Ralph Karnes would have killed me.

After a bit, Penelope spoke, just loud enough for me to hear. "Mr. Sackett? Are you all right?"

Well, now, that was a foolish question. Did she figure that I'd be just a-lyin' here if I was all right? I tried to speak, and finally made a kind of weak sound. Then I tried to move. I made a real effort, and I felt a sort of spasm go through me, but nothing else happened.

Then I heard her coming. At least, I hoped it was her.

She came down over the rocks as if she was born to them, and she kept looking around to see if anybody was closing in on her. Then she was standing near me and looking down, and I looked right into her eyes.

"You're alive then," she said, and then she kind of bent down close to me. "We can't stay here," she said. "He'll be back with the others. He knows you're hurt."

She pulled my arm across her shoulder and tried to pull me up, but she wasn't strong enough.

My lips worked, and finally I managed to shape words. "Horse . . . get my horse."

She got up quickly, and as quickly was gone.

Meantime I tried to move my head, and managed it, then wrapped my fingers around a rock and tugged. The rock held, and I moved myself a little. With care, I managed to work that hand up the side of a slab of rock, but I had no strength at all in it, and it fell back to my side. I couldn't seem to make my fingers work as they should, and my head was starting to ache with a dull, heavy throb. I didn't think I was seriously hurt. Maybe I just didn't dare think so, for to be badly hurt here was almost the same as being dead; yet I had been shot, hit in the head, it seemed, and had been temporarily shocked into some kind of paralysis.

To a man who has spent his life depending on his muscles and his reflexes, there could be nothing more frightening than the state I seemed to be in now. I'd made my living with strength, and with my skill in any kind of shooting, and without that, I had nothing. I'd never had no chance for schooling, and if I couldn't count on my muscles there'd be nothing left for me.

I found I could work the fingers of the other hand like a claw, opening and closing them. I got my hand on an edge of rock and tugged myself up, one-handed, to a kneeling position.

I knew I had to get out of here. Those murdering Karneses would be coming a-hunting me. If I was dead, they'd be wanting to see the body; and if I wasn't, they had to know it and finish me off.

Penelope was coming back, leading the dun. I was surprised he had let her come up to him, he was that shy of strangers. But that girl had a way about her . . . and nerve too.

When the dun came alongside me he snorted nervously, smelling blood, which was trickling down my face now. I spoke softly to him. "Easy, boy, easy now."

With my one working hand I reached out and caught hold of the stirrup leather. Penelope slipped her arm around my waist, and with her lifting and my grip on the stirrup I managed to pull myself erect. But when the horse took a step, I almost went to the ground; it was only Penelope's tight grip that held me up.

We started to move off, my feet trying to work but dragging. We hadn't made more than twenty feet before Penelope, glancing over her shoulder, let go of me, and I grabbed wildly with my one good hand to hang onto the stirrup.

Her rifle went to her shoulder and she fired in the same instant. Then she fired again. The dun was still walking dragging me toward the brush. "Go, boy, go!" I said to him, and he went.

A shot came from somewhere and a bullet hit sand near me. Another shot, and it struck somewhere above me and the dun jumped, but I hung on until we got into a clump of juniper. Then I let go, and fell face down in the sand.

Penelope shot once more, and then I heard her scrambling in the rocks. After that silence.

The dun had stopped among the trees, nostrils wide. My face was wet with blood and sweat, and I was trembling all over. My Winchester was in the boot, but I couldn't reach it.

Had Penelope been shot? Everything was so quiet. The sun was hot. I could smell dust and blood and sweat. Reaching back, I got the thong off my Colt and fished it out and up where I could shoot.

Nothing moved, and there was not a sound. The dun switched his tail, nosed at some brush, then pricked his ears to listen. Struggling, I managed to lift my head. All I could see was roots and rock. Underneath me there was blood on the sand, my blood.

What had happened to Penelope? And where was Loomis? For some reason I hadn't given a thought to him, nor to Flinch.

It was the Karneses who worried me. It must have been the Karneses shooting. And where was Steve Hooker and his outfit? For they must have heard the shooting if they were anywhere within miles, for sound carried on those wide plains.

Reaching out, I caught my fingers over a root and tugged myself closer to the trunk of a tree. It was a mighty slim tree, but I was in no position to argue about cover.

The worst of it was, I couldn't see a thing. I had cover of a sort, but I couldn't even see if anybody was moving out there.

Was Penelope alive? Was she hurt? I'd no way of moving to find out—all I could do was lie there and wait, gun in hand.

The dun stamped his feet. Somewhere a pebble rattled. I shifted my gun and wiped my palm dry on my shirt. After a minute I put the gun down on a piece of bark and started to knead the muscles of the other arm, trying to get some life into it. My head ached heavily, but the bleeding seemed to have stopped. Presently I took up the gun again, fearing to risk any more time with it out of my hand.

The throbbing in my head had me wrinkling my brow against it, and my throat was dry, needing water. There was water in the creek, and in my canteen on the saddle, but one seemed as far off as the other.

Reaching out now, I gripped the trunk of the tree and pulled myself further along. It was much too quiet out there, and I was scared for Penelope.

Looking out over the low brush and rocks, I searched for her, but could see no sign of her. I looked across the mouth of the canyon, and let my eyes move slowly across the rocky wall and the scattered boulders at the canyon's mouth, then down on the tree-dotted flatland that sloped away toward the creek.

Nothing . . .

And then behind me I heard a faint movement. Turning my head, I looked across the small clearing among the trees and brush. The dun was standing head up, nostrils wide, looking toward my right. Stiffly, I turned my head.

Andrew was standing very still in a narrow space between two clumps of mesquite, a prickly pear almost waist-high in front of him. He was holding his rifle up, ready to shoot, and his eyes were moving along the thicker brush on my side, looking for me.

And when he shot, he would shoot to kill.

Chapter 9

Andrew Karnes was no more than sixty feet away, but I was drawn back under the low-growing juniper and it was not easy to see me. His eyes were shifting around quickly, like a weasel's eyes, hunting something to kill.

My pistol was in my right hand, and I was looking back over my left shoulder. To shoot, I'd have to swing around, and that would make a noise. I had watched Andrew, and I knew he was quick as a cat—and there was no way I could move without giving him the first shot. I didn't want to chance it at that range. So I just lay there, hoping he wouldn't see me.

He came forward a step. His eyes went to the horse again, then began again their restless search for me.

I was going to risk it, I would have to. When his eyes got down to the farthest rocks, I would roll over and fire. I wouldn't be in the best shooting position, but I had no choice. It was him or me.

The dun stomped his hoof, and Andrew looked in that direction. Not wanting to take my eyes from him, I moved my left hand to a position under my left shoulder and pushed up, then I moved my right arm under my body.

Actually, I hadn't an idea whether I could do it. Each movement was a gamble, and each might be my last. My left hand started across my body. My eyes were on Andrew; my right hand was coming forward . . . and then he saw me.

He must have failed to believe what he saw. Or maybe the shadows were thick enough so what he saw was indistinct, for there was an instant when he froze. And then the rifle whipped to his shoulder.

Even as he moved, I moved; my left hand slapped the ground and my right thrust forward. My gun must have gone off an instant sooner, or perhaps he shot too fast, for the bullet *whapped* into the ground right where my body had been before the half-turn was completed.

My own shot was high. It cut a furrow across the top of his shoulder and his involuntary move jerked the rifle out of line. He levered another bullet into the chamber, but my second shot went right through his face. It was a miss, for I'd shot at his body, but the bullet went in under his eye and came out the back of his head.

He fell forward, all sprawled out, into that mess of prickly pear. The rifle, thrown forward as he fell, dropped into the sand beyond the patch of cactus. I held the gun on him, ready for another shot, even after I realized the back of his skull was gone.

Working feverishly, I poked the two spent shells from the cylinder and slipped two others in place.

I listened, but I heard no sound. Catching hold of the branches of the tree, I pulled myself up, and was surprised that I could do it. The shock that had temporarily put me out of action was wearing off.

My first move was for his rifle, for my own was on the dun, and I had no idea where brother Ralph was. Staggering, I got to the rifle and picked it up, then looked carefully around.

All was quiet again. How many ears had heard those shots and were now listening, I did not know. I only hoped that somewhere out there Penelope was able to listen.

My head still ached, and every step I took was made with caution, for I had no idea how bad a shape I was in. My fingers went to my skull. There was a deep furrow above my ear that had cut the scalp almost to the back of my head. Leading my horse, for even if I could stay in the saddle I would be too easily seen, I started down the gradual slope, which flattened out toward the creek. From time to time I paused, careful to conserve what strength I had.

Before riding away, I studied the area carefully, but there was no sign of life, no movement. What worried me most was that I had no idea what was going on, nor where anybody was. Penelope had been out there in the rocks somewhere, but she had vanished as if she had never been. And across there in the trees Ralph might still be waiting, to say nothing of that poisonous flower, Sylvie.

There were big old cottonwoods and willows along the creek, and there was water. Once under the trees, I got down and took a long drink. I was hungry, but to risk a fire was to risk my neck. I wasn't that hungry. More than anything else, I wanted to find a place under a safe tree and sleep, but there was no chance of that.

Near me was a huge old cottonwood whose thick leaves rustled and whispered endlessly. Glancing up, I noticed the huge branches and the idea came suddenly.

After tying my horse to a shrub, I rigged a quick sling for my rifle from a couple of piggin strings and then reaching up, I caught the lowest limb of the big tree. Its leaves and the other trees around me offered concealment, and I climbed carefully until I was about twenty feet off the ground and could see all around me.

The first thing I saw was a dust cloud. It was some distance off, downstream, and whoever was causing the dust was out of sight beyond the rocks. My guess made it about half a dozen riders.

Not far away I could see some bones, lying time-whitened under the sun. Were these the bones of Nathan Hume's mule train? I remembered that there had been another battle, a hundred and fifty years before, when an army of Spanish pioneers whipped a huge band of Comanches at this place.

It was very still. The only sound was the gentle rustling of the cottonwood leaves, which never seemed to be quiet. After a few minutes, just as I was about to get down from the tree, I saw Sylvie Karnes come down from the rocks riding a bay pony.

Now where had she gotten that horse? As I watched, she was followed by Steve Hooker, Tex Parker, and two other men whom I did not recognize. This looked to me like too much activity around for one lone Tennessee boy, even if he was a Sackett. My better sense kept telling me I should pull out of here, and fast.

Sylvie by herself was a package of dynamite, and I wanted no part of her. When they discovered Andrew dead—for it was likely they still did not know about it—they would have another reason for hunting me down.

Gold is a hard-won thing, and hard-kept, and when Nathan Hume bought smuggled gold from the Spanish miners in the San Juans he little knew what he was starting. Those old Spanish miners preferred to sell their gold in secret to traders like Hume, rather than have a big part of it taken from them by the Spanish or Mexican governments, to say nothing of the governors of New Mexico. What Hume had started was being played out now, right here.

The group rode out on a little meadow about a quarter of a mile back from the creek and dismounted. They looked as if they were going to camp.

Carefully, I climbed down the tree. My neck was stiff and my head still throbbed with a dull, brow-wrinkling pain, but my muscles seemed to have loosened up. Mounting up, I walked my horse down through the willows and across the creek, which here was only eight to ten inches deep.

The rest of the day I scouted around, searching for the box canyon. All I knew was that it was somewhere north of Rabbit Ears, which was little enough to go on. And during all that day I stayed clear of the Karnes outfit, riding wide around. Now that they had tied up with Steve Hooker and the boys from Coe's gang, my troubles were multiplied. Of course, I couldn't wish the Coe gang any worse luck than making a deal with Sylvie. She was likely to poison the lot when she got the gold . . . if she got it.

When night came I was far out to the north, and I rode on a few miles and camped on a little creek that emptied into the North Canadian. As I was eight or nine miles from the Rabbit Ears I figured to be pretty safe, so I built myself a fire I could have covered with my hat, and made coffee and broiled myself a steak. I had plenty of fresh meat now, for earlier that day I had killed a yearling buffalo well over to the east.

Just as I was about to pour some coffee, the dun, who was drinking at the creek, suddenly jerked up his head, water dripping from his muzzle, and looked across the creek into the darkness.

Before you could say scat I was back in the darkness with my Winchester cocked and ready.

"Hold easy on that trigger, son. I'm huntin' help, not trouble."

I knew that voice, and while I lay quiet trying to place it in my memory, it spoke again.

"That horse knows me better'n he does you. I gave him to you."

"Come on out then. Show yourself."

"You'll have to give me time. I'm hurt."

Well, I taken a long chance. That voice did sound familiar and only one man could know how I got that horse. So I went down to the creek and crossed it.

The old man lay in the grass on the far side of the creek, and he was in bad shape. He had been shot more than once, and his left hand was a bloody mess, but he was game. There was no quit in that old man. His kind come from away up the creek, and he was a tough old mossy-horn with a lot of life in him yet.

So I just picked him up and carried him back to camp. He couldn't have weighed more than a hundred and thirty soaking wet, and I'd never seen the day when I couldn't pick up three times that much.

He was in bad shape, but it was his left hand that gave me the turn. Every fingernail was gone, and his fingers all bloody . . . and that could have been no accident.

"Comanches?" I asked.

"In-laws," he said grimly. "Sometimes they can be worse."

"You ain't related to that Karnes outfit?"

"You met up with them?"

"Uh-huh."

First off, I filled a cup with hot, black coffee and held it for him to drink. He was shaky, and he needed something to pick up his spirits a mite. He drank it, taking it in his right hand, while I put on some water to heat up to clean him up with.

"Looks to me as if ever'body on the Staked Plains is related," I said, "and all of them after Nathan Hume's gold."

"I got a claim to it, better than any of the rest."

"Better than Penelope?"

"You don't say. She here?"

"Unless they've killed her, she is. She saved my bacon yesterday, and a fine girl she is."

After he'd drunk the coffee he laid back while I washed out a couple of bullet wounds, neither of them serious, beyond the blood he'd lost. At least, I'd seen men survive worse ones. I always made shift to pack a few wrappings of bandage, for a man on the dodge can't go running to no doctor. So I fixed up the wounds as best I could, and that hand along with it.

The fingernails had been missing for a while, but crawling through the brush he'd evidently torn open the wounds.

"You must have known something they wanted almighty bad."

"I should smile, I did. I knew where that gold was. And I know just where that box canyon is."

"I wonder they let you live."

"They fired my place and then rode off, leaving me hog-tied in the house. I was out cold and they never figured I'd get out alive. Well, I fooled 'em."

"Seems like everybody in the country started after that gold all to once."

"What would you have me do?" the old man said. "I worked with old Nathan when I was a boy, and I had me a mighty good idea where that gold was, but as long as the widow was alive I didn't figure I had a right to it.

"Others hunted it, but most of them had no idea where to look. I knew how old Nathan thought, and I was sure I could hand on the gold. The old man was my cousin, blood-kin, and I was the only one of his flesh who had worked with him. Many a time I went into the San Juans to meet up with the gold traders.

"Them Karneses, they didn't know where I was until you fetched up to their wagon. When they saw that brand on the dun, NH Connected, they knew it for old Nathan Hume's brand, and knew that I was somewhere about. That was one of the reasons they wanted to do away with you."

"Why didn't you try to get the gold before now?"

He glanced up at me. "You ain't seen that place yet, nor heard the stories. Well, I heard 'em. Ain't no Indian alive who will spend a night in that canyon and mighty few who will even go into it. Evil spirits, they say, and maybe there is."

"You ain't told me your name?"

"Harry Mims. Now don't get me wrong. It wasn't ha'nts kept me out of that box canyon. Mostly it was Comanches. Why, I've lost my outfit twice and nearly lost my hair a couple of times, too.

"One time I was lucky and got right up to the canyon before they come on me. Well, they took my pack outfit and got so busy arguing over the loot that I sneaked off and hid until things quieted down. Took me two weeks to get back to Las Vegas, and when I got there I hadn't enough money for a meal. I got a job swamping in a saloon, then they moved me up to bartender. Took me six months to get myself an outfit again, what with gambling an' all."

"How'd you get clear up here now?"

"A-hossback—how'd you figure? They stole some horses off me, scattered the rest, but those horses come on home, and I caught up a few, saddled up, and rode. I taken me some time, but here I am."

He lay back, resting. He was in such bad shape I didn't feel much like asking him more questions. Somebody had been shooting at him more than a little, and he'd wasted away some, riding all that time. It gave a body the shudders to think what that old man had gone through in getting here.

"What do you figure to do now?"

"You ask a fool question like that? I'm going to get that gold, or stop them from getting it, and by the Lord Harry, I'll kill that Ralph Karnes."

"What about her?"

Harry Mims was still for a while, and then he looked up at me. "Sackett, I know she needs it, but I can't bring myself to kill no woman. Why, she was the worst of all when it came to thinkin' of things to do t'me. It was her thought of the fingernails, and she did part of it herself."

I could believe that of Sylvie.

After a while Mims dropped off to sleep, and I covered him up better. He hadn't told me where his outfit was, but it must be somewhere back in the brush. He couldn't have come far in the shape he was in, not afoot, anyway.

The death of Nathan Hume's widow, way back in Virginia, had opened a fancy show out here on the grasslands of the Panhandle. Everybody and his brother was heading right for the gold, and all at the same time. It was just my luck to land right in the middle of it; and here I was, saddled with an old man who needed help the worst way, and maybe with a girl, if I could find her again.

What about those Indian stories? Now, I was never one to doubt anything an Indian told me. Folks would say they were superstitious and all, but behind most of what they believed there was good common sense. I know one time down Mexico way Indians told me they would never go near a certain place, because there were evil spirits around. Come to find out, there had been a smallpox epidemic there, and that was the Indian way of quarantining the place. They thought evil spirits had caused the smallpox. . . . Well, maybe there was something odd about that box canyon too.

After I'd found Mims's horses—he had four of them . . . two pack animals and a spare saddle horse—I went back to the fire and drank some more coffee, then let the flames die down to the coals. Then when it was fairly dark, I moved my bed back into the darkest shadows, where I could see the old man and the firelit space, and where I'd be unseen by anybody scouting the camp.

Several times during the night I awakened, and each time I lay listening into the night. Finally, near daybreak, I decided not to go back to sleep. Many a night before this I had stayed awake for hours, for in my kind of life a man never knew when he would have to come up shooting.

A long time I lay there thinking of other nights in other places when I had stayed awake listening to the night sounds. It wasn't much of a life, being on the dodge all the time.

After a while I began to hear something. At first it wasn't really a clear sound, only of a sudden my ears seemed to sharpen, for something was moving out there, something that made no sound I could rightly make out.

I looked toward the fire . . . a few red coals still glowed there, and Harry Mims, wrapped in two blankets and a ground sheet, lay dark and silent beside the fire. I could hear his faint breathing.

I reached out with my left hand and took up the edge of the blanket that covered me and put it back carefully. The moccasins I always had with me were close by. Holding my pistol in my right hand, I picked up the moccasins with my left and eased my feet into them.

Picking up a small stone, I tossed it at Mims. It struck his shoulder and his breathing seemed to stop, then it went on again. Was he awake? I had a hunch he was, awake and as ready as a body in his shape could be.

All was quiet, yet with a different sort of quiet now. In the area north of our camp even the night sounds had stopped. Then I heard a faint whisper—the sort of sound a branch can make scraping the side of a man's jeans. Somebody was approaching—perhaps more than one.

I came smoothly and silently to my feet and took a careful step backward, where I was nearer the tree and partly shielded by its branches. Now, even if my bed was seen, I myself was blended into the darkness of the tree.

That gun felt good in my hand, but suddenly I put it back in its holster and drew my knife.

A knife was better for quiet work, in close.

Chapter 10

I waited there in the darkness, knife in hand, thankful its edge was razor-sharp. I held it low, cutting edge up.

Down in the creek there was a rustle of water. Cottonwood leaves whispered softly to the breath of wind. I could smell the wood smoke from the fire, the faint aromatic scent of crushed leaves. Whoever was approaching moved with great skill, for there was not another whisper of sound.

My leg muscles grew tired, but I did not want to shift my feet in a movement that might make even the slightest sound. Anyone who moved as silently as this unknown one would also listen well, for the two are one, to listen and to be conscious of others listening.

Then I saw a shadow where no shadow had been before. I had to look a second time to be sure my eyes were not tricking me into believing something had changed. But the shadow was there. I made a slight move forward, and then my name was breathed. "Mr. Sackett?"

It was Penelope.

My relief was so great that all I could say was, "Where have you been?"

She did not answer, but came swiftly toward me. "Who is that by the fire?"

"Harry Mims. Have you heard of him?"

"I know of him. You'd best awaken him. We must go quickly, before it is light."

"What's happened?"

"Have you ever heard of a man called Tom Fryer? Or Noble Bishop?"

"Are they in this now?"

"Sylvie brought them in. I don't know where she found them, but from all I hear, this only makes things worse."

"Is Ferrara with them?"

"There's a slim, dark man. I didn't hear his name. They came into camp tonight, and they seemed to know you."

They knew me all right—it could not have been worse. There were not three more dangerous men west of the Mississippi than those three.

"You are right," I said. "We'd better move."

Mims was sitting up. As we neared the fire he used his good hand to help himself up. "I heard. Let's get out of here. Let's get the gold and run."

It took only a few minutes to roll up our beds and to bring up the horses. Penelope would ride Mims's extra horse, for she didn't have one of her own.

We led our horses to the stream, then mounted and crossed. Mims took the lead, for he was sure he knew where the box canyon lay.

I didn't like the sound of a box canyon, for that meant a trap—a canyon with only one entrance, and the chances were it had steep sides. It smelled like trouble—but then, everything smelled like trouble. I wished again that I had had sense enough to ride out of here before this.

Penelope was close beside me. "You're no tenderfoot," I said. "You couldn't move like that if you were."

"I grew up in the woods in Virginia. I was stalking deer before I was ten."

She'd had no right to make me feel she was helpless, I told myself. It was downright dishonest. Why, she was as good in the woods as I was myself. And she had saved my bacon.

"You pulled me out of trouble." I said it a little grudgingly, for I wasn't used to being bested by a woman. "Thanks."

"That's all right," she said.

"Where's Loomis?" I asked.

"Somewhere around. I lost track of him."

It seemed to me she was neither worried nor sorry. Maybe she already had him figured out. But how about me? How did she know I wouldn't take all that gold and run? I gave her an uneasy look. Could be I was guessing wrong all the way around. But one thing I felt pretty sure of— she wasn't anything like Sylvie Karnes.

When my thoughts turned to Ferrara, Fryer, and Noble Bishop, I felt a chill. Any one of them was bad enough. All three at once I wanted no part of.

Noble Bishop was a gunman. They told it around that he'd killed twenty men. Cut that by half and it might be true—at least, those killed in known gun battles. Whoever he might have dry-gulched I'd never be knowing, although that sort of thing was more to the taste of Fryer than of Bishop. As for Ferrara, he was a knife man.

All three were known men, hired killers, men for whatever was needed when there was violence to be done. No doubt Sylvie had gotten wind of them through Hooker or one of the others, and she had wasted no time in hiring them.

Harry Mims was old, and he might be crippled now, but he led us as swiftly through the trees as though he could see in the dark. We followed, and when he brought up the canyon's mouth we came up close to him.

"I don't like it," he said. "The place worries me."

"You're scared?" I was surprised, for that old man was tough. At any other time he might have gone for his gun at the very question.

"Call it what you like. Maybe the Indians know what they're talking about. I don't like that canyon, and never did."

"You've been here before?"

"Yes. . . . It's a litter of bones in there. More than one man has died in that place."

"Sure. Nathan Hume's pack train died there, or most of them. Their bones will be there—what else would you expect?"

"There's others," he said soberly. "I tell you, I don't like the place."

"Let's get the gold then, and get out. If we don't do that, we might as well leave right now, because they'll be coming and I'm not one to fight without cause."

The dun didn't like the canyon either. He tried to turn away, fought the bit, and did all he could to avoid entering. The other horses were nervous, but none of them behaved as badly as the dun.

We rode in, darkness closed around us. Up ahead of us, Harry Mims coughed, and then drew up. "Like it or not, we'll have to wait until daylight. There's a pool covered with green scum, and there's some holes around here too. God knows what's in them, but I'd not like to be."

We sat our horses then, no one of us wanting to get down from the saddle, though no one of us could have said why. It was simply an uneasy feeling we had, and the way the horses acted. I know I had no wish to trust the dun with me out of the saddle, unless he was strongly tied.

Presently a saddle creaked. "I'm getting down," Penelope said. "I'm going to look around."

"Wait!" I spoke sharply. "This may be a damned trap. Get back in your saddle and wait."

Well, I expected a quick answer, but none came. She got back into the saddle and sat quietly. By now the sky was growing gray, and it would not be very long until it was light enough to see.

Nobody said anything for several minutes and then it was Mims who spoke. "Say I'm scared if you like, but I can't get shut of this place fast enough."

Rocks and brush began to take shape, and we could see the walls of the canyon. Nobody was going to ride out of here unless he went out the front way. Or so I thought then.

"I could do with a cup of coffee," I said.

"Not here. Let's get the gold and get out."

"It won't be that easy," I said. "It never is."

Nevertheless, I was as eager to be away as he was, for the canyon was a depressing place. Bones lay about, and not all of them seemed old enough to be the remains of Nathan Hume's pack train.

We all saw the pool, which lay close to Penelope's horse. A still, dead place covered with a scum of green. Penelope leaned over and stirred the surface with a branch she broke from a dead tree. The water under the scum was oily and dark.

"You notice something?" Harry Mims said suddenly. "There ain't no birds in here. I've seen no insects, either. Maybe them Indians are right."

The place was beginning to give me the creeps. "All right," I said. "From what I've heard the gold should be somewhere yonder."

We worked our way around the fallen rocks and over to the spot. There were bones enough, all right. A mule's jaw, white and ancient, lay near a shattered rib cage. But the skeletons weren't pulled apart, the way they often are after wolves or coyotes have worried at them.

I could see that the canyon walls were too steep for any horse to climb, in some places too steep for a man. Yet the first sign of life I saw in the canyon were the tracks of wild horses. Several horses had come through here not long since, but there were older tracks, too, which were headed toward the back of the canyon. On a hunch, I swung my horse around.

"You hunt the gold," I said. "There's something back there I've got to see."

Without waiting for a reply, I started off on the trail of those mustangs, and believe me, the dun was ready to move. He just didn't take to that box canyon, not at all.

Those wild horses headed right back up the canyon and into a mess of boulders tumbled from the rock wall above. They wound around among the rocks and brush, and of a sudden I found myself on a narrow trail going up a steep crack in the rocks, scarcely wide enough for a man on horseback. It went straight up, then took a turn, but I had no doubt but that it topped out on the mesa above.

So there was another way out.

Suddenly I heard a faint call, and turned in the saddle to look back. I hadn't realized I had come so far, or so much higher. I could see Penelope back there, a tiny figure waving her arm at me.

When I reached them Mims was down on the ground. He was lying on his face, which I saw had a faint bluish tinge when I turned him over. "Let's get him out of here," I said quickly. "If they come on us with him out—"

I'd no idea what was wrong with him, but it looked as if he'd fainted from some cause or other, and his heart seemed a mite rapid, but was beating all right. I got him up in the saddle and lashed him there, then led the way down the canyon and out. We rode at once toward the shelter of the trees but saw no one, and soon were back among the cottonwoods and willows along the creek.

By that time the better air outside the canyon, and maybe the movement on the back of his horse, seemed to have done him some good. I took him down from the saddle, feeling uncommonly helpless, not knowing what to do for him; but after a moment or two he began to come around.

"You given to passing out?" I asked. "What happened back there?"

"I don't know. All of a sudden I felt myself going. I tell you one thing —I want no more of that box canyon. There's something wrong about that place. Call it whatever you like, I think that place is ha'nted."

After a while he sat up, but his face was uncommonly pale. When he tried to drink he couldn't keep it down.

"Whatever we do had best be done quickly," I said. "There are too many others around. They'll find the place if we waste time.

"Maybe I'd best go after the gold. I can take along one of the horses and pack some of it out, and I can get the rest on my horse."

Penelope stood there looking at me, and then she said, "Mr. Sackett, you must think I am a very foolish girl, to let you go after that gold alone."

"No, ma'am. You feel up to it, you just go along by yourself—maybe you'd feel safer that way. But I figure one of us ought to stay by Mr. Mims here."

"I can get along," said Mims. "You can both go."

To tell the truth, I'd no great urge to go back there at all, and even less so if I went along with Penelope. She had helped me out of a fix, but she needed my help. I didn't figure it would be easy to get that gold out, and I wanted nothing else to worry about—especially not a girl I had to look after. I said as much.

"You look after yourself," she told me, speaking sharp but not what you'd call angry. And with that she got into the saddle and I followed.

To see us, you wouldn't figure we were going after a treasure like three hundred pounds of gold. We didn't act very willing, and the closer we came to the mouth of that canyon the slower we rode. I didn't like it, and neither did she.

Harry Mims was a tough old man, but something had put him down, and it was nothing we could see. Maybe there was a peculiar smell, time to time. I never mentioned it, not really knowing whether it was imagination, or something more.

It was almost at the mouth of the canyon that we rode right into a trap.

Penelope might have had an excuse, but there wasn't anything like that for me—I should have known better. All of a sudden, there was Sylvie, standing right out in front of us, and when we both drew up, men started stepping out from the rocks and brush.

They had us, all right. They had us cold. And a prettier lot of thieves you never did see. Bishop was there, and Ralph Karnes. Hooker was there, too, his arm in a sling. And there was Charlie Hurst and Tex Parker and Bishop's men.

"Well, Mr. Sackett," Sylvie said, "it looks as if we can pick up the chips."

"Don't figure on it."

She just smiled at me, but when she looked at Penelope she was not smiling. "And now I've got you," she said, and there was an ugly ring to her voice. "Right where I've wanted you."

"Where's that canyon?" Bishop asked.

It sounded like an odd question, for from where he sat he could almost have thrown a rock into the mouth of it, but the way it looked we were about to ride right past it. The reason was that you had to ride to the far side before you could get past the big boulders at the mouth.

"Canyons all around, Noble. You take your pick." I gestured right toward the canyon. "Like that one, for instance."

He grinned at me. "You already checked that one," he said. "We found your tracks coming out. If you left that canyon the gold can't be there. So you show us."

"I wish I knew. How's a man going to pick one canyon out of all these around here?"

"You'd better find a way," Bishop said.

"Don't be a damn fool, Noble. Look, we've been up here a few days now. How long does it take to pick up that much gold and run? If we knew where it was, we'd have been off and running. Nathan Hume was supposed to have hidden some gold up here. We know that two men got away from the massacre. Maybe some others did, too."

"Two?" Sylvie spoke up. She hadn't known that.

"Sure, there was a Mexican got away—he was a packer for Hume. But the governor of New Mexico was after anybody who worked for him. Somebody tipped off the governor that Hume was smuggling gold out and paying no percentage to the government, or whatever they had to do in those days.

"That Mexican lit out for Mexico, but he got his back broke down there and never could come back. But that doesn't say some of his folks mightn't have come back."

"Are you trying to tell us the gold isn't there?" Ralph demanded incredulously.

"I'd say it isn't," I replied. "Bishop, I don't know about you, but Fryer worked the mining camps in Nevada and Colorado. He'll tell you hidden gold is usually gone, or nobody ever finds it. There's men who have spent their lives hunting for treasure like this, and never found anything."

"That's nonsense," Ralph said. "The gold is here . . . we know it is."

"Lots of luck. I only hired on to guide these folks into this country. You find it, you can have it. And you'll know the place by the bones."

"Bones?" It was the first time Ferrara had spoken.

"Sure. A lot of men died there when Hume was killed, and a lot have died since. The Comanches and the Utes say that box canyon is cursed. No Indian will spend a night in the canyon, and none will ride through if they can help it."

"See?" Hooker said. "That was what I was tellin' you."

"Take their weapons," Sylvie said. "We will make them talk."

"Noble," I said, "nobody ain't about to take my guns. Do you think I'd shuck my iron, with what I know's ahead? I've got nothing to tell you, so there'd be no end to it. You boys want what I'm holdin', you're going to have to buy it the hard way."

"Don't talk like a fool!" Ralph said. "Why, we could blow you out of your saddle!"

"Likely. Only Noble here knows me, and he knows I wouldn't be goin' alone. I seen a man one time who was still shooting with sixteen bullets in him. At this range I know I'm going to get two of you anyway—maybe three or four."

And they were going to help me do it, for if trouble started I was going to jump my horse right in the middle of them, where every shot they fired would endanger everybody else in their party.

Now, Noble Bishop was no damn fool. He'd used a gun enough to know that you don't just shoot somebody and they fall down. If a man is mad and coming at you, you have to get him right through the heart, right through the brain, or on a big bone to stop him. On the other hand, a shot that's unexpected can drop a man in his tracks; although any expert on gun-shot wounds can tell some strange stories about what can happen in a shooting.

Bishop knew I'd been wild and desperate. He knew I was reckoned to be a fast man with a gun, and a dead shot; and he knew if it came to shooting, somebody was going to get killed. In such a melee it could be anybody. And like I'd hinted, the gold might not even be there.

Bishop, Fryer, Ferrara, and maybe Parker were canny enough to guess what I'd do, and they weren't having any of it. After all, why start a gunfight when they could pick us off one at a time with small risk? Or let us find the gold and then take it away from us? I knew how they were thinking, because I knew what I'd think in their place.

Bishop spoke calmly. "He's right as rain." He wasn't going to turn this into a wild shooting where anybody could get hurt, and maybe nothing accomplished in the end.

Time and numbers were on their side. All the help I had was a girl and a crippled-up old man, but both of them could scatter a lot of promiscuous lead at such close-up range as this.

"There's nothing to be gained by shooting it out here," Bishop went on. "You ride on your business and we'll ride on ours."

Sylvie was about to protest, then said, "Let him go. Just kill the girl. She has claim to that gold." You never did see anybody who looked so beautiful and was so poison mean as she did when she said it.

"Nobody gets shot," Bishop said. "You all turn and ride out of here."

We turned and started away, but as I went past Bishop, I said to him in a low voice, "Noble, if you find that gold, don't drink any coffee she makes."

Then we went on by, but when I glanced back he was still watching us. After a minute, he lifted a hand and waved. That was all.

"I thought surely there would be shooting," Penelope said.

"Nobody'd been drinking," I said dryly, "and nobody was crazy. We'd have wound up with some of them shot up, and nothing settled."

All the same, nothing was settled anyway. Noble Bishop and me would have it to do, come the right day.

And I had an idea the day was not far off.

Chapter 11

Sylvie Karnes must have made contact with Bishop in Romero, I was thinking. But murderous as Bishop was, he did his work with a gun, which in my book was something altogether different from using poison. Yet he was none the less deadly, for all of that.

"How'd you get shut of Loomis?" I asked as we rode along.

Penelope shrugged. "Who said I was? We got separated, that's all."

Now, I didn't really believe that, nor did I believe that I'd seen the last of that stiff-necked, hard-mouthed old man.

"Whatever we're going to do," I added, "had best be done soon." Even as I said it, I had no stomach for it. I'd a sight rather face Bishop with a gun than ride back into that box canyon.

And Mims was in bad shape. He had lost blood, leaving him weak as a cat, and he could only fumble with his bad hand. It was no wonder he had passed out up there in the canyon, but the idea stayed with me that it had been something worse than mere weakness.

The shadows were growing long as we rode along the stream and then crossed to a low island covered with willows. It was no more than sixty or seventy feet long and half as wide, but there was concealment of a sort there, and some grass.

Swinging down, I helped Mims from the saddle, and felt him trembling with weakness. I spread his blankets, and got him over to them, and he let himself down with a deep sigh.

"We'd better make some coffee," Penelope said. "We all need it."

The stars were out while I gathered driftwood along the island's low shore, and the water rustled pleasantly. Behind the trunk of a huge old cottonwood deadfall, I put together a small fire. The wind was picking up a little, and it worried me, for the sound of the wind would cover anybody trying to approach us.

Nobody talked. All of us were tired, and on edge. We all needed rest, Mims most of all. When I looked at the old man it gave me a twist of pain inside. And it gave me a sudden turn to think that though I was young and strong and tough now, this was the way a man could be when he grew old. It was old age I could see in the face of Harry Mims now.

He drank some coffee, but refused anything to eat, and soon he fell into a restless sleep. Off to one side I said to Penelope, "All the gold in this country ain't worth that man's life. He's a good old man."

"I know." Then she was silent. I sipped black coffee and tried to reach out with my thoughts and picture what tomorrow would bring.

"I need that money, Nolan," she went on. "I need it badly. Say I am selfish if you will, but if I don't get the gold, I'll have nothing, nothing at all."

There didn't seem much of anything to say to that, and I kept still. But I kept thinking about the gold.

We were not far from the canyon. As I thought about it, I wondered if I could find my way around in there in the dark. The trouble was they would probably have somebody watching. Tired as I was, I wanted to get it over with and get out of there.

That canyon worried me. A man who lives on the rough side of things learns to trust to his instincts. The life he leads calls for a kind of alertness no man living a safe and regular life would need; his senses become sharper and they make him alive to things he can't always put into words. I was not a superstitious man, but there was something about that canyon that was all wrong.

After a bit of contemplating, I decided not to go there by night. It would be hard enough to come upon the gold in the daylight, let alone prowling among boulders and rock slides in the dark, and maybe falling into a hole, nobody knew how deep.

Most of all I wanted to get shut of Loomis and Sylvie and Ralph, and I got to thinking about what kind of people they were. With western folks a body knew where he stood. I mean, things were mostly out in the open, for the very good reason that there was no place to hide anything. People were scarce, the towns were small, and whatever a man did it had to be pretty well known.

Things were beginning to change, though, because with the railroads a new kind of folks were coming west. The cheats and the weaklings that hard times had weeded out in the earlier years could now ride west on the cushions.

Jacob Loomis was a man who might have come at any time, though he wouldn't have been any great addition to the country. Sylvie and Ralph would not have come west at all but for the gold they thought they'd come by in an easy way.

Bishop might try to shoot me, I knew. Fryer might try dry-gulching me, but that was to be expected, more or less; anyway, this was Indian country where a man had to be on guard. Poison was another matter, and Sylvie and Ralph . . . well, there was something wrong about them, something evil, something twisted in their minds.

Finally I went to sleep, though I knew when I closed my eyes that I would wake up to a day of guns and gunsmoke. There would be blood on the rocks of the Rabbit Ears before another sundown.

The last stars hung lonely in the sky, and a low wind trembled the cottonwood leaves when my eyes opened and my ears reached out for sound. One by one I heard the sounds—the rustling leaves, the low murmur of the creek water, the pleasant sound of horses cropping grass. Out in the creek a fish jumped.

Picking up my boots, I shook them out—centipedes or scorpions have a way of crawling into boots at night—and then I tugged them on, stood up, and stamped them into place. My hat was already on, of course. First thing any cowhand does of a morning is put on his hat. I slung my gun belt and settled the holster into place, then tied the thong about my leg.

It was not yet full daylight. A single red coal showed in the fire. I stretched the stiffness out of me, wiped the night sweat from my Winchester, and went down to the creek to wash and to brush my teeth with a frayed willow stick.

Moving quietly, I went to the dun and rubbed his ears a mite, talking to him in a low, friendly tone. Then I saddled up, rolled my bed, and made ready to move out.

The old man was sleeping, breathing evenly. That tough old man, all bone and rawhide, would pull through all right. As for that girl Penelope—

She was gone. Her bed was there, but she had slipped away. Her horse was gone too.

My mustang hadn't made any fuss because she came from within the camp, she was one of us, and she had a right to go. And for once I slept so sound I'd missed her going.

She had no business slipping off that way, but I had no business sleeping so sound that she could do it. The truth was, it made me mad to think anybody could slip out of camp without me knowing—but it worried me, too. My life depended on never sleeping that sound.

Kneeling down, I touched Mims on the shoulder. He opened his eyes right off, sharp and clear as if he had never slept.

"That girl kin of yours slipped off. No telling what's happened to her."

He sat up and reached for his hat. "She'll have gone to that misbegotten canyon. We'd better get over there."

Whilst he got himself up, I slapped a saddle on his horse, and only minutes after he opened his eyes we had all gear packed and ready, and rode out of camp.

We walked our horses out of the creek and started up through the trees. The Rabbit Ears bulked large and dark against the sky. A quail called somewhere out in the brush. I knew we were riding to a showdown, and for once I wished it was over.

We kept to low ground, seeking all the cover we could find, and riding out in the open only when we reached the canyon mouth. There seemed to be plenty of tracks, but we could make nothing of them. As before, the dun wanted no part of the box canyon, but at my urging he went ahead hesitantly. I could see that several horses had entered the canyon since we had come out of it.

The first thing we saw was Steve Hooker, and he was dead. He lay crumpled on the ground, one knee drawn up, his six-gun still in its holster, the thong in place.

"Look!" Mims said hoarsely. He was pointing at Hooker's tracks.

He had been walking along, taking slightly shorter strides than a man of his height might have been expected to take, which made me sure he had come in here after dark. Walking on uneven ground, unfamiliar to him, a man will usually take shorter steps.

He had fallen after a few staggering steps and had gone to his hands and his knees. He had gotten up and gone on; and then had fallen again. This time when he had risen he took not more than two or three steps before he collapsed.

"Something last night," Mims spoke in a low, awed tone. "Sackett, I'm riding the hell out of here."

"You wait just a minute," I said. "No use goin' off half-cocked."

Nothing seemed any different from yesterday except for the body of Hooker. I stepped down from the saddle and turned him over. There was no sign of a wound, no blood. His face looked puffy and had a kind of bluish color to it, but that might have been the effect of the early light, or it might have been my imagination.

The low clouds that had come with daybreak hung over the Rabbit Ears, and tails of mist drifted past them. The canyon was a gloomy place at any time with its dark, basaltic rock and the uncanny stillness. I heard no sound at all, and saw no birds, no small animals.

What was it the Mexican had told me that night on the Neuces?

The gold had been pushed into a hole under a boulder, and rocks had been caved in over it. A cross had been scratched on the rock. Forty years or more had passed since the day that happened—I didn't have a sure idea when it was that Nathan Hume had been caught in this trap and massacred.

"Look for a white cross, Mims," I said, keeping my voice low, not knowing who there might be listening. "The sort of thing a man would scratch on a rock if he was in a hurry."

We both saw it at the same moment and started our horses toward it.

The gray clouds seemed darker and lower still, and there was a hint of dampness in the air. I did not like the feel of it; I did not like anything about this strange, haunted place.

Dropping my Winchester into the boot, I swung down from the saddle, and tied the dun to some stiff brush nearby. I loosened the thong from my six-shooter, then walked into the hollow where the boulder stood. At the base of it, below the scratched cross, was a jumble of tumbled rock.

I looked all around. "Keep a sharp lookout, Mims," I said. "Don't watch me—watch for them."

"I wonder where that girl is?" Mims said in a worried tone. "She'd no call to go traipsing off like that."

"Let's get the gold. Then we'll hunt for her. I've got a hunch she can take care of herself."

The hiding place was logical enough. Men defending themselves from Indians would probably retreat to just such a place as this. It would have seemed a good place to make a stand, although Indians up on the rim could have covered them with rifle fire.

One by one I started moving the rocks, most of them slabs, or boulders from head-size on up. I worked as fast as a body could, but I was trying to make as little noise as possible. It was not so much that I suspected anybody was close by, but there was something about that canyon that made a man want to walk softly and speak in a low tone.

My head, which had only stopped aching the day before, started in again now, and my breathing was bad. After a bit I left the hollow and scrambled up beside my horse, to lean against him. It was a surprising thing to know how much a wallop on the head could take out of a man.

Mims looked worried. "You feel all right? You sure don't look so good."

"Headache," I told him, "from that knock on the head from Andrew's bullet."

He looked at me thoughtfully. "Now, you never did tell me how come your head was like that. Andrew, hey? What become of him?"

"Come to think of it, it wasn't Andrew who shot me, it was Ralph. It was Andrew who came in to finish the job."

The air was better up there beside my horse—only a few feet difference, too. After a few minutes I slid back down and went to work again, but I had moved only a few boulders when my head began to buzz and I felt very peculiar. I was going to have to quit.

"If there was a swamp around here," Mims said, "I'd figure you were getting a dose of marsh gas. It'll sometimes do that to a man. Cuts his wind."

Crawling up again, I staggered to my horse, took my canteen and rinsed my mouth with water, and then emptied some of the water over my head. After a moment or two I felt better and went down into the hollow once more. Almost at once I found the gold.

It had been dumped into a natural hollow in the rock underneath. Wasting no time, I began to get it out.

Mims, despite his weakness, got down and started to help. Our excitement carried us on, with me passing the ingots up to Mims, who put them in the prepared packs on his two lead horses.

There was no question of silence any more. I was coughing and choking, and couldn't seem to stop. But I knew that at any moment the others might come.

When the last of the gold was loaded, I climbed up to where the horses stood, not more than six or eight feet above where the gold had been hidden. I fell down, pulled myself up, and then untying my horse, I got a leg over the saddle.

The dun wasted no time, but started for the steep trail up the mountain. It was that which saved us.

I was coughing so hard I could scarcely do more than stay in the saddle. Harry Mims was right behind me with the gold. We had started up the trail when far back behind us we heard a clatter of hoofs and saw several riders come into the canyon. The first thing they saw was Hooker, and then the marks of our horses' hoofs where they had waited while we loaded the gold. They saw the hollow among the rocks, where I'd climbed down to get at the gold, and they saw the empty hole. While they were flocked around it our horses were still scrambling up the steep trail.

We were still within rifle range when they saw us. The gold had been there . . . and now they were seeing it slip away from them.

Which one of them fired the shot, I will never know, nor how many of them there were. I know Tex Parker was there, or somebody riding his horse, and a man wearing a Mexican sombrero, who might have been

Charlie Hurst. There was no sign of Bishop, nor of Penelope. All that I saw at that one quick glance, for I never got another.

One man whipped his rifle to his shoulder and fired, I saw the leap of flame from the muzzle, and then the whole world seemed to blow up in our faces. There was a tremendous explosion and an enormous flame shot up out of the canyon.

I hit the ground with a jarring thud, and I never knew whether I was blown from my saddle or thrown by my startled horse. Only I lit on my hands and knees, looking down into the canyon but well back from the edge.

Flame was streaking out in rushing streams from the point of the explosion, seeming to seek out every hollow, every low place among the rocks, and then it hit a three-foot-wide hole in the rocks. We'd seen that hole, but we hadn't gone near it.

Now the mouth of the hole was a great jet of flame, and the air was filled with a terrible, continuing roar.

Pulling myself to my feet, I staggered away, filled with horror, and trying to get away from the sound of the roaring.

There was no sign of my horse, and none of Harry Mims or the pack horses, but for several minutes the only thing I could think of was that I wanted to get away.

I climbed up, and had gone almost half a mile before I saw Mims. He was still in the saddle, and he had the pack horses with him. He was trying to round up the line-back dun, but the mustang was frightened and would have none of him.

Slowly, I limped along the mountainside toward them. The dun shied several times, but finally he stood still and let me get into the saddle.

We rode straight away toward the west, with no thought in our minds but to get away from that dreadful sight and that terrible sound. I'd seen men die before, but never like that.

And where . . . *where was Penelope?*

Chapter 12

Neither of us felt like talking. We rode straight ahead, but we had no destination in mind. It was simply that we wanted to get away from the box canyon, away from that awful scene.

It was Mims who finally spoke. "Must be some kind of gas . . . or oil. You hear about that feller back in Pennsylvania who drilled him an oil well? Supposing something like that caught fire?"

I didn't know the answer, but it seemed as if it must have been something of the sort. Even the fact that we had the gold, three hundred pounds of it, was forgotten in the shock of what had happened in the canyon.

What brought me back to myself was the thought of Penelope. . . . Where was she? Loomis, I was sure, had not been among those in the canyon. There had been at least four or five men down there, and Fryer and Ferrara might have been among them, or perhaps some other friends of Parker and Hurst.

"We've got to get under cover," I said, "and we've got to stash this gold somewhere."

I was still coughing from whatever it was I'd gotten into my lungs down there—the same thing probably that had killed Steve Hooker. It might have been worse for him at nighttime, or maybe his heart was bad. We'd never know about that, and I wasn't giving it much thought. It was the living I was concerned with.

Steve Hooker had charted his own course, followed his own trail. If it led him to the death he'd found, he had probably saved himself from a bullet or a noose, for he was headed for one or the other. When a man begins a life of violence, or when he decides to live by taking something away from others, he just naturally points himself toward one end. He can't win—the odds are too much against him.

We kept heading west, riding at a steady gait for about four miles, and then I let Mims go on ahead with the pack horses while I did what I could to wipe out whatever trail we had left through the bunch grass.

When I came up to him again, walking my horse up Cienequilla Creek, he had stopped at a place barren of cover—a sandy bank rising a few feet above the shore of the creek. It was just what we wanted. We unloaded the gold and put it down close to the bank, then caved the bank over it. The sand was dry, and when we had finished there was no sign that this spot was any different from any other place along the banks where small slides or cave-ins were common. Wiping out our own tracks, we started back.

It was early—the sun wasn't more than an hour above the horizon. The sky was darkened by the pall of smoke above Rabbit Ears, but the smoke seemed to be thinning out some, we thought.

We had to find Penelope, if she was alive, and I was surely thinking she was. She just had to be.

Slipping off in the middle of the night like that . . . it made no kind of sense unless she figured to get to the gold before we did, or anybody else.

But what happened to her? She had not been in the canyon, of that I was sure, so something must have stopped her, or turned her aside.

Presently I said to Mims, "I never figured to see you again after you loaning me that horse. Main thing I wanted then was distance."

"They had a rope for you, all right, and I never did see such an outfit." Mims chuckled. "Mad? They were really scratching dirt and butting heads. Fact is, they talked some about lynching me on general principles."

"What stopped 'em?"

"I had me an old ten-gauge shotgun in the cabin. After you taken off I just went back and loaded her up. Time or two I've noticed that a ten-gauge shotgun is quite a pacifier. Folks who get riled up and want to twist somebody's tail sort of calm down when they see one.

"Well, they rode up, just a-stompin' and a-chawin', so I showed 'em the shotgun and told 'em you wanted a horse in a hurry and I let you have one.

"I just wished I'd of had that shotgun ready when Sylvie showed up. I never did shoot no woman, but there's one I figure I could shoot with a clear conscience."

By now we had picked up Rabbit Ears Creek and were working our way around to the south side of the mountain, all the while scouting for tracks. And soon we found them.

They were buckboard tracks, leading north past the east side of the mountain. We slowed our pace and followed, riding with rifles ready for trouble.

We found a camp that had been used for a couple of days, but was deserted now. We could be only a few miles from the box canyon, and their next camp must be close by. We were getting smoke from the fire in the canyon now; it was thin, but there was a-plenty of it.

Harry Mims drew up. "Nolan, I ain't much on the scare, but we're sure askin' for trouble. That outfit's got to be close by, and they'll be in a sweat to get that gold or our hides."

"That girl needs help," I said, "and I can't ride off without seeing her safe. It ain't in me."

"What kinda outlaw are you?"

"I ain't figured that out yet, but I surely ain't riding away until she's safe."

We had started on again, keeping under cover of brush and trees, and pulling up every now and again to listen.

Suddenly we came upon the buckboard—or what was left of it. It had been pushed off a little bank, brush thrown over it, and then set afire. There was little left but the wheel rims, the hubs, and some charred spokes. A smell of smoke still hung over it.

Neither of us could make much out of the tracks except that somebody had charged off the side of the hill and stampeded the buckboard horses. There had been a fight, for we found some empty shells, a bullet scar on a tree, and the earth churned up by the hoofs of several horses.

"I'll bet they didn't get Flinch," Mims commented. "From what you tell of that breed, he'd be a sly one."

It was mid-afternoon now. We listened but there wasn't a sound.

We rode on under a low sky made darker by the oily smoke still coming from the fire in the canyon. We held to the bottoms, alert for trouble. How Mims felt I could guess, and I knew that I was all in. Seemed like we'd been running and riding forever. What I wanted now was some sitting-around time and eating three square meals a day. I wanted coffee I didn't make myself, and some restaurant-cooked grub.

We had come up the east side of the Rabbit Ears and had reached the creek again. Now we smelled woodsmoke, and we took our horses down to the damp sand along the edge of the creek.

There was a peck of trouble standing out for us somewhere close ahead, and we both knew it. You just don't ride up to a crowd like that without expecting trouble. And there'd be one woman there, maybe two. The women worried me most of all. You might figure out what a man would do, but never a woman.

An old outlaw told me one time, "Look out for the women. You never know whether they're going to scream, or faint, or go for a gun."

And they were there, all right, both of them. When we rode up the two of them were facing each other alongside the fire.

Jacob Loomis was sitting on a rock facing toward us, his blanket roll beside him. Noble Bishop was there, his face still, eyes watchful, missing nothing. And Fryer . . . I'd sort of figured him for one of those who died back in the canyon, but here he was, big as life and twice as ugly. And the Mexican was beside him.

Flinch worried me most of all. He wasn't there.

Loomis' eyes took on an ugly shine when we rode up through the trees. Bishop looked at me, but he made no move of any kind. With Bishop and me it was a cut-and-dried thing. Each of us had a reputation as a fast man with a gun, and each of us knew that if it came to shooting somebody was going to get hurt. Neither was eager to try the other, but each of us knew that events might push us that way.

What was going on when we rode up I didn't wait to find out, but I knew it was something that had to be stopped.

"Penelope," I said, "it's all over now. We'll ride with you to Santa Fe."

Bishop turned his eyes to me. "What happened over there?"

"That canyon must have been full of gas from oil underground. It seeped out and, being heavy like, it held close to the ground in the low places. Me an' Harry here, we were up on the rim, and one of them—I don't know who—got skittish and fired a shot.

"You know how this black powder is. A flame jumped from the muzzle when he shot, and the whole canyon blew up all to once, with streamers of fire wherever gas had gathered. Those men never had them a chance."

"We rode over that way," Bishop said. "We couldn't make out much, and we didn't stay long. All we could see was rocks blackened by fire and that hole in the rocks shooting out a jet of fire."

"How long do you reckon it will burn?" Fryer asked.

"Who knows? Years, maybe. It'll burn as long as there's anything left to burn."

"What about the gold?" Ralph Karnes demanded.

I shrugged. "What about it? Looks to me like nobody's going to get at that gold for a good long time."

"Unless," Sylvie said, looking right at me, "somebody got it out before the fire started."

"There's always that," I admitted. "But it looked to me like all those fellows got it to once. I don't think any of them got out alive."

"I wasn't thinking of them," Sylvie said. "I was thinking of you."

Nobody said anything for a minute, but Penelope was looking at me, her eyes bright with the questions in them. I was hoping they would wait.

"Well," I said, smiling easier than I felt like, "if I had that gold I'd be splittin' the breeze for Denver right now. I surely wouldn't be wastin' time talking to you folks."

"Neither would I," Fryer said. "What would he come back for?"

"For her," Sylvie said. "Can't you see he's got an itch for Penelope?"

They were all looking at me, and I just shrugged. I wasn't looking at Pen when I spoke. "You're funnin' me, Sylvie. With all that money no man's going to have to look for women; he'll just have to look out for them. Why, if a man rides into Denver with all that gold he'll be combin' them out of his hair.

"Now, Penelope here is a nice girl. We promised to see her safe into Santa Fe. Mims here is a relative of hers."

I knew about where we stood. Fryer believed me easy enough, and so did the Mexican. Bishop . . . well, he was holdin' court in his mind—he hadn't come to any decision yet. Sylvie and Loomis, they were so crooked they wouldn't believe anybody and they were suspicious of everybody. Sylvie, I knew, would never let us ride out of there if she could figure some way to do us in. And I knew that, money or not, Jake Loomis wanted Penelope. He wanted her right out in those hills with nobody around. I could see the purpose in him, and the cruelty.

Right then, I guess, I made up my mind it was going to be a shooting matter.

The last thing I wanted was to swap lead with Bishop in that crowd. Likely he felt the same way, but Sylvie or Ralph or maybe Loomis would surely trigger trouble unless we could get out of here quick.

"Mount up, Pen," I said, "we're riding out."

Even as I spoke my mind was laying out the whole scene, taking everything in.

The bank of the creek was low and flat, just rising a mite near the edge of the trees that surrounded the clearing. There were a few good-sized boulders close by. Some of their horses were back on the left, standing under the trees. Penelope's horse, loaned her by Mims, was over with the team from the buckboard. The harness had been stripped off and both of them now wore Indian-style bridles, made by Flinch, I'd bet.

"She's not going," Sylvie said. "This is family trouble, and we'll settle it here."

Bishop wasn't talking. I wanted to know where he stood, but as long as I didn't make a point of it he could wait and listen.

"There's no reason for trouble," I said, "family or no family. You and Ralph go your own way and she can go hers."

"We found Andrew," Ralph said.

Well, here it was. The whole thing was shaping up now just the way I thought it would, but had hoped it wouldn't.

"You shot me, Ralph," I said, "and Andrew figured to finish the job. He didn't quite make it."

"I think you've got the gold," Loomis said. "Why else would you be so ready to ride off?"

I shrugged. "Why waste time around here? The show's over."

Sylvie suddenly seemed to give in. "All right. Let's forgive and forget. We were just getting ready for supper. Get down and I'll pour some coffee."

This had gone on long enough. "I don't like your coffee, Sylvie. It comes out a mite strong for my taste. Pen, you get your horse. We're leaving . . . now."

Pen started toward the horses and Sylvie sprang at her. All I needed was to move in to help her and somebody would take a shot at me.

But Pen didn't need any help. Sylvie tried to grab at her hair with both hands, but Pen wasn't having any. She let her have it.

Well, I couldn't believe it. Seemed I'd never learn. Here was that girl I was always for protecting, and she needed no more protection than a mountain lion. Sylvie sprang at her, hands up-raised, and Pen hit her right in the stomach with a doubled-up fist. When Sylvie gasped for breath and brought her hands down, Pen slapped her across the mouth with a crack like a pistol shot. Then she caught up the reins of her horse and swung up.

"Stop her!" Loomis shouted. "Bishop, you stop her—or give me a gun and I will!"

Bishop never moved. He just glanced over at Loomis and said, "You better be happy, old man, that you ain't got a gun. Nolan Sackett would kill you."

So we rode out of there and started west again. But I was worried. Noble Bishop would be wanting that gold, and how much of my story he believed I didn't know. Only thing I was sure of was that he hadn't wanted a shoot-out down there by the creek. There were too many people and too many guns, and it would be a matter of luck, not skill, if a man survived. There were too many chances of a wild bullet doing what you didn't mean an aimed bullet to do.

We rode fast. We were going to pick up that gold and ride out of there, and I was hoping I'd seen the last of all of them.

We were northeast of the Rabbit Ears now, and the peaks were red with the dying sun. There was a dull glow over the canyon and we could hear, even at this distance, the roar.

We headed for Rabbit Ears Creek, and from time to time I turned in my saddle, but nobody was following us that I could see. By the time we were due south of the mountain the stars were coming out and it was well on toward dark.

"They won't leave it alone, Sackett," Mims said. "They'll come."

"Sure, they will."

Penelope had not done any talking, and I was just as pleased. I was still mad over her riding out and leaving us in the night that way.

Taking the bulk of Cienequilla del Barro Mountain for a landmark, I kept on west and when it was well after dark I changed direction several times until we were close under the shadow of the mountain. Then we switched and turned northeast toward the creek where the gold had been buried.

Mims drew up suddenly. "Sackett, I don't like the smell of this. Something's wrong."

Of course it was . . . but what? It had gone off too easy, altogether too easy. I was sure we had not been followed, but what if there had been no need? Supposing we had been observed earlier in the day? Observed in the vicinity, even if not while burying the gold.

Maybe they knew approximately where we had gone, but not exactly. There was a good deal of smoke, the clouds were low, and there might have been intervening trees or brush. As I thought of it, it was plain enough to me that they might have been watching from up on the Rabbit Ears.

"What's wrong?" Penelope asked.

"Mims has got a hunch we're walking into some kind of a trap."

"How could that be? They're all back there."

"Are they?"

A faint breeze stirred across the bunch grass levels, but it brought with it none of the canyon's smoke, for that was all to the east of us now. The clouds were heavy and it was now full dark. A horse stamped impatiently. The horses wanted water, they wanted rest, and they wanted grass. I had a feeling it would be hours before they were that lucky.

"All right," I said, "let's go on."

Moving ahead, I walked the dun slowly, pausing often to listen, but there was no sound beyond those to be expected—the sound of the horses' hoofs in the grass, the creak of saddle leather.

We were within two hundred yards of the Cienequilla when I drew up again, but again I heard no sound.

Flinch would have been the one on the mountain, of course, whether it was their idea or his. He would have been Indian enough to go up on the Rabbit Ears where he could watch everything that took place. He could not have seen us get the gold, but he could draw some conclusions from the way the pack horses moved.

So what would they do now? Wait in hiding until we had the gold out and loaded again? That would be what Bishop would want, but would the others be patient enough for that?

Suddenly I knew what I was going to do.

Chapter 13

"Harry, do you know the peak called Sierra Grande? Due west from here?"

"I know it."

"Six or seven miles south of it there's an outcropping of lava and there's a peak there about four hundred feet high. When we get the gold loaded, you and Pen head due west for that lava flow and hole up somewhere south of the peak.

"You can water your horses on the Middle Fork of the Burro, but water won't be a problem. There are scattered ponds all over that country. Go on to the Carrizo if you want to, but it's about thirty miles, probably nearer forty the way you'll have to go to the peak. I wouldn't go out of my way if I can help it."

"What about you?" Penelope asked.

"It's dark. You move off quietly and they'll never know. I'll stay behind and tumble rocks around, cave in the bank here and there, make them think we were digging or hunting for the place. I figure I can give you an hour's start before they close in."

"And after they close in?"

"Why, there's liable to be a little difficulty, Penelope. I sort of doubt if they'll take my word, but I figure to be convincing."

"And then?"

"I'll come and join you."

There was a long moment of silence, and then she said, "There will be six of them—seven counting Sylvie . . . and just you."

"Maybe I can slip away before they close in."

"Why are you doing this?"

"That's a lot of gold."

"Wouldn't it be easier just to shoot Mr. Mims and me? There's only two of us."

"We're wastin' time talking like this. Anyway, I was never much on doing things the easy way. We'll ride in now. If we're lucky we'll get the gold loaded and you out of here before there's trouble."

With that, I turned my horse and rode on to the creek. I felt pretty sure that they were close by, and that they would wait until we had the gold uncovered . . . it all depended on that. But you couldn't be sure about Sylvie and Ralph. Nobody knew when they'd go off half-cocked.

We dug the sand away with our hands, loaded the pack horses, with me counting the ingots as I had when we hid them. When they were all on the pack saddles I pushed Mims's shoulder as a signal for him to go.

Then, loud enough so a listener might hear if close enough, I said, "I tell you it was further this way!"

"You try it," Harry said, catching the drift. "I'll look down the creek."

Penelope had stopped beside me, and I turned and, putting my lips close to her ear, whispered: "Go on! I'll need every minute!"

She turned her head then and kissed me quickly on the lips, and I was surprised as if she'd stuck a knife into me . . . which I was half expecting.

Then she was gone.

Reaching up, I caught hold of a rock stuck in the sand at the top of the low bank, tugged it loose, and let it fall with a little cascade of sand.

"Ssh!" I hissed. "You want to start the whole country moving?"

Then I fumbled around in the dark, managed to step on a dried branch, to tumble some more dirt, and with a piece of the broken branch I dug at the dirt.

"Over further," I said. "It was over the other side about ten feet."

The minutes dragged. All of a sudden I knew myself for a damned fool. This wasn't going to fool anybody anywhere near long enough. My eyes went to the dun.

The horse was standing there, ground-hitched. One quick jump and I'd be in the saddle and riding out of here. How much was money worth, anyway? A man's life? Particularly when it was my life?

Suddenly, I heard a faint stir of movement on the far bank. Without waiting, I moved toward my horse. There was that movement again. After all, I had no friends over there. I palmed my six-shooter and let drive a shot right at the sound. Then I dropped to the sand, scuttled quickly five or six feet and came up running as two guns crossed their fire toward the point I'd just left.

There came a sudden crackle of flame and the brush across the creek exploded. Somebody had dropped a match into a dead juniper. The flames soared high, and the area was brightly lit. Instantly I heard the hard bark of pistols, the sharper report of a rifle, and a spout of sand leaped in front of me. Just behind me something slapped the water sharply and, turning, I saw a leaping figure and fired.

The man, whoever he was, caught in mid-jump, jerked oddly, and fell. He started to get up, then rolled off the bank into the shallow water.

Something seemed to tug at my sleeve, and then I was running, falling, running again. Another tree burst into flame ahead of me, and just beyond it I saw my horse.

Starting up the sloping bank from what was evidently a ford on the stream, I saw Ferrara. He had a rifle, and was taking aim, not more than sixty feet away. My six-shooter was in my hand, and I simply fired, threw myself to one side, and fired again. He went down, tried to bring the gun around, but I had ducked from sight and was back in the stream bed running for my horse. Crawling up the bank, I grabbed the reins and jumped for the saddle, mounting without touching a stirrup.

The dun, not liking either the flames or the shooting, took off at a dead run. Behind me there were a few wasted shots, and then silence.

Riding north, I headed for the breaks along the North Canadian, knowing my first problem was to try to lead them away from Penelope and Mims, and the gold.

Also, I was going to have to find rest for my horse. Any wild mustang will travel for days, run a good part of the time, and get along on very little water, but carrying a rider is another thing.

After a brief run I slowed the dun, changed direction, and then reloaded my pistol and rifle. An hour or more later I holed up in a little hollow on a creek that fed into the North Canadian, stripped the gear from the dun, let him roll and then picketed him where he could reach the water. When I stretched out on the grass where I'd spread my blanket, I told myself I would not be able to sleep. A minute later I must have proved myself a liar, for when I awakened it was bright sunlight and I could hear the birds twittering in the willows.

For a long time, I lay still, looking up to where the sunlight fell through the leaves, and listening. There was a magpie fussing on a branch nearby, but after a few minutes he flew off. I sat up, put on my hat, shook out my boots, pulled them on, and stood up.

Slinging my gun belt around my hips, I buckled the belt, then walked over and talked to the dun for a while, all the time listening for whatever my ears could pick up. I tied my gun down with the rawhide thong around my leg, and went back and rolled up my blankets and ground sheet. Then I dug into my saddlebags for a busted box of cartridges and filled the empty loops in my belt.

I was hungry, but the little grub I'd had was used up, except for a little coffee, and I had no urge to hunt anything and draw attention by shooting. It wouldn't be the first morning I'd ridden off with no breakfast, nor would it be the last. I went to the creek and drank, watered the dun again, and saddled him up.

Riding west along the Corrumpaw Creek, I held to a line that would skirt Sierra Grande on the south. The clouds of the last few days were finally giving up some rain, which began to fall in a cold, steady shower, and I put on my slicker. From time to time I studied my back trail but saw nothing.

Had they gone off after Penelope and Mims, then? The two had a fair start, but with two heavily loaded pack horses they were not going to move very fast. However, Harry Mims was an old-timer, and a man who should know something about losing pursuit.

On the other hand, the hits I'd scored on two men might have cooled the others off somewhat. They could not know I was not with Penelope and Mims, or about to join them. I had no idea what the results of my shooting were. Both men were hit, and I hoped they were not killed, though wounded men are a sight more trouble than the dead.

That night, just before sundown, I sighted a sheep camp. There must have been over a thousand sheep in the lot, and three Mexican herders, with their dogs. The three were well-armed men, for this was Indian country, although we were getting closer to the settlements. I joined them, and soon learned that they were out of Las Vegas.

After I'd eaten I told them I was pushing on a ways. "No reason for you to get into grief," I said. "There may be some men following me."

One of the Mexicans grinned slyly. "Si, amigo. Men have followed me also. Vaya con Dios."

Leaving them, I followed the south branch of the Corrumpaw until it lost itself in the steep slope of Sierra Grande, and made camp for the night. When daybreak came I found a bench and worked my way along it around the base of the mountain until the lava beds and their lone peak were due south of me.

The bench was five hundred feet or so above the land below and gave me a good view of the country toward the lava beds and the peak. Seated on a flat rock, I gave myself time to contemplate the country around that peak, which was a good five miles from where I sat. And that was a good mile south of the peak of Sierra Grande.

It was still early morning. Nothing moved down there. No dust clouds . . . nothing. When I'd watched for at least an hour, I mounted up again and let the dun find his own way down the mountain. We rode across the valley floor, raising as little dust as possible; after the light rain of the day before, that was no problem.

When I reached the lava beds I rode with caution, with my Winchester ready to hand.

There was nobody there . . . and no tracks.

Either they had never gotten here, or the tracks they'd left had been wiped out by the rain. For a while I scouted the country, and only once did I find anything like a track, and then it was only a slight indentation under the edge of a bush, such as a horse might have made in stepping past the bush.

Finally, I rode back to the peak. I'd told them to hole up somewhere south of the peak, so I tied my horse to a mesquite bush and climbed up on the lava.

I knew what lava would do to a pair of boots, and mine weren't in very good shape as it was. Scrambling around over lava, those boots could be done for in an hour or two, so I simply climbed the highest bulge I could find short of the peak and looked around.

The first thing I saw was an empty cartridge shell, bright in the sun. And a little beyond it, projecting from behind some brush, I sighted a boot and a spur.

It needed only a couple of minutes for me to get there. It was Harry Mims, and he was dead.

He had been shot in the back at fairly close range, but he was a tough old man with a lot of life in him and he had crawled—his scraped and bloodied hands showed that—trying to get away over the lava.

He must have lost his gun when they shot at him. I didn't see it anywhere around and did not look for it. They had followed, caught up with him, and then standing over him had emptied a gun into his chest.

There were no other bodies, no horses, no gold, no Penelope.

Penelope? . . . A little chill caught me in the chest. Suppose she had killed him? Suppose it was she who'd shot him in the back, then followed him up and shot him in the chest to make sure of his death?

Who else could get that close? . . . And where was Penelope?

I left the place and rode to the west, cutting back and forth for sign. Almost a mile out I found where several horses, two of them heavily loaded, had crossed a wash, their heels sliding in the mud.

At intervals then I found sign; but I'd been following for scarcely another mile when, in glancing around to study my back trail, I thought I saw another trail off to the right. Riding over, I did find another trail—a

lone rider keeping well off to one side, and often stopping beside a mesquite bush. Obviously, somebody had been scouting along the trail of the
bunch of horses. I had no idea who the lone rider might be, but I knew
Penelope had the horses, and I was sure there were no strange tracks
among that lot.

Of the original group against us, I did not know which ones had survived, and were able to ride. Perhaps all of them.

It was just shy of noon when I found the other trail.

Chapter 14

The new trail showed four riders coming in from the south, and a couple of the tracks were familiar ones. They belonged to some of the Bishop crowd. Who, then, was the lone rider following Penelope?

The trail held steadily west, then suddenly it ended in a maze of tracks. Drawing up, I stood in the stirrups and gave study to the ground.

The pursuers had lost Penelope's trail, and in trying to find it again had chopped up all the ground with hoof marks. Circling, I tried to pick up the trail of the lone rider again. From the way he had been acting I had an idea that he was a good tracker, and as he had been ahead of them, he was most likely to discover where Penelope had gone.

She had ridden into a belt of soft sand where tracks leave no clear impressions. Then she had evidently seen some herders coming with a flock of sheep and had simply ridden on ahead of them, keeping track of the direction they were taking and staying ahead so their tracks would wipe hers out.

The herd had been headed west, which was her direction, but I wasn't satisfied. She would not want to go north, for in that direction it was too far to any town where she could be sure of protection from the law. West was all right for her, but it was almost too obvious. Cimarron was over west, and she might head for there . . . but she might not. I found myself wishing I knew what she and Mims had talked about before he was killed. That old man knew this country and he had probably told her a good deal.

Those sheep were a good cover for her tracks, but it was likely Loomis, Bishop, and the rest of them would follow right along until they caught up with the sheep, and then they'd find her tracks. Yet I could not be sure of that. Suppose she turned off?

This girl was showing herself uncommonly smart. She was all alone now with three hundred pounds of gold, two pack horses, and a spare saddle horse, for she must have Mims's mount with her. She would outfigure everybody if she could, and I had a hunch she would leave that sheep herd at the first chance. She was, without doubt, riding a good way ahead of it. With that much gold she would be suspicious of everybody and taking no chance even with the herders.

So I held to the south edge of the herd, keeping an eye out for tracks. The herd was heading for a patch of junipers and piñon that lay ahead. There was good grass and a lot of good grazing on the slopes around those trees. A mile or more this side were twin peaks, with a low hill standing north of them.

When I got to that low hill I drew up and studied the gound. The sheep had passed north of it, but there were scattered tracks out from the flock, as there always are, and dog tracks among them. There was no sign of a horse track, but somehow I was not convinced.

Skirting the hill, I rode up between the two buttes that lay south of it. I'd been on the dodge too many times myself to ignore such a place. If she turned off between those buttes the sheepherders would have their view of her cut off until they passed the buttes, and by that time she could be under cover. They would not know which way she had gone.

On the far side of the buttes I suddenly came on several horse tracks, one of which I recognized. Yet I had gone on half a mile farther before I found more. She was using every bit of soft sand or hard rock she could find, and she left practically no signs.

Now the thing to figure was where she would be going. Cimarron was closest; if she by-passed that she could go through the mountains and turn north to Elizabethtown, or ride on to Taos. Each mile of this would be dangerous, but she had nerve, and evidently she had a plan. It was my hunch she would skip Cimarron.

Well now, here was a girl out of the East who was making fools out of the lot of us. One young girl, all alone, with four horses and three hundred pounds in gold, cutting across wild country toward . . . where?

Her trail was plain enough, so I lifted the dun into a canter and followed as rapidly as possible. She was hours ahead of me when she crossed the Canadian, but she was moving her pack horses too fast. Carrying a dead weight such as gold was harder than carrying a rider.

We were riding in cattle country now, and sooner or later she was sure to come up with some cowhands. Sure enough, she had, and did the smart thing. She swapped her horses for three fresh and better ones. But before she did the swapping she left her gold cached out in the hills.

She'd been gone less than an hour when I came into their camp. Right off, I noticed her horses in the remuda. They were beat, for they'd been ridden hard, and she had been smart to trade them off.

Me, I asked no questions at all. Like always, they invited me to set and eat, and whilst eating I made a swap for my dun. I was in no mind to let the dun go, and told them so, and they let me have a fresh horse that I could swap back for the dun at any time, they said. And that I meant to do.

"Ridin' far?" one of them asked.

I shrugged. "Yeah. Headin' to Mora to visit kinfolk. Name of Sackett."

"Heard of them." They looked at me with interest, for Tyrel and Orrin were known men in New Mexico.

The last thing I wanted those cowhands to know was that I was following Penelope Hume. They'd never tell me anything if they knew, for they'd all be on the side of a pretty girl, for which I'd not blame them.

"Seen a party of men north of here," I volunteered. "Look to be huntin' somebody."

The horse they traded me was a short-coupled black with some Morgan blood, and a good horse by any man's standards.

Riding out of their camp, I came upon the place where she had left the gold hidden while making her horse trade. She had loaded up, pack saddles and gold, and lit out as if the heel-flies were after her. Likely knowing she'd lost time, she wanted to get on with it.

Now I thought of Fort Union . . . she was headed for Fort Union. There were soldiers there, and she would be safe. The difficulty was that there would be a lot of questions asked about a young girl traveling across the country with all that gold.

But her tracks led right by the Fort, and by then I was actually within sight of her from time to time. I had no idea whether she had seen me, but if she had she knew she was headed for a showdown. I still wanted to know who had killed Harry Mims—shot in the back, at close range. Of the lone rider I had seen nothing in all this time. Nor had I seen anything of the others.

Suddenly I knew exactly where she was going. She was headed for Loma Parda.

The little town on the Mora River was rough and bloody, a resort for the soldiers at Fort Union, and for any number of drifters, male and female. They knew me at Loma Parda, but for her to ride into Loma with gold was like a lamb going to visit a lot of hungry wolves.

When she reached the town I was no more than four or five miles behind her, but there was simply nothing I could do. By the time I got to the town her horses were turned into a corral and Penelope had disappeared. It seemed the last person she wanted to see was me.

Avoiding the saloon, where I knew Penelope would not be, I went to a Mexican eating place down the street from Baca's. It was an off hour, and they were glad to see me. They knew me there, and the woman who came to wait on table shook her head when she saw me and said, "Señor Nolan, what do you do to yourself? You are tired!"

Glancing around, I saw myself in the mirror, a big, rough, bearded man who needed a shave, a bath, a haircut, and new clothes. He also needed about three nights sleep.

"Señora," I said, "have you seen a girl—a girl with several horses?"

"Ah? It is a girl now? Si, I see her. She rode in today, only a little while ago."

"Where is she? Where did she go?"

"Go? Where can you go in Loma Parda? She did not go, she is here."

"Where?"

The señora shrugged. "Here . . . somewhere. How should I know?"

From where I sat I could look down the street and see anyone who moved, so I ordered a meal and stayed there, eating and drinking coffee and trying to stay awake.

There was not much out there in the street at this hour. In a little while the town would wake up, the soldiers would come in in one of the rigs that carried them over from the Fort, or they would hike, as many preferred to do. The town would be wide open. It was a town where killing was the order of the day, where the idea of gold would set the place afire. And somewhere in the town was Penelope, and three hundred pounds of gold.

Where did I fit in, anyway? I had given her a chance to get away, given Mims the same chance; but he was dead, murdered. And Penelope had not wasted any time looking for me, nor left any sign for me. And she had come here, to the least likely place. I couldn't even imagine her knowing of this place.

Rightfully, a piece of that gold was mine. I was the one who'd found it, I got it out of there, and now here I sat with about four dollars in my pocket and a nasty scar on my scalp to show for all I'd been through.

And then for the first time I remembered the money I'd been paid for guiding Loomis and Penelope. Fifty dollars . . .

I wasn't broke, then. Fifty dollars was nigh onto two months' pay for a cowhand, and I'd known a few who had worked for less.

While I sat there thinking about it, I saw Noble Bishop ride into the street. Jacob Loomis was with him, and Ralph and Sylvie Karnes. They come riding up the street, looking right and left, dusty and beat-looking, their eyes hot with the fire that only gold can light.

They did not see me sitting there, and if they went to the corral the big black horse would not be familiar to them.

But where was Penelope, and where was that gold?

And then I started to get really mad.

I'd been riding my fool head off, a good man had been killed and a couple of others less than good, and all for what? So one big-eyed girl could walk off with the lot, a girl with no more claim to it than any one of us. What if Nathan Hume was a relative? The gold had been buried for years, and without me she would never have had it.

I got up from the table so fast I almost upset it, dropped a half-dollar beside my place, and started for the door.

The señora ran after me. "Wait a minute, señor! Your change!"

"Keep it. Feed me sometime when I come in here broke."

It was hot outside in the late afternoon sun, but I did not care. I strode up the street and pushed open the bat-wing doors of Baca's saloon. Baca himself was standing at the bar, and I saw his eyes turn to me, narrowing slightly.

"Baca," I said abruptly, "there's a girl in town who came in this afternoon, and she's hiding out somewhere. You know everything that happens in this town—I want that girl, and I want her quick!"

"I am sorry. I—"

"Baca, I'm Nolan Sackett. You know me."

He hesitated. Within call he might have fifteen, twenty tough men. If he called them I was in for one hell of a fight. But right then I didn't care, and I think he realized it.

"She's down at Slanting Annie's. Not her crib—her cabin. You take your own chances. She's got a gun, and I hear she's ready to use it."

"She won't use it on me." But even as I said it, I wasn't sure.

I walked outside. The sun's glare hit my eyes like a fist, and I stood blinking. The anger was still in me, and I wanted only to see Penelope and know the truth. I had fought for her, helped her escape, found the gold for her—and then she had gone off on her own.

Mims was dead. Had she killed him? How else could anyone have come up on him? These thoughts went through my head, but in the back of my mind I didn't want to believe it.

Slanting Annie's cabin was under the cottonwoods on the edge of town. I walked down the dusty street, wishing I had a horse. No cowhand worthy of the name ever walked far on a street if he could avoid it, but there was no time to get a horse and the distance was short. All the time I knew that Bishop and the others were in town and would be hunting the girl, and me as well.

Annie herself came to the door. Slanting Annie had worked in a dozen western towns, and I had known her in both Fort Griffin and Dodge.

"Annie, I want to see Penelope Hume."

"She isn't here, Nolan."

"Annie," I said roughly, "you know better than to tell me something like that. I know she's here, and she'd better know that Loomis, Bishop, and all of them are in town."

"Let him come in," Penelope's voice said.

Annie stepped aside and I came into the shadowed room and removed my hat. Penelope was wearing a gray traveling outfit of some kind, and she was actually beautiful. I hadn't realized before just how beautiful she was, although I figured her for a mighty pretty girl.

"Mr. Sackett, I thought you were dead!"

"Like Mims, you mean?"

"Poor Uncle Harry . . . he never had a chance. Flinch did it."

"Flinch?"

Now, why hadn't I thought of him? There was Injun enough in him to be able to close in on a man without his knowing it.

"You expect me to believe that?" I said.

"Of course I do. You can't believe I would kill that fine old man!"

"You seem to manage pretty well when the chips are down." I dropped into a chair and put my hat on the floor beside it. "We've some talking to do."

She glanced at Annie. "Not now."

Annie looked at her, then at me. "You want me to leave so you can talk? You're perfectly safe with him," she added to Penelope.

I grinned at her. "Now that's a hell of a thing to say!"

"I mean that you're a gentleman. An outlaw, maybe, but a gentleman."

"Well . . . thanks."

"I'll go up the street. I want to see Jennie, anyway."

She took up her hat, pinned it on, and went out and closed the door.

"You're pretty good at getting across country," I said grudgingly. "That was a neat trick with the sheep."

"It didn't fool anybody."

"Yes, it did. It fooled them." I looked hard at her. "It didn't fool me."

"As for getting across the country, I had a good teacher. Probably the best."

"Who?"

"Who else? You, of course. I watched you when you minded us, watched everything you did. You're a very careful man."

She was watching me with a curious expression that I couldn't quite figure out. "You haven't asked about the gold," she said.

"I was coming to that."

"I'm afraid you're not much of an outlaw, Mr. Sackett. I imagine a really successful outlaw would have asked about the gold first."

"Maybe."

I looked around the room. It was a small room in a small adobe house, but it was well furnished—there was nothing tawdry about it. I didn't know a lot about such things, but now and again I'd been in enough homes to know the difference between what was right and what wasn't.

"How'd you happen to know Annie?" I asked.

"Her aunt used to sew for my mother. I knew she was in Loma Parda, and I knew of no one else I could go to. I suppose you think a nice girl shouldn't even recognize Annie."

"I think nothing of the kind. Annie's all right. I've known her for quite a spell . . . in a manner of speaking.

"You know what would happen if anybody realized you had that gold? It would blow the lid off this town. And right at this moment they're hunting you."

"Annie knows a freighter. She was going to get him to help me get to Santa Fe." Then she said, "I had just made coffee—would you like some?"

While she went into the kitchen for the coffeepot and some cups, I sort of eased back in that plush chair. I didn't rightly trust the furniture. Benches and bunks or saloon chairs were more what I was used to, and I'm a big man. This sort of fine furniture didn't seem exactly made for my size. But it was a comfortable place and, looking around, I admired it. Even to the butt of the gun that showed from under a bit of sewing on the table.

Penelope returned with the coffee, poured some for me, and then seated herself, near the gun.

"The freighter was to leave tonight," she said. "He has ten wagons. Annie is arranging for me to have one of them."

"Where's the gold?"

She didn't answer that, but said, "I want you to have a share of it. After all, without you I might never have found it, and certainly I couldn't have kept it."

"Thanks," I said. "I can't set here waiting for them to come. I've got to find Loomis . . . and Flinch."

"Be careful of him. I had to run, you know. After Flinch killed Mr. Mims there was nothing for me to do. I was afraid of him."

I still held my coffee cup, but I was doing some fast thinking. Not that I don't trust folks, but it began to seem to me that she had been out of the room after that coffee just a mite longer than she should have been. I swallowed some coffee, put the cup down, and stood up.

"You're not going?"

"You'll be seeing me around. And when the time comes for that freighter to leave, I'll be back here."

Bending over, I picked up my hat. Her hand was near the gun—was that just accident? I took my time straightening up and saw she was looking at me, all bright-eyed. The trouble was, I wanted to trust her and almost believed that I could, but just wasn't able to gamble on it.

I went past her quickly and into the kitchen, opened the kitchen door, and stepped outside. On the small back porch I turned my eyes to the sun, and blinked a couple of times before stepping clear of the porch.

Back here there was a small stable, and the yard and the house were shaded by the cottonwoods. Somebody moved swiftly inside the house, and then I was at the front corner, looking across the street and up and down it. The first glance was swift, to locate any immediate danger, the second slower, carefully searching each possible hiding place.

It was a faint whisper of movement behind me that warned me. Turning sharply, I was in time to see Loomis lifting a shotgun. I palmed my gun and shot him through the middle, and both barrels of his shotgun emptied into the ground with a dull roar.

Instantly I was back under the cottonwoods and ran behind a long building, slowed down, and then walked out into the street to join a few others from the saloons.

"What happened?" somebody was asking.

"Shooting down the street," I said. "Maybe somebody killed a turkey."

I turned and walked up to Baca's, where things were stirring around. But there was no sign of Bishop.

The corral was my next stop. I got the black out, saddled him up, and left him tied outside the corral but well in the shadows.

A thought came to me, and I looked around the corral. Her horses were there, including the pack horses. But I saw no sign of the pack saddles. I had not been far behind her when she rode into town, and she must have known that. She could not have known where Slanting Annie lived, so she could not have taken the gold there. A young girl riding through Loma Parda's street with three horses, two of them pack horses, would have aroused interest, and this she would have guessed. So what then?

She would not have brought the gold to the corral, for she would have to unload it by herself, piece by piece . . . unless she just loosened the cinches and let the saddles fall. She could not have done that in town for fear of the packs bursting, or somebody seeing them and becoming curious at their weight.

So the gold must be somewhere out of town, quickly unloaded and left there before she rode in.

Chapter 15

Standing with my hand on the saddle, I thought back along the trail. The sort of place she would need to hide the gold, where it could not accidentally be discovered, would be rare. Moreover, I had followed her trail in to Loma Parda, so how could she have veered off without my being aware of it?

Then I recalled that I had not actually followed her trail all the way into town. When her tracks merged with those of others coming or going, I had ceased to follow them and had merely taken it for granted that she was going on into town.

Stepping into the saddle, I skirted around the far side of the corral and rode down the alley toward the edge of town, and so out of sight of any watcher not in the stable itself.

There was another trail, I remembered, that led westward from Loma Parda toward the Sangre de Cristo Mountains, and then went south to Las Vegas and so on to Santa Fe. That trail was occasionally used by freighters, I knew. Supposing Penelope had skirted the town, come up close to that trail, and hidden the gold there?

In less than ten minutes I was riding along that trail, looking for possible hiding places. If I wanted to dump a heavy load, to be easily picked up again, where would I leave it?

It was still light, but the sun was down and it would soon be dark. My horse made no sound in the soft dust of the trail. But look as I would, I could find no place such as I sought.

Then at the last moment, with darkness closing around, I saw a patch of grass pressed down and almost yellow, some scattered pine needles and cones upon the grass. Drawing up, I studied the place. Something had been on that spot, something that was there no longer.

The mark, I saw, had clearly been made by a fallen pine tree, a tree no more than ten feet high that had been blown down or broken off and had rested there.

The tree was there, but it was now a few feet over to one side, still fastened to the stump by a strip of wood and bark. Somebody had picked up the top end of the tree and pulled it to one side, leaving uncovered the place where it had originally fallen and where it had been lying for at least several weeks.

Leading the black off the trail, I left it tied, and went over to the tree. When I had pulled it aside I found the pack saddles, fully loaded and not more than a few feet off the trail the freighters would take. Each saddle held a hundred and fifty pounds of gold.

Reaching down, I caught hold of a loaded saddle with each hand and straightened my knees. I walked off about fifty feet and paused, resting the saddles, and then after a moment went on. Twenty minutes or so later I returned and rode my horse all around the area, trampling out all the tracks. Then I rode back to town and tied my horse to the hitch rail in front of a store, now closed for the night.

Carrying those three hundred pounds had been no trick for me, for I'd grown up swinging a double-bitted axe, wrestling with a crowd of brothers and cousins, and then going on to handling freight on a river boat. After that I'd wrestled mean broncs and thousand-pound longhorn steers. I guess I'd been born strong, and anything I could pick up I could carry away . . . and often had.

But moving that gold would only help me for a matter of hours. By daylight there'd be other folks hunting it. However, if a freighter was pulling out with a train of wagons, I figured to be along. I'd driven a team a good many times, and handled a jerk-line outfit as well.

Standing in the darkness alongside my horse, I checked my gun and my knives, for if ever a man was bucking for a fistful of trouble it was me. If there were freighters about I figured they'd be in Baca's saloon, and it was there I went.

The place was already half full of soldiers from the Fort, mingling with Baca's dance-hall girls, and he had him a plenty of them. Here and there some tough-looking Mexicans stood around, and they were Baca men, not to be taken lightly.

Baca's eyes found me as soon as I came in, and they watched me as I worked my way through the crowd. When I stopped near him I ordered a drink. "Gracias, Baca," I said. "I found her."

He shrugged. "Bueno. Annie tells me you are a good man."

"One thing, Baca. If any trouble starts around here, I want none with you. I've no argument with you, and want no trouble."

"Si, it is understood." He motioned for a glass and poured me a drink. "To you, señor, and good fortune." We drank, and then he placed his glass carefully on the bar. "Noble Bishop is in town. He was asking for you."

"I'm not trying to prove anything, Baca. If he wants me he's got to come asking."

"Is it about the señorita?"

Better for him to think that than to start wondering. "She's a pretty girl," I said, "and a lady."

"So I am told."

"Frankly," I said, "I'm hunting a job. Something to sort of keep me out of sight for a while. Riding or driving a freight team. But not a stage . . . nobody sees a freighter, but everybody sees a stage driver."

"There is a man in town—his name is Ollie Shaddock. He is taking some wagons out tonight, picking up more at Las Vegas."

I moved to a table near the wall, where I sat down and waited for Shaddock to come in. Most times I was a patient man, but now I was impatient, for gold makes a heavy weight on a man's thinking. It worried me that I had not seen Bishop, or Sylvie or any of that lot.

When Shaddock came in he was motioned to my table by Baca. I've no doubt Baca wanted to get shut of me.

Ollie Shaddock was a broad, cheerful man whose blond hair was turning gray. He thrust out a hand. "Anybody by the name of Sackett is a friend of mine. I'm from Tennessee, too."

"You know Tyrel and them?"

"I brought their ma and younger brothers west. I'm from the Cumberland."

"Me, I'm from Clinch Mountain."

"Good folks over there. I've some kin there. What can I do for you?"

"I want to hire on as a driver, or I'll drive for free. Only I want to be driving the last wagon when you pull out tonight."

His face sobered. "You tied up with that girl?"

"Sort of. I'll load what she thinks she's going to load. She'll get her share in Santa Fe . . . only I want to be sure I get mine."

"You're a Sackett. That's enough for me." He motioned for a bottle. "Nolan, I was the one who started Orrin in politics. In fact, it was because I was sheriffin' back in Tennessee that the boys came west.

"Tyrel, he wound up their feud with the Higginses by killin' Long Higgins. It was up to me to arrest him, and he went west to avoid trouble . . . me bein' a friend of the family, and all."*

---

* *The Daybreakers.*

"Well, can you leave me a space for a couple of loaded pack saddles in the middle of the wagon?"

"Sure enough." Shaddock filled his glass. "You know Tyrel and them?"

"No. Heard tell of them."

By now the place was going full blast and I wanted to get out; besides, I wanted to see if Penelope was all right. That girl worried me. I couldn't figure whether she was a-fixin' to get me killed or not. Maybe she'd been out in that kitchen pourin' coffee . . . but she might have been signaling Loomis.

Ollie Shaddock got up after a while and left, telling me where to meet them. It was sheer luck that he had turned out to be a friend of the family, and a man from the Tennessee hills. I'd heard of him before this, but only as being a man who operated several strings of freight wagons in New Mexico and Arizona.

After a few minutes I got up, paid what was asked, and eased out of a side door. Baca watched me go, no doubt glad to see me leaving. Not that fights were unusual in Loma Parda, for the town had been the scene of many a bloody battle, with many kinds of weapons.

The night was cool and still. Stars hung large in the dark sky, the cottonwoods rustled their leaves gently. I stood there, hearing the voices from inside and the tinpanny sound of the music from the music box. There was a smell of woodsmoke in the air.

I moved to the side of the door, where I waited, breathing easy of the night air and letting my eyes grow accustomed to the darkness. The last thing I wanted now was trouble. I had the gold hidden, I had a way of getting out of town, and in a matter of less than an hour we would be leaving.

When I moved, it was along the wall toward the street, and when I reached it I paused in the darkness looking both ways. Down the street I could see a light in Slanting Annie's window, and I wanted to go that way. Annie would be at work by now, but Penelope would be there, waiting as I was.

She wouldn't be caring about seeing me, I knew, for I was no likely man to attract a girl's eye. Lifting my hands, I looked at them. Fit for handling guns or tools, fit for the hardest kind of work, for lifting the heaviest loads, but they'd found no call to gentleness, nor were they likely to. A girl as pretty as Penelope . . .

No use thinking about that. She had gone off and left me, leaving no sign. She might have murdered Harry Mims, and set a trap for me.

Maybe it was like she said, that after he was killed she was afraid to be alone, but I couldn't trust her. The trouble was she looked so warm and friendly, so soft and lovely, that every once in a while my good sense went a-glimmering.

Somewhere around there was Sylvie and that brother of hers, and I'd given too little thought to Sylvie. But she'd probably given a lot of thought to me, and the chances were that she'd been working on Noble Bishop.

I stepped out on the street, which was partly lit by the light from the windows around, and walked toward the place where I'd left my horse.

The black nickered a mite and snuffed at my hand with delicate nostrils. I'd picked up a lump of brown sugar, and I fed it to him. Then I untied him and led him away into the darkness.

Well, it would soon be over. In a matter of minutes I'd be sitting up on the seat of a freight wagon, rolling out of town. Then I'd pick up the gold, put it aboard, cover it well, and we'd be rolling on toward Las Vegas and Santa Fe.

What would Penelope do when she found the gold gone? Would she come along, or would she stay behind and try to find it?

With these thoughts in mind, I mounted up and circled the town, working around to where the wagons were. Penelope should be there soon.

The wind was cool off the Sangre de Cristos, cool and fresh to the lungs, carrying the scent of pines and the memory of snows. Alongside the church I drew up and looked along the street. A wild Texas yell came to me from one of the saloons, then a shot . . . some celebrating soldier or cowhand. On the hills back of the town a coyote talked to the stars, complaining of something, by the sound of him.

When I reached the wagon I drew up alongside the last one and tied my horse to the tail-gate. I took my Winchester from the saddle boot and placed it behind the seat, but within easy grasp of my hand.

A man came down the line of wagons. "Sackett?" he said.

"Here."

He moved over beside me, his cigar glowing redly. "You set store by that girl?"

"Some."

"She ain't showed, and it's getting nigh to time. You think she'll back out?"

"Not likely." I considered. Was this another trap? She had told me she was going tonight. Was I now supposed to go looking for her? Or had Sylvie and Ralph finally caught up with her?

"How soon you want to go?" I asked.

"Fifteen minutes. I'm waiting for another wagon, loading over yonder."

"I'll go get her."

Ollie Shaddock said, "You better wait here. She wants to come, she will."

"I'll see."

"Sackett, I've heard talk around town. You better walk careful. Somebody has been hiring guns. You know how Loma is . . . you can get anything here you can pay for, and some things come cheap, like killings."

"Who's hiring?"

"No idea."

The wind off the mountains felt good on my face. It was no time for a man to die. Oddly enough, I was thinking less of that gold I would be picking up than of the wind in my face, or the girl. I had no meeting ground with gold. When it came to me I spent it and had little enough left to remember.

"Are you in love with that girl?" Ollie asked.

Was I? I didn't think so. I wasn't even sure I knew what love was, and I'd always guarded myself against any deep feeling for a girl. After all, who would want to live with me? I was a big tough man with two hard hands and a gun . . . that was me.

If it had been someone else I'd have answered with some scoffing thing; but it was Ollie, and he knew people of my blood, and he was from Tennessee. "Ollie, I just don't know," I said. "I don't altogether trust her. The other one, that dark-eyed Sylvie, she's pure poison. Her I know. But Penelope? Well, I can't make up my mind."

"You step light, boy. Step light."

He meant it one way, but I decided to take it two ways, and I walked back to my horse and switched my boots for moccasins.

"Ollie, I'll be back. You just hold tight."

It wasn't more than a hundred and fifty yards to Annie's house, and I walked along under the edge of the cottonwoods. My mouth felt dry and my heart was beating heavy—I wasn't sure whether it was because I expected trouble or because of that girl. I told myself I'd no business feeling like that about any girl, but all the telling did no good, none at all.

I could hear music at Baca's; there men were singing and drinking and laughing, men playing cards and looking at girls and chinking coins or chips in their fingers. I could see the horses standing three-legged at the hitch rail, and I saw a man come from the walk in the darkness and cross toward Baca's, a man wearing a big sombrero, spurs jingling.

In the shadows under a big old tree I stood and looked at Slanting Annie's house. Lights in the windows, all cheerful and bright. Yet bright as they were, I felt an emptiness in me, a sudden longing for lighted windows of my own, and a coming home to them, opening the door to warmth and comfort and a woman waiting. Well, no use thinking of that, an unlikely thing for Nolan Sackett.

My moccasins made no slightest sound as I moved along under the trees. Long ago I'd learned to move like a wild animal in the wilderness. Boots would have made sound, but with the moccasins I could feel the branches under my feet before stepping down hard, and so shifted my step.

When I got to within fifty feet or so of the house I stopped again, holding myself close to the trunk of a cottonwood. There was no sound from within the house, and I moved closer and edged up to a window.

Penelope sat at the table, pouring coffee, and across the table from her sat Sylvie Karnes!

Shoulder to shoulder with Sylvie was Noble Bishop. Ralph Karnes was coming in from the kitchen with a plate of cakes. Just as he put them down I heard Penelope say something about the time. All their heads turned toward the clock.

Penelope finished pouring coffee and sat back, taking up her own cup. There they sat, who were supposed to be enemies, talking together like at a tea party. I never saw the like. Maybe, after all, I was the only fool in the lot.

Then Penelope put down her cup, said something to Sylvie about the dishes, and went over and took up her bonnet. She turned and spoke to them all, obviously saying good-bye.

Like a ghost, I faded back into the trees and walked back quickly to the wagons. Ollie was waiting impatiently.

"She'll be along," I said.

"Did you talk to her?"

"No, but she's coming."

"She'll be in the wagon right ahead of you, since both of you wanted to stop."

"Who's driving hers?"

"A good man . . . Reinhardt. He's been with me a couple of years." Ollie looked around at me suddenly. "Never thought to tell you. Orrin Sackett is a partner in this outfit. He owns a third of it."

"He's done well, I guess."

"Yes, he has. I'd say he was one of the strongest political figures in the Territory."

Leaning against the wagon, waiting for Penelope to come, I reflected bitterly that Orrin had no more start than me when he came west. They had educated themselves. Tyrel and him, and both of them were big people in this country, while all I had behind me were a lot of dusty trails, barroom brawls, and lonely hide-outs in the hills.

The fact that I was about to pick up enough gold to make a man wealthy for life meant little when a body figured on it. What mattered was what a man made with his own hands, his own brains. Whatever I got out of this was from sheer chance and a fast gun. And right at this moment I didn't even have the gold.

She came walking up out of the darkness. "Oh, Mr. Shaddock, I'm sorry to be late, but some friends dropped in and I just had to talk for a few minutes. Are you ready to leave?"

"Yes, ma'am. If you'll get up in your wagon, ma'am. This here is Oscar Reinhardt. He'll be your driver."

"Thank you." I could see her eyes straining toward me, a figure she could only dimly make out.

Ollie turned and gestured toward me. "Nolan Sackett will be driving the last wagon."

Ollie walked away toward the front of the train, and Penelope came back to me. "You're here then? I'm glad." She hesitated. "I'll have to admit that I'm glad to be leaving." Then she went on quickly. "I want to get away from this . . . this killing." She looked up at me. I could see the pale oval of her face in the darkness. "Poor Mr. Loomis was shot. He's not dead, but he was badly hurt. I can't imagine how it happened."

"This here is a dangerous country," I said. "Somebody might have seen him wandering around in the dark and figured he was hunting for them. I heard about the shooting. There were two shots fired, weren't there?"

"I don't know." She turned away from me and walked up to her wagon, where Reinhardt helped her in. After a few minutes I heard the first wagons moving out. As with all such freight outfits, they wouldn't really be moving as a unit until they were on the trail. Some of the wagons were standing off the side of the road, and they would be falling into place one by one. The movement would be a lot of stop-and-go until they finally got lined out. The stopping of a wagon would attract no attention for many of them would be stopped briefly while other wagons pulled in ahead of them.

Reinhardt's wagon moved out, and I let them get a start. I was driving a team of big Missouri mules, eight of them, and they handled nice. I'd always liked handling the straps on a good team.

We moved slowly while getting lined out, slower than a man could walk. I was watching for the marks I'd chosen and it was not many minutes after the wagons pulled out that I drew up. The wagon ahead was rolling on. I listened for a while, but there was no sound.

My hands wound the reins around the brake and I got down carefully, as quietly as possible.

Penelope might be in with Sylvie and them, but if she wasn't they would certainly be watching the wagon train move out. They would know that she had the gold, and that she must pick it up somewhere along the line. Would they be watching me too?

Climbing down the small bank off the road, I went into the trees, pausing from moment to moment to listen. I heard no sound that seemed out of place, and I stooped to pick up the pack saddles. Behind me I thought I heard a faint stir among the pine needles and junipers. Crouching, I listened, but heard nothing more.

I reached down into the hollow and lifted the first pack saddle out, then the second. I had been going to carry them both, but if I did I would be helpless if attacked. It was not so quick a thing to let go of such a weight and grab a gun. . . . One at a time then.

Picking up the first, I swung it to my shoulder and, keeping my free hand on my gun, walked back to the bank. There I needed the free hand to help me climb. I scrambled up and placed the pack saddle and its gold in the wagon, then went back for the second.

As I crouched by the second load, I listened again. I could hear the now distant, subdued sounds of the wagons—there was no special sound from Penelope's wagon. But I thought I heard something stirring up ahead. Taking up the second load, I lifted it to my shoulder and walked slowly and carefully to the bank. I put the gold down on the bank and, turning, looked all around, listening.

Nothing moved. Getting up on the roadbed quickly, I picked up the gold and lifted it into the wagon, then drew the tarpaulin over it and tied it in place.

I was standing beside the mules when I heard someone walking along the road. As he came up I saw that it was Reinhardt.

"Sackett? That girl's been out there ten minutes or more. What's this all about, d'you know?"

"I guess she had some packages she wanted picked up. Things look different in the dark and she's probably looking for them."

"Is that all?"

He was a good man, Ollie had said, and an honest man, no doubt. "Look," I said, "you better stay by your team. There's trouble in this, and there's no use in your getting shot over something that's no part of your business."

"Hell, I'm not afraid."

"Of course you're not, but that's not the point. You could get killed out there, and to no purpose."

"If that girl's in trouble—"

"Take it from me, she can handle it. Or I can. You sit tight." One hand checked my gun. "I'll go get her."

I had no urge to go down into that black patch of juniper with Penelope down there, and the Lord only knew how many others. The smart thing to do was to stay right where I was and let her get out under her own power.

All I would get down there was trouble. Nevertheless, that girl was down there alone, and like a damned fool I went after her.

At this point there was no bank—the road was level with the woods. Knee-high brush grew alongside the trail and I tried to step over it to avoid sound, but I made a little.

First off, I headed for that broken-off tree where she'd had the gold hidden. When I was almost there, something moved near me, and I smelled a faint perfume.

"Penelope?"

A body moved against mine and a hand took my arm, a woman's fingers closing gently on my wrist. Suddenly those fingers tightened and my wrist was jerked back, and at the same time I felt her body move close to mine with a quick, violent movement.

My wide silver buckle that held my gun belt saved me, that and my own reaction, for as the point of the knife hit the silver and was deflected upward, my hand swept down in a blind, instinctive action and struck her arm on the inside of the elbow.

Like I said, I'm a big man, and mighty strong, and that sudden blow must have numbed her arm. She dropped the knife and I heard it hit the ground. The next instant the whole place was lit by a tremendous blaze of light. Somebody had dropped a match into the top of that dead pine.

Now, anybody who has ever seen fire hit dead pine would know what happened then. It went up in one tremendous burst of crackling, spitting flame, lighting the entire area. And across the space in front of me was Ralph Karnes, and not far away Noble Bishop.

In the instant the light leaped up, Bishop saw me and I saw him, and both of us knew the cards were on the table. His hand dropped for his gun, and my instinct must have triggered my muscles even before my brain realized the necessity, for my gun sprang to my hand . . . a split second faster than his.

I felt the sharp whip of the bullet as it cut by my neck, and I saw Bishop crumple and begin to fall. He caught himself with his left hand on a tree branch and started to bring his gun around on me. I shot into him again.

Karnes shot, but he was no gunfighter and he shot too quick. He must have pulled the trigger instead of squeezing, because he missed me. I didn't miss him. He backed up, clawing at his chest and spitting, then fell into the leaves, where he threshed around like a wild animal for a moment, then was still.

The brief burst of flame was dying down, and I looked around for Penelope. She was standing where the gold had been, almost as if unaware of all that had happened, just standing there saying over and over again, "It's gone . . . it's gone."

From the direction of town I could hear excited yells, and I saw a lantern bobbing in the distance as someone came toward us.

Without a word, I picked up Penelope and carried her to my wagon. "Get rolling!" I said to Reinhardt. "Try to catch up with the others. I'll take care of her."

"She all right?"

"Sure . . . now get going. I want to get out of here."

Reinhardt moved ahead and swung to his wagon. I put Penelope on the seat of mine, then climbed up beside her and took the reins from around the brake handle.

Reinhardt was moving out, and we followed. Mentally I counted my shots. Two bullets left in the pistol, no chance to load while driving the mules. The rifle was right behind me, within reach of my hand.

Suddenly, as the wagon began to move, Penelope came to life. "No, no! I can't go! The gold is back there! I've got to find it!"

"It isn't there," I said calmly. "It was moved within a short time after you hid it."

She turned on me. "How do you know that?"

"Relax," I said. "It's a long ride to Santa Fe."

"I don't want to go to Santa Fe! I want that gold!"

"They wanted it, too—Sylvie, Bishop, and them. Look what it got them."

Reinhardt's wagon had stopped again, then after a moment it started on.

"I need that gold," she said stubbornly. "I've got to have it. I don't know how to make a living, and there aren't any jobs for women."

"You could get married."

"When I marry I don't want it to be because I need someone to take care of me. I want to marry for love."

"Romantic," I said coolly.

"Well, I don't care—it's the way I feel!"

"You have all that gold, somebody would marry you because he wanted somebody to take care of him."

Reinhardt was sure doing an erratic job of driving. He had stopped again. I sat there, holding the lines, waiting for him to get going again.

"You couldn't find that gold now anyway. That place back there will be overrun with folks trying to figure out who shot who. If you figure to go back, you'd better wait a few weeks."

We drove on for a short distance, and then I said, "Did you have a nice talk with Sylvie last night?"

She turned sharply around on me. "You were spying!"

"Sure. A man has to know what's going on. I like to know who my friends are."

"And you don't think I'm your friend?"

"Are you?"

She was silent for a minute. Then she said, "I ought to be. You've done more for me than anyone else has. I don't think I'd even be alive but for you."

"You saved my bacon when I was down and hurt. You kept Ralph off me." I urged the mules a little faster. "And you did pretty well coming across the country alone."

"If you hadn't been coming somewhere behind me, I couldn't have done it. I knew you had to be back there, and I tried to do what you would have done."

"You did it well."

Neither of us said anything for a good while, just listening to the rumble of the wagon wheels on the road, watching the stars. But I was listening for other sounds too. By now my ears knew the sounds the wagon made, and the harness and the mules. I knew what sounds came from up ahead, and what the right night sounds were around me.

There was a missing piece somewhere. . . . Did Penelope have a knife ready for my ribs?

"That Sylvie," I said, "she tried to knife me."

"Where is she?"

"Back there. She may have a sore arm for a while, but she's going to live . . . worse luck."

"She's mean."

"I sort of gathered that. Sure as shootin', other folks will die because of her. I just hope we can stay shut of her."

That "we" sort of slipped in there, but Penelope didn't seem to notice it.

Then she said, "What could have happened to the gold?"

"Things look a lot differently by night. You probably mistook the place."

"But that tree! I know it was under that dead pine!"

"There's lots of dead pines," I said carelessly.

"You certainly don't seem very upset about it."

"I'm not. I never had that much money in my life, so if I never see it again I ain't a-going to miss it."

We drove on, talking a bit from time to time, then she dropped off to sleep. It was daybreak when she sat up and began to push her hair into place and try to straighten her clothes.

"Where is the wagon train?" she asked. "We've fallen way behind."

"That Reinhardt! He's been taking it almighty slow. I didn't know until it got light that we were so far behind the rest of them."

Suddenly the wagon ahead pulled up. Nobody moved—the wagon just stood there. I got down and walked up to it. "Reinhardt," I said, "what's the matter? You gone to sleep?"

I looked into the muzzle of a gun, behind it the black, heavy-lidded eyes of Flinch.

"The belt," he said. "Unbuckle."

With this man I took no chances. Moving my hands with infinite care, I unbuckled the belt and let it fall to the trail.

"The bowie . . . take it out of the scabbard and drop it . . . fingertips only."

"Where is Reinhardt?"

Flinch jerked his head toward the wagon. "He is all right."

"How do you fit into this, Flinch? You working with Karnes?"

"I work for Flinch. My grandfather . . . he was in fight at Rabbit Ears. He was Indian. He tell me the white chief hide something there. A long time after he went back to look, but could not find. When I hear talk in Fort Griffin about Rabbit Ears, I get a job."

The way the wagons stood on the trail, Penelope could not see us. I heard her getting down from the wagon and heard the sound of her feet.

"You too," Flinch said as she came up. "You stand over there. Beside him."

For the first time his thin lips smiled. "Now, after all, the Indian gets the gold."

"The gold isn't here, Flinch," Penelope protested. "It's back there, at Loma Parda."

"The gold in his wagon." He nodded toward me. "I follow him. I know he will find it, so I follow, watch him when he hide it, watch him when he load it in wagon. It is better for me to have the wagon for a while . . . the gold is much heavy."

Penelope stared at me. "You had that gold all the time? You mean you had—"

"Now I am going to kill," Flinch said. "First you, then her."

"Let her take my horse and go."

He did not even reply. I took a half-step toward him. "Up!" he said. "*Manos arriba!*"

I lifted my hands as high as my ears. He kept his eyes on me, wanting me to see the effect of his words. "I kill you. I keep her until tomorrow."

"They'll hang you," I said. "Look here, Flinch, let's—"

My right hand, only inches from my collar, moved suddenly. The knife slung down my back slid into my hand, the hand whipped forward, and he fired. I felt the slam of his bullet, heard the thud of my knife. It had gone into the hollow at the base of his throat, up to the hilt.

His mouth opened in a great gasp and blood gushed from it. He fell forward to his knees, grasping at the hilt, fumbling to get hold of it with both hands, but I had thrown with all my strength and the knife had gone in hard.

He struggled, choked, then fell over on his side, the knife coming free in his hand.

Stooping down, I took the knife from his fingers and sank it twice into the sandy earth to cleanse the blade. Penelope was looking at him, her eyes filled with horror.

"See what happened to Reinhardt," I said sharply. "Be quick!"

Startled, she turned and hurried to the wagon. When I looked back at Flinch, he was dead.

Belting on my gun again, I stripped Flinch's gun belt and tossed it into the wagon.

Reinhardt came out from under the wagon cover, rubbing his wrists. "He wouldn't have killed me, I think," he said. "I staked him a couple of times when he was broke."

"We'd better move on. Ollie Shaddock will be wondering what happened."

He glanced at me, then at the dead man. "What happened? He was sure enough going to kill you."

I reached back and drew the knife again. "This," I said. "I learned it south of the border."

I started back to the wagon. Penelope joined me, and I helped her up. Reinhardt was already moving off.

We had been traveling for some time when she said, "You had the gold all the time!"

"Uh-huh."

"What are you going to do with it?"

"Been contemplating on that. Likely I'll give half of it to you."

"You'll *give*—!"

"And I'll keep the other half myself. That way," I continued, "you'll be free to marry for love. But with half of that gold, I won't need anybody to take care of me, either, so you won't be married for what you have."

She didn't say anything to that, and I didn't figure she needed to, the way things were shaping up.

"I thought you got hit back there," she said presently.

So I showed her where the bullet had hit my cartridge belt right on my left hip. It had struck the lead noses of two bullets, fusing them into one. "I'll have a bad bruise, the way it feels, but I'm the luckiest man alive."

Only thing was, I surely wished I had a shave. And before we got to Santa Fe she was wishing it, too.